Barbara Taylor Bradford is the bestselling author of *A Woman of Substance, Voice of the Heart, Hold the Dream, Act of Will* and *To Be the Best. A Woman of Substance, Hold the Dream, Voice of the Heart* and *Act of Will* were hugely successful television series.

Barbara Taylor Bradford was born in Leeds, and was a journalist in Yorkshire and Fleet Street before moving to New York, where she lives with her husband, Robert Bradford. She is published in thirty-three countries and nineteen languages.

D1149650

Barbara Taylor Bradford

THE WOMEN
IN HIS LIFE

GRAFTON BOOKS

A Division of the Collins Publishing Group

LONDON GLASGOW
TORONTO SYDNEY AUCKLAND

Grafton Books
A Division of the Collins Publishing Group
8 Grafton Street, London W1X 3LA

Published by Grafton Books 1990

This is a work of fiction.
The situations and scenes described, other than
historical events, are all imaginary. With the
exception of well-known historical figures, none
of the characters portrayed is based on real
people, but were created from the imagination
of the author. Any similarity, therefore, to those
living or dead is purely coincidental.

A CIP catalogue record for this book is
available from the British Library

ISBN 0–246–12984–0
ISBN 0–246–13826–2 (Pbk)

Printed in Great Britain by
William Collins Sons & Co. Ltd, Glasgow

Grateful acknowledgement is made for permission to
reprint lines from the following songs:

'There'll Always Be an England' (Parker/Charles)
Copyright © 1939, Dash Music Co. Ltd, 8-9 Frith Street,
London, W1V 5TZ
Used by permission. All rights reserved.

'The White Cliffs of Dover' (Kent/Burton)
Copyright © 1941, Shapiro Bernstein & Co. Inc., USA
Reproduced by permission of B. Feldman & Co. Ltd,
London WC2H 0EA.

'I'll Be Seeing You' (Fain/Kahal)
Copyright © 1938, Marlo Music Corp., USA
Reproduced by permission of Francis Day and Hunter Ltd,
London WC2H 0EA.

Extract from *Rich: The Life of Richard Burton* by Melvyn
Bragg is reprinted by kind permission of Hodder &
Stoughton Ltd.

This book is for Bob, who means all the world to me, and without whom it could not have been written.

PART 1

MAXIMILIAN

LONDON – NEW YORK

1989

A man who stormed and captured so many citadels which in his boyhood and youth must have seemed as fantastical and unobtainable as Ali Baba's cave. A man of many lives.

Rich: The Life of Richard Burton
by Melvyn Bragg

ONE

He came out of the imposing house on the corner of Chesterfield Hill and Charles Street and stood for a moment poised on the front step. It had rained earlier and the dampness lingered and the air was raw on this chilly Thursday evening in January.

Normally oblivious of the weather, he found himself shivering and turned up the collar of his black trenchcoat. The weather underscored his morose mood, his sense of desolation. For a long time there had been a deep sadness inside him; tonight, for some reason, it seemed more acute than usual.

Pushing his hands in his pockets, he forced himself to stride out, heading in the direction of Berkeley Square. He walked at a rapid pace along Charles Street, his step determined, his back straight, his head held erect. He was dark-haired with dark-brown eyes, tall, lean, trimly built. There was an athletic hardness about his body, which was echoed in his lean and angular face, its raw-boned sharpness softened by a deep tan. He was an exceptionally handsome man, in his early fifties: his name was Maximilian West.

He cursed mildly under his breath, wondering at the heaviness he felt and suddenly regretting that he had agreed to this meeting set for such a late hour. He had done so impulsively – he who was rarely impulsive – out of deference to his old schoolfriend, Alan Trenton. Alan had made his presence sound so vitally important. But eight-forty-five was late even for him, renowned as he was for being ready to do business at any time of day or night, any day of the week, especially since he had another appointment that evening. What saved the situation for him was the fact that Alan's office was only a stone's throw away from the late-night dining club where he had a table booked for nine-thirty.

He circled Berkeley Square, dodging the traffic as he made for the far side, wondering why Alan needed to see him, what this was all about. When Alan had telephoned the house earlier his voice had vibrated with urgency, yet he had been curiously reticent. Intrigued, Maxim had agreed to stop by, but now he was acutely aware of the time, reminding himself that Alan was talkative, could be a bit long-winded on occasion. He would have to keep his eye on the clock, move the meeting along quickly if he was to stay on schedule.

Oh what the hell, he thought, as he reached the corner of Bruton Street. Alan's been special to me most of my life. I owe him . . . we go back so far, he knows so much – and he's my best friend.

Crossing the street, his eyes focused on the Jack Barclay showroom on the opposite corner, and when he reached the plate-glass windows he paused to admire the sleek Rolls-Royces and Bentleys gleaming under the brilliant spotlights. He was always promising himself one of these super-deluxe models, but he never seemed to get around to buying it. On the other hand, he did not have much need for a car for his personal use anymore. Corporate jets that sped around the world were more his style these days, and when he *was* on the ground there were always company limousines at his disposal.

He walked on past the Henley car showroom and Lloyds bank, and pushed through the doors of Berkeley Square House, the best commercial address in town and a powerhouse of a building. Here, floor upon floor, were housed the great international corporations and the multi-nationals, companies that had more financial clout than the governments of the world. Maxim thought of it as a mighty treasury of trade, for it did hundreds of billions of dollars' worth of business a year. And yet the buff-coloured edifice had no visible face, had long since blended into the landscape of this lovely, leafy square in the very heart of Mayfair, and most Londoners who walked past it daily were hardly aware of its existence. But it was the British base for an amazing number of mega corporations and the spot where the big bucks stopped.

Maxim crossed the richly-carpeted, white-marble hall, and nodded to the security guard who touched his cap in recognition. He stepped into the elevator and rode up to Alan Trenton's offices on the sixth floor. Trenton's secretary of many years responded to his knock and opened the door. She smiled warmly when she saw him standing there. 'Good evening, Mr West. Oh dear, I'm so sorry, do excuse me. I mean, Sir Maximilian.'

He swiftly brushed aside her apologies, flashed a dazzling smile. 'Hello, Evelyn,' he said, stepping inside briskly, shrugging out of his trenchcoat.

She took it from him, ushered him towards Trenton's inner sanctum. 'He's waiting for you.'

Maxim nodded, went in.

Alan Trenton was standing next to a carved mahogany console of Chippendale design, pouring Roederer Cristal Brut into a silver tankard. He was Maxim's age, yet appeared older. His figure was stout, he was of medium height, fair of colouring, and slightly balding above a ruddy face.

'Maxim!' he exclaimed, his pale-blue eyes lighting up with the most obvious pleasure. He put the bottle of Cristal down with a clatter, hurried across the faded but highly valuable Aubusson carpet, grasped Maxim's hand, put an arm around him, half embraced his oldest and dearest friend.

Maxim returned the gesture.

'It's good to see you,' Trenton said.

'And you, Alan. It's been too long this time. My fault.'

'No problem. I understand.' Alan's face filled with sudden glee, and he beamed. 'I know I've said it on the phone, but I feel I must say it to you in person . . . congratulations, Maxim, on your great honour.'

'Thanks, Stubby,' Maxim said, reverting to his old nickname for Trenton from their schooldays. He grinned hugely, punched Alan lightly on the arm. 'Who'd have thought it, eh?'

'*I* would, Duke, that's who,' Alan shot back, following Maxim's lead, using the name *he* had bestowed on the other man some forty-seven years before. 'And thanks for coming at such short notice, I know how pressed you are.'

'And why *am* I here?' Maxim's gaze turned quizzical. A dark brow lifted.

Trenton did not at first respond. He stepped over to the console, lifted the bottle. 'A drop of bubbly, old chap.'

'Thanks, but not really,' Maxim said, then instantly changed his mind, realising the champagne was in his honour. He added quickly, 'Of course, why not? But do make it a *drop*. A quarter of a tankard, please, not a full one like yours, Stubby.'

Maxim watched Trenton dispensing the champagne, waiting for him to open up, but when nothing was said about the reason for his presence, he casually strolled into the middle of the room and glanced around.

Alan had recently finished redecorating his office and Maxim liked the new ambience. A sense of elegance and warmth had been created with pine-panelled walls, fine English antiques and bucolic landscapes of the English countryside hanging in elaborate carved and gilded frames. All bespoke Trenton's life-long predilection for ancient objects and artifacts, which had developed into a very serious and consuming hobby. He had become a well-known collector, an avid bidder at mighty auctions. All that oil money to spend, Maxim commented to himself. North Sea oil money. Big Texas oil money. He had encouraged Alan to pursue his own ideas, to expand the family business after he had taken over from his father, had backed him to the hilt in every way, giving him moral and financial support. The combination had worked, and Alan's great prosperity over the past fifteen years pleased him greatly.

A moment later Trenton joined Maxim, handed him the champagne.

They clinked tankards. Alan said, 'Here's to your title. Wear it in good health, old chap.'

Maxim couldn't help laughing. 'Thanks. And here's to you, Stubby. *Your* good health.' Maxim savoured the icy Cristal, liking its dryness. He took another sip, then said, 'So, Alan, what *is* this all about?'

Trenton eyed him speculatively. 'How would you like to be a white knight?'

Maxim stared. A dark brow lifted again. This was the last thing he had expected.

There was a small silence.

'To come to the rescue of Lister Newspapers, I presume,' Maxim said at last.

Trenton was taken aback. 'Someone else has already approached you!' he exclaimed, managing to make his words sound like both statement and question.

Maxim shook his head emphatically, the expression in his dark eyes denying. 'Not at all. But that's the only company in London facing a hostile takeover bid, at least that I'm aware of. Anyway, how come you're involved?'

'Actually, I'm not,' Trenton was quick to say. 'I'm sort of – ' he paused, half laughed, groped for a word, came up with ' – a go-between. It's John Vale, my merchant banker, who is the one involved. The merchant bank acts for Lister Newspapers and John is very close to the chairman, Harry Lister, and is seeking to help him. He's aware we're old friends and asked me to arrange this meeting.'

'But it's hardly my bailiwick, I'm not interested in – ' Maxim abruptly broke off, looked towards the door as it flew open.

'Ah there you are, John,' Trenton said, hurrying to greet the newcomer, his genial hand outstretched. 'Come in! Come in!'

'Hello, Alan,' John Vale said, shaking Trenton's hand. He was in his late thirties, of average height, wiry, very English in appearance, with a fair skin, streaky blond hair and light grey eyes behind thick tortoiseshell glasses. He allowed Trenton to propel him across the room to its centre, where Maxim stood.

'Maxim, I'd like to introduce John Vale of Morgan Lane,' Trenton said. 'And, of course, this is Sir Maximilian West, John.'

'Glad to meet you.' Maxim thrust out his hand.

'It's my very great pleasure, Sir Maximilian,' John Vale responded, almost wincing at Maxim's vice-like grip, staring at him, yet trying to conceal, as best he could, his avid curiosity. Maximilian West was one of the world's most brilliant tycoons, a buccaneer like Sir James Goldsmith and Lord Hanson, both shrewd operators in the takeover game.

West more than outmatched them, at least in John Vale's considered opinion.

Leaving the two men standing together, Alan went over to the console, exclaiming, 'Champagne coming up immediately, John.'

'Thanks,' Vale replied. He turned to Maxim and smoothly began to make small talk, all the while studying him surreptitiously. West had the effluvium of power; it seemed to emanate from him. Vale had not expected such a good-looking man, though. There was something rather spectacular about that wide engaging smile, the very white teeth, the dark eyes filled with vivid intelligence. And that tan! It was the golden tan of a playboy garnered in some exotic winter playground, not that of a workaholic conglomerateur who spent the majority of his time cooped up in boardrooms and circling the globe in his private jet. The clothes were equally unexpected, hardly the usual drab garb of a typical businessman. More like movie star clothes, Vale thought, eyeing the grey, pure-silk shirt, the pearl-grey silk tie, the superbly-cut black gabardine suit that hung on West with such precision that it had undoubtedly been engineered by the world's greatest tailor for a large quantity of money. John Vale recognised at once that there was an intense glamour about Maxim West which had just as much to do with his personal magnetism as his dashing appearance.

Trenton's voice, booming out suddenly, interrupted Vale's thoughts and the discussion he was having with Maxim West about the filthy English weather and other trivialities.

'Here you go, John, a drop of the old bubbly for you,' Alan cried. 'And now we can get down to business. At least the two of you can. Although I've brought you and Sir Maximilian together, I intend to sit back and be the observer. The silent observer.'

Maxim chuckled. 'The day you do that I guarantee it'll snow gold bricks. You haven't drawn breath since you uttered your first word,' he said, but there was no hint of criticism in his voice, only warmth and great affection.

Alan threw back his head and roared. 'I suppose there's some truth in what you say. And *you* should know – after the years we've been together.' He ambled across the floor, brought the tankard of champagne to Vale. 'Good health,' he said.

The three men drank, and Trenton gestured to a group of chairs around a Georgian occasional table. 'Shall we sit?'

Once they were settled, Trenton again glanced at John Vale, and continued, 'I told Maxim why I asked him to come over this evening. I think you should elucidate further.'

Vale nodded, gave his attention to Maxim. 'Firstly, I'd like to know whether you *would* be interested in being the white knight for Lister Newspapers?'

Maxim frowned. 'I *honestly* don't know. Just as you were arriving, I had started to say to Alan that I didn't think a newspaper empire was my bailiwick exactly.'

'But why not, Maxim?' Alan demanded peremptorily, forgetting his vow of silence of a moment ago. 'Surely it's a perfect acquisition for you at this stage of your career. Think of the added power and influence you would have if you controlled Lister. A national daily, a national Sunday newspaper, and a galaxy of prestigious magazines.'

Maxim threw Alan a swift look but did not respond. Instead he addressed John Vale. 'What makes you think I'd be acceptable to the stockholders?'

'Harry Lister is certain of it; so are the other members of the Lister board. I agree with them, as do the directors of Morgan Lane.' Vale perched precariously on the edge of his seat, leaned forward, fixed his bespectacled, earnest gaze on Maxim. 'You have the name, a formidable reputation, and an extraordinary track record. You're not an asset stripper, far from it. The companies you have taken over have flourished under your good management. These things are tremendous points in your favour. Quite frankly, you're impressive, very impressive indeed, and that's why we're absolutely positive you'd be acceptable to the stockholders. Incidentally, so are Birch, Rider, stockbrokers for Lister Newspapers. They're as enthusiastic about you as we are, in point of fact.'

'Those *are* very kind words. Thank you,' Maxim murmured, and paused, steepled his fingers, brought them up to his mouth. He was thoughtful, then continued, 'Arthur Bradley's International Publishing Group has tendered an offer of five hundred million pounds for Lister Newspapers. As a white knight I would have to top that offer by at least two hundred million pounds.'

'Not necessarily,' Vale shot back. 'It could be less.'

'Two hundred million pounds, one hundred million pounds, what's the difference . . . it's still a big ticket,' Maxim remarked coolly.

'True,' John Vale agreed, nodding his head. 'But look at it this way, you stand to make a lot of money.'

'I don't always consider how much I might make,' Maxim replied in a quiet voice. 'Rather, I ask myself how much can I *lose*?'

'Oh I'm certain you wouldn't lose,' John asserted, sounding confident. 'I would like to give you some relevant information regarding Lister Newspapers, a few facts and figures.'

'Go ahead.' Maxim settled back in the chair, ready to listen.

At this juncture, Alan Trenton rose.

'If you'll excuse me, I'll attend to a bit of my own business,' he murmured and went to the far side of the office where he sat down behind his desk. He studied the faxes and telexes from New York, which had come in earlier, wrote succinct replies to be dispatched in the morning, perused other urgent papers, making notations on them.

Once he had finished, he looked at Maxim and John Vale. He saw they were still deep in conversation, decided to leave them to their own devices for a short while longer. There was nothing pertinent he could say, little he could contribute to their discussion. It was best he remain out of it altogether.

Swivelling the desk chair, Alan sat gazing out of the window which overlooked Berkeley Square. His thoughts drifted aimlessly for a few seconds, and then inevitably they settled on Maximilian West, as they generally did when Maxim was in close proximity. It was difficult not to focus on him, so powerful was his charisma and his presence.

It delighted Alan to see him in such great form, such good spirits. If one judged him by his appearance, Maxim looked as if he led a life of ease and pleasure in one of his many beautiful houses or on his floating palace of a yacht. Nothing was farther from the truth. He worked around the clock, was never off a plane, kept up the most killing pace – and yet somehow managed to remain remarkably unscathed. In fact, Alan often thought that Maxim thrived on it all. In the past nine years Maxim had been under excessive pressure and not so readily available socially, travelling the world at large as he did. Also, London was more of a stopping off point for him these days, even though he had his head office here and the house in Mayfair. Greener fields, in the shape of Manhattan, beckoned most beguilingly.

And Alan sorely missed Maxim.

He wished he saw more of him. They spoke frequently on the telephone, grabbed a quick bite or a drink together occasionally, but this was not quite the same as lunching and dining in a leisurely fashion, the way they had in the past. They had been inseparable as boys, equally close in their teens, and their friendship had continued into full manhood.

Best friends 'til the day we die, they had sworn at boarding school, and curiously enough this boyhood vow was holding true. And that's all that matters in the long run, Alan thought. To know in our hearts that we're always there for each other, that we can rely on each other no matter what the circumstances.

Spinning the chair again, Alan peered the length of his office, fixed his eyes on Maxim, observed him carefully for a few seconds. His old friend appeared to be quizzing John Vale, asking some hard questions, no doubt.

Vale was responding alertly, looking suitably impressed by his inquisitor. But then there was nothing unique about that. Everyone was impressed by Maximilian West. Startled, too, more often than not, when they first met him. He was *never* what anyone expected him to be. Nor did he *ever* do what people anticipated he would do. He had always been a maverick.

In his mind's eye Alan suddenly saw Maxim as he had been at fifteen, remembered that ghastly day when two boys from another school, bullies both, had picked on Maxim, sneered at him, called him filthy names, been immeasurably cruel as only the young can be cruel. Maxim, ashen-faced, his dark eyes blazing with rage, had instantly turned combative, had raised his hands like a boxer about to go on the attack. Ready to do battle for his best friend, he had brought his hands up too, wanting to fight at Maxim's side. And then the unexpected, the unanticipated, had happened, startling the crowd of boys, and him most of all. Maxim had dropped his arms to his sides and had walked away without uttering a word, his head held high, his immense pride, his uncommon dignity forming an unassailable shield around him. The group of boys who had been watching and jeering had fallen silent, had parted ranks with docility to let him pass, intimidated by the cold, implacable expression on Maxim's face, his lofty demeanour.

Alan recalled how he had run after Maxim, wanting to give him comfort, to make him feel better. But Maxim had not needed sympathy; he had even refused to discuss the matter, had turned morose and moody for the rest of the day. It was only later that night, after lights-out in the dormitory, that Maxim had finally mentioned the incident. As if in answer to Alan's unspoken question, he had hissed in the dark, 'I walked away because those cowards weren't worth fighting! I didn't even want to soil my hands by touching them!' He had expressed his contempt and disgust for the likes of the two bullies, and had gone on to proclaim, 'One day I'll be cock of the walk, just you wait and see, Stubby.' And then in a fierce whisper he had added vehemently, 'I'm nobody now! I have nothing now! But no matter how long it takes, I promise you I'm going to be *somebody*. And I'm going to have *everything*.'

He was. And he did. He had made it come true, perhaps beyond even his own wildest dreams.

Maximilian West was a man with the world in his arms.

Consequently he was envied by most men. Alan did not envy him. He was filled only with admiration for Maxim. He knew what a hard and difficult road he had travelled, the enormous leaps he had made, the chances he had taken. His was an extraordinary success story, an epic story, really, quite fantastical. He was a great magnate, his name was one to be truly reckoned with on the international business scene, and in the last fifteen years he had gone from millionaire to multi-millionaire to billionaire.

And only a couple of weeks ago, on the last day of December, the Queen's New Year Honours List had been announced. Among those titles and honours put forward by the Prime Minister for the Queen's approval was a knighthood for Maxim. It was for his enormous contributions to British industry at home and abroad, and he was now Sir Maximilian West, and could be thus addressed, even though his investiture at Buckingham Palace was not for three more months to come, in March.

Cock of the bloody walk *indeed*, Alan thought. And smiled. It was a deep smile, one of genuine pride and the greatest satisfaction. He revelled in Maxim's successes and triumphs, was always there on the sidelines, applauding. Maxim had been his hero at school. In a way, he still was. Alan supposed he always would be.

He glanced at Maxim again, and admiringly so. How wonderful his dear old friend looked. No, he doesn't, Trenton suddenly thought, startling himself, sitting up with a little jolt. He peered harder at Maxim. The dazzling facade was intact, but now, instinctively, he knew there was something terribly wrong. It was not possible to be close to a man for nigh on forty-seven years and not know him inside out. There was a shadow at the back of Maxim's eyes that he had not seen there for years; he wondered why he hadn't noticed it when Maxim first arrived. Perhaps because he'd been too busy congratulating him on his knighthood. Maxim's got trouble, serious trouble, Stubby decided. Is it the women? I hope to God not, he's had enough trouble with women to last him a lifetime. Well, whatever's wrong, and there is something, I'll offer to help. That's what a best friend is for.

Now Alan looked quickly at the watch on his wrist, the gold Patek Philippe which Maxim had given him last year for his fifty-fourth birthday. He saw that it was exactly nine-fifteen. Earlier, on the phone, Maxim had said he would have to leave by nine-twenty. Alan knew that in one second, certainly not much longer, Maxim would stand up, make his goodbyes and be gone. He was precise in many ways, and punctuality was one of his strongest suits.

Anticipating Maxim's imminent departure, Alan rose, went over to join him and Vale, as Maxim was saying to John Vale, 'The figures you've given me are interesting. However, I'm still uncertain whether or not I want to jump into the fray, make a counter offer for Lister. I really will have to give the matter some thought.'

Vale swallowed hard, striving to hide his deep disappointment that this meeting had not been more conclusive. 'Yes, of course, I understand perfectly, and I'm sure you understand that speed is of the essence. Lister are wide open right at this moment, exposed in so many ways. They're a sitting target for other corporate raiders. That's what worries us the most, that someone else, another company, might enter the bidding and go after Lister.' Vale exhaled heavily. 'You know what that could mean.'

'Only too well. *A bidding war.*' Maxim stood. 'If you drop the documents off at my house tonight, as you suggested, I'll study them later.'

Vale also rose, nodded. 'Yes, I will. And thank you very much for your courtesy and for listening.' He extended his hand, added, 'I'm most appreciative, Sir Maximilian.'

Maxim took Vale's hand. 'Now, if you'll excuse me I really must leave.' He glanced conspiratorially at Alan, winked, said as an afterthought, 'I have a dinner engagement and I would hate to keep the lady waiting.'

'I'll walk you to the lift, Duke,' Alan said, taking hold of Maxim's arm in a proprietary fashion, ushering him out. He wanted to get Maxim alone, to ask him what was the matter, what he could do to help.

When Alan Trenton returned to his office a few seconds later, John Vale peered at him myopically. Anxiety underlined his voice, as he asked with some urgency, 'Well, what did he say?'

'Nothing. At least not about Lister Newspapers and his intentions. He wouldn't, you know, not even to me. He's very secretive about his business, always has been. I can tell you for a fact that he shreds every document that passes through his hands. Afraid of leaks, I suppose.'

'Nobody knows him better than you, Alan. What is your assessment? What do you think our chances are?'

Trenton pursed his lips, pondered briefly. 'I honestly don't know.' He sat down heavily and looked off into the distance, a reflective expression invading his face.

John Vale followed suit, sat across from Alan Trenton, waiting patiently.

At length Trenton said, 'If it *feels* right to him, he'll go with it.'

'What do you mean exactly?'

'That's what Maxim has always said to me . . . that a deal's got to feel right. He goes on instinct. Gut instinct. He ignores analysts, reports, valuations, advisers. Gut instinct, that's what guides him.'

'Do you really believe that?' Vale sounded doubtful.

'Oh yes, I do! More importantly, Maxim believes it. But what he really means, of course, is that he relies on his *experience*, his *expertise*, his *great knowledge*. Plus his instinctive feel for the particular deal, the particular situation.'

Trenton picked up his silver tankard, swigged the last of his champagne, looked as if he was mulling something over.

'You asked me what my assessment is, John,' he went on at last, 'and it's this. If Maximilian West feels right about making an offer for Lister Newspapers he will do so. And if he feels wrong, or if he has no feeling about it whatsoever, then he'll pass. That's the way he is. Very cut and dried. *Precise.* It's his nature. Certainly he won't keep you dangling. You'll get a decision, and an answer, very quickly.'

'That's good to know at least. And by the by, Alan, whatever the outcome is, I'm indebted to you. I don't know how to thank you for arranging this meeting.'

'Very easily, old boy. Take me to dinner as you promised. *Now.* I'm starving.'

John laughed. 'That makes two of us. I booked a table at Mark's Club. Let's stroll over there, and after we've dined I'll leave the papers at Maxim's house in Chesterfield Hill. He said you'd give me the exact address.'

'Of course.' Alan pushed himself up. 'I'll clear my desk, then we can be off.'

Vale followed him across the room, hovered about.

At one moment, he remarked, 'I hadn't expected him to be such a handsome man. I've seen photographs of him in newspapers and magazines and none of them do him justice.'

'No, they don't. But then a lot of Duke's appeal lies in his personal charisma. I don't suppose you can take a photograph of that.'

'Why do you call him Duke?' Vale asked curiously.

'After Archduke Maximilian of Austria who became Emperor of Mexico in 1864,' Alan explained. 'Maxim was being a bit imperious with me one day at prep school, and I dubbed him that. He thought it was hilarious . . . anyway, the name stuck.'

'I see. Is it true what they say about him?'

'They say a lot of things . . . what in particular are you referring to?'

'That Maximilian West cares about only four things. The Prime Minister. The United States. Making money. And screwing.'

Alan glanced up, started to laugh. Recovering himself after a brief moment, he said, 'I know he holds Mrs Thatcher in the highest regard, is a great admirer of her policies, especially when it comes to business. And let's face it, old chap, he's flourishing under her regime. She's just had him knighted. Most certainly he loves the United States, he's been straddling the Atlantic for a decade or so. He spends as much time there as he does here, you know.'

A mischievous gleam entered Alan's eyes. 'And for as long as I can remember, Maxim's been very intense about making money, *and* making love to the ladies. Oh yes, he's a bit of a lady-killer, our Maxim is. As for the ladies, they, of course, find him quite devastating. Drop like ninepins at his feet.'

'All those wives, all those mistresses,' Vale murmured, a hint of awe echoing. 'How on earth has he managed to juggle them, and apparently with such adroitness?'

'I wouldn't know.'

'Haven't you ever asked him?'

'Good Lord, of course I haven't! I've never had the nerve,' Alan lied. He had no wish to discuss Maxim's unorthodox personal life any further with John Vale. He had said enough as it was. Certain things must always remain private. There had been a great deal of gossip about Maxim over the years and he was hardly going to add to it. That would be the worst kind of betrayal.

I know far too much, Alan thought, dropping his eyes, locking the top drawer of his desk. *All those confidences Maxim has shared over the years. And continues to share. But his secrets are safe with me. And he knows that, knows I will take them with me to the grave.*

TWO

For the second time that evening Maximilian West found himself shaking off a feeling of heaviness as he traversed Berkeley Square, heading back in the direction he had walked earlier.

Directly opposite Alan Trenton's office building, on the other side of the plane trees in the park in the middle of the square, was number forty-four. This was his destination. Here, in the basement of the beautiful old house, was one of the most exclusive nightclubs in Europe – the famous Annabel's.

Founded in the summer of 1963 by Mark Birley, and named after his wife Lady Annabel, from whom he was now divorced, it was *the* chicest of watering holes for the rich and famous, where the international jet set rubbed shoulders with movie stars and magnates and members of the British royal family. For the past twenty-six years it had remained very much the *in* spot, yet it had now gone beyond being merely fashionable. It had become legendary. And it was Maxim's favourite place to dine in London.

Within minutes of leaving Alan's office, Maxim was nodding to the uniformed doorman who hovered outside, ducking under the green awning and hurrying down the flight of steps into the club.

A bevy of familiar, smiling faces greeted him as he entered, and after shedding his trenchcoat he went over to the reception desk where Ted was waiting to welcome guests, as he was most nights of the week.

Maxim accepted Ted's quietly-spoken congratulations, exchanged pleasantries with him, signed the book, sauntered through into the bar-sitting room. Glancing quickly about, he saw that it was still relatively empty, and he took a small table in the corner, to one side of the brightly-burning log fire.

A waiter was instantly by his side, and he ordered vodka straight with ice and a chunk of lime, then settled into the squashy sofa, enjoying the comfort and warmth and the sense of ease that always came to him here.

He had been a member since the club had first opened its doors, and he liked the atmosphere, the intimacy that sprang from the blazing fire, the soft lights and deep sofas, the cheerful feeling created by the masses of fresh flowers in antique containers, the dark-red Oriental rugs and the pumpkin-coloured walls covered with a diversity of paintings. Wonderful dog portraits, cartoons by Landseer, Munnings and Bateman, oils of elegant women, some nude, some clothed, hung cheek by jowl, and at first glance seemed to have been put together with some sort of careless abandon. Yet there was nothing haphazard about their placement, if one looked a second time and a bit more carefully. They never ceased to delight his eye, to amuse him, and they were a source of constant pleasure, frequently brought a quick smile to his face.

To Maxim, Annabel's was more like an extension of Mark Birley's own house than a restaurant and nightclub, and perhaps this was the key to its enormous success. The bar area had the feeling of a country drawing room in a manor house, could never be mistaken for anything *but* an English drawing room at that, what with its mixtures of chintzes and paintings and flowers, its mellowness and charm. Quite aside from the inimitable and inviting ambience, there were the gracious staff to be thankful for, the excellent service they gave, and finally the type of unpretentious food Maxim preferred to eat. For the most part, English cooking at its best with a few continental dishes thrown in.

In his opinion there was nowhere in the world quite like Annabel's, and it was one of the things he sorely missed about London when he was away. He had not been in town for some weeks and he was glad to be back in his special haunt. Invariably, the tensions of the day left him the instant he stepped through its portals. He felt insulated against the world when he was at the club, cocooned within the familiar, pleasant surroundings,

attended to by the discreet and congenial staff. A home from home, he
thought, then added sardonically to himself: Except that I prefer this place
to home. But I don't have a home any more, do I?

Reaching for the drink, he took a quick swallow, leaned against the
cushions, forced himself to focus on the meeting he had just had in
Stubby's office.

He was curiously ambivalent about going after the Lister newspaper
empire, and he wondered why. Before he had a chance to focus on this
properly, ponder the reasons further, he saw Louis, the manager, coming
through the bar-sitting room, heading in his direction. Louis's face was
wreathed in smiles. They were old friends, had known each other for
over thirty years, ever since the days Louis had been the *maitre d'* at the
Mirabelle Restaurant in Curzon Street, just around the corner from the
club. There was a camaraderie between them that sprang from the past,
many shared experiences, the genuine affection they held for each other.

Maxim jumped up, beaming.

They greeted each other warmly, shook hands. Louis congratulated him
on his knighthood, and they stood chatting, catching up with each other's
news. After a few minutes, Louis was summoned to take a phone call in
the dining room, and he excused himself. Maxim sat down on the sofa
and picked up his drink, but no sooner had he done so than he found
himself rising once more as his personal assistant came floating into the
bar-sitting room on a cloud of perfume.

Graeme Longdon was an American, thirty-seven years old, tall, bean-
pole thin, with curly brown hair shot through with a hint of auburn and
the brightest of green eyes. Not classically beautiful in the given sense
of the word, she was, nonetheless, a lovely young woman, very arresting,
with a broad brow, high cheekbones above rounded cheeks, and a full,
wide mouth that was forever smiling. She was from Richmond, Virginia,
was independent, feisty, and outspoken.

Maxim considered her to be one of the smartest people he had ever
known, and she was his good right hand.

Tonight she was dressed in a superlative black velvet suit, which to his
discerning eye was most obviously an *haute couture* number from Paris.
The excellently-styled jacket above the pencil-slim skirt was trimmed
across the shoulders and yoke with jet-bead embroidery and silk tassels.
Her long, shapely legs were encased in sheer black hose, her feet elegantly
shod in a pair of black satin pumps. The only jewellery she wore were
large diamond earrings shaped like flowers, and, on her wrist, a narrow
diamond watch designed by Cartier in the thirties.

Maxim went to meet her, took hold of her elbow, guided her over to
the corner table.

'You look lovely,' he said, forever appreciative of a pretty woman, always full of genuine gallantry, ready with a compliment.

'Why thank you,' she said, turning to him, widening her smile. It lit up her face. 'I always feel I must get myself done up in my best fancy duds to come to this place. So I dashed back to the Ritz to change. That's why I'm late. Sorry, Boss,' she said with her usual breeziness and casual style.

'There's no need to apologise,' he replied, returning her smile, as usual faintly amused by her irreverent manner, her persistence in calling him *Boss*. When she had first come to work for him and had started to address him in this way, he had been irritated, had tried to make her stop. But she had ignored his protests, or they had flown over her head, he wasn't sure which, and *Boss* it had remained since then. He had grown used to it by now, no longer minded. It was of no consequence to him, really. And he admired her for being herself, for not compromising her personality to suit somebody else's idea of the proper corporate image. She was honest and forthright and rather blunt, unnervingly so at times. He laughed to himself. Graeme had nicknames for everyone in the company, at least those she dealt with on a day-to-day basis. Most of the names were highly appropriate, and some disconcertingly so.

'What's a few minutes between us,' Maxim remarked as they sat down. 'In any case, you're worth the wait, Graeme. You're positively blooming tonight. Let's settle down, relax, have a drink before dinner and you can tell me what happened after I left the office. What would you like? A glass of champagne, as usual? Or something else?'

'Champagne, Maxim, please.' Graeme put her black velvet evening purse on the table, made herself more comfortable on the chair opposite him, crossed her legs, adjusted her skirt. There was an air of expectancy about her; it was as though she could hardly contain herself.

Once he had ordered her drink, she bent forward, her manner suddenly grown confidential, her vivid eyes more alive and eager than ever, her intelligent face aglow, flushed pink with excitement. 'I've come to a conclusion about the Winonda Group, after being on and off the phone with Peter Heilbron in New York for the last couple of hours,' she exclaimed, her tone rising slightly. 'I think we should go for it, Boss, make a bid! It's a cinch for us. The perfect company for a takeover despite what appear to be certain problems. I've studied the last two faxes I received from Peter and – '

'If they're sensitive, I presume you've shredded them,' Maxim cut in swiftly.

'Of course! How can you think otherwise!' She sounded astonished, looked at him askance. 'Am I not your clone, Boss?'

Maxim bit back a smile, made no response.

Graeme rushed on, 'Winonda has a number of unprofitable divisions, but these would be easy to liquidate. We would keep the profitable divisions, of course, and simply reorganise them, give them a bit of the West International streamlining.'

She paused when the waiter brought the flute of champagne to her, waited until they were alone before continuing, 'What makes the deal so attractive to me is the real estate Winonda owns just outside Seattle. It looks worthless at first glance, and especially so on paper. Undervalued, actually. It's run down, and it's in a very bad area. However, I know it has *great* value, that it's a big *asset*.'

Maxim raised a brow.

Graeme explained. 'It's an asset because a Japanese company wants to buy it. They're in the process of buying up the entire area, actually, and they want the Winonda real estate so that they can tear down the existing buildings, redevelop the land by constructing a hotel, a shopping mall, and offices on it.'

'Then why hasn't Charles Bishop sold?' Maxim's brow furrowed. 'That strikes me as particularly odd. He's extremely shrewd, usually very fast on the draw.'

'He turned them down flat. Didn't want to know, apparently. And not because they weren't offering plenty. I believe they went as high as two hundred and seventy million dollars.'

'What's the catch?'

'There isn't one. At least, not for us. If we owned Winonda we could sell the real-estate holdings tomorrow. And to the same Japanese company. They're standing in the wings. Waiting. They'll wait in vain, of course, as long as Bishop's the president of Winonda. You see, his father died in a Japanese prisoner-of-war camp, that's why he won't strike a deal with them.'

When Maxim said nothing, Graeme remarked in a low voice, 'Put very simply, he's letting his personal feelings get in the way.'

Maxim was thoughtful. After a moment he glanced at her. 'You have good vibes about this deal, don't you?'

'Absolutely, Boss!'

'So do I. And I have from the beginning, ever since you put forward Winonda as a possibility for us. Call Peter tomorrow, tell him to get the acquisition team moving at once. And good for you, Grae. I'm impressed. You must have done a great deal of research.'

Graeme shook her head. 'A little, but not as much as you probably think. By one of those odd coincidences, my cousin Sara lives in Seattle now. She's with a bank. I asked her about Winonda, after you'd told me to go ahead and analyse the situation. She mentioned that some Japanese company had been sniffing around. She'd heard about their interest in the Winonda real estate through her boyfriend, who's a partner in an accounting firm. There was a nasty leak from somewhere, I suspect.'

She grinned at Maxim. 'I guess you're right about shredding machines, Boss. You can't be too careful. In any event, I ran with the information Sara had passed on to me and had it checked out. It proved to be correct.' Graeme stopped, cleared her throat. 'The stockholders of the Winonda Group might not be too happy to learn that their president passed up millions of dollars for a parcel of real estate that nobody else seems to want. Poor judgement on Bishop's part, wouldn't you say?'

'I can understand his reasoning in some ways. But yes, I suppose in the final analysis you're right, Graeme.'

'As the president and CEO of a public company he ought to have put personal sentiments aside,' she stated in a voice that was surprisingly cold and deliberate.

Maxim gave her a swift look. He knew how tough, even ruthless, she could be at times. But her assessment of Bishop seemed harsh. Fleetingly, a faint shadow crossed his face. He frowned. 'Yes,' he said laconically, having no wish to continue this conversation, and reached for his glass.

Graeme sat back, gazed at him through appraising eyes. A muscle twitched on his cheek and he appeared strained all of a sudden and she wondered why. She was about to ask him if something was wrong and then changed her mind immediately. He was a very private man, never revealed much about himself or his feelings, and he hated anyone to pry, to try to winkle their way behind that powerful facade of his.

She lifted her flute of untouched champagne. 'Cheers,' she said. 'Here's to the Winonda Group. May it soon be ours.'

Maxim said, 'To Winonda.'

She took another long swallow of the Dom Perignon, began to relax for the first time that day. They fell silent for a short while, both caught up in the complexity of their own thoughts. It was Graeme who spoke first, breaking the momentary lull. 'How did your meeting with Alan Trenton go?'

'It wasn't with Alan. Oh, he was there, of course, but he wanted me to meet his merchant banker, John Vale of Morgan Lane, who had a proposition for me.'

'What kind of proposition?' she asked, her eyes instantly lighting up. Like Maxim she was excited by business, and the prospect of cutting a new deal thrilled her. It gave her a high in much the same way it did him.

'To come to the rescue of Lister Newspapers,' he said.

Graeme let out a long, low whistle that was audible only to Maxim. 'My, my, that *is* something,' she said in a soft voice. '*And?*'

Maxim began to tell her what had transpired earlier that evening, leaving nothing out.

Graeme listened avidly, giving him her full attention, not once interrupting him, knowing how he detested interruptions, but at the same time wondering what he would do, asking herself whether he *would* go after the Lister empire. Her mind raced. He was tough-minded, fearless when it came to business, but not really a gambler. He was too cautious to be that. And Lister might well prove to be something of a gamble. Rectitude and prudence he had in abundance, and she admired those traits in him. Yet, when she looked back over the seven years she had worked for him, there had been times when he *had* taken chances, and now, on reflection, it occurred to her that they had been rather big chances at that. Would he consider Lister Newspapers worth the risk? One never knew with him. He was so hard to read accurately – and to second guess. He might do anything, jump either way. He called her his good right hand. The problem was, most of the time she never knew what his left hand was doing.

Perhaps it was the contradictions, the unexpected in him that she found so fascinating – and irresistible. She stifled a sigh. She had always been a little bit in love with him, even though he had never displayed one iota of interest in her. Not as a woman, at any rate. Oh, he paid her lovely compliments about her appearance, said flattering things about her work, but that was as far as it went. She was his executive assistant, and therefore forbidden. He was far too involved with his business ever to mix it with anything that remotely smacked of pleasure, sex or love.

And besides, he was married – of course! And there were hints of another woman.

Still, there were times, like now, when they were not in a work environment, when she sat looking at him, listening to his mellifluous voice, enjoying his company, that she fell completely under his spell, became hopelessly vulnerable to him. He was the most dangerously attractive man she had ever met. It was not only his face, his powerful dark gaze, his elegance and distinction, but the enigma of him. For there *was* something extremely mysterious about Maximilian West.

And of course there was his charm. Maxim had fatal charm, the kind that makes women commit terrible indiscretions. He was a natural born lady-killer who, without doing one single thing, had women flinging themselves at him. Then again, on yet another level, there was the intellect, the brains, the drive, the energy, the ambition and the success. It was a combination that spelled one thing – power. And power was exciting to her, an extraordinary aphrodisiac like no other she had ever known.

'You look as if you're drifting off into Never-Never Land with Peter Pan and Wendy,' Maxim exclaimed somewhat sharply for him, giving her a hard stare.

'I'm right here and standing to attention, figuratively speaking that is,' she said, forever swift on the draw and ready with a riposte. 'If I appear to have a glazed expression it's only because I'm concentrating on your words, Boss. And truly, I *have* heard everything you've just said.' She offered him a bright, reassuring smile. 'Let me sum up for you – John Vale of Morgan Lane wants you to be the white knight for Lister. Everyone involved wants it.'

'That's right,' he said more mildly, sounding mollified.

'And you're not interested, are you?' she went on, hoping to prove to him that she *had* indeed been listening, had picked up the nuances implicit in his voice. Her eyes held his.

'No, I don't think I am,' he admitted.

'Are the figures that poor?'

'On the contrary, they're quite impressive. In fact, the company's in great shape.' He let out a sigh. 'It's *me*, Grae. I'm just not excited about it, I guess. Not *enough* excited, anyway. No fire in my gut. I don't believe I want to pick up my sword and go into combat for a newspaper empire. That's more up Rupert Murdoch's alley. Come to think of it, John Vale ought to have asked Rupert to be the white knight, not me.'

Maxim stopped, laughed ruefully. 'Vale is dropping the Lister accounts off at the house later, and I suddenly wish he weren't. I don't think I can summon up the energy to look at the wretched things, never mind study them.'

'Do you want me to do it for you, Maxim?'

'We'll see.'

He motioned to one of the waiters, ordered two more drinks, then turned to her, put his hand on her arm. 'I'm not staying in London for the weekend after all, Grae.'

'That's no problem. I can be ready whenever you say. I'm half packed. When are we leaving? Tomorrow or Saturday?'

'*I'm* leaving tomorrow. On the morning Concorde.'

From his emphasis on his first word she knew he was leaving alone. He rarely did that when they were together on business, and unable to disguise her surprise she stared at him. 'Oh,' was about the only word she could muster.

'Normally I would say come back on Concorde with me, but I'd like you to stay in London this trip, to follow through on a few things for me, Grae. You should be able to finish up by the end of the day tomorrow. You can fly back to New York on the company jet whenever you wish.

Tomorrow night, Saturday, Sunday or even Monday. The plane's at your disposal.'

'London at the weekend doesn't appeal to me especially,' she murmured, 'but maybe I will stay in Europe. I could go to Paris for a couple of days. It might be fun.' There was a moment's hesitation on her part before she leaned across the table and said in a low conspiratorial voice, 'No problems at the New York office, I hope, Boss?'

'No, no, of course not! You'd be the first to know. I'm going back a little earlier than I'd planned because there's a personal matter I must attend to, and I want to get it out of the way this weekend.'

Instantly she thought: *It's a woman and he's got trouble with her.* She said, 'What is it you want me to do for you here in London?'

'There're a couple of banking matters you'll have to attend to, also, rather than cancelling it, I'd like you to take my place at the meeting with Montague Reston and Gerald Sloane. There'll be no problem, you'll handle yourself well.' A faint smile touched his mouth. 'And handle them well, I might add.'

'Okay, whatever you say, Boss. But I'd like a briefing about the Reston deal.'

'Of course. We'll discuss it later. Now, shall we order dinner? I see Louis heading in our direction.'

THREE

It was one-fifteen in the morning by the time Maxim got back to his house on the corner of Chesterfield Hill and Charles Street.

He had escorted Graeme to the Ritz Hotel after their dinner at Annabel's, and had then walked home, crossing Piccadilly and heading through Half Moon Street into Mayfair. There was no longer any hint of rain, the air was crisp and dry and usually he would have enjoyed the short walk. Yet all evening he had been fighting this feeling of weight, almost of oppression.

He let himself in, locked the front door behind him, hung his black trenchcoat in the hall cupboard, and paused for a moment, listening.

Nothing stirred. The house was quiet, perfectly still. The staff had gone to bed, were no doubt already fast asleep, and the only sound was the hollow ticking of the antique grandfather clock in the imposing marble foyer where he stood.

Turning off the light, Maxim went up the curving staircase more slowly than usual to the second floor. He crossed the landing, went into the master bedroom where he shed his clothes and put on pyjamas and a dressing gown. He did everything with swiftness before hurrying through into the study which was part of the master bedroom suite, wishing he felt better.

Marco, the butler, aware of Maxim's nocturnal habits of working late, studying documents and balance sheets well into the early hours, had turned on the lamps and banked up the fire before retiring to his own quarters. The silk-shaded lamps cast a roseate glow throughout and the logs burned brightly in the grate behind the mesh fire screen, threw off welcome warming heat. Maxim seated himself at the French *bureau plat*, glanced at the telephone messages Marco had placed under a glass paperweight and put them to one side. None were of any great importance, could be dealt with before he left for the airport in a few hours or so. Picking up a pearl-handled paper knife, he slit the manilla envelope which John Vale had dropped off earlier and took out the sheaf of papers.

It was with only the smallest degree of interest that he looked over the accounts of Lister Newspapers which he had fanned out on the desk in front of him. One of Maxim's greatest assets was his ability to read a financial statement well, and to size up a company quickly with his own special brand of business acumen. This he did now, understanding at once that Lister Newspapers was indeed a good buy, by anybody's standards. Excellent, in fact. And yet he felt no quickening of his pulse, no excitement in his veins, no thrill at the thought of going after it. Indisputably, his attitude had not changed since the meeting in Alan Trenton's office. He simply was not interested in making a play for this company. Or was that true for *any* company?

It struck Maxim, with some force, that he was not particularly interested in the Winonda Group either, and this brought him up in the chair with a small start, instantly made him scrutinise his sudden change of mind.

He had told Graeme to go ahead earlier for a variety of reasons. It was one of her bigger deals; he knew how much it meant to her, he had no wish to disappoint or discourage her. Also, right at the outset he had recognised that Winonda would be an important acquisition for them, an enormously valuable asset to West International when it came to the overall picture of the conglomerate. But he had to admit that he much preferred her to handle the deal herself – with the help of Peter Heilbron and the financial team in the New York office. Certainly he did not want to be the chief combatant in the actual battle, had no interest in being out there on the front line. He would give advice from the trenches. His troops would have to do the hard hand-to-hand fighting.

Maxim frowned intently, wondering about his reluctance to put himself in the middle of the action. He had always been a big part of it in the past, the pivotal point. Surely business wasn't beginning to bore him, was it? How could that be? Business was his life, wasn't it? Anastasia had always said so. He winced at the thought of his first wife.

A weary sigh escaped, and he ran his hands through his hair distractedly, conscious that he had not been himself of late. He kept up the facade, of course, the facade of charm and magnetism that the world had come to expect. But inside, at the very core of his being, he felt empty. There was a bleakness in his soul, he was joyless for most of the time, and increasingly he was held in the grips of a terrible melancholia he could not fully comprehend. Nor, indeed, explain.

A peculiar feeling began to settle over him, one of claustrophobia. No, oppression. He felt as if he was gagging, suffocating, and he had the most pressing urge to get out of the room, a compulsion to run and not stop running until he had put great distance between himself and this place. He wanted to be far, far away.

A chill coursed through him, and he shivered; it was as though someone had walked over his grave. With this strange thought, goose flesh speckled his arms and his face and he was startled at himself, unaccustomed as he was to feelings of discomfiture, of uneasiness.

Maxim swung his head, glanced around the study, asked himself why he wanted to escape this room. He did not understand. It was his favourite spot in the entire house, filled as it was with treasures from which he had constantly drawn enormous pleasure. Each item had been so lovingly placed here by Anastasia and himself, and he recalled the satisfaction they had derived when they were searching out the antiques, the objects of art and the paintings in England and on the Continent.

The ancient oak *boiserie* that panelled the walls had been found in an old manor house in Normandy. The French writing desk where he now sat was discovered in an *antiquaire*'s shop in the Rue du Bac on a weekend trip to Paris. The wall sconces were picked up when they had been travelling through Tuscany, while the remarkable horse paintings by Stubbs had been bought from a peer of the realm whose country seat was in Yorkshire. Altogether it was an eclectic mixture that somehow worked, mostly because the pieces were compatible with each other and shared one important quality, that of excellence.

Although the possessions in his study were beautiful, not all of the items were of great value. Yet they had always meant a lot to him. Now, seemingly, they no longer mattered, since, for some reason he could not understand, he was regarding them through jaundiced eyes.

Irritated with himself, and also baffled, Maxim rose, walked over to the handsome William and Mary inlaid chest under the window, opened a bottle of carbonated water and poured himself a glass. He took a long swallow, carried the glass back to a chair in front of the fire, and sat staring into the flames, a look of abstraction settling on his face.

After a while, as if his mind had been flooded by bright light, he began to see things as they actually *were*. With a rush of clarity he understood the change in himself, understood his dilemma.

He was a man in crisis.

This sudden self-knowledge came from the deepest, innermost part of his psyche and it gave him a bitter jolt. He sat up straighter, his eyes flaring, and then he closed them convulsively, momentarily stunned.

But it was *true*. There was no point in denying it anymore, as he had been doing for so long. He was at the most critical point in his life . . . he could not go on any longer . . . could not live the way he had been living . . . and yet he did not know what to do about himself . . . or about his life.

He was immobilised by uncertainty. Rendered helpless by indecision. Hamstrung by the situations he himself had created. Held in limbo by the people who populated his life.

Placing the crystal tumbler of water he was clutching on the small table next to the chair, Maxim dropped his head into his hands. He was brimming with dismay, completely at a loss. For once he had no solutions for his problems. After a few minutes he lifted his head, smoothed back his hair with one hand, forced himself to relax. And he began to ruminate on his life.

His dear old friend Stubby truly believed he had everything. The world believed he had everything. In reality he had nothing. Oh yes he had immense success, immense power, fame of a kind, money to burn and houses galore and a luxury yacht and a slick private jet and the other grand accoutrements of privilege and great wealth. And he hobnobbed with those who were as rich and renowned as he was. There was his knighthood, a great honour bestowed on him by the highest in the land, an honour he had never sought, nor tried to buy, but which had come to him through his own merit. And whilst he would never belittle its importance to him, was proud of it, in fact it did not fill the terrible void in his life.

He was alone. And lonely.

He was estranged from the women he was involved with, who no longer brought him the remotest bit of joy. His children were lost to him: perhaps only temporarily, but nevertheless they were lost at this moment. And now he was facing the possibility that his work, the most enduring of all his passions, and his greatest pleasure, was beginning to pall on him. The idea was insupportable. He balked at the mere thought of it. In all truth, it frightened the hell out of him.

And when he added up all of these points, the bottom line was very telling indeed. *Dismal*. He was in the red on every personal level . . . emotionally bankrupt.

He was an unhappy man, flailing around in an over-abundance of misery. That was the crux of it. But then had not happiness been an elusive stranger for the best part of his life, transient at best?

A cynical laugh rose in Maxim's throat and he choked it back, thought: What an overworked word it is, happiness. And who the hell is happy? At least for very long, anyway? Some fortunate people did know *contentment*, others gained a certain *peace*. But that was about it. Unluckily he was not blessed with either state of mind.

Rising, he began to pace the floor restlessly, his mind careening around in dizzying circles.

Eventually he was able to calm himself sufficiently in order to look at things as clearly as he possibly could. He regrouped his thoughts and redirected his focus, concentrated on the women in his life.

Two women to be exact.

Adriana. His wife. *Blair*. His mistress.

Blair was pushing for marriage. Adriana would not acknowledge that such a word as divorce even existed. And he was caught between the two of them, like a fly trapped in amber.

He was not so sure he wanted to continue living with Adriana. On the other hand, did he really want to divorce her? What were his true feelings about Blair? And would marrying her solve his problems? He remembered something, and it made him laugh out loud. A famous wit had once said that when a man married his mistress he created a job vacancy. If he married Blair would he then be tempted to fill the vacancy? Find himself a new mistress to replace the one who had become his wife?

What a cynical thought *that* was. He laughed again, but still without a trace of mirth. Was he the kind of man who would always need a mistress whatever the circumstances in the marriage? Perish the thought, he added under his breath.

In his mind's eye, Maxim pictured the people who occupied his life, who were important to him. How did *they* view *him*? He did not have to ponder that for more than a split second.

To Adriana I am the faithless husband wanting to escape the marital bonds.

To Blair I am the lover grown ambivalent, distracted, less caring, in my preoccupation with my business.

To Anastasia I am her best friend, but only a friend, nothing else.

To my children I am the busy tycoon who has no time for them. I have been cast in the role of the heavy. I am important because I pay their bills, but in their eyes I am no longer the loving father they once adored.

To my mother I am the son she is the most proud of, her favourite perhaps, and yet half the time she is disapproving of me because she cannot condone my private life, my personal behaviour.

But I am *not* the person they think I am, he said to himself. None of their perceptions of me is accurate. They don't really know me. On the other hand, I don't know myself. Not anymore. I have no sense of my own identity. I don't know who I am, why I'm here, what my purpose is on this planet, or what it's all about in the last analysis. I'm confused, lost, adrift, floundering.

These admissions were so staggering, so unacceptable to Maxim that they made him catch his breath in surprise, and he paused in his pacing, endeavouring to squash them. He had no wish to validate them by giving them any kind of credence whatsoever.

Ultimately, though, he was unable to banish these unprecedented and shattering self-revelations. All were inescapable truths. And no matter which way he twisted and turned everything around in his head he finally had to admit to himself that he would have to face up to them, tackle them head-on sooner or later.

It was three o'clock by the time Maxim went to bed.

He did not really sleep, merely dozed fitfully on and off for several hours. Finally, around six, he got up, went into the bathroom to shower and shave. Once he was dressed, Marco brought him a pot of coffee and toast, and whilst he had his light breakfast he wrote a detailed memo to Graeme, explained what he wanted done in London, and outlined strategy for the meeting she was to have with Montague Reston.

At exactly eight-thirty he left the house carrying his black trenchcoat and a briefcase, his only piece of luggage, and was driven off to Heathrow in one of West International's limousines. At the airport he was swiftly checked in, and went immediately to the Concorde departure lounge, where he sat reading the morning newspapers until he and the other passengers were boarded at ten o'clock.

Fastening his seat belt and settling down, Maxim glanced around and was relieved to see the plane was not as jam-packed as it had been on the last few occasions he had flown it. He had chosen to go on to New York by Concorde rather than travel on his personal Grumman Gulfstream jet because it was much faster, only three hours and forty-five minutes, even less time if there were no strong headwinds.

Maxim opened his briefcase, took out a sheaf of papers and buried his head in them for the first hour of the flight. He accepted a cup of tea, refused all other drinks and snacks, and gave his entire attention to his business papers, hardly glancing up, so intense was his concentration. When he had done as much work as he could, he locked the folders in his briefcase, pushed this under the seat, made himself comfortable and closed his eyes. He found it impossible to sleep, but did manage to relax sufficiently enough to rest his tired body. Half an hour later Maxim roused himself, sat up, looked out of the window.

They were floating through a vast stretch of cumulus clouds, soaring higher and higher above the Atlantic. He stared into the infinite space, contemplated Alix, his daughter. *She* was the reason he had decided to return to New York a few days earlier than he had originally planned. He wanted to see her, to talk to her, to spend the weekend with her. He desperately needed to put things right with his first-born child. They were both at fault, she more than he in so many ways. Nevertheless, he was quite prepared to take full blame for the rift that had developed between them. He would apologise, ask her forgiveness, if necessary. In fact, he would do just about anything to win her trust again, to have her back in his life.

FOUR

A female voice he did not recognise answered the telephone. 'Alix West's office. Can I help you?'

'I'd like to speak to Miss West, please,' Maxim said.

'I'm sorry, but Ms West isn't in today,' the young breathy voice went on to inform him. 'May I ask who's calling?'

'This is her father. To whom am I speaking?'

'Oh good morning, Sir Maximilian,' the voice said in a tone that now sounded a little awed. 'This is Geraldine Bonnay, her new assistant. Alix flew to California this morning. On business.'

'I see. When will she be returning to New York?'

'Hopefully on Monday, Sir Maximilian. It's a quick trip. She has a meeting with a client in Beverly Hills tomorrow and is flying right out again on Sunday. Unless there are unexpected problems, of course. She *will* be calling me sometime tomorrow. Can I give her a message?'

'No, not really,' Maxim began, and paused, thought quickly. 'As a matter of fact, Miss Bonnay, I'd rather you didn't say I telephoned today. I have something special for her . . . a surprise,' he improvised. 'So please, not a word, it would only spoil everything.'

'Of course I won't tell her!' Geraldine Bonnay assured him, her genuine sincerity echoing down the wire, 'and just in case you do change your mind and want to talk to her tonight, or on Saturday, Alix is staying at the Bel-Air Hotel.'

'I think not . . . the surprise, you know. But thank you for the information anyway.'

'Oh it's my pleasure, and it's been lovely talking to you, Sir Maximilian.'

'Likewise, Miss Bonnay. My thanks again. Goodbye.'

'Goodbye.'

Maxim let his hand rest on the phone for a moment, fighting back his disappointment that Alix had left New York the very same day he had arrived. He had so wanted to see her, to spend time with her. He ought to have checked with her about her plans, he supposed, made sure she was going to be in the city for the weekend. Obviously that would have been the most intelligent and sensible thing to do. On the other hand, if he *had* phoned from London he would have alerted her to his arrival and she, more than likely, would have fled. Or found innumerable reasons why she was not able to see him. Surprise was always the most successful technique to use with her he had discovered long ago.

He sighed under his breath. There was no doubt in his mind that Alix still harboured all manner of grudges, even though she persisted in denying this. He was equally convinced that her smouldering dissatisfaction with him was more than likely being fanned into a roaring bush fire by her brother. Michael had always had enormous influence over her, ever since their childhood, more so than anyone else and in an infinite number of ways. Furthermore, his son had his own axe to grind these days, filled with grievances and resentment as he was, and not a little anger. Maxim was patently aware of that anger, and the frustration in Michael, even though he, too, denied there was anything wrong just as his sister did. Children, Maxim muttered to himself. Why do they want to make things so difficult? As if life isn't hard enough without having them inventing problems and blowing things out of all proportion.

Shifting slightly in the chair behind his desk, Maxim turned his head, allowed his gaze to rest on the photograph of Alix that stood framed in silver on the ebony table near the window along with other family portraits. This had been taken six years ago to commemorate her twenty-first birthday, and it struck him yet again what a lovely young woman the tomboy of a child had grown up to be, so fair and creamy of skin, with delicate bone structure in a face whose expression was invariably so serene, so calm it made him catch his breath. But most beautiful and striking were her eyes. Widely spaced and enormous, they were an unusual pale grey-green and filled with pellucid light. Alix was tall, as he was, and lissome, with a fine athletic body, and she moved with considerable grace and elegance. Aside from her great looks, his daughter had a quick, intelligent mind, and was extremely clever, most especially when it came to business and finance. In fact, she was as smart as her brother, perhaps even a fraction more astute than he, which was saying a great deal for her since Michael was brilliant.

Alix had wanted to come and work with him since her teens. He had been thrilled at the idea of having his daughter in the business, and everything had been planned most carefully. And then four years ago, just before she started at the New York office, they had quarrelled badly. It had been about her entanglement with a man whom he considered to be highly disreputable, amongst several other things which now seemed too petty to recall, and she had gone off in a huff and started a business of her own.

Without as much as batting an eyelash, she had opened an office in the middle of Manhattan, had set herself up as an art and antiques broker, working primarily with English and European dealers and leading art galleries.

She bought and sold only the most sought-after items, the kind of rare, precious and costly objects and paintings that generally made it to the auction floor of Christie's and Sotheby's. Some few years earlier she had taken several courses at Sotheby's in London, and her knowledge of paintings and *objets d'art* was considerable. Also, she had been gifted with the beady, critical eye of a true expert who recognises excellence instantly and can just as quickly and easily spot a fake. These attributes, plus her extraordinary taste and natural head for business, had proven to be an invaluable combination. She had been successful right from the start and he was inordinately proud of her. Nonetheless, he still hankered after her presence at the office, wished she worked alongside him.

Perhaps it was not too late. Maybe he could still lure her into West International – once they had made their peace. And he was determined to do that. He heard his mother's voice reverberating in his head . . . 'It's never too late to repair the damages of the heart, Maxim. It's never too late to start over again, to come back to a loved one by mending a quarrel.' His mother had said that to him countless times over the years and he had always believed her. He still did. He had to, because that belief reinforced his hope that he *would* win Alix back, that they would be as close as they were before their ghastly row.

He had never missed anyone as much as he missed his daughter.

Alix's absence from his life was so acutely felt it was a genuine physical pain in the region of his chest. A savage ache that rarely if ever dissolved. He hurt in a way he never had before. No, that wasn't strictly true. He had once experienced this same kind of longing, this yearning for someone a long, long time ago.

It had been for Ursula.

Once again Maxim's eyes strayed to the photograph of Alix.

She had the same fine blonde hair and flawless complexion as Ursula, the same lovely, luminous eyes full of dreaminess and tranquillity.

Ursula. He had thought of her so often recently; he began to wonder why she had been so much on his mind of late. Was it because his painful feelings about Alix echoed his feelings about *her*, the other one he had loved with such intensity and so completely? These feelings had been buried for so long, and buried so deep at that, he had been momentarily startled a few weeks ago when *her* face had sprung wholly formed into his mind for the first time in years. His memories of Ursula were very clear . . . unalloyed.

Maxim unlocked the top drawer of his desk and reached into the back, took out the black leather wallet which he kept there for safety. He opened it and gazed at the picture of Ursula held therein. It was a black and white shot, faded now, but time had not dimmed the lustrous eyes, the bright curving smile so full of trust and hope.

The wallet was worn, the leather cracked in places. He smoothed his hand over it, remembering. It had belonged to Sigmund . . .

Eventually he slipped it back into the drawer and he was surprised at the tightness in his throat, the way his eyes smarted, were unusually moist.

Resolutely pushing away this unexpected rush of profound emotion, Maxim stood up and walked across the cream-coloured stretch of carpet. He stood gazing out through the metal-mesh curtain that covered the plate-glass window of his office high up in the Seagram building, focused his attention on Park Avenue far below, but he hardly saw anything, so puzzled was he. The troubled mood that had beset him in London in the early hours of the morning seemed somehow to persist, and now, to cap it, he found himself dwelling on his past. Tearing his mind away from Ursula, Maxim brought his concentration to bear on the present. He had come to New York for the weekend hoping to see his daughter. But Alix was not available until Monday, perhaps even Tuesday. Today was Friday. The whole weekend stretched ahead.

What to do? More precisely, where to go?

He had a variety of choices. None appealed. There was his beautiful apartment on Fifth Avenue. If he went there he would undoubtedly be confronted by Adriana, whose sole purpose in life these days was to fight with him. He could go to the house he owned in Sutton Place, where he had installed Blair. If he did he would be exposing himself to a weekend of Blair's nagging and veiled threats, except that they were not particularly veiled any more. There was his bucolic farm in Connecticut, but Adriana might conceivably get wind of his arrival in New Preston and come rushing out – to fight with him in the country instead of the city. She was certainly combative enough at the moment.

What he really wanted was to be alone.

Entirely alone.

There was only one place for that, and it was the perfect place. His beach house in East Hampton. Closed for the winter though it was, the house was more or less kept ready for his sudden arrival at any moment. It was a year-round house, proofed for the cold weather, and in the winter months the heat was kept on a low temperature at all times. Elias Mulvaney, his gardener and handyman, watched over the house, checked on it every day or so. And Mrs Mulvaney went in to dust once a week. All he had to do was telephone Elias and instruct him to go over to the house later that afternoon to turn up the heat, and arrange for Mrs Mulvaney to come in on Saturday and do a few chores. It couldn't be simpler.

Maxim swung away from the window, strode back to his desk, well pleased with the idea of driving out to East Hampton for a couple of days. He would be able to indulge himself in that rare commodity – solitude. And do nothing except listen to music, take long walks on the beach. Mostly, though, he would do some very serious thinking, endeavour to bring a semblance of order to the chaos in his head.

He had an unconventional private life. It had long needed to be put in order. Yet he had not been able to commit himself to any action. Perhaps the time had come to do this, to normalise things. Also, he must make some decisions about Adriana and Blair. Only then would he be able to take himself in hand, get to the root of the personal crisis that threatened to engulf him, and in so doing solve his own inner conflicts.

The decision to go to the Hamptons for the weekend galvanised him, brought him out of the introspection that had held him in its grip since the previous night.

He opened his address book, picked up his private phone and dialled Elias Mulvaney's number on Long Island. It rang and rang. No one answered. Maxim glanced at the clock on the desk. It was just turned eleven. No doubt Elias was making his daily rounds, checking on other homes, doing odd jobs for the permanent residents in the village who also employed him on a part-time basis. And Mrs Mulvaney was more than likely out marketing for the weekend groceries.

No problem, Maxim murmured to himself. I'll reach one of them sooner or later. He pressed the intercom. 'Douglas, would you come in, please.'

'Right away.'

Within a couple of seconds, Douglas Andrews, Maxim's private secretary at the New York office, hurried in carrying a sheaf of papers. A New Yorker born and bred, Douglas was about thirty-three, short, fresh-faced, dark-haired, with a pleasant, outgoing disposition and a willingness to work around the clock for Maxim. He had been his private secretary for five years and was devoted, loyal and fiercely protective.

'Here are the legal documents on the Mystell deal which you asked me for. Peter Heilbron's secretary just dropped this memo off for you. It's regarding the Blane-Gregson takeover,' Douglas said. As he reached the desk, he placed the papers in an empty chromium tray on the right-hand corner, then seated himself in the chair facing Maxim, his notebook in his hand, his pencil poised.

'Thank you,' Maxim said, glancing at the pile in the tray. 'I'll attend to those shortly. There's a couple of things I'd like you to do, Dougie. Rent a car for me, please, and have it outside at four o'clock, and send one of the secretaries over to Bloomingdale's food department to buy some provisions for me. A cold chicken, potato salad, a piece of Brie, some French bread and a carton of milk. That should do it. Okay?'

'Yes, I'll get on it right away.' Try though he did, Douglas could not quite keep the surprise out of his voice, and he gave Maxim a curious stare. 'Are you going somewhere?'

An imperceptible smile flicked onto Maxim's face. '*Obviously*, Dougie. To my beach cottage in East Hampton, to be precise. For the weekend. Alone. I want a bit of peace, some quiet time to think. And I don't want *anyone* to know where I am. *Understand?*'

Douglas nodded. 'I do. Absolutely. I'll deal with the car and send Alice over to the store, but are you sure that's enough food for you? Maybe she should buy more.'

'No, no, the chicken and the salad will do me fine for tonight. I can easily pick up some groceries in East Hampton village on Saturday morning.'

'You're pretty brave, leaving at four o'clock,' Douglas volunteered, frowning. 'You'll have all that commuter traffic on the Long Island Expressway to contend with. It might be a better idea to drive out to the Hamptons later, say around six or so.'

'Oh it's not all that bad in winter, Dougie.'

'I guess not. Still . . .' Douglas's voice trailed off. He could see that Maxim was already thinking about something else, and so he got up, headed for the door.

Maxim reached for the documents in the chromium tray, and called across to Douglas, 'Please ask Peter if he can have a quick lunch with me. And if he *is* available, you might let the Four Seasons know that I'd like my usual table today, if that's possible. Around one.'

'Yes, Sir Maxim,' Douglas murmured, opening the door, closing it quietly behind him, wondering if Maxim really was going to spend the weekend alone. Or did he have an assignation with some new lady love? Lucky devil, Douglas thought, he's got it all. And then some. What I wouldn't give to be in his shoes.

But would I really? Douglas asked himself as he sat down at his desk a moment later. Would I want that bitch Adriana for a wife? And as for the girlfriend over on Sutton Place, she's not much better. More than once he had seen a look in Blair Martin's baby blues that had immediately alerted him to her scheming ways. Graeme Longdon called her Miss Greedy Guts behind her back. Spot on, Graeme was.

How did such a lovely guy, such a *prince* of a guy, like Maxim West get hooked up with those two barracudas? Douglas sat shaking his head in bafflement. He came to the conclusion, as he had so often in the past, that men who were brilliant in business were not necessarily very smart when it came to the women in their lives. Fools rush in, he thought.

Still shaking his head, Douglas lifted the phone, dialled Peter Heilbron, head of West International's acquisition team.

The phone was answered after one ring. 'Heilbron here.'

'It's Dougie. The boss wants to know if you can have a quick lunch with him today. Downstairs. At one. I hope you can, because he seems a bit down in the mouth to me.'

'I'm free . . . at least I'll make myself free,' Peter said quickly. 'And what exactly do you mean by *down in the mouth*, Dougie?'

Douglas heard the concern in Peter's voice, the anxiety surfacing. He said, 'When the boss walked in off the Concorde this morning I thought he looked really lousy. Preoccupied. No, troubled is a better word, and a bit sad, or so it seemed to me. And that's not like him. You know what an expert he is at veiling his feelings.'

'Yes, I do. Business? Or personal, Dougie?'

'I'm not sure . . . personal most probably.'

'It has to be. There are no problems here, or at the London office that I know of . . . and I'd know – ' Peter bit off the end of his sentence. I hope to God those two women are not on the rampage again, he thought, dismay rising. He cleared his throat and said carefully, 'Whatever it is, it can't be too serious, Dougie. He would have mentioned it to me, if only in passing. I'm sure it's merely tiredness.'

'Yes,' Douglas agreed, deeming discretion to be the wisest policy when it came to the subject of the boss. He had no intention of speculating, gossiping with Peter. 'I'm sure you're right,' Dougie continued. 'He *has* been travelling a lot these past few weeks. By the way, nobody knows he's in town except you and me and your secretary. I have a feeling he wants to keep it that way.'

'I get your drift, Douglas, my boy,' Peter responded. 'That's my other line ringing. Please tell the boss I'll pick him up in his office just before one.'

FIVE

It took Maxim two and a half hours to drive from Manhattan to East Hampton.

By the time he reached the charming old village on Long Island the bleak January sky, so cold and remote and colourless, had long since deepened into curdled grey then quickly turned the colour of pitch. Only a few stars littered the horizon far out over the black and endless sea, and the orb of a moon, clear, high-flung, and silvered, was constantly obscured by scudding dark clouds.

Maxim glanced at the clock on the dashboard as he turned off Ocean Avenue into Lily Pond Lane, noted that it was almost six-forty-five. Not bad going, he thought, as he drove on, heading towards the Georgica Beach end of the lane where his cottage was located.

He had bought the house twelve years earlier. It was his private little retreat. At least that is the way he thought of it, and referred to it, and apparently his message had been clearly received by Adriana and Blair, both of whom knew better than to descend on him without an invitation, and these he rarely issued. He mostly stayed there by himself, or with his colleagues from West International.

Within a few minutes he was pulling up outside.

The cottage had grey shingles, white-painted shutters, a black door, and neat, squared-off chimneys. Set a little back from the road, it was fronted by sloping lawns, now covered with a sprinkling of hoary frost, along with a number of giant oaks which offered privacy the year round and plenty of cool leafy shade in the heat of the summer.

Although it was not a large house by Maxim's standards, it more than adequately suited his needs, the type of bachelor life he led when he came out to the island. It was spacious without being sprawling, and the layout was well planned; the hall, big family kitchen, dining room and study were at the front of the house, the living room, which flowed into a library, was at the back. These two adjoining rooms overlooked the swimming pool, a small pool house and flower gardens; nestling at the far end of the rear lawn, beyond the flower beds, was a copse of trees that afforded the property additional privacy on this side of the house.

The upstairs consisted of two floors. On one were Maxim's bedroom, bath and dressing rooms; on the other, two guest rooms with their own bathrooms, plus a third, larger bedroom which had been converted into an office, equipped with two modern desks, a typewriter and a computer, plus fax, xerox and shredding machines, as well as a battery of telephones.

Because of this super-efficient office, which Maxim thought of as a command post, he could come to the cottage whenever he wished, yet still be in touch with his business empire around the world. Often he brought along Douglas Andrews and Graeme Longdon, sometimes Peter Heilbron, to work on pending deals, especially in the summer months when they were glad to escape from the sweltering heat of the city for a few days at a stretch.

After parking against the kerb, turning off the ignition and the lights, Maxim took the Bloomingdale's shopping bag from the back seat and alighted from the rented Jaguar.

It was a bitter night, with an icy wind blowing in from the Atlantic. He glanced about. The lane was in total darkness; there was not the slightest glimmer of friendly light from any of the other houses. But as he strode rapidly up the path between the lawns, the moon came out from behind the banked-up clouds, bathed the cottage and the path with silvery radiance. For a few moments it was like daylight.

Out of the corner of his eye Maxim noticed the station wagon parked a bit further along, wondered who it belonged to, instantly dismissed it as he hurried around to the side entrance of the cottage. He let himself in through the kitchen door, retrieved the bag of food he had dumped on the back step, and switched on the lights. Pushing the door closed with his foot, he carried the bag over to the circular table which stood in the centre of the floor.

The blue-and-white tiled kitchen was spotless. Everything gleamed brightly, was in its given place, and the room looked as if Mrs Mulvaney had only just cleaned it.

Perhaps she *did* do it today, Maxim thought. He had not succeeded in reaching either of the Mulvaneys before leaving the office, and aware of their diligence and reliability it now struck him that they might easily have been here when he was ringing their home.

Maxim shivered, became conscious of the chill in the air. The heat was on as usual but he realised that it needed to be turned up on a cold night such as this. Still shivering, he headed in the direction of the front hall, where the controls for the heating system were located in a cupboard under the stairs.

Pulling open the door leading into the hall, Maxim suddenly stopped in his tracks, one foot poised on the step. There was a faint noise, a pinging sound like metal hitting metal. It was barely discernible, but because Maxim's hearing was extremely acute he always picked up the slightest sound wherever he was.

Puzzled, he stepped out into the hall.

Light from the kitchen streamed around him, and he could not fail to miss the television set standing on the floor, along with various pieces of equipment from the office upstairs.

Once more there was that odd pinging sound, then a small crash, a muffled curse.

The noises were coming from the living room, and immediately all Maxim's senses were alerted to trouble. There was apparently someone in the house beside himself, an intruder, no doubt about that.

Moving with stealth, noiselessly crossing the hall, Maxim opened the door a crack. The living room was dark, as was the adjoining library. The latter was in his clear line of vision and he instantly saw the pinspot of light from a flashlamp, which was being trained around the room.

Deciding that surprise was his best bet, Maxim struck the master switch on the wall. Instantly, six table lamps in the two rooms blazed fully to life, flooding the area with brilliance.

Startled, the intruder swung around, saw Maxim. He was not very tall and slightly built, dressed entirely in black. He was holding a large black nylon laundry bag that bulged and was obviously filled to the brim with loot.

The burglar stood gaping at Maxim.

'Drop that bag!' Maxim yelled irately, his expression one of furious anger. The man did nothing, continued to gape. There was a dumbfounded look on his face, and he appeared to be momentarily paralysed.

With a rush, Maxim sprinted across the floor, heading directly for the intruder, confident he could tackle and overpower him before calling in the police to apprehend him.

Just before Maxim reached him, the burglar pulled a gun and fired.

Maxim heard the report, felt the bullet slam against his chest. He went down at once with a thud, sprawling between the living room and the library. The look of astonishment on his face changed to one of stunned shock.

Maxim thought: *This can't be happening to me . . . it can't be ending like this . . . not after all I've been through . . . I can't be dying at the hands of a petty thief . . .*

The burglar stood stock still, listening.

He wondered if anyone had heard the shot, then dismissed this idea at once. There was nobody around. These houses were summer places. That's why he had headed for the area earlier. He'd already pulled two other jobs down the block. Easy pickings they'd been. He hadn't had to waste anybody in the other houses though. No one had walked in and surprised him, that's why. Shame about the guy who just had. But he'd had to protect himself. The guy was big, powerful, could've taken him easy.

The burglar walked over to the body, looked down at it dispassionately. The man he had shot was lying on his side. He did not stir. Blood stained the front of his pale blue shirt, was already seeping onto the grey carpet, turning a patch of it a funny rust colour.

Shoving the gun back into the waistband of his trousers, he pivoted swiftly, returned to the library, grabbed a few more silver trinkets, threw them into the laundry bag. There was a pinging sound as they struck the items he had stolen from other homes in the vicinity. Glancing about, satisfied that he had ripped off the best of the small stuff here, he left the living room, switched off the lights as he headed out. He went through to check the kitchen, doused the lights there, returned to the hall.

He stood listening again.

The darkened house was as silent as the grave. So was the street. Nothing moved. No cars drove past. Methodically, he began to carry the pieces of equipment and the television set to the front steps. Once everything was outside, he dropped the latch on the door and pulled it tightly shut behind him. Still moving with speed and expertise, he went up and down the path until all of his booty had been stowed in the station wagon. Sliding in behind the wheel, he drove off without a backward glance.

He did not see one solitary person, nor any traffic, as he sped down Lily Pond Lane. He knew he was safe. Nobody ever came out here in this kind of freezing weather in the dead of winter. The body would not be found for weeks. And anyway, he couldn't be linked to the man's death. He had been smart, cool. He'd not left a single fingerprint, not even half of one. He knew better than that. He always wore gloves when he pulled jobs.

*

Elias Mulvaney sat at the kitchen table in his small, comfortable house behind the railway station in East Hampton. He was enjoying the warmth of the blazing fire, his second cup of coffee and a jelly doughnut on this icy night, and thinking about the afternoon he and Clara had just spent at their daughter's house in Quogue.

It had been a red-letter day for them, visiting their first grandchild, revelling in her good health and prettiness, and in Lola's happiness. She and Mickey, her husband of ten years, had been waiting a long time for this baby. Yep, it's been the grandest day, Elias thought, and it has given Clara a real boost, made her forget her rheumatism. Clara had stayed on in Quogue for the weekend. Elias was certain she would be fussing and bustling, playing mother hen to the child and Lola, but he didn't think there was any harm in that. None at all. Do her good, he decided, and picked up his mug, drank the rest of his coffee.

The shrilling of the telephone broke the silence in the kitchen, made Elias sit up with a small start. He rose, ambled across the floor to answer it.

'Mulvaney here.'

'Good evening, Elias, this is Douglas Andrews.'

'Hello, Mr Andrews!' Elias exclaimed warmly, his grizzled, weather-beaten face lighting up. Douglas Andrews had been a favourite of his for several years. 'How've you been?' he asked, genuinely interested.

'Very well, thanks, Elias. And you?'

'Can't complain,' Elias replied.

'I'm calling you because I've been trying to reach Sir Maximilian at the cottage, but there's no reply. I was wondering if you'd heard from him this evening?'

'Well, no I haven't,' Elias said, sounding surprised. 'Been in Quogue all day, didn't get back until seven. I didn't even know Sir Maxim was out here.'

'He did try to get hold of you several times today. Obviously, since you were in Quogue, there was no answer. Sir Maxim left the city around four-fifteen. I rented a Jaguar for him and he was driving himself. I figured it would probably take him about three hours, or thereabouts, and I started to call him around seven-thirty. I have a number of messages for him. I don't understand why he's not there, since it's now turned eight already.'

'Yes, Sir Maxim should have reached East Hampton by this time,' Elias agreed. Because Douglas Andrews sounded so worried he tried to reassure him. 'Mebbe the line is wonky in some way or other, it's been mighty cold and windy out here these last few days, and we've had a lot of rain.'

'Yes,' Douglas said and paused. He took a deep breath, then continued, 'I must admit, I'm growing concerned. I hope he hasn't had an accident on the road.'

'Oh I'm sure he hasn't!' Elias exclaimed. 'Sir Maxim's a careful driver, you know that. Now don't you worry none, there's more'n likely a good explanation.'

'It's very important that I speak with him tonight, Elias, and I wonder if you'd mind going over to the cottage, checking things out for me?'

'Sure, I'll go immediately, that's no problem. Just give me your number so I can call you the minute I get there.' As he was speaking Elias picked up the pencil near the message pad, licked the end, quickly scribbled down Douglas's number as it was reeled off to him.

'Thanks, Elias, I'm very appreciative,' Douglas finished.

'I'm glad to be of help, Mr Andrews. Now remember what I said, don't you worry none, you hear?'

'I'll try not to,' Douglas replied, knowing that he would.

They hung up, and Elias hurried out into the passageway. He opened the top drawer of the chest, took out his bunch of house keys and slipped them into his trouser pocket. Hanging on a coat stand near the door were his down-filled parka, a woollen scarf and a cap with ear flaps, and these garments he took down and put on. He picked up his gloves and left at once, anxious to get over to Maximilian West's place as fast as he possibly could.

The pickup truck Elias used for running around the village was parked in front of his house, and he clambered in more agilely and swiftly than he usually did, and drove off down the street with a screeching of tyres.

Once he had crossed the railway tracks he sped through the village, heading for Lily Pond Lane, driving through streets unimpeded by traffic this evening. East Hampton was deserted, and it looked as if every one of the locals had left along with the summer residents. Within minutes Elias arrived at the grey-shingled cottage.

Alighting from the pickup truck, he walked briskly to the Jaguar parked immediately in front of him, shone his flashlight on the windows, peered inside. The car revealed nothing.

Elias swung around, began to walk up the path between the frost-covered lawns. As he approached the house he suddenly experienced such a strange sense of apprehension he was startled, and he stopped, taken aback at himself. He had been born and brought up in East Hampton, and in all of his sixty-five years of living here he had never felt uneasy or afraid.

But at this moment he was filled with a certain trepidation, and he did not understand why. It was eerie.

Elias looked up at the house.

The moon was high, a great chunk of silver shining vibrantly, casting its bright glow across the lines of the roof, the chimneys, the towering trees. The cottage was thrown into relief against the dark backdrop of the sky and the copse, and it looked unnaturally gloomy and sombre, almost sinister. No welcoming lights winked in the windows as they normally did when Maximilian West was in residence.

If Sir Maxim is inside then why are all the lights turned off? Elias asked himself, and continued to stare at the house worriedly. He knew Sir Maxim had arrived because of the Jaguar parked in the street next to his pickup truck. He wondered if Sir Maxim had had a heart attack or a stroke, and was lying somewhere in the house stricken and unable to phone for help. Sir Maxim was a young man, and he looked healthy enough, but you never knew about anybody these days. On the other hand, he could have gone for a walk. Elias dismissed this idea the moment it entered his mind. Who would go wandering around the neighbourhood on a freezing, bitter-cold night such as this? It then occurred to him that someone driving their own car could have picked Sir Maxim up and taken him out to dinner.

This last theory was the most reasonable explanation so far, and a feeling of vast relief washed over Elias. He hurried up the path, strode purposefully around to the side of the house and halted at the kitchen door.

Even though he was now convinced that Sir Maximilian West had gone to dinner with a friend, Elias nevertheless rang the doorbell several times. When there was no answer he took out the bunch of keys, found the right one, and let himself into the house. He switched on the lights, closed the door behind him, and, walking into the middle of the floor, he called out, 'Hello, hello, anybody home?'

His question was greeted by total silence, but this did not particularly surprise him. He swung his eyes around the kitchen, spotted the Bloomingdale's shopping bag, went and looked inside, saw that it was filled with provisions for the weekend. Nodding knowingly to himself, he then strolled over to the door leading into the main entrance hall, determined to investigate further on the off chance that Sir Maxim *had* been taken ill.

When Elias opened the door, such a strong sense of foreboding assaulted him again, the hackles rose on the back of his neck, and he shivered. Telling himself he was being a stupid old fool, and clamping down on this unexpected feeling of dread, which he considered to be ridiculous, he put the light on, glanced about, saw that there was nothing untoward here in the hall.

Reassured, Elias walked across to the double doors leading into the living room, flung them open, and flicked down the master switch. Instantly he saw the body on the floor.

He gasped, then exclaimed out loud, 'Oh my God!' His chest tightened, and for a split second he was rooted to the spot, unable to move, his eyes staring, the expression on his face one of mingled horror and alarm.

After a moment or two Elias managed to take hold of himself and he walked over to the body. The shock he experienced was like a violent punch in the belly, and he gazed down at Maximilian West disbelievingly, feeling as though his legs were turning to jelly. He thought he was going to keel over, and he gripped the back of a chair, took several deep breaths, trying to steady himself.

Eventually he was a little calmer and he stepped closer, saw the blood, the gunshot wound, and his heart sank with dismay. The injury was serious. He knelt down, peering into Maxim's face worriedly. It was ghastly, the colour of bleached bone. Elias searched for signs of life, brought his head nearer to Maxim's chest. He was breathing. Just barely. Elias took hold of his wrist, felt for a pulse. It was faint but it was there.

Elias straightened, his face stark, his eyes glassy with shock. Who had done this? And why? Rage flooded him, and he thought of searching the house looking for clues. Instantly he changed his mind. Whoever had shot Sir Maxim had doubtless fled without leaving any telltale evidence. Besides, it was vital that he get help immediately, act with speed if he was to save Sir Maxim. He went to the desk, picked up the phone and dialled.

'East Hampton Village Police. Officer Spank speaking.'

'Norman, it's Elias here. I'm at the West house out on Lily Pond Lane. Sir Maximilian West has been shot,' he said in a voice that was both shaky and shaken. It faltered slightly as he continued, 'I just found him. Call Southampton Hospital for an ambulance. He's alive but he looks as if he's lost a lot of blood. So tell them to hurry. And you'd better get here as fast as you can.'

'As soon as I've contacted the hospital I'll be over,' Norman Spank said. As an afterthought, he added brusquely, 'Don't touch anything, Elias,' and promptly hung up.

Elias sat down heavily in the chair near the desk, fumbled in his pocket, pulled out the piece of paper on which he had written Douglas Andrews's phone number in Manhattan. He dialled it, and as the number began to ring he braced himself to give the young man the terrible news.

Maxim floated in space . . . in a great white void . . . in a vast nothingness.

He wanted to open his eyes. He could not. He felt as if they were permanently sealed. It was as if the top and bottom lashes were glued together.

Where was he?

He did not know. He hardly cared. His body, which a moment ago had seemed weightless, now felt as heavy as lead, and immovable.

Gradually he became aware of voices. A man's voice, clear, resonant, a voice he had never heard before. The man was saying something about blood transfusions, a bullet which had lodged near the heart.

And then Maxim heard a woman speaking. Her voice filled the air . . . it was light . . . musical . . . and it seemed familiar, yet he could not quite identify it.

'He's not going to die, is he, Doctor Morrison?' the woman asked.

'We're doing everything to save his life,' the man replied. His tone was sombre. 'He lost a lot of blood at the time of the shooting, and, as I have explained, the operation to remove the bullet has been delicate, complicated. He *is* in a very serious condition, I'm not going to mislead you about that.'

'But he does have a chance, doesn't he?' the woman persisted.

The doctor did not answer immediately. Then he said, 'Fortunately, Sir Maximilian is a healthy man, strong, robust. That's an important factor. And he is in the best of hands here at Mount Sinai. He's getting superior care and treatment, and he is being monitored night and day.'

Maxim made a supreme effort and finally he managed to lift his eyelids. He blinked, adjusted to the light.

The room where he was lying was quite large.

He saw a man in a white coat. That must be the doctor.

Then he became aware of the others standing at the bottom of the bed.

The women.

They were grouped in a semi-circle. He was conscious of five pairs of female eyes focused on him intently, watching him, waiting. *His mother. His first wife. His third wife. His mistress. His daughter Alix.*

All of the women in his life were assembled here, keeping vigil over him.

He snapped his eyes shut. He did not want to see them, nor deal with them.

Everything suddenly came back to him. He remembered driving to Long Island in the rented Jaguar, going into the cottage in East Hampton, surprising the intruder. Then the man had pulled a gun and shot him. He could not remember anything after that.

The doctor in the room had just mentioned Mount Sinai. So he had

been brought to New York. How long had he been here? He had
no idea.

He wondered if he was going to die. He didn't want to die. He wanted
to live.

Teddy. Where was Teddy?

Maxim tried to open his eyes but the effort to do so was far too great.

*He wanted Teddy. She could save him. She had always saved him in
the past.*

He could not die now. He must live. He had so much to do. So much
to put right.

Maxim tried to speak but the words would not come out of his
mouth.

Teddy. Oh Teddy where are you? Help . . . help . . . me . . .

He felt himself drifting back into the vast white nothingness, that great
vaporous void that had engulfed him before, and he fought it, but it was
too strong for him in his weakened state and it overwhelmed him.

And finally he succumbed to it, fell into a deep unconsciousness
once more.

PART 2

URSULA

BERLIN

1938

Thou shalt not be afraid for the terror by night; nor for the arrow that
flieth by day; Nor for the pestilence
that walketh in darkness; nor for the
destruction that wasteth at noonday.
A thousand shall fall at thy side, and
ten thousand at thy right hand; but
it shall not come nigh thee.

Psalm 91: The Bible

SIX

The woman stood before the Empire-style cheval mirror in the bedroom, staring hard at her reflection.

Slowly she turned, studying the gown. She had bought it on a trip to Paris three years ago and it was by Jean Patou, her favourite couturier. She had worn it only once since then and now she saw that it had retained its incomparable style and elegance, as had the other Patou creations she owned.

Tonight she had wanted to wear a simple dress, which was why she had chosen this particular one, a floor-length column that fell in fluid lines from shoulder to hem. The sleeves were long, the bodice plain, the neckline high, skimming across the throat, while the back was worked into a draped-cowl effect. Made of matte crepe and cut with superb skill, it was the colour, nevertheless, that caught the eye. Called Patou Blue, it was almost, but not quite, violet.

This vibrant shade was the ideal foil for the woman's Nordic colouring. Her hair was a shining silver gilt, her skin creamy, her eyes a misty grey-blue, luminous, fringed with thick blonde lashes. She was of medium height, but her slender figure and long coltish legs made her look taller. Her feet and ankles were delicate, well shaped, and she had aristocratic hands, slim, with tapering fingers. It was the combination of her physical attributes, her ability to wear clothes well and her inherent good taste that gave her an elegance of appearance that was quite singular. Gentle of manner, the overall impression she projected was a mixture of femininity, great breeding, and intelligence. Her name was Ursula Westheim. She was thirty-four years old.

Satisfied that the gown was appropriate not only for the reception and dinner at the British Embassy, which she was to attend that evening, but that it also suited her mood of reserve, her sense of restraint, she slowly walked across the floor in the direction of the dressing table. But when she came to the white marble fireplace she paused, stood warming her hands at the huge log fire that blazed up the chimney and took the chill out of the air on this cold winter night.

After a moment she found herself turning inward, sinking down into her myriad thoughts, as she was wont to do of late. Introspective of nature though she was, this characteristic had grown and magnified, become more pronounced in the past year. She had to watch herself rigidly, particularly at social functions, since she had developed a habit of drifting off, carried along by her thoughts into a place known only to her, and where no one else could follow. Her husband Sigmund endeavoured to understand; he was infinitely patient with her and gentle, but she was conscious that his family, most especially his mother and his sister Hedy, found her remote, impenetrable. She could not help this. Her thoughts were like inchoate monsters in her mind, forever present yet not wholly formed and therefore all the more troubling.

She lived with a nagging anxiety that never seemed to leave her these days. Moreover, she no longer felt safe anywhere, except perhaps when she was in this house. It was her haven, her place of beauty, her bastion against the ugliness in the world outside its doors, her strong citadel. There were moments when she truly wished she did not have to leave it, and, in a certain sense, there was very little for her beyond these walls.

The Berlin she had been born in, and where she had grown up, no longer existed. Today it was a city of fear, of brutality and thuggery, of treachery and betrayal, of grimness and virulent rumour. It was teeming with the Gestapo, the Secret Police who stalked the streets, the beer halls and the cafés; frozen-faced SS men were everywhere one looked, as were Hitler's unholy gang of thugs, posturing and ridiculous in their operetta uniforms, screaming shrilly and striking theatrical poses, for all the world like toy soldiers playing war games. Except that their games were deadly, dangerous, and of course they were not toy soldiers, not even soldiers, but murderers with evil intent in their hearts.

Last year she had been at a reception at the French Embassy on the Pariserplatz when Hitler had walked in suddenly, flanked by Göbbels and Göring and several of his other cronies. She had been startled to see how small they were, unimpressive rather ordinary little men who looked quite different in reality than they did in their photographs in newspapers, which made them seem invincible. She had thought they appeared a bit foolish in their fancy-dress uniforms, and it was, for a brief moment, difficult to take them seriously as they hurried past, strutting, arrogant, vulgar, and bloated with self-importance. But that moment had been fleeting, and indeed she took them seriously. *Very seriously*. The power they embodied was only too real. And it was a terrifying power.

She was forever asking herself how such a large number of people had allowed themselves to be led by the nose by a man like Hitler, a former vagabond and derelict who wasn't even a German, but a jumped-up, uneducated Austrian corporal who could not speak the German language properly. Yet, amazingly, many believed he had only the welfare of the German nation at heart, had fallen under his spell, had been duped by him, considered him to have extraordinary brilliance and ability, not to mention great magnetism, and they were mesmerised by him and by his demagoguery. Weren't they aware of the frighteningly ruthless aspects of his terrible creed? How could they possibly think he was their saviour? He was leading them down a road to hell.

She had voiced these thoughts to her dearest friend Renata von Tiegal recently, and Renata had said, 'The Germans have a tendency to love false Gods, to worship false idols. And don't let any of us forget that.'

And then Renata's husband Reinhard had remarked in a regretful voice, 'Hitler should have been stopped years ago. The Western Alliance could have done it. But they didn't, and now I'm afraid it's too late. For us. For them.' Kurt von Wittingen, who was also present that evening, had finished softly, 'The British, the French and the Americans failed to understand one basic fact. That the Nazis didn't want power because of the economic situation. They wanted power.'

Well, they had power, didn't they? Ultimate power. Ursula shivered involuntarily, gripped the mantelpiece, and rested her forehead on her hands. She closed her eyes. *What to do? What to do?* This question was her constant companion, endlessly reverberating in her head. Panic flooded through her, but after only a moment she got a grip on herself. What she would do, what they would all do, was simply keep going. That was the only answer. There was no alternative. One day at a time, she told herself, I'll get through one day at a time.

After a short while she lifted her face, and her eyes swept the room. How normal it looked and therefore so reassuring. Her bedroom was truly beautiful, such a tranquil setting with its mixtures of pale greens in the watered silks that splashed over the walls, hung at the windows, covered chairs and a chaise longue. The furniture was French, finely-scaled antiques from her favourite Louis XVI period, and here and there were scattered elegant and exquisite trinkets and small objects which she had collected over the years or had inherited from her family. Rose-quartz boxes, miniature watercolours, antique porcelain snuff boxes and vinaigrettes, Meissen figurines, and silver-framed photographs of family and friends, those dearest to her and whom she loved the most.

And everywhere there were bowls of fresh, hot-house flowers spilling their bright colours and fragrant scents into the room, which glowed at this hour with the muted light from crystal lamps shaded in pink silk.

The superb bedroom was made all the more superb by the art. Her eyes came finally to rest on the paintings by Auguste Renoir, and she admired them yet again, and as usual she was awed. How magnificent they looked against the pale green walls. Two were paintings of nudes, another was a portrait of a mother with her two daughters, and the fourth depicted a garden in summer. To Ursula their tints were breathtaking: shell-pink and pearl, deep rose and lustrous gold, soft pastel blues and greens and the most glorious of yellows. All were light-filled, warm and sensuous, quite wondrous to behold. They were part of the Westheim Collection which had been started by Sigmund's grandfather Friedrich in the late nineteenth century, immediately following the historic first Impressionist showing in Paris in 1874, and she considered it a privilege to have them hanging here in her home.

Sighing under her breath, Ursula roused herself, aware that Sigmund had returned from the bank some time ago, and that he was already dressed in his evening clothes and waiting for her downstairs. Now she must hurry. Punctual himself, he disliked tardiness in others. She went to the Venetian mirrored dressing table positioned between two soaring windows that floated up to the high ceiling, opened the black leather case resting on top of it, glanced at some of the magnificent jewels which lay glittering on the black velvet.

Automatically, almost without interest, she put on a pair of simple, diamond earrings, slipped on her diamond engagement ring next to her gold wedding band, and closed and locked the case. She would wear nothing else, none of her important pieces. She loathed ostentation at the best of times and these were the worst. And why encourage the envy of others, she added under her breath.

Stepping away from the dressing table, Ursula gave herself a final cursory glance, smoothed one hand over her short, wavy blonde hair before turning, walking over to the wardrobe where her coats and capes were kept.

There was a knock on the door, and before she could respond it flew open and her personal maid Gisela hurried into the room. 'You are ready to leave, Frau Westheim? Which fur will you wear?'

Ursula's smile was as lovely as her face, and in her low, cultured voice she said, 'I'm not taking a coat. The velvet wrap will do nicely, Gisela. If you would be good enough to get it out for me, please. Oh, and I will need a pair of white kid gloves. If you'll excuse me for a moment, I'll be right back.'

'Yes, Frau Westheim.'

Ursula stepped out into the bedroom corridor, pushed open the door exactly opposite hers and went inside. A night light on the bedside table glowed faintly in the dim and shadowy room. She tiptoed over to the bed, looked down at the small boy sleeping there so peacefully with one of his small chubby hands resting under a pink cheek. Bending over him, she stroked his blond hair, gave him a light kiss.

The boy stirred. A pair of eyes opened and a sleep-filled voice murmured, 'Mutti? I've been waiting for you, Mutti.'

Ursula filled with a rush of surging warmth, and she smiled inwardly. She experienced such infinite joy when she was with this child. There was a chair near the bed and she pulled it closer, sat down, took his other hand in hers. 'I was dressing, Mein Schatzi. Papa and I have to go out this evening.'

'Papa came to kiss me. He's buying me a pony next summer,' her small son confided, suddenly wide awake. His brown eyes gleamed brightly with excitement as they fastened so intently on hers.

Ursula leaned forward to kiss him again. He nuzzled his warm little face against her cheek and a pair of tender young arms went around her neck and he clung to her. She held him close, stroking his head with one hand. She loved this four-year-old boy so very much. Her only child. Her heart. *She was so afraid for him. Nothing must happen to him. She must protect him with her life.*

Pushing away the troubled thoughts with which she now lived on a daily basis, she took a deep breath and said, 'Your pony will be waiting for you when we go to the villa in the Wannsee next summer. Papa will have it taken there for you.'

'Mutti?'

'Yes, Maxim?'

'Will Papa show me how to ride it?'

'Of course he will,' she said, smiling.

'What's the pony's name?'

'I don't know. We haven't found the right one for you yet. But we will. Come now, it's time to go to sleep.'

Still holding her child in her arms she leaned forward, laid him against the snowy linen pillows, but he did not want to let go of her, clung to her more tightly than ever, almost fiercely. Gently she unclasped his arms, straightened her back, and sat up. Touching his face lightly with her fingertips, she spoke to him with great tenderness. 'You're such a good little boy, Maxim, a sweet boy, and I love you very, very much.'

'I love you, Mutti.'

'Goodnight, Mäuschen, sweet dreams,' she murmured against his cheek.

'Night.' He yawned and his eyelids began to droop, and Ursula knew he would be fast asleep before she even reached the door. She crept out on silent feet, returned to her bedroom where she collected her wrap, gloves and evening bag from her maid.

'Goodnight, Gisela,' she said, pausing in the doorway and turning around. 'And please don't wait up for me.'

'But Frau Westheim, I always help you to – '

'No, no, it's not really necessary,' Ursula interrupted softly. 'I can manage by myself, but thank you anyway.' With these words she walked along the corridor to the staircase.

This swept grandly down to the vast baronial entrance foyer of the Westheim house, a mansion on the Tiergartenstrasse, near the Tiergarten, in a charming residential area of Berlin.

Halfway down the stairs, Ursula stopped, stood stock still listening, her head on one side.

Sigmund was playing the piano in the music room, and the melodic strains of Beethoven's *Moonlight Sonata* came wafting to her on the warm air. It was beautiful . . . delicate . . . but so ineffably sad. Her throat ached with unexpected emotion, and inexplicably tears sprang into her eyes. And she realised that tonight for some reason this particular piece of music seemed to move her especially, perhaps more than it ever had before.

She stood for a moment longer, composing herself and marvelling at Sigmund's touch. It was magical. If he had not been an investment banker she believed he could easily have become a classical concert pianist, such was his talent. But banking was in his blood. Centuries of it. Passed down from father to son, ever since Jacob Westheim, the founding father of the dynasty, had opened the original merchant bank in Frankfurt in 1690. The entire family had moved to Berlin over a hundred years ago, and the Westheim private investment bank in the Gendarmenmarkt, Berlin's financial district, dated back to 1820. Like his father and their illustrious forebears, Sigmund had a brilliant financial brain, and he loved the bank and his work, but had he been born into any family other than the Westheims he might easily have turned out to be a musician by profession.

The clock in the foyer began to chime and the pendulum struck six times, announcing the hour and cutting into her thoughts. She hurried down the stairs, deposited her things on an antique loveseat underneath a Gobelin tapestry, then crossed the black-and-white marble floor, heading in the direction of the music room. Here she paused in the doorway, stood regarding her husband, thinking how handsome he looked in his dinner jacket and black tie.

The moment he saw her, Sigmund stopped playing, sprang up, came swiftly to meet her. Brown-haired with bright blue eyes and a warm, sincere smile, he was about five foot eleven, slender, compact of build, a good-looking man with a strong, well-defined face. He was thirty-six years old, and he had been married to Ursula for fifteen years.

Ursula walked towards him.

They met in the middle of the room.

He took hold of her hands, pulled her to him, put his arm around her, brought his lips to her cheek. They had known each other all of their lives, and their parents had always hoped they would marry; when they had, two elite German families had been united. But it had not been an arranged union. Theirs was a true love story. They had fallen in love as children and they had never wanted anyone but each other. It was a perfect match.

Sigmund broke their embrace, held her away from him and looked down into her face. 'You are very beautiful tonight, Ursula.'

A faint smile touched her lips and her eyes signalled her deep love for him, but she made no response, merely inclined her head graciously.

He put his arm around her, walked her back towards the foyer. 'I was going to have a glass of champagne with you before we left, but I'm afraid that's no longer possible. I think we must leave. I promised Irina we would meet her at the reception, and I don't want to keep her waiting since she's going there alone.'

Ursula nodded. 'Of course, I understand.'

Her voice was so low it was barely audible and Sigmund came to a standstill, glanced at her swiftly, then tilted her face to his. He frowned when he saw the worry in her eyes and the gravity which had suddenly settled on her face. 'What's wrong? What is it?'

'I wish we didn't have to go, Sigmund.'

'But you were enthusiastic when the invitation came. Why this change of heart at the last minute?' He sounded puzzled.

'I was never *that* enthusiastic,' she replied. 'Not really.'

'It's important that we make an appearance, you know. The Ambassador *is* expecting us.'

For a moment she did not speak, and then she said slowly, 'There will be Nazis there.'

'That's true, yes. But then there are Nazis everywhere these days. You mustn't let it concern you.'

Again she was briefly silent before saying, more vehemently than was usual for her, 'But it does concern me, Sigi. We're Jews.'

'And Germans, Ursula. *Real* Germans, just as our forefathers were for centuries before we were born. Remember, we are both from great and ancient families, and furthermore, as an investment banker, I am extremely important and useful to the Government and State, as I have so often pointed out to you. You *know* they need me to help them build the economy, and for my foreign connections, the bankers and industrialists I'm acquainted with, and also for the foreign currency and gold the bank deals in.' He put his arm around her again, held her close to him, finished confidently, in a reassuring voice, 'We are not at risk, Ursula, please believe that.'

She leaned away from him, looked up into his face, gave him a penetrating stare. 'The Nazis fill me with dread. I detest being anywhere near them, or having to even breathe the same air.'

'*I know, I know.* But, Ursula, many of our good friends will be present this evening, and you'll be with *them.* Renata and Reinhard, Kurt and Arabella von Wittingen, and Irina . . .' His voice trailed off. He was not sure how to make her feel better at this moment.

'Yes, many of our friends *will* be there, Sigi,' she concurred softly, 'including those who are now members of the Nazi Party. I'm uncomfortable with them, too, these days.'

His swift nod indicated that he acknowledged the truth of her comments, and he grimaced, then cleared his throat. 'But I'm afraid we can't possibly cancel at this hour, and we really must leave. *Now,* darling. Quite aside from not wishing to keep Irina waiting, I don't want to offend Sir Nevile Henderson by being late.'

'Yes, of course,' she said at once, forcing a smile, putting on a bright face, instantly trying to change her demeanour. There was nothing to be gained by upsetting him further. 'I'll be fine, Sigi, please don't worry about me.'

Looking relieved, he smiled into her eyes, took her arm, squeezed it, and together they hurried out of the music room into the foyer, where Sigmund picked up her wrap. He was placing it around her shoulders when Walter, the butler, came through from the servants' quarters at the back of the house. When he saw his employers, to whom he was devoted, he inclined his head respectfully, went immediately to the clothes cupboard, took out Sigmund's overcoat and brought it to him.

'Thank you, Walter, but I think I'll carry it,' Sigmund said.

The butler nodded, carefully folded the coat, handed it to him, then ushered them out.

SEVEN

The car was waiting in front of the house.

Karl, the chauffeur, greeted them cordially, held the door open for them, and helped them inside. Sigmund told him they were going to the British Embassy, and a second later Karl pulled away from the kerb and headed along the Tiergartenstrasse in the direction of the Hofjägeralle.

Ursula glanced out of the window as the car sped past the Tiergarten, the lovely public park which had once been the private hunting forest of the Brandenburg princes several hundred years ago. How forbidding it looks tonight, she thought, bringing her face closer to the glass. The trees were stark, bereft of leaves, skeletal black images silhouetted against the cold and fading sky of early evening. She felt suddenly chilled and nestled deeper into her velvet wrap.

And then in her mind's eye she pictured the park as it was in the summer months. At that time of year the Tiergarten was breathtaking in its beauty, the rolling expanses of grass, the abundant weeping willows, the limes and the horse chestnut trees lushly green, the planted beds bordering the paths bursting with flowers of every hue, the flowering bushes in full bloom. The lilacs were her favourites, dripping their plump May blossoms of pink and white and mauve, filling the air with a delicate, evocative fragrance.

Laid out in the manner of a natural English park, landscaped in parts, and scattered with artificial ponds and flowing streams, the Tiergarten had majesty and serenity; it was a place of happy memories for her. She had gone riding through it as a child and a young girl, still rode there when the weather was good, and she had always been partial to walking along its winding paths beneath the panoply of cool and shady trees. In the past it had been with Sigmund; now she went there with Maxim and his nurse; occasionally she would stroll through this gentle green enclave by herself, when she wanted to be alone or to think. It was, for her, still a place of peace and safety amidst the turbulence of life in Berlin today, always a refuge. And the beauty and simplicity of nature soothed her, were a balm to her troubled spirit.

Sigmund made a remark to her about his mother, and she turned to him at once, searched his face in the dimness of the car, put a hand on his arm lovingly, knowing how concerned he was about her. For a few seconds they discussed the senior Frau Westheim, who had been in precarious health since her husband's death two years before. They went on to talk about his sisters Hedy and Sigrid and their relationship with their mother, and chatted briefly about the happenings of the day, before lapsing into silence again.

For a short while they were caught up in the intricate webs of their own private thoughts.

Ursula, who adored Sigmund, and respected him, wanted desperately to believe that he was correct in his assertions about their situation, as far as the Nazi regime was concerned. On the other hand, her intelligence and her woman's intuition were at odds with his assurances. *They* were saying entirely different things to her, were alerting her to trouble. Her deepest instincts told her that something horrendous was coming, although what this was, what form it would take, she could not say. She sat up straighter in the corner of the car, stiffening slightly. Was it this awful foreboding that was at the root of her anxiety and apprehension? She was convinced it was. She felt an overwhelming sense of anticipatory despair and her blood ran cold. She sank down into herself and her gaze turned inward.

For his part, Sigmund's thoughts were also somewhat troubled. It was perfectly true that he felt reasonably secure in Berlin, despite the climate of the times, for although measures had been taken against Jews, the entire Westheim family had been left alone. This was also the case with other prominent and wealthy Jewish families who were important, and useful to the State. Then again, not one piece of Westheim property had been touched and the bank had not been closed down. Nor had he been forced to take on Aryan partners, as some Jewish businessmen had. And yet, lately, he had been assailed by worry, had started to harbour a disturbing suspicion that the situation was going to change for every Jew living under the rule of the Third Reich.

Only a few minutes ago he had been reassuring his wife, speaking brave words to her, having no wish to underscore her smouldering anxiety. But *he* must confront the possibility that they might soon be in danger. Not to do so would be sheer folly. Perhaps it would be wise to leave Berlin, to leave Germany, as so many already had. He was a wealthy man. Conceivably he might be able to buy their way out, purchase exit visas and new passports. But he would need assistance to do that, the right introductions to those who could produce the necessary documents. He was fully aware that bribery, graft and corruption were commonplace in the Third Reich; it was only a question of knowing exactly *who* to go to in order to get what he needed. He had friends who could probably guide him in this, ease the way for him. But would they? And whom could he trust? He ran a few names through his head, pondered them carefully.

Karl swept off the Hofjägeralle, took the car around the circle that was the Grosser Stern, passed the Siegessäule, the winged victory column that dominated its centre, and headed down towards the Brandenburg Gate.

Ursula stared in front of her as they drove under the triumphal arch of the gate, focused her eyes on the Unter den Linden ahead. The Nazis had defaced this wide and stately avenue, the most glorious and beautiful of all the boulevards in Berlin, by erecting rows of soaring columns down its centre and along its sides. Each one of these columns was surmounted by a giant Nazi eagle, and because the columns were floodlit they were thrown into relief, stood out dramatically against the darkening night sky.

Typical Nazi theatrics, Ursula thought, loathing what she saw. To her the columns were towering reminders of the domination, tyranny and menace the Third Reich represented. She averted her eyes.

They were passing the Pariserplatz. Her parents had owned a house on that elegant square, and she had grown up there, had been married to Sigmund from that house, and it was there that her mother had died in 1935, and then her father, only last year. The square had played such an important part in her life: it evoked a time past, the Berlin she loved and which, tragically, was now gone forever.

She sighed under her breath and tried to shake off her despondency. Karl had turned right and was driving up the Wilhelmstrasse where the British Embassy was located at number seventy. They were about to arrive at their destination, and she adjusted her expression, fixed a smile on her face as she had learned to do.

There was a lineup of cars in front of theirs. Some were official and from various ministries, others were diplomatic and bore stiff little flags on their bonnets; she recognised the colours of Italy and America and Spain.

A moment later Ursula was alighting from the car, and in the split second she waited for Sigmund to come around from the other side, she glanced up the Wilhelmstrasse. Only a few doors away from her stood the Reich Chancellery where Hitler was ensconced around the clock with his sinister henchmen, and she could not help wondering what diabolical schemes they were hatching at this moment. Her insides shrivelled at the thought, and a shudder ran through her.

And then Sigmund was by her side, smiling down at her, and she tried to smile back, but it was rather faltering. If he noticed this he showed no sign of it, simply took hold of her elbow firmly and led her forward through the huge doors above which the Union Jack fluttered in the cold wind.

The sight of the red, white and blue flag lifted her spirits. It was not merely a banner of coloured cloth that was the national emblem of Great Britain, but a symbol of freedom, democracy and justice.

Sir Nevile Henderson, His Britannic Majesty's Ambassador in Berlin, stood in the hall situated between the two reception rooms at the top of the broad staircase, greeting his guests as they arrived. He was his usual smiling self, debonair and full of charm.

Sigmund and Ursula edged along slowly behind the other guests, until at last Sir Nevile was shaking her hand and warmly welcoming her, before turning his attention to Sigmund. Ursula stood by, waiting. The two men exchanged pleasantries for a few moments, and then together she and Sigmund stepped away, and headed for one of the two rooms where drinks were being served before dinner.

The reception was already in full swing.

The room was thronged and there was a sense of glamour about the gathering, a feeling of tension and excitement in the air, as there generally was at such affairs in Berlin these days. This was especially so at the foreign embassy parties which tended to be international in scope and peopled with interesting characters.

Shimmering crystal chandeliers blazed from the high ceiling, masses of flowers were banked around the room, adding to the festive mood, and a small string quartet played quietly in a corner. White-gloved waiters in tail coats were fleet of foot amongst the crowd, expertly balancing immense silver trays which held either glasses of champagne or assorted canapés. And gazing down on the scene was the life-size portrait in oils of King George VI, newly crowned last year, who had stepped into the breach after his weak and shallow brother, Edward, had abdicated and rushed off to marry Mrs Simpson, the American adventuress.

'It's quite a turnout this evening,' Sigmund murmured in Ursula's ear, escorting her into the room, glancing about as he did.

Instantly, a waiter came to a standstill in front of them, offered them champagne. Sigmund thanked him, took two flutes, handed one to Ursula and clinked his glass to hers. He looked about. 'I don't see Irina, do you?'

Ursula followed his gaze, swiftly surveyed the gathering. 'No, I'm afraid not, Sigi. Perhaps she's in the other reception room. And you're correct, it *is* a crowd tonight.'

She saw that the diplomatic corps was present in full force, spotted several ambassadors she knew by sight, as well as the familiar faces of two British foreign correspondents who were talking to their American colleague, William Shirer. Mingled in amongst them were Government ministers, military officers, high ranking Nazis, members of the German aristocracy and prominent Berliners.

Some of the young internationals who lived in Berlin were also present. She knew from Irina that they were popular with the staffs of the British and French Embassies because they were charming, entertaining and good looking, and enlivened these formal diplomatic functions. The majority had titles and were Hungarians, Slavs, Lithuanians, Austrians, Poles, Rumanians, or White Russians like Irina. With their families, they had been displaced from their homelands by the erratic swings of political power in a shifting Europe inexorably changed some twenty years ago, first by the Russian Revolution and then the collapse of the Austro-Hungarian empire.

Ursula's eyes roved the room and she noticed how well dressed everyone was. Elegance was the order of the evening, it seemed. The men wore dinner jackets or military uniforms; the women were decked out in their finery, and most of them boasted a certain chic, a stylishness that was eye-catching. A few women clinging to the arms of some of the Nazis looked out of place, flashy in their gaudy dresses splattered with sequins or diamanté, their hands, arms and throats plastered with vulgar jewellery.

In the crowd she saw a familiar burnished head, a piquant smiling face in which vivid blue eyes danced, a small hand waving in greeting to her.

Ursula's face instantly lit up. 'Sigi, Irina's over there!'

'Yes, I just saw her myself. Come on, darling.'

He took hold of Ursula's arm and they hurried over to their friend. Irina came to meet them half way, her black lace dress of ballerina length swirling around her slim ankles, and a moment later they were hugging and kissing each other, and laughing.

Irina had a gay effervescent personality and was full of *joie de vivre*, and again it struck Ursula that her extraordinary life, marked by tragedy, upheaval and turbulence, had done little, perhaps nothing, to scar her. Princess Irina Troubetzkoy and her mother Princess Natalie had fled Russia after the Bolsheviks had murdered Prince Igor Troubetzkoy in 1917, when the Romanov autocracy fell. Irina had been six years old, her mother twenty-five, at the time. The Troubetzkoys had lived as refugees in Lithuania, Poland and Silesia before journeying to Berlin and settling in the city ten years ago, which was when Ursula and Sigmund had first met them. Recently Princess Natalie had married a widowed Prussian baron, and for the first time in their twenty-one years of exile from Russia the two women had a real home at last.

Irina, Sigmund and Ursula were talking about her mother and the change for the better in her fortunes when Irina began to chuckle.

Sigmund stared at her, raised a brow, asked in perplexity, 'What is it? Have either of us said something which amuses you?'

Irina shook her head. 'No. I was just thinking that my mother has now acquired a degree of respectability since her marriage to the Herr Baron.' She looked around, then dropped her voice. 'As far as the Nazis are concerned, that is. How ridiculous when one considers that she has always been a woman of rectitude and impeccable moral character, with a spotless reputation, quite aside from the fact that she's of royal blood and is a cousin of the late Tsar.' Irina leaned closer to them, confided softly, 'Incidentally, Göbbels just attached a label to us foreign exiles. *International garbage* he calls us.'

'Ah yes, Doctor Göbbels – ' Sigmund began, and bit off the rest of his sentence.

A pair of SS officers, very typical of their breed, cold-faced and blue-eyed with short-cropped blond hair and ramrod-straight postures, were drawing to a halt in front of them. They clicked their heels together, made elaborate bows and focused their penetrating eyes on Irina. Both flashed her smiles, and one of them said, '*Guten Abend, Prinzessin.*'

'Good evening,' Irina responded, repeating his greeting politely, even proffering a smile. But her eyes, which were the colour of violets, turned almost black and they were glacial.

The officers inclined their heads courteously, and moved on, perfectly in step like carefully programmed robots.

'And that's *Nazi garbage,*' Irina whispered. 'A couple of Heydrich's hatchet men. I felt like spitting in their faces.'

Ursula put a gentle hand on her arm, murmured, sotto voce, 'Please, do be careful what you say, Irina, you never know who's listening.'

'Yes, informers are all over the place,' she muttered in agreement. 'One doesn't know who to trust these days.' Irina now spoke in a voice so inaudible the Westheims had to draw closer to her in order to hear what she said as she added, 'But a foul regime such as theirs needs informers in order to function, to flourish.'

Renata von Tiegal, who had been scanning the reception room from the entrance, saw them and hurried over. She was always dramatic looking, and tonight more than ever, gowned in scarlet silk, this vivid colour most effectively setting off her inky-black hair and ivory skin.

'Hello!' she cried. 'I was looking for you. How is everyone?' Her dark eyes and her wide smile radiated affection.

'We're all well,' Sigmund said, answering for the three of them. 'And you look superb this evening, my dear.'

'Why thank you, Sigi,' she said.

Ursula slipped her arm through Renata's and asked, 'And where's Reinhard?'

'In the other reception room.' Renata glanced about her with quickness, brought her gaze back to her friends. 'What a happy crowd it appears to be tonight.'

'But everyone is happy in Berlin,' Irina said very, very softly, her voice dripping sarcasm. 'They're full of relief that Hitler averted war when he signed the Munich Pact with the British Prime Minister and the French Premier in September.'

'Berliners have their heads stuck in the sand,' Renata responded, and made a sour face. 'How can anyone think that that odious little man has stopped a war?' she asked in an even lower key, sounding scornful. When Irina was silent, she turned to Sigi. 'Do *you* believe he has?'

'I'm hoping against hope,' Sigi answered.

Irina looked over her shoulder to make sure no one was eavesdropping on their conversation, saw that they were quite isolated where they stood, then remarked quietly, 'Hitler might have duped Chamberlain and Daladier, bluffed them into thinking that he wants peace as they do, but he hasn't convinced me and my mother, or the baron for that matter. Helmut thinks he aims to go against the Western democracies next year.'

Renata said, 'I suspect your stepfather's not far from the truth.'

'I pray that Helmut is wrong.' Sigmund's voice was as sombre as the expression on his face.

Renata began to shake her head. 'I tremble at the thought of the poor Czechoslovakians. When Hitler marched into the Sudetenland last month *they* were finished.'

'Please, don't let's talk politics tonight,' Ursula whispered. 'Not even here in the relative safety of the British Embassy. It makes me nervous.'

'You're absolutely right,' Sigmund agreed. 'It's a dangerous game anywhere these days.' Out of the corner of his eye he noticed that the von Wittingens had just arrived, and wanting to bring this conversation to a close, and needing an excuse to speak privately to Irina, he said, 'Come along, Irina my dear, let's go over and have a word with Kurt and Arabella, and find ourselves a drop of champagne on the way.'

Irina nodded in consent, and they both excused themselves and sauntered off in the direction of the prince and princess.

Left alone together, Renata faced Ursula, frowning slightly. 'Are you feeling all right, Ursi?' she asked, peering at her friend. 'You look so very pale tonight.'

Ursula was silent for a moment, and then she gave Renata a direct look and, suddenly wanting to unburden herself, she confessed, 'I live with the most corrosive anxiety, Ren. It's perfectly awful. So debilitating. And although I try desperately to control myself, I'm filled with terrible apprehension most of the time.'

Renata's face reflected her sympathy and her understanding. 'We all feel the same way, and with good reason. We're in the hands of criminals. Let's face it, the German Government is being led by a bunch of gangsters.'

'Keep your voice down,' Ursula cautioned in a whisper, 'the Gestapo's everywhere. Even at this party, I'm sure.'

'Yes, you're probably right,' Renata replied dully, adopting the same whispering tone.

Automatically they both edged further into the corner, and Renata stared at Ursula in dismay and let out a weary sigh. 'I wonder why we bothered to come here tonight, knowing the place would be seething with *them* and the SS and God knows who else?'

'To be together in a friendly atmosphere at a friendly embassy where there are still a few civilised people left to talk to, and to have a pleasant evening with each other, I do believe,' Ursula murmured, and squeezed her arm, wanting to reassure her friend.

'Hello, you two,' a husky, very cultured, very English voice said, and knowing that it was Arabella von Wittingen standing behind them they swung around and greeted her lovingly.

She was an English aristocrat, the former Lady Arabella Cunningham, and the sister of the Earl of Langley. Tall, slender, and elegant this evening in a bottle-green brocade dinner suit composed of a long skirt and a tailored jacket, Arabella had light-blue eyes and a skin like a peach.

Her manner was insouciant, and her pretty mouth twitched with amusement when she said, 'I can hardly believe my eyes! A member of the Ambassador's staff must have gone slightly *mad*. What an invitation list! Some of the raciest ladies in Berlin are present this evening, not to mention those *cuties* over there, the ones draped all over the Nazi officers.' She laughed uproariously. 'The three of them look as if they've just stepped out of Madam Kitty's front door,' she continued, referring to the most famous brothel in Berlin. 'Out of several *beds* in Madam Kitty's, I should have said,' she added as an afterthought, and laughed again.

Renata also laughed. 'You are wicked.'

Ursula chuckled with them, and exclaimed softly, 'And you're as irreverent as ever and brutally honest, but then that's why we love you, Belle darling.'

Ursula spoke the truth.

These three women did love each other; they had been devoted friends for the past eighteen years. They had met in 1920 when, at the age of sixteen, they were pupils at Roedean, the famous English girls' school near Brighton. In the two years they had attended the school they had been considered a daunting trio – intelligent, confident, self-assured, independent and, at times, rebellious. The friendship had continued after their schooldays, and Renata and Ursula had gone frequently to stay with Arabella at Langley Castle in Yorkshire, which was the family seat; Arabella had journeyed to Berlin to visit both girls at different times. In 1923 she and Renata were bridesmaids at Ursula's marriage with Sigmund. After the wedding, Arabella had gone with Renata to stay at the home of her fiancé, Graf Reinhard von Tiegal, at his Schloss on the edge of the forests of the Spree in the Mark Brandenburg, a country area outside Berlin. It was there that she had met Prince Rudolf Kurt von Wittingen, with whom she had fallen in love, and he with her. They had been married a year later, after which Arabella had come to live in

Berlin permanently. The three women had drawn closer than ever, and from this day forward were as inseparable as they had been at school in England in their teens.

Their irrepressible laughter broke the tension Ursula and Renata had been experiencing a few moments ago, before Arabella's arrival. Now Renata motioned to a waiter. 'Let's have another glass of champagne,' she suggested to her closest friends, her expression brightening considerably.

'That's a good idea,' Ursula said, and after helping herself to a flute of the wine, she went on, 'It's ages since we've had a quiet moment together without our children. Why don't we go and sit over there and talk for a few minutes.'

'Splendid thought,' Arabella said, and Renata agreed with her. They strolled over to a group of chairs arranged in front of a window, where they made themselves comfortable and began to talk about inconsequential things. Each of them wanted desperately to create a sense of normalcy about their lives in these most abnormal times, and they drew comfort from each other, and a feeling of greater security from being together.

They did not move until their husbands came to escort them in to dinner. And later they agreed that for them this short interlude had been the best part of the evening at the British Embassy.

EIGHT

'I'm glad you told Henrietta we had to leave,' Theodora Stein said, looking across at her boyfriend Willy Herzog, who stood on the other side of the small foyer, putting on his overcoat. 'I have to get up early tomorrow.' She made a face at the thought.

Willy nodded as he reached for his hat. 'We'll only get a few hours' sleep, that's true, it's an early start for me, too. It was a grand party and I enjoyed myself, but it's going on a bit too long.'

'Yes, I agree, Willy.'

Theodora glanced at the door which led into the living room and through which could be heard varied sounds – voices raised in revelry, and laughter, and gramophone music. She lifted her shoulders in a shrug. 'But then, how often are you twenty-one, Willy?' Since this was a rhetorical question she did not expect an answer, and she rushed on, 'I suppose Henrietta wanted to make the most of this very special birthday. And I don't blame her. I know I will when *I'm* twenty-one. I plan to have a fancy party too.'

Willy flashed her a wide grin. 'Will I be invited?'

'*If* you're still around, Willy Herzog. *If* you haven't sailed off to America as you keep threatening to do,' she shot back, giving him a flirtatious look. 'Are you still planning to go over there to join your Uncle Nathan in Brooklyn and study to be a dentist?'

'*Doctor*,' he corrected. He frowned. 'It's the getting of the American visas, Theodora. *Very* difficult it is. They're extremely hard to come by, I think I told you that before. Anyway, my father has a friend in Frankfurt who has a friend who knows a consular official who *might* be able to help us. For the right price. That's why my father went to Frankfurt yesterday, hoping to bribe this man and get the three visas we need. For himself, and for my sister Clara and me.'

Willy cleared his throat. 'I'd like to go to America . . . want to go . . . but . . .' He hesitated and cleared his throat again, looked down, studied his shoes. When he looked up he fixed his gentle, hazel eyes on Theodora. 'I don't want to leave *you*,' he announced, surprising himself and startling her. There, it's out at last, he thought. He had finally said it, had had the courage to tell her what had been on his mind for weeks. Relief surged through him as he stood gazing adoringly at Theodora.

Stupefied, and totally at a loss for words, she gaped back at him, amazement registering on her face.

Willy flung down his hat, leapt across the foyer, pulled her into his arms and held her close. 'I love you, Teddy,' he said against the top of her head, kissing her silky fair hair. 'I do, I love you.'

'Oh . . . Oh . . . Is this a proposal then?'

There was a small silence.

He said at last, 'Do I want to marry you? Yes . . . *yes* . . . and *yes*, it's a proposal.'

'*Oh Willy!* I don't know what to say, I'm only nineteen and you're only nineteen. We're so young and – '

'Don't you love me?'

Now it was Theodora's turn to be silent.

She wondered if she did love him. She wasn't sure. Perhaps she did. He was very nice looking and quiet and studious, and serious about studying medicine, and he had lovely manners. Mrs Mandelbaum, Henrietta's mother, was always saying Willy was a real *mensh*. And it was true, he was a *haimisher mensh*, so easy to be around, very comfortable. Yes, Willy was a good man, and he went to *shul* regularly, and in the year she had known him he had never done a thing to upset her, had never put a foot wrong. But *marriage*? She hadn't thought about *that* before. But she could do worse. Much worse. Besides, she didn't mind it when he kissed her. In fact, she liked it. He had soft warm lips and sweet breath and he always smelled fresh and clean, of soap and *Kölnisch Wasser*. And he was gentle with her, never tried to force her, or make her do anything wrong. When he kissed her she always got a funny feeling inside, and her heart pounded, and she grew warm and flushed. Yes, Willy *was* special, now that she *really* thought about it. She didn't want to lose him. Quite suddenly she knew she would never find anybody who was *better* than Willy.

She said slowly, 'I *think* I love you, Willy.' There was a little pause, and she said more firmly, 'Yes, I do love you.'

'Oh Teddy! That makes me so happy. And *will* you marry me?'

There was another fractional pause before she acquiesced. 'Yes, Willy Herzog, I will.'

He put his hand under her chin and lifted her small heart-shaped face to his, kissed her pretty upturned nose, her eyelids and finally her sweet lips. They held the kiss, making it last, and they clung to each other tightly until they had to break away to catch their breaths.

Willy pressed her head against his shoulder and stroked her hair and in silent communion they lingered in their embrace. They knew that a commitment had been made, by the one to the other, and it was a serious moment, very meaningful and precious to them both, and they did not want to let it go.

Finally Theodora gently pushed Willy away, extracted herself from his arms. 'Look at the clock, Willy, it's almost midnight. We must leave. I'll hardly get any sleep before I have to be up to take care of Maxim. The little one's always awake early.'

'Yes, we had better go. Come on.'

'Let me put my hat on first. It's a cold night, and even colder on the back of your motorbike.'

Turning to the coatstand, Theodora took down her green-and-blue tartan tam o'shanter and looked at herself in the Biedermeier mirror as she put it on, then tightened her matching scarf around her neck. She fished a woollen glove out of each pocket of her navy-blue winter coat, and said, 'I'm ready then.'

They let themselves out of the Mandelbaums' apartment and Willy closed the door behind them; pausing on the landing, he took hold of Theodora's shoulders and gently turned her face to him. 'So, we have an understanding, Theodora? You *will* meet me under the *chuppa* and become my wife?'

She nodded solemnly and her expression was serious, but her light green eyes were shining and they danced with happiness. 'Yes, Willy. *Yes* to both your questions, and I shall write to my Aunt Ketti to tell her. As my only living relative she'd want to know that I'm . . . engaged . . . to be married.'

'That's true. And I shall inform my father, when he gets back from Frankfurt, and I shall also tell him that I can't go to America. Not without you. We'll have to get a visa for you, Teddy. I'll stay in Berlin until we can *both* go to Brooklyn to my Uncle Nathan's.'

She smiled and nodded and took his hand in hers and together they went down the steep flight of stairs and crossed the vestibule of the apartment building.

As Willy opened the door leading into the street, Theodora stiffened alertly, grabbed hold of his arm. 'Listen! Isn't that the sound of breaking glass?'

'You're right, it is. I hope it's not a burglar trying to get into Mr Mandelbaum's jewellery shop. I'd better go and see. Wait here.'

'No! Don't go out, Willy! It's dangerous!' she cried.

He paid no attention to her warning, hurried into the narrow street, where he immediately collided with a stormtrooper who stood staring up at the building.

The stormtrooper grabbed Willy by the shoulder and swung him to one side. 'Hey you! Watch it! Watch where you're going, you clumsy dolt!'

'I'm very sorry, sir,' Willy said politely, struggling to break free from the man's grip, but it was tenacious. 'Please, let go of me.'

On hearing this request the stormtrooper tightened his hold, peered at Willy in the pale light coming through the door's transom from the vestibule. 'Why should I let go of you? You might be a Jew for all I know. *Is* this a Jewish house? *Are* you a Jew?'

Theodora, who had been listening with growing alarm behind the door, could no longer contain herself. She rushed outside before Willy had a chance to answer – and perhaps unwittingly say the wrong thing altogether.

'Let him go!' she yelled, drawing to a stop right in front of the stormtrooper. 'Let him go at once!' she repeated, her voice rising shrilly. 'We haven't done anything.'

'You have if you're Jews. Are you stinking shitty Jews?' He grinned sadistically and twisted Willy's shoulder back so far Theodora cringed and sucked in her breath.

Willy was stoic. He gritted his teeth and he did not cry out once, despite the sharp pain.

'Come on, confess it,' the stormtrooper snarled, 'this *is* a Jewish house, and you're *both* Jews.'

'We are not Jews! What kind of a thing is that to say!' Theodora exclaimed. And with immense hauteur she drew herself up to her full height of five foot five, and glared at him. She was as bold as brass as she faced him down unflinchingly.

'My name is Theodora Marie-Theresa Schmidt and this is Wilhelm Braun, and we're both good Catholics and good Germans.' She gulped, took a deep breath. 'And good Nazis, yes, we are indeed that. *Heil Hitler!*' She thrust her arm straight out in front of her in the Nazi salute. '*Heil Hitler!* Long live our magnificent Führer! Long live the Third Reich!' She saluted again.

The stormtrooper gaped at her in astonishment.

And so did Willy. When she had rushed out into the street his heart had almost stopped and he had been terrified, more for her than for himself. But now he knew she was going to get away with this act because of her insolence, her aggressiveness and her effrontery. He'll believe her, Willy thought, because he's certain no Jew would dare to confront him like this, or shout at a Nazi stormtrooper the way she is shouting at him. Her anger and her arrogance were so perfectly simulated, and she spoke with such conviction, who could doubt that she was telling the truth? It was quite a performance she was giving. Willy marvelled at it, and at her audacity.

Theodora continued to rail at the man. 'You've got a flashlight in your hand,' she bellowed. 'Shine it on us. Shine it on Willy. Go on, do it! You'll see he's not a Jew!' Before the stormtrooper could stop her she leaned forward and snatched the flashlight out of his hand, turned it on and levelled it at Willy.

Willy held his breath, once again petrified for her, for them both.

'Take your hat off, Willy!' She spoke so authoritatively, he did as she said, pulling off his hat with his free hand, whilst praying under his breath.

'Look at him!' she ordered the stormtrooper. '*Look at him!* Willy has sandy-red hair and more freckles than you've ever seen on anybody, and hazel eyes. Is that a Jewish face? No, it's an Aryan face.'

Dramatically, she turned the flashlight on herself.

'And just look at me. I'm the Nordic type personified.' She pulled her long hair over her shoulder. 'See, I have fair hair and green eyes and skin the colour of a rose. Do I look semitic? *Of course* I don't, because I'm not.'

At last the stormtrooper found his voice. 'Looks can be very deceptive,' he snapped. Nonetheless, some of the harshness and bluster had gone out of him, and he seemed uncertain in the face of her anger and her torrent of words uttered in such superior and confident tones. But he continued to hold on to Willy, even tightening his grasp.

Theodora drew closer and said with icy imperiousness, 'What you say is true. Looks *can* deceive. And perhaps *you* are not all *you* appear to be. I said *Heil Hitler* before. Why didn't you respond in the same way, as you're supposed to? I hope you're a loyal Party member.' She threw back her shoulders proudly, and tossed her head, spoke more arrogantly than ever. 'My father is SS Gruppenführer Schmidt. He is a good friend of Reichsführer Himmler. He knows him very well.' Summoning every ounce of her nerve, Theodora now waved the flashlight in front of the startled stormtrooper's face. She stared at him, as if committing his face to memory. 'What's your name, corporal?' she asked, her eyes narrowing.

The stormtrooper reacted as she had expected he would, furiously pushing her arm away. 'Get that light out of my eyes!' he yelled, and leaning towards her he grabbed the flashlamp from her with great roughness.

Unperturbed, Theodora said, 'Did you hear me, corporal? My father is a friend of *Himmler's*, and he's a powerful man in the SS. He's not going to be happy when he knows we've been detained by *you* in this way. I asked you your name, corporal. *So, what is it?'*

It was apparent the stormtrooper had believed everything Theodora had said thus far, and this second reference to Himmler, who was head of the SS, seemed to both frighten and galvanise him. Abruptly he let go of Willy.

Instantly Theodora took hold of Willy's arm and pulled him close to her side. 'Come on, let's go,' she said.

'Yes, you'd better get off,' the stormtrooper exclaimed sharply, stepping back. 'Go on, go home! A lot's about to happen. Soon it won't be safe on the streets. We're after Jews tonight.' As he said this he laughed raucously and slapped his thigh, as if it was a huge joke, and, without so much as another word or a glance, he turned from them indifferently, walked on down the narrow street, shining his flashlight on other shop windows.

Willy gasped, 'Look what he did to Mr Mandelbaum's store front – '

'Hurry, Willy! *Hurry!*' Theodora hissed, and catching Willy's hand in hers she turned, dragging him with her, and together they ran in the other direction, away from the apartment building and Mandelbaum's jewellery shop, and out into the Kurfürstendamm.

As they hit this street they immediately saw that havoc was starting to break loose everywhere, and so they went on running as fast as they could, their feet pounding the pavement until they reached the lamp post where Willy had parked his motorbike earlier. They were thankful and relieved to see that it was perfectly secure and had not been touched, but they knew they had reached it just in time. The two of them clambered on, their breathing laboured as they settled themselves on the saddle.

'Hold tight!' Willy ordered, and she wrapped her arms around his waist as the bike leapt forward and headed down the Kurfürstendamm at breakneck speed.

Vans and trucks were now pulling up all along this wide avenue lined with shops and cafés and apartment buildings. Stormtroopers, rowdies and thugs were spilling out, brandishing hatchets, guns, clubs and truncheons. Like fevered maniacs they were rushing in every direction, smashing the windows of Jewish-owned stores, throwing goods out into the street, destroying the fronts of cafés and hacking at the doors of apartment buildings. Combined with the ear-splitting noise of shattering glass were the sounds of splintering wood and the blood-curdling cries of triumph from the frenzied mob led by stormtroopers.

Theodora was shaking. Holding onto Willy tighter than ever, she shouted in his ear, 'Faster! Faster! Get us out of here!'

He did not bother to respond, simply gunned the bike forward with a screeching of tyres, and within minutes they were leaving the Kurfürstendamm behind them. Willy was making for the Stülerstrasse, which flowed into the Tiergartenstrasse where the Westheim mansion stood. It was there that Theodora lived and worked as the nanny to young Maxim.

They were on the Fasanenstrasse now.

Just ahead of them was the lovely old Central Synagogue, and as they approached it they were horror-struck. The building was being completely demolished by thugs and stormtroopers, who were breaking all the windows and setting it alight with flaming torches.

Willy accelerated his speed considerably, dangerous though this was, and shot ahead, racing through the mêlée and away from this scene of violent wholesale destruction. But not before they had seen the scrolls of the Torah and the ark of the covenant lying amongst the debris in the street. And alongside were torn prayer books and shawls, and all were being trampled underfoot by the wild mob who were shrieking with hysterical laughter, and shouting obscenities about Jews to each other.

'I can't believe they're burning down the synagogue,' Theodora wailed in Willy's ear, and she began to sob and pressed her face into his back.

Willy desperately wanted to stop in order to comfort her, but he did not dare, not until they were out of this area and in a safer part of Berlin. With a terrible relentlessness he pushed the motorcycle harder, as hard as he could, and eventually he was cutting across the Kantstrasse and speeding down the Budapesterstrasse. This was a long and curving avenue which led directly into the Stülerstrasse. With enormous relief he saw that the latter was quiet, entirely deserted as he entered it; in fact, it might well have been on another planet, so peaceful was it. And so he slowed his speed at last, finally came to a stop. After braking, he parked by the side of the road in the shadow of some trees and jumped off the bike.

Theodora was still weeping, now shaking her head from side to side, her hands pressed to her streaming eyes. 'God forgive me! God forgive me for denying my heritage, for denying my religion, for denying myself and all that I am!'

Willy took her to him, and she sobbed uncontrollably in his arms, cleaving to him. He stroked her back, trying to calm her.

Eventually, he said with great gentleness, 'God does forgive you. I know He does. You saved us, didn't you? With your quick thinking and your cheek. You've got a good Jewish *kop* on your shoulders, Teddy. And *chutzpah*. A lot of *chutzpah*. That's what saved us.'

'I shouldn't have denied we are Jews,' she whimpered. 'It was wrong, Willy.'

'It saved us. *And that's all that counts.*'

She drew away from him slightly, looked up into his grave face, asked tearfully, 'Why, Willy? *Why?* Why are they doing this? And why are they burning down the synagogue?'

He was briefly silent, and then he said in a voice that was anguished, 'The Nazis have turned prejudice into hatred, and tonight we are witnessing a Nazi rampage against us and our homes, our businesses and our places of worship. They are torching, vandalising and desecrating everything that belongs to Jews, because they hate us with a terrible, *terrible* vengeance.'

'*Oh Willy.*'

He held her close to him again so that she would not see the sudden tears misting his eyes.

Theodora was trying to stem her sobs, heaving and catching her breath in little spasms, and after a short while she was quieter, in control. 'Willy?'

'Yes, Teddy?'

'They want to murder us all,' she whispered against his shoulder.

He did not respond. He knew she was right. And he was afraid.

NINE

Theodora felt considerably safer once she was inside the Westheim mansion on the Tiergartenstrasse.

She locked and bolted the door behind her, and then leaned against it, trying to compose herself. She was no longer wracked by sobs, the tears had dried on her face, but, nonetheless, she was still disturbed and upset. The violence she had just seen on the streets, the ferocity of the attack on the synagogue, were indelibly imprinted on her mind forever. And, like Willy, she was frightened.

After taking several deep breaths and steadying herself, she walked quickly across the black-and-white marble foyer, the metallic click of her heels against the marble floor the only sound in the huge and silent house. Obviously everyone was sleeping soundly, unaware of the riots outside. The mobs had stayed away from this exclusive residential district, occupied mostly by wealthy Gentile families, and had apparently concentrated their attacks around the area of the Kurfürstendamm, at least as far as she knew.

An antique porcelain lamp on a chest to one side of the Gobelin tapestry had been left burning for her, by Frau Westheim, upon her return from the dinner at the British Embassy, she had no doubt about that. It illuminated her way up the grand staircase.

When she reached the landing at the top of the stairs, she turned on the lights and made her way along the main corridor. She stopped at Maxim's door, stood listening, then opened it gently and peeped inside.

The tiny night-light on the bedside table made a faint glow, and it comforted her to see that the child was sleeping so peacefully. Closing the door carefully, so as not to awaken him, she swung around, and, rather than going to her own room which was next to Maxim's, she stepped over to his parents' bedroom instead. Lightly, she rapped on the door.

She waited several moments, and was about to knock again, when the door was opened by Sigmund dressed in his pyjamas and a dark silk robe.

Taken by surprise that it was she, and not one of the servants, he stared at her, frowning. 'Theodora! What is it? What's wrong? You're as white as chalk.' He squinted at her worriedly in the dimly-lit corridor.

He was about to say something else, when Theodora put her finger to her lips, shook her head, and glanced over at the child's room. 'Shhhh,' she whispered, 'we don't want to awaken Maxim.'

Sigmund nodded his understanding, opened the door wider, and ushered her into the bedroom.

Ursula was out of bed and slipping on her peignoir, worry clouding her smoky-blue eyes.

When she saw Theodora's white face and the shock in her eyes, the girl's distress instantly communicated itself to her. 'Teddy, whatever is it? Why, you've been crying. What has upset you so?'

Theodora stood in the centre of the extraordinarily beautiful bedroom with its green watered-silk walls and many exquisite objects and great works of art, and wondered where to begin, how to tell this refined and aristocratic couple about the hideous violence and destruction she had just witnessed out there in the centre of the city. And for a second she could not find the words.

She stared at Ursula. Her mouth trembled.

Ursula returned the girl's unblinking gaze, her eyes puzzled, her expression one of concern. Theodora was her charge, whom she had taken into her home three years ago, after the death of Frau Rosa Stein, Teddy's mother and widow of Doctor Johann Stein. Until his death in 1933, the doctor had been the Westheim family's physician for many years, and devoted to them. When Teddy had come to live with them at the age of sixteen, Ursula had been fulfilling a death-bed promise to Teddy's mother to look after her until she came of age, or got married. Ursula took this promise seriously, and although Teddy was Maxim's nanny, the girl was treated with great kindness and consideration, and was almost like a member of the family. Her welfare was of importance to Ursula and Sigmund.

Now Ursula said gently, 'Teddy dear, please tell us what has happened to you.'

Theodora nodded, and words began to tumble out of her, a little breathlessly and in a great rush. 'Out there. In the streets. The Nazis have gone crazy. They're doing terrible things. Demolishing Jewish property. Smashing store windows, café fronts. Battering their way into apartment buildings. And they've burned the Central Synagogue. *Burned it to the ground.* I saw them doing it with my own eyes!'

'Oh dear God! Dear God!' Ursula cried. Her face lost all of its colour. She turned ashen, and an internal shaking seized her. Reaching out, she got hold of the back of a chair to steady herself, and that sense of dread, which she had pressed back for weeks, rose up in her and lodged like a stone weight in her chest.

Anxiously she looked at Sigmund. They stared at each other disbelievingly. They were appalled and aghast at what they had just heard, and considerably alarmed.

Turning back to Teddy, Ursula said, 'Thank God you weren't hurt. You're not, are you?'

'No, I'm not, Frau Westheim.'

'You weren't out alone tonight, were you, Teddy?' Sigmund interjected.

'I was with Willy, Herr Westheim.'

'Willy?' he repeated, his gaze quizzical.

'Professor Herzog's son,' Ursula cut in swiftly. 'He's studying at the university, and he's been taking Teddy out on her days off for about a year.'

'Yes, of course, now I remember.' Sigmund focused his bright blue eyes on Teddy again. 'How did you get home? How did you manage to get through the demonstrations unscathed?'

'On Willy's motorcycle. He drove like a maniac. But he had to. It was awful, frightening, especially on the Ku'damm and the Fasanenstrasse.'

'Oh Teddy, Teddy,' Ursula said, her voice low and strained, 'I've warned you not to stay out late at night. These are terribly dangerous times we're living in.'

'I know. And I'm sorry, Frau Westheim. I know you worry about me. But Henrietta's birthday party went on much longer than we expected. We kept trying to leave. Finally we got away around midnight. The havoc was just starting to break loose.'

Ursula frowned, thinking that their unimpeded journey across the rioting city was something akin to miraculous, and she probed, 'No one bothered you? Stopped you? Shot at you?'

'No, not when we were riding the motorbike. But . . . well . . . there was a little incident as we left the apartment. Willy accidentally barrelled into a stormtrooper outside the Mandelbaums' building, and he grabbed hold of Willy, started to question – '

'*Stormtrooper!*' Ursula's eyes opened wider. She brought a hand up to her mouth. Civilian mobs were one thing; the involvement of stormtroopers meant something entirely different – and much more threatening.

'Yes, a stormtrooper,' Theodora said, and speaking swiftly and graphically, she recounted exactly what had transpired between herself and the Nazi when she had rushed out to confront him on the street. And she did not leave out one single detail.

Ursula was aghast throughout this recital, and when Teddy had finished, she exclaimed, 'What you did was terribly, *terribly* dangerous! The consequences for you and Willy could have been disastrous. *Horrendous.* The stormtrooper could have beaten you up, or killed you. What's perhaps even worse to contemplate, he could have dragged you both to Gestapo Headquarters for questioning. People who have been made to take forced trips to the Prinz Albrechtstrasse haven't always come out of there alive. And *if* they have, they've often been mindless wrecks because of the torture inflicted on them.'

Teddy went cold, realising that everything Ursula Westheim said was true. She bit her lip, responded quietly, in a chagrined voice, 'I just reacted . . . without thinking. I was certain my insolence and superior manner would convince him I was not Jewish. I *was* right about that, Frau Westheim, and he really did believe my father was in the SS, and that he was a friend of Himmler's.'

'Teddy did what she thought was the best thing, I'm absolutely sure of that, and certainly she used her wits,' Sigmund said to Ursula. Then he glanced across at Theodora and shook his head. His kindly eyes were grave when he murmured, after a slight pause, 'I don't think you should tempt providence again. It might not work a second time.'

'Yes, now I realise that,' Teddy admitted. 'Willy was scared when I was shouting at the stormtrooper. Scared for both of us, he told me later.'

'And where is Willy?' Sigmund asked. 'Is he downstairs?'

'No, he went home. His father's away and he was worried about his sister Clara being alone in their flat.'

'But it's dangerous out on the streets,' Sigmund responded with a show of concern. 'You should have insisted that he stay here tonight.'

Ursula said, 'I'm certain Willy is all right, Sigi. He lives not far from here, just behind us, near the Landwehrkanal.'

'Willy *must* be safely home by now,' Teddy asserted, and explained, 'It would only take him a few minutes on the motorbike, and everything was quiet in the neighbourhood when he dropped me off.'

Sigmund went across to one of the windows, parted the silk draperies and anxiously looked down into the Tiergartenstrasse. He saw that the street below was indeed empty, and this reassured him that the boy had undoubtedly made it home easily and without running into trouble. Nevertheless, he swung around, and gesturing to the phone on Ursula's writing desk, he said, 'I think we will all feel much better, Teddy, if you ring Willy.'

'Yes, Herr Westheim,' Teddy replied and did as he asked, walking over to the small desk and dialling. The phone in the Herzogs' apartment was picked up after only two rings, and Willy was on the line. 'Yes?' he said warily.

'It's Teddy here,' she answered. 'Herr Westheim asked me to ring you up, Willy, to check that you'd arrived home all right.' He told her that he had done so without any sort of incident and without seeing one single person, then they said goodbye.

Teddy replaced the receiver, turned to Sigmund. 'He's fine, he said he got home in a few minutes. The streets around here *are* quiet, Herr Westheim.'

Sigmund nodded. His immense relief showed on his face.

'Stormtroopers,' Ursula said and looked at Sigmund, then addressed Teddy. 'So apparently the Government is no longer simply turning a blind eye to these anti-semitic demonstrations. *Now*, seemingly, it is actively involved in them.'

'That's the way it looks,' Teddy responded. 'I saw a lot of stormtroopers on our way home. They were leading the mobs – ' Theodora broke off as a wave of nausea unexpectedly swept over her and she brought her hand up to her eyes. She swayed slightly on her feet, and wondered if she was going to faint.

Ursula ran to her immediately, put an arm around her to give her support. 'Come, *Mein Kind*,' she murmured, 'come, my child, take off your things and let's sit down until you feel better.' She helped Teddy remove her coat and tam o'shanter, mothering her as she would Maxim. Taking hold of her hand, Ursula led her over to the fireplace where a few embers still glowed in the grate. Glancing over her shoulder at Sigmund, she said, 'I think a glass of cognac would help Teddy. Her hands are icy.'

'Of course. I'll get it right away.'

Sigmund strode into the adjoining room. This was his upstairs study where he sometimes worked, and where there was a small but well-stocked liquor cabinet.

Meanwhile, Ursula and Teddy seated themselves on the chaise and Ursula continued to hold the girl's hands, rubbing them between her own, trying to warm them.

Theodora looked at her suddenly, and exclaimed, 'They were so *vicious* when they smashed the synagogue, set fire to it. I couldn't believe such a dreadful thing was happening.' This scene stood out with such agonising clarity in her mind that she began to weep, and the tears rolled down her cheeks unchecked.

Ursula brought her hand up to Teddy's face, and gently wiped the tears away with her fingertips, and endeavoured to comfort her.

Sigmund was back within seconds, carrying a silver tray upon which there were three liqueur glasses of brandy. 'I think we *all* need a drop of this,' he said, coming over to the chaise, offering the tray to his wife and Teddy.

Theodora took a big swallow of the brandy and she felt the warmth of it in her throat at once. She took another swallow, and put the glass on a nearby table, looked from Ursula to Sigmund. 'Thank you,' she said softly, her expression one of deep gratitude. 'Thank you for being so kind to me always.'

Sigmund had tossed back his small glass of cognac in one quick gulp, and now he said, 'I must go and make several phone calls . . . to Hedy, to make certain she and my mother are all right. I'm absolutely positive they are, out there in the Grunewald. Sigrid, of course, is in Hamburg with Thomas on business, so we don't have to be concerned about them. And then I must reach the night guard at the bank, check out the situation in the Gendarmenmarkt.'

'Yes, you had better do that,' Ursula concurred.

Sigmund nodded, and disappeared in the direction of his study.

Theodora, who had been fumbling around in the pocket of her blue wool dress, pulled out her handkerchief and blew her nose. 'I'm sorry I broke down before, Frau Westheim. But I couldn't help it. This has been the most terrifying experience. I know one thing . . . I'll never forget the ninth of November . . . Henrietta Mandelbaum's twenty-first birthday and the night the Nazis torched the Central Synagogue. No, I'll never forget it,' she finished vehemently. 'Not as long as I live.'

'I don't think anyone will,' Ursula replied.

She rose, walked over to a window, drew open the draperies and stood looking out at the sky. It was jet black and littered with bright stars, and on the horizon she could see a jagged patch of red flaring upwards. *Fire*, she thought. *They're burning something else in another part of the city. Another synagogue perhaps. Or someone's home. Or both. Where will this end? Dear God, where will this end?* She felt chilled to the bone, icy.

Sigmund did not remain on the telephone for very long, and he soon returned to the bedroom, saying with obvious relief, 'I spoke to Hedy. The Grunewald is as peaceful and sleepy as it always is, and the night guard at the bank tells me nothing untoward is happening down there in the financial district. So perhaps the demonstrations on the Ku'damm and the Fasanenstrasse are simply isolated incidents, started by the rowdies and thugs who are so frequently out of control – '

'I doubt that,' Ursula remarked in the softest of voices. 'Not when there are stormtroopers involved. This is much more serious than anything we've ever seen before.'

'Perhaps,' Sigmund muttered noncommittally. Privately he agreed with her, but he did not want to foster her alarm; nor did he wish to frighten Theodora further, who had been through enough as it was this night.

Abruptly, Ursula said, 'It's the beginning.'

'The beginning of what, Frau Westheim?' Theodora asked.

There was a silence before Ursula replied. 'The beginning of the end of the Jews in Germany.'

After Theodora had gone to bed, Ursula and Sigmund sat together on the chaise, talking quietly, sharing their thoughts, trying to analyse the dramatic events of that night, trying to understand what they meant, and what they predicted for the future.

At one moment, Ursula turned to him, and said slowly, 'Stop trying to protect me by not telling me what you *truly* think, Sigi. I'm far too intelligent to be duped, especially by my own husband, a man I've known since childhood.'

'Yes, you are,' he said with a faint sigh. 'And I only meant the best for you.'

She tried to smile, unsuccessfully. 'As always, my dearest Sigi, as always.'

Taking hold of his hand she held it very tightly in hers and after a while she said in a voice choked with emotion, 'We have to leave, Sigi . . . leave this house . . . leave the villa in Wannsee . . . leave the bank . . . leave the art collection . . . leave all of our possessions . . . and go. We have to leave Berlin, Sigi. We have to get out of Germany.'

'Yes, I know,' he said with resignation. 'I've known it for a long time, really, but I suppose I haven't wanted to face it.' He sighed again. 'The entire family must get out. And Theodora. We cannot leave her behind, that would be unthinkable. She will come with us, and I must get exit visas for everyone, and entry visas for another country.'

'How?'

Indeed *how*, he thought, but said, 'To be honest, Ursula, I don't know . . . *yet*. But I will. And very soon. Certainly I've got one thing in my favour.'

'What is that, Sigi?'

'Money.'

TEN

'*Entschuldigen Sie, gnädige Frau*,' the butler said, excusing himself for disturbing her.

Ursula looked across at him from the Louis XVI writing desk at the far end of the bedroom, where she sat working on some papers. 'That's perfectly all right, Walter. What is it?'

'*Die Gräfin von Tiegal ist da, gnädige Frau.*'

Ursula was momentarily startled. 'The Countess von Tiegal is here?' she repeated, making it sound like a question.

Walter nodded. '*Ja, gnädige Frau.*'

'Please show her into the library, and I'll be down in a moment. Offer her coffee, and I'll have a cup, too. Thank you, Walter.'

'*Gnädige Frau*,' he murmured, inclining his head, backing out, and quietly closing the door behind him.

Ursula slid her papers into the top drawer of the desk, locked it and pocketed the key. She rose, smoothing down the skirt of her dark-grey woollen dress with both hands as she walked over to the dressing table, where she glanced at herself in the mirror. Her face was drawn, her mouth pale and tense, and there were dark circles under her eyes. This hardly surprised her, in view of the events of the previous night. She had not slept, had lain awake until the first light, worrying and pondering their predicament and their future. Sigmund had not slept either; he had risen at six and gone off to the bank very early. He had already spoken to her on the telephone several times since leaving the house, keeping his promise to stay in touch, to inform her of any new developments after the night of havoc in the city.

She ran a comb through her short blonde hair, smoothed a hand over it abstractedly, then walked to the door, looking at her wristwatch as she did. It was still early, not quite nine o'clock. There was no question in her mind why Renata was downstairs, asking to see her. She had come out of genuine concern for them, and Ursula was immeasurably touched by the gesture.

A moment later she was hurrying down the stairs, crossing the vast hall and pushing open the double doors which led into the library.

Renata was standing looking out of the window, and she swung around when Ursula entered and ran to meet her. She caught hold of her almost roughly, hugged her close, saying, 'Oh, Ursi, Ursi,' several times before releasing her. 'Forgive me for bursting in on you like this, unannounced,' Renata went on, 'but I wanted to speak to you urgently, and our phone isn't working. For some reason, it seems to be out of order this morning.'

'It was good of you to come, Ren, and I'm glad you're here. You always make me feel better. Walter is bringing us coffee. Come.'

Arms linked, the two of them walked over to the Biedermeier sofa, where they sat down. Drawing back and looking at her closely, Renata said, 'Of course you know that last night's riots were not only in Berlin, but took place all over Germany and Austria as well. Yes, I can see from your face that you do.'

'The whole thing is incredible. Hard to believe.'

'And even harder to stomach! You've seen the newspapers? Heard the radio?'

'The papers yes, but I haven't listened to the radio.' Speaking quickly, Ursula explained how they had learned about the demonstrations from Theodora in the middle of the night, and recounted the girl's experiences.

Renata had paled as she listened, and she exclaimed, 'Teddy and her friend were extremely lucky, they could easily have been killed. Quite a few people were.'

Ursula stared at her. '*Jews* were killed.'

'Yes.' Renata leaned closer. 'Listen to me, Ursula, you must – ' She broke off as Walter knocked, opened the door, and came gliding in with the coffee tray.

'*Danke schön*, Walter,' Ursula said.

The butler deposited the silver tray on the occasional table in front of the sofa and discreetly withdrew.

In hushed tones, Renata continued, with some urgency, 'You must make plans to leave Germany. It's not safe for you here anymore.'

'I don't think it has been for a long time. We should have gone last year, even the year before, perhaps. But we believed in German law and order, and we thought we were safe. We also drew comfort from the belief that Hitler couldn't last, couldn't possibly stay in power. Many Germans did, and not all of them Jews, you and Reinhard included. But we were all wrong. Now I don't think there is any turning back. This is the end. For Jews anyway.'

'For us all.' Renata looked at her intently, her dark eyes very bright, and blazing with sudden anger. 'That damned megalomaniac Hitler is leading us into a dark abyss of brutality and murder. Germany is being destroyed from within by him and his depraved cohorts. Why, they're nothing but terrorists, for God's sake!'

'I read in the papers that the Nazis are saying last night's demonstrations were spontaneous. *That they were provoked,*' Ursula said. 'And all because of that seventeen-year-old German Jewish refugee living in Paris, Herschel Grynszpan, who shot and killed Ernst vom Rath, the third secretary at the German Embassy in Paris. You see, Renata, they're blaming the Jews yet again.'

'We read that story, but Reinhard is convinced the riots were not spontaneous, that they were cleverly and expertly orchestrated by Heydrich and the SS. And he's right, I'm certain. What's more, we both believe there are bound to be additional demonstrations, and many other acts of brutality directed against Jews.' Renata shook her head, finished in a worried voice, 'We think Hitler wants to kill every Jew in the land, Ursi.'

'But that's inconceivable,' Ursula stammered. 'How can Hitler kill an entire people? Millions of people. No one could do that . . .' Her voice trailed off helplessly.

'He aims to try.' Renata's tone was more apprehensive than ever. 'Read *Mein Kampf* again. And believe it this time.'

'We are *Germans,*' Ursula began, and stopped abruptly.

She clenched her hands together and took a deep breath. 'Our families, Sigi's and mine, have been here for hundreds and hundreds of years . . .' Once more she came to a halt as her voice cracked, and she looked away, steadying herself. 'But we must leave our country . . . yes . . . we must leave this country we love . . . if we are to survive . . .'

Feelings of compassion and loving friendship washed over Renata, and she reached out, put her hand on Ursula's arm consolingly. Ursula turned, stared into her face, and they shared a look that was very direct and intimate and full of truth.

Tears welled up in Renata when she saw the anguish casting a deep shadow across Ursula's face, the profound sorrow darkening her soft, grey-blue eyes. 'I don't want anything to happen to you!' she cried fiercely, her voice choked with anxiety. 'I love and care for you, and for Sigi and little Maxim. So does Reinhard. We will help you in any way we can, do anything to help you leave Germany safely. And you must leave, darling, you know you must . . . to save yourselves.'

'Yes.' Ursula sat staring into the distance, her eyes focused on the pale blue sky outside the tall window, and with an unexpected rush of clarity she finally came to understand what it was that had haunted her for so long a time. For a while she was unable to say anything, so shaken and alarmed was she, but at last she turned her head and looked deeply into Renata's eyes once more.

Renata felt as if Ursula was staring into her soul, and she shivered slightly, and said, 'Why are you looking at me like that? Whatever is it?'

'A moment ago I said that it was inconceivable . . . that Hitler cannot kill an entire people. *But he can.* Oh yes, he can. *I know that now.* The knowledge is deep within me, in my bones, in the very pores of my skin. For months I've had desperate feelings gnawing at me . . . the ones I've spoken to you about. I thought they were feelings of apprehension and dread, but they weren't. What I've harboured within me all this time is an overwhelming sense of doom. *We are doomed, my family and I.*'

'My dearest, my most beloved friend – ' Renata found she was unable to continue, so overcome was she by the pain she felt for Ursula. What she was facing was monstrous: upheaval, flight, exile. But if she and Sigi and little Maxim stayed they would be hounded, persecuted and ultimately harmed. The evil and injustice of it filled Renata with rage, and the rage swamped her and she cried passionately, 'Those Nazi bastards! This shouldn't be happening! It shouldn't! It's wrong!'

'Don't, darling. Please don't. We'll be all right. Somehow.'

Renata reached for Ursula's hand and clasped it in hers; they sat quietly, neither of them able to continue the conversation for a while.

Eventually Ursula cleared her throat and said in a voice that was oddly calm, 'Sigi does have a plan of action, you know. He's working on it right now. He has a good contact, apparently. He's hoping to buy exit visas for us. And new passports.' She paused, then went on, 'You see, last month we had to take our passports to be stamped . . . with a J . . . for Jew.'

Startled and shocked, Renata looked at her in consternation. 'How ridiculous! What evil nonsense!'

'Yes, but the Nazis have made this a law, and we had to comply.'

Renata made a supreme effort to suppress her immense anger, control her flaring emotions, thinking that if Ursula could be so brave, so contained, then so must she. She even managed to push a smile onto her face, when she said, 'Reinhard and I want you to come out to the Mark Brandenburg and stay at the Schloss. Until you leave Germany it will be much safer for you at our country estate than in Berlin.'

When Ursula did not immediately respond, Renata said, 'Look,' and took hold of her arm, brought her face closer to her friend's, 'it could take Sigi several weeks to get the necessary documents together, to arrange everything to facilitate your departure.'

'It might, that's true. And thank you for inviting us to the Schloss. It's so kind and thoughtful of you. But I can't leave Sigi alone here in Berlin. You know how much he needs me. We've never really been apart since we were children, except when I was at school in England with you and Arabella.'

'He can see you at weekends. He can drive down to the Mark with us every Friday afternoon. Please say yes.'

Ursula remained uncertain. 'Let me think about it, and I'll discuss it with Sigi.'

The telephone began to ring and Ursula rushed to answer it, wanting to pick up before the butler did.

'Hello?' she said, fully expecting to hear her husband's voice, but it was Arabella von Wittingen at the other end. She listened for several moments, then murmured, 'Thank you, Belle, and I'm all right, really.' She listened again, then quickly explained, 'Their phone is out of order. Ren is here. Do you wish to speak with her?' Ursula stood with the receiver pressed to her ear, nodding her head several times before she said, 'Yes, Arabella, that's fine. Goodbye.'

'She's coming over here, isn't she?' Renata stated as Ursula put down the phone.

'Of course. I suppose we both knew she would. And I'm sure you've gathered that she's been trying to telephone you.'

Renata nodded.

'Arabella is in her most Bolshy and defiant mood this morning,' Ursula confided. 'She insists that the three of us go out to lunch. To the Adlon Hotel.'

Straightening up on the sofa, Renata threw her a questioning look. 'Are you up to it? And do you think we *should*?'

Ursula was thoughtful, wondering whether or not it would be a wise thing to do. And then she, who of late had sometimes been fearful about going out, suddenly had no qualms at all. Her own sense of defiance and her pride made her say, 'Of course I'm up to it. And why shouldn't we go to lunch at the Adlon? We're as entitled as anyone else, aren't we?'

'Indeed we are!' Renata agreed. 'Let's do it!'

Ursula walked back to the sofa, stood looking down at the silver tray, shaking her head. 'We've been so busy talking we never drank the coffee, and now it's probably quite cold. Shall I ask Walter to brew some more?'

'Not right now, thanks. Let's wait until Arabella gets here. You know what she's like about her morning tea. She's bound to ask you for a pot, so we might as well share it with her.' Renata rose, strolled over to the window, glanced out into the Tiergartenstrasse, then swung to face Ursula. 'I heard on the radio earlier that the Nazis have already given last night a name. They're calling it *Kristallnacht* . . . crystal night. Because of all the broken glass, I suppose.' Renata shuddered, and grimaced in utter disgust. 'How despicable the Nazis are! Imagine using a pretty and poetic name like that to describe a night of such unspeakable savagery!' She shuddered again. 'It's beyond comprehension.'

'Everything that's happening is beyond comprehension,' Ursula said.

ELEVEN

The Tiergarten was deserted.

As Sigmund walked down the path he realised it would not be anything *but* deserted in bitterly cold weather such as they were having in Berlin this December. And that was *precisely* the reason it had been chosen for the rendezvous. A park without people was a safe park.

He had no idea whom he was to meet.

Irina had slipped a note to him two nights ago, during drinks at the von Tiegals' house, where he and Ursula were attending a small dinner party. Within seconds of pocketing it he had excused himself, hurried to the bathroom in order to read it, impatient to know what it said.

The note had been brief and to the point.

Tiergarten. Saturday. 11 a.m. Hofjägeralle side. For identification your contact will say: The blue gentians are not in bloom today. Destroy this note.

After reading the note a second time, he had set fire to the bit of paper with his cigarette lighter, held it until it was almost burnt through, then dropped it into the toilet bowl and flushed it away. Returning to the living room, he had found Irina in conversation with Reinhard, and he had simply touched her elbow, as if by accident, to let her know he had read the note and destroyed it. He knew better than to discuss anything in front of others, even their closest and most trustworthy friends. A slip of the tongue might put others in grave danger.

Sigmund had asked Princess Irina Troubetzkoy for help the evening he and Ursula had attended the reception and dinner at the British Embassy, which had been the ill-fated night of the Nazi riots – *Kristallnacht* – as it turned out.

Without ever having been told, he knew intuitively that Irina was closely tied to one of the secret movements which aided Jews, Catholics, Protestants, dissidents, and so-called 'political offenders' of all kinds, who sought to flee Germany and the persecution of the Third Reich. From a few things he had picked up, here and there and at different times, he was aware that there were several such movements operating in Berlin; all were run by German aristocrats, for the most part, although some of the young international émigrés were also apparently involved. All were opposed to Hitler and his regime, and violently anti-Nazi.

When he had approached Irina four weeks ago he had not made any reference to the various resistance movements, deeming it wiser not to do so, and had merely asked her if she could put him in touch with someone who might help him get exit visas. She had replied that she would see what she could do, and a week later she had invited them to dinner with her mother Natalie and the baron, at the baron's house on the Lützowufer. She had found an opportunity to get him alone for a moment, had murmured that the matter was in hand, and that there was no need for him to approach anyone else. 'Patience, Sigi. Trust me,' she had said softly, before gliding away to speak to another guest. Three more weeks had gone by until she had finally passed the note to him on Thursday. He had been vastly relieved, and had hardly been able to contain himself until today.

As he continued along the same path that ran parallel with the Hofjägeralle, walking in the direction of the Siegessäule, Sigmund saw a man coming towards him. He was tall and thin, dressed in a dark-green loden coat and a Tyrolean hat, and he was striding out purposefully, swinging a walking stick. He seemed oddly familiar to Sigi, who within seconds was filled with dismay. He had recognised the man; it was Kurt von Wittingen. The last person he wanted to run into when he was on this kind of delicate mission was a friend who would engage him in conversation, and in the process most probably scare off his contact. But Sigmund knew there was nothing he could do. He was trapped. He could not turn around and walk in another direction because Kurt had already seen him, was raising his stick, waving it in greeting. There was nothing for it but to act in the most normal way, chat for a few minutes and then walk on. Fortunately the weather played in his favour. It was so icy he was sure Kurt would not wish to linger.

A moment later the two men were drawing to a standstill, greeting each other warmly, and shaking hands.

After the initial greetings were over, Kurt said, 'It's far too bitter to stand here chatting like this.'

Relieved to hear him make this comment, Sigmund instantly agreed. 'Yes, it is. Very nice running into you, Kurt, give my love to Arabella, and we'll see you next week. I must be on my way.'

Kurt said, 'I'll walk with you.'

Sigmund's dismay spiralled into alarm. When his contact saw him with a companion, he or she would not dare to approach him, but would simply disappear, he was quite convinced of that. For a split second panic rendered him speechless. He stood staring at Kurt, desperately wondering how to get rid of him courteously, and without giving offence.

'It's all right, Sigi,' Kurt said. 'Relax. *The blue gentians are not in bloom in the Tiergarten today.*'

Sigmund was not sure that he had heard correctly, and he continued to stare at Kurt, looking slightly dumbfounded.

'Let's start walking,' Kurt said swiftly, and set off at a brisk pace.

Recovering himself immediately, Sigi fell into step. 'Why didn't Irina tell me *you* were my contact?'

'She wasn't sure it *would* be me. So why risk exposing me unnecessarily, albeit to a very old and reliable friend?'

'I understand.'

'The eight exit visas you require are for Ursula, Maxim and yourself, and your immediate family. And Theodora. I am correct am I not?'

'Yes. I would like to get new passports for all of us. Passports not stamped with a J.'

Kurt threw him a quick glance and frowned. 'I am *positive* I cannot get new passports, Sigi. Does it really matter that they're stamped with a J?'

'No, I don't suppose so.' Sigmund cleared his throat. 'But I was hoping that if you *could* get them, they could be issued under a different name. At least, for the Westheims.'

'Why a false name, Sigi?'

'Look, I've not been touched so far, nor has the bank been taken over by them, because I've been extremely useful to the Government in various financial transactions, notably those to do with foreign currencies and such. And I'm still very useful to them. Frankly, I just don't think they'd like it if I tried to leave Germany at this time. They might even try to prevent me from going, if they got wind of it. And so obviously if I were travelling out under a different name I would not be so easily spotted.'

'Yes, of course, I see what you mean. But I know I cannot get you the new passports. I'm so sorry, but that's not something *my* contact could pull off.'

'All right, never mind.'

'Arabella tells me that you and Ursula are coming to supper on Monday night. You must bring the eight passports with you then. I will need them for the exit visas. Put them in the inside breast pocket of your overcoat. I will take them out of your coat at some point during the evening.'

'No problem. I'll collect the passports from my family tomorrow.'

The two men walked on in silence for several seconds and then Sigmund said worriedly, 'Are you sure you can procure the exit visas?'

'I won't lie to you, Sigi, I don't know that I can,' Kurt said. 'It won't be easy. But I have a good source and I am extremely hopeful. Let's just say that I'm ninety per cent certain.'

'I have money on me, in my overcoat pocket. A great deal of cash. Do you want it now?'

'No, I don't, but thank you for offering.'

'What about entry visas to another country?'

'They're not going to be easy to get either.'

'Have you any idea which country we might be able to go to?'

Kurt shook his head. 'Not at this moment. I doubt that it will be America, though. The US Congress doesn't seem willing to modify the immigration laws, to allow any more Jewish refugees from Germany to enter the country. Nor does Roosevelt seem prepared to act.'

'What about England?'

'I believe that's your best chance, since the British have been very generous about taking in Jewish refugees from Europe for some time. And anyway, my influence and contacts are much stronger with the British diplomatic service. Never fear, I will pull every string available to me.'

'I know you'll do your damnedest. Where will we actually *go* when we leave Berlin?'

'To one of two cities, Lisbon or Paris. But more than likely it will be Paris, where you could pick up your entry visas from the British Embassy, if you didn't have them in your hands when you left Germany.'

'Have you any idea when that will be?' Sigi asked.

'I daren't promise anything, or give you a specific date. But I don't think it will take much longer than a month to get the documents. Let's say early January.'

Sigmund nodded. 'I *can* tell Ursula, can't I? Just to alleviate her awful worry about Maxim's safety.'

'Yes, but do warn her not to discuss your plans with anyone outside the family. And don't tell her who is helping you. The less you say, and actually the less you know, the safer it is for me, Irina and our friends. And for you too, in the long run,' Kurt said.

'You have no cause to worry, Kurt. I will be discreet, and so will Ursula. And not one member of my family will know any of the details, only that we are going to leave. I realise that there will be hefty pay-offs involved, and I would simply like to add that money is no object.'

'I know that, Sigi. I also know that it is now impossible for Jews to transfer any assets abroad. I hope you took care of that some time ago.' Kurt gave him a questioning look.

Sigmund nodded. 'I managed to get some money out.'

'But not enough, perhaps. You must have Ursula sew her most valuable jewellery into the linings of the clothes she will be travelling in, such as a suit jacket and its skirt, her top coat, even under the lining of her hat. That is the best way to get valuables out undetected. And have your mother and sisters do the same thing.'

'I will.'

'Oh, and one other thing, they must do this themselves. I'm not suggesting for one moment that your servants are disloyal, but it's wise to be cautious. One never knows about anyone these days. Brother is informing on brother, so just be careful in front of the servants. The last thing you want is the Nazi guards at the border alerted that you are carrying valuables. They would confiscate everything.'

'I am quite positive our servants are trustworthy, they have been with the family for years. However, I will naturally heed your advice,' Sigi promised.

'And also be careful what you say on the telephone . . . at home and at the bank. Phone-tapping has become a favourite Nazi pastime,' Kurt remarked in a disdainful tone.

'Do you think my phones are tapped?' Sigmund asked swiftly.

'I'm not sure. Possibly they are at the bank. Just be *aware*, that's all.'

'I have been for a long time.'

'Good. That's it for now. We will go our separate ways. And when we meet again socially we will obviously not discuss this meeting, or anything else pertaining to the matter.'

'Absolutely not,' Sigi concurred.

'Once I have the documents in my hands, I will arrange a rendezvous for us. We will meet somewhere exceptionally safe,' Kurt said, then went on to explain, 'And you must be prepared to travel immediately, of course. So be ready. And you must travel light. Take only one suitcase each, if possible. If it's not, then do not take more than two each, at the most.'

'I understand.' Sigi came to a halt, turned to face the other man. 'I don't know how to thank you, Kurt, I really don't. I am overcome with gratitude for what you're doing for me and my family. The words *thank you* somehow don't seem to be quite enough.'

'Thanks are not necessary, my dear old friend. I am glad to help you. And for your own sakes, I'm glad you're going. It's obvious, after *Kristallnacht*, that this country is in the hands of mass murderers.' Kurt's sensitive, gentle face filled with a terrible sadness and he sighed heavily. There was a slight pause before he went on quietly, 'Stay calm. Try not to worry. Everything is in hand. With a bit of luck you'll soon be out of Germany. In the meantime, just continue to go about your business in the most natural way.' He thrust out his hand.

Sigi took it, clasped it strongly. 'Thank you again, Kurt, and from the very bottom of my heart. I will never forget this, never as long as I live. You are a true friend.'

The two men parted company.

Sigmund stood for a moment watching Kurt's retreating figure. Then he turned up the collar of his overcoat, thrust his hands in his pockets, swung around and walked in the direction they had just come. He could not wait to get back to his house on the Tiergartenstrasse to tell Ursula the good news.

His thoughts turned to Prince Rudolf Kurt von Wittingen as he hurried along the path. He trusted Kurt implicitly. And if anyone could pull this off, then he could.

For several years Kurt had been a senior consultant to Krupp, the German armaments king. As such he roamed all over Europe, frequently travelled to England and the United States, handling top-level negotiations, entertaining foreign dignitaries and acting as a sort of roving ambassador for the Krupp organisation.

Sigi now realised that this job was the perfect cover for Kurt. He was able to come and go almost as he wished. He had access to all kinds of important people, who in turn were extraordinary sources of information, and probably privileged information at that.

This aside, Sigmund knew for a fact that Kurt was an anti-Fascist, an idealist who happened to be a realist, in that he viewed the totalitarian dictatorship that was Germany through clear, unblinkered eyes. Naturally he would be involved in some sort of resistance movement because of his convictions.

Sigmund wondered why he had never thought of this before. Perhaps because of the Krupp connection, which was undoubtedly the *real* reason why it existed in the first place. It was a red herring to throw people off the scent. A protection for Kurt. He was above suspicion as Krupp's envoy.

And then there was Graf Reinhard von Tiegal. Sigmund considered his other close friend. The count was also an aristocrat, from an ancient Prussian family of *Junkers*, the conservative landholders who were descended from the Teutonic knights. And so by reason of birth and upbringing Reinhard also detested everything the Nazis stood for, and believed them to be criminals of the worst kind.

Was Reinhard involved in the resistance to Hitler? Sigi asked himself. More than likely, he decided after only a moment's thought. And although he knew how dangerous it was for both men, the knowledge that they were fighting the Nazis with whatever means they had was immensely comforting to him.

As long as there were men of honour and humanity in Germany then Hitler and his evil regime would eventually be overcome and ultimately destroyed.

Ursula looked up quickly as Sigmund walked into the library and angrily threw the newspaper she had been reading down on the floor.

'I don't know why I bother with the papers anymore!' she exclaimed, gesturing to the pile of discarded journals at her feet. 'They're only full of Hitler's vile lies and propaganda, courtesy of Göbbels!'

Sigmund sat down on the sofa next to her. 'I suppose we all keep reading the newspapers hoping against hope that we'll glean a little bit of real news.'

'Yes, you're right, darling,' she agreed.

Sigmund took her hand in his and smiled into her drawn face. '*I* have some *news*, Ursula,' he said softly. Moving closer to her, he kissed her cheek, then whispered against her hair, 'I saw my contact a short while ago. The plans are progressing. We're getting out. Hopefully within the next four to five weeks if all goes well.'

'Thank God! Oh thank God!' she gasped, holding onto him tightly. 'Maxim's going to be safe. Our little boy is going to be safe, and that's all that matters, Sigi.'

TWELVE

Maxim stood outside the library, listening.

The door was open a crack and he peeped through it. Just as he thought, his grandmother was sitting near the fireplace in her favourite chair, the one in which she always sat when she came to visit them. She preferred its straight back, he had heard her say that to *Mutti* and Papa many times.

She sat staring into the fire, her hands resting on top of her black cane with its polished silver handle that gleamed brightly in the firelight.

He liked her cane. It had belonged to his grandfather.

His Grandfather Westheim had died two years ago. He remembered many things about him, and he missed him very much. When his Grandfather Westheim used to come to visit them he would lift him up on his knee and tell him stories, and sometimes he would take him for a drive in his big black motorcar with Manfred, the chauffeur, at the wheel. *They* would sit on the back seat together and talk of many Important Things, like The Bank, where he would work with his Papa when he grew up, and which would be his one day. After their drive they always stopped at Grandfather's favourite *Konditorei* and had an ice cream and sometimes cake as well, and his Grandfather Westheim would smoke a cigar and sip a small cup of strong coffee, very black and very sweet, which he was not allowed to have.

He wished his grandfather would come back. But dead people never came back. Not ever. Being dead meant that you had gone to Heaven to live with God, his Papa had told him that. His Grandfather Neuman was dead, too. He had died last year, and *Mutti* had been very sad and had cried a lot, and he had cried too, partly because she was crying and that made him sad. But he had loved his Grandfather Neuman as much as he had loved his Grandfather Westheim.

Suddenly he wondered if the grandfathers ever met each other in Heaven and sat and smoked their cigars and drank cognac and talked about Important World Matters, as they had when they had not been dead. He hoped they did. He wouldn't like them to be lonely in Heaven. His Grandmama Neuman was another dead person, but he had never known her. At least, he had only been one year old when she had died, just a little baby, not grown up like he was now that he was four, and so he couldn't remember much about her, not really. There was only Grandmama Westheim left. 'We must treasure her,' his mother kept saying.

Maxim bent over and pulled up his sock which had slithered down around his ankle.

As he straightened he heard the rustle of silk and a small sigh, and he smiled inside, waiting. Then he heard it . . . the low whistle like a bird chirping in the Tiergarten. He pursed his lips and gave a little whistle himself, and waited again.

The trilling response came almost immediately, and he pushed open the big double doors with both hands and bounded into the room, laughing as he rushed to her, exclaiming, 'I am here, Grandmama! I am here!'

She laughed, too, as he drew to a standstill in front of her and leaned forward, proffering her cheek to him.

He gave her a big kiss, then stood back regarding her, rocking on his heels. His grandmother was dressed in a black lace and silk dress, as she usually was, with the long string of shiny white pearls like fat peas hanging around her neck and the sparkly clips on her ears. She had lots of silky white hair piled on top of her head, with tortoiseshell combs pressed in at each side to hold it there. Her skin was funny, all wrinkly like scrunched-up paper, but she had smooth, pink apple cheeks and bright shining eyes that reminded him of round blue pebbles.

He loved her a lot.

'Don't do that, Maximilian. Don't rock backwards and forwards in that fashion,' his grandmother scolded, but her voice was gentle.

'Sorry, Grandmama.'

She took the box which lay on her lap and handed it to him. 'This is from Auntie Hedy. She wasn't able to come tonight, but she sent this to you and many kisses as well.'

'Oh thank you, Grandmama!' he cried, taking the box from her. Excitedly he tore off the fancy coloured paper, lifted the lid and looked inside.

'Oooh!' he cried when he saw the six candy pigs lying side by side in the box. They were plump and rosy, with beady eyes and yellow bows, and they looked delicious. His mouth watered.

'They're made of your favourite marzipan,' his grandmother said, smiling at him indulgently. 'But you're not to eat even *one* before dinner. Your mother will be cross with both of us, if you do.'

'I won't, I *promise*, Grandmama,' he said, as always a polite and obedient boy. After putting the lid back on the box, he placed it on a nearby table, picked up the torn paper from the floor, crumpled it in a ball and threw it into the fire.

Then he stepped closer to his grandmother, put one of his small, chubby hands on top of hers and began to pat it. 'Gangan,' he said, reverting to his babyhood name for her. 'Can I ask you something?'

'Anything in the whole world, Maxim.'

He held his head on one side and wrinkled his nose. 'How do you know when to whistle?'

'What do you mean?'

'How do you know I'm there, outside the door?'

Her mouth twitched in amusement but she kept a serious face and said, 'Well, I don't *really* know that you're there. I *hope* you are . . . I suppose I sort of *feel* that you are . . . because I love you.'

He nodded solemnly. 'I *like* our game, Grandmama.'

'So do I.' Margarete Westheim leaned back in the chair and studied her only grandchild for a moment. She loved him so much she sometimes thought her heart would break from it. The knowledge that she would have to leave him was an agony. Her only regret about dying, and die she must one day in the not-too-distant future, was that she would miss all those years of his growing up, the wonderful years. He was such a beautiful boy, full of life and laughter and mischief, and so bright, and intelligent beyond his years. She prayed to God every night that Sigmund would succeed in getting the child out of Germany. Like her son and daughter-in-law she was terribly afraid for him. A pestilence stalked this land. A shiver ran through Margarete, and she wondered where God was in this Godless nation. But then what could *He* do? Evil was man's invention, not God's.

'Is something hurting, Gangan?'

Startled out of her brief reverie by his piping child's voice, Margarete looked at him quickly. 'No. Why do you ask that, darling?'

'You have a funny look on your face, a puckery look, like you're going to cry.'

'I'm fine,' she reassured him with a swift smile, suddenly aware of the worry in his child's eyes. She opened her black beaded evening bag, reached inside, took out a small item wrapped in silver paper and handed it to him. 'Here you are, Maxim, here is your Friday pocket money.'

'Oh, Grandmama, thank you, *thank you.*'

He unwrapped the silver paper, his eyes shining as he stared down at the coins in his hand. *Four marks.* His Gangan always gave him four now. Last year he had received three. Next year she would give him five. She had told him that. One mark for every year he had been born. He leaned closer to her, kissed her cheek, and beamed into her face as he slipped the coins in his pocket, playing with them for a moment, liking the way they jingled.

The door opened and Maxim turned his head. When he saw his father standing in the doorway he flew to him at once, crying, 'Papa! Papa!'

His father caught him, swung him up and kissed him, and carried him in his arms as he strode across the floor.

'Good evening, Mother,' Sigmund said.

'Good evening, Sigi,' she responded, her clear blue eyes so like his lighting up at the sight of him. He was her youngest son, the third one she had borne. His two elder brothers were both dead over twenty years now. Killed in the trenches of the Somme in the Great War when only boys. Two sons she had sacrificed for the Fatherland.

Sigmund put Maxim on the sofa, went to kiss his mother before sitting down next to his small son. He said to her, 'I understand from Ursula that

Hedy is not coming this evening, that she's not feeling well. Nothing too serious, I hope?'

'A cold, Sigi, that's all.' Frau Westheim sighed. 'There's always *something* with Hedy these days. That girl would be better off living in a warmer climate, I do believe.'

'Wouldn't we all,' Sigmund murmured, and continued, 'She's not seemed well since she broke off her engagement to Paul.'

'No, she hasn't,' Frau Westheim agreed, and turned her head, looked into the fire, a faraway expression flicking onto her face.

Watching her, Maxim thought: Gangan looks unhappy. I wonder why? He glanced up at his father, his wonderful Papa, and smiled at him adoringly.

Sigmund stared down into the small, bright face upturned to his, smiled back, and said, 'Do you remember what I told you last Friday evening? When I was speaking to you about the standards I want you to have when you are a big boy, and when you are a man?'

'Yes, Papa, you said a gentleman never tells a lie.'

'That's correct, Maxim, but now I'm afraid I must amend that statement.'

'Oh.' Maxim looked surprised. He was not sure what the word amend meant, but he was reluctant to admit this, so he kept silent.

'I don't suppose you know what amend means, do you?' Sigmund said, as if reading his mind.

'No.'

Sigmund took his child's hand lovingly. 'I thought as much. It means to *change* or *revise*. And I wish to revise what I said to you last week, change my opinion . . . I believe it is perfectly all right for a gentleman to tell a lie, if it is a matter of life and death . . . if it is to save his life. Or the lives of others, of course.'

Maxim nodded.

'Do you understand me?'

'I think so, Papa.'

'Very good, Maxim. You're a clever boy, I know that, and you are learning quickly. Now . . . there is something else I want to tell you, and it is this. A man must have valour, honour and nobility if he is to be of great character. I want you to remember that when you grow up.'

'Yes, Papa, I will.'

His grandmother said, 'Your father's brothers Heinrich and Peter had valour . . . they were very courageous . . . they went to fight for their country in the Great War and they were not afraid. That is what valour means.'

'The dead uncles . . . they were *brave*,' Maxim said with a little frown.

'Yes, the dead uncles were,' his grandmother answered. 'And your grandfathers were both men of honour because they never did anything that was cruel or wicked, unjust or dishonest – '

'Dinner is ready everyone,' Ursula announced from the doorway. 'Marta is waiting to serve.'

'We shall come at once, my darling,' Sigmund said, rising immediately. 'Now, Maxim, run along with your mother. We will follow.' He lifted him down from the sofa, then reached into his pocket and took out a slip of paper. 'Here you are. I have written out the new words for you, as well as their meaning.'

Maxim took it, put it safely in his pocket. He kept all of these pieces of paper which his father had been giving him for the last few weeks. 'Thank you, Papa, and I *will* remember. Always.'

Sigmund gazed down at him, marvelling at the beauty and brightness of the boy. He really was exceptional, highly intelligent and articulate for his age, an extraordinary child. He smoothed his hand over Maxim's blond head, and then went to help his mother out of the chair, escorted her slowly across the room.

Maxim ran ahead to Ursula, who stood waiting in the doorway.

She took his hand in hers and together they crossed the baronial marble entrance hall, walking in the direction of the dining room.

'And what was Papa telling you tonight, my darling?'

'He said that when I grow up I must be a man of valour, honour and nobility.'

Ursula said, very softly, 'If you are, then you will be exactly like your father.'

Maxim shut his eyes tightly and listened as his mother performed the ritual of blessing the *shabbat* candles.

'*Baruch-ata Adonai Elohaynu, melech ha-olam asher kid'shanu b'mits-votav v'tsivanu l'hadlik nayr shel shabbat,*' she said slowly in her light clear voice which he always loved to listen to, and most especially when she spoke Hebrew. She made the words sound like music.

'Amen,' he sang as she finished, joining in with everyone else. And then he opened his eyes.

They all sat down around the large table with its snow-white cloth and silver candelabra and crystal goblets which sparkled in the candlelight. Papa was at the head, *Mutti* at the other end facing his father, and he and Theodora sat together opposite Grandmama.

Now it was his father's turn to perform the ritual.

He blessed the red wine in a little silver cup and said the *Kiddush* in Hebrew, and then he murmured another blessing, this time over the *chollah*, the two twisted loaves of bread in the silver basket under the embroidered linen napkin.

Once the blessings were finished, his father lifted the napkin, made a little ceremony of breaking the bread, and passed it around to everyone at the table. And at last Marta was allowed to serve the food, which Frau Müller had been cooking all afternoon in the big kitchen. Marta always served the dinner on Friday because it was Walter's night off, when he went to see his daughter and her children. *He* knew a lot about the butler's grandchildren. Walter told him many things when he sneaked into the kitchen on baking days. Walter would sit him at Frau Müller's baking table and give him a *Berliner Pfannkuchen*, oozing jelly, and a glass of milk, and talk to him, and slip him another jelly doughnut when no one was looking. Except that Frau Müller always noticed. 'You spoil that child,' she would tell Walter, who fortunately never paid any attention to her. Walter and he were *very* good friends.

Maxim settled back in the chair, waiting.

Everything always happened the way he knew it would, and as it had for as long as he could remember. 'The rituals of the sabbath are important to us all, and should be properly observed,' his mother had often told him. He liked rituals and looked forward to them. They were special, somehow.

Friday was his most favourite night of the week, and for lots of reasons. For one thing, he and Teddy were permitted to have dinner with his mother and father in the grand dining room, instead of eating alone together in the nursery as they generally did, except on Teddy's day off. For another, he was with *Mutti*, Papa, Teddy and Grandmama, the four people he loved the most in the whole wide world; also, he got to stay up *late*; and finally the things he enjoyed the most were served. Piping-hot chicken soup, then a roasted chicken, all golden and crisp on the outside and juicy on the inside, or beef flanken or perhaps steamed carp, and there would be little potato pancakes and apple sauce, or sweet shredded carrots and potato dumplings. And at the end of the meal there was always something wonderful, such as apple strudel which melted in his mouth.

Yes, Friday was the *best* night of the week. It was like the beginning of a holiday. His father did not go to The Bank on Saturday and Sunday, and so they did many things and had such a lot of fun together. Friday night was . . . was . . . *festive*. Yes, that was it exactly. Except that tonight no one seemed very festive. His mother was quiet, so very still. She had been like this for ages, and he kept wondering why. He had asked Teddy, just the other day, and she had not really given him an answer. All she had said was that his mother had *things* on her mind, and even though he had pestered her a lot she had not told him anything else.

Mutti did not laugh very much any more, and her beautiful face was sad, like when Grandfather Neuman died. He thought she was cross with him, but Teddy said this wasn't so, and he believed Teddy. She always told him the truth. Besides, he hadn't been a bad boy. In fact, he had been an angel lately, so Teddy said.

The tantalising aroma of chicken soup floated delicately on the air, and Maxim's nose twitched when Marta placed one of the steaming porcelain bowls in front of him.

'*Danke schön*, Marta,' he said, and picked up his silver spoon. He dipped it in the clear golden liquid, scooped up a sliver of carrot and a curly bit of noodle, and took his first mouthful. It tasted delicious. This was *definitely* the soup he liked the best. He wished they had it every day.

His father and his grandmother talked non-stop about this and that, and occasionally his mother joined in, but he and Teddy were as quiet as mice, as they always were, not speaking unless they were spoken to, when they had to reply.

After they had all finished the soup, Gerda, the other downstairs maid, took the bowls away and Marta came gliding in from the kitchen carrying a silver platter on which there lay a huge steamed carp.

Maxim could see the fish if he sat up really straight in the chair and craned his neck. Marta showed the fish to his mother, who nodded and said, 'It looks wonderful, Marta. My compliments to Frau Müller. Please be kind enough to serve it.'

'It seems to me that it would be a nice change for you if you went to stay with Renata at the Schloss for a few days,' Sigmund said, looking down the long stretch of table at Ursula as the dessert was being served. 'And I'm sure Maxim and Teddy would enjoy it too.'

At the mention of his name, Maxim sat up in the chair and looked from his father to his mother alertly. His dark eyes gleamed, and before he could stop himself, he exclaimed, 'Oh yes, *Mutti*, please let's go!'

Ursula glanced at him. A faint smile touched her mouth. 'Would you really like to do that, *Mein Schatz*?'

'I would, *Mutti*, and so would Teddy. Wouldn't you, Teddy?' He turned to Theodora, gave her a pleading look.

Teddy said, 'I think Maxim would benefit from a change of air, a few days in the country.'

Sigmund smiled. He was delighted to have his son and Teddy as his allies. He had been quite certain that Ursula would object, that she would not wish to go away, although in his opinion she truly needed a break from

Berlin and its tensions. Maxim's enthusiasm would undoubtedly sway her, he now believed.

Just as Sigmund had thought, Ursula nodded her assent. 'All right, Maxim, we'll go in the middle of next week, let's say on Wednesday.' She focused her gaze on Sigmund, and added, 'But only if you promise to join us on Friday, Sigi.'

'I do promise,' Sigmund said at once. 'I understand from Reinhard that Renata is going to invite Arabella and the children if you accept, so it will be nice for Maxim to be with them.'

'Yes, it will,' Ursula agreed. The thought of the trip to the Mark Brandenburg and being with her two best women friends cheered Ursula, and she suddenly felt lighter in spirit. Turning to Maxim, she said with a loving smile, 'It's been snowing in the Mark so we'll be able to play outside with the other children. We'll go tobogganing and perhaps we can even skate on the lake.'

Maxim nodded excitedly. The prospect of this trip thrilled him and it showed on his animated little face. Laughing gaily, he cried, 'And I will build you a beautiful snowman, *Mutti*, and one for *you* too, Teddy.' He looked from one to the other, and his mother smiled at him as Teddy murmured her thanks, and this made him glow inside.

As he picked up his fork and cut into his apple strudel, he thought he was going to burst with happiness. Friday night had been *extra* special this week. They were going to stay at the big old castle where he always had fun with Gretchen, Diana and Christian, and his mother was smiling again, which was the most important thing of all.

THIRTEEN

The forests of the Mark Brandenburg, once the domain of the conquering Teutonic knights, stretch for miles in the marshy region of Prussia where they are located. Drained by three rivers, the Havel, the Spree and the Oder, this area has many lakes and is also crisscrossed by countless canals and little waterways which connect its quaint villages.

At the edge of one such old and charming village stands the great Schloss of Graf Reinhard von Tiegal. The back facade of this ancient and picturesque castle faces sloping lawns and formal gardens, and beyond these are the pine forests which are part of the immense von Tiegal estates, owned by the family since the sixteenth century.

On this Sunday morning, early in January of 1939, these forests looked quite magical, completely garbed in white. Snow and dripping icicles covered the trees, weighted their branches down in places, and underfoot the narrow, winding paths were obscured by new layers of snow which had fallen during the night and then frozen. In the brilliant, golden sunlight streaming in through the trees everything glistened as if it had been dusted with silver.

The only sound in this vast and silent white wonderland was the crunch of heavy boots sinking into the crisp snow as Sigmund and Kurt ploughed forward through the forest on their morning walk. Both men had come to the Schloss to join their wives for the weekend, Sigmund driving down to the Mark from Berlin on Friday evening, Kurt on Saturday afternoon.

Heavily bundled up though they were, in thick green loden coats, Tyrolean hats, woollen scarves and gloves, and with their trousers tucked inside their ski boots, they nevertheless moved at a relatively brisk pace since there was an icy, cutting wind.

Neither of them spoke for a while, wrapped in their own thoughts yet perfectly comfortable in their mutual silence, as old friends frequently are.

It was Kurt who finally broke this silence when he said, 'I have news for you, Sigi.'

Sigmund looked at him alertly. 'You do? Please, tell me quickly.'

'I will have the exit visas for you tomorrow or on Tuesday. However, there has been a slight snag. I can only get three.'

'Oh no!' Sigmund's heart sank. He came to an abrupt standstill and stared at Kurt, unable to keep the dismay from showing on his face. 'What happened? What went wrong?'

'Nothing went *wrong*. Very simply, my contact feels he must move carefully. For the moment, at least. To avoid arousing suspicion.' Kurt took hold of Sigmund's arm. 'Come, let's keep walking. We don't want to freeze to death out here.' The two men set off again, and the prince continued, 'Eight visas are a lot to get all at once, Sigi, and especially since only a week or two ago my contact managed to help a large family leave, after numerous delays. *Nine* people, actually. But quite aside from his own sense of caution, *his* contact at the Foreign Ministry is somewhat nervous just now. Nonetheless, my friend promises to have three more exit visas for you in a couple of weeks, and the last two by the end of the month. *No later*. Please don't worry, it's going to be all right. Now, we need to know who will be using the first three visas. I presume you want to get Ursula and Maxim out immediately. Will you go with them?'

'Ursula and Maxim *must* go at once. But I cannot,' Sigmund said without hesitation. 'I must stay behind until everyone else has left.'

'I rather thought you'd say that,' Kurt murmured. 'So who will accompany Ursula and Maxim? Your mother?'

Sigmund shook his head. 'My mother wouldn't go, not without my sisters. She would never leave her daughters behind, I can assure you of that. She will tell me that she is an old woman, that her life is virtually over anyway, and she'll refuse. *Adamantly*. And so I think it will be best if Theodora travels with Ursula and Maxim. In two weeks, when you have the second set of visas, Sigrid, her husband, and Hedy can leave. I will take my mother out with me at the end of the month.'

'I guessed you wouldn't even contemplate leaving Germany until the entire family was safely in another country,' Kurt said. 'I should have the three relevant passports back in my hands by Tuesday, Wednesday at the latest. I will bring them to you at the house.'

'Thank you very much, Kurt. Ursula is prepared, and she can leave immediately. Your contact – ' Sigmund broke off, hesitating, then said, 'Your contact *is* fairly certain he can get the other visas, isn't he?'

'Yes.' Now it was Kurt's turn to stop, and he swung to face Sigmund. The look he gave him was one of great directness. '*He is absolutely sure*, I promise you, Sigi.'

Sigmund returned his friend's gaze unwaveringly.

Their eyes locked and held.

For a fleeting moment Kurt thought he saw a flicker of doubt or worry, or perhaps a mingling of both, at the back of Sigmund's light blue eyes, and he said, 'You must believe me, my source is extremely reliable. He wouldn't say he could get the visas if he thought he couldn't, if he had any reservations whatsoever.'

There was a small silence; finally Sigmund nodded. 'As long as *you* have confidence in him, Kurt, that is good enough for me.'

Even though they were now in the depths of the forest, Kurt dropped his voice to a lower pitch, more from habit than anything else, and said, 'Look, to make you feel more secure about everything I will tell you who is helping me. And you. It's Admiral Canaris.'

Sigmund's jaw dropped. He was thunderstruck and he gaped at Kurt. '*Wilhelm Canaris!* But he's head of the Abwehr.'

'Yes. As head of German Military Intelligence he is invaluable to me. And in many more ways than I can ever tell you.'

'*Canaris*,' Sigmund repeated wonderingly.

It was patently obvious to Kurt that Sigmund was genuinely stunned by what he had just told him, and he said, 'By birth, upbringing, tradition, instinct and conviction, Admiral Canaris detests Hitler and all that he stands for, as do many of the men who work under him. And, incidentally, there isn't one ministry in the entire Government that doesn't have two or three men, sometimes even more, who feel the same way.'

'Like the admiral's contact in the Foreign Ministry?'

'*Exactly.*'

'I must admit, you startled me, took my breath away, when you mentioned the admiral,' Sigi said. 'Who would guess he is an anti-Nazi?'

'His hatred of them is quite known . . . in a select circle. You could say it's a sort of . . . well, it's an open secret really. And there happens to be a number of generals who think exactly as he does. But it would be useless for them to work *openly* against Hitler, not to mention extremely foolhardy. Each of them would find himself swinging at the end of a rope if he did.'

'So Canaris and the others are fighting Hitler from within . . . on the inside,' Sigi asserted.

'That's correct. Canaris believes that Hitler will eventually bring about the total collapse of Germany. I happen to agree,' Kurt said with a heavy sigh. 'And he and I are both convinced that Hitler will definitely go to war with Britain sometime this year . . . a lot of people believe that, actually. He wants to engulf the West.'

'You sound ominous, Kurt.'

'I feel *very* ominous.' The prince shook his head. 'The future looks bleak, very bad; war *is* inevitable. And Germany must lose that war if it is to survive as a nation, and regain its humanity.'

'Yes,' Sigi said laconically, in the quietest of tones.

They walked on together, each of them momentarily preoccupied with dire thoughts, but after only a few seconds Sigi volunteered, 'If Hitler forces Chamberlain's hand and Britain *does* go to war, France will join in the fray as England's long-standing ally, and co-signer of the Munich Pact.'

'Undoubtedly.' Kurt shook his head and cursed mildly under his breath, before exclaiming, 'That fool Chamberlain! He always buys Hitler's talk of appeasement . . . empty words . . . of no value. There's only one politician in England who genuinely understands Hitler's warlike intentions, his eventual aims, and the overall situation, and that's Winston Churchill.'

'But he's a lone voice, Kurt. No one is listening to him,' Sigmund pointed out.

'*Unfortunately*. It's a great pity Churchill isn't Prime Minister.' Once more Kurt expelled a sigh of frustration, and then went on rather rapidly, 'But to get back to Ursula's travel plans. I do think it would be a good idea to have her leave by the end of this coming week. I want you to buy train tickets for Paris, Sigi. *Return tickets.*'

'Yes, I will. But what about the entry visas for England?'

'We decided that it would look better if Ursula appears to be taking Maxim on a vacation to France, hence the return tickets. Therefore she *cannot* have the entry visa for England in her passport when she leaves Germany, and obviously neither can Maxim or Theodora. Ursula will be able to pick up the documents they require at the British Embassy in Paris. I have arranged everything, and she will get the entry visas immediately, without any problem, rest assured.'

Sigmund nodded. 'I have every confidence in you, Kurt, and again I thank you for all that you are doing for me, and for trusting me enough to tell me about Canaris. And of course I realise the necessity for total secrecy about the admiral and his activities.'

'I know you will be discreet, and after all the years of close friendship we have enjoyed our mutual trust in each other goes without saying. Now perhaps we ought to return to the Schloss and join Reinhard. I believe he's expecting Adam von Trott for lunch. He's staying with friends nearby. You know Adam von Trott zu Solz, don't you?'

'Not very well. I've met him with Reinhard a few times. Weren't they at Oxford together?'

'Yes. Adam is a Rhodes Scholar.'

'He's half German, half American, isn't he?'

'That's correct. He had a rather *famous* American ancestor, as a matter of fact. John Jay, the Supreme Court Judge who became the first Chief Justice of the United States, was his great-great-grandfather. Jay was also a statesman and diplomat of great repute.'

'I didn't know that. It will be nice to see Adam again,' Sigmund said. 'If I remember correctly, he's with the German Foreign Office.'

'Yes,' Kurt said.

FOURTEEN

A rambling, centuries-old castle standing on a small rise, its turrets and towers and onion-shaped cupolas glittering in the radiant sunshine. Dark-green pine forests frosted with ice, encircling the white-stone Schloss, rising up behind it like a giant ruff. Children brightly dressed, playing in the snow under a sky so crystal clear it looked like polished blue glass.

Such was the scene that confronted Sigmund and Kurt as they tramped out of the lower forest, where they had been walking and talking for the past half hour. And it was a scene of such simplicity, gentleness and innocence both men stopped to stare, momentarily entranced, carried back to their own childhoods, and then they glanced at each other, sharing identical thoughts.

Sigi said softly, as though to himself, 'Nothing must happen to those children, Kurt. They must not come to any harm.'

'They won't. Not if I have anything to do with it,' Kurt vowed vehemently. His own children, thirteen-year-old Christian and nine-year-old Diana, were helping Maxim to build a huge snowman, which dwarfed the smaller boy somewhat, although this did not seem to bother him. Eight-year-old Gretchen von Tiegal was pushing a wheelbarrow full of snow over to her nanny, Irmgard. The latter stood with Teddy, and both young women were fashioning an ice castle for Gretchen, working intently at their task, completely absorbed in what they were doing.

'Cooee, all of you!' Kurt called. He and Sigmund waved to the group as all eyes swung towards them.

'Cooee!' the children and the nannies chorused in unison, waving and laughing before turning back to their sculptures of snow.

'They want to finish before lunch,' Sigmund laughed. 'So that we can come and admire their handiwork.'

Kurt also chuckled and nodded, and the two men veered to the left, took a path that led up to a side wing of the castle; the path had recently been cleared of snow by one of the gardeners and they were able to cover the distance at a rapid pace.

Once inside the little entrance hall, with its wood-panelled walls and blue-and-white tiled floor, they shed their outer garments, replaced their ski boots with shoes, and climbed the narrow, twisting stone staircase that spiralled up to the floor above, and Reinhard's study.

The door was ajar. Sigmund pushed it open and walked in, followed by Kurt closely on his heels.

Adam von Trott zu Solz had already arrived and he and Reinhard were standing in front of the blazing fire, drinking champagne. Greetings were exchanged, and Reinhard then said to the newcomers, 'A glass of this? Or would you prefer to fortify yourselves with something stronger?'

'Champagne for me, please,' Sigmund said. 'How about you, Kurt?'

The prince nodded. 'I'll have the same, thanks.' He took a gold cigarette case out of his tweed shooting jacket, offered it to Sigi and Adam. Sigi took one; Adam declined.

As he lit his cigarette, Sigi looked across at Adam von Trott. He had forgotten how good-looking Adam was. Tall, rather rangy in build, he was very personable, with a great deal of natural charm, Sigi recalled.

In contrast to him, physically at least, Reinhard was shorter, with dark-brown hair and eyes, and a somewhat burnished, weatherbeaten complexion, that of a man who spends a lot of time outdoors. He was exuberant and outgoing by nature, and full of easy laughter, although that laughter had been mostly absent in the past year.

His face was very serious now as he carried the crystal goblets of sparkling wine over to Sigmund and Kurt. They thanked him, and he went to retrieve his own glass from the mantel of the huge stone fireplace. He lifted it in the air. *'Prost!'*

'Prost!' the others said.

After a few sips of champagne, Reinhard said, 'I think Hitler is losing his self-control. I understand from certain sources of mine that there have been a lot of mad outbursts lately, in the inner sanctum of the Reich Chancellery. And then there's *Kristallnacht* to consider. I lay the blame for that unconscionable brutality entirely at his door. Nobody will ever convince *me* that he didn't sanction it, indeed encourage the riots. And it seems to me that his megalomania is getting out of hand. Frankly, I believe it's started to take him over, and who knows what he'll do next, what atrocities he'll commit if he isn't stopped.'

Kurt frowned. 'What are you leading up to, Reinhard?'

'Tyrannicide. He won't go willingly, so he has to be assassinated.'

'Do be careful!' Kurt hissed quietly, striding over to the door which was still ajar, looking out into the corridor. To his relief it was deserted, and he closed it firmly before he rejoined the others at the fireplace. 'Careless talk can do a lot of harm to a lot of people,' he said, giving Reinhard a cautionary look. 'I know you are going to say that you trust the servants and everyone else living under this roof, but we must all be circumspect in what we say, *wherever* we are.'

'I'm not planning to assassinate Hitler. I'm only theorising about it,' Reinhard pointed out. 'But you're absolutely right, Kurt, of course.' There was a slight pause on his part before he said in a much lower voice, 'Don't you all agree with me that tyrannicide *is* the only answer?'

The other men were silent.

Sigi spoke at last. 'It's not enough to assassinate Hitler. His evil partners in crime would have to be killed as well.'

'That is correct,' Kurt agreed swiftly. 'Killing a tyrant is one thing, but here there's a whole Government to be taken into consideration. Any plot to kill Hitler would have to be very comprehensive in scope. There would have to be plans to seize power instantly, the minute he was dead. A list of men to run the Government would have to be drawn up beforehand, and they would have to take control immediately.'

'Yes,' Reinhard said thoughtfully. He walked over to the window, stood looking out, then swung around to face his guests. 'I want democracy for Germany, not dictatorship.'

'Of course you do. That's what we all want,' Adam said.

'I know that.' Reinhard shook his head. 'And we'll never have it as long as the Nazis are in power. To get rid of the Nazis effectively, we have first to cut off the head of the beast, the master of the vermin. Which brings me back to my first point . . . there are a lot of committed anti-Nazis around . . . someone's got to formulate a plan for killing Hitler.'

'Yes, but – ' Kurt began and stopped with abruptness at the sound of knocking.

The men exchanged worried glances only a split second before the door flew open.

Renata stood on the threshold.

'You startled us!' Reinhard exclaimed.

'Oh, I'm sorry, I didn't mean to,' Renata apologised. 'Are the ladies allowed up here for a glass of champagne before lunch, or shall you come down to join us?'

'We'll be down in a moment,' Reinhard told her.

'Very well, darling.' She smiled and disappeared, quietly closing the door behind her as she left.

'You see what I mean? That could have been anyone,' Kurt was quick to point out. 'I think we would be wise to drop this conversation, for the time being at any rate.'

Reinhard nodded in agreement, pivoted, looked out of the window again, and exclaimed, 'Now who can this be arriving just before lunch? A fellow on a motorcycle, no less, and he doesn't look remotely familiar to me.'

'Motorcycle,' Sigi repeated, instantly thinking of Willy Herzog. 'It might possibly be Theodora's boyfriend. Sunday is her day off when we're in Berlin,' he murmured, hurrying over to the window. He glanced down, saw that the young man was already parking the motorbike. 'Yes, that *is* Willy,' Sigi said. 'I suppose he's come to make his usual Sunday call.'

'Teddy! Teddy! Look, there's Willy!' Maxim shouted to her, and he began to wave at the young man standing on the wide flagstone terrace which ran along the back facade of the Schloss.

Theodora glanced across at Maxim, then looked up towards the terrace and exclaimed, 'Good Lord, it *is* Willy, and I thought you were teasing me, Maxim.' Thrusting the garden trowel into a snowdrift, she climbed the slope, carefully straightening her tartan tam o'shanter as she did.

Willy grabbed hold of her when she reached him, hugged her tightly and kissed her cheek, not giving her a chance to say a word. When they finally drew apart, she cried, 'Goodness, Willy, whatever are you doing here?'

'I came to see you.'

'I realise . . . but such a long way, Willy.'

'Not so long. It only took me a few hours on the bike. When you told me on the phone yesterday that Frau Westheim planned to stay on at Schloss Tiegal for several more weeks, I thought I should come. I've something to discuss with you, and it's always better to talk in person, Teddy, isn't it?'

'Is something wrong?' Anxiously she searched his face.

He shook his head. 'Do you think I could go to the cloakroom, and also get a cup of hot coffee or tea, please? It *was* a bit cold riding the bike.'

'Of course, Willy. How rude I'm being. First I'll show you to the cloakroom, and then I'll ask Cook for something hot. And you must stay to lunch with us. I know Frau Westheim and Countess von Tiegal will insist that you do . . . I hope you won't mind eating with the children and Irmgard, as well as me?'

'No. And thanks, I'd like to stay. Who's Irmgard?'

'She's the nanny here,' Teddy explained, and moving to the edge of the terrace she called out, 'Maxim!'

'Yes, Teddy?' he responded at once, raising his little face, looking up the slope, shielding his eyes against the sun with one hand.

'I'm taking Willy to the kitchen . . . to get a hot drink.'

'Can I come?'

'No, Maxim! You stay here and play.'

'But I want to say hello to Willy!'

'You'll see him later. He's going to have lunch with us.'

'Hooray! Hooray!' Maxim cried, waving his spade in the air. Willy was his friend. He liked him.

'Don't worry,' Irmgard called. 'I'll keep an eye on Maxim for you.'

'And so will I, Teddy,' nine-year-old Diana von Wittingen volunteered.

'I'm not a baby!' Maxim shouted.

'Thanks, to both of you,' Teddy cried, and swinging around she dashed over to Willy and took hold of his arm. 'Come along, let's go and get that cup of coffee for you. You can drink it in Irmgard's sitting room, which I'm sharing with her. There's a big fire in there, and you can get warm in front of it. You must be frozen.'

'I am,' Willy admitted.

Theodora gave him a penetrating look. 'And then you can tell me what's troubling you *so much* it brought you all this way to talk to me.'

'It's like this,' Willy said, looking across at Theodora. 'My father hasn't been able to get entry visas for America, as you know. But he has been promised *one* for Palestine by a Jewish organisation in Berlin, which will also obtain an exit visa. He should be getting both in a week or two.'

'And he wants you to use them, Willy, isn't that so?'

'Yes,' Willy muttered, sounding as miserable as he looked.

'Then you must.'

'I can't,' Willy exclaimed. 'Don't you see, I can't go without you, Teddy.'

'You *must*, Willy dear. You have no alternative,' Teddy said very gently, leaning forward, putting her hand on his arm affectionately.

'I won't leave you behind in Berlin,' he protested, his voice suddenly shaking.

He seemed close to tears, Teddy thought. But she was fully prepared for such a moment as this, fully prepared with all the right words – and lies, if necessary. In November, when Herr Westheim had asked her for her passport, and had explained that he was hoping to get his family and her out of Germany, he had sworn her to secrecy. 'No one must know,' he had said. The Nazis might stop the Westheims from leaving if they discovered their plans, because of his importance to the Ministry of Finance and the State, he had warned. She had understood everything, and had given her word to him.

It was on this same Saturday afternoon that she had told the Westheims about her unofficial engagement to Willy, had confided that Willy hoped the two of them would be able to go to America eventually, along with his father and sister. The Westheims had immediately exchanged worried looks, and Frau Westheim had said, 'Of course we can't force you to leave with us, Teddy, nor would we. However, don't forget that you are my charge. I promised your mother I would look after you, and it would distress me to leave you behind. Very honestly, I think you should get out when you can. Just as Willy should, if he has the opportunity, even if it means going without you. In any case, there's no guarantee that Professor Herzog is going to succeed.'

Herr Westheim had then interjected: 'It's highly unlikely that he will, Theodora. The United States is not going to admit any more European Jews. The quota is used up.' On hearing this dismal news she had looked from Herr Westheim to Frau Westheim, and had exclaimed, 'But I can't just *disappear*! Willy would be worried.' Ursula Westheim had taken her hand, had said, 'Yes, you can, Teddy. And when we arrive at our destination, you can phone Willy to explain everything. He will be *relieved* to know you are safe. Trust me, he will.'

Quite suddenly she had realised that what Frau Westheim said was true. Anyway, Willy had a far better chance of making it safely out of Germany alone, without her hampering him. Something else had instantly struck her that afternoon, and she had wondered out loud what she would say to Willy if he asked for her passport. 'He won't,' Herr Westheim had assured

her, 'the Americans are not issuing any more entry visas. But should he do
so, then you must simply say you have sent your passport in for renewal.
Don't say I have it, and remember, don't mention our plans, whatever you
do.' For a second time she had promised not to reveal a single thing.

In the end, of course, the Westheims had managed to convince her to
abide by their wishes. After all, her mother had had great faith in them,
and had entrusted her well-being to them until she was twenty-one, and
she must respect that. They were older and cleverer than she, and they
knew best.

And as the weeks had slowly passed she had begun to acknowledge
to herself that they had indeed been correct in what they had said to
her. Chanukah had come and gone, and then Christmas, and finally
New Year's Eve. It was suddenly 1939 and Professor Herzog had still
not heard a word from his friend in Frankfurt who had a friend who
knew an American consular official. Inevitably, Willy had confessed to
her one night that he had given up all hope of the American visas ever
being issued. Several times she had been on the verge of confiding that her
Aunt Ketti in London was trying to get a British entry visa for her, but she
had always remained silent, always curiously inexplicably tongue-tied on
this subject.

Now here was Willy at the Schloss with his latest news.

As she looked into his pale, stricken face her heart went out to him.
He was concerned about leaving her behind, and yet there was no way
she could alleviate his worry by revealing the truth. Certainly she could
not tell Willy about Sigmund Westheim's plans for them. Nothing on
this earth would make her put the family in jeopardy. She trusted Willy
Herzog, trusted him with *her* life. On the other hand, it was not up to
her to put little Maxim and his parents at risk in any way whatsoever.

And so she must convince Willy to take advantage of the visa his father
had been offered and leave Germany, whatever lies she had to tell him to
accomplish this end.

Rising, she went and sat next to him on the sofa in front of the fire.
She got hold of his hand and squeezed it, then brought it up to her face
and rubbed it against her cheek in a gesture of tenderness and love.

After a moment, she said, 'I want you to go to Palestine, Willy. In fact, I
insist that you go. Listen to me. Frau Westheim is planning to stay at the
Schloss *indefinitely*. When you phoned yesterday, I said we'd be staying a
few weeks because I didn't want to upset you. But actually we won't be
coming back to Berlin for a very, very long time. The Westheims believe
it's safer here in the country. And it is. We'll be fine, living with the von
Tiegals. And once you get to Palestine you can try to get entry visas for
your family. And for me. And as soon as you do, I'll come and join you.'

'It worries me to leave you behind, and – '

'You'll have a much better chance of getting those visas in Palestine than you would here,' she cut in swiftly.

'I don't know about that,' Willy said, his expression doubtful.

'Oh yes, you *will*. Honestly, Willy. Herr Westheim told me it's easier to get a visa for a country when you're actually in that country. You know, a visa for someone else. He understands these things. He's a banker, don't forget.' Teddy paused, took a deep breath, 'My Aunt Ketti in London is trying to get me an entry visa for England,' she blurted out, telling him at last, knowing that she must now use this as a weapon of persuasion.

Genuinely startled by this last announcement, Willy stared at Theodora. 'Why didn't you tell me about your Aunt Ketti's efforts?'

Teddy bit her lip. 'I'm sorry, Willy, I should have.' She sighed. 'I suppose I was reluctant to tell you that I might leave Berlin before you, and also I don't like discussing such things, in case they don't happen. I'm a bit superstitious in that way. Aunt Ketti is hopeful though, very hopeful indeed.' This last statement was not strictly true, but Theodora gave him the benefit of a huge smile, and warming to her subject, she went on, 'I will give you Aunt Ketti's address before you leave this afternoon, just in case. Listen, by the time you get to Tel Aviv or Jerusalem, or wherever you're going, I could be sitting in Belsize Park Gardens with my aunt. Think about that, Willy. It should cheer you up.' She sat back, beaming at him confidently, her face a picture of truth and sincerity.

Willy studied her carefully. His eyes narrowed. 'Are you *sure* your Aunt Ketti can get a British visa for you?'

'*Absolutely!* She has all the right connections,' Teddy lied adroitly. 'So you see, you must go to Palestine, Willy dear. We'll meet up when this mess is over . . . Herr Westheim says there's going to be a war.' When he did not respond, she exclaimed in a cheery voice, 'Look, Willy, either you'll come to London, or I'll come to Palestine, and together we'll go to America!'

For the first time since he had arrived at the Schloss Willy smiled. '*America!* Oh Teddy, that's where our future is. And it's a wonderful dream to hold onto . . . something to look forward to, and keep us both going while we're apart.' He put his arm around her and drew her close to him. 'You will write to me, won't you?' he asked anxiously, holding her even tighter.

'Every week,' Theodora promised, filling with relief that she had managed to persuade him to go to Palestine without her. And she was happy in the knowledge that once he was there Willy Herzog would be safe.

FIFTEEN

Maxim sat on the carriage seat gazing up at his father.

'Why aren't you coming with us, Papa?' he asked tremulously. Until this moment of departure he had not known that Sigmund was staying behind in Berlin, and his young face was charged with disappointment and sudden worry flickered in his brown eyes.

'Because they need me at the bank next week, Maxim. But as soon as I finish my work I shall come to Paris,' Sigmund explained, wanting so much to reassure the child.

'When, Papa?'

'In about two weeks, and when I arrive we shall go away immediately for our seaside holiday.'

'Where, Papa?'

'To the south of France . . . to Monte Carlo or Cannes. Or perhaps we'll go to San Remo in Italy, possibly even Corsica. But I'm certainly going to choose a warmer climate so that *Mutti* can rest, and you and I will have a fine time together.'

A smile touched the boy's mouth, but it was fleeting, and he said in a plaintive voice, 'Please come soon, Papa. *Please.*'

'I will, I *promise*,' Sigmund said. 'Now, let me take off your overcoat, it's rather warm in the compartment.' He lifted Maxim down, removed his coat, and handed it to Teddy, who stowed it away on top of their three suitcases in the luggage rack above.

Sigmund bent forward and picked Maxim up in his arms, held him tightly, pressing the boy's head into his shoulder, loving him so much. He drew back after a moment, smiled into his face as he put him down on the seat, and then he reached out and straightened his little blue tie, smoothed the same loving hand over his fair head.

Still smiling at him, Sigi said, 'I want you to be a good boy, Maxim, and you must take care of *Mutti* for me, and Teddy too, until I can get there.'

Maxim nodded, looking very solemn. 'Yes, I will, Papa, but don't be long, will you?'

'No, I won't.' Sigmund leaned closer and kissed Maxim, who put his arms around his father's neck and clung to him. He had never been separated from him for longer than a day or two, and knowing his father was staying in Berlin now alarmed and frightened him, even though Teddy and his mother were with him on the train.

Sigmund hugged his son once more, then released him and turned away, clearing his throat and blinking rapidly. His eyes were suddenly wet and it took him a moment to compose himself. Once he had done so, he swung to Teddy, offered her his hand. She clasped it tightly, and then impulsively Sigmund pulled her to her feet and enveloped her in a warm, avuncular hug.

'Look after them for me, Teddy, and take care of yourself,' he said quietly, when they drew apart.

'I will, Herr Westheim, and please try not to worry.'

Sigmund nodded, and glanced down at his little son whose eyes were fastened on him so intently. 'You'll enjoy the train journey, Maxim. It'll be like an adventure for you, and before you know it, you'll be in Paris . . . on holiday. *Mutti* and Teddy will take you to see the Eiffel Tower and all the other sights.'

'Yes . . . Papa, will Gangan come with you?'

'She will indeed.'

A joyful smile suddenly lit up Maxim's face. It made him happy to know that his grandmother was coming on holiday with them. Soon everyone he loved in the whole wide world would be with him. He settled against the seat and picked up the small wooden horse his Papa had given him yesterday. It was exactly like the pony he was going to buy for him. He had told him so. 'And you'll have it very soon, I promise,' his Papa had added. He could hardly wait. It would be lovely to have the pony. He had wanted it for so long. In the summer he would ride it in the garden in Wannsee.

Sigmund saw that Maxim was occupied with the little carved horse, and he left the carriage rapidly, wishing to curtail these prolonged goodbyes which were painful to him and everyone else. His heart was very full, and he was aware that Ursula was on the verge of tears. She followed him out of the carriage and onto the platform, where they stood together talking.

Maxim pressed his nose to the window, watching his parents. But he could not hear what they were saying, and so he went back to examining the wooden horse, banging his heels against the bottom of the carriage seat until Teddy told him, rather sternly, to stop at once. He did.

Despite the bustle and din on the crowded platform, Ursula spoke very quietly, not wanting to be overheard. She took Sigmund's hand in hers. 'I wish I hadn't agreed to this. I hate to leave you behind. I think we should all go together. Please, Sigi, let me take Maxim and Teddy off the train now, whilst there's still time.'

'No, absolutely not,' he replied in a low but emphatic voice. 'I told you, I don't want you to wait until the end of the month. I think it's better this way, that we go out in twos and threes, less noticeable, for one thing. In ten days or so Hedy, Sigrid and Thomas will be joining you in Paris, and then I will follow with Mother.'

'Yes, Sigi, I know. But I loathe leaving like this, I really do. I'm worried about you. Apprehensive. Anything could happen,' she whispered.

'Nothing is going to happen. I want you and Maxim out of Berlin. I'll breathe a little easier knowing that you and the child are safe.'

The train started to hoot loudly, emitting clouds of steam and smoke which enveloped them, and a guard was hurrying along the platform holding his red flag and blowing his whistle. The departure of the Berlin –Paris train was imminent and last-minute passengers pushed past them, intent on boarding at once.

Sigmund and Ursula were jostled closer together and he took her in his arms and kissed her. 'I love you, Ursula.'

'I love you, Sigi, with all my heart.'

He heard the tremor of emotion in her voice and he put his hand under her chin and lifted her face to his, gazing into her smoky-blue eyes. 'Come now, no tears, my love. I'll soon be with you and Maxim. You and he are my life, and nothing is going to separate us. Not for very long, at least.'

'Yes,' she said, striving for control, clutching him to her fiercely. All of their lives they had loved each other, all of their lives they had been together, had hardly ever been apart, except for their school years. Leaving him like this made her feel as if part of her body was being wrenched away from her.

'You'd better board,' Sigi said, and added sotto voce, 'And be careful on the train. *Wary*, darling. Keep your eyes and ears open, and say very little to anyone. Just be polite, that's all that's necessary. No complicated conversations.'

'Yes,' she murmured.

'It looks as if the train's thick with SS officers, army personnel and Gestapo, but there's nothing very unusual about that, so don't worry. Some of them are probably going on leave, others following military orders.'

She nodded.

Sigi went on quickly, in the same undertone, 'And remember, there will be police at the border, as well as immigration and customs officials. And Gestapo agents. But that is quite normal these days. *Routine*. As long as you remain your usual calm self everything will be all right.'

'Yes, Sigi, I understand.' Ursula's throat was tight and she was incapable of saying anything more. She pivoted swiftly and walked to the train.

Sigmund followed her, took hold of her arm, helped her up the steps. 'Go on,' he said, 'go to the carriage.' He banged the door shut, but immediately she pushed down the window and reached her hand out to him. He grasped it in his.

Slowly the wheels began to turn, grinding and screeching against the iron tracks, moving at a snail's pace at first. He walked along the platform, still gripping her hand, staring up into that face he had known and loved since he had been a boy. The lovely face was pale now, but the valedictory smile she gave him was brave and he smiled back, but then her smile slipped and her face crumpled and the tears she had been holding back trickled down her cheeks.

'Don't, darling, don't,' he said, squeezing her hand encouragingly, reassuringly, but when the train picked up speed he had to let go of her fingers.

He raised his arm in a farewell salute as the train slid out of the station, and he stood quite motionless on the platform, staring after it until it had completely disappeared from sight.

Only then did he finally turn away and leave the Schlesischer Bahnhof, making for the Westheim bank in the Gendarmenmarkt.

SIXTEEN

Ursula hung out of the window for as long as she could see Sigmund. But when the train rounded a bend and he was lost from view, she closed it and turned away.

She hurried along the corridor until she found a toilet. She went in, locked the door and leaned against it, pressing her handkerchief to her streaming eyes. But within seconds she had managed to calm herself, knowing that Maxim and Teddy would be wondering where she was, and that Teddy in particular would be worrying about her.

When she looked in the mirror above the washbasin she saw that her face was streaked with tears, her nose shiny. Rummaging around in her handbag she found her compact, took it out, powdered herself, added a touch of rouge and outlined her mouth with pink lipstick. Next, she placed her fedora-style hat in the washbasin along with her bag, ran a comb through her short blonde hair, replaced the hat, and stood back to review her own image.

She nodded to herself, perfectly satisfied that she looked quietly elegant, dignified and dull, which was exactly what she and Sigi had intended.

The most important thing on the journey to France was not to draw attention to herself. This was the reason she had chosen the tailored, heather-coloured tweed suit with a plain white silk blouse, the dark-grey fedora and a heather-tweed topcoat. Her jewellery was austere: her gold wedding band, a utilitarian watch, and simple pearl studs on her ears were the only things she wore.

Ursula had helped Theodora to select her own clothes equally carefully, and together they had picked out a navy-blue wool suit, a matching sweater and a navy topcoat. As always, Teddy wore her dark green-and-blue tartan tam o'shanter, from which she refused to be parted.

'Don't you remember, Frau Westheim, my Aunt Ketti gave it to me three years ago when I went on holiday to London. She bought it for me at the Scotch House, and it's my lucky hat,' Teddy had explained when they were packing. And she had answered, 'Of course, Teddy dear, wear it by all means.' And Teddy had.

Ursula picked up her handbag, slung it over her arm and left the toilet. She walked down the corridor somewhat unevenly, swaying from side to side, occasionally stretching an arm out to steady herself against the wall as the train hurtled along the tracks at gathering speed.

She, Maxim and Teddy had been the only occupants of the carriage when she had left it to follow Sigmund onto the platform. Now, when she opened the door and stepped inside, she saw that it was full. But of course it was; Sigi had told her the train was completely booked. He had been unable to get them a compartment to themselves, or sleepers. In fact, he had considered himself lucky to find three tickets available when he had, and for the day he wanted them.

Excusing herself to the other passengers as she moved past them, Ursula took her seat between Maxim and Teddy.

Maxim was engrossed in one of his picture books, but he looked up as she sat down. 'Where were you, *Mutti*?' he asked.

She leaned closer to him, and whispered, 'I had to powder my nose, darling.'

Teddy had a book on her lap, but she was not reading it. She looked extremely relieved to see Ursula, and gave her a faint smile.

Ursula smiled back.

Teddy nodded imperceptibly, picked up the novel, opened it and buried her face in it.

Ursula allowed her gaze to wander discreetly around the carriage.

Sitting in the window seat, immediately facing Maxim, was a middle-aged officer dressed in the field-grey uniform of the German army. From the insignia on his highnecked tunic she saw that he was a colonel. He had a briefcase open on his knee and he was studiously perusing a sheaf of papers, appeared to be totally absorbed in them.

Seated next to him was a thin young woman who looked to be in her early thirties. She had a narrow face and was nondescript in appearance, except for her eyes, which were a startling blue and extremely piercing. She sat rigidly in her seat, her face stony, staring across at Ursula with unblinking intensity.

Ursula shivered involuntarily, finding those eyes unbearably cold and calculating, and she glanced away at once, wondering if the woman was with the colonel. If she was, he was paying scant attention to her.

Now Ursula focused on the SS officer in the corner, who sat opposite Teddy. His face looked as if it had been cut from cold steel, his mouth had a cruel set to it, and his expression was disdainful. Oh what a typical Nazi *he* is, she thought. Perhaps the young woman was with him. Two of a kind, she added under her breath. The SS officer also had a briefcase open and he was reading documents, and then, as if he were aware of Ursula's gaze resting on him, he suddenly raised his eyes and looked at her, frowning slightly.

Quickly she averted her face, looked out of the window. The train was now slowing, pulling into the Friedrichstrasse Bahnhof, its second stop in Berlin, to take on additional passengers. Within a few minutes it was steaming out again, but it would stop one more time, at the Zoologischer Garten station, before heading in the direction of Hanover, Cologne and beyond.

Leaning her head against the seat she closed her eyes, trying to relax her muscles, which were stiff with tension. It was difficult for her to believe that they were actually sitting on this train, which today and tonight would push its way through the very heart of Germany on its journey west to France. Everything had happened so fast she still felt slightly disoriented, and a bit breathless. Less than a week ago, at the Schloss in the Mark on Sunday night, Sigmund had told her they must return to Berlin the following morning, explaining that they would soon be leaving the country. And then on Wednesday evening, not long after arriving home from the bank, he had asked her to join him in the library for cocktails. She had thought nothing of it, and had gone downstairs a few minutes later, to be confronted by Kurt von Wittingen looking extremely serious, and an equally concerned Sigi.

Without much preamble, Kurt had taken her fully into his confidence and had told her everything. He had then handed the three passports to her; when she saw that Sigmund's was not amongst them she had protested violently, and had refused to leave without him. Despite her terribly fierce opposition to the idea, Kurt had eventually managed to convince her that she must go, even though it had taken him several hours to do so.

Last night she had endeavoured to talk Sigi into allowing her to remain until the entire family could leave together, but he had been adamant, would brook no argument from her. And so she had had no alternative but to do as her husband said in the end. She desperately wished he were here with them on the train, and that . . .

'Please present tickets, passports and any other travel documents.' A man's loud, gruff voice shattered the quietness of the carriage.

Ursula's eyes flew open and she sat up straighter on her seat, her attention directed on the doorway. The conductor was framed in it, and standing immediately behind him were two official-looking men dressed in dark coats and snap-brimmed hats.

She pulled her passport, and Maxim's, out of her handbag, along with the train tickets, and offered them to the conductor. Teddy did the same thing.

The conductor glanced at the tickets first, then opened Ursula's passport. His eyes rested on it for a moment, and he stared at her closely, before handing it to the man nearest to him without making any comment. Next, he examined Maxim's, passed it on whilst carefully scrutinising the child, and then opened Teddy's, giving it the same attention as the others. This, too, was handed over at once.

Whilst the men studied their papers, the conductor collected the travel documents belonging to the other passengers; he flipped through them and held them out to his companions. These papers were given only a cursory glance before being returned to the conductor, who immediately distributed them to their owners.

Ursula looked across at the conductor, now fully expecting their documents to be passed back to her.

He stared at her icily and with the two men stepped out into the corridor, where they stood conferring with each other. Several times they turned their heads to look at her, peered at the passports they were holding, and went on talking between themselves.

Gestapo, Ursula thought. She was unnerved.

She gripped the frame of her handbag tightly in order to stop her hands from shaking. A feeling of enormous panic swept over her. But she could not afford to panic, not under any circumstances, and so she immediately made an effort to push it aside, to still her nerves. Keep a cool head, Ursula, stay calm, she cautioned herself, remembering Sigi's instructions to her. She tried to take comfort from the fact that their passports and exit visas were in order, and that their tickets, from Berlin to Paris and back, were valid. The only thing was, their passports were stamped with J for Jew. So what, she thought. All the Nazis can do is harass me, humiliate me on this train. I can live with that quite easily. I am taking my child to safety and freedom and that overshadows everything else.

They can do much more than harass me, she thought, stiffening on the carriage seat. Alarm seized her, and in an instant that alarm turned to sudden fear. They could take her and her child and Teddy off this train at any point during the journey and arrest them, if the whim struck. *Kristallnacht* had unleashed additional ugliness and brutality, cruelty and pain for so many. Jews all over Germany had been sent to concentration camps. They were still being sent, and property, businesses and possessions were being confiscated daily by the Third Reich.

She thought of her jewellery stitched into her clothes and tightened her hands on her bag, conscious that they were beginning to shake again. God knows what the Nazis would do to her if they did arrest her, and found the diamonds in the hem of her skirt and inside the lining of her jacket. The consequences were unthinkable. But she thought of them: *imprisonment, most certainly. Torture and death, perhaps.*

Those men were taking far too long examining their papers. Her heart shifted within her. Oh dear God, dear God, don't let them interfere with us, don't let them take me away. I must get Maxim and Teddy to France where they will be safe. That's all that matters.

She swallowed, fixed her eyes on the wall opposite, forcing herself to think of Arabella and Renata and their schooldays at Roedean together. 'Focus on good things, positive things which will make you feel truly strong,' Sigi had said last night. 'And most especially when you feel nervous,' he had thought to add.

And so that is what she did, remembering those youthful days and her dearest friends with the greatest of love and affection. She had spoken to Ren and Belle yesterday, talking only about inconsequential things. Her trip had not been discussed; the three of them knew better than that these days. So many phones were being tapped by the Gestapo. In any case, Ren and Belle would have learned from their husbands that she was leaving. Nothing else needed to be said between them.

Ursula continued to stare at the wall. Her face was without expression. She was determined not to display any signs of weakness, or look in the direction of the Gestapo agents, who continued to have their powwow. And Gestapo they most certainly were. She had no doubt.

Paris. That was another positive thought and she hooked in to it. The first thing she would do when she arrived at the Plaza-Athénée Hotel tomorrow was telephone Sigi in Berlin. If he had reminded her of this once, he had done so half a dozen times in the past twenty-four hours. But she had not needed to be reminded, as she had pointed out to him. How relieved he would be when they were in *la belle France* at last. Her dearest Sigi. She loved him so.

The conductor was standing in front of her.

His sudden presence made her jump. Her heart began to clatter in her chest, and she gaped at him speechlessly, wondering what was coming, steeling herself for the worst.

He handed her the tickets and passports without uttering a single word.

'*Danke schön,*' she heard herself saying, and she was surprised how steady her voice sounded.

The conductor nodded curtly, and moved on to Teddy, who also thanked him politely when her documents were returned to her.

And then he was gone, striding down the corridor with the Gestapo agents hurrying after him.

Teddy and Ursula exchanged looks, and then Ursula put her arm around her child, bent her head, sat staring at the drawings in his picture book without seeing anything at all.

Her mind was still fogged by fear, and she acknowledged that it was going to take her a while to entirely recover her equilibrium. She had a strong desire to expel a sigh of the most profound relief, but she did not dare, thinking that even this might betray her in some way. A wave of nausea rolled over her and she suddenly felt quite weak in the legs, and she realised that the last few minutes had been an ordeal. But her shakiness would disappear in a short while, all she had to do was sit here quietly until it did.

Everything was going to be all right. Unexpectedly she felt quite certain of that. *They were going to make it.* She must hold these thoughts to her. They gave her additional strength.

About an hour after the departure of the conductor, the door slid open again. This time a steward in a white jacket was standing there, and he quietly announced to the occupants of the compartment that those who wished to partake of lunch could now be seated.

Immediately Ursula stood up, took Maxim's picture book away from him, and lifted him down off the seat. 'Come along,' she said softly, taking him by the hand. Teddy rose and the three of them filed out of the carriage.

They swayed their way down the corridor in the direction of the dining car, and paused when they came to the first vacant toilet. Teddy opened the door, ushered Maxim inside, and instructed him to wash his hands.

'Yes, Teddy,' he said and closed the door behind him.

The moment they were alone Teddy spun to Ursula, took hold of her arm anxiously. She exhaled heavily, peered into Ursula's face. 'I was so worried, Frau Westheim,' she whispered. 'I really thought we were going to have trouble with those men. Do you think they're Gestapo?'

With a swift nod Ursula affirmed this, and she brought her finger to her lips, warning the girl to be absolutely silent.

Teddy inclined her head, indicating that she understood.

Lunch passed uneventfully.

After Ursula and Teddy had finished their coffee they all returned to the compartment. Maxim soon began to doze, feeling sleepy after his lunch and lulled by the movement of the train. Teddy read her book, and Ursula let herself drift with her thoughts. None of the other occupants of the carriage addressed a single word to her, and she did not speak either. She was relieved not to have to communicate, and to be left alone.

Although the behaviour of the conductor and the two Gestapo agents had unnerved her earlier that morning, she had managed to take hold of herself, and had remained quite calm, a model of self-possession. Assiduously, she had schooled herself not to contemplate what might happen when they reached the border town of Aachen very early the next morning, and, thus far, she had been most successful. She simply continued to focus on plans for the future, as always heeding Sigi's advice to hold only positive thoughts in her head.

SEVENTEEN

Later that evening, at seven o'clock, the same steward appeared in the doorway of the carriage and announced that dinner was about to be served.

Ursula, Maxim and Teddy wended their way down the corridor, all three of them glad to stretch their legs – and escape the confines of the compartment and the cold and watchful faces of the other passengers with whom they shared it.

By the time they entered the dining car it was filling up, but a large table for four was still available. The pleasant waiter with the friendly smile, who had served them at lunch, showed them to it, then went on to explain that they would most probably have to share it with someone else.

Ursula, Maxim and Teddy had only just settled into their places when another passenger *was* ushered to the table to be seated. It was a grey-haired, middle-aged woman dressed in black.

'*Guten Abend,*' the woman said as she sat down.

Both Ursula and Teddy said good evening in response, and they turned their attention to the menus. Before Ursula had a chance to suggest something to Maxim, he tugged at her sleeve. 'Yes, darling, what is it?' she asked, looking at him.

'I'd like chicken soup, please, *Mutti.*'

'Oh dear, I don't think there is any.' She scanned the menu again. 'There's lentil, though.'

'Chicken soup's my favourite.'

'I know. But if it's not on the menu, I can't order it for you. Have the lentil soup. I'm going to, I think.'

Maxim nodded. 'All right.'

Teddy said, 'That's what I'll have, please.'

'I'm sure it's excellent,' Ursula murmured. 'Now, Maxim, what will you have after the soup? There's – '

'Chicken or carp, *Mutti.*'

She shook her head. 'I'm afraid not, darling, neither are on the menu. But here's *Wiener Schnitzel, Bratwurst* or – '

'But we always have carp or roast chicken on Friday. And where are the *shabbat* candles, *Mutti*? You have to bless them,' he cried in his ringing child's voice.

Ursula blanched and threw a quick, worried look at the woman who sat next to Teddy. She had been watching them surreptitiously, and listening.

Helplessly, Ursula gazed across the table at Teddy who was as startled as she, and had turned deathly pale. They both began to talk at once, in order to drown out Maxim's voice as he began to prattle innocently again about the *shabbat* candles.

Eventually he stopped talking since neither his mother nor Teddy were listening, or paying any attention to him.

Ursula said, 'I'm sorry, Teddy, I didn't hear you.'

'I said I thought I would have the *Bratwurst*, please. And that perhaps Maxim should have the veal sausage too, since it's the lightest thing on the menu.'

'That's a good idea.' Ursula cast another glance in the woman's direction. She was now diligently studying her menu.

Maxim said, 'But I don't want – '

'Listen, darling, there's one thing on the menu which you really love. *Apple Strudel.* You can have it for dessert,' his mother said.

A happy expression spread across his face and he nodded enthusiastically. 'But where are the candles – '

'Now, Maxim!' Ursula exclaimed, instantly cutting him off. She turned into him, so that her body hid him from view, and bent down, said in a low voice, 'Shhh, *Mein Schatz*, I don't want you to discuss the things we do at home. Those are private matters, and are not talked about in public. Do you understand me?'

'Yes, *Mutti*.' He looked up at her and smiled that funny little smile of his that always tugged at her heartstrings.

Ursula smiled at him and said, 'That's a good boy.' She straightened, and shared a knowing look with Teddy. And then craning her neck she looked down the restaurant car, finally caught the eye of their waiter and motioned to him. Within seconds he was standing to attention at their table, his pencil poised above his order pad.

Ursula told him they would all like to have the lentil soup, the *Bratwurst* with mashed potatoes and red cabbage, and that two would have the *Strudel* to follow. 'No dessert for me, thank you,' she said. 'Just a cup of black coffee.'

The waiter nodded, said they had made good choices, and then gave his attention to the fourth person at the table. The woman asked him a question about the *Kasseler Rippchen*, a pork dish, and he started to explain that it was served with *Sauerkraut*.

'Speak up, speak up, please,' the woman shouted, leaning closer to him, cupping a hand around her ear.

The waiter immediately bent down and began to explain about the dish carefully, and in a much louder voice.

It was obvious to Ursula and Teddy that the woman was stone deaf. Teddy rolled her eyes heavenwards, and then looked across at Ursula pointedly.

Ursula exhaled quietly. She was relieved the woman hadn't heard Maxim's reference to the *shabbat* candles. Many Germans were antisemitic and had been brainwashed by the Nazis into believing the Jews were responsible for all of their troubles. The woman was obviously just another passenger, with no special powers, as far as they were aware. On the other hand, if she knew they were Jews she might conceivably make a fuss, insist on changing tables, and so draw unwanted attention to them. If she were prejudiced that is – not every German was. Still, thank God she was deaf. Now they had a chance to relax if only for a short time over dinner. Ursula was not particularly hungry, but Maxim and Teddy needed their nourishment, and she wanted them to eat in peace.

Another thought struck Ursula all of a sudden and she frowned to herself. What if the woman weren't deaf at all, merely pretending to be? But why would she do that? There was no reason. She was a stranger on the train who did not know them. And so Ursula dismissed the idea at once, refusing to become paranoid.

She began to talk to Teddy and Maxim about Paris, an innocuous subject, one that was perfectly safe.

They listened to her most attentively.

Ursula led Maxim down the platform, holding him tightly with one hand. In the other she carried her suitcase.

Teddy walked along next to her, carrying her own case and Maxim's. They stepped forward quickly, since it was cold on this early morning, following the other passengers who were making for the German customs and immigration shed at the far end of the platform. They had reached the railway station at the border town of Aachen about ten minutes ago, and the conductor had gone down the corridor of the train, opening carriage doors, telling the remaining passengers to take all of their belongings when they alighted. And to have their papers ready. The crowd ahead of them was not very large, and it was apparent to Ursula that many people had left the train during the night, when it had stopped at different towns.

She paused abruptly and Teddy immediately followed suit and threw her a questioning look.

'Give me your ticket and passport, Teddy dear,' Ursula said, putting her case down, holding out her hand. 'I think it will be easier if I deal with our papers. You can look after Maxim.'

'Yes, Frau Westheim,' Teddy said, placing the two cases on the platform, opening her bag and taking out her passport and ticket. She gave them to Ursula, who thanked her and put them inside her own purse. Ursula held Teddy's eyes and mouthed silently, above Maxim's head, 'Stay calm.'

Teddy nodded.

As the two women and the child started walking again, the SS officer who had occupied their carriage dashed past them at breakneck speed, veered to the left, and went barrelling out through the exit door. Ursula was glad to see the back of him. Although he had paid no attention to them, he had somehow been a sinister presence on the entire journey.

Upon entering the customs and immigration shed, Ursula saw that there were three tables. Behind each one sat a member of the border police, all of them identifiable because of their uniforms. But hovering in the background, under the windows set high on the wall, were several men in civilian clothes. She was quite certain they were Gestapo.

Sigi had told her the secret police were everywhere, and that she should not worry, so she took a deep breath and marched forward determinedly. Her face was calm, her expression neutral, but her light-blue eyes were wary, missing nothing as she drew to a standstill behind a young couple. She glanced over her shoulder and gave Teddy a warm smile, one that she hoped was reassuring.

When it was finally her turn, Ursula stepped up to the table, looked steadily at the uniformed policeman, opened her bag and gave him their three sets of papers.

The policeman spread them out before him on the table and examined them for a moment or two, then he lifted his head, eyed her coldly. 'What is the purpose of your journey to France, Frau Westheim?'

'I am taking my child, and his nurse, Fraulein Stein, on a holiday.'

'You have return tickets for Berlin. When do you plan to return to Germany?'

'In several weeks. About four weeks, to be precise.'

He said nothing as he cast his eyes over the three of them, scrutinising them fixedly for the longest minute. Eventually he asked, 'Are you taking any valuables out of Germany?'

'No. No, I'm not,' Ursula said in a clear, strong voice. 'We are not. No, no.'

'Put the suitcases up here on the table. I want to see inside them,' the policeman ordered.

Ursula did as he bid, lifting her own onto the table first. He made a thorough search, rummaging through her clothes, feeling the sides and bottom. He then went through the other two cases, before asking for their handbags. The contents were tipped out of her bag and it was carefully checked, as was Teddy's, before everything was put back.

Once again, the border policeman studied their passports, finally stamped each one with a sharp thud, and handed them back to her with a curt nod of dismissal.

'*Danke schön*,' Ursula murmured, picked up her own suitcase and the one belonging to Teddy. Turning to her, she said, 'Let's go. Attend to Maxim, and I'll handle these.'

'Yes, Frau Westheim.' Teddy took Maxim's hand in hers, lifted his suitcase, and together they followed his mother, although it was a trifle difficult to keep up with her. Ursula was hurrying so fast she was almost running out of the customs and immigration shed.

Thank God, thank God, it was easier than I imagined it was going to be, Ursula thought. Her heart soared. They were free. Well, *almost*. Nevertheless, she could not keep the happy smile from invading her face.

As she came out of the shed and turned right, about to walk along the platform and back to their carriage, Ursula found herself face to face with the army colonel who had been seated opposite Maxim all the way from Berlin.

He was blocking her path.

She moved slightly to one side, attempting to walk around him, but he moved also, and so blocked her path once more. The smile on her face congealed. Swiftly, she glanced back, checking on Teddy and Maxim.

They were only a few steps behind her, but Teddy was now standing perfectly still, watching her uncertainly, and grasping Maxim's hand more tightly than ever. Her expression was frightened, her eyes stark in her white face.

Swinging back to the officer, Ursula gasped, 'Please. We must get on the train. We have been through customs. And immigration. Please. Let me pass.' She was terrified that this man was going to prevent them from leaving Germany.

'Frau Westheim,' the colonel said.

Aghast, Ursula could only stare at him. My God, he knew her name! Who was he? What did he want? She opened her mouth. No words came out.

Pitching his voice to a lower key, he said, 'Don't be alarmed. My name is Oster. Colonel Oster of the Abwehr. I am a friend of Kurt's.'

For a split second Ursula did not comprehend what the colonel was saying, and she continued to gape at him blankly.

'You'll be crossing the border into Belgium in a short while, and within the hour you'll be in France,' he went on softly. 'You are safe, Frau Westheim. Good luck.' He half smiled, and then clicking his heels together and lifting his arm he said in his normal voice, 'Heil Hitler!'

'Heil Hitler!' Ursula responded automatically, suddenly understanding everything. She swung her head, motioned to Teddy to join her and then turned back to look at the colonel. To her astonishment he was not there. Her eyes searched for him on the platform, but he had disappeared. Literally into thin air.

'Is everything all right, Frau Westheim?' Teddy asked, hurrying up to her with Maxim in tow.

'Yes,' Ursula said. '*Very*. Now, let's go and get on that train that's taking us to Liège, and from there to Paris.'

'What did that man want, *Mutti*?' Maxim asked.

'I'll tell you later,' she said.

It was not until they were settled in the carriage and rolling slowly out of the railway station that Ursula realised something. The army colonel called Oster, who had wished her luck, had done so in English.

EIGHTEEN

The Berlin–Paris train thundered into the Gare du Nord, and came to a shuddering stop with a screeching of wheels on the iron tracks when the engine driver braked.

Ursula glanced at her watch. It was six-thirty a.m. With typical German efficiency the train had arrived exactly on time. She rose, and as she did she realised that the tension which had built up inside her on the journey was now beginning to evaporate.

Maxim was safe. Teddy was safe. She was safe. Soon the entire family would be safe. The rest of them would come to Paris by the end of the month and they would all go south for a holiday in warmer climes. And then they would embark for England afterwards and the start of a new life there. The future looked very bright to her, and she felt happier and more optimistic than she had for several years.

Moving swiftly, Ursula pulled their suitcases off the rack and then bundled Teddy and Maxim down onto the platform, handed out the suitcases one by one to Teddy, and alighted herself.

A porter was quickly found, and trundling their luggage ahead of them on a rickety barrow he led them out of the immense and cavernous old railway station to a taxi stand.

Within minutes the three of them were squashed together in the back seat of an ancient taxi cab and rumbling their way across Paris to the Plaza-Athénée Hotel on the Avenue Montaigne.

Paris, Ursula thought. *Paris.* I can hardly believe I'm actually here. She glanced out of the window, just to reassure herself that she was. Even in the cold, wintry light of early morning the city had a unique kind of beauty – muted, gentle, misty, a mingling of pale greys and darker anthracites and smudged blacks. Like a painting in grisaille, she thought.

Maxim rested his head against her arm and snuggled into her body. She glanced down at him. My poor little boy, she thought, he must be exhausted after the long, overnight journey. She was worn out herself, and grubby, and she suspected that Teddy felt exactly the same way.

Ursula turned her head and caught Teddy stifling a yawn. 'I know how you feel,' she said, 'but we'll soon be arriving at the hotel. I think we should have a light breakfast and then go to bed for a few hours. We need to rest after sitting up all night on the train.'

'Yes,' Teddy agreed, and peered at Maxim. She saw that his eyes were closed, and added softly, confidingly, 'It was the strain that was the worst, Frau Westheim. We were both so worried something would go wrong, weren't we?'

'Yes.'

Teddy continued in the same soft voice, 'The army colonel who spoke to you at the border station gave me a fright. For a minute I thought something awful was going to happen, that in some way he would prevent us from leaving Germany.'

'So did I.'

'I was afraid to speak about it on the train,' Teddy now admitted, 'even after we crossed the border into Belgium. But I couldn't help wondering about him, Frau Westheim. I mean, it was so peculiar, wasn't it? He never spoke to you once during the entire journey, and then suddenly he approaches you at the station in Aachen.'

'But only after we had passed customs and immigration, Teddy, don't forget that. Perhaps he didn't dare reveal himself to me before then, certainly not on the train in front of the SS officer and that strange young woman. He is a friend of a friend, and I'm positive he was on the train to keep an eye on us.'

'Oh!' Teddy exclaimed, looking surprised. 'Do you mean he was there to intervene, if we ran into . . . trouble?'

'I'm not sure. Perhaps he couldn't have done that exactly. But who knows, maybe he could. He told me his name was Oster, and that he was with the Abwehr.'

Teddy looked at her quickly. 'He was our guardian angel.'

'Perhaps he was.'

The two women fell silent, and not long after this conversation the taxi pulled up outside the Plaza-Athénée. It took Ursula only a few seconds to pay the driver and organise their luggage, and then she ushered Maxim and Teddy into the lobby. Here Ursula was immediately greeted by the head concierge, who knew her from her previous visits over the years, and by the manager, who hurried forward to meet her. He chatted amiably as he escorted her over to the reception desk, and once she had registered he showed them to their rooms on the sixth floor.

As they entered the elevator he told her she would be occupying her usual suite, but that an adjoining second bedroom had been opened up to accommodate the three of them. Having their old suite pleased Ursula, brought a smile to her face, albeit fleetingly.

'Yes, yes, Sigi, everything is fine!' Ursula cried, her voice rising slightly to compensate for the static on the line, the poor connection to Berlin. 'The journey was quite uneventful.'

'And you're comfortably settled in?' Sigi shouted back.

'Yes, we are,' Ursula responded, watching her words, knowing she must be absolutely circumspect in what she said, in case the line at the house in the Tiergartenstrasse *was* tapped. 'I'm in our old suite,' she added, thinking that at least there was no harm in saying this to him.

She heard the pleasure enter his voice as he said, 'I'm glad you are. Familiar surroundings are important. Now you must relax, have a pleasant holiday.'

'Yes. Is everything all right with you, Sigi?'

'Things are just the same as they were yesterday, when you left. Give Maxim my love, kiss him for me, and say hello to Teddy.'

'I will.'

'Goodbye for now. We'll speak in a few days.'

'Goodbye, Sigi. Take care.'

Ursula replaced the receiver slowly. She stood for a moment by the bed, her hand resting on the phone. Before she had left they had agreed that their calls must, out of necessity, be brief and to the point, but how unsatisfactory this was, she had now just discovered. She had wanted to tell him about Colonel Oster being on the train, their guardian angel, as Teddy had called him, and talk about a few other things as well. Never mind, she thought, I will be able to tell him everything when I see him.

Ursula hurried through into the sitting room, crossed it, and entered the second bedroom of the large suite. Teddy had Maxim's suitcase open on one of the twin beds that stood side by side, with a small night-table between them, and she was unpacking his clothes; Maxim hovered near the washbasin in the adjoining bathroom, drying his hands on a towel.

'I just spoke to Herr Westheim, Teddy. He says hello to you.'

Teddy smiled and nodded and went on taking out the child's underclothes and jumpers, placing them on the bed in a neat pile.

Maxim ran to his mother, and she bent down and kissed his cheek, and gave him a big hug. 'That's from Papa. And he sends his love to you,' she said.

'Is he coming soon?' Maxim asked, looking up at her.

'Yes, *Mein Schatz*.'

'I'm hungry, *Mutti*.'

'We shall have breakfast immediately. Soft boiled eggs and bread and butter and jam and hot chocolate. Would you like that?'

'Yes please, *Mutti*.'

'And you, Teddy dear? What will you have?'

'The same, thank you, Frau Westheim.'

'Once I've ordered breakfast, perhaps you should put a call through to Willy Herzog in Berlin,' Ursula went on, looking at her. 'To let him know that you are here in Paris.'

'He had to go to Frankfurt on Thursday with his father and sister,' Teddy explained. 'They'll be away for a week. I thought I'd write to him today, or tomorrow, and post it immediately, so that it'll be there waiting for him when he gets back.'

'All right. But remember, the rest of our family are still in Berlin, so do be most careful what you say.'

'Oh I will!' Teddy cried. 'I was just going to tell him that I was on my way to see my aunt. He'll understand exactly what I mean at once. He knows I only have *one* aunt, and that she lives in London. Yes, he'll understand that I've left Germany for good, that I'm safe, Frau Westheim.'

'I'm sure he will. He's very intelligent.' Ursula picked up the phone and called room service; once she had ordered breakfast, she took Maxim by the hand and led him into the sitting room.

'Papa and I have always stayed in this suite when we've been in Paris, and there's something I want to show you,' she said, going over to the tall window. She let go of his hand to open this, and stepped out onto a small terrace which overlooked the trees on the Avenue Montaigne and where she and Sigi had so frequently breakfasted in summers past. 'Come along,' she said, beckoning to Maxim.

The child clambered out onto the terrace and she picked him up in her arms and then turned around, so that the two of them were facing the River Seine. 'Look, Maxim, over there! Do you see it? The Eiffel Tower.'

That most extraordinary edifice made of interlocking steel girders soared up into the sky, dominating it, and glittering brightly in the clear morning sunlight that now streamed out from behind the banked-up grey clouds.

Maxim caught his breath in surprise. 'It's so tall, *Mutti*, the tallest building I've ever seen!'

'We can go to the very top of it, if you wish.'

'*To the very top!*' he cried, turning his head to look at her, his dark, soulful eyes huge in his little face.

'Yes, and you can see the whole of Paris from there. I once went up to the top with your papa, and it was a most wonderful sight.'

'When can we go?' he asked, his excitement growing.

'Tomorrow, Maxim, I promise.'

She put him down on the terrace and gave him a gentle push forward. 'Go along inside, darling. It's chilly out here, and I don't want you to catch cold.'

Ursula sat at the *bureau plat* in the sitting room, staring down at the list in front of her. It did not seem possible, and yet it was. Everything she had set out to do had been accomplished.

They had been in Paris for six days, and for most of that time she had behaved like a whirling dervish, never still for a single moment, and rushing from place to place, attending to her business. Of course on Sunday, the day after they had arrived, she had devoted herself to Maxim. She had taken him and Teddy to the top of the Eiffel Tower, as always keeping any promise she made to him, and afterwards to see some of the other famous sights in Paris. In the afternoon they had gone for a drive through the Bois de Boulogne, before eating an early dinner at a charming bistro on the Left Bank. On Monday morning, bright and early, she had gone to the British Embassy in the Rue Faubourg St-Honoré, where she had met with Mr Stiles, a consular official who had been expecting her. He had had the three entry visas for Great Britain waiting for her when she arrived at the appointed hour, and had presented them to her at once. He had been a pleasant man who had told her to get in touch with him if she needed anything else during her stay in Paris.

After lunch, on that same day, she had visited a luggage store where she had purchased extra suitcases, explaining to Teddy that since they had brought so little with them they were going to go shopping for clothes later in the week.

On Tuesday morning she had kept the appointment she had previously made with Monsieur André Mallet, head of the Banque Mallet, which was situated in a side street just off the Place Madeleine. After discussing a variety of financial matters with him at great length, she had withdrawn a substantial amount of money from the Westheim account to cover her current expenses. And then, once the business appointments were out of the way, she occupied herself with shopping for two days. Maxim and Teddy had been taken to numerous shops and department stores, where Ursula had purchased warm and attractive winter clothes for them and good strong shoes guaranteed to keep them dry in the rainy English weather.

Now, this afternoon, she planned to select a few outfits for herself. But she had no intention of visiting Jean Patou or any other famous dress designers, for that matter. Haute couture clothes were an extravagance she could no longer afford, but actually this did not trouble her in the least. She had much more pressing and important priorities these days: her family's survival, to mention only one.

The telephone next to her on the desk began to shrill loudly, and she picked it up at once. The hotel operator told her she had a call from Berlin coming through, and would she please kindly hold on. A few seconds later Sigi was on the line, asking her how she was.

'What a wonderful surprise!' she exclaimed, her heart lifting on hearing his dear, familiar voice. 'I thought you wouldn't call until tomorrow, or Sunday. I am well, we are all well. How are you?'

'I am fine. And things at the bank are fine, just the same as usual.'

She knew instantly, and instinctively, that things weren't fine at all, that there was something dreadfully wrong. His voice was flat, very tense, and the strain in it was pronounced.

'Sigi, what is it?' she cried, sitting up in the chair, holding herself stiffly.

'It's Mother. I'm afraid she's quite poorly. She had . . .'

His voice faded away and there was a great deal of static on the line and a peculiar, hollow echoing sound as if they were talking down a long tunnel. It was another bad connection.

'Sigi! Sigi! I can't hear you! What did you say?'

'I . . . mother . . . had a stroke . . . in the early . . . Thursday . . .' His voice disappeared, then came back. 'I spent most of yesterday with her . . . Sigrid . . . Hedy . . .'

'Oh, my God! Your poor mother! Oh no! Not Margarete! Oh Sigi, I'm so sorry.' She clutched the phone tightly. Her heart was in her throat; she could hardly speak, so stunned was she and filled with dread. Swallowing hard, she asked urgently, 'What do the doctors say? What's the prognosis?' She held her breath, silently praying as she waited for his answer.

' . . . not sure . . . cannot be moved . . . she cannot join the boy . . .'

'Sigi, you keep fading away. *Can you hear me?*'

'Yes . . . I can.'

'Will she get better?' Ursula screamed down the phone.

'We think so. We hope so.' His voice was now quite distinct and very close, as though he were in the next room. The line was finally clear. 'But she cannot take her holiday just yet. *Do you understand me?*'

'I do. Can the others?'

' . . . don't want to . . .'

'*You?* Can *you*, Sigi?'

'I . . . hopefully . . . as planned. I have to go now, my darling. I . . .' The static obliterated his voice completely.

'Give my love to your mother!' Ursula shouted. 'To everyone. I'll wait for your next call. And Sigi – '

The line was abruptly cut at the Berlin end of the wire.

Ursula was left holding a dead phone in her hand. She replaced it and sat staring at the wall for the longest time, reeling from Sigi's bad news, so unexpected, so shocking, thinking of her mother-in-law. Poor Margarete. How tragic and distressing that she had had a stroke at this time in her life. Sigi's mother had never completely recovered from her husband's death and her health had been faltering of late. And surely this stroke was too much for a frail old lady to bear. Ursula was extremely fond of Margarete, and her compassionate, loving heart now went out to her, and to Sigi. Her husband had always been close to his mother . . .

Ursula froze in the chair.

A terrible truth came to her. As long as his mother was ill and incapacitated and could not be moved, Sigi would not leave Berlin. Not the Sigmund Westheim she knew. He had too much integrity and responsibility and devotion to abandon the mother he loved, to flee to freedom and safety without her.

NINETEEN

Ursula crossed the Rond-Point at the bottom of the Champs-Élysées and walked down the Avenue Montaigne, shivering slightly, even though she was wearing a thick, cream-wool suit, a heavier wool cream-and-coffee plaid cloak to match, and a tight-fitting cream felt cloche that entirely covered her silver-gilt hair.

It was an exceptionally cold afternoon early in February. A biting northern wind was blowing down from the plains of eastern Europe, and she quickened her step, craving the warmth of the hotel after her long walk back from the Banque Mallet near the Madeleine.

When she had set out earlier, Maxim had wanted to accompany her, but she had insisted he stay inside today. She was relieved now that she had been adamant with him, had remained unmoved by his cajoling and pleading to come with her. He had developed a slight head cold and, despite the radiant sunshine and the blameless, vivid blue sky, the weather was pernicious; the last thing she needed was for her child to become sick.

It was exceedingly worrying to her, and dismaying, that illness was dogging the Westheims at this time. Margarete was still paralysed from the stroke that had felled her in the middle of January, and only a week ago Hedy, Sigmund's youngest sister, had fallen on the front steps of the house in the Grunewald and broken her shoulder. As a consequence of these health problems, none of the family had yet come to Paris, and the longer she sat waiting for them the more anxious, nervous and frustrated she became. She continually willed herself to be patient, but this was a hard task for her, especially under the present circumstances. She had always been a person of decision and action, and she had lately discovered that playing a waiting game was debilitating, since it was alien to her nature.

As she drew closer to the hotel, she sighed to herself, then tried to push to one side the dismal thoughts which had preoccupied her for most of the day, and which now jostled for prominence in her mind. Ursula felt it was her duty to have a positive demeanour, to be cheerful around her child and Teddy. Not that Teddy needed any cheering up at the moment. Her worry about Willy Herzog had been completely alleviated with the arrival of Willy's long letter from Palestine, which had been forwarded to her from London by her Aunt Ketti Berners.

'He's out! He's safe! He's in Tel Aviv!' Teddy had shrieked with her usual exuberance, waving the letter in the air, before hurrying to her room to reply to it at once. Ursula had been as joyful as the girl on hearing this good news. It was always heartening for her to learn that another person had managed to escape the Nazi tyranny, had made it out of Germany to freedom in another country.

The uniformed doorman touched his cap and acknowledged her with a friendly nod when she approached the hotel. He opened the door for her, and she swept into the lobby, crossing it briskly.

Ursula stopped at the desk, where Charles, the head concierge, greeted her with a bright smile. 'A gentleman was here a short while ago, looking for you, Madame Westheim,' Charles said. 'He went into the Relais Plaza for tea. He asked me to tell you that he would wait there for you.'

Ursula was startled, and she frowned. 'Did he give you his name?'

'No, Madame.'

'Thank you, Charles,' she murmured, pulling off her gloves and going directly to the Relais Plaza to look for her mysterious visitor, wondering who it could possibly be. Pushing open the door, she entered the small restaurant linked to the hotel by a short corridor, and paused in the doorway, scanning the room.

He saw her before she spotted him.

He rose and came quickly to meet her.

Ursula caught her breath in happy surprise and her face lit up at the sight of the tall, thin, fair-haired man in the dark business suit who was smiling broadly at her. There he was, larger than life, their dear, dear friend Prince Kurt von Wittingen.

'Kurt!' She moved forward, both hands outstretched to him.

He took them in his. 'Hello, Ursula,' he said, leaning into her, kissing her cheek. 'Come, my dear, let us sit down.' As he spoke he led her to his table in the corner, and after motioning to a waiter and ordering a pot of the China tea which he knew she preferred, he went on: 'I'm sorry I wasn't able to let you know in advance that I was coming to Paris. I arrived early this morning from Berlin, and I was picked up at the Gare du Nord by an associate, who took me directly to a business meeting. After that there was a luncheon, and another meeting, and I was never alone for a single moment. It was quite impossible for me to telephone you.'

'Oh Kurt, that's all right. It doesn't matter, really. It's just so wonderful to see you. I'm glad I returned to the hotel when I did, it would have been an enormous disappointment to me if I had missed you, just awful, in fact.'

'I would have waited for you, my dear. I wouldn't have left without seeing you.'

She nodded, gave him a small smile. 'How is Sigi?' she asked, anxiously searching his face. 'Have you seen him?'

'Yes, a few days ago. And he is well. I told him I would most likely be in Paris this week, and he sends his dearest love to you and Maxim. Ursula, he especially asked me to tell you that you must not worry. He is doing the best he can, and he hopes his mother will be well enough to travel soon. She is now improving, and very rapidly, it seems. He wanted you to know this.'

'Thank God! I've been so concerned about them, and sitting here waiting is dreadfully nerve-racking, as I'm sure you can imagine. And, of course, the phone calls are extremely frustrating. We're both afraid to say too much, for fear the phones at the Berlin end *are* tapped, as you suggested they might be. But quite apart from this, the connections are terrible. Half the time we can hardly hear each other. Still, I do live for those calls.'

'So does Sigi. They have kept him going.'

'As they have me, Kurt. Do forgive me, I'm being so rude, not asking about Arabella and the children. How are they?'

'In fine form, and Arabella sends her love, as do Renata and Reinhard. We miss you very much, you know.'

Her lovely luminous eyes filled with tears. 'Oh Kurt, I miss all of you,' she murmured, her voice husky with emotion.

He took her hand in his and held it tightly, his gentle face sympathetic, his eyes reflecting his inherent kindness. 'I know, I know. It is terribly hard for you in so many different ways, but you are in the best place at the moment. Believe me, you are.'

'Yes.' She picked up the pot of tea which the waiter had brought whilst they had been talking, and poured herself a cup. There was a tiny silence, and then she glanced at Kurt and confided in a low voice, 'I had hoped that at least Sigrid and Thomas would join me here, but I suppose Sigrid doesn't want to leave her mother, and certainly Thomas won't leave without his wife.'

'You are quite correct, and of course Sigrid feels she's needed in Berlin more than ever at the moment, because of Hedy's broken shoulder.'

'Poor Hedy, she's always been accident-prone, and her injury must be excruciatingly painful. But I gathered from Sigi that she *is* mending.'

'So I understand.'

Ursula now said in an even quieter voice, 'Where do the family stand, as far as exit visas are concerned?' Her grey-blue eyes held his.

He returned her gaze steadfastly. 'The three I was expecting in the middle of January were given to me then, and they have been passed on. And I received the last two at the end of last month. Sigi already has them in his possession.'

'So everyone could travel now?'

'Yes, if Frau Westheim were well enough.

A relieved smile touched her mouth. 'Well, that is certainly good to know.' She reached out, touched his arm affectionately. 'Thank you, Kurt, for everything you've done for us. You have been so very caring, and a true friend.'

'You know I will always do anything to help you and Sigi.'

Leaning closer, Ursula said, 'There was a man on the train . . . a Colonel Oster. He said he was a friend of yours . . .' Her voice trailed off, and she gazed at him questioningly.

'Indeed he is.'

'*You* arranged for him to be on that train. It wasn't a coincidence, was it?'

'No, but I didn't actually arrange it. I simply asked my contact if someone could be in your carriage, certainly nearby you, in order to keep an eye on you until after you passed border controls.'

'And Admiral Canaris agreed?'

Kurt von Wittingen nodded.

'The admiral has also been wonderful to us,' Ursula said. 'He's another person we will never be able to thank enough. Not ever, as long as we live.'

'You have thanked him actually, and in a very special way.'

'How?'

'Sigi gave me quite a lot of money for a fund the admiral controls . . . a fund that he uses to help people without money get out of Germany

... Jews, Catholics, political refugees. So you have done your bit, so to speak. The admiral was very grateful to Sigi.'

'I am glad we were able to help with such a positive gesture. It's very important to come to the aid of other people who are in trouble, especially those who are less fortunate than oneself.'

Kurt smiled at her, then glanced at his watch. He grimaced and shook his head sadly. 'I'm afraid I haven't got much longer, Ursula. I must keep my last business appointment at the other side of Paris before I take the night train to Zurich.'

'Oh Kurt, it's been so quick, such a short visit ...' She broke off, glanced away so that he would not see the tears starting to gather in her eyes. She longed desperately to detain him, needing his understanding, his warmth and his friendship so much at this moment. He had played an important role in her life because of her relationship with Arabella, and his presence had been particularly reassuring, had brought her such a great measure of comfort this afternoon.

Kurt asked for the bill and when it came he put enough money on the table to cover it, rose and helped her up from the banquette where they were sitting. He lifted his briefcase and overcoat from the chair nearby, and led her out into the lobby.

They paused for a moment and turned to face each other.

Kurt said, 'I have a few minutes to spare, Ursi. May I come up to the suite to see Maxim?'

'That would be lovely, Kurt.' She broke into smiles. 'Maxim will be so thrilled to see you.'

'Then let's go,' he said, putting one hand under her elbow, guiding her in the direction of the elevator.

'Uncle Kurt! Uncle Kurt!'

Maxim slid off the sofa where he sat with Teddy reading one of his books, and hurtled across the sitting room.

Kurt quickly placed his briefcase and overcoat on a chair in the small foyer, and swept the boy up into his arms when he reached him and hugged him close.

A second later he put him down on the floor, lowered his lanky frame into a hunkering position in front of him and looked into Maxim's flushed face. 'Hello, Maxim, I came all the way from Berlin to see you.'

'Is Papa here?' Maxim asked excitedly, looking past him to the door. 'Did you bring my papa?'

Kurt shook his head. 'No, old fellow, I didn't,' he said in a gentle voice. 'But I did bring much love and many kisses from him, and he told me to tell you that he will be here in no time at all.'

Maxim beamed with happiness on hearing this news. 'Soon? Will Papa come soon?'

'Indeed he will.' Kurt straightened and stood up, took hold of Maxim's hand, and together they walked into the sitting room. After greeting Teddy, Kurt seated himself on a chair, picked up the four-year-old boy and settled him comfortably on his knee.

Maxim peered into his face. 'Did Christian come? And Diana? Are they here?'

'No, they're not, Maxim. They're with their mother in Berlin.'

'I wish they were here, then I could play with them, couldn't I?'

'Yes, you could. Now, tell me what you've been doing in Paris, old fellow.'

Maxim, who was an articulate child, started his recital by explaining that he had been to the top of the Eiffel Tower with his mother and Teddy, went on to enumerate the other sights they had seen, and listed everything they had done since they had arrived in Paris. The prince listened most attentively, nodding, and smiling lovingly at the boy.

From the doorway, Ursula stood watching them, her eyes bright with pleasure. Kurt von Wittingen's unexpected visit had been an enormous boost to her flagging morale. But, perhaps even more importantly, his news from Berlin about her mother-in-law's improved condition had given her renewed hope that she and Sigi would soon be able to travel. Ursula was now convinced that they would be with her in the next couple of weeks, and her spirits soared.

TWENTY

'How is your aunt?' Ursula asked Teddy when she returned to the sitting room of the suite in the Plaza-Athénée, after making her weekly telephone call to Ketti Berners in London.

Teddy gave her a vivid, happy smile and sat down opposite her. 'Aunt Ketti is very well, and she can't wait for us to go to London, Frau Westheim. She's looking forward to meeting you and Maxim, and she told me, once again, how grateful she is to you for everything you've done for me, and most especially for getting me out of Germany.'

'I never had any intention of leaving you behind,' Ursula replied. There was a small pause before she went on, 'You haven't told me very much about your aunt, except that she's your father's sister and that she's a widow.'

'Yes, my Uncle Harry died two years ago. Aunt Ketti is about sixty-one, and she has one daughter, my cousin Rachel, who lives in Brighton. Rachel's married and has a baby girl called Harriet.'

'Your aunt has lived in London for a long time, hasn't she, Teddy?'

'Over thirty years or more. She married my uncle in 1904, when she was twenty-six, and that was when she moved to England. She's English now, an English citizen, I mean.'

'And was your uncle an Englishman?'

'Yes, but of German extraction. My Uncle Harry once told me that his parents left Berlin in about 1860, when there was apparently a big influx of the Ashkenazim into England, and he and his two brothers were born in London. You'll like Aunt Ketti when you meet her, Frau Westheim, she's a fine woman.'

'If she's anything like your father, she must be very special indeed.' Ursula rose, walked over to her bedroom, opened the door quietly and slipped inside. She tiptoed over to the single bed next to hers, where Maxim lay curled up under the covers, satisfied herself that he was sleeping soundly, and immediately returned to the sitting room.

Teddy had picked up her embroidery whilst Ursula had been out of the room, and without lifting her head, she said, 'He *is* fast asleep, isn't he?'

'Yes,' Ursula murmured, and leaned back against the chair and closed her eyes.

Teddy glanced up from her needlework, on the point of making a comment about Maxim, but when she saw that Ursula Westheim was resting she refrained. In repose Ursula's face looked weary and vulnerable, and a little sad. She's tired, Teddy thought, tired of waiting all these weeks for the family to come, tired of marking time since January. It's just not in her nature to be so inactive. Still, there's very little she *can* do except sit and wait. At least I have Maxim to keep me busy with his lessons and his walks and his care in general. Poor Frau Westheim is lost. If only we were in London, she could be looking for a home for us, a flat or a house, and getting it furnished and ready for Herr Westheim and the rest of the family, keeping herself busy. This awful waiting and the inactivity are destructive to her.

Teddy sighed under her breath, and dropped her eyes, plied her stitches neatly, thinking of the way Ursula had led her life in Berlin. There she had had two houses to run, the mansion in the Tiergartenstrasse and the rambling old villa out in the Wannsee, and the servants to deal with, plus her various charity committees to attend and friends to see and a social schedule to organise. It struck Teddy that there had never been a single moment when Ursula Westheim had not been busy. How different was her life in Paris . . .

Quite suddenly Ursula bestirred herself, opened her eyes and sat up. 'Teddy?'

'Yes, Frau Westheim?' Teddy said and looked across at her.

'What is your aunt's house in London like? Is it large?'

'Fairly large. She rents out the flat in the basement, as well as the one at the top of the house in the attics, which she had converted recently. But she still has two floors to herself, and a lovely garden at the back with a lawn and a rockery and an apple tree. She lives in Belsize Park Gardens, in a pleasant area near Hampstead.'

'It sounds very nice indeed. Teddy – ' Ursula paused and hesitated briefly, then plunged on, 'do you think your aunt would let you and Maxim stay with her for a few weeks?'

Teddy glanced up from her embroidery, and although she was startled by this question, she nodded. 'I'm sure she would. But why do you want us to stay with her?'

'Because I'd like to send you and Maxim to London ahead of me. I would then follow later this month.'

'Oh,' was about all Teddy could think of to say, and she stared hard at Ursula, her eyes full of questions. After a moment, she asked, 'Why aren't you coming at the same time as us, Frau Westheim?'

'I came to a decision the other day,' Ursula began and stopped. After a second, she went on slowly, softly, 'I'm going back.'

Teddy frowned. '*Back*,' she repeated, looking puzzled. 'I'm sorry, I'm not following you.'

'I'm going back to Berlin.'

Teddy was so flabbergasted she was speechless. However, she found her voice very quickly, and cried in a fierce whisper, 'You can't, Frau Westheim! You can't!'

'Yes, Teddy, I can.'

'But it's not safe in Berlin,' the girl exclaimed heatedly.

'Perhaps it isn't. Nevertheless, I have to return, to help Herr Westheim. He needs me. Instinctively, I *know* he does. Together, we must bring his mother out. And his sisters. It's the only way. We must do it *somehow*.'

Teddy was not only startled by Ursula's sudden and dramatic announcement, but exceedingly frightened by it. Memories of *Kristallnacht* still lingered. They were extremely potent, vividly etched on her brain, and they continued to fill her with dread whenever she remembered that horrifying night, reluctantly cast her mind back to it. And certainly things had not improved in the Third Reich since then. If anything, they must have worsened. She wondered how to convey her own terror to Ursula, how to convince her not to return there, but she was at a loss. Teddy knew Ursula Westheim well, knew how stubborn she could be, and difficult to dissuade once her mind was made up.

Ursula leaned forward and pinned her gaze on Teddy.

'I realise you're wondering how to talk me out of my plan, but you can't. Look, it's already March and soon it will be spring, and I can't just sit here waiting, leaving things to chance. I'm frantic about the family, I've no idea what's happening anymore. You've heard me on the phone to Herr Westheim. The calls are hopeless, frustrating, since neither of us dare speak openly to each other. However, one thing I'm certain of – he needs assistance with his mother. His sisters are lovely women, but, unfortunately, they have never been very decisive, and under the present circumstances I don't believe they are of much use to him. *But I can be.* And I know Prince and Princess von Wittingen will be as helpful as *they* possibly can . . . they'll do whatever is necessary to get us out, with the cooperation of Admiral Canaris and Colonel Oster of German Military Intelligence.'

Teddy remained silent, and so Ursula hurried on, 'And there's another thing. We both know from what we've read in the French newspapers that war is inevitable between Germany and England, and France is bound to join in. We don't know when it will come . . . the situation gets more explosive by the day, and obviously I don't want the family to get stuck in Berlin . . . I *must* act now whilst there's still time.'

Leaning back in the chair, Ursula waited for Teddy to respond. But yet again no words were forthcoming, and so she added quickly, in a more insistent tone, 'I'm *needed* in Berlin! Don't you see that?'

'Yes, I suppose so,' Teddy mumbled, desperately trying to quieten her fears, although without much success.

'I knew you would understand. I really would appreciate it if you would telephone your aunt tomorrow morning and ask her if you can stay with her for two weeks. And I will have a word with her myself, of course, Teddy.'

'She'll try to talk you out of it!'

'No, she won't, because I'm not going to tell her about my trip to Germany. I shall merely say that I have business in Switzerland, and that I think it would be more suitable for you and my son to go to England. That *is* the wisest thing to say, don't you agree, Teddy?'

'Yes, Frau Westheim,' Teddy said miserably, her voice a whisper.

Ursula jumped up, unexpectedly full of energy and vigour after days of lethargy and despair, and hurried over to the desk, opened the top drawer and took out two envelopes. These she brought to Teddy, and after showing them to her, she continued in the same brisk and businesslike tone, 'I shall give these letters to you on the day you leave for London, and in the meantime they'll be locked in the desk here. The first is addressed to Mr Henry Rossiter, of the Rossiter Merchant Bank in London. I have already spoken to him on the telephone, and he is expecting to hear from you, once you have settled in at your aunt's house. You must go to see him and give him my letter. It confirms in writing my verbal instructions to him, which, in essence, are to give you money as and when you need it. Our funds here in France are in the process of being transferred from the Banque Mallet to the Rossiter Merchant Bank. I arranged this transaction several days ago. I want you to remember that you have access to those funds for yourself and Maxim until we arrive.'

'I don't need any money, Frau Westheim,' Teddy protested. 'My aunt will provide for us whilst we're staying with her.'

'I realise that, Teddy. However, it makes me feel better, easier within myself, knowing that you can draw on the money in case of an emergency.'

Teddy nodded, realising that there was no point in arguing with her.

Ursula rushed on, 'The second letter is addressed to you. However, you must not open it unless something happens to me and my husband. If I should die, and he survives me, then you will give him the letter. I have asked Mr Rossiter to provide us with a safety deposit box at the bank, and you will place the letter in it for safe keeping.'

'Yes, of course. But nothing is going to happen to you or Herr Westheim!' Teddy announced emphatically, forcing a smile and inwardly praying that she spoke the truth.

'There's something else I must mention,' Ursula went on. 'When we left Germany, some of my jewellery was stitched into my travelling clothes. Mostly my diamonds and sapphires. After we arrived in Paris I took the jewellery to Monsieur André Mallet of the Banque Mallet, who has been keeping it in a safe for me. Tomorrow it will be on its way to the Rossiter Merchant Bank in London. Monsieur Mallet is sending it by bonded courier. The jewellery must also be put in the safety deposit box with the letter, and before you leave I'll make a list of everything for you.'

Teddy nodded.

'There's one last thing. I know you are very capable, Teddy, and that you speak good English, but Mr Stiles at the British Embassy here in Paris is going to have someone from the British Foreign Office waiting for you, when you pass through immigration in England. Just in case you need help with any of the formalities.'

'Thank you,' Teddy said and looked closely at Ursula. 'You didn't tell Mr Stiles you were going back to Germany, did you?'

'Of course not!'

'If you had, he would have objected too, and *he* would have perhaps tried to stop you!' she exclaimed with her special brand of feistiness.

Ursula was silent, realising this was true.

After a moment she rose and joined Teddy on the sofa.

Taking hold of her hand she squeezed it, then said quietly, but with an air of immense confidence, 'Try not to worry, everything's going to be all right. I just know it is, Teddy dear.'

'Yes,' Teddy answered swiftly. 'Yes, it is. I know that, Frau Westheim.'

Four days after this conversation had taken place, all of the necessary arrangements had been made for Teddy and Maxim to travel to England.

Aunt Ketti Berners had immediately agreed that they could stay with her until such time Ursula and Sigmund arrived in London.

'I will be at Victoria Station to meet the boat train from Paris,' she told Teddy, and had repeated this to Ursula, before going on to say how excited and delighted she was they were coming, and that she was truly looking forward to receiving them in her home.

Nonetheless, Ursula knew there was no point in denying to herself that she was going to miss her child, because she was. On the other hand, this was the right course of action, the only course.

For several weeks, Ursula had wrestled with the problem of what to do for the best for them all, and she had been caught on the horns of the most agonising dilemma, torn up inside. She loved her child and her husband equally, and it had never been a question of choosing between them, but rather of deciding on the best measures to take: measures which would ultimately guarantee that they would be reunited.

Sigi, seemingly, was immobilised in Berlin, but for what reason she did not know. Nor did she have any means of finding out, unless Kurt von Wittingen passed through Paris on business again and brought her news. Yet this was most unlikely; he had told her as much when he had dropped in unexpectedly for tea, over a month ago now.

At one point last week she had considered telephoning either Arabella or Renata, but had dismissed the idea instantly. Their phones had more than likely been tapped for the longest time, and she had no wish to create difficulties for her two dearest friends. And anyway, she was not sure what they could have told her, even if she had telephoned. Certainly no more than Sigi was saying when he called, for, like him, they would have been afraid to speak out.

And so finally she had made the decision to go back to Berlin. Her aim was to aid Sigi in moving the family as soon and as rapidly as possible. There was no question in her mind that together she and he could do it. They had always been a good team, even as children.

Sigi already had the five exit visas from Admiral Canaris, and once she was there she would literally force Sigrid and her husband, Thomas Mayer, to leave at once. She had worked it all out in her head in advance and it was a good plan: the Mayers would tell their servants they were going to Hamburg on business, as they frequently did, and they would take Hedy with them. As a companion for Sigrid, the story would be. As soon as the three of them reached Hamburg they would book passages on any boat leaving for England, even a cargo steamer if there was nothing else available. Hamburg was a busy North Sea port and there would be no problem for them to find some kind of vessel.

Meanwhile, she and Sigi would take his mother to Switzerland, ostensibly for medical reasons. Her idea was that they would travel by car, taking the route from Berlin to Frankfurt and on to Stuttgart. From there they would go to Mannheim and Konstanz, sleeping overnight at most of these places, and resting whenever necessary, to give Margarete a respite from all the travelling. They would cross the German border into Switzerland near Konstanz, which would bring them relatively close to Zurich, where they had Swiss banking friends who would assist them, if this was required.

Ursula was absolutely convinced that Admiral Canaris would be willing to help them one last time, and that he might also be able to facilitate an easy crossing at the border. Hopefully without too much close scrutiny from the German border police.

There was no doubt in her mind that Maxim would be safe whilst she and Sigi were engaged in these activities, and she drew comfort from this knowledge. She had implicit faith in Theodora Stein. The young woman was responsible and trustworthy, and loving Maxim the way she did, as if he were her own child, she would never let anything happen to him. Teddy would protect him with her life, in the same way she herself would. And so she had no qualms about sending him to England in her care, and England *was* the best place for him, a democratic and civilised land where justice and fair play were common everyday standards, a country whose treatment of Jews had always been less harsh and far more generous than most other places in the world.

Furthermore, she was satisfied that Ketti Berners was a solid, upstanding woman. Certainly the several conversations she had had with her on the phone over the past few days had only served to reinforce the feeling that she was as admirable as her late brother, Doctor Johann Stein. There was not the slightest question in Ursula's mind that Maxim and Teddy would be well looked after by this woman, who sounded unusually loving and the personification of kindness.

And yet on the morning they were to leave, Ursula felt a heaviness descend on her. There was a terrible ache in the region of her heart, a constriction in her throat as she buttoned Maxim's jacket after breakfast, getting him ready for the journey. He was such a little boy, only four-and-a-half years old, and still a baby in so many ways.

For a moment she wavered, almost changed her mind, realising that she could hardly bear to let him out of her sight for a single second, never mind several weeks. But then she remembered what was at stake in Berlin, and she swallowed, took firm control of her emotions.

'Come and sit on the sofa with me for a moment, *Schatzi*, I want to talk to you,' she said gently, lovingly, smiling at him.

'What about, *Mutti*?' he asked, staring up at her through those large, liquid brown eyes that always touched her heart, and never more than they did today.

'About the trip to England,' she answered as they settled on the sofa next to each other. Through the corner of her eye she could see Teddy on the phone in the adjoining bedroom, undoubtedly calling the concierge for porters to help with the many suitcases.

Clearing her throat, Ursula continued, 'Teddy is going to take you to London by yourself, Maxim. You're going to stay with her Aunt Ketti. I can't come today, but I shall be there very soon.'

Alarm instantly struck his small face. His eyes opened wide and he cried fretfully, 'But why aren't you coming with us, *Mutti*? I want you to come too!'

'Sssh, sweetheart, there's no reason to get upset.' Wishing to calm and reassure him, she took his hand in hers and held it tightly. 'I have to go to Berlin tomorrow, to help Papa. We must bring your grandmother to England. Remember, I told you she was ill, and Papa cannot manage to do everything for her himself. He needs me to take care of Grandmama on the journey; she's an old lady, and she needs properly looking after, you know.'

'I don't want to go without you!' Maxim wailed. His top lip began to tremble and he flung himself against her body and promptly burst into tears as he clutched her.

Ursula wrapped her arms around him and held him close to her, stroking his hair, hushing him gently. It was hard for her to part with this child, even for so short a time. They had waited so long for him, for so many years of their marriage, and she loved him so very much. He was part of her . . . her heart.

Tears welled, she was unable to speak, so she simply sat there holding her little son in her arms, rocking him to and fro, her love enveloping him.

Finally, when she was composed enough, she said, 'I'll be with you in

ten days, not much longer, *Mäuschen*, and then we'll be together again
. . . you and me and Papa . . . just like we always were in Berlin.'

The child drew away from her and peered into her face, and then he
put a chubby hand against her cheek and stroked it. 'Promise, *Mutti*,' he
whispered, his voice still tearful.

'I do. *I promise*.' Ursula took a handkerchief out of her suit pocket and
wiped his damp cheeks. 'There, that's better, my little love,' she said,
smiling at him. 'No more tears. We won't be separated for long, and you
have sweet Teddy to look after you until I get there.'

Maxim nodded and gave her a faint watery smile in return. 'And when
you come, will you bring Papa and Gangan with you, *Mutti*?'

'Of course! That's why I'm going back . . . to get them.'

He gazed at her thoughtfully and then he tilted his head on one side,
and said, 'You won't lose me, will you, *Mutti*?'

Taken aback by this question, and instantly noticing the worry settling
on his face, she exclaimed, 'How could I lose you! Whatever makes you
say a thing like that, darling?'

'Teddy read me a story once . . . about a boy called Hans . . . his mother
lost him . . . and she couldn't find him . . . not ever. I don't want to be a
lost boy. Don't lose me, *Mutti. Please.*'

'Never, darling! *Never, never, never!* You're far too precious. And I love
you far too much.' She reached out for him again and brought him close
into her arms and hugged him, and he clung to her tenaciously, with all
his might.

The sudden sound of knocking on the door made Ursula release him
and she stood up quickly. At this moment, Teddy came hurrying into the
living room exclaiming, 'That must be the porters!' She went through into
the foyer and opened the door, asked the two bell boys standing there to
come inside.

'Maxim, would you like to take them into the bedroom, show them
the suitcases which are to be taken down to the lobby?' Ursula suggested,
wanting to distract him and also to speak to Teddy alone for a moment.

'Oh yes, I would!' Maxim cried, jumping down off the sofa and running
over to the bell boys.

The two women watched him usher them into the bedroom, and then
turned to look at each other.

Ursula said in a very low voice, 'I won't leave for Berlin until I
know you've arrived. I'll wait here at the hotel until I hear from
you.'

'I'll telephone you as soon as we get to Aunt Ketti's.'

'You do remember everything I've told you, don't you, Teddy?'

'Every single thing . . . all of your instructions. I have the two letters in my handbag, along with the cash you gave me, and the list of your jewellery.'

'I have great faith in you, Teddy, and your abilities. If anything should go wrong – ' Ursula's throat closed and she glanced away, unable, suddenly, to continue. But shortly she was able to proceed, and she did so in the same quiet tone. 'If we don't make it to England, you will look after Maxim for me, won't you? For as long as it's necessary.'

'You know I will!' Teddy caught hold of Ursula's arm reassuringly. 'But you'll be looking after him yourself. You'll be with us soon. Everything will go according to your plan.'

'I hope so.' Ursula stepped closer and embraced Teddy warmly. 'Take care of yourself, and of Maxim,' she said.

'I will, Frau Westheim, and remember, you have nothing to fret yourself about.'

'I know. Now, I think that perhaps we should get off to the Gare du Nord. Although I'm going to miss you both most dreadfully, I'm glad I'm putting you on that boat train to London.' There was a pause, and she stared into Teddy's face, and the smile she gave her was brave. She finished softly, 'You'll be safe there, the two of you.'

PART 3

There shall no evil befall thee, neither shall any plague come nigh thy dwelling. For he shall give his angels charge over thee, to keep thee in all thy ways. They shall bear thee up in their hands, lest thou dash thy foot against a stone.

Psalm 91: The Bible

TWENTY-ONE

It was a perfect summer evening on the last day of August.

The brilliant sun had disappeared, its last flickering rays painting the rim of the sky with liquid crimson bleeding into saffron and amethyst and the palest of lilacs before dropping down behind the dim horizon. The sunset had been one of such incredible beauty Theodora had caught her breath in surprise and delight. Now the sky was turning a deep pavonian blue and filling with dusky clouds; twilight was rapidly descending, casting pearly and opalescent tints over the verdant green lawn, the old apple tree, the fragrant rose bushes and the rockery scattered with pretty alpine flowers.

In the garden spread out in front of the stone-paved terrace where she sat all things appeared transfixed. Nothing moved. Not a blade of grass nor a leaf nor any living creature stirred, and there was a hush over everything, as if the little garden lay under a vast body of pale, transparent water that was entirely motionless.

Teddy rested her head against the back of the canvas deck chair, listening to the silence, enjoying the peace which drifted around her. There was a heaviness in the air, but she did not find this unpleasant; it was a balminess really, and it added to the tranquillity she was feeling.

Theodora had had such a hectic day she was glad of this brief respite before she started to prepare supper. Maxim and his school friend Alan Trenton, who was staying with them for a few days, had kept her busy since early morning. Walking on Hampstead Heath – *exploring*, they called it; racing down to the Two Blues Tea Room in Hampstead village for a mid-morning snack of tea and biscuits; afterwards up to the heath again, to sail their boats on Whitestone Pond, and finally back down to the house for lunch.

She had made them sausages and chips and baked beans, their particular favourites at the moment, and there had been the rare luxury of two fresh eggs, which the grocer, Sam Giles, had let her have the day before. She had queued up for half an hour, standing in line outside the shop along with the other women waiting patiently to buy their groceries for the weekend. When it was her turn, Mr Giles had glanced at her three ration books, leaned over the counter and whispered conspiratorially, 'You've got enough coupons left for two eggs, Miss Stein,' and then he had brought out a brown paper bag surreptitiously, and, with sleight of hand, had quickly passed it to her. 'Put this in your basket, ducks, and don't say a word to anyone. I don't want a riot on my hands, I've only got nine eggs in the entire shop, and two dozen women wanting them.'

Teddy had thanked him profusely, and had carefully carried the precious eggs back to the house, gratified that Sam Giles liked her, and that she had been a favoured customer over the years. Everything was scarcer than ever these days, especially fresh eggs, sugar, meat and imported fruits. They had not seen an orange, a banana or a grapefruit in the shops for years, and food rationing meant dreary meals most of the time. Something rare was therefore the greatest of treats, and it had given her immense pleasure to observe the way the boys' eyes had gleamed at the sight of the eggs, when she had put their plates in front of them.

In the afternoon, Aunt Ketti had provided yet another treat. She had taken them to a matinée at the local picture house, to see Claude Rains in *The Phantom of the Opera*, which had come around for the third time since it had opened the previous year. The four of them had enjoyed it enormously. The technicolor film had been just ghoulish enough, and sufficiently scary, for the ten-year-olds to take great delight in it, and on the way home they had pranced ahead of Teddy and Ketti, pulling grotesque faces and aping Claude Rains emoting in the bowels of the Paris Opera House.

Ten years old, she mused. How the time had flown since they had come to England five years ago. Her only regret was that the Westheims had not been able to join them yet. Their whereabouts, their well-being and their safety were forever on her mind. Not a day went by without her thinking of them, and every night before she went to sleep she prayed for them, for their deliverance. Sometimes she found it hard to believe that Maxim was already ten, but he was, and he was grown up in so many different ways. She supposed this came from being away at boarding school with boys of his own age, out on his own, in a certain sense. He had become much more independent this past year. But that was all to the good. Whilst *he* was the centre of *her* life, she did not want Maxim to become a namby-pamby boy, permanently attached to her apron strings, forever reliant on her. Steadfastly, she had encouraged him to stand on his own two feet, and, much to her satisfaction, he had done so.

Academically, Maxim was brilliant.

When he was eight he had passed the entrance exam for Colet Court with the greatest of ease, and had won such high marks even Aunt Ketti had been suitably impressed. Teddy was particularly proud of the way he had handled the exams without blinking an eyelash, since the scholastic standards of the famous old school were extremely high, and also because she herself had tutored him.

After they had arrived in England in March of 1939, she had sent him to the little elementary school in Belsize Park near Aunt Ketti's house, on her aunt's recommendation. He had started in the September, a few months after his fifth birthday on June the twelfth, and he had settled in at once, had swiftly adapted himself, chameleon-like, to the English and their curious ways. There had never been any problems with him at the local kindergarten, nor at Colet Court thus far.

She had taught him English in the first five months they had lived with Aunt Ketti, before he had started at the kindergarten, and he had proved to have an aptitude for languages. He now spoke flawless English with the most perfect of English accents, and he was becoming fluent in French as well, which he was learning at the preparatory school.

Even though he had only been five when he had started at the kindergarten, Teddy had realised almost at once that the curriculum was not challenging enough for him, for he was an exceptionally clever boy, a quick study, and light years ahead of his age. And so she had begun to teach him herself at weekends, giving him lessons in more advanced English history, geography and mathematics. The latter, even at that age, had been his favourite subject and he had a unique affinity for, and an understanding of, numbers. Since attending Colet Court, maths had become his forte, and his teacher considered him to be a mathematical genius, only echoing what she herself had believed for a very long time.

The sudden shrill, insistent wailing of the air-raid siren disturbed the peace and tranquillity of the garden. It cut off her ruminations about Maxim, brought her up out of the deck chair with a leap, the war insinuating itself in her consciousness once again, as it did at some point every day.

There was a clattering sound behind her, and when she swung her head she saw that her aunt, Maxim, and Alan were rushing through the French doors which led from the back parlour out into the garden.

'Doodlebugs again, Teddy!' Maxim cried, using the common nickname for the V1 flying bombs which were being systematically launched on England by the Germans, from sites across the English Channel. As he spoke he was solicitous of Aunt Ketti, carefully helping her down the stone steps.

'That's one thing I'm *absolutely* certain of!' Teddy called back pithily, turning around, beckoning to them urgently. 'Let's take to the safety of the shelter at once. Get a move on, the three of you! *Please.*'

'We're right behind you, lovey,' Aunt Ketti assured her.

Teddy raced ahead to the air-raid shelter at the bottom of the garden, which had such a large quantity of sandbags protecting its roof of corrugated-iron and earth that it looked like a dugout in the trenches on the front lines.

Running down the three steps and wrenching open the door, she picked up the flashlight which was kept on the floor immediately inside, turned it on, made for the table straight ahead of her. Three large white candles in jam jars and two kerosene lamps stood on this, and she had just finished lighting them when Aunt Ketti came in with the boys.

Ketti closed the door firmly behind her and crossed the floor to her usual chair, sighing under her breath as she did so. Five years of war, of bombings and peril and fear, of deprivations and anxieties of all kinds, plus living in the shelter on a daily basis, had wearied her in a variety of different ways.

The Anderson air-raid shelter was of reasonable size, and there was ample room for the four of them. The local air-raid warden, Jock Philips, and two of his helpers, had built the shelter for Aunt Ketti. This had been in September of 1939, not many days after the British Government, ultimately provoked to the limit of their patience by Hitler's ruthless invasion of Poland, had declared war on Germany finally, as had France.

The three men had done an excellent job of erecting the shelter, which was actually pre-fabricated and came in sections. To be effective, the tunnel-shaped shelter had to be partially sunk into a hole in the ground. Its walls, floor and curved ceiling were made of the corrugated-iron panels, and these were joined together to form the whole. Earth was then piled on the roof outside and covered with sandbags for that extra protection.

Two bunk beds, stacked one on top of the other, stood against a wall, and there was a cot aligned along another; aside from the table holding the candles and the lamps, such items as two chairs and a worn Oriental rug added small but welcome touches of comfort. A paraffin stove occupied a corner, and this provided necessary heat for them in the cold weather.

Placed against a third wall was their all-important storage cupboard. Aunt Ketti and Teddy had stocked this to the hilt with tinned food such as Fray Bentos corned beef, Spam, Heinz tomato soup, baked beans, bottled fruits, tins of cocoa, Ovaltine, powdered milk and powdered eggs, and many Tizer bottles, emptied of their soda-pop and filled with water in case the mains were hit and there was a water shortage. A primus stove for cooking, several pans, a whistling kettle, plates, mugs, cutlery, and a thermos flask were ranged along the top of the cupboard, whilst a tea chest next to it contained a first-aid box and extra gas masks for them, just in case the Germans did use poison gas after all; a second tea chest held soap, toothpaste, and other toiletries, plus towels, hot water bottles, thick wool blankets, sweaters, scarves, woollen caps and gloves.

The two women had endeavoured to stock the air-raid shelter with the basic necessities of daily life. These were the essentials they knew they would require, should the house suffer a direct hit in one of the many bombing raids, when they would then be forced to live in the shelter permanently. Or until they could make other arrangements, at least.

Maxim, who had led Alan over to the cot, now said, 'Sit here, Stubby old thing, I've got a new jigsaw puzzle, and we can have a go at it, if you like.'

'Bang-on, Duke!' Alan exclaimed, flopping down on one end of the cot unceremoniously. He lolled back on an elbow, stared up at Maxim, and asked, 'What's the subject this time?'

'A good one,' Maxim answered, taking the puzzle out of the tea chest. 'St George and the Dragon, and it looks jolly difficult.'

'It won't be for you, Genius,' Stubby shot back, grinning. 'Come on, don't dawdle! Open it, and let's start putting it together.'

'You open it, Stubby.' Maxim dropped the box on the blanket, and added, 'I'll get the tin tray from under the cot, so that we can set the puzzle up properly on a solid base.' Once Maxim had produced the tray, the boys bent their heads over it, and soon they were so completely engrossed, sorting through the hundreds of pieces of the jigsaw puzzle, they were entirely oblivious of Teddy and Aunt Ketti and even the air raid outside.

During the boys' exchange, Teddy had seated herself in the chair opposite Aunt Ketti, and she said to her softly, 'I hope we're not in for a long night of it again.'

'You never know with the V1s. It depends how many they're going to fire at us in the next few hours,' Ketti answered dourly. 'Hitler's secret weapon has turned out to be a rather diabolical one, hasn't it, Theodora?'

'Yes, it has . . . so many people killed these past few months, hundreds in the London area alone. It makes my heart ache just to think about it.' She shook her head. 'I remember what Mr Churchill said on the wireless in July . . . that civilian deaths from the flying bombs have been on such a scale there's been nothing like this since the Blitz. The way those bombs suddenly zoom over unexpectedly is horrible, and so frightening to everyone. I know they petrify me, Aunt Ketti.'

Ketti shuddered, made no verbal response, merely nodded. But she grimaced angrily to herself as she reached for the knitting bag she kept in the shelter, cursing the Mad Austrian, as she called Hitler, and the Nazis, under her breath. Heaving a small sigh, she took out the Fair Isle sweater she was making for Maxim, and within seconds her knitting needles were rapidly clicking away.

At sixty-six, Ketti Stein Berners was a most handsome woman, who did not look her age. Perhaps this was because she had led a good life in England, a sheltered life, wrapped in a cocoon of love and tender care and comfort by her late husband. Snow-white though her hair was, her face was plump, pink-complexioned and almost without a wrinkle. Certainly it belied her age, as did her trim figure, her considerable vigour and vitality. She had sympathetic brown eyes, a warm, outgoing nature and a cheerful disposition. Her only regret in life was that her beloved Harry had died of a heart attack long before his time. Harry Berners, the only man she had ever loved, had left her comfortably off; his two brothers, his partners in the clothing manufacturing business he had founded, continued to pay her his full salary and his share of the profits, and they would do so until the day she died. After that, her daughter Rachel would receive a share of the profits for as long as the Berners brothers remained in business.

Abruptly, Ketti stopped knitting, lifted her head, listened alertly.

So did Teddy and the boys.

A loud roaring noise drew closer, became deafening. It alarmed them considerably since it was immediately above their heads, and they exchanged apprehensive glances. They knew it was a flying bomb, and their fear showed on their faces. The roar of the engine reached a crescendo, then cut out, and there was a sudden deathly silence for a second or two, followed by a crash and the most shattering explosion.

'Oh my God, the house!' Ketti shrieked, panic registering, her eyes widening. 'We've been hit! The house has suffered a direct hit!'

'No, it hasn't, Aunt Ketti,' Maxim said. 'The explosion would have been ten times louder if the doodlebug had dropped on our house. I think it fell a few streets away.'

'Maxim's right, Mrs Berners,' Stubby asserted, as always agreeing with Maxim. 'I bet there's a big crater, too, wherever it fell. There always is.'

'Poor souls. Poor, poor souls,' Ketti murmured, shaking her head with the greatest of sadness and compassion. 'Every night ... nothing but death and destruction. And grief for so many ...' Her voice trailed off miserably, and her expression became more dolorous than ever.

She thought of her daughter Rachel and her little granddaughter Harriet in Brighton, and she prayed to God that they were safe in their own air-raid shelter. She also prayed for her son-in-law Gerald, who was somewhere in Italy with General Alexander and the British army. Keep them safe, dear God, she said in the silence of her heart. Keep my family safe ... and keep all of our brave fighting men safe, wherever they might be.

'A flying bomb is the size of a Spitfire,' Maxim suddenly remarked, startling Ketti, making her sit up with a jerk.

She looked across at him, frowning slightly, as he went on to tell her, 'It's a pilotless aircraft, Aunt Ketti, and very large. That's why it makes such a gigantic crater when it crashes.'

Stubby nodded, his pale blue eyes and his little freckled face growing very serious. 'My father says we'll beat 'em yet though, beat the Jerries and the Eyeties. Our fighter planes and anti-aircraft guns are shooting down a lot of flying bombs, and we're building new anti-aircraft sites all along the coast of the English Channel.'

This was said with such authority, Ketti glanced at Stubby in surprise. 'Such knowledge for children to have!' she cried, genuine horror reverberating in her voice. 'Such a *terrible* knowledge ... of guns and fighter planes and death ... Ach! ... I can't stand it! I cannot wait for this horrendous war to be over, so that our children can forget about aeroplanes and bombs and tanks and guns and bullets, and go back to being children, playing children's games.'

Teddy nodded. 'I know exactly what you mean, Aunt.'

'My father says the war *will* be over soon,' Stubby now announced. 'He says we'll be having victory celebrations next summer.'

'And let's hope your father is right, Alan,' Teddy murmured succinctly. She rose and went over to the storage cupboard. 'How about a nice cup of tea to calm your nerves, Aunt Ketti?'

'My nerves don't need calming, Theodora. On the other hand, I wouldn't mind a rosy lea. You know I rarely say no to that.'

'I could do with one myself.' Teddy picked up the Tizer bottle, poured water from it into the kettle, lit the primus stove, and placed the kettle on it to boil.

'A rosy lea, *a cup of tea*. A twist and a twirl, *a girl*. Apples and pears, *stairs*. Whistle and flute, *suit*,' Stubby recited in a gleeful voice, grinning at Maxim.

Maxim burst out laughing. 'I love the Cockney rhyming slang. You promised to teach me more of it, so go on, let's hear it.'

'Trouble and strife, *wife*,' Stubby began, and stopped, his repertoire instantly petering out.

'*And?*' Maxim pressed, staring hard at his dearest friend, raising a brow questioningly.

Stubby made a face, shrugged, and admitted, 'That's all I know, Duke.' His smile was a bit rueful, as he added, 'I'll try and rustle up some more next week, before we go back to school. I'll ask Mrs Threscoe, you know,

our char lady. She's a real Cockney, born in the sound of Bow bells . . .
that's where you have to be born to be a Cockney, in case you didn't
know.'

'I *did* know, because you keep telling me. Listen, Mrs Threscoe promised to take us to see the costermongers, to meet the Pearly King and
Queen. But she never did, did she?'

'That's because the Pearly King of the costermongers is in the Royal
Navy, off fighting the war. She'll take us though, when the Jerries have
surrendered and he comes home to the East End. That's where the costermongers live, down the Mile End Road, Duke. But come on, let's keep
going with the jigsaw, it's great fun.'

'All right,' Maxim agreed, searching through the pieces on the cot,
looking for one which might complete the dragon's head.

'Would you boys like something to drink?' Teddy asked as she poured
hot water over the tea leaves she had just measured into the large brown
teapot, the one Aunt Ketti insisted produced the best cup of tea in
the world.

'Yes, please,' Maxim said and glanced at his friend. 'How about you,
Stubby? Would you like a dandelion and burdock?'

'Whiz-O! That's smashing!' Stubby burst out, and then instantly
remembered his manners, added swiftly, in his most polite voice, 'If I
may, Teddy, please.'

She nodded. 'Very well, but only one glass each, I don't like you drinking too much of this bottled pop. It's not good for you.'

TWENTY-TWO

Teddy sat sipping her tea, endeavouring to ignore the air-raid which was
still raging outside.

This was difficult to do, however, for the continuing bombardment
and explosions, the anti-aircraft guns, the high-pitched whine of the
ambulances and the loudly-clanging bells of the fire engines created a
cacophony of sound that easily penetrated the corrugated-iron walls of
the shelter, and it was nerve-racking.

She dreaded to think of the havoc in the streets, of those who were dead
or dying or injured, or who had lost loved ones or their homes. Every night
it was the same, lives torn asunder by this foul and senseless war.

At one moment she glanced around, thinking how well this shelter
had served *them* so far. All through the Battle of Britain, during those

long and dreadful months of 1940 when England had stood alone after the fall of France. London and most of the big provincial cities had been turned into piles of rubble by the thousands of bombs which had been dropped on them, and thousands of people had been killed or maimed. Everyone had suffered terribly through those days and nights of relentless pounding by the Dornier and Heinkel bombers of the Luftwaffe, never knowing whether or not they would live to see another day.

But eventually those brave boys of the Royal Air Force, heroes all, had finally beaten back the Luftwaffe, described by journalists as 'the greatest air fleet ever assembled by any nation'. Summer had turned to autumn, winter had come and gone, and at the start of the new year, 1941, the British were still surviving, and they had continued to survive for three more years.

How lucky *they* had been, not to suffer so much as a single scratch. Now their Anderson shelter was protecting them once again, this time against the lethal flying bombs which had started to rain down in a never-ending torrent in June, taking the whole country by surprise and filling them all with perpetual fear.

Teddy prayed constantly that Maxim, Aunt Ketti and she would live to see the end of this war. The danger was not over for them and the rest of England yet; on the other hand, she was inclined to agree with Stubby's father's prediction that the Allies would be victorious by next summer. The defeat of the Third Reich, which she had once believed to be an impossibility, miraculously now seemed imminent. Much had happened lately to send their hopes soaring, lift their spirits high, and gladden their weary hearts.

Two months ago, on the sixth of June, a great Armada of ships had sailed from England to France, and British and American troops had stormed the beaches of Normandy. D-Day had been an outstanding success for the Allies. And just a week ago, at noon last Friday the twenty-fifth of August, the Free French army, led by General Leclerc, and backed up by American infantry, had poured across the bridges of the Seine in an endless stream. French tanks had rumbled into the city, the foot soldiers taking possession of the streets, and within hours General Leclerc had liberated Paris from German occupation and domination. Later that same evening, the commanding German General Dietrich von Choltitz was captured, and the last of the German troops finally surrendered.

General von Choltitz had then handed the French capital back to the French.

The following morning, General Charles de Gaulle had marched down the Champs-Élysées from the Arc de Triomphe to the Place de la

Concorde, leading a triumphal parade amidst the tumultuous cheers and rejoicing of the exultant, flag-waving French citizens.

She, Maxim, Aunt Ketti and Stubby had seen these joyous and memorable events on the Movietone News at the local cinema on Tuesday night, and the liberation of Paris had also been much reported in the British newspapers. Teddy kept herself well-informed about the progress of the war by reading the *Daily Express*, and several other papers every day, and she and Aunt Ketti listened to the daily news bulletins on the wireless, most particularly when Winston Churchill broadcast to the nation.

Teddy revered Winnie, as he was affectionately called by the British people, and she had ever since he had become Prime Minister on May tenth 1940. She remembered that date very well indeed, for it happened to have been the day following her twenty-first birthday.

To Teddy, Churchill was a man of honour and bravery, and the pure embodiment of all that was best in this island race of Britons . . . robust, stoical, strong, determined, and just. He was an inspiration to her and every other ordinary person in England, and to those in the fighting forces, and he gave each and every one of them a bit of his tremendous courage, imbued in them his own strength of will to keep on going against all odds.

In part, he did this through his extraordinary rhetoric and magnificent oratory, which never failed to touch and move her. In fact, his words captivated her, and they forever reverberated in her head. Much of what he had said at different times she knew by heart, and she frequently found herself drawing strength from his words. And repeatedly she garnered hope from them when things looked bleak, or when she was filled with despair.

Her mind slid back to the time she had first heard him speak, in the summer of 1940, just after Dunkirk, when he had said, 'We shall fight on the beaches, we shall fight on the landing grounds, we shall fight in the fields and in the streets, we shall fight in the hills; we shall never surrender.' And as she had listened to the radio that day, her own courage had been fortified and renewed because of him.

In that same month of June, not long before France fell, when the world had wondered out loud what England would do, Winston Churchill had vowed that the English would battle on alone. And he had told his countrymen and women, in that majestic and sonorous voice of his, 'Let us therefore brace ourselves to our duties, and so bear ourselves that, if the British Empire and its Commonwealth last for a thousand years, men will still say, "This was their finest hour."'

And she, German Jewish refugee that she was, had wept as she had listened to him. For her deepest emotions had been stirred, and she was filled with pride and love for this man who was setting such an awesome and valiant example for them, and for the rest of the world. She had taken great heart after hearing this speech, for she had come to understand fully that, with a leader like Churchill, Britain could not fail to win the war. However long it took, they would inevitably succeed, because *he* was determined to lead them to victory.

And in this summer of 1944 they *were* winning.

It will soon be over, Teddy thought. The hostilities will end finally, and we will be able to start leading normal lives again . . . and we will be able to pick up the threads of the past . . .

The sound of the All Clear signal going off roused her at once, brought her instantly to her feet, as it did Aunt Ketti, who pushed her knitting into its bag and off-handedly threw this onto the chair she had just vacated.

But the boys remained glued to their jigsaw puzzle, not bothering to lift their heads as Teddy flew across the floor to the door. She jerked it open, peered out, and turned back to her aunt. 'There it goes again, Aunt Ketti! The All Clear at last, thank God! We can go back to the house. Come along, Maxim, Stubby.'

'May we bring the jigsaw puzzle with us, Teddy?' Maxim asked, looking up at last.

She nodded before stepping outside into the garden.

Lifting her head, Teddy stared up into the heavens from which the murderous bombs had so recently fallen. The ink-black velvety sky was incredibly beautiful, glittering with brilliant stars and swept by searchlights which continued to crisscross the dark clouds with giant beams of blazing white light. Here and there, the sky glowed scarlet from the many fires burning where bombs had fallen in different areas. Tonight, as on so many other nights, London was aflame.

Casualties and pain, grief, despair and devastation, Teddy said to herself, that's all we live with on a daily basis. She felt a sudden heaviness settle on her when she realised that they would have much, much more to live through before peace came to this turbulent world so riven by fighting.

She began to walk up the garden path at a rapid pace. The muggy August air was acrid with the smell of smoke, high explosives, burning wood and metal. Despite the warmth of the evening, she could not help shivering when she envisioned the damage which must have been done only a few streets away from where they lived. The sound of ambulances and fire engines only reinforced this assumption, led her to believe that there were obviously many losses on every level. And she knew that the Red Cross, the St John Ambulance Brigade, and other emergency units would be at work throughout the night.

Climbing the front steps, she pushed open the door to the back parlour, and paused on the threshold of the darkened room. Earlier, when the air-raid siren had sounded, Aunt Ketti had run out and left the wireless on in the kitchen. Now, along the corridor floated the familiar voice of the Forces Sweetheart, as Vera Lynn had come to be known through her radio show *Sincerely Yours*.

Teddy leaned her head against the door frame, listening to Vera's rendition of one of the most popular songs of the war years. *'There'll always be an England, while there's a country lane, wherever there's a cottage small beside a field of grain. There'll always be an England, while there's a busy street, wherever there's a turning wheel, a million marching feet.'*

Teddy's throat tightened as she continued to stand there for a moment longer, listening to Vera finishing the song. And she found herself unexpectedly confronting an inescapable fact: *she did not want to live anywhere else but England.*

Almost immediately her thoughts swung to Willy Herzog, and her heart sank. He wanted to go to America more desperately than ever, at least so it seemed to her from his letters these days. Perhaps there was a way to persuade him to change his mind, to convince him to settle here in London. Certainly she must try. It struck her that this was imperative, and then with a rush of genuine insight into herself she realised how much this country had come to mean to her. She felt safe here, secure; she had become very anglicised in the last five years, as had Maxim. She knew this was partially because of Ursula Westheim, who had wanted them to love this country, and who had never stopped talking about England when they were in Paris in 1939. Ursula had forever extolled its virtues, telling them it was the best, the fairest, the most democratic and civilised place in the world, and she had discovered this to be true. Then again, there was her Aunt Ketti, who in the forty years she had lived here had become a true Londoner.

Teddy had to admit that becoming so English herself was her way of denying Nazi Germany, of negating the country of her birth in her mind because its anti-semitism was so painful to her. And as far as Maxim was concerned, he wanted to be like the other boys at school. She was well aware how much children hated to be singled out as being 'different' from their peers. They wanted to conform.

She heard her aunt behind her on the stone steps, and crossed the parlour, hurried down the corridor to the kitchen. After checking that the blackout curtain was properly drawn, she turned on the kitchen lights, pushed aside her worrisome thoughts about Willy and the future, and set about the task of preparing supper.

It had become the custom for Ketti and Teddy to sit down together in the back parlour at the end of the day, to share a pot of tea and chat for a while before retiring.

Tonight was no exception to this rule.

After Maxim and Stubby had gone upstairs to bed, Teddy and Ketti washed the dishes and put everything away, and then Ketti retreated to the other room to wait for her niece, who always made the tea.

'It's such a warm night,' Teddy said a few minutes later, coming into the parlour carrying the silver tray of tea things. She placed this on the antique butler's tray table near the fireplace, and went on, 'Shall I turn off the lamps and open the French windows?'

'Why not, Theodora, it's very humid, isn't it?'

After she had given Ketti her cup of tea, Teddy doused the lights, drew back the heavy blackout curtains, and flung open the glass doors leading into the garden.

There was a high, full moon riding the dark crest of the clouds, and it silvered the apple tree, the rose bushes and the rockery filled with alpine flowers that was Ketti's pride and joy. A slight breeze had blown up and it rustled the leaves of the old tree, and swept the heady fragrance of the last of the summer roses towards them on the pleasant, night air.

The two women sat in silence, looking out at the garden, beautiful now in the moonlight and uncommonly peaceful. Once more, the war seemed remote to them both, far, far away after the air-raid of earlier; at this moment it might not have even existed. They sipped their tea, not talking at all, lost in the complexities of their own reveries.

It was Ketti who finally spoke first, when she said quietly, 'Children know too much about too many things these days, and well before they *should*, in my considered opinion.'

'I suppose they do,' Teddy acknowledged. 'It's the times we're living in, I'm afraid.'

'That's true, and between the wireless and the newsreels at the picture house and the newspapers, it's not possible to hide anything from them these days, I'm sad to say,' Ketti added.

Teddy was silent, and she did not speak for a while, caught up in her thoughts as she was, until she suddenly blurted out, 'Where will I find the wisdom to raise him, to bring him up properly, Aunt Ketti?'

Ketti put her cup back in the saucer with a clatter, startled by these words which she found quite extraordinary. They literally took her breath away. 'What *ever* makes you ask me a thing like that, Theodora?' she demanded, her voice rising slightly to a higher pitch.

'I can't *help* asking it, when I think of Maxim and the way he is these days,' Teddy replied. 'He's so clever, and he has such brain power. I don't have to tell *you* that he's a quite remarkable little boy, since you know that already. But I wonder if you've ever realised how much he is aware of?' She did not wait for a response, rushed on, 'His teachers at Colet Court keep telling me that he's a brilliant student . . . and imagine, I used to think I was prejudiced because he's mine and I love him so much, but I've discovered I'm not prejudiced at all. Maxim *is* unique, Aunt Ketti, and sometimes I think he knows more than I do. About almost everything, too. So who am I to bring him up . . .' Her sentence trailed off and she sat back, staring at her aunt, looking glum in the dim light.

Ketti did not immediately reply.

She rose and went over to the glass doors, which she closed. After attending to the blackout curtains and switching on a lamp, she sat down again and examined Teddy closely through narrowed eyes. 'This is the first time you've ever spoken so negatively, Teddy dear. You sound as if you think the Westheims won't be bringing him up themselves.' There was a moment's hesitation on Ketti's part before she leaned forward, clasped Teddy's hand in hers, asked urgently, 'Have you had bad news from Germany? Is there something you're not telling me?'

Teddy shook her head, but nevertheless she sounded worried as she said, 'No, I haven't had any news, good or bad. You'd be the first to know if I had. However, I'm not stupid, and even if they weren't arrested and taken away to one of those hideous camps and are still in Berlin, how could they possibly be *alive*? Berlin has been razed to the ground by British and American bombers. You know the raids have been far heavier than usual of late, and on a non-stop basis.'

'The raids in London have been just as grim and *we're* alive, aren't we? So you see, we mustn't give up on the Westheims. And even if they *were* taken to a camp, they may well be surviving.' Ketti paused, took a deep breath, and finished emphatically, 'Certainly *I* will not give up hope for them.'

'I try to believe they're alive, Aunt Ketti! *I do!* I have to, for the child's sake. But it's been so long since we've heard anything . . . *years*. And Arabella von Wittingen hasn't been in touch for ages either. I can't help wondering if that's because she knows something *new* . . . something she's afraid to tell me.'

'Nonsense, Theodora! The princess is a true aristocrat, and as such she would never shirk her duty, even if that duty meant she had to be the bearer of bad tidings!' Ketti exclaimed. She squeezed Teddy's hand more tightly, and her voice was strong as she asserted, 'I know in my heart of hearts that Ursula and Sigmund Westheim are alive. You must believe that too, Teddy dear. You must have *faith*, as I do.'

Her aunt's positive attitude seemed to have the right effect on Teddy, and she immediately brightened. 'Yes, you're right, Aunt Ketti, it's ridiculous of me to be so pessimistic, I realise that,' she said, 'especially since I've nothing to go on. Besides, Ursula Westheim is a clever and resourceful woman. If anyone can survive under difficult and extreme circumstances, she can. I agree with you, I'm sure she and Herr Westheim are all right. And the rest of the family. She would see to that.'

'Maxim's grandmother might have passed on, God rest her soul,' Ketti murmured softly.

'She *was* frail, yes, and the stroke she had five years ago paralysed her . . .' Teddy did not have the heart to continue.

Ketti inclined her head slightly, sat back in the chair, and sipped her tea.

A silence fell between them yet again.

Teddy, in particular, was lost in her thoughts, and an abstracted expression glazed her face as she drifted off, endlessly caught up in her concerns for the Westheims and Maxim.

Ketti cast a glance in her direction and then picking up the teapot she poured herself another cup, nibbled on a ginger biscuit and carefully observed her niece, reflecting about her. She's a good girl, Ketti thought. The best. So straightforward and honest. There's not a devious bone in her body. And she's strong of heart. And loyal and kind and loving. She loves that child too much, though. Yes, she's building a tragedy for herself, thinking that Maxim's hers. He's not, and his parents will come and take him away one day, and then where will she be? Heartbroken, I've no doubt. *Oy vey is mir*, such *tsuris* will we have when that happens, oh yes, trouble and then some. What she needs is to be married. That will help to soften the blow when the Westheims take him away from her, as they will once the war ends. After all, he is *their* child, not hers, whatever she might think. Yes, marriage is definitely the solution. Marriage, and babies of her own to love.

Ketti cleared her throat and ventured carefully, 'Talking of absent friends, what about Willy Herzog? I haven't heard you mention him lately.'

Teddy looked at her aunt swiftly, then lifted her shoulders in a light shrug. 'I had a letter from him the other day. Opened by the British censor, of course, because of the foreign postmark. But they needn't have bothered. There was very little in the letter, and Willy didn't have much to say about anything.' She let out a small sigh. 'I'll never understand why

Willy left Palestine and went to Shanghai. I realise it's an international city, but what can that possibly *mean* to Willy?' She shook her head in bafflement and instantly answered her own question. 'It means nothing to him, that's what! His moving there has never made the remotest bit of sense to me.'

'Nor to me, Teddy. It always seemed to be a *meshuggeneh* thing to do, a crazy idea, if you want the truth,' Ketti said quietly, and added, 'China is so very, *very* far away.'

'So is America,' Teddy muttered.

'What do you mean, dear?'

'You know very well Willy wants to live in America when the war is over.'

'So you've told me. But I thought you were keen to go there too.' Ketti gave her a questioning look.

'I was, when Willy and I were in Berlin,' Teddy answered quickly. 'But it struck me tonight, very forcibly, that I don't want to leave London. I'd like to spend the rest of my life here, Aunt Ketti. I feel comfortable with the English, and you're here, and you're the only family I have. Besides, Maxim likes living in England. He loves Colet Court, and he can't wait to go to St Paul's when he's thirteen, and later to Oxford when he's old enough. So I couldn't go to America with Willy anyway, because of Maxim.' She paused and glanced at her aunt. 'Well, I couldn't, could I?'

Ketti stared at her, dumbfounded by her statements, and perturbed about her attitude towards Maxim. She said slowly, pointedly, 'When the Westheims get here you can do anything you want, Teddy, since they will be raising their own child.'

'Oh yes, I know they will. But look, don't misunderstand me, Aunt Ketti, when I say this ... but if something *has* happened to them, God forbid, then I am responsible for Maxim until he's grown up. I *promised* Frau Westheim I would bring him up until he could take care of himself. And even looking on the positive side, and believing they *will* come to London eventually, I would still prefer to live in England. Aside from anything else, I want to be near Maxim, to visit him at school, and see him from time to time. That's only natural, under the circumstances, isn't it?'

'Perhaps,' Ketti said in a low voice.

She was thoughtful for a few seconds, and then she murmured in her most gentle and loving tone, 'I hope you don't mind me saying this, but from the way you're speaking, *bubeleh*, it sounds to me as though Maxim means more to you than Willy Herzog.'

Teddy opened her mouth to say something and then, obviously changing her mind, she instantly closed it.

Ketti probed. 'Don't you love Willy?'

'I don't know,' Teddy said after a moment, speaking the truth. 'And I'm not even sure that I want to marry him any more.'

'You told me he is a real *mensh*, and a good Jew who goes to *shul* regularly, that he is reliable and studious, and all these things seemed to please you. But if I recollect correctly, and I *do*, you have never actually used that most important word in relation to Willy. The word *love*, Teddy. You've never said to me that you *love* Willy.'

'I was never entirely certain that I did, I suppose,' Teddy said, sounding regretful. 'I was young then, back in Berlin. Only nineteen, and I thought I wouldn't find anyone who was nicer than Willy, *better* than he is, because he *is* a good person, and that's why I said I'd marry him . . . I think.'

Ketti was quiet, but her mind was turning with great agility and rapidity. What I need is a *shadchen*. Ach! What good will a matchmaker do me, when all the nice Jewish boys are off fighting this terrible war? Never mind. I must go and talk to Rebecca Cohen. And Sarah Levine. Tomorrow. I'll go tomorrow. Fine sons they both have. Fine sons their sisters have. All single. A fine Jewish boy *I* will find for my Theodora, my only niece, my brother's only child. An English Jew to be her husband. That's what I need for her.

'Is something wrong, Aunt Ketti?'

'No, no, why do you ask?' Ketti cried, sitting up with a jerk, looking across at her niece, proffering her the sweetest of smiles.

'You look troubled, that's all.'

'I'm all right, Theodora. Perfectly all right. I was just thinking about . . . er . . . thinking . . . *Thinking* that five years is a long time for you to have been separated from your Willy Herzog. And these past five years have changed you, Teddy. Living here has changed you, the war has changed you, being entirely responsible for Maxim and making all the decisions about his education has changed you. And you've grown up a *little*. No, I correct myself, you've grown up a whole lot. You're twenty-five now, not nineteen, and Willy is also twenty-five, and I'm quite positive that he, too, has been changed by his experiences and the life he's lived in Palestine and Shanghai.'

Ketti paused and gave Teddy a meaningful look as she finished slowly, 'Why, you could say that you and he will be like total *strangers* when you meet again.'

'Yes,' Teddy said, her voice almost a whisper. 'I've already thought of that.'

TWENTY-THREE

'Can we go to Lyon's Corner House for lunch?' Maxim asked, looking at Teddy.

She returned his glance and nodded as she reached into her bag for money and their clothing coupon books. 'Yes, we can, and I think we'll have it next, before we look for that raincoat for you. As Aunt Ketti always says, I'm feeling a bit peckish. Aren't you?'

'Yes, I am.'

Teddy and Maxim stood together at the counter in the boys' clothing department in Selfridge's, waiting patiently for the young woman who was serving them to check if she had a third shirt in Maxim's size. The girl soon returned, shaking her head and grimacing. 'Sorry, madam, but those *are* the last two in your boy's size. Would you like to look at some jerseys perhaps?'

'No, thank you very much. We'll take the two shirts and leave it at that for today,' Teddy said, and handed her the clothing coupon books and a pound note.

The girl made out the bill, clipped the coupons out of the ration books, counted Teddy's change, and gave it to her, along with the books and the bill. After putting the white shirts in a paper bag, she said, 'Here you are, madam,' and passed the bag to Teddy.

'Thank you,' Teddy said.

The girl grinned at Maxim and remarked, 'Summer hols never seem to last very long, do they? Now it's back to school, eh? Grim thought.'

'I like school,' Maxim told her.

The girl gave him a glance that was entirely sceptical, and raised an eyebrow rather expressively. With a small smile she moved along behind the counter and began to attend to another customer waiting with her young son.

Teddy winked at Maxim conspiratorially, put an arm around his shoulders and hurried him through the boys' clothing department, across the main hall of the large store, and out into Oxford Street.

The two of them walked towards Marble Arch, where Lyon's Corner House was located, not talking as they hurried along, dodging in and out between the other pedestrians. It was a Saturday morning at the beginning of September. The sky was a radiant blue, without a cloud and shimmering with pale sunlight. It was a soft day, balmy, and unusually warm for September, a day for the garden rather than the hard city streets.

Teddy wished they were sitting in the shade of the old apple tree, sipping a cool lemonade and reading. But there had been no avoiding this shopping expedition, since Maxim had to return to school in a few days, and certainly he needed the extra shirts and a new raincoat. He was growing so rapidly, sprouting every day. All arms and legs, or so it seemed to her; he was tall for ten.

Maxim suddenly said, in a slightly indignant voice, 'That girl who served us in Selfridge's didn't believe me when I said I liked school.'

Teddy looked at him through the corner of her eye. 'Not everyone does, you know. Unlike you,' she said, and started to laugh.

The laughter instantly froze on her lips and abruptly she stopped walking and looked up at the sky fearfully. Maxim did the same thing, as did the other people hurrying along both sides of Oxford Street.

The high-pitched roaring noise was only too familiar and frightening to Londoners. It was a flying bomb, one of the pilotless aircraft, and it was zooming across the blue sky towards them at a relatively low level. The air-raid siren was already wailing in unison, and the combined noises were obliterating the sound of the traffic.

For a moment Teddy and Maxim were mesmerised as they stared up into the clear, wide arc of the sky. The bomb was flying at a level so low they could easily see the insignia of the swastika painted on its fat underbelly.

People began to scream, and they scattered in all directions, running in search of shelter or some form of protection.

Teddy grabbed hold of Maxim's hand, shouted, 'Come on!' and dragged him out into the middle of the road, as far away from the store fronts as possible. The bomb was now casting a giant shadow over Oxford Street and the crowds, and then its engine cut out, which always happened before it started to fall. Reacting with her typical alertness and presence of mind, Teddy instinctively pushed Maxim down onto the ground and flung herself on top of him, shielding his body with her own.

Other people were also dropping to the ground in a similar fashion, hoping to protect themselves as best they could from the flying bomb. A bus screeched to a standstill; passengers jumped off, along with the driver and the conductor, all of them seeking to take cover, or to at least minimise the risk of injury by lying prone.

A taxi swerved, and came to a halt close to Teddy and Maxim, and braked. The cabbie leapt out, flattened himself on the road next to Teddy, and shouted to her, 'Crikey! It's a bleedin' Jerry buzz bomb, an' right over our bleedin' heads!'

The cabbie wrapped his arms around his head and hissed at her, 'Do the same as me with your arms, ducks. Protect yourself, as well as your lad. Against the glass. It's the shattering glass from the store windows does the most bleedin' harm. Folks get slashed to ribbons by the flyin' glass.'

'I know,' Teddy yelled back, and took the cabbie's advice, covering her head with her arms.

'Look after yourself as well as me,' a muffled voice from underneath her body instructed, and she replied, 'I'm fine, Maxim, don't worry.' But her words were drowned out by the sound of the crash and, a split second later, a terrific explosion.

The cab-driver was the first to raise his head and look around. He stood up, briskly brushing down his trousers as he did so. 'We was lucky, ducks,' he said to Teddy. 'It could have come down right on top of us. But the bleeder fell somewhere behind the Cumberland Hotel. Down Edgware Road. Poor buggers, whoever it was that got it.'

Teddy looked at him speechlessly, willing the shaking in her limbs to stop, and for a moment she was unable to get up off the ground so shaken was she.

In the distance there was the sudden roaring sound of another flying bomb, and like the first it was heading in their direction. Everyone looked at the sky, immediately anticipating further danger, and the screaming started all over again.

The cabbie gave Teddy his hand, and pulled her up, and Maxim scrambled to his feet. The cab-driver said, 'The bleedin' Germans don't know when to stop! Take your lad and run to the tube, ducks. This bloomin' raid ain't going to be over for a bit, mark my words.'

'Yes, that's where we'll go,' Teddy exclaimed. 'And thanks.'

Without giving his abandoned taxi a second glance, the cabbie began to sprint towards Marble Arch. Teddy retrieved the paper bag of shirts, took hold of Maxim's hand, and together they ran as fast as they could, hard on the heels of the friendly cab-driver, following him to the tube station at Marble Arch.

The cheery little cabbie had disappeared in the crowds thronging the underground station by the time Teddy and Maxim raced down the steps.

The platform was jammed with people, mostly women and children who had been visiting the shops, out on a Saturday morning jaunt. There were a few men, but not many. Most of the menfolk of England were with the fighting forces . . . in the army, the navy or the air force.

Panting and heaving, and considerably out of breath, Teddy and Maxim stopped at the bottom of the stairs. They were lucky enough to find a corner spot near the flight of steps and they sat down and wedged themselves close together, to make room for someone else.

They were both unnerved by the ordeal they had just gone through, had not really recovered from their narrow escape, and for a long time they sat in silence, calming themselves, collecting their scattered senses.

'Don't be afraid, Maxim, we're safe here,' Teddy said to him at last.

'I'm never afraid when I'm with you, Teddy,' Maxim replied, and took a handkerchief out of his pocket. He spat on it and began to pat his knee with the damp corner of the hankie.

Leaning forward, Teddy exclaimed, 'Did I hurt you when I pushed you to the ground?'

Maxim shook his head and grinned at her. 'It's just a graze, and it doesn't smart, honestly. Well, not really.'

She frowned and bent over him, examining his knee. 'It doesn't look bad; still, it ought to have some iodine on it . . .' She raised her head and scanned the crowd. 'Usually there are Red Cross nurses covering all of the underground stations during a raid. But I don't see one, do you?'

He shook his head. 'Anyway, I'm not hurt. Please don't fuss, Teddy, I'll wash my knee in the men's toilet at Lyon's Corner House. We're still going there for lunch, aren't we?'

'At this rate, if the raid keeps up, it'll be more like tea that we'll be having,' she muttered.

Maxim did not respond. He leaned back against the base of the steps, stretched out his legs and sat staring at his shoes for the longest time, his young face preoccupied, and thoughtful. At last he turned his dark eyes to hers, and said in a low voice, 'Thanks for shielding me the way you did.'

'I will always protect you, Maxim. For as long as I live. You're my boy, and I love you very much.'

'I love you, Teddy.'

Maxim did not say anything after this, and neither did she. But in a short while his hand crept into hers and he drew even closer to her, rested his head against her bare arm. And they sat quietly, feeling safe together, knowing that whatever happened they had each other.

Suddenly, unexpectedly, the lone voice of a stranger rang out in the underground, a woman's beautiful soprano reaching high to the ceiling as she began to sing, 'There'll be bluebirds over the white cliffs of Dover, tomorrow, just you wait and see. There'll be love and laughter, and peace ever after, tomorrow, when the world is free.'

As the woman went on singing, people began to join in, lending their own voices to hers as she picked up the verse, and soon the whole underground station reverberated with the wonderful sound of the crowd singing their hearts out, Teddy and Maxim included. *'The shepherd will tend his sheep, the valley will bloom again and Jimmy will go to sleep in his own little room again. There'll be bluebirds over the white cliffs of Dover, tomorrow, just you wait and see.'*

Once the song was finished, the woman stood up and shouted, 'We're not going to let the Jerries get *us* down, are we?'

'NO!' the crowd bellowed back.

'Then let's keep on singing!' the woman shouted.

'How about *Pack Up Your Troubles In Your Old Kit Bag*?' an elderly lady cried.

'You've got the wrong war, ducks!' their little cabbie retorted, unexpectedly popping up next to Teddy and Maxim, and grinning at them.

'Let's have *I'm Gonna Get Lit Up When The Lights Go Up In London*,' another person called out.

The crowd roared its approval of this suggestion, and the soprano started them off. They followed her lead, and once this number was finished she began another, and then another, and another after that, and the crowd sang along for the next hour.

Teddy and Maxim joined in, enjoying themselves, the raid certainly not forgotten but pushed to one side for a while. And they found themselves enveloped in the extraordinary warmth and friendliness of these Londoners with whom they now shared a common fate, and the common bonds of courage, perseverance, cheerfulness and defiance.

It was an air-raid warden who broke up the sing-song when he pushed his way down the crowded steps, blowing his whistle enthusiastically. Voices fell silent at once and dozens of pairs of eyes were focused on him intently.

'The All Clear has just gone off,' he called to them. 'You can leave, it's safe now. But file out in an orderly fashion, please. We don't want any accidents down here. There's enough trouble up there.'

Maxim sprang to his feet, stretched out his hand, and helped Teddy to get up.

'I'm going to have beans on toast,' he said to her as they slowly mounted the steps, following the hordes of people out of the underground. 'What are you going to have for lunch?'

'The same I suppose. There's never much choice these days, lovey, is there?' she answered, and realised that she was quite hungry. Survival, she thought. That's what it's all about. I must make sure we survive until Hitler is defeated and the world is a free place again.

TWENTY-FOUR

Maxim placed the two new shirts on top of the other clothes in the suitcase on his bed, closed the lid, locked it, and carried the case to the door.

Then he turned around and walked back to the chest of drawers near the window, where he stood for a moment looking at the photographs. He always did this before returning to boarding school, and over the past two years it had become something of a little ritual.

There were three pictures, large, framed in silver, and carefully arranged in a semi-circle on the chest. One of them in particular held Maxim's attention and he stared at it intently. It was his favourite because whenever he remembered the day the picture had been taken he experienced a surge of happiness, and the sadness inside him went away for a while.

The photograph was of the four people he loved the most in the whole world. He was in it, too, and it had been taken on his fourth birthday in 1938, in the garden of their country villa in the Wannsee, near the two lakes of the same name, on the outskirts of Berlin.

Aunt Hedy had been the photographer, and she had arranged the little family group exactly the way she had wanted, had seated them on the lawn underneath the linden trees down by the edge of the little lake, the *Kleiner Wannsee*.

He sat between *Mutti* and Papa. His grandmother was next to his father, and Teddy was on the other side of his mother, and they were all smiling and their faces looked radiant in the bright sunlight filtering through the leafy branches of the trees. It was a happy picture, just as the day had been a happy one, and it had remained etched in his memory since then.

When he closed his eyes, as he did now, he could picture *everything* exactly the way it was that afternoon, could conjure it up, so that every nuance was vivid, every detail crystal clear, and he could relive it again . . .

He was four years old today.
He stood in the vast garden shielding his eyes against the bright yellow

sun. The day was beautiful. The sky was blue, filled with puff-ball white clouds, and down at the bottom of the sloping green lawns the lake glittered like glass and the big white sails of their boat billowed about in the wind.

His nose twitched. He caught a whiff of lilacs mingled with the scent of roses, and the tangy smell of brine wafted up from the lake. He ran across the lawn to the table under the weeping willow tree. It was spread with a white damask cloth and set for eight with his mother's fine bone china. Nearby, on another table, were piled many beribboned boxes, full of fanciful toys and games and picture books, he was quite sure of that.

He heard his mother's voice calling him and suddenly she and Papa were standing there next to him, smiling, and hugging him, and out of the corner of his eye he saw Aunt Sigrid and Uncle Thomas walking across the lawn to join them. Behind Uncle Thomas walked his chauffeur, Heinz, who was carrying a very large object wrapped in brown paper. Heinz put the package down in front of him, and Aunt Sigrid cried, 'It's for you, darling!' and she helped him to rip the paper off; and then before his eyes stood the most beautiful rocking horse he had ever seen, with a golden mane and flaring nostrils and a polished saddle trimmed with silver bells.

Papa placed him on the rocking horse and pushed him, and he rode it excitedly for a while, and Aunt Hedy took many photographs of him until finally his father said, 'Enough,' and lifted him down. Next, everyone gave him the other presents in the pretty boxes, and Aunt Hedy said, 'Now I want a family group,' and she led them to the linden trees and they sat down, whilst she snapped and snapped her camera.

Walter suddenly appeared on the terrace, and led the way down the steps and across the lawn, carrying the big silver tea tray, and behind him came a small procession composed of Marta, Gerda and Anna, the three maids from the mansion in the Tiergartenstrasse, and even Frau Müller, the cook, was in the little procession. The trays the four women held out in front of them were laden with tea, sandwiches and fancy cakes and marzipan pigs and a Schwarzwälder Kirschtorte oozing rich brown chocolate and cherries and whipped cream, which Frau Müller had made specially for his birthday as an extra treat.

His grandmother took hold of his hand and led him to the table. 'You have the place of honour, sweetheart,' she said, and then they ate the special birthday tea and everyone chattered and laughed and was happy.

Not long after tea was finished, Walter came walking down the terrace steps again, this time bringing a birthday cake with four red candles on it, and everyone sang the special birthday song, and he sang it too, which made them all laugh. And when the song was finished he huffed and puffed and blew out the candles and made a wish, just as Mutti had told him to do, and everyone kissed him and hugged him again, and it was the best day, the happiest day he had ever spent . . .

After a few seconds, Maxim opened his eyes and stared again at the photograph taken on his fourth birthday. It had been the last one he had spent with his parents. They had planned to be in London with him and Teddy to celebrate his fifth, but they had not come because Gangan was so sick and they had been unable to travel. And then the war had started and they were trapped in Berlin. He had celebrated six more birthdays without them and this had made him very sad.

He thought about his parents every day, wondering where they were and what they were doing, and he worried a lot about them. He knew bad things were done to Jews in Germany. Teddy had told him that when he was seven. 'You're old enough now to know,' she had said, and had gone on to explain that this was the reason his father had wanted them to leave Germany in the first place. But he was sure his parents were safe. He had always been close to them, and he would have *known* if something terrible had happened to them, would have *felt* it in his heart if they were dead. And so, like Teddy and Aunt Ketti he truly believed they were still alive.

He loved Teddy very much, and he knew she loved him. When he had been small, and *Mutti* had not come, he had cried a lot, and Teddy had rocked him in her arms and comforted him, and made him feel safe. He did not know what he would do without Teddy, she was the most important person in his life after Papa and *Mutti*. When his father and mother finally arrived they would all live together in a big house here in London, perhaps in Regent's Park or Hampstead. He supposed Aunt Hedy would live with them too, but he did not know whether his grandmother would, since he was not sure whether or not she had died. Gangan had been a very, *very* old lady even six years ago, and then she had fallen ill, and perhaps by now she had gone to Heaven to be with Grandfather Westheim. He would miss her if she had.

Maxim's glance shifted to the other photographs.

One was of his parents in 1935. Teddy called it 'the portrait' because they were posed together in evening clothes, his mother in a white satin gown with a little cape and glittering diamond necklace, his father in white tie and tails.

The third photograph was of *Mutti* and Teddy and him standing outside the Plaza-Athénée Hotel in Paris; it had been taken by the head concierge who was always so nice to them.

Stepping closer to the chest, Maxim now pulled open the top drawer, took out Papa's black leather wallet which he had given to him the day before he and *Mutti* and Teddy had gone to Paris. He opened it and took out the enlarged snapshot of *Mutti*, which was his father's favourite.

His mother was standing on the jetty at the villa in Wannsee, with the lake shimmering in the sunlight behind her. How beautiful she was with her halo of blonde hair, her bright, curving smile, her lovely, lustrous eyes. He kissed her face and then quickly slipped the picture back into one side of the wallet. In the other section were the pieces of paper his father had given him when he was little, but he did not take them out because he knew the words very well by now. 'These are the standards by which to live your life,' Papa had told him. He had not understood some of the things his father had written down, at least not *then*, for he had been only a little boy, only four. Now that he was ten and grown up, he knew what the words meant, and he intended to live by those standards, which were his father's.

Returning the wallet to its given place in the drawer, Maxim picked up the carved wooden horse which his father had also given him just before he had left Germany. He touched the little horse gently, thinking first of Papa and then of *Mutti*, loving them so much.

He shut his eyes tightly, squeezing back the tears that suddenly pricked behind his lids. 'Be safe,' he whispered out loud. 'Be safe. Come back to me, *Mutti* and Papa. Please, please come back to me.'

He stood there for the longest time, clutching the little horse and swallowing his tears as the sadness returned and once again filled him up inside.

'Maxim! Maxim!' he heard Teddy calling from downstairs. 'It's time to go!'

He put the horse next to the wallet in the drawer and closed it, and gave the photographs a last lingering glance before running over to the door. Picking up his suitcase, he took a deep breath, threw back his shoulders, and went out.

'I hate railway stations!' Maxim announced vehemently as he and Teddy walked down the platform at Victoria.

Teddy glanced at him swiftly and although she made no comment her heart shifted inside her.

'You always have to say goodbye at railway stations,' he muttered, and stopped walking abruptly.

She also came to a standstill and turned to look at him. His fresh young face, so healthy and rosy and lightly tanned by the summer sun, had suddenly set in rigid lines and she saw his mother's stubbornness in his tightened mouth and in the proud tilt of his little chin.

'I know, darling,' she said softly, putting the suitcase down, reaching out and squeezing his shoulder.

'I had to say goodbye to Papa at the railway station in Berlin and to *Mutti* in Paris, and whenever I go back to school it's *you* I leave behind, and I don't like the feeling it gives me inside.'

She pulled him to her and hugged him close to her body. 'I'm not going anywhere, I shall always be here for you, and anyway you're clever enough to know there *is* a difference when *we* say goodbye. The circumstances *are* different from those other times.'

'I suppose . . . but I still hate railway stations!'

'It'll be different soon, Maxim. Once the war is over Colet Court and St Paul's won't need to be evacuated any longer and will return to London, and you'll be able to become a day boy and live at home.'

He nodded and his face began to brighten. 'Stubby's father says that our two schools have played a big part in the war effort. After all, Colet Court houses recruits, and St Paul's is General Montgomery's headquarters. He's an old boy of St Paul's, don't forget.'

She laughed. 'How could I! Neither you nor Stubby are likely to let me. In any case, once things return to normal the two schools will be housed in their old buildings in Hammersmith again. And talking of Stubby's father, isn't that Stubby himself standing over there looking rather forlorn?'

'Gosh, it is! I wonder where Mrs Trenton is? She usually brings old Stubby to the station herself. Come on, Teddy, let's go and see what's up.' So saying he hitched his satchel of books over his shoulder and hurried off, looking behind him once and beckoning urgently to her.

'Don't trail your new raincoat on the ground!' she shouted after him, following more slowly, hampered as she was by the large suitcase, her purse and a carrier bag full of sandwiches and buns for their lunch.

'Hello, Teddy,' Stubby said politely as she drew closer.

'Hello, Alan. Where's your mother?'

'She had to dash off. She's got an appointment in Whitehall this morning. At the Ministry of Works. Something to do with Dad's business. She's been sort of trying to run it since my uncle had a heart attack, while Dad's in the RAF. She knew you were bound to arrive any minute with Duke, and that you'd see me safely on the train.'

'And here comes the train for Crowthorne now!' Teddy exclaimed. 'As well as a few of your school fellows, it seems. Isn't that nice? You'll be able to sit together.'

Maxim and Stubby followed her gaze and groaned loudly and in unison when they saw the stragglers coming down the platform.

'We don't want to sit with *them*,' Maxim muttered, rolling his eyes heavenward. 'They're too *young*, Teddy. Can't you see that?'

'Last term's new boys,' Stubby explained.

'We'd like a carriage to ourselves,' Maxim said. 'We can, can't we, Teddy?'

'I suppose so. There aren't many people waiting for the train, and certainly not as many boys as I'd expected.'

'A lot went back yesterday,' Stubby told her and grinned hugely. 'I expect their mothers wanted to get rid of the ugly blighters!'

'And you two are beautiful, is that it?' she asked, raising a brow, looking amused.

Typical ten-year-olds that they were, they made ugly faces for her and she began to laugh, enjoying them, and her spirits lifted at the sight of their youthful antics. She was pleased that Maxim's mood had changed. He'll be all right, she thought, more than all right.

But sitting on the bus going home to Belsize Park Gardens, Teddy wondered if she had made a mistake sending him away to school. In view of the Westheims' absence, perhaps it would have been wiser if she had kept him by her side.

On the other hand, he was such a brilliant boy he deserved to be in the best school. Aunt Ketti had recommended St Paul's and its preparatory school, Colet Court. The prep school and the college, being connected as they were, welded the juniors and the older boys together as a unit. Also, the ancient public school had a great liberal tradition, seemed to be totally without prejudice, and there were a number of German Jewish refugee boys at the school.

Henry Rossiter, of the Rossiter Merchant Bank, had wholeheartedly endorsed Ketti's suggestion, and had said that the Westheims would certainly approve of her choice of schools for their son. He had also pointed out that she had plenty of money for the school fees, books, and the uniform, although the latter was not mandatory at the moment because of clothes rationing.

And so she had sent him there, and it had hardly been her fault that the two schools had been evacuated to Wellington College in Surrey in 1942, just when Maxim was starting at Colet.

I did the right thing, she reassured herself, sat back in her seat and opened the *Evening Standard* she had just bought at the railway station.

The headlines brought a happy smile to her face. The Allies were in the process of liberating the whole of France.

TWENTY-FIVE

'I'm so glad you came, Theodora!' Lydia Pell exclaimed, her face lighting up at the sight of Teddy on the doorstep of her mother's house in Hampstead. 'Come in, come in, don't stand outside in the cold.'

'Hello, Lydia,' Teddy said, smiling affectionately, stepping inside. 'I said I'd try my best to come, and here I am,' she went on, taking off her scarf, shrugging out of her coat, putting them into Lydia's outstretched hands.

'It was Aunt Ketti who was being a bit difficult, but only because she'd arranged for me to go with her to Mrs Levine's house for supper tonight. But without telling *me*,' Teddy explained. 'She finally came around to seeing my point of view and she understands now that it's not fair to accept invitations for me, without first finding out if I'm free.'

Lydia gave Teddy a swift look and asked, 'Does Mrs Levine have a son?'

'Yes. Two, in fact. They're both in the services. Why?'

'I bet one of them is home on leave,' Lydia said and chuckled. 'Knowing your Aunt Ketti, she's more than likely trying to fix you up with a nice young man.'

'Oh she wouldn't do that!' Teddy exclaimed, looking at Lydia askance.

'I wouldn't be so sure, if I were you,' Lydia retorted, still chuckling. She hung Teddy's coat and scarf in the coat closet, linked her arm through her friend's, and said, 'Let's go in and join the others.'

Together the two young women strolled across the entrance hall in the direction of the drawing room.

From behind its closed door came the sound of a piano being played with superb skill, and Teddy instantly thought of Sigmund Westheim, who had been such a virtuoso himself, and her throat filled with unexpected emotion. She could not help wondering where he and Ursula were at this moment, and if they were all right. And then Lydia pushed open the door and led her inside, and she quickly clamped down on her troubled thoughts, arranged a bright smile on her face.

Teddy knew this room very well. She had spent many enjoyable evenings here with Lydia since they had first met four years ago, and she always felt comfortable and at home in it.

Mellow, and filled with a certain kind of old-world charm, it had strong echoes of a country house in its decoration, and was warm and welcoming with soft creamy walls, heavy, red-brocade draperies, a matching red carpet stretching wall to wall, with an Oriental rug in front of the fireplace. The sofa and chairs were covered in a floral chintz that had once been vivid and colourful but which had long ago faded into softer tones, and scattered about were antique pieces of furniture made of ripe old woods. There were good oil paintings and watercolours on the walls, and a beautiful Queen Anne mirror hung above the fireplace.

In the grate, a huge log fire burned brightly, crystal vases brimmed with gold and bronze chrysanthemums, and a brass jug on the baby grand was resplendent with burnished copper beech leaves. All contributed to the feeling of autumn which abounded throughout, and on this chilly October night the room appeared more inviting than ever.

There was a small group gathered around the piano.

Archie, Lydia's brother who was in the Royal Air Force, stood with his arm around his girlfriend, Penelope Jardene. Two of his former schoolfriends from Eton, Tom Andrews and Victor Spencer, both fighter pilots like Archie, were leaning over the piano, and so was Victor's current girl, Daphne Hodges.

Lydia announced, 'Here's Theodora at last!' and whoever it was playing the piano instantly stopped, and the others turned around to greet her warmly, and she smiled back at them and said, 'Hello, everyone.'

Propelling Teddy across the room, Lydia murmured to her, 'The only person whom you don't know is the chap who was just playing the piano so exceptionally well. He's with the No. 32 Squadron at Biggin Hill in Kent – Archie's squadron. His name is Mark Lewis.'

On hearing his name mentioned, Mark pushed back the piano stool, stood up and strode around the group of friends to meet Theodora.

Lydia said, 'Teddy, this is Mark, and Mark, meet my very dear friend, Theodora Stein.'

'Hello, Theodora,' Mark said, stepping towards her, his hand outstretched.

Teddy put her hand in his, said, 'Good evening, Mark,' and stood staring into his face, one of such boyishness he did not look old enough to be a fighter pilot. And then she became aware of his eyes. They were of a brown so dark they were almost black, and there was an expression in them that was quite unfathomable. Old eyes in a young face, she thought, old eyes that have already seen too much killing and death and destruction. And it was then that she recognised the enigmatic expression for what it was – a mingling of pain and sadness.

'I've been playing favourite songs for the chaps,' Mark told her, breaking the silence between them. 'What's your's, Theodora?'

'I'm not sure,' she replied, suddenly feeling rather shy and tongue-tied with him. She slid her hand out of his, and took a step backwards, realising that he was having a peculiar effect on her.

'No requests then?' he asked softly.

She shook her head, still incapable of speech.

He half smiled, turned away, walked over to the piano and took up his seat once more.

Daphne said to him, 'If no one has a request, please play my second favourite, Mark. It's *I'll Be Seeing You.'*

'All right,' Mark said, and grinned. 'Providing you sing it, Daphers.'

'Agreed!' Daphne cried. 'We'll all sing it, won't we, chaps?'

'Of course we will, Daphers,' Victor said, and as Mark struck up the refrain this is exactly what they did.

Whilst the sing-song was underway, Teddy went and sat in a chair near the fire, and a few seconds later Lydia came over, bringing her a glass of white wine.

'Don't you want to sing along with them?' Lydia asked, handing Teddy the crystal goblet, sitting down on the arm of the chair.

'Thank you,' Teddy said, accepting the wine, and went on, 'Sing-songs are very nice, and jolly, and usually I enjoy them, but I just don't feel like joining in tonight. Don't ask me why.'

'Neither do I, to tell you the truth,' Lydia confessed. 'The sing-song seems to be the most popular pastime there is these days, and it certainly puts a stop to any decent conversation, doesn't it?'

'It does,' Teddy agreed. 'Still, *we* must seem rather aloof, even a bit churlish, sitting over here by ourselves. Perhaps we ought to join them, we don't *have* to sing, I suppose.'

'Come on then,' Lydia said, standing up. 'I'd hate anyone's feelings to be hurt.'

Teddy stood with Lydia near the piano, listening to Mark playing. His immense talent as a pianist was undeniable, and for the second time that evening she was reminded of Sigmund Westheim. Poignant memories assailed her and she was carried back to the music room in the mansion on the Tiergartenstrasse; for a moment she was wrapped in sadness and her sense of loss was so acutely felt it resembled a sharp physical pain. She took a deep breath, willing the pain to go away, reminding herself that the war would soon be over now, that in due course the Westheims would come to England, and that they would be together. Things would again be the way they had been in Berlin. The past would become the present – and the future.

This thought, hardly a new one, immediately cheered her, as it usually did, and she took a sip of the wine and looked over the rim of the glass at Mark Lewis.

As the young airman continued to play she studied him surreptitiously, filled with enormous curiosity about him. He was good-looking, with smooth, round cheeks, a wide brow, and a full and generous mouth. His hair was dark brown and wavy, brushed straight back from his forehead, and he had thick, curving brows above those soulful, expressive eyes. Broad-shouldered and muscular, he had towered over her when they had been introduced, and she decided he must be all of six feet, perhaps more than that. Even sitting down on the piano stool he looked tall.

Unexpectedly, he lifted his head and stared at her. Their eyes locked. Try though she did, Teddy discovered she was unable to look away. The intensity of his gaze held her. And it unnerved her, made her heart begin to pound in a most unreasonable and unfamiliar way, and she felt the colour rushing up from her neck to flood her face.

She was finally able to avert her gaze, but within a split second her eyes were inevitably drawn back to his. The look he gave her was more direct than ever and seemed full of hidden meaning.

Teddy dropped her eyes, trying to compose herself. When she looked up again, she saw that he was watching her closely. Then he smiled at her, and it was the loveliest of smiles; it seemed to reach deep inside her to touch her heart, and she understood that something important was happening between them at this moment, and she was afraid.

Lydia whispered in her ear, 'I'm going to the kitchen to give my mother a hand with supper. Excuse me a moment,' and she moved away from the piano as she spoke.

Teddy immediately swung around and hurried after her friend.

Drawing alongside her, she murmured, 'I haven't said hello to your mother yet. I'll come with you, and perhaps I can also be of some help.'

'I'm quite sure Mother has done everything, Teddy dear, but by all means come along, and at least we can carry the food into the dining room for her.'

Teddy followed Lydia out into the hall. They were making their way down the corridor to the kitchen at the back of the house, when Teddy said quietly, 'Mark is tremendously talented, isn't he?'

'Yes, he is,' Lydia agreed. There was a short pause and then she came to a halt, glanced at Teddy over her shoulder. 'I think he is very taken with you, my dear.'

'What do you mean?' Teddy asked, her eyes widening.

'He was looking at you, Teddy, you know, in that way.'

'What way?'

'The way a man looks at a woman when he's attracted to her, and very interested in pursuing her.'

'Oh,' Teddy said, at a loss for words.

'Do you *like* him?'

'I hardly know him, Lydia!'

'What I meant was, do you like the look of him?'

'Yes,' Teddy admitted, and then shyness seized her and she stammered, 'I – I – I think he's very good-looking, actually, and he seems very nice, very pleasant.'

'Mark's quite something, in my opinion. I wish he were interested in me, but he isn't. I suppose I'm not his type.' Lydia eyed her, and a smile spread across her face slowly. 'But I believe *you* are, and that's why I wanted you to come this evening.'

'Do you mean you're *matchmaking*?' Teddy probed, frowning, and then giving her friend a hard stare.

Lydia grinned, 'Yes, I'm afraid so. But look, why not? What's wrong with getting two people together?'

Teddy was silent, and then she suddenly said, 'I hope Mark doesn't think you're doing that. I'd feel awful if he did. I'd be very embarrassed.'

'He has no inkling. *Truly*. By the way, quite aside from being such a nice person, Mark's a war hero. He has the DSO, and the DFC, and oodles of other decorations.'

'But he's so young!' Teddy exclaimed in surprise. 'Still, I can well imagine that he is brave and full of valour.'

'Yes, so can I. He has a certain look about him,' Lydia murmured thoughtfully. 'A special look, one I can't quite define. And I understand from Archie that he's very true blue and dependable and patriotic. Incidentally, he's not as young as he *looks* and you *think*.'

'How old is he?'

'Twenty-five, a year older than Archie. Your age, actually.'

'I see.'

'He's one of The Few, you know.'

'A Battle of Britain pilot!' Teddy exclaimed, impressed. 'Then that explains all the medals,' she added, and thought of Winston Churchill's words about those young men, none of them much older than twenty, who in 1940 had defended England in the skies. '*Never in the field of human conflict was so much owed by so many to so few*,' Churchill had said, and ever after that speech to the House of Commons, those valiant Battle of Britain fighter pilots had been known as The Few. Being a Battle of Britain flyer had become a special kind of honour in itself, even for those who had not won medals.

TWENTY-SIX

Julia Pell was peering inside the Aga oven when Lydia and Teddy walked into the spacious, family-style kitchen. She straightened and swung around at the sound of footsteps on the tiled floor.

Her face instantly lit up at the sight of the two young women. She was extremely fond of Teddy, and she cried, 'There you are, Theodora! I'm delighted you are here tonight after all.'

'So am I, Mrs Pell,' Teddy responded, walking over to her friend's mother and embracing her. Mrs Pell returned the loving gesture with genuine warmth, and when they drew apart Teddy asked, 'What can I do to help?'

'Nothing right now, my dear, but thank you so much for offering. Do go and sit at the kitchen table and finish your wine, and you, too, Lydia. Everything's under control. In a few minutes I'll start taking the food out of the oven, and then you can both pitch in, good sports that you are.'

So saying, Mrs Pell hurried over to the pantry, went in, came out immediately carrying a large glass bowl, which she placed on one of the counter tops, and then returned to the pantry again.

Watching her move around the kitchen with speed and efficiency, yet also with lithesome grace, Teddy could not help thinking how much Lydia resembled her, and in so many ways.

Julia Pell was tall, willowy, a striking woman with dark-red hair, cornflower-blue eyes and hundreds of freckles on her creamy-toned skin. Lydia had inherited her height and figure, her sparkling blue eyes and fiery hair, as well as her elegance of movement, her happy-go-lucky disposition. It struck Teddy that tonight more than ever they seemed like sisters rather than mother and daughter. She was extremely fond of both women, who had proven to be good friends to her over the past few years. When she and Lydia had first met they had taken to each other at once, and Mrs Pell's response to her had been as spontaneous and warm as her daughter's.

Julia and her husband Michael were both descended from ancient Anglo-Irish Catholic families and had been born and brought up in Ireland. Although they had lived in London for their entire married life, and their children had been born here, they still maintained a home in Donegal, the house which Michael had inherited from his father, and where, until 1939, they had spent their summers. 'When the war is over and we can all travel again, you must come and stay with us at Dromlochan, and for the whole summer,' Mrs Pell had said on frequent occasions to Teddy, and she had graciously included Maxim, Aunt Ketti and even the Westheims. Teddy had been touched by this generous invitation, and she hoped they would all be able to go to Dromlochan one day. For a long time she had itched to visit Ireland, and it had become one of her ambitions for the future. The Pells had two other children, Siobhan, who was in the Women's Land Army in Scotland, and Niall, an officer with the merchant marine on the Russian convoy run, and they were equally as unorthodox, friendly and easygoing as the rest of the family.

Mrs Pell made a final trip to the pantry, came out carrying another cut-glass bowl, and closed the door behind her.

'Well, my darling,' she said, swinging around to face Lydia, 'I've blown every one of our ration coupons on this supper for Archie and his friends! However, I do think it's been worth it, and certainly your brother is about to savour some of his favourite dishes.'

Lydia laughed and said, 'They're undoubtedly Daddy's favourites, too. I wish he weren't up North tonight. He'd enjoy them as much as Archie.'

'Yes, that's true, he would, but what can one do, my darling?' Julia did not wait for an answer and rushed on, 'He had to be at the munitions factory in Leeds today, come hell or high water, and the trains are so *frightfully* slow at the moment he would never have got back in time for supper anyway. So it's much better he spends the night at the Queens Hotel in Leeds, and travels home comfortably tomorrow.'

'That's true,' Lydia murmured.

Teddy said, 'Whatever's in the oven smells delicious, Mrs Pell.'

Julia beamed at her. 'Doesn't it just,' she agreed, and continued in a confiding manner, 'The butcher let me have some ground beef – in exchange for all of our ration coupons for the next few weeks, of course! And with it I've made a huge cottage pie, Archie does love that so. And I've got an apple tart baking as well. I had some bottled apples put away, you see, for a rainy day or a special occasion, and tonight seemed as good a time as any to use them.'

Lydia said, 'I thought you were making a trifle, Mummy.'

'Oh but I did, my darling!' Mrs Pell glanced at the glass bowls. 'Two actually, though I am rather *afraid* they're very much war-time trifles, since there are no bananas available. Or any of the other fruit I need, for that matter. Oh well, never mind.' Julia Pell shrugged and let out a chuckle. 'Thank goodness for sponge cake, jelly, Bird's Eye custard powder, and sherry. Lots of the latter, I might add. It does give a trifle a special flavour.'

'Good Lord, Mummy, you haven't gone and done it again, have you!' Lydia exclaimed, and groaned loudly. She looked across the kitchen table at Teddy, rolled her eyes and grimaced most theatrically, and explained, 'My mother has recently acquired this knack for making sherry-drenched trifle that gets us all positively squiffy, truly and absolutely pie-eyed!'

Julia Pell instantly and vociferously protested this statement, but before Teddy could think of an appropriate comment, Archie's ginger head appeared around the kitchen door.

'How much longer until supper, Mother?' he asked. 'The troops are getting more ravenous by the minute. I won't be able to restrain them soon . . . they'll be descending on you like the Mongol hordes.'

'Actually, Archie my darling, supper is ready now,' Mrs Pell answered her son with a bright, beaming smile. 'Do show your friends into the dining room, please. Lydia and Teddy are about to bring everything in, and they will help me to serve.'

'Whiz-O!' Archie yelled, gave a blood-curdling war cry, and disappeared.

There was a feeling of jocularity in the air.

Supper at the Pells' was always a boisterous affair when Archie was home on leave, and most especially when he invited his chums along for the evening.

And as usual the boys of the Royal Air Force took over. They recounted hair-raising stories about flying, gave vivid accounts of the narrow escapes they had had, told all kinds of jokes, laughed a lot, ribbed each other and everyone else unmercifully, and in general kept the womenfolk well and truly entertained throughout the meal.

Teddy, who could hold her own with anyone, and was spirited and vivacious, found herself silent for once, almost withdrawn. She was aware that this was because of Mark Lewis. He sat next to her at the dining table, and she was acutely conscious of his presence. Several times he had addressed remarks to her, and she had responded politely, but she had not initiated any conversation with him, even though she longed to do so. Her own reticence surprised her, for she was outgoing, gregarious by nature, and friendly. Yet she was rendered completely tongue-tied by this man.

Her problem was herself, she knew that, and she was endeavouring to come to grips with her inner feelings. From the moment she had met him she had responded to Mark Lewis on every level as a woman. She found him overwhelmingly attractive and physically appealing, and on the surface he was genial and charming. Yet she knew he was also a young man of character, one who was strong and brave, and intuitively she felt there were hidden depths to him, sensed that he was a person of feeling, sensitivity and gentleness, and, not unnaturally, he fascinated her.

In the five years she had been living in London, Teddy had met several young men who had shown an interest in her, and who had wanted to take her out. Each time she had declined, and she had never dated anyone since leaving Berlin. This was not only because of her commitment to Willy Herzog, but because she had not been attracted to those other men. In consequence, her fierce response to Mark had shaken her considerably, and she was taken aback at herself. There was no possible way she could deny that she was as interested in him as he was in her, because she was, and she wanted to see him again, to be alone with him, to get to know him better.

Earlier, when he had pulled the chair out for her at the dining table, he had accidentally brushed his hand against hers, and she had almost jumped out of her skin. His fingers on hers had been like an electric shock, and she had pulled her hand away quickly, even though she had not wanted to do this at all, had wanted to entwine her fingers with his.

Mark Lewis was having the most profound effect on her, and she was flooded with emotions which were unusually strong – and wholly unfamiliar. She realised she was feeling off-balance, that she had never experienced anything like this before in her entire life. Not even with Willy. Her fiancé. Poor Willy. Just a short while ago her thoughts had swung to him, so far away in Shanghai, and she had admitted that there was no future for them together, whether Mark Lewis was around or not. *He* had nothing whatsoever to do with her sudden self-revelations. Her aunt had said that she and Willy would be like total strangers when they met again after their long, five-year separation, and she acknowledged to herself that Aunt Ketti was correct.

All of her instincts told Teddy that Mark Lewis would ask to see her again, and she had every intention of doing so. He might turn out to be a flash in the pan for her, and she for him, and in all truth she had no idea what would happen between them, if, indeed, anything at all. But she was *certain* of one thing. She did not love Willy enough to marry him, harboured only sisterly affection for him and she now understood that this was all she had ever felt. She had not been in love with him in Berlin in 1938, but in love with love, in love with the idea of marriage, and that was why she had said yes to Willy. But those were the wrong reasons to marry anyone.

'How long have you known the Pells?' Mark asked, startling her. He pushed his chair away from the table slightly, turned to face her, crossed his long legs.

'About four and a half years,' Teddy replied.

'I suppose you met them through Lydia?'

'Yes, we do war work together.'

'War work,' he repeated and stared at her, frowning. 'You can't mean you both work in a factory. Or do you mean that?'

'No. I was referring to the work we do at the first-aid station on Haverstock Hill, and as volunteers for the Red Cross,' Teddy explained.

'Oh, I see. So you don't have a job then?'

'No ... well, not really,' Teddy hesitated, wondering whether to tell him about Maxim, and decided against it. 'Both Lydia and I are involved in our volunteer war work on a full-time basis,' she murmured.

Mark nodded. 'And do you live near here, Theodora?'

'Yes, in Belsize Park Gardens.'

'With your parents?'

'Do you always ask so many questions when you first meet someone?' Teddy asked quietly.

He had the good grace to laugh. 'No,' he admitted, and flashed her his most charming smile, showing his even white teeth. He sat back in the chair, draped one arm over it in a nonchalant manner, and gave her a long, very meaningful look. 'Only when I'm intrigued by someone,' he said in a low, husky voice.

Teddy could not fail to miss the innuendo, and she was at a loss for words. She tried to look away from those dark, piercing eyes focused so unblinkingly on her, and she discovered she could not. And then she began to blush under his close and fixed scrutiny, and was mortified with herself. Teddy was wondering how best to steer the conversation in another direction when Mrs Pell saved her the trouble.

'Let's have coffee in the drawing room,' Julia Pell announced, pushing back her chair, rising from the table, sweeping through the door into the hall.

Everyone else did the same thing, and trooped out of the dining room after her.

At the end of the evening Mark asked Teddy if he could drive her home and she accepted his offer.

Now the two of them sat in his red MG sports car cruising down the hill from Hampstead Village in the direction of Belsize Park Gardens. For one who had asked so many questions earlier, Mark was curiously uncommunicative on the short drive to her home. And Teddy herself was as quiet as she had been at the Pells', hardly opening her mouth except to give him directions.

Finally when Mark came to a standstill outside her aunt's house and braked, he swivelled around in the seat to face her and said, 'I'd like to see you again, Theodora. Will you come out with me?'

'Yes.'

'Such a weak little yes,' he said gently. 'You are the shy one, aren't you?'

'I'm not really. It's just that – ' She broke off, looked at him in the murky light of the car, took a deep breath and said, 'I'd like to go out with you. I *want* to . . . very much.'

'Good, I'm glad,' he said, sounding pleased, his deep-timbred voice full of warmth. 'What about tomorrow evening?'

'I can't. I promised a visit to a friend who is sick, and it wouldn't be very nice to disappoint her.'

'I understand. Unfortunately, I'm busy on Friday.'

'So am I.'

'I hope you're free on Saturday, Theodora, because my leave is up on Sunday.'

'Oh yes, I'm free, Mark.'

'Then we'll go dancing,' he said, smiling at her in the darkness of the car.

TWENTY-SEVEN

He took her to the Savoy Hotel in the Strand.

They had dinner in the beautiful room overlooking the River Thames, and danced to Carroll Gibbons and his orchestra.

Teddy thought she had never seen anyone as handsome as Mark Lewis. Tonight he wore his blue Royal Air Force uniform with his decorations on the left side of his jacket, and it was a shock to see that boyish face above those war hero's emblems which proclaimed his bravery as a fighter pilot.

Several times during the evening she had noticed that men as well as women cast admiring glances in his direction, and at one moment an older gentleman in a dinner jacket, dancing with his wife, had spoken to them on the dance floor.

'It's young men like you for whom we have to be thankful,' the stranger had said approvingly. 'Well done, well done, your country's very proud of you.'

Mark had murmured something appropriate, and had smiled at the man and his wife, but he had made no comment to her as they had continued to move around the floor to the strains of *Besame Mucho*. And then, quite unexpectedly, he had tightened his grip on her, pulled her closer to him, much closer than before, and she had trembled in his arms and worried that he would hear the sound of her rapidly beating heart. But of course he had not. How could he? Only she heard it.

Now they were sitting at their table, sipping the champagne he had ordered to go with dessert, and talking in a desultory fashion. So far this evening they had spoken only in generalities. They had shared their mutual worry about the V2s, the horrendous new German flying bombs which did far more damage than the V1s, and which were currently being hurled upon London. They had discussed the progress of the war, the Allied victories in Italy and other parts of Europe, and Mark had echoed what everyone was saying – that the war would be over by next summer. But they had not touched on anything else. It was almost as if they were both reluctant and afraid to take the initial step of asking the first truly personal question of each other.

Teddy continued to be thrown off balance by Mark Lewis, and her emotions were churning inside her, just as they had at the Pells' several nights ago. Yet she was determined not to allow her nervousness to show, and she had been skilful in masking this, outwardly appeared to be cool, contained, and very much in control.

'I'm sorry the pudding is taking so long,' Mark said, making an apologetic face. 'Would you like to dance whilst we're waiting, Theodora?'

She shook her head. 'Not at the moment, if you don't mind. And you can call me Teddy if you want, Theodora's such a mouthful.'

He smiled at her. 'No, it isn't, I think it's a beautiful name. Thee-o-dor-a . . . it's very melodic to me. Of course, Teddy is more . . . cosy. In any case, I shall call you by both names, sometimes Theodora, sometimes Teddy.'

She nodded, leaned back in her chair, took another sip of the champagne, and gave him a lovely smile. Then she turned her head towards the orchestra, sat listening to the music, tapping her foot under the table, glad that she had spent the five pounds on the smart new evening dress, which was long and svelte-looking and in the latest colour called Dusty Pink. She knew it was flattering. She had seen it in the model room at Harrods, and had known at once that it would suit her. With the gown she wore a strand of pearls, pearl studs in her ears, and an amethyst bracelet, all of which had been her mother's, and her mother's engagement ring was on her right hand.

Earlier that evening, when she had finished dressing and had come downstairs, Aunt Ketti had caught her breath and told her she looked beautiful, but she hadn't believed her – well, not really. And then Mark had said exactly the same thing when he had arrived to collect her, and she had believed *him*, because she had wanted to, she supposed.

She had taken him into the drawing room to meet Aunt Ketti, who had immediately asked him to take off his overcoat, sit down and have a drink, but thankfully he had declined. He had quickly explained that he had a cab waiting and that the cab-driver was a bit bolshy and wanting to be on his way back to the West End, and so they ought to hurry.

When they had stepped into the cab a few minutes later Teddy had given a little sigh of relief that they were out of the house and on their way to dinner. Aunt Ketti had previously asked her a multitude of questions about Mark, which she had been unable to answer, and she had not wanted her aunt to start probing again, asking *him* awkward questions about his family and, even worse, his religion. She did not care what he was. He was the most fascinating man she had ever met, and, as far as she was concerned, that was all that mattered.

Although Teddy had no way of knowing it, Mark Lewis was as overwhelmed by her as she was by him, and now, as *she* sat lost in her thoughts, a dreamy expression on her face, *he* was doing his level best to keep cool. His main concern was to conduct himself like a mature man and not a schoolboy having his first crush who was out on his first date with the object of his infatuation, even though he did seem to fit this role.

He lit a cigarette and sat back, looked across the table at Teddy in the candlelight. She had a face that was positively angelic; he had never seen a woman as beautiful as she, except perhaps for Ingrid Bergman in one of her recent movies, *Casablanca*, whom she strongly resembled. Teddy had a well-rounded face, high cheekbones, a small, straight nose, and a wide mouth with a full, voluptuous bottom lip. Although her hair was fair, her brows were dark and thick, and natural in shape, thankfully not fashionably plucked into ugly thin lines.

Her eyes were large and of the clearest green and heavily lashed. They were not only lovely eyes, but bright with intelligence which convinced him there was a quick, keen brain behind that madonna-like face.

Mark picked up his glass and took a gulp of champagne, suddenly wishing it were something much stronger. Teddy unnerved him. She also intrigued him, and he longed to know more about her, yet he did not dare ask her anything. She had already implied he was being nosy and he had considered himself rebuked by her at the Pells' on Wednesday

Was it only Wednesday that they had met?

Mark felt as though he had always known her – odd really, under the circumstances. He had thought about her incessantly over the past few days, and dreamed about her every night, and he was patently aware that she was the most dangerous woman he had ever met. Dangerous because he could so easily fall in love with her, become serious about her. He had known quite a few women in the past five or six years, but he had never experienced these kinds of feelings, or felt like this before . . . so . . . so . . . *undone.*

Theodora Stein was different from those other women in his past, infinitely different. There was something about her that tugged at his heart strings, made him want to protect and cherish her as well as possess her physically. *Theodora Stein* he repeated to himself. He wondered if she were Jewish; his mother had wondered the same thing out loud at lunch today.

'With a name like *Stein* she has to be,' his mother had said. He had explained that he didn't know, and why did it matter what she was? Jew or Gentile, it made no difference to him. It was a remark he instantly regretted, should have known not to utter. 'You had better find out. You know what your father's like,' his mother had warned, and he had groaned to himself, wishing he had never mentioned Teddy to her. But he had, and she would tell his father, had probably already told him over dinner, and tomorrow at Sunday lunch there would most probably be an inquisition. There always was when he showed an interest in a woman. This was because he was the elder son now. His brother David, his most beloved darling David, whom he had hero-worshipped all of his life and had adored, had been killed in the North African campaign. And he was supposed to take his place. As if anyone could take the place of another human being who was unique unto himself. But he was expected to do just that, and go into the family business, as David had been going to do. And he was also expected to do the right thing by the family by marrying the right kind of woman one day.

Oh bugger it, Mark thought, I'm going to go out with whomever I wish, and marry the woman I *love*, when I find her and when the time comes, whether she's Jewish, Catholic, Protestant or Hindustani. I must please myself as well as the old man. After all, it's my life not his, and I can't *be* him, just as I can't *become* what David was. I *shall* do as I want. *Unto thine own self be true.*

The thought of his father galvanised Mark into verbal action, and leaning forward he took a deep breath and plunged in. 'I want to get to know you better, Teddy,' he said, 'and I want you to know me, too, but that will never happen if we just sit here listening to the music and smiling at each other. However, I must admit, I do hesitate to ask you about yourself, because you sort of rebuked me the other evening, and I – '

'Rebuked you! But I didn't mean it to sound that way!' Teddy exclaimed, cutting in peremptorily, looking at him askance. 'I hope I didn't offend you?'

He smiled at her, and shook his head. 'No, you didn't. Anyway, now it's your turn ... you must ask me anything you wish and I'll answer you truthfully, I promise.'

'No, Mark, it's *you* who must ask *me* ... I owe you that for making you feel so badly on Wednesday.'

'All right, if you say so.' There was a little pause and he levelled his eyes on her as he asked slowly, 'Is there anyone that you're going out with, Teddy, a sweetheart who's perhaps away in the forces?'

'No,' she answered at once, giving him a very direct, straightforward look. 'There *was* a boy ... once. But I haven't seen him for almost six years. He lives abroad. He's become ... just a friend.'

'And you haven't dated anyone in all this time?'

'No.'

'But a beautiful girl like you! Why, Teddy, you must have had a few admirers, surely?'

'Yes, I have,' she replied somewhat shyly. 'But I didn't go out with any of them ... I wasn't interested in them.'

He stared hard at her, reached out and put his hand on hers. He felt it trembling under his, and this pleased him. He leaned closer and whispered, 'Are you interested in *me*, Theodora?'

She was so overcome by her feelings for him she could not speak, and she swallowed several times, merely gazed back at him, her lips slightly parted. Then finally she nodded her head.

A glow spread through him and he tightened his grip on her hand, and said in the same low voice, 'You simply can't imagine how very happy that makes me. And, Teddy, I'm terribly interested in you, but then you know that.'

She continued to gaze at him, and her eyes were shining with joy, and there was a faint blush on her cheeks.

Eventually Mark said, 'It's your turn to ask me a question.'

'What about you?' she said in a faintly quavering voice after a short pause. 'I mean, is there someone you've been seeing?'

'Absolutely not! Look, there have been women, I'm not going to deny that, of course. But there's no one special, and there hasn't been for the longest time.' Not ever, if the truth be known, he thought. Not in comparison to you, my darling.

At this moment the waiter arrived with the dessert course, which he began to serve. Their conversation was momentarily curtailed as they watched him spoon out the piping hot bread-and-butter pudding, which they had both ordered and were now no longer interested in eating.

Once the waiter had departed, Mark said, 'I thought I might meet your parents when I came to collect you tonight. Were they out?'

'My parents are dead, Mark,' Teddy replied very quietly.

'God, how stupid I am! And so very clumsy. Do forgive me. I'm so sorry – '

'Please, it's all right, you weren't to know. In any case, they've both been dead for a very long time.'

'And that's why you live with your aunt?'

'Yes. What about your parents? Are they alive?'

'They are. Do you have any brothers and sisters?'

She shook her head. 'I was an only child. Do you?'

'A younger brother, Lionel. He's away at school. At Harrow.'

'Harrow! That's a marvellous school! Winston Churchill went to Harrow.'

'So did I,' Mark said.

'Did you really! Have you ever met Winston Churchill?' she now asked in an eager voice.

'Once.'

'How lucky you are. I wish I had. He's the greatest man in England. In the world, actually, at least in my opinion. He's my hero.'

Mark smiled at her, and he wanted to say he wished *he* were her hero, but restrained himself. Instead he asked, 'And where did *you* go to school, Theodora?'

'I went to a school you couldn't possibly know . . . in Berlin.'

Mark was taken aback by her answer and he stared at her, frowning slightly. 'What on earth were you doing in Berlin? Were your parents living there for some reason at the time?'

'They were Berliners. I am a Berliner. I was born there.'

'You are a *German*?' Mark's voice reverberated with incredulity.

'I am.'

'But you don't sound it. What I mean is that you don't have a German accent. You speak perfect English, and beautifully, I might add.'

Teddy explained, 'My mother taught me English when I was small. She spoke it well herself, and we came frequently to England to see Aunt Ketti before the war, when I was growing up. You see, she's lived here for forty years. Her late husband, Uncle Harry, was an Englishman. Anyway, I've spoken English since I was five years old. Perhaps that's the reason I have no accent. When children learn a second language at a very young age they generally do speak it without any kind of accent.'

Mark continued to stare at Teddy and suddenly something clicked in his mind. 'How long have you lived here?'

'Five years. I came here in the spring of 1939, via Paris.'

He nodded, wondering if what he now suspected could possibly be true.

Teddy saw a look cross Mark's face, and it was an expression she could not quite fathom. She was not certain if it was one of perplexity or confusion or worry, or a combination of all three.

'I'm Jewish,' she blurted out, and then she sat back in the chair and returned his stare, wondering if this was going to make any difference to him. She fervently hoped it wouldn't, that he was not one of those hateful people who were prejudiced.

Mark did not at first respond. He just sat looking at her in amazement. And then he smiled an odd little smile before he stretched his hand across the table and took hold of hers. 'So am I, Teddy,' he said. 'As my father would say, our family is also of the Mosaic persuasion.'

TWENTY-EIGHT

They sat staring at each other across the dinner table, both of them equally engrossed in everything the other had to say.

Mark spoke about his family, and then talked at length about the family businesses. He told her that he was expected to go to work in the organisation with his father when the war ended, and that he would take over when his father retired. He went on to explain that music had only ever been his hobby, that he had never intended to make a career on the concert platform; swiftly he pointed out to her that he was therefore not one bit disappointed about his future, that the world of business excited him, which was the absolute truth.

In turn, Teddy filled him in with details of her early life in Berlin and her sojourn with the Westheims at the mansion on the Tiergartenstrasse. Then she carefully recounted the experiences she had had just before she had left Berlin, along with a blow-by-blow description of *Kristallnacht* on November the ninth, a date she would never ever forget. She even told him about her relationship with Willy Herzog, leaving nothing out. After touching on her stay in Paris with Ursula Westheim, she ended up speaking about her subsequent journey to England with Maxim, the life she had made for them in London, and finally she confided her concerns about Maxim and the future.

Mark listened most attentively to everything she had to say, and when at last she finished he reached out, took her hand in his, and his face was on the sober side when he asked, 'And Frau Westheim and her husband are still in Germany?'

'Oh yes, I'm sure they are,' Teddy responded. 'I would have definitely heard from them if they had managed to leave. And there would have been some sort of message from Princess von Wittingen, if anything . . . if anything *awful* had happened to them. But there's been nothing but silence.' Teddy's smile was confident as she concluded, 'They're in hiding somewhere and they're quite *safe*, of that I'm convinced. And Aunt Ketti agrees with me.'

Mark nodded. It was on the tip of his tongue to bring up the heavy Allied bombing raids on Germany, also mention the concentration camps, both dire threats to the safety of the Westheims, but he bit back his words. He had no desire to alarm her, or spoil their wonderful evening together, by raising unpleasant facts which neither of them could do anything to alter. Instead, he raised his glass of champagne to her, and said, 'I toast you, Teddy! I'm full of admiration for you. It strikes me you're a wonderfully loyal girl, and a very courageous one, quite aside from being the most beautiful I've ever known.'

'Thank you,' she said, smiling with happiness, flattered by his compliments. 'I don't know about courage, though, I just do what I have to do. As for my looks, well, I'm not all *that* beautiful, Mark.'

'To me you are . . . ' He paused, eyed her carefully, added in a lower tone, 'You're also very dangerous.'

'*Dangerous!*' She gave him an odd look through narrowed green eyes and frowned at him. 'I can't *imagine* what you mean!'

'I say *dangerous* because I could so easily become serious about you, Teddy.'

Speechlessly, she gaped at him, at a loss to know how to respond to this declaration. And then quite suddenly she admitted to herself that she felt exactly the same way about him. When she had first met him she had been afraid of him – because she had sensed *his* danger to *her*, had understood her own vulnerability to him.

Mark had been studying her and now he leaned across the table, put his hand over hers again. 'I've never said that to anyone else, Theodora, you do believe me, don't you?'

'Yes, of course.'

'Do you think . . . could *you* become serious about *me*, Teddy?'

'I could, Mark,' she answered in a voice that was clear and firm and strong, and she gave him the benefit of a loving smile.

He squeezed her hand, thrilled at her response and by her reaction to him. 'Come on, darling,' he said, using this term of endearment for the first time. 'I want to hold you in my arms and dance with you,' and so saying he led her away from the table, her hand gripped in his.

The lights were very dim in the room, and on the dance floor they were virtually non-existent, and so the atmosphere was highly conducive to romance, and perfect for young lovers caught up in the fears and dangers and tensions of war.

Mark took Teddy in his arms when the Carroll Gibbons orchestra began to play one of the most sentimental love songs of the times. As they moved slowly around the room to the music, holding each other tightly, Teddy sang the chorus softly, in a low voice which only Mark could hear: *'I'll be seeing you in all the old familiar places that my mind and heart embraces all day through. In that small café, the park across the way, the children's carousel, the chestnut trees, the wishing well. I'll be seeing you in every lovely summer's day, in everything that's light and gay, I'll always think of you that way, I'll find you in the morning sun, and when the night is new, I'll be looking at the moon, but I'll be seeing you.'*

She did not know the verse, and so she hummed the rest of the number, now pressed so close to him she could feel the brass buttons of his uniform hard and sharp against her body. And she thought: I'm falling in love with him, I knew I was going to at the Pells'. And she had no regrets; she was filled with the most total kind of happiness she had ever known.

Mark glanced down at Teddy.

Her face was upturned to his and he saw the radiant joy reflected on it, and he drew even closer still, brought her head against his shoulder and kissed her hair tenderly. He would never forget this moment or this song for as long as he lived . . . he had just realised he had found the woman of his life.

He brushed his lips against her cheek without breaking the rhythm of their steps, and they danced around the floor once again.

And they went on dancing for the rest of the evening as if in a dream.

They walked along the Embankment in silence, holding hands.

It was a cold, clear night without a cloud and there was a full moon, and even though the wind blowing up from the Thames was sharp with frost neither of them noticed.

Teddy was bundled up in her aunt's sheared beaver coat, borrowed for the occasion, with a pink, lacy-mohair scarf covering her hair, and Mark wore his heavy RAF overcoat, peaked officer's cap and white silk flyer's scarf wrapped around his neck.

But quite aside from their warm clothing, they were both too preoccupied with themselves to be aware of such a mundane thing as the weather, were oblivious to all else except their entrancement with each other and their emotions.

The stretch of the Embankment behind the Savoy Hotel, which they had just left, was as dark as pitch because of the blackout regulations; not a crack of light was visible from the hotel windows, and all of the street lamps were doused for the same reason. But the bright moon lighted their way, and at one moment Mark lifted his eyes to the sky and said, 'It's perfect weather for flying, Teddy. I'd love to be up there with you in my plane, taking you for a spin right now. It's so breathtaking on a night like this, awe-inspiring, really.' As he spoke he turned his head and looked down at her and caught his breath.

Teddy was gazing up at him as raptly as she had been on the dance floor. In the moonlight her face was clearly illuminated, and once again he saw her adoring expression, instantly recognised her enchantment with him shining forth from her eyes, and his heart missed a beat. Without so much as a second thought he pulled her to him almost roughly, wrapped his arms around her, brought his face down to hers and kissed her fully on the mouth.

She returned his kiss ardently, wanting this as much as he did, and she clung to him, and when they managed to let go of each other at last, and drew apart, they were breathless, thrown off balance by the impact of their first real physical contact. They stared at each other wonderingly, both discovering that they were slightly dazed.

'Oh Teddy, my darling . . .' he began, and then fell silent. It was his turn to be inexplicably tongue-tied, and he simply stood staring at her in the moonlight, marvelling at her beauty and the feelings she aroused in him.

But within seconds Mark drew her to him again and whispered against her hair, 'You know, I've been wanting to kiss you all evening. In fact, ever since the first night I met you at the Pells', if you want the truth.'

'And I've wanted you to kiss me,' she answered without the slightest bit of guile, in her honest fashion.

This admission thrilled him, and, unable to resist her, Mark began to kiss her even more passionately than before, his mouth warm, loving, seeking. And she responded with equal passion, wrapping her arms around his neck and parting her lips at last to let in his insistent tongue. He allowed it to rest there for a moment of quiet and profound intimacy, and then he began to caress her tongue with his own, slowly, languorously.

With a sudden, swift movement he brought both of his hands up to her face and cupped it between them, and began to devour her mouth with a hunger that was surprising to him as well as to her.

She grew more excited and inflamed, and an extraordinary heat suffused her entire body, settled in the pit of her stomach, and she swayed slightly in his arms, overcome by strange new feelings and urgent desires and longings hitherto unknown to her.

For his part, Mark was slightly dizzy himself, and their passionate kissing was arousing him to such a degree his legs were shaking, and he thought for a moment that they were going to buckle under him. He could hardly contain himself, and so he withdrew his mouth from hers, albeit reluctantly, and took a deep breath of the frosty air, endeavouring to calm his racing heart, his flaring sexual desire for her. In a short while he slackened his grip on her, released her from his embrace, and said gently, 'It's cold out here, and late, Theodora darling. I'd better get you home. Your aunt will be wondering where you are. Worrying.'

'It's all right,' she responded, touching his arm. 'I am twenty-five, you know, and quite grown up. I don't have to answer to my aunt.'

'I know that,' he said with a quirky smile, looking suddenly amused. He continued, 'But I wouldn't want to find myself in her bad books. That wouldn't bode well for the future, now would it?'

'No,' she agreed, pleased by his words.

Mark now took charge, purposefully tucked her arm through his, and falling into step they set off at a brisk pace, soon left the Embankment behind them and made their way up the Strand, all the while looking for a cab. They had reached Nelson's Column in Trafalgar Square before they found one, the only one in the vicinity, in fact.

'Belsize Park Gardens, number forty-three,' Mark told the driver, helped Teddy to get in, jumped inside after her, and slammed the door. They sat close to each other on the seat, holding hands tightly as the taxi rumbled on its way, making for north London.

Mark wanted to take her in his arms, to start kissing her again, but he resisted the temptation, knowing that under the circumstances this would not lead anywhere, and that he would only end up feeling more frustrated than he already did. There was even a brief moment when he thought of telling the cabbie to turn around and drive to Farm Street in Mayfair, where his mews house was located, but he did not. With any other woman he would hardly have hesitated, and once there he would have had little or no compunction about seducing her. But he would not do that to Teddy. She was different. She was special. She was going to be his wife.

The streets were relatively empty of traffic, not only because it was now turned one o'clock in the morning, but also due to petrol rationing which kept motorists at home. In consequence, there were few vehicles on the road, and in a very short time they were pulling up outside her aunt's house and alighting together.

Mark took Teddy's arm and led her up the flight of steps. After she had inserted the key in the front door, he turned her to face him.

'Thanks, Teddy, for coming out with me. I had a grand time, and it's really meant a lot. More than I can ever say actually, darling.'

'It's *I* who should be thanking *you*, Mark, and I do.' She stood on tiptoe and kissed his cheek. 'And this evening's meant a great deal to me, too.'

'I'm so glad.' He looked serious, almost concerned, when he added, 'There's something I've been wanting to ask you for the last couple of hours.'

'What is it?'

'I want you to be my girl, Teddy. You will, won't you? I haven't misread your reaction to me, have I?'

'No, you haven't, and of course I'll be your girl.' For always, she thought. For the rest of my life. But she did not voice these thoughts, just stood and smiled at him instead.

'Thank God I've found you!' he cried and swept her into his arms, kissed her on the lips and hugged her hard. When he let her go, he said, 'I told you I have to have lunch with my parents tomorrow. But I'll ring you up before I go back to Biggin Hill.'

'I'll be in all day, Mark, I'll wait for your call. Goodnight now.'

'Goodnight, darling.'

He ran lightly down the steps. Before he stepped into the waiting cab he turned to wave, and she waved back, and then she went into the house and closed the door behind her.

Teddy stood for a moment in the darkness of the hall, trying to catch her breath, to quieten her rapidly beating heart. She was reeling from the impact of him, still felt startled by the power of their physical attraction for each other. She had not realised she was capable of such intense passion, or that such strong and overwhelming feelings could even exist between a man and a woman.

TWENTY-NINE

After hanging up the sheared beaver coat in the hall cupboard, Teddy crept gingerly up the stairs, having no wish to disturb her aunt.

But when she reached the landing at the top she smiled to herself. She might have known that Aunt Ketti would not go to sleep before she arrived home. Her aunt's bedroom door stood ajar and lamplight was streaming out onto the darkened landing. Teddy crossed the floor in several swift strides, popped her head around the door, and exclaimed, 'I'm home, Aunt Ketti! And you certainly didn't have to wait up for me!'

Ketti was propped against the snowy, antique linen pillows in her large comfortable bed, holding a library book in her hands. She put this down and smiled at her niece. 'Hello, Teddy dear, and I know I didn't, but I wasn't at all tired. In any case, I wanted to hear all about your evening. I also thought it would be nice if we had our usual cup of tea before going to sleep. We've never missed our little ritual yet, except when I've been in Brighton visiting Rachel.'

'I'll run downstairs and make a pot immediately.'

'Everything's ready for you in the kitchen, dear. All you have to do is boil the water.'

'I'll be back in a jiffy,' Teddy said, and hurried off.

True to her word, she returned after only a few minutes, carrying the silver tea tray, which she placed carefully on the window seat. After pouring two cups, she carried these over to the bed, passed one to her aunt and then sat down with her own cup in an easy chair nearby.

Ketti took a sip of the tea, put the cup and saucer on the bedside table, and gave Teddy a long and careful look. 'Did you have a lovely time?' she asked at last. 'Where did Mark take you?'

'To the Savoy Hotel, for dinner and dancing, and yes, I had a marvellous time.'

Ketti studied her thoughtfully for a moment. 'Mmmmm. Stars in your eyes, I see.'

Teddy nodded, and all at once her face became serious, grave almost. 'Yes, that's true, very much so, Aunt Ketti. Mark is absolutely wonderful – ' She broke off, looking as thoughtful as her aunt, then confided, 'I think I'm falling in love with him.'

Ketti clucked sharply under her breath. Her expression altered slightly; worry settled in her eyes. She said in a voice that had become rather fretful, 'Teddy, Teddy, all this is going too *fast*, most assuredly it is. Yes, *far* too fast, in my opinion.'

'No, it isn't! I know how I feel, so does Mark!'

'I don't want you to get hurt.'

'What do you mean?'

'You hardly know him! Why, Teddy dear, you only met him three days ago – '

'Mark will *never* hurt me, I'm sure of that!' Teddy exclaimed heatedly, cutting her aunt off. She rose, crossed to the bed and sat down on the edge of it. Clearing her throat, she went on more softly, in a gentler tone, 'Well, there's one thing that should please you, at least.'

'And what's that?'

'He's Jewish.'

It was immediately obvious from Ketti's face that she was indeed delighted to hear this news; her expression instantly changed for the better, and her eyes brightened. 'That's a blessing! When people are of the same religion it saves a lot of heartache in the end. Is he Orthodox or Reform?'

'Reform. However, I got the impression Mark isn't especially religious himself, although he did say his father was constantly worried that he might marry out of the faith.'

'Don't tell me he's proposed to you already!' Ketti cried, sitting up straighter in the bed, her eyes flying open in surprise and alarm.

'No, of course not! Don't be so silly!' Teddy retorted, and shook her head, amazed that her aunt would even think such a thing. 'We were simply telling each other about our lives,' she continued, and then suddenly she began to laugh. 'But just now, on the doorstep, he *did* ask me to be his girl. And I accepted.'

'*Naturally.*' Ketti drank some of her tea, replaced the cup in its saucer with a clatter, and probed, 'What else did Mark tell you about himself and his family?'

'He has a brother, Lionel, who's at Harrow, and he went there himself. He was just starting at Oxford when he joined the RAF at the beginning of the war. Oh, by the way, Mark is fourth-generation English, his great-great-grandfather came here from Odessa in the early 1880s.'

'Russian, eh? And Ashkenazi! Good, very good.' Ketti nodded to herself, looking pleased as she mulled this information over. 'More than likely their original name was Lewenstein, before it got shortened and anglicised to Lewis. I have a friend, Riba Lewis, whose family also came from Odessa years ago. Goodness me, could it be that *she's* a relative of *theirs*? What does his father do? Did Mark mention that?'

'Yes, he did. They have a company called Lewis and Sons, which his father runs. They're diamond merchants in Hatton Gardens. And they have several other related businesses, including a jewellery shop in Regent Street – '

'Not Tannen and Graf!' Ketti interjected, giving her niece a swift glance. 'Now don't tell me that Mark comes from *that* family.'

'Why yes, he does, Aunt Ketti. You've got a peculiar look on your face. Is something the matter?'

'Is something the matter, she asks me,' Ketti muttered and sighed to herself. 'Oh dear no, nothing's the matter. At least, I don't believe it is. Tannen and Graf, eh? So, Mark is a grandson of old Isadore Tannen.'

'Do you know his grandfather, Aunt Ketti? Tell me about him, tell me more about the family,' Teddy cajoled eagerly.

'Ach, such a long *megillah* that is! But, since you ask, I'll try, and I'll make it as brief as possible. Isadore Tannen used to own Tannen and Graf, and *he* inherited it from *his* father, who in turn got it from *his* father. Mark's mother, Isabelle, is Isadore's only child, and the store is hers now, given to her by her father, of course, some years ago. Isadore is a very old man. Very old, yes, in his nineties, and the store has been run for a long time by Isabelle's husband, Charles Lewis, who is Mark's father. The Tannens were German Jews originally, Tannenbaum was their actual name, shortened years ago to Tannen – easier for the English to pronounce, and much more English-sounding. But Isadore Tannen is what I term a *fancy* Jew, extraordinarily rich, living in grand houses, full of pretensions, and one who likes to call the English aristocracy his *landsleit*,' she finished, a hint of sarcasm echoing in her voice.

'And the Lewises? Do you know anything about them?'

'Now there's a different kettle of fish. Intellectuals, thinkers, musicians, painters, although I must add that they've always been rich, too, and a trifle fancy, like the Tannens. But they've also been great philanthropists. As Mark told you, they came from Russia a century ago, and some of them seemingly set themselves up as diamond merchants, which they had been in Russia. And other members became money-lenders and bankers, still others went into the arts. They're a big family, with many branches, if I remember correctly.'

'I see . . . have you ever met Mark's parents?'

'Very briefly, at a charity event once. I will say this for Isabelle Lewis, she is a doer of good works, and has given millions to deserving causes, mostly to do with children and the sick. Her husband is equally philanthropic, like his father before him.'

'And how do you know so much about the Tannens and the Lewises, Aunt Ketti?'

'We Jews in London *do* know a lot about each other,' she answered. 'In a certain sense, it's a small community, and anyway, I suspect we all make it our business to know about each other. But actually, if you want the real truth, my friend Riba *is* related to Mark's family, and most of my knowledge about them comes from her. She's a second cousin of Mark's father. Riba is married to one of the Levines, and, in fact, I think you might have met her with me.'

'I believe I have, Aunt Ketti. Isn't it a small world?'

Ketti nodded.

There was a little pause, and then Teddy asked, 'Why were you looking so strange a moment ago? Don't you like Mark's family?'

'What's to like or dislike, since I don't *know* them personally? I only know *of* them. Good heavens, my dear, they don't socialise with the likes of me.'

'I'm not following you.'

'They're very snobbish, have their own little clique.'

'I see.'

'And they're very anglicised,' Ketti added.

'But so are you, Aunt Ketti! You've been here for thirty-odd years or more, and I can't think of anyone who's more English than you. You're a *real* Londoner.'

'That's true, yes, but *I* wasn't born here, nor do *I* have English-born ancestors. Also, I come from a different echelon than they do. I'm sort of ... well, middle-class, wouldn't you say? They're the upper crust. Why, one might say they're more English than the English.'

'I've heard that before!'

Ketti lifted a brow. 'Now it's my turn to say what do you mean?'

'The German Jews were more German than the Germans.'

'Sadly, yes.'

A sudden thought occurred to Teddy and she exclaimed, 'Do you think Mark's family might not consider me good enough for him? Is that what you're implying?'

'Certainly not! You come from a fine, highly-educated family, with doctors and professors as your antecedents. You're good enough for anybody, as far as I'm concerned. Seemingly, Mark thinks the same thing.'

Teddy smiled. 'Yes, Aunt Ketti, I believe he does.'

Ketti returned Teddy's smile. 'And what have you told Mark about *your* life?'

'*Everything.*'

'Have you now! And does he know about Maxim?'

'Of course he does!' Teddy looked at Ketti aghast. 'Why wouldn't I tell him about Maxim?'

Ketti merely shrugged and did not answer.

Teddy continued, 'Mark thinks I'm sending Maxim to *exactly* the right school, and he wants to meet him at Christmas, or before, if that's possible. And I know they're going to like each other very much. In fact, they're going to get on like a house on fire.'

'I'm sure they will,' Ketti soothed, fully aware that Teddy's voice had risen an octave. She now stifled a yawn, glanced at the carriage clock on the mantelpiece. 'Good heavens, we *have* been talking a stream, haven't we? It's turned two o'clock, already. Come, Teddy dear, give me a good-night kiss and let's go to sleep.'

Dutifully, Teddy bent forward and embraced her aunt affectionately, and then she got up off the bed and gathered the tea cups together. 'I'll take these downstairs and rinse them before I go to bed.'

Ketti nodded and leaned back against the pillows, and once Teddy had left and closed the door she turned off the lamp and settled down for the night.

However, Ketti soon discovered she could not fall asleep. Her mind was suddenly alive with thoughts of the Tannens and the Lewises. She could not help wondering what their attitude would be if Mark became seriously involved with Teddy and wanted to marry her. She knew enough about them to understand that the two clans were ambitious and class-conscious, and had always set their sights high when it came to marrying off their young. They were the elite of English Jewry and prominent in society, and they were not likely to let anyone forget that.

A nice English Jewish boy she had wanted for her Theodora. One so high-born she had not quite bargained for.

As he had promised, Mark telephoned Teddy on Sunday, before he returned to Number 32 Squadron at Biggin Hill. And he did so almost every day thereafter.

On the days he did not ring her, she knew he was on a flying mission somewhere over Germany, and her heart was in her mouth until she heard his voice again. A responsible and devoted person by nature, Teddy was always concerned about the welfare of those she loved. She now had another person's well-being to occupy her; along with Maxim, the Westheims and Aunt Ketti, Mark Lewis was added to her list. But quite aside from their telephone calls, Teddy and Mark wrote to each other on a regular basis, quickly got to know each other better, and drew closer and closer as the weeks sped by.

Unexpectedly, in late October, Mark managed to get a twenty-four-hour weekend pass, and rushed up to London. Since he wanted to see his parents and Teddy, and did not really have the time to do both, he decided on the most practical solution. He took the three of them to dinner at Claridge's on Saturday night.

As it turned out, Isabelle and Charles Lewis were just as enchanted by Teddy as was their smitten son. His mother appreciated her natural beauty and air of refinement, her obvious innocence and lack of sophistication, and saw her possibilities at once. Isabelle Lewis decided that this young woman looked as if she would bear children well, and made up her mind about Theodora on the spot. It seemed to her that she would make her son an excellent wife – if it went that far.

As for Mark's father, he too was full of enthusiasm for Teddy. Like his wife, he thought she was quite lovely. This was a major consideration in his son's case, since he knew how necessary physical beauty was to Mark who had always fallen for a pretty face. Charles was well aware, just from looking at her across the dinner table, that Teddy would satisfy Mark on every physical level. But what delighted him most was Teddy's wholesomeness. The other young women Mark had brought home in the past had always struck him as being racy, and had dripped with 'war paint', as he termed cosmetics. Good in bed, no doubt, but unqualified disasters in the drawing room, he had always thought privately to himself. And, of course, Theodora Stein was Jewish, a fact that was of vital consideration to Charles Lewis. If his son was as serious about this girl as he appeared to be, then marriage would be the inevitable outcome of the relationship. And he could not have borne it if Mark had married out of the faith. So he gave Teddy his stamp of approval, albeit silently at this moment.

The minute she met Isabelle and Charles Lewis, Teddy knew that Mark's parents were not *quite* the way Aunt Ketti had painted them to be, when she had heard about the dinner earlier in the day. They did not seem to have any pretensions of grandeur, nor did they strike her as being snobs. Teddy thought they were a pleasant, charming couple who appeared to be fair-minded and not a bit judgemental, and they showed a warm interest in her. Furthermore, they put her at ease immediately. She liked them a lot.

And so the evening at Claridge's was an enormous success, and the future looked bright for the young lovers.

Having jumped the hurdle of meeting Mark's parents, Teddy could not wait for Maxim and Mark to be introduced. And luckily it just so happened that Mark's next weekend leave fell at the same time as half term at Colet Court, when Maxim was home from prep school.

From the moment Mark walked into the back parlour at number forty-three, looking so dashing and heroic in his RAF uniform, and shook Maxim's hand, the two were fast friends. Within only a few minutes Mark asked the boy if he would like to go for a spin in the MG, and perhaps to sail his boat on Whitestone Pond in Hampstead, and Maxim accepted with alacrity and enthusiasm.

All through that weekend, as Teddy watched them enjoying so many different things together – talking animatedly about football, cricket, flying, aeroplanes and sports cars – she came to understand how much Maxim must have missed a masculine influence in his life at home, with only she and Aunt Ketti for company. And momentarily she was sad, thinking once again about Sigmund Westheim. He and Ursula were rarely far from her thoughts, and she prayed every day for their safety and longed for the war to be over so that they could come at last to England.

On Sunday night, after Mark had gone back to his squadron, Teddy and Maxim had their supper together in the dining room. They were alone, since Aunt Ketti had gone to play cards with Sarah Levine, and he suddenly looked across at her and said, 'Is Mark your sweetheart, Teddy?'

Coming out of the blue as it did, the question startled her, and for a second she was silent. And then she said, with a small smile, 'I suppose you could call him that.'

'Does that mean you're going to marry him?'

Giving Maxim a very direct look, she said carefully, 'I don't know, darling, he hasn't asked me.'

'But if he did ask?' Maxim insisted.

'I might.'

There was a short pause, and then the boy asked so quietly she could hardly hear him, 'What would happen to me?'

'Nothing would happen to you,' Teddy exclaimed, sitting up in her chair, frowning. 'You'd be with me. And in any case, if I ever did decide to marry Mark, or anyone else for that matter, I certainly wouldn't do so until your parents were here. Surely you know that.'

Maxim nodded. 'You've always said we'd live together. You and me and *Mutti* and Papa. If you married Mark, I suppose you'd have to live with him, wouldn't you, Teddy?'

'Yes. But we'd find a house or a flat very close to your parents, and I'd see you every day, and nothing would be very much different,' she reassured him quickly, sensing his insecurity. She looked across at him, smiling, her love and devotion reflected in her eyes.

'I know,' Maxim said, but nevertheless a glum expression settled on his face and he glanced down at his plate.

Teddy was now watching him closely. She was suddenly worried about him, wondering how to make him feel better, when he lifted his head and stared back at her. There was such bereftness in his eyes, such a stricken expression on his face, she sucked in her breath in concern and her chest tightened.

'Maxim, whatever is it? Don't you like Mark Lewis?'

'Yes,' he muttered. 'He's nice . . . '

'But?'

'No buts, Teddy.'

'Well then, what is it, darling?'

His voice was very small and it quavered slightly when he said slowly, 'What if *Mutti* and Papa don't come? What if . . . what if something's – ' The boy broke off, unable to voice his fears about his parents, and he sat back in his chair, biting his lower lip, fighting the sudden rush of emotion filling his throat.

Teddy was alarmed by his words, and she immediately jumped up and went to sit in the vacant chair next to his. She put an arm around him and held him close.

After a moment, she said gently, 'They're safe, Maxim. Try not to worry. And they *will* come to London, once the war ends and things get back to normal. But whatever happens, I want you to remember that I will always be here for you, and I'll look after you, until you're grown up if necessary. I've told you that many times before, now haven't I?'

'Yes,' he whispered against her shoulder, fighting back his incipient tears.

'You're *my boy*, don't forget, and I love you very much.'

'I love you, Teddy.'

THIRTY

Maxim's half term was over a few days later, and he returned to Colet Court, and Teddy went back to her voluntary work at the local Red Cross office.

It seemed to her that after this the weeks rushed by at breakneck speed, and almost before she could catch her breath Maxim was home again in December for the holidays. Christmas and the New Year were the best they had spent in years, they both agreed wholeheartedly on that. This was not only because of Mark, who was with them for part of the festivities, and made a great fuss of Maxim and Teddy, but because the news about the war grew better and better every day, and filled them with hope.

As January of 1945 turned into February, Allied troops were spreading out across the whole of Europe, and the entire country was betting that peace would come in the spring.

One day, towards the end of April, as Teddy stood in the kitchen preparing breakfast for Aunt Ketti and herself, she could not help thinking about Stubby's father's prediction. It suddenly struck her that Mr Trenton *had* been right in the end. All of the British newspapers were saying that the collapse of Nazi Germany was only a matter of weeks, and Arthur Trenton had constantly told her and the boys that they would be celebrating victory well before Maxim's eleventh birthday in June.

Teddy sighed to herself as she put the cups and saucers on the big wooden tray. There were times, like this morning, when she could hardly bear the waiting . . . her mind was forever focused on the Westheims. It had been a long time . . . six years since Paris, when Ursula had put them on the boat train to Victoria Station. How proud she and Sigmund would be of Maxim today. What a truly remarkable boy he had turned out to be. So brilliant at school, yet not at all vain or boastful about his scholastic achievements, and he was such a nice boy as well, and so very normal. At Christmas, when Mark's mother had met him for the first time, she had said he was a little gentleman, and this had caused Teddy to fill with pleasure; her pride in him knew no bounds. His parents would be surprised, of course, when they saw him. He had sprung up even more than ever in the last couple of years, and he was rather tall for his age, looked older than he was.

Teddy heard the rattle of the letter box in the front hall, and she wondered if it was the post or the newspapers which had been pushed through. After carrying the tray of breakfast china into the dining room, she walked down the hall to the front door; the morning papers were on the floor, and she picked them up along with the post, which lay underneath.

The postman came early today, she thought, tucking the newspapers under her arm, and shuffling through the envelopes, hoping to find a letter from Mark.

Her face lit up at the sight of his handwriting, and, wasting no time, she hurried back to the kitchen, flung the newspapers and the mail down on the kitchen table and ripped open his letter. As always it was loving and romantic, and full of plans for his next weekend leave, and for the future. She read it through twice, and, still smiling, she slipped it into her pocket.

As she swung around, intending to fill the kettle for the tea, her eye caught the *Daily Express*, which lay front-page up on the table, and the smile on her face congealed.

Stepping over to the table, she grabbed the paper, stood staring at the headlines and the photographs, her eyes widening with shock, her face freezing into rigid lines of horror.

Names of places leapt off the page at her. *Ohrdruf . . . Belsen . . . Buchenwald.* The most fearful words stabbed at her eyes. *Death camps . . . atrocities . . . inhumanity . . . extermination . . . Jews . . . millions murdered . . . genocide.*

She lowered her eyes to the pictures. They stunned and horrified her, so graphic were they in the foul, inhuman story they told of the most unspeakable brutality and cruelty, a terrible testament to the pitiless torture and mass murder of innocent people.

Teddy's hands began to shake uncontrollably, and she had to put the newspaper down on the table. She snapped her eyes shut, not wanting to see or read anything else, but then she forced herself to open them at once. *She had to know more.*

She stood with her head bent over the table, her eyes scanning the photographs. Half-naked people, emaciated beyond recognition as human beings, were living skeletons, hollow-eyed and hairless, staring vacantly out from behind the barbed wire fences of the camps. And yet more photographs ... of gas ovens and torture chambers, of heaps and heaps of bodies dumped haphazardly like so much rubbish in mass graves, of experimental medical laboratories, and lampshades made of human skin, and mountainous piles of discarded false teeth and eye glasses and shoes, and more bodies, and still more, of men and women and little children and even babies, all victims of the Nazi death machine.

Teddy brought her hands up to her mouth as the first sob broke free from her throat. Scalding-hot tears fell down her face and splashed onto the newspaper, and she wrapped her arms around her body, rocking backwards and forwards, crying out, 'Oh God, no! Oh my God, no! It's not possible! It just can't be ... it *can't* have happened!' But she knew it had.

She fell into a chair, her legs collapsing under her weakly, and she doubled over in anguish, clapped one hand over her mouth once more, to stifle the scream of pain and outrage rising in her throat.

After a while, Teddy was able to calm herself sufficiently to reach for the other newspapers. She was fully aware that to read on would be harrowing, yet she was unable to resist. It was imperative that she knew everything there was to know.

The *Daily Mail* carried as many photographs as the *Express*, as did the *Daily Telegraph*, and the accounts she read in all three papers were virtually the same, reporting the ghastly and horrendous facts. British and American troops had entered camps in western and eastern Germany in the last few days, and what they had found there had been overwhelming in its indescribable horror. The first camp to be liberated was Ohrdruf near Gotha, and there the Americans had discovered ditches filled to overflowing with four thousand bodies, including Jews, Russian prisoners-of-war and Polish slave labourers who had been systematically starved to death, or so neglected and denied medical treatment they had died of disease, or had been most cruelly murdered. When the British had entered Belsen they had been outraged, shocked and appalled by what they had found, and the Americans, who had liberated Buchenwald, had reacted in the same way, stunned by the scenes which had greeted them. General Bedell Smith, General Eisenhower's chief of staff, was quoted as saying that among the newly liberated camps, Buchenwald was 'the acme of atrocity'.

Waves of nausea washed over Teddy, and she swayed slightly in the chair; she thought for a moment that she was going to vomit, to be violently sick, but the feeling eventually passed. She put the *Telegraph* on the table with the other papers, reeling from what she had read, her mind unable to absorb any more.

Teddy sat for a while at the kitchen table, staring blankly into space, but finally she roused herself, rose and put the kettle on, stood near the stove waiting for it to boil. Once it had, she made the morning tea in the brown pot which Aunt Ketti preferred, put a cup and saucer and a small pitcher of milk on a tray, doing everything by rote. All she could think of were the horrifying reports in the papers.

Carrying the tray upstairs, she pushed open the door to her aunt's room and went inside. Light was filtering in through the blackout curtains. She glanced at the bed, wondering whether her aunt was awake, when Ketti said in her usual bright voice, 'Good morning, Theodora. This *is* a treat, getting a cup of tea in bed.'

'Good morning,' Teddy replied quietly, hardly trusting her own voice, placing the tray on the window seat. She then drew back the curtains swiftly, and brilliant sunlight streamed into the bedroom, making her blink.

Teddy carried the cup of tea over to her aunt, who now sat propped up against the pillows.

'Thank you,' Ketti said, and instantly noticed that Teddy's hand was shaking slightly as she passed her the cup. She glanced at her face, saw that it was white and drawn. 'Teddy, you look awful. Whatever is it? Is something wrong?'

Teddy could only nod.

'It's not Mark, is it? Nothing's happened to him, has it?' Ketti cried, filling with alarm, sitting bolt upright.

'No, it's not Mark,' Teddy said, and sat down heavily on the edge of the bed. Not knowing quite how to begin, she started in a roundabout way, saying slowly, 'Aunt Ketti . . . that committee you're on, the refugee committee affiliated to the synagogue . . .'

'Yes, what about it?' Ketti asked with a tiny, puzzled frown.

'You've told me stories, horrendous stories, which came from some of the European refugees your committee has been trying to help.'

Ketti nodded. 'You're referring to the dreadful things they said happened in the concentration camps, aren't you?'

'They're true. *Absolutely true,*' Teddy whispered hoarsely. 'And they're *not* concentration camps, they're *death* camps. The proof is in this morning's papers, proof for the whole world.'

Ketti pulled back slightly, staring at her niece, finding it difficult to comprehend what she was saying. 'I don't understand,' she muttered, shaking her silvered head from side to side.

Teddy explained. 'British and American troops have started to enter those camps, liberate them, in the past few days, and what they've found is so ghastly, so horrifying, it's beyond understanding. Unbelievable cruelty, and human degradation of such enormity it staggers the mind. Millions have been slaughtered. Jews, Russians, Poles, Slavs, and Gypsies, but mostly . . . Jews.'

The cup and saucer Ketti was holding began to rattle violently in her trembling hands, and Teddy leaned forward, took them from her, placed them on the bedside table before she spilled the tea all over herself.

'It doesn't seem possible,' Ketti whispered, her skin turning the colour of putty, her eyes wide and staring in her stark face. 'They couldn't . . . they wouldn't *dare* – '

'They did!' Teddy said in a low, fierce voice. 'And the British newspapers are calling it genocide.'

Later that day Ketti went looking all over the house for Teddy, concerned about her.

She found her in Maxim's room, sitting in a chair, staring at the photographs of the Westheims on the chest of drawers. Teddy swung her head and looked around, as the door was pushed open, and Ketti knew that she had been weeping.

'Are you all right, dear?' Ketti asked.

'Yes.'

'Am I intruding?'

'No, come in.'

Ketti did so, and sat down on the edge of the other chair. She was aware that Theodora was filled with worry about the Westheims, but she had been afraid to mention them thus far today. She still hesitated to do so even now, for fear of upsetting Teddy further.

Almost as if she knew what her aunt was thinking, Teddy said, 'Ursula and Sigmund have been the focus of my thoughts ever since I read the newspapers, Aunt Ketti, as I'm sure you probably realise.'

'I do, Teddy. You care for them deeply, so it's obvious you would be more worried than ever about them after . . . after what we've read.'

'I haven't been able to get the newspaper photographs out of my head ... those heartbreaking images are indelibly imprinted on my brain. Oh Aunt Ketti!' she cried, her voice anguished. 'What if Sigmund and Ursula *did* end up in one of those monstrous places?' Her voice faltered and her eyes filled. 'I'm so afraid for them, in agony about them, and I don't seem able to think straight, to function properly.'

Ketti said, 'I know it's hard, but you must be *hopeful, positive*. And you must remember that the last message you received from Arabella von Wittingen was very reassuring.'

'But that was such a long time ago, several years now.'

'Never mind.' Ketti bent forward urgently, and continued in her most reassuring voice, 'The princess hasn't been in touch since then, I know that; on the other hand, this only leads me to believe that things are status quo. She told you then, when she telephoned from Switzerland, that the Westheims were staying with the von Tiegals at the Schloss Tiegal in the Mark Brandenburg, where they were safe. And you've said over and over again to me that they *would* definitely be safe there.'

'Yes, and the von Tiegals could easily be hiding them. There are dozens of passages and dungeons underneath the castle, which is centuries old. I think there are even some secret rooms and corridors.' Teddy looked across at her aunt and went on, 'I don't doubt they're all right if they're at the Schloss. But I can't help wondering if they remained there. This has always been my worry ... that they left for some reason, went back to Berlin. Once in the city, they could have been arrested and sent ... to a camp, or they could have been killed in an Allied bombing raid.'

'We've gone over this so many times before, Teddy dear, and I'm not trying to dismiss your concern or diminish your reasons for it. God only knows, you have good cause to worry about Ursula and Sigmund. But you must hold the thought that they are surviving, wherever they are, whatever their circumstances. If you don't, you'll drive yourself mad.'

Teddy was silent.

Ketti said slowly, softly, 'And Teddy dear, there's Maxim to think of. The boy needs you so very much.'

'I'll never give up hope for them,' Teddy said. 'I will go on believing they are alive until I have proof ... proof that they're not.'

THIRTY-ONE

The red-white-and-blue Union Jack hung out of every window, fluttering in the breeze.

People danced in the streets, cheering and singing, laughing and crying, and they hugged and kissed each other, friends and strangers alike, filled with jubilance, happiness and pride.

Corridors of brilliant light streamed out of windows no longer blacked-out against enemy bombers, and bonfires blazed the length and breadth of the land as effigies of Hitler were devoured in their flames. And the pubs were filled to overflowing with the revellers, who toasted the boys in blue and khaki, and each other, and cried, 'Long live Winston, he's brought us through!'

It was the night of Tuesday, May the eighth, and the whole of England was rejoicing. The day before, in the early hours of Monday, May the seventh, at two-forty-one a.m. precisely, General Alfred Jodl, the representative of the German High Command, and Grand Admiral Karl Doenitz, the designated head of the German State, signed the act of unconditional surrender of all German land, sea and air forces in Europe to the Allied Expeditionary Force and simultaneously to the Soviet Union. The war with Germany was suddenly, and finally at an end.

Great Britain was victorious.

And the British were celebrating Victory Day in Europe. They had taken to the streets to do it, and what better place to share their joy with their ecstatic fellow citizens on this national holiday, which would forever after commemorate the destruction of the most evil regime in the history of the world.

Teddy and Aunt Ketti were amongst the thousands of people who stood near the House of Commons, waiting for the Prime Minister to make a speech. He had spoken to the nation on the wireless at three o'clock that afternoon, but the crowds still wanted to hear more from this British bulldog, their beloved Winnie, their great leader – possibly the greatest leader their country had ever known – who had brought them to a victory hard won and honourable.

The roar of the crowd and the cheering were overpowering, deafening, when he appeared on the balcony of one of the Government buildings at ten-thirty that night, wearing his 'siren' suit and giving his famous V for Victory sign with his right hand.

A sea of faces stretching for miles stared up at him. And as he began to speak Teddy and Ketti and the thousands swarming around them fell silent, and the most extraordinary hush of reverence and respect descended on the streets of Whitehall.

'My dear friends,' Winston Churchill began, 'this is your hour. This is not victory of a party or of any class. It's a victory of the great British nation as a whole. We were the first, in this ancient island, to draw the sword against tyranny. After a while we were left all alone against the most tremendous military power that has been seen. We were all alone for a whole year. There we stood, alone. Did anyone want to give in?' Churchill paused and in answer to this question the crowd roared, 'No!' 'Were we downhearted?' the Prime Minister demanded. 'No!' responded thousands in one voice.

The Prime Minister said, 'The lights went out and the bombs came down. But every man, woman and child in the country had no thought of quitting the struggle. London can take it. So we came back after long months from the jaws of death, out of the mouth of hell, while all the world wondered. When shall the reputation and faith of this generation of English men and women fail? I say that in the long years to come not only will the people of this island but of the world, wherever the bird of freedom chirps in human hearts, look back to what we've done and they will say, "do not despair, do not yield to violence and tyranny, march straight forward and die if needs be – unconquered". Now we have emerged from one deadly struggle – a terrible foe has been cast on the ground and awaits our judgement and our mercy.'

Teddy discovered that tears were streaming down her cheeks unchecked, and she fumbled with her handbag, opened it and searched for her handkerchief, mopped her wet cheeks.

'Are you all right, my dear?' Ketti asked, taking Teddy's arm, peering into her face, concerned.

'I'm fine, Aunt Ketti.' Teddy blew her nose and blinked back her tears. 'Mr Churchill always manages to move me with his words. He speaks such truths in his own very special way, and he's so reassuring and inspiring. There's no one like him, really.'

Apparently the thousands in the streets listening now to the end of his speech agreed with her. As Winston Churchill finished speaking they began to shout and cheer, and they cheered him until they were hoarse, and then they started singing For He's a Jolly Good Fellow and Land of Hope and Glory. Ketti and Teddy joined in, warbling like full-blown Cockney sparrows. And it struck Teddy suddenly, as she sang, that this war had been punctuated by rousing Churchillian speeches and by singing, and that somehow his words and the popular songs had kept them going, had been their mainstay when the future looked bleak.

The Prime Minister waved and left the balcony, and slowly the crowds began to disperse and stream away, and the two women moved with them. It was growing late, and Teddy and Ketti had had a long and busy day, one that had been exciting, even thrilling, but also a trifle wearing. Near Victoria Station they managed to find a taxi, clambered in thankfully and settled on the seat together. They were glad to be by themselves at last, and away from the milling crowds.

Teddy glanced at her aunt, and despite the dim light in the cab she noticed how worn out she looked, and exclaimed, 'Why, Aunt Ketti, you're absolutely exhausted!'

'I'm afraid I am a bit, aren't you?'

'Yes,' Teddy admitted. 'But it's been worth it, celebrating the downfall and defeat of the Nazis and the Third Reich.'

It was Theodora's twenty-sixth birthday the following day, May the ninth, and that afternoon Aunt Ketti gave a small tea party for her, to which Ketti invited Teddy's dear friends, Julia and Lydia Pell.

They came promptly at four, each carrying a prettily-wrapped present, which Teddy opened, as always touched by their thoughtfulness. From Mrs Pell she received a hand-painted silk scarf in pretty tones of lilac, magenta and pink, and from Lydia a string of amethyst beads which were quite beautiful. 'You spoil me, and you're far too extravagant,' Teddy said, first kissing Mrs Pell and then Lydia. 'Thank you both very much.'

A short while later, Aunt Ketti brought in the silver tea tray and the four women sat down around the Queen Anne tea table which was laden with a mixture of thin finger sandwiches, scones, and an iced birthday cake boasting a single candle. They were halfway through the tea party when the doorbell rang shrilly.

'Who on earth can that be?' Ketti asked, frowning. 'We're not expecting anyone else, are we, Teddy?'

'No, I'll go and see who it is,' she volunteered, springing up, hurrying down the corridor to the front door. She jerked it open to find Mark standing on the doorstep, much to her surprise.

'Happy birthday, darling!' he exclaimed, stepping inside the hall, hugging her, picking her up and swinging her around so furiously her feet left the ground.

'But you've already wished me that on the telephone,' Teddy said, as he put her down on the floor at last and planted a kiss on her cheek.

'But I wanted to say it in person, and with this,' he explained, presenting her with the package he was holding. He added, 'It's a bottle of Dad's best pink champagne.'

'Oh how lovely of you, Mark, thank you. Come on, Aunt Ketti is with Lydia and Mrs Pell in the drawing room. We're having tea. Perhaps you'd like a cup, and a piece of birthday cake?'

'No thanks,' he said with a huge grin. 'I much prefer the champagne.'

The others were equally surprised to see Mark when Teddy ushered him into the room, and after he had greeted them in his genial way he set about opening the bottle. 'It's cold enough to drink now,' he assured Teddy as she took the champagne flutes out of the china cabinet. 'My father always keeps a few bottles on ice for emergencies, and I bagged one from his cellar for this very special occasion.' The cork in the Dom Perignon popped like a gun going off, and some of the frothy wine rushed up and spilled out of the neck of the bottle. 'Whoops!' he exclaimed, quickly pouring the champagne into the flutes. 'I mustn't waste any of *this* precious stuff.'

Mark lifted his glass and toasted Teddy, and so did everyone else. They clinked glasses and sipped the wine and then Mark put his flute down, and turned to her. 'May I speak to you alone for a moment?' he asked.

'Of course, Mark,' Teddy replied, throwing him a swift glance, wondering if something was wrong. He sounded unexpectedly serious, even grave.

They excused themselves, and Mark escorted her down the corridor, through the back parlour and out into the garden without enlightening her, and she wondered what this was about.

Mark was aware that Teddy liked to sit under the old apple tree reading or sewing in the warm weather, and it was to this favourite spot that he now led her, holding her hand in his.

Once there he turned to her and gazed down into her baffled face.

'You know I love you, Teddy, that I want to marry you, and I know you love me. But you've never agreed to become engaged. You've said over and over again that you wanted to wait until the war was over. Well, it *is* over now. Please say *yes*, please become my fiancée today.'

'Yes, I will, Mark,' she said after the merest hesitation. Her sudden joy was muted by her nagging worry about the Westheims, but she did not allow this to show. She looked up into his adoring face and the smile she gave him was radiant.

He reached into the pocket of his flying jacket, took out a black leather box and handed it to her without a word. But his eyes were fastened on hers and he watched her closely.

Teddy slowly opened the box. A breathtaking square-cut emerald ring with diamonds on either side nestled in the folds of the white satin. 'Oh Mark, it's beautiful!'

'As are you, my Teddy,' he said, and then asked, 'Do you really like it?'

'How could I not! It's magnificent!'

'Emerald is your birth-stone, as well as the colour of your eyes, and that's why I chose it. And happy birthday again, darling.'

'Thank you, Mark.'

He took the ring out of the box and slipped it on the third finger of her left hand. 'Now it's truly official,' and so saying he swept her into his arms and kissed her on the mouth.

After a short while the two of them walked slowly up the garden path holding hands, and went back into the house to announce their engagement to Aunt Ketti and the Pells. Neither her aunt nor her friends seemed in the least bit surprised to hear this news. They congratulated them warmly, and Ketti said, 'We've been expecting it, you know, for ages. And the three of us were only just saying that we've never seen anyone more in love than you two.'

Everyone laughed at this comment, and the newly engaged couple thanked Ketti and the Pells for their good wishes, and another toast was made.

Mark immediately put his glass down after only a sip and said, 'I have to go, Teddy. I've got to get back to Biggin Hill. My pass is for a few hours, that's all. Courtesy of a very romantic squadron leader, who agreed you should have your ring on your birthday. And who, by the way, insists on being present at the wedding.'

Teddy said, 'Then we must invite him.'

Mark took his leave of Aunt Ketti and the Pells, and Teddy accompanied him to the front door, where she stood on tiptoe to kiss him goodbye.

When they drew apart, Mark murmured softly, 'Let's set a date for the wedding.'

Teddy's face instantly changed. 'You know I can't, Mark! Not until I hear from the Westheims, find out when they're coming. I've always told you I couldn't get married without Maxim's parents being present.'

'But it might be months before you hear anything from them! Things are a mess in Germany, there's nothing but chaos over there right now!'

'I understand that, Mark, but knowing Ursula Westheim, I'm quite certain she'll find a way to be in touch with me soon. Or someone else will be, on her behalf.'

'All right,' Mark said in a resigned voice. 'We'll wait for a while before we get married.' He smiled at her and Teddy smiled back and she did not notice the uncertainty in his eyes. Nor did she realise at this moment that she would wait in vain to hear from the Westheims. In the weeks that followed there was no news from them. And they did not come.

THIRTY-TWO

She went back to Germany to find the Westheims and felt like an alien in an alien land.

She did not recognise the city where she had been born and had lived until she was almost twenty. There was nothing left standing to recognise. Berlin looked like some strange and distant planet, a moonscape covered with deep craters and weirdly-shaped mountains made of debris.

The city had been turned into a wasteland by Allied bombers which had flattened five hundred thousand buildings, a third of those in the city, and in so doing had destroyed most of central Berlin. What had not been laid to waste by Allied bombs had been demolished on May the second when the city had fallen to Marshal Zhukov and the advancing Red Army. Ruthlessly, the Russians had turned twenty-two thousand guns on what remained, a barrage of unprecedented intensity, and had thus reduced everything left standing to rubble, dirt and dust.

Teddy was stupefied by what she saw. Addicted to newspapers, and a voracious reader of international news, especially news about Germany, she had followed the events of the past few months scrupulously. Nonetheless, she had not envisioned that the city would be as ravaged as it was, or that it would have an air of such desolation about it.

She returned at the beginning of October, travelling from London to Berlin by train. The many arrangements for her journey had been made with the help of Mark's father and Julia Pell. Charles Lewis had made certain that all of her papers were in good order, and had insisted on paying for the trip, even though she had not wanted him to do so. He had won his argument, and she had given in gracefully.

It was Lydia's mother who had found her accommodation in Berlin. Julia Pell had arranged for her to stay with a woman called Anne Reynolds, who held an important administrative position with the International Red Cross, and had been a friend of Julia's for over twenty years. Now a widow, Anne Reynolds had lived in Germany with her husband before the war, spoke fluent German and also knew the country well. These were just two of the many reasons she had been selected for her high-powered job.

According to Julia Pell, Mrs Reynolds had been sent to Berlin in July, when the British, American and French troops had entered the city to join with the Russian Army in the four-power control of Berlin. She had been allocated a small apartment in Charlottenburg, which was one of the areas in the British Zone, and she had written back to Julia Pell to say that although her quarters were not very large, Theodora was most certainly welcome to stay as long as she wished. In her letter she had added that she constantly travelled around the British Zone of West Germany on Red Cross business, and that it was more than likely Teddy would have the place to herself most of the time. And as it happened, this was the way it turned out.

After greeting her cordially when she arrived at the flat on Sunday afternoon, and showing her around, Anne Reynolds apologetically explained that she had to depart almost immediately for Frankfurt, on an assignment.

'I'm afraid I only have time for a cup of tea with you before I leave,' she said as they sat down together in the sitting room.

'That's all right, Mrs Reynolds, I do understand,' Teddy said, taking to her at once. A tall, striking woman in her late forties, with blonde hair and a typical English-rose complexion, she had a friendly smile and a commanding yet sympathetic way about her.

'Please make yourself comfortable, whilst I brew a pot,' Anne Reynolds went on, 'and I'll be back in a moment.' Then she suddenly changed her mind and said, 'Now that I think of it, why don't you come to the kitchen with me? I'll show you where everything's kept, and we can chat at the same time.'

'I'd like that, Mrs Reynolds, and thank you so much for letting me stay here. It's very generous of you to take in a stranger like this,' Teddy said warmly, her gratitude very much apparent on her face.

Anne smiled at her, and as she led the way to the tiny kitchen, more like a large walk-in closet than a room, she remarked, 'Julia Pell cares about you a great deal, thinks of you as another daughter. And since she's one of my oldest and dearest friends, I was delighted to be of help to someone who obviously means so much to her. Besides, there are no hotels left standing, so I don't know where you would have found accommodation. The Kaiserhoff, the Eden and the Adlon have been destroyed beyond recognition, and so have most of the smaller hotels. Rooms are at a premium.' She sighed heavily, and added, 'Most Berliners are living in cellars, or are camping out in the ruins. The city's in a mess, and refugees are still pouring in every day.'

'Where from?' Teddy asked swiftly.

'Everywhere really. Mostly they're returning Berliners who left during the war, but there are refugees coming in from other parts of Germany, who think they will be better off here.' She shook her head, and grimaced. 'They're not, of course. Conditions are terrible, and I've never seen such overcrowding in my life.'

Anne Reynolds now struck a match, lit the gas under the kettle and told Teddy, 'We have our work cut out for us, I don't mind telling you. Almost all of the hospitals are gone, blown apart in the bombing raids, and those that are left are very badly damaged. There's also a shortage of medicines, food and fuel. The hospitals are full, jammed actually, and tuberculosis, typhoid and diphtheria are the cause of most deaths.' Anne paused, swung her head to face Teddy, and asked matter-of-factly, 'By the way, you *were* immunised for the last two, weren't you? I told Julia you *must* be.'

'Yes, I was,' Teddy replied. She thought of Ursula and Sigmund, and wondered where they were, if *they* were amongst the refugees streaming back into Berlin. She was about to mention them to Anne Reynolds, then changed her mind, decided to do this later when they sat down for their cup of tea.

'Disease is rampant in the city, Theodora,' Anne informed her. 'You could say it's in the very air we breathe, since there are still thousands of dead bodies which have not yet been buried.'

'My God, that's appalling!' Teddy cried, horrified by what she had just heard. 'Where are they?'

'In the rivers, under the piles of rubble, and lying in very shallow graves in gardens. Not conducive to a healthy atmosphere at all. And, of course, there are rats everywhere.'

Teddy shuddered and her skin crawled at the thought of the vermin. 'It must be very, very grim out there in the streets.'

'I'm afraid it's really quite ghastly,' Anne answered, concern flooding her eyes. She shook her head sadly. 'We have an immense task, but we do try to do our best. For everyone.'

'I know from working with the Red Cross in London how extraordinary the international division is,' Teddy said. 'I don't know what the world would do if our organisation didn't exist. I'm so proud to be associated with it.'

'So am I,' Anne murmured, and began putting cups, saucers and a small bowl of powdered milk on a tray. Once she had done this, she opened two cupboards, turned to Teddy, and explained, 'Here are utensils, china, those sort of things. In here are basic staples, and food. There's plenty of that, mostly tinned stuff, though, such as corned beef, spam and soup.'

She closed these doors, opened another, and went on, 'There are a few luxuries here . . . tinned fruit, sugar and chocolate biscuits, courtesy of the PX and a friend of mine who's a major in the American army. He very kindly keeps me supplied, on a regular basis, so do feel free to use whatever you wish.'

'Thank you, Mrs Reynolds,' Teddy murmured. 'You're being extremely kind and I'm very appreciative.' It struck her now that she would have been floundering in Berlin without the help of Anne Reynolds, and she could not help thinking how lucky she was to have friends like the Pells, and a future father-in-law as caring as Charles Lewis. Between them they had made her personal search for the Westheims possible, and certainly easier than it would have been otherwise.

Later, as they were drinking their tea in the little sitting room, Teddy was about to bring up the subject of the Westheims when her friendly and hospitable hostess began to enlighten her about everyday living in Berlin. Teddy had no alternative but to bide her time.

'After Germany capitulated to the Allies, the Russians soon got certain services working again,' Anne explained. 'Such as gas and electricity. Plus the underground, trams and trains, so we're able to get around the city. There are also a few ramshackle old taxis, but not many, because of the petrol shortage. But stay in the British Zone,' she cautioned, 'don't wander into the Russian Zone by mistake, it's dangerous, there's still a lot of rape going on.'

'I understand.'

'The telephone service isn't what it should be yet,' Anne added with a wry smile. 'Sometimes it works, sometimes it doesn't. If you want to call your aunt later, to let her know you've arrived safely, you could give it a try. I can't guarantee that you'd get through, though.'

'That's very kind of you, and I will attempt to call Aunt Ketti tonight, if you don't mind,' Teddy said, 'but I insist on paying for any calls I make.'

'Don't be so silly,' Anne murmured dismissively.

Teddy now said, 'You haven't mentioned the Westheims, so I assume the International Red Cross hasn't turned up anything regarding their whereabouts yet. Or come across any other information about them.'

Anne shook her head. 'No, I'm afraid not, I would have told you the moment you walked in, if I'd had any news.'

Teddy bit her lip tensely, looking troubled.

'Try not to be downhearted,' Anne said with sudden gentleness, softening her rather efficient manner, wishing to be supportive. 'Even though there is no information so far, in actuality this doesn't mean very much. Things are terribly chaotic, as I've already explained. Millions of displaced people are on the move in Europe, about ten million to be precise. Records have been destroyed, either in the bombing raids, or by the Nazis when they realised defeat was upon them. Then again, many of the agencies which might be able to help you locate them are understaffed. It truly is a herculean task, trying to trace missing people, so it may take a while. But you will find them, I feel sure of that.'

Teddy nodded, praying that Mrs Reynolds was correct in her assumption that she would succeed in what she had come here to do.

Anne gave her another reassuring glance, then swung around in her chair, and motioned to the desk near the window. 'I've written down the names and addresses of the agencies you must visit tomorrow, as well as my office number. Elizabeth Jefford, my secretary, is efficient, knows her way around the British and American Zones very well, so don't hesitate to call her if you need any kind of help. And there's a set of keys to the flat on the desk alongside the pad.'

'Thank you, Mrs Reynolds, thank you for everything.'

'Thanks are not necessary,' Anne said, 'I'm happy to be of some help. As a matter of fact, I wanted to tell – '

'There's one other thing,' Teddy said, swiftly cutting in. She leaned forward with a show of urgency and rushed on, 'If I don't have any success with the agencies here in Berlin, I would like to go to the Schloss Tiegal in the Mark Brandenburg. I realise it's in the Russian Zone, but perhaps I – '

Now it was Anne's turn to interrupt. 'You don't have to go there, Theodora,' she said. 'I was about to tell you that Julia wrote to me some weeks ago, explained that the Westheims were staying at the Schloss when you last had news of them. And so I asked my American friend Major Evans to have the Schloss checked out. Fortunately he was able to do so, managed to cut through the usual Russian red tape. He discovered that the Schloss hadn't been damaged in the war, even though Potsdam and Brandenburg had been badly bombed.'

'That's wonderful news!' Teddy cried, her eyes instantly brightening.

'Yes, it is. Since the Schloss wasn't bombed, we know the Westheims couldn't possibly have been killed in a raid there. However, the Schloss is uninhabited, deserted except for a caretaker who was put in by the Russians. They have requisitioned it, and I understand from Major Evans that they are going to turn it into a barracks.'

'And this caretaker had no information to offer?' Teddy asked quickly, fixing her intent green gaze on Anne.

'None. Apparently all he said was that everyone had gone away.'

'It seems as if the Westheims have disappeared without a trace, doesn't it?' Teddy muttered in a glum voice, her excitement of a moment ago completely evaporating.

'Yes, that's true,' Anne agreed. 'On the other hand, there is no reason to believe they're dead.'

Anne now rose and went out into the small foyer, where she took her overcoat from the cupboard. Slipping into it, she said, 'I'm afraid I really must leave for Frankfurt. Keep your spirits up, and try not to fret, Theodora. And don't forget, my secretary is there if you need anything, she'll do her best to help you. I'll see you at the end of the week.'

'Goodbye, Mrs Reynolds, have a safe trip,' Teddy said.

The following morning Teddy left the flat in Charlottenburg early, and took the underground to the Bahnhof Zoo, which was the station closest to the Tiergartenstrasse.

It did not take her long to arrive at her destination, and after alighting from the train she walked up the Budapesterstrasse and into the Stülerstrasse, heading in the direction of the Tiergarten, the lovely old park which she had so often frequented with Maxim and Ursula.

Teddy hurried along at a brisk pace on this misty and drizzly October day, glancing from side to side, filling with dismay when she saw the devastation all around her. She wondered whether there was any point going to see if there was anything left of the Westheim mansion. No buildings were standing on these two streets, so why should the Tiergartenstrasse be any different, she asked herself. Berlin was a ruined city. She had seen that with her own eyes yesterday, and Mrs Reynolds's descriptions had only confirmed that *everything* had been blown to smithereens.

Drawing closer to the Tiergarten, she came to a sudden abrupt stop, and she could not help gasping in astonishment. She was astounded by what she saw. Not a single tree was left standing, and the denuded park looked barren and desolate under the curdled grey sky.

After a moment, Teddy became aware of a curious chip-chip-chipping noise that sounded like metal hitting stone, and she swung her head, wondering what it was.

A few yards away a woman was working amongst the piles of rubble littering a stretch of waste ground where once there had been a house. The woman was hacking at a brick with a broken chisel, removing ancient plaster from around its edges. And then she placed the brick into an improvised wheelbarrow made from a pair of small wheels and an old wooden box strung together with string and bits of wire.

Teddy walked over to the woman and addressed her politely. '*Bitte . . .* what happened to the trees in the park? *Please,* can you tell me why the park is so ruined?'

The woman glanced at Teddy, looked her up and down through wary eyes, not responding at first. Then she said in a clipped, harsh tone, 'You must be a stranger to Berlin to ask a question like that.'

'Yes, I am. The trees in the Tiergarten,' Teddy repeated. 'What happened to them?'

'They were cut down,' the woman said flatly. 'For firewood. The Berliners needed to keep warm during the war. There was no other fuel.'

'Yes, I see, I understand,' Teddy said. '*Danke* . . . thank you very much.' She inclined her head and walked away rapidly, conscious of the woman's hostility.

Within the space of a few seconds Teddy was at the centre of the Tiergartenstrasse where the Westheim's beautiful mansion had been. Her steps slowed and she stood gazing across the dirt and the mud and the puddles to the pile of rubble it had become.

Memories rushed at her, bright and sharp and in focus, and for a fleeting moment she was carried back in time to the old days, and she thought of the happy hours she had spent in that house with Maxim and his parents.

And she saw them then in her mind's eye.

Ursula, so lovely in her blonde freshness, refined and elegant, moving about the house and the garden with such grace; Sigmund, so handsome, kind and gentlemanly, sitting at the piano in the music room, playing his beautiful music. And Maxim running to them, calling their names, his young face shining with adoration for them. The memories were bittersweet, for she was caught between the past as it had once been, and the present as it was in all its pain and ugliness. She felt a strangling sensation in her throat, and tears pricked behind her lids, but she blinked them away at once, and breathed deeply.

It was ridiculous to think about that house. It had only been bricks and mortar, and therefore of small consequence. What truly mattered was the couple who had owned it and who had made it into such a wonderfully loving and happy home for their child. And also for her.

Teddy turned away, sadness swamping her, slowly retraced her steps down the Tiergartenstrasse and swung off it at the intersection between the Hofjägeralle and the Stülerstrasse, making for the Lützowufer. The latter was where the von Tiegals had lived, in an apartment overlooking the Landwehrkanal. Willy Herzog's home had been close by as well.

But before she even reached the Lützowufer she saw that this area was another blighted wasteland, and so she pivoted sharply, and walked back to the Bahnhof Zoo station. There was nothing for her here.

I cannot linger in the past, she thought, or dwell on the memories. The present is the only thing that counts now. My objective in Berlin is to find the Westheims, and that is what I must do.

Teddy held this thought for the rest of the day as she visited the various agencies on Anne Reynolds's list. These included several Jewish refugee groups and Zionist organisations dealing with missing persons, and the Society of Friends, run by the American Quakers, who were doing relief and reconstruction work in the war-torn city. Everyone she met was as helpful as they could possibly be. Each agency gave her long lists of names of those who had been sent to camps or deported by the Nazis, or who had been reported as dead. The Westheims were not on any of them.

'Don't give up hope,' the American woman at the office of the Society of Friends said. 'And check all the agencies daily, since new names are constantly being added.'

Teddy thanked the helpful Quaker and returned to the flat in Charlottenburg. She made a light supper and then went to bed, determined to start her search again tomorrow.

THIRTY-THREE

It drew her back like a magnet, that area of the Tiergarten and its environs where so much of her life had been spent in the past.

After her first visit, on that drizzly Monday morning, she had returned several times, enticed by a place she found irresistible, because it was both familiar and loaded with poignant memories. But on each occasion she had found nothing worthwhile, and certainly nothing which would help her in her search for the Westheims. And she had always come away from there brimming with frustration and heightened anxiety, vowing never to return.

But one Saturday afternoon, two weeks after she had arrived in Berlin, Teddy took herself off to the Tiergartenstrasse yet again. The difference was that today she had a purpose, a real reason for being there. Elizabeth Jefford, Mrs Reynolds's secretary, had suggested to Teddy that she talk to the *Trümmerfrauen*, the rubble women, who worked the city in groups, cleaning up the debris, and collecting the bricks which could be used again, once the rebuilding of Berlin commenced.

Elizabeth had explained to her on the telephone last night that the *Trümmerfrauen* had developed their own intricate networks, had their own grapevines, and thus were extraordinary sources of information about everything – from the black market to missing people. The women apparently worked in and around the streets where they had previously had homes, and where most of them still lived in makeshift quarters.

Elizabeth had pointed out to Teddy that perhaps one of them might have seen something or met someone or heard gossip which could be useful to her, and aid her as she continued to look for Ursula and Sigmund.

And so she had come here again. *Just one more time,* she had said to herself a short while ago, as she had taken the underground train which had brought her to the Bahnhof Zoo station. Now she walked along the Tiergartenstrasse at a slow pace, all the time glancing around alertly.

It did not take her very long to realise that there were no women working the rubble today. Her disappointment was so acute she suddenly understood how high her anticipation had been since her conversation with Elizabeth last night.

Just as Teddy was giving up hope of finding any of the *Trümmerfrauen,* she spotted three of them standing near a pit on a piece of land that had been partially cleared of rubble. They were talking amongst themselves and sharing a cigarette.

Teddy came to a stop a short distance away, stood watching them with interest for a few seconds. Each woman took several deep drags of the cigarette, then handed it to the next one, and Teddy saw at once how much they were enjoying this little luxury, making the most of it.

Elizabeth had warned her not to go empty-handed. And so in her bag were a packet of Lucky Strikes and three chocolate bars from the special store cupboard in the flat, gifts Mrs Reynolds had undoubtedly received from her boyfriend, the American major. Mrs Reynolds was in Bonn with him this weekend, and Elizabeth had told her to take the items with her today, assuring her that Mrs Reynolds would not mind. Teddy was now very glad she had listened to her, that she had this extremely precious supply on hand. A bribe of cigarettes or chocolate would surely help to loosen tongues which otherwise might remain still.

The women stopped talking when Teddy approached, and turned to look at her. Their faces were closed and inscrutable, their eyes cold, and she remembered the blatant hostility of the only other rubble woman she had spoken to about the lack of trees in the Tiergarten. She hoped these three would be a little more friendly.

'Please . . . can you help me?' Teddy said.

The women simply stared at her, made no response.

She began again. '*Bitte* . . . I'm looking for some friends, or information about them . . . a couple I used to know before the war. They lived along there – ' Teddy paused, swung her head, pointed down the Tiergarten-strasse. 'In one of the big houses, one of the grand houses. Herr Sigmund Westheim, Frau Ursula Westheim. They had a small son, a boy called Maximilian.'

Three pairs of eyes bored into her. Not one pair blinked, nor did a single eyelash flicker.

Teddy focused on the woman nearest to her. 'Perhaps you knew the Westheims?'

'*Nein.*'

'Did *you* know them?' Teddy said to the woman who was poised in the centre of the trio, and who was at this moment drawing on the cigarette. The woman exhaled, shook her head. '*Nein.*'

Teddy decided there was not much point in asking the third woman. These *Trümmerfrauen* were obviously not going to be of any help to her. At least, not without a little encouragement. She opened her bag, took out the packet of Lucky Strikes.

'*Die Zigarette?*' Teddy asked, offering the packet around. Each of them took one, said, '*Danke*' – but only thanks, nothing more – and carefully stowed the cigarette in their pockets.

'*I must find these people,*' Teddy began again, more emphatically, hoping for success this time. 'If you know anything at all, or have heard *anything* about them, please tell me. *Please.*' She let her intense gaze rest on each woman individually, and her eyes were full of entreaty.

There was a long moment of silence, and at last one of the women spoke. She said, 'That mansion was bombed like all of them on this street, you can see that for yourself. No one survived.'

'Some people who lived on the Tiergartenstrasse *did* survive,' one of the women swiftly contradicted, and then she volunteered, 'There's a rubble woman who works on the Lützowufer. She knew lots of people in this area before the war. Go and talk to her.'

'I will!' Teddy exclaimed, her face lighting up. 'Who is she? What's her name? How will I recognise her?'

'I don't know who she is, or her name. I've only heard about her,' the friendliest of these three now said. 'Ask around, one of the other *Trümmerfrauen* will point her out.'

'Thank you! Thank you so much!' Teddy cried. 'You've been most helpful.'

Buoyed up by renewed hope, Teddy set off at a rapid pace, and by the time she reached the bridge that led over the Landwehrkanal into the Lützowufer she was almost running. Finally, she came to a halt, and stood catching her breath, looking up and down the street. To her dismay, and further disappointment, it was even more deserted than the Tiergartenstrasse. And it was eerily silent.

Because there was little or no traffic in the Berlin streets these days, human voices were most audible, as were footsteps. But these sounds were strangely and most noticeably absent this afternoon. So was the constant chip-chip-chipping noise made by the countless *Trümmerfrauen* cleaning up the bricks and stones they were salvaging.

Teddy exhaled heavily, wondering where the rubble women were; Elizabeth had assured her that they worked seven days a week. Since she was here she decided she might as well investigate the area further, and she set off again, shivering slightly and huddling into her topcoat. A chill wind was blowing across from the Landwehrkanal, and within seconds she understood why the street was deserted. The wind was whipping the dust from the rubble up into the air. It swirled around her, settling in her hair, on her cheeks and her lips, and she blinked rapidly as it got into her eyes.

There's no point walking through *this*, she thought, it's like a sandstorm. I might as well return to the flat in Charlottenburg. And so she swung round and hurried down the Lützowufer the way she had just come, heading for the bridge. She suddenly wished she had not bothered to make this little excursion after all. It had only been a wild goose chase like the others.

The silence was suddenly broken by a piping child's voice ringing out clearly across the rubble. 'Here, Grandfather! Here's another one!'

Teddy stopped, looking around, listening.

There was no one in sight.

Then there was a burst of harsh incessant coughing, and after a moment an old man's raspy voice said, 'We have a good pile of tiles, Wilhelm. We have done very well today.'

'*Ja, ja!*' the child responded, and he sounded excited.

Teddy had no way of knowing where these disembodied voices were coming from, but they had sounded quite close. She hesitated, wondering exactly where to begin looking for the old man and the boy in this rubble, when she heard the old man's coughing again. It came from a small mountain of debris a little way ahead of her, to the right. She guessed the old man and the boy were working behind it.

Leaving the path, Teddy ventured into the rubble-strewn wasteland, and picked her way across the messy ground until she arrived at the mound. She walked around it to the other side, and stepped forward. 'Excuse me,' she said.

The old man and the boy were startled by her sudden appearance as if from nowhere; it was obvious from their faces that they had not heard her approaching.

They gaped at her, and the old man said quickly, in an aggressive, hostile voice, 'Who are you? What do you want?'

Teddy detected a certain amount of fear behind the hostility, and wanting to put him at ease she said mildly, 'I am a stranger from another city. I am looking for one of the rubble women who works here on the Lützowufer.'

'*Why?*' the old man asked.

'The *Trümmerfrauen* on the Tiergartenstrasse said she might be able to help me.'

The old man laughed with some coldness. 'How could a poor rubble woman help *you?*' he asked scathingly, his eyes running over her, swiftly assessing her, taking in her well-fed appearance, her cleanliness, and her good clothes.

'She might be able to give me information about certain people who once lived here,' Teddy explained in the same soft tone. 'I am looking for these people. The woman I seek . . . well, I understand that she knew everyone there was to know in this district before the war.'

'Maybe she did,' the old man snapped. 'I don't know. Nor do I know which rubble woman you mean. *Many* work this street, you can see what a mess it is. And they are not here today. You can also *see* that for yourself, you're not blind. *Go away!*'

'Will the women be here tomorrow?' Teddy asked patiently, with her usual persistence.

'How do I know! I am not their keeper!' the old man angrily muttered, and dropped his eyes, began to fiddle with the stack of chipped white tiles in front of him, which he and the boy had obviously been diligently collecting.

The boy had been listening attentively and closely watching Teddy during this conversation. He said plaintively, '*Bitte* . . . do you have something to eat? I'm hungry.' He put his hand out to her in a begging gesture, his expression pleading, and said again, '*Please*, do you have anything?'

Teddy looked back at him. His dark eyes were sunken hollows in his little white face, and she could not help thinking of Maxim. But this boy was not as healthy a specimen; he was small and thin and undernourished. Starving most probably, she thought. She put his age at about seven or eight, but his eyes were much older and knowing and very weary.

She opened her bag, took out a bar of chocolate and handed it to the boy without saying a word.

'*Danke!*' he cried excitedly, ripped off the silver paper and pushed the chocolate into his mouth wolfishly with both hands.

Only then did Teddy truly understand how ravenous he was.

But after only a mouthful the boy called Wilhelm suddenly stopped eating, and looked at his grandfather. He took the chocolate bar out of his mouth, broke it in two and gave half to the old man. 'Here, Grandfather, you are also hungry,' the boy said.

'*Danke*, Wilhelm.' The old man smiled at his grandson, took the chocolate and began to munch on it.

Teddy stood watching them devouring the chocolate. She had mixed feelings about the Germans these days. Her eyes came to rest on the old man and she thought: Where were *you* on *Kristallnacht*, I wonder? Where were you when they were shoving my people into the gas ovens and the torture chambers and onto the deportation trains? And what would you say now if I asked you these questions? Would you deny having been a Nazi? Would you protest that you had not known about the terrible things they did to the Jews? *But you all knew.* You and every other German were aware the camps existed. Not a single German alive today can deny that. And what would you do if you knew *I* was a *Jew*? Would you continue to eat my chocolate? Eat the chocolate of a dirty *Jew*?

Teddy curbed these thoughts immediately, before they ran on and on and got out of hand and made her angry, as they generally did once they were ignited. After all, not every German had been a Nazi, and the average person had been powerless, unequipped to do anything against Hitler and his band of gangsters. Nor had anyone understood or guessed how far these criminals would go in their persecution of the Jews. No one had anticipated the massacre of millions. To everyone, Jew and Gentile alike, the systematic killing of an entire people had been unthinkable, had seemed downright impossible.

Shifting her gaze to the little boy, Teddy also reminded herself that one should not punish the children for the sins of the fathers. Opening her handbag, she brought out the other two bars of chocolate and gave one to the boy, one to the grandfather. They both seemed startled and surprised by her generosity, although happily so, and they smiled at her and thanked her profusely.

And then the old man suddenly bowed to her in the most elaborate way, and said in a gruff voice, 'The *Trümmerfrauen* take their bricks to the storage place every Saturday afternoon. That is why they are not here, they get paid today. But they should be back again tomorrow.' There was a little pause and he finished with a thin smile, 'You see, they have nowhere else to go.'

'Come tomorrow,' the boy Wilhelm said with a huge grin, showing her his chocolate-covered teeth.

Teddy smiled at him. 'Yes, I will,' she answered, and then turning to the old man, she added, '*Danke*.'

'And we thank you, *gnädige Frau*,' the old man said with great politeness, and bowed again.

There was only one rubble woman working on the Lützowufer when Teddy returned the following morning. Deciding not to procrastinate, Teddy walked over to her purposefully and said, '*Guten Morgen.*'

The woman was standing near an old pram, piling bricks into it. She glanced up and looked at her, and then she smiled, much to Teddy's amazement, and considerable relief.

'*Guten Morgen*,' the rubble woman said, returning her greeting graciously.

Encouraged by the woman's pleasantness and approachability, Teddy went on, 'I am hoping you might be able to help me.'

'I will be happy to if I can,' the woman replied with the same courtesy as before.

Teddy said, 'Yesterday I was talking to the *Trümmerfrauen* on the Tiergartenstrasse, asking them for information about people who used to live on that street. They told me to look for a woman who worked the Lützowufer, who may well have been acquainted with them, and who might know where they are now.'

'I certainly know all of the women who clear the rubble in this vicinity. What is her name, the one for whom you are looking?'

Teddy shrugged and said, 'That's just the problem, I don't know her name . . .' Her voice trailed off lamely as she realised how ridiculous she sounded.

The woman was again bending over the decrepit pram, covering the bricks with a piece of torn linoleum. She straightened up, threw her shoulders back and tossed her head slightly, and gazed at Teddy, focusing vivid blue eyes on her. 'Then I'm afraid I cannot be of help,' the woman murmured.

To Teddy there was something strangely familiar about the voice, the sudden gesture of the head, and she gave the rubble woman a penetrating stare, swiftly noting everything about her as a distant memory stirred.

Like the other *Trümmerfrauen*, this woman had covered her hair with a scarf, had wrapped it turban-style around her head, and she wore an assortment of odd clothes. And yet despite her worn, patched coat and the man's boots on her feet, she had a distinct air of breeding about her, a certain dignity that commanded attention, and then again there were the good manners, the pleasant demeanour.

It came together in a flash all of a sudden, clicked into place in Teddy's mind, and she had to stifle a small cry of recognition. Her heart tightened and she held herself perfectly still, hardly daring to breathe, as she said slowly, 'Actually, *gnädige Frau*, I think *you* are the person I am looking for.'

The rubble woman frowned and arched a brow. 'I?' she said. 'Oh no, I don't think so. I'm sure not, in fact.'

Teddy was now absolutely certain who she was and said. 'Yes, I *do* know you. And *you* know *me*. I am Theodora Stein, Maxim's nanny!'

The rubble woman was flabbergasted and for a moment she could not speak, and then she gasped, 'Is it *you*, Teddy? Is it *really* you?'

'Yes, it's me!' Teddy cried, and she stepped forward and took hold of the chapped, work-worn hands of Princess Irina Troubetzkoy.

THIRTY-FOUR

Teddy and the Russian princess stood clasping hands and staring at each other incredulously. They were hardly able to contain their excitement, and their delight and amazement at finding each other in the devastated and war-torn city was reflected on their faces.

After a moment the princess took a sudden step forward, put her arms around Teddy and embraced her warmly, and the two women clung together in the midst of the debris on the ruined Lützowufer.

When at last they drew apart the princess exclaimed, '*Maxim*. How is he? Is he all right? He must be quite grown up by now.'

'Yes, he is,' Teddy answered. 'He's the most wonderful boy, a brilliant student. He's at a good school in England.' Teddy stared hard at the princess, and clearing her throat she said in a voice that sounded suddenly strained, 'I came to Berlin as soon as I could, to look for his parents. Do you know what happened to them?'

The smile on Princess Irina's face faded and she shook her head rapidly.

'When was the last time *you* saw them, Princess Irina?'

'In September of 1941, when they were staying with the *Graf* and *Gräfin* von Tiegal at the Schloss near Brandenburg,' Irina replied. 'This was just prior to my falling ill with bronchitis, Teddy. When I recovered, and was finally able to leave my bed, I discovered they had disappeared.'

'Had they gone into hiding somewhere? Or had they simply left the Schloss?'

'I honestly don't know. It was . . . well, it was a mystery.'

'Didn't the Count and Countess von Tiegal know anything, *Prinzessin*?'

Again Irina Troubetzkoy shook her head, and her face filled with overwhelming sadness. 'They had also vanished – as if into thin air.'

Teddy met Irina's steady gaze with alert and questioning eyes. 'Did they vanish at the same time as the Westheims? Or later?' she probed.

'Actually, I am not certain. All I know is that the four of them were not at the Schloss in November of 1941, which was when I went there hoping to see them again.'

'But surely the von Tiegals' servants knew something. There were quite a few servants, I remember, and Gretchen had a nanny, Irmgard was her name.'

'Yes, I know,' Princess Irina replied, leaning closer, giving Teddy a very direct look. 'But by 1941 all of the male servants who had been employed at the Schloss had gone off to fight the war, and the maids were in the munitions factories, or doing other war work. There was only an old housekeeper left when I went to the Schloss that day in November. She told me the *Graf* and *Gräfin* had returned to Berlin some days before, that I would find them at their flat . . . the flat *here* on the Lützowufer where we are standing now, but I didn't find them, no one was there, not even servants.'

'And the von Tiegals never showed up? You never heard from them?' Teddy asked quietly, her eyes not leaving the other woman's face.

'No. Nor did I hear from Sigmund and Ursula. Not ever again. The house on the Tiergartenstrasse had been badly bombed earlier that summer, and so obviously they had not returned there. I went next to the villa in the Wannsee to look for them, but it was deserted. Locked and shuttered.'

Teddy said, 'I visited the villa at the lake last week. My friend Mrs Anne Reynolds, who is with the International Red Cross, drove me out. I didn't expect to find the Westheims, but I felt I had to check the villa, just for my own satisfaction. Mrs Reynolds and I both spoke to the woman who is living at the villa now. We didn't get anything out of her, and she denies any knowledge of the Westheims.'

The princess nodded, and gave Teddy a pointed look. 'The villa was taken over later by a high-ranking Nazi,' she told her. 'Things like that happened all the time in those days. Bigwigs in the Third Reich stole so much from so many.'

'And especially from Jews,' Teddy said, and hesitated for a moment before murmuring more softly, 'But Princess, didn't you try to investigate the disappearance of the Westheims and the von Tiegals? Check things out through . . . through the underground, the resistance?'

'*I* was a member of one of the resistance movements, Teddy, and naturally I tried to find out if my friends had managed to leave Germany. Or if they had been arrested by the Gestapo. But I wasn't able to turn anything up, no one was. We all drew a blank. But it was not *unusual* for people to simply disappear without leaving a trace. Millions did, *millions*, Teddy. And millions are *still* missing, their fates unknown.'

'What about the rest of the Westheim family? Do you have any idea what happened to them?'

'Mrs Westheim, Sigmund's mother, died in the spring of 1940. Of natural causes . . . heart failure. She had been ill for a long time, as you know. That same year, Sigrid and her husband Thomas Mayer were killed in a bombing raid, when they were in Hamburg, and poor Hedy was in the house in the Tiergartenstrasse when it was hit in the summer of 1941. I'm afraid she died with the servants who were in the house at the time.'

On hearing this news Teddy became very quiet. She stood staring at the princess, incapable of making any sort of response. Sadness filled her and tears came into her eyes when she thought of Maxim's aunts and his Uncle Thomas. They had been so young, all of them in their twenties.

A deep sigh escaped Teddy's lips, and she said in a sorrowful voice, 'How tragic that they're *all* dead. I was fairly certain Grandmother Westheim would be gone by now – she was old and frail. But the others . . . I had hoped that one of them would still be alive . . . Oh God, it's so *hard* to accept!'

'I know it is,' the princess agreed and shook her head. Her expression was as mournful as Teddy's. 'Nobody wanted this war,' she exclaimed, anger surfacing. 'It was started by a madman, and it was so futile, so *unnecessary*, need never have happened. And look how it's taken its toll on the whole world. Millions are dead, or maimed for life, we are all suffering terribly because of it in countless different ways. Great cities throughout Europe have been destroyed, so much has been lost . . . so much is gone . . . forever.'

Teddy nodded, shifted on her feet slightly and looked off into the distance, caught up in her worried thoughts. Then she swung to face the Russian aristocrat again, and confided, 'I don't know what to do anymore, *Prinzessin* – ' She broke off, lifted her shoulders in a gesture of helplessness. 'I've been to all the appropriate agencies, the International Red Cross, Jewish and Zionist organisations, and the Quakers, to no avail. I've studied their many lists, gone over list after list of names, in fact, and neither the Westheims nor the von Tiegals are on any of them. It's so strange, it doesn't make any sense, how can they have just . . . *vanished*?'

'So many did, Teddy, I've tried to explain that.' The princess touched her arm lightly, and continued, 'Let us not stand here like this. It would be much better if we went to my little abode to talk.' She swung around, put her red, chafed hands on the old pram and began to push it ahead of her, saying, as she trundled it along, 'We will go to my house. It is not a grand place, but it is reasonably comfortable and it will certainly be much warmer than standing out here.'

'Yes, it's colder this morning than it has been since I arrived in Berlin,' Teddy remarked, and followed the princess through the rubble, glancing around, looking for any sort of dwelling, however humble. But there were no houses standing, nor any other kind of structures visible for that matter.

As she drew alongside her, Teddy could not help saying, 'And where do you live, Princess Irina? Where is your house?'

'Oh you can't see it from here,' Irina Troubetzkoy answered with a curious little laugh. 'I call it my *house*, but my little abode is actually a hole in the ground.'

'*Oh.*' Teddy was so startled to hear this she was completely at a loss for words.

They had not gone much farther when the princess suddenly drew to a halt, and pointed to a crater a few steps in front of them.

'*That* is my hole! I live down there . . . like a troglodyte.' Irina looked at Teddy through the corner of her eye and went on, 'Don't be alarmed, it's not quite as dreadful as it sounds. Now . . . I shall leave my bricks here for the moment, and deal with them later.'

The princess pushed the pram over to a heap of debris near the crater, knelt down, and began carefully to wedge stones around the front wheels.

Teddy also knelt, helped to put the stones in place, and stole a glance at Irina as she did. '*Prinzessin?*'

'Yes?'

'Why are you a rubble woman?'

Irina Troubetzkoy lifted her head, rather proudly, and rested her bright blue eyes on Teddy. She said, very simply, 'Because I have nothing else to do.' She gave a little sigh, then explained, 'Besides, I get paid for the bricks, and I also get extra food rations.' With a small smile, she went on, 'And there is another reason, another consideration. I feel as though I am doing something useful and worthwhile, something for the future, by reclaiming the bricks with which Berlin can eventually be rebuilt. It gives me, and the other rubble women too, a sense of purpose. And a stake in the future.'

'Yes,' Teddy said, nodding her head. 'Yes, yes, I see what you mean.' But she could not help thinking how different Princess Irina Troubetzkoy's life would have been if the Russian Revolution had not happened. Her mother, the Princess Natalie, had been born a Romanov and was the cousin of Tsar Nicholas, and Irina would have led an existence of ease and comfort and privilege at the Russian court. She certainly would not have been scrabbling around in the ruins of Berlin, salvaging bricks and living in a hole in the ground.

The princess scrambled to her feet, stared down at Teddy who had remained kneeling in the rubble, and beckoned. 'Come!' she cried, and moving to the crater she stepped over the edge and disappeared from view.

Teddy stifled a cry, jumped up and ran after her, looked into the crater with trepidation, and saw that there was a steep flight of stone steps leading to the bottom. The steps were half-shattered, and she realised that they had been badly damaged by bombs. The princess was carefully manoeuvring her way down them.

Taking a deep breath, Teddy followed her.

'These steps used to lead from the kitchen to the cellars in my step-father's house when it was standing,' Irina informed her. 'And as you can see they're all that's left of the Herr Baron's mansion now, except for my little home, of course, which is through the door straight ahead.'

THIRTY-FIVE

The princess pulled an iron key out of her coat pocket and opened the heavy wood door. 'Wait here for a moment, please Teddy, whilst I light the oil lamps,' she said, and stepped inside.

A moment later the princess was calling, 'Come in, come in,' and Teddy entered.

She found herself standing in a little cellar.

This was illuminated by the lamps which had just been lit by Irina, which flickered brightly in the murky light of the interior. Teddy blinked several times, adjusting her eyes, and then looked around, filled with curiosity.

The ugly cellar was furnished sparsely. An ancient threadbare sofa with sagging springs was set against the back wall, flanked on either side by small, dark wood tables on which the oil lamps stood, and a couple of armchairs faced the sofa. In the centre of this grouping was a large wooden packing crate with a lace doily on top of it, and apparently this served as a coffee table. Against another wall rested an old-fashioned sideboard which had seen better days; on its top were a pile of books, a fat white candle in a carved wooden candlestick, and some chipped, white china cups and saucers.

It seemed to Teddy that the princess had tried to give the cellar some warmth and cosiness, a few homely touches. A worn Oriental rug covered the concrete floor, several stained and crumpled red-velvet cushions dressed up the dark-blue brocade sofa, and a faded plaid blanket was thrown over the back of one of the armchairs. On the packing crate stood a bedraggled little bunch of artificial flowers in a jamjar. There was something pathetically touching about these grubby imitations of the real thing, and Teddy's eyes lingered, and for a reason she could not explain a lump came into her throat as she looked at them.

The princess had been keenly observing Teddy, and moving forward into the centre of the cellar, she said swiftly, in a brisk voice, 'It's not much, I know, but it's better than what most Berliners have these days. Many of them are walking around carrying their possessions in paper bags, and camping out in the ruins, the best way they can. *I am lucky.* This place is dry, and, most importantly, it's safe. And I soon get it warm with the paraffin stove. Are you cold, Teddy? I will light the stove, if you are.'

'No, no!' Teddy exclaimed. 'I don't want you to waste your precious fuel on me. I'll keep my overcoat on.'

'So will I,' the princess said, 'such as it is.' She chuckled, glanced down at the shabby, oversized man's coat that was far too big for her, pulled it around her tightly, almost possessively, and added, 'This belonged to my stepfather, and I look dreadful in it, but it *is* warm.' Gesturing to a chair, she hurried on, 'Now, Teddy, please do sit down. I would like to offer you some sort of refreshments, however I don't really have much. Still, let me see what I can find.'

'Thank you, but I don't want anything, Princess Irina, really I don't, I'm fine,' Teddy assured her, and sat down in one of the chairs, took off her woollen gloves and stuffed them in her pocket, unwrapped her long tartan scarf, let it dangle loosely around her neck.

The princess took a seat on the sofa, opposite Teddy, and airily waved one hand around the cellar. 'This was a storage room, a vault really. The baron used it for silver, porcelain, and household valuables of that sort,' she explained. 'Through there – ' she motioned to the door near the sideboard ' – is the wine cellar, although there's no wine in it anymore. The bottles were smashed in the raids, and the wine cave is now . . . my bedroom!'

Teddy nodded, eyeing everything with interest, and then asked, 'Did you manage to salvage this furniture from the wreckage of the mansion?'

'Oh no, there wasn't much left of the house, or its contents, not after the Allies had bombed us eighty-two times in as many days. These sorry pieces were already down here. My stepfather had turned the two storage cellars into air-raid shelters for us, and the household staff, in 1940. So you see, my little abode was ready and waiting for me after the house was hit the last time. That was when it was completely demolished.'

'The baron . . . Princess Natalie . . .' Teddy stopped, suddenly wondering if she ought to continue. Perhaps the princess's mother and stepfather had been killed; she had no wish to upset her.

Immediately recognising Teddy's dilemma, Irina said hastily, 'It's all right, they are perfectly well, thank goodness. My mother and stepfather are living in the gardener's cottage on one of the baron's estates near Baden-Baden in the Black Forest. Naturally, the castle itself is closed up for the time being, it's too difficult for Helmut to run it without staff, fuel and other supplies.'

'I'm glad to hear they're both in good health, and were not hurt.' Teddy glanced around the dank, gloomy cellar, and suggested quietly, 'Wouldn't you be better off living in the country with them, Princess Irina?'

'Not at all!' Irina shook her head vehemently, and frowned at the mere idea of this. Unexpectedly, a peal of laughter broke free, and she said, through her chuckles, 'They are an odd couple, the Russian princess and the Prussian baron. They are like . . . a couple of love birds, yes, I do believe that is the best way to describe them. And they much prefer to be on their own, I am quite certain of this. Besides, the cottage is small, and, as they say, three's a crowd.' Irina sat back, crossed her long legs, thought to add, 'I like being in Berlin, in the centre of things, difficult though living here is these days. And at least I'm not in the Russian Zone.'

'Mrs Reynolds told me there's still a lot of rape going on, that it's not safe for women in the Red Sector.'

'And especially a White Russian such as myself! Can you imagine how the Bolsheviks would treat me!' Irina cried. 'When they first captured the city in May, I was terrified. I hid in here for weeks, until the British, French and Americans came in to occupy their zones . . . Enough of this, I am safe now.'

Teddy looked thoughtful for a moment, before saying, 'But things are not especially easy for you, Princess Irina, even though you do have a roof over your head. I know food is short and I would like to come tomorrow with some groceries, a few luxuries. I know Mrs Reynolds will gladly give them to me, she will want to help you, too, when she knows of your plight.'

'That's not necessary, but thank you anyway, Teddy, it was kind of you to offer. I do manage fairly well, and when I feel the need I occasionally make a purchase in the Tiergarten.'

'The Tiergarten?' Teddy repeated, sounding puzzled, giving the princess a quizzical look.

'There is a very active black market in the park,' Irina explained. 'For a price, one can buy butter, coffee, tea, chocolate bars, cigarettes and toothpaste. Many things.'

'Even so, I would like to bring you some of those items. It's no trouble, really it isn't. I want to do *something* to help you. Please let me,' she begged.

'Very well, Teddy, and thank you.' The princess inclined her head graciously and a pleased expression settled on her face. 'That is very, very kind of you. But then one does have to rely on the kindness of friends in times of great difficulty such as these,' she said, and smiled warmly.

Teddy returned her smile. 'I have wonderful friends in London who helped me to come here to look for Herr and Frau Westheim. Do you have good friends, Princess? I mean in Berlin?'

'One or two are still left. Unfortunately, and very sadly, most of my friends have not survived the war.' Irina leaned her head against the back of the sofa and closed her eyes, and when she opened them they were dark with pain, and sudden tears glistened on her lashes.

Teddy could not miss the look of suffering on Irina's face, now so pale and drawn in the lamplight, and her heart went out to her. 'I'm so sorry,' she said. 'So very sorry, Princess Irina.'

'My friends were murdered, tragically murdered – ' Irina Troubetzkoy's voice started to tremble and she faltered, was unable to continue speaking. She began to weep silently. After a second or two, she reached into her pocket and pulled out a piece of grubby rag, wiped her eyes with it.

'Forgive me,' she apologised, forcing a smile, but it was a weak one. 'I didn't mean to break down this way, but your kindness touched me, and when I thought of my poor friends – ' Irina cut herself off, closed her eyes once more, repeatedly sighing to herself, as if her sorrow was too much for her to bear.

Teddy sat watching the princess, waiting for her to recover her equilibrium, knowing there was not much she could do or say to help her assuage her grief. And for the second time that morning she could not help thinking what a hard and painful life this aristocratic Russian woman had led. Scrutinising her face in the lambent light, Teddy noted its fine structure, the good bones, the perfectly shaped mouth and chin, and the smooth, wide forehead, the symmetrical auburn brows above those startlingly blue eyes. There were webs of fine lines around her eyes and her mouth now, but she was still a beautiful woman. Teddy guessed she must be thirty-three or thereabouts, yet she looked older. No wonder, Teddy thought, after what she's been through.

Suddenly the princess sat up straighter and threw Teddy a quick glance. 'Kurt von Wittingen and I worked together in the resistance, and we had a good friend, Admiral Canaris . . . Wilhelm Canaris. It was the admiral who helped to get Ursula, Maxim and you out of Germany. Did you know that?'

'Frau Westheim told me.'

'Wilhelm Canaris is dead,' Irina announced quietly. 'He loathed and detested Hitler, and everything that that criminal stood for, and inevitably he paid for his beliefs with his life.' She focused her attention on a distant corner of the cellar, momentarily lost in her own ruminations, and a few minutes elapsed before she carried on slowly, 'The admiral certainly took breathtaking risks in order to help the resistance, to help us aid those victims of the Nazis whom we were so desperately trying to save – ' Irina broke off, left her sentence unfinished.

Teddy was watching her closely, and she saw an agonised look cross her face. She suddenly knew that the princess harboured some awful knowledge that she did not dare guess at, and she felt a shiver run through her. She held herself very still, waiting.

Rising jerkily, all of a sudden, Irina crossed to the sideboard, opened a drawer and took out a packet of cigarettes. Swinging to face Teddy, she asked, 'Do you smoke? Would you like one of these?'

Teddy shook her head. 'No, thank you, and please take this.' Opening her bag, Teddy took out a packet of Lucky Strikes, and put them on the packing crate next to the jamjar of faded silk flowers. 'I hadn't realised you smoked, I would have given them to you before.'

'My thanks, Teddy,' Irina said, gratefully accepting the precious little gift. She walked back to the sofa, sat down again, lit one of the Lucky Strikes, and started to speak about Wilhelm Canaris. 'The admiral was arrested last summer, the summer of 1944, and accused of treason against the Third Reich.' There was a short pause as she puffed on her cigarette, and in a low voice she told Teddy, 'He was hanged at Flossenburg concentration camp in April of this year, ironically just a short time before the Allies liberated the camp.'

'How tragic that the Americans arrived too late to save him. It's heartbreaking even to think about,' Teddy said, and immediately fell silent, pondering on the sad demise of this courageous man.

The princess was also quiet for a few moments, drawing on her cigarette, lost in her thoughts, surrounded by a haze of smoke. Eventually she took a deep breath, and remarked in a precise and careful voice, wanting to give weight to her words, 'I hope they are beginning to understand in England that there were some very brave men in Germany, men who fought Hitler and his henchmen with all their might and tried to stop them. Men of great honour and integrity who wanted to save others from being destroyed by that foul regime of evilness and tyranny, who tried very hard to overthrow Hitler and the Nazis, and who ultimately lost their lives in so doing.'

'Yes, they do know now,' Teddy assured her. 'I've recently been reading things in the papers about the German resistance, and I also read about Admiral Canaris's execution. The British papers called him a hero, *Prinzessin*.'

'He was indeed.'

'Maxim and I owe him our lives,' Teddy said softly.

'True, yes, you do. But other people were involved in helping you to escape. Do you remember the colonel who travelled in your compartment on the train from Berlin to Aachen?'

'Colonel Oster,' Teddy said. 'Frau Westheim told me who he was, after we crossed the border into Belgium.'

'He was on the train to keep an eye on you, to make sure all of you were safe, and that you got away. He, too, was a brave man. He was the admiral's assistant in German Military Intelligence, close to him, and most especially so because of their mutual hatred of the Nazis.'

Irina stubbed out her cigarette, sat back, folding her hands in her lap. She stared down at them. The events of the past few years were forever fresh and vivid in her mind, could never be forgotten. Without looking up, she confided, 'There was a plot to assassinate Hitler in 1944 – imagine, just last year, yet it seems so long ago now, perhaps because so much has happened lately. It was called the July Twentieth Plot and it did not succeed, went horribly awry, unfortunately. Hitler was only *wounded*, not killed, as had been planned, even though Count Klaus von Stauffenberg placed the briefcase holding the bomb only twelve feet away from him. Despite his injuries, Hitler survived, and some of the plotters were captured immediately. Colonel von Stauffenberg was shot that same evening . . . at midnight in the courtyard of the War Ministry.'

The princess reached for another cigarette, and proceeded with her story: 'The Gestapo thought Colonel Oster was involved, and he was arrested that month, held at Gestapo Headquarters in the Prinz Albrechtstrasse. We were sure he was being horribly tortured. In fact, we were quite positive they were all being tortured . . .'

'Who were the others?' Teddy asked in a whisper, hardly able to breathe.

'Adam von Trott zu Solz, Gottfried Bismarck, Fritzi Schulenberg, many others. None of those men broke under torture, they did not give our names or implicate us. No, they did not give us away . . .' Irina Troubetzkoy stared into Teddy's eyes, and confessed, 'I was deeply,

deeply involved with the plotters, who were all my friends, but I was never arrested. They died protecting me, and other men and women as well.'

'Oh, Princess Irina, how courageous of you! But you could easily have been killed yourself!' Teddy cried, and then she remembered that Irina had always appeared intrepid to her, and had carried her fearlessness like a proud banner in the past. Ursula Westheim had called her an heroic woman.

Irina nodded. 'Yes, I could have died,' she agreed. 'But I didn't. *I was left to mourn.*'

There was a little silence; the cellar was deathly quiet.

Teddy wanted to mention Prince Kurt von Wittingen, to ask about his fate, but before she could, Irina started to speak again, as if it was a great relief to unburden herself to someone.

She said, in the softest of tones, 'So many of my friends *were* executed in the end, and some died most horribly. Adam von Trott was hung from a meat hook with piano wire, and died very slowly of strangulation, in Plötzensee Prison in August of last year. And, Teddy, can you believe that they actually took photographs and made films of the meat-hook deaths to show to Hitler. *Sadists!* Hans Oster was hanged in Flossenburg this past April, at the same time as Admiral Canaris. My heart bleeds for them all. I will never forget any of them. I think of each one every day, and I will, until the day *I* die.'

Teddy was so shocked, so profoundly affected by the things she had just heard, that she could not speak for a while, and when she did her voice was choked. 'What a tragic, tragic waste. The world must be told about these horrendous deeds as they have been told about the camps. And it must never be allowed to happen again.'

'No, it must not. None of it.' Turning to look at Teddy, Irina took a deep breath, and said, 'At least Hitler is dead. Although I can't help wishing he hadn't committed suicide in his bunker in April, that he could have been arrested by the Allies, and properly tried for his crimes against humanity, along with the other criminals. The four-power international tribunal begins in Nuremberg next month, and the whole world is watching. *Justice must be done.* It *must* be done, in the name of those millions who died, to ensure that they did not die in vain.'

'It will be, don't worry,' Teddy said confidently. 'Those monsters are not going to walk, to get off scot free. They're all going to be punished, to swing at the end of ropes. Hanging is too good for them, in my opinion.'

'An eye for an eye, a tooth for a tooth,' Irina muttered almost to herself.

Leaning forward urgently, Teddy focused her eyes on the other woman and said tremulously, in a worried tone, 'You haven't mentioned Prince Kurt von Wittingen . . . *he* wasn't captured and executed as well, was he?'

'Not by the Nazis.' Irina's bright blue eyes clouded over, and she took a long draw on the Lucky Strike she was holding before elucidating further. 'Actually, Teddy, no one really knows what has happened to him. Kurt was in Berlin this summer. I didn't see him myself, but another member of our resistance group, Wolfgang Schroeder, did. Wolfgang exchanged greetings with Kurt, and a couple of days later he saw him again. This time talking to some Russian officers in that part of Berlin which is now the East Zone. But Kurt has never been seen by anyone since then. He just vanished.'

'Like the Westheims and the von Tiegals did.'

Irina made no response to this comment at first, then she murmured quietly, 'It wasn't quite the same.'

'Do *you* think the prince is dead?' Teddy asked.

'He might be. When Kurt did not surface at the end of the war, we thought that perhaps he had been injured in the last-ditch fighting. Some of it was still going on, even after the Russians had overrun the city and taken it. And so we searched every hospital. Berlin was turned upside down, and many people were questioned. Another member of our resistance group, Dieter Müller, made a second and more thorough search, but Kurt was never found. Nor was his body.'

'Could it . . . could the prince's body be buried under the rubble?' Teddy ventured, recalling what Anne Reynolds had told her about the bodies rotting in the ruins of the city and in the river.

'That's always possible, of course,' Irina conceded. 'But Dieter Müller has another theory. He believes that Kurt was arrested by those Russian officers whom Wolfgang Schroeder spotted him with. Perhaps on that very day.'

Teddy sat poised on the edge of her seat. She had listened attentively and was full of questions. But she asked the princess the most obvious one. 'Whyever would the Russians want to arrest Prince Kurt von Wittingen?'

'Perhaps because they thought he was a spy,' Irina suggested. 'More precisely, a spy for the Americans, and that would surely make him an enemy of the Soviet Union. They're very paranoid, you know, these Bolsheviks, especially about the Americans. In that respect they take after their leader, Josef Stalin, another tyrant with blood on his hands.'

'And *you*? What is *your* opinion? Do you believe that the prince was arrested?'

'I simply don't know, Teddy. I wish I did.'

'I went to the von Wittingen house the other day . . . and of course you know that it is no more. Like the rest of Berlin, it's a pile of rubble. Is Princess Arabella in Zurich?'

'Yes, she is. She came back to Berlin as soon as she could this summer, but with Kurt missing, her home destroyed and nowhere to live, there was nothing here for her. She returned to Switzerland with Diana and Christian.'

'I thought perhaps she had done.'

'Arabella is . . . Well, to be truthful, she's not herself anymore. Since Kurt's disappearance, her mind has – she's a little confused at times.'

Teddy looked stricken. 'How *dreadful*. I'm very sorry to hear that. Poor woman, she's such a good person, and she's always so nice with everyone. Anyway, at least she has the children.'

'Diana and Christian are a great comfort to her, yes.'

The two women did not speak for a while, drifted with their own thoughts. Finally, it was Irina who broke the silence which had settled between them.

'Oh dear, all we have spoken about are sad things, Theodora. Painful things. And when we haven't seen each other for six very long and trying years. It's my fault, of course, I'm the one who's been doing most of the talking.' Irina sat forward with a certain eagerness, and suddenly, with a lovely smile, exclaimed, 'I want to hear all about you and Maxim and the life you've made in London! *Everything* now, you mustn't miss anything out.'

'I won't,' Teddy promised, also smiling. 'And actually I do have a lot to tell you.' She reached into her bag, searched for the packet of snaps, and when she found this she glanced up and said, 'I have some beautiful photos of Maxim, I brought them with me for his parents. They're going to be so proud of him when they see him again. He's very grown up, the most wonderful boy.'

Irina Troubetzkoy could not speak.

She stood up unsteadily and walked across the floor to the sideboard where, with shaking hands, she made a pretence of looking for something in a drawer. It was imperative that Teddy did not see the anguish on her face, the tears which blinded her.

THIRTY-SIX

It was late in the afternoon when Teddy returned to the cellar on the Lützowufer the following day.

The princess had obviously been waiting for her and the door was opened instantly, after only one knock. Teddy found herself being greeted cordially and ushered into the little abode, as the princess insisted on calling the cellar.

To Teddy it was a miserable hole in the ground, dark, damp, fusty and insanitary, and she could not bear to think of anyone living there, especially Princess Irina Troubetzkoy. Yet Teddy knew she was powerless to help her change her lot in life, at least at this moment. She had spoken at length about the princess to Anne Reynolds last night, who had promised to keep an eye on her, and if possible make her life a bit easier whenever she could, and this had pleased Teddy.

Irina had lit the paraffin stove earlier and the cellar did not seem as cold and as damp as it had been yesterday, even though it was a rainy day; the candle and the two oil lamps burned brightly and added to the feeling of warmth, the illusion of cosiness.

After helping Teddy off with her coat, Irina said, 'I thought you might like a little *Schnaps*. It will warm you, Teddy, it's awfully cold out there this afternoon.' She waved her hand in the direction of the sideboard, and then carefully placed Teddy's coat over a chair back.

Teddy glanced at the sideboard and saw that the princess had put out two chipped crystal glasses and a much-depleted bottle of *Kirschwasser* from the Black Forest. 'Thank you, that would be nice,' she answered, even though she did not feel like cherry brandy right now. On the other hand, she did not want to offend the princess, who had obviously gone to a lot of trouble to spruce up the cellar, make it more inviting. And the precious *drop* of *Kirschwasser*, which was all there was left in the bottle, was yet another kind gesture from a woman in the most pitiful of circumstances.

'However, before we have a drink I would first like to give you this,' Teddy said, picking up the shopping bag which she had put down on the floor when she had entered the cellar. 'I *was* able to get a few things for you, Princess Irina.'

'How kind of you, Teddy,' the princess said, her eyes lighting up.

Carrying the bag over to the sideboard, Teddy began to take out some food, saying as she did, 'Here's a packet of Typhoo tea, real coffee, chocolate biscuits – delicious American ones, too – a loaf of bread, and a quarter of butter. Then there's some tinned items. Spam, corned beef, salmon, and sardines, all from the American PX, and a tin of powdered egg, one of powdered milk. Plus a few other things in the bottom of the bag. Come and look.'

'My goodness!' Irina exclaimed, sounding flabbergasted. She had not expected such a large quantity of food stuff, and her face was a picture of gratitude as she joined Teddy near the sideboard. Almost reverently, she touched the items which Teddy had already unpacked before peeking into the bag. Then she turned to Teddy in astonishment. 'Toothpaste, toilet soap, and . . . Oh Teddy, how wonderful! A tube of Max Factor lipstick and Apple Blossom toilet water! Thank you, thank you.' She took a step closer and embraced Teddy affectionately, gave her a warm smile.

Teddy said, 'I'm glad to help you in any way I can, Princess Irina.'

'And where in heaven's name did you get all of these wonderful things?'

'From Mrs Reynolds, of the International Red Cross, the lady I told you about, and her secretary, Elizabeth Jefford. They both gave me some of their own rations, and Mrs Reynolds was also able to get a few extra things for you from her friend, Major Evans, who's with the American Occupation Forces. It was the major who contributed the red lipstick, Princess. And Mrs Reynolds gave me the toilet water for you.'

'How very generous and kind of them. You must thank them all for me. Imagine, lipstick!'

'I think you're more thrilled about the lipstick than the food,' Teddy exclaimed and began to laugh.

Irina also laughed. 'Not really,' she said. 'But it's a treat to have something truly feminine after all this time, and years of deprivations of all kinds. Now, shall we have the Schnaps?'

'That would be nice.' Teddy walked over to the sofa where she seated herself, and sat watching the princess pour the cherry brandy into the liqueur glasses.

This afternoon Irina Troubetzkoy looked more like the woman she had been before the war, almost her old self, Teddy thought. She wore a black wool dress, old-fashioned, very dated and obviously from the 1930s, thick black stockings and sturdy black walking shoes. Nonetheless, despite the drabness of the clothes, there was a certain elegance about her, a special kind of dignity which had a lot to do with her aristocratic bearing. Her hair was as magnificent as it had always been – a wonderful, burnished auburn, and, surprisingly, there were only a few sprinklings of silver amongst its luxuriant waves. She found a way to wash it today, Teddy thought. Irina's face was also scrubbed and shining, not dust-covered as it had been the day before when Teddy had found her working in the rubble. And the princess looked her real age, not a woman in her late forties which she had appeared to be yesterday; in the flickering lamplight she was as beautiful as she had ever been.

Irina gave Teddy the glass of Kirschwasser, and said, 'I would like to toast you, Teddy, to say many, many congratulations on your engagement to be married.' She clinked her little glass against Teddy's, and added, 'I was so pleased when you told me about it.'

'Thank you very much.' Teddy took a swallow of the liqueur, being careful not to drink from the chipped side of the glass.

The princess also sipped her drink, then went and sat down in one of the chairs facing the sofa.

Reaching forward, Teddy put her glass on the packing crate, opened her handbag and took out a small photograph in a leather frame. 'I only had snaps of Maxim with me yesterday,' she explained. 'This is Mark, my fiancé.' As she spoke she handed the picture to the princess.

'And what a nice looking young man he is too, Teddy,' Irina said, looking at the photograph. 'And obviously very brave, if these decorations on his uniform are anything to go by.'

'He was in the Battle of Britain.'

The princess nodded and handed the frame back to her. 'After you left yesterday morning, I remembered that you had been going out with Professor Herzog's son before the war. I believe they lived further down on the Lützowufer. As I recall, the young man went to Palestine in 1939 . . . whatever happened to him?'

'Willy is his name, and he didn't stay very long in Palestine. He moved on, went to Shanghai. He's still there, but hoping to go to America one day,' Teddy told her. 'We wrote to each other regularly, and I never thought of another man until I met Mark. He and I truly fell in love, and it was only then that I realised I had to write to Willy and end our unofficial engagement.'

'And was Willy Herzog heartbroken?'

Teddy shook her head and gave a little laugh. 'No, he wasn't. He was rather relieved. He wrote back to congratulate me and explained that he, too, had met someone else, and had been wondering how to break the news to *me*. So, no broken hearts, and we have remained good friends. Actually, I should think Willy is married by now.'

'And when are you planning to marry, Teddy?' the princess asked, and took a sip of the cherry brandy she was holding.

'Oh not yet for a while. I couldn't possibly get married without Frau and Herr Westheim being present. Mark understands that we have to wait until I find them, or until they get in touch with me, as I know they will.'

Irina Troubetzkoy sat straighter in the chair, gaping at Teddy. She did not say a word, simply sat there staring blankly, and her face turned very pale.

Teddy noticed the sudden change in her and asked in a concerned tone, 'What's the matter? Are you ill? Don't you feel well?'

Still the princess did not speak, and then, at last, she said faintly, 'No,
I don't. But I'll be all right. Just give me a moment . . .' She placed the
chipped liqueur glass on the packing crate and she saw that her hand
trembled as she did so. Clasping her fingers together to stop them shaking,
she bent forward from the waist, focused her gaze on Teddy.

Returning the princess's gaze, Teddy couldn't help thinking that her
eyes looked more startlingly blue than ever and very beautiful. Then
she noticed they were glittering with tears, and that her face had turned
whiter, was as white as chalk.

'Princess Irina, what's wrong? Whatever is it?'

'I have not told you the truth,' the princess said in a voice pitched low.
'Whilst I have not exactly lied to you, I have been less than honest.'
She shook her head and made a small, self-deprecating grimace with her
mouth. 'Why do I make excuses for myself? Why do I say that I have not
lied to you, when I have? I have lied by omission.'

'What . . . do . . . you . . . mean?' Teddy asked nervously, slowly
dragging the words out. They seemed to be stuck in her throat. She
leaned forward herself, and frowned, examining the princess's face. And
at that moment she had a premonition and a terrible sense of dread swept
over her.

'I omitted – ' The princess stopped, took a deep breath, continued in a
quick rush of words, 'I omitted to tell you something, Teddy. Something
I know about Sigmund and Ursula. Something I ought to have told you
yesterday. I was going to several times, but my courage failed me.'

'What?' Teddy cried, her voice rising shrilly. 'Tell me! Oh please
tell me!'

'Teddy dear . . . Teddy . . . you're not going to find them. And they won't
find you, as you keep insisting they will. Ursula and Sigmund are not
refugees trying to get back to Berlin, and they're not about to be released
from the camps.' Irina said very shakily, 'They're not coming back. Not
ever coming back.'

The princess now rose quickly and went to sit on the sofa, and she
took Teddy's hand in hers, wanting to help her.

Teddy's mouth had begun to tremble and her eyes were wide and staring
in her face, which was strained, pale with shock. She grabbed Irina's hand
strongly and peered deeply into her eyes, and said in a strangled voice,
'They're dead, aren't they? Ursula and Sigmund Westheim are dead.'

The princess inclined her head. 'Yes,' she acknowledged in a whisper,
and drew Teddy into her arms, held her close, with one hand pressed to
her head.

Teddy was weeping uncontrollably. 'I knew, really . . . deep down
inside. I think I always knew,' she sobbed, choking on her words. 'I

was always so afraid for them. They had a million to one chance of making it. I knew they wouldn't . . . but I couldn't admit it.'

Irina cradled Teddy like a child and tried to soothe her, to console and comfort her, and the two women clung to each other. But at one moment Teddy pulled away and cried out, '*Oh God, why them? Why did it have to be them?*'

Irina Troubetzkoy shook her head. She had no answer for her, just as she had no answer for herself.

The sobbing of the two women slowly began to lessen, and finally it stopped completely. They drew apart, sat up, and wiped their eyes.

Teddy asked quietly, 'Where . . . where did they die?'

Brushing her damp cheeks with one hand, Irina said, 'Sigmund died in Buchenwald. In 1942.'

'Are you sure?'

The princess nodded. 'Kurt von Wittingen found out. Somehow . . . through the Krupp works at Essen . . . a group of inmates from Buchenwald were sent to work at one of Krupp's slave camps. Mostly women. One of them, a Polish countess, had known Sigi in Berlin. She had seen him in Buchenwald, and passed on word of his execution. He was shot.' Tears filled Irina's eyes again, and she pressed one hand to her mouth, choking back a sob. After a moment, she managed to say, 'Kurt was able to find things out all the time. But he couldn't always do anything about what he knew. Only occasionally could he do that.'

Teddy pressed back her tears, and asked, '*Ursula?* Was she in Buchenwald?'

'No. Ravensbrück. She died there in 1943.'

'You're sure?'

'Yes, I am. A member of our resistance group, Maria Langen, was imprisoned in Ravensbrück from 1943 until the summer of 1944, when she was unexpectedly released. She knew Ursula and Renata in the camp. They were there together. Renata died in Ravensbrück too.'

'Were they shot? How did they die?'

Irina bit her lip and began to blink. She averted her head, swallowing repeatedly, sat gazing straight in front of her, and she held herself very still.

'*Please,*' Teddy said. '*I must know.*'

Irina swung to face her, gave her a very direct look, and the tears could no longer be held back. They fell out of Irina's eyes and splashed down her face onto her hands in her lap.

In a voice that was barely a whisper, Irina said, 'She was beaten to death.'

'Oh my God, no! No! No! No! Not Ursula,' Teddy shouted, half rising from the sofa. 'Oh God, no, I can't bear it! I can't bear it!' She was seized by a terrible weeping as the horror of Ursula's agonising death struck at her, and at the thought of her suffering Teddy doubled over, in agony herself, and wrapped her arms around her body. And she went on weeping until there were no tears left to weep, rocking backwards and forwards, filled with pain.

Irina sat with her arm resting around Teddy's shoulders, endeavouring to comfort her whilst knowing there was no comfort to give. And the two women mourned for Ursula and Sigmund, and shared their overwhelming grief.

It took Teddy a long time to calm down, but eventually she was able to take control of herself and her swimming senses. She reached for the *Schnaps*, and after swallowing some of it she asked softly, in a subdued tone, 'How did Renata von Tiegal die? Was it . . . the same way? Do you know?'

'Renata *was* badly beaten. But she died from a burst appendix. It was neglected, she had no treatment, peritonitis set in and she was suddenly gone. This was a few months after Ursula had died.'

Teddy bit her lip, and looked away, at last managed to ask, 'And what about Reinhard von Tiegal?'

'We never found out what happened to him.'

'Then he could still be alive,' Teddy suggested, hope rising.

'I doubt it. Renata told Maria Langen in Ravensbrück that the four of them had left Schloss Tiegal because they had been warned they were going to be arrested. Sigi and Ursula because they were Jews, Renata and Reinhard because they were sheltering Jews. And also, because the Gestapo apparently believed Reinhard was a member of one of the resistance groups, which he was, of course.'

'And they didn't make it to a safe place,' Teddy stated quietly.

'No, they didn't. They only got as far as Potsdam, when they were arrested. Renata and Ursula were taken to Ravensbrück. They never found out where Reinhard and Sigi had been sent.'

'But why weren't any of their names on the lists with the various agencies I visited?' Teddy wondered out loud, looking at Irina, frowning in bafflement.

'I don't know,' Irina answered, and shook her head very slowly, helplessly lifted her shoulders. 'We all know how zealous the Nazis were about making lists of those they arrested, lists of the numbers they had tattooed on the wrists of their victims. But in the same way, they were equally zealous in destroying their lists, once defeat was upon them, and when the Allies started liberating the camps.' She repeated, 'I just don't know how to explain it, Teddy. Their names had to have been on the camp lists which were destroyed by the Nazis.'

'Yes.' Teddy looked at Irina alertly. 'Your friend Maria Langen from the resistance group . . . is it possible . . . could I go and see her, talk to her? Perhaps she could tell me more . . .'

'Unfortunately she died earlier this year. God knows how she survived as long as she did. Poor Maria had been so mistreated she never properly recovered.'

Teddy leaned against the sofa and said nothing.

Suddenly there was nothing to say.

She closed her eyes and fell down into her memories; she saw Ursula's lovely face, heard her sweet and gentle voice, and a cry rose in her throat. She pushed it back and squeezed her eyes more tightly shut, holding back the tears. She could not bear to think of the horrifying way Ursula had died, so cruelly beaten and tortured beyond endurance. And she knew then that she would never be able to expunge the brutality of Ursula's death from her mind. It would haunt her for as long as she lived.

THIRTY-SEVEN

'You'll be quite comfortable in here, Miss Stein,' Mr Johnson of the Rossiter Merchant Bank said, showing her into the small private room. 'And if you would kindly sign this card, I will bring your safety deposit box to you immediately.'

'Thank you, Mr Johnson,' Teddy said, and, sitting down at the table, she signed the authorisation card he put in front of her, and gave it back to him.

The bank official smiled pleasantly and went out.

Teddy sat back in the chair, waiting for him to return, staring at the painting on the wall opposite, but not really seeing it. The conversation she had just had with Henry Rossiter occupied her thoughts.

Mr Rossiter had been saddened to hear the dire news she had brought back from Berlin, but she realised now that he had not appeared to be unduly surprised to learn that the Westheims were dead. After offering her his condolences in a gentle and concerned way, he had told her that she was now Maxim's guardian until he was twenty-one years old.

'This was Mrs Westheim's express wish,' the head of the bank explained. 'The letter which you brought to me from her, when you first arrived in England in 1939, confirmed a telephone conversation which she and I had about this matter, just a week prior to your arrival. I thought you would like to see that letter now.' Henry Rossiter had passed it across the desk, she had perused it quickly, and had handed it back to him. 'Is everything clear?' he had asked, and she had nodded. After this, she had told him she wanted him to continue advising her about the investment of the Westheim funds, had thanked him for the guidance he had given her thus far. He had smiled in his kindly way, assured her that he would help her however he could, and had agreed to handle Maxim's money.

Teddy's thoughts were interrupted as the door of the private room flew open and Mr Johnson reappeared. He hurried in, carrying her safety deposit box, which he placed on the table. 'There you are, Miss Stein. Take your time,' he said, and disappeared before she had a chance to thank him properly.

This was the first time Teddy had gone into her safety deposit box since the day she had acquired it, over six years ago, when she had locked the contents inside. She sat staring at the box for a very long moment, before taking the key out of her handbag, opening it and lifting the lid.

Ursula Westheim's jewels filled the box. The pieces were wrapped in the soft, velvet-lined jewellery rolls which Ursula herself had purchased in Paris in 1939, on one of the days they had gone shopping together. Teddy picked up one of the rolls, opened it, gazed down at the wide diamond bracelet which lay there glittering brilliantly in the light.

She touched the bracelet, remembering the last time she had seen Ursula wearing it in Berlin, and her throat tightened with emotion. The occasion had been a small dinner party at the mansion on the Tiergartenstrasse in 1937, and Ursula had never looked more beautiful. That night she had worn a burgundy velvet evening gown that had set off her fair skin, her pale blonde hair, her ethereal beauty. Teddy felt the tears rushing to the surface, but she blinked them away, clamped down on her grief for the dead woman.

Ever since Princess Irina Troubetzkoy had told her about Ursula's death a week ago, she had lived with nightmares, had rarely been able to close her eyes without seeing images of Ursula, a bruised and battered Ursula, tortured and beaten to insensibility by her Nazi tormentors in Ravensbrück. Only in the last few days had she begun to realise that the only way she could cope was to remember Ursula the way she had been in all her loveliness, and hold this picture in her head. But frequently the other horrifying images insinuated themselves into her mind, and when she imagined the agony Ursula must have lived through she was in torment herself. She wondered if she would ever obliterate those images.

I must, she thought, for Maxim's sake, for my own sanity, and for Mark and our future life together.

After fastening the roll and laying it on one side on the table, Teddy removed all of the other jewellery until she came to the envelope which lay in the bottom of the safety deposit box.

Ursula Westheim had given this envelope to her in Paris on the day she had taken Maxim and herself to the boat train bound for England. Across the large brown envelope Ursula had printed in bold block letters: PRIVATE AND CONFIDENTIAL: TO BE OPENED IN THE EVENT OF THE DEATHS OF SIGMUND AND URSULA WESTHEIM.

And then underneath, in her flowing script, Ursula had written: *Miss Theodora Stein.*

Miss, Teddy repeated to herself, and thought, she was already making me English, even then. Swiftly she opened the brown envelope. Inside were two smaller, white envelopes; one had her name on the front, the other was addressed to Maxim.

Teddy opened her own letter, and saw that it was written on the stationery of the Plaza-Athénée Hotel.

> *Paris*
> *March 10th, 1939*

My dear Teddy

If you are reading this letter then my husband and I are already dead. I return to Berlin knowing there is a great possibility that neither he nor I, nor any of the Westheim family, will survive the persecution of the Third Reich. And if we do not die at the hands of the Nazis, there is always the strong probability that we will be killed in the war between Germany and the Western Alliance, which we all know is now an inevitability.

I therefore feel that I must write to you about a matter of tremendous importance regarding my son, Maximilian. I know that what I am about to say is going to come as a great surprise, and it may even shock you, but I want someone to know the truth, in the event that I do not survive. And it can only be you. Before I go any further, I must tell you that the words which I am about to write are for your eyes only. No one else must ever know the contents of this letter, unless, of course, you wish to tell Maxim when he is old enough to understand everything. However, I leave that decision to you. You must use your discretion, and you may come to believe that it is better he never knows.

Perhaps it is wrong of me to burden you with this responsibility, but there is no one else I can entrust with this secret. And I do trust you implicitly, Teddy. I cannot advise you, I am afraid, for I have never really been sure what I myself would do, when Maxim was old enough to be told the truth. You are strong and clear thinking and sensible, and I am certain that the decision you make will be the right one for my son, whom I know you love very much, as I do.

To begin my story, I must go back in time, to 1931. It was then that . . .

Teddy's eyes raced down the page, absorbing line after line which Ursula had written so carefully in Paris, six years ago. The letter continued for another page, and when she had finished reading it Teddy sat back in the chair. She was stunned, and her face was a picture of disbelief.

She fervently wished that Ursula Westheim had never written this letter to her.

Teddy left the Rossiter Merchant Bank and walked across Berkeley Square. It was a crisp, sunny winter's day, and she hoped that the fresh air would help clear her head. The letter she had just read troubled her considerably, but she knew she must put it out of her mind for the time being. There was something much more pressing and important with which she had to deal. Maxim was coming home from school for the weekend, was probably already there now, and she *must* tell him about his parents. But she had no idea what she would say to him . . . she balked at the thought of it.

Near Marble Arch she hailed a cab and got in, and all the way back to Belsize Park Gardens she wrestled with her terrible problem. By the time she was alighting at Aunt Ketti's house she was certain of only one thing . . . that no matter what else she said, she could never tell Maxim exactly how his mother had died. To burden a child with that awful knowledge would be unconscionable.

He must have been waiting for her, watching the street from his bedroom window, for as Teddy came into the house Maxim was already clattering down the stairs.

'I'm here, Teddy!' he cried, racing along the hall, flinging himself against her body, and hugging her. She hugged him back, and then looked up and saw Aunt Ketti standing in the doorway of the back parlour, observing them worriedly, her eyes anxious.

'Let me take my coat off, darling,' she said to Maxim, swung around, went swiftly to the coat cupboard.

Ketti said, 'The train was on time for once, Teddy. Mrs Trenton was at the railway station to meet Stubby. She invited Maxim for lunch tomorrow. But Mark rang up just before I left to say he has a pass for the weekend. You'll have to let Mrs Trenton know what you want to do about Saturday lunch.'

'Yes, Aunt Ketti, I'll ring her up later, and thank you for collecting Maxim from the station for me.'

Maxim said, 'Gosh, if Mark is coming up for the weekend, I'd like to see him. I mean, I see old Stubby all the time, don't I? And I have lunch with him every day at school.'

'That's true,' Teddy said, walking over to Maxim. 'Perhaps Stubby can join *us*. It would be nice to spend the day with Mark.'

She put her arm around his shoulder, and they continued down the hall together. Teddy paused at the door leading into the small den, and said, 'Come in here for a moment, there's something I want to talk to you about.'

'Gosh, you do sound serious!' he cried, frowning. 'I hope it's not anything to do with school. Old Mr Helliwell – '

'It doesn't have anything to do with school. You haven't done anything wrong,' she said, pushing open the door and going inside.

Teddy sat down on the sofa and patted the cushion next to her. 'Sit here with me, Maxim.'

He did so, continuing to look at her with curiosity.

Teddy said, 'I've been away for a couple of weeks. I've been to Berlin.'

His dark eyes widened. 'And you didn't tell me!' he said swiftly, sounding hurt, even a little accusatory.

'I went there to look for your parents, and I didn't want to get your hopes up.'

'Did you find them?' he asked, sudden excitement flaring.

'No, I'm afraid not.'

'Didn't you find *anything* out?' he demanded, his eyes impaling hers.

She swallowed. 'No, not really. At least, not very much.'

'But *what* exactly?'

'That they were with the von Tiegals at the Schloss in 1941, and then the four of them disappeared. Vanished.'

'But we already knew that!'

'That's all I could find out.'

'I don't believe you,' Maxim said, his face settling in rigid, stubborn lines. 'I know you, Teddy, I've known you all my life. And you're far too clever not to have found out something else. I just *know* you *did*,' he insisted.

'I didn't,' she protested, shaking her head.

He was silent, staring at her.

Teddy could almost hear his mind working, and she held her breath.

He was only eleven years old, but he was a boy of great brilliance and
precocity, and therefore far too bright to be deceived. He would probe and
probe. Her mouth went dry, and she wondered where she would find the
words to tell him. Her eyes filled, and she blinked.

He noticed this immediately, and said, 'Are they . . . are they . . .
dead?'

'I'm so sorry, darling, so very, very sorry,' she murmured, her voice full
of love, and she reached for his hand.

He took it, held onto it tightly, and said in a small voice, 'How did
Mutti and Papa die?'

Teddy could not speak.

'In a bombing raid or . . . or . . . in the camps?' he asked hesitantly, his
voice growing even smaller.

Teddy was still incapable of saying anything, but the tears spilled over
the rims of her eyes and trickled down her cheeks unchecked.

'It *was* in the camps,' he whispered, so softly now she could hardly hear
him. '*Mutti* and Papa died in the camps, didn't they?'

'Yes.'

'Which one?'

'Your father in Buchenwald . . . your mother in Ravensbrück.'

'*How*?'

'That I don't know. I really don't know. I promise you, I don't know
how they died, Maxim,' she said, her tone quietly vehement.

He sat looking at her speechlessly. His face was grey and his eyes had
turned black with shock and anguish.

'Oh Teddy . . . Teddy . . .' he cried at last, and his face crumpled.

She reached for him as he reached for her, and she held him in her
arms as he sobbed out his raw pain and grief for his mother and father.
She rocked him to and fro, and tried to comfort him, to give him
consolation. She whispered: 'I will look after you always, and so will
Mark. I know it's not the same, but you will have us. You will be
our boy.'

He did not respond, but she knew he had heard her, and that he had
understood, even though he went on weeping as though his heart was
breaking.

Later, when he was calmer, she made him sit up on the sofa. After she
had wiped his wet face with her handkerchief, she reached into her jacket
pocket.

'The day we left Paris in 1939 your mother gave me a brown envelope,
Maxim. Do you remember?'

He nodded.

'This was in it,' she explained, and handed him the smaller white envelope with his name written on the front in Ursula's hand.

He took the letter from her and gazed at it. After a moment, he whispered, 'I'd like to go to my room, Teddy. Do you mind?'

'No, I understand,' she said. 'I understand everything.' She leaned back against the sofa and watched him walk slowly across the floor, and her heart ached for him. He was still such a little boy in so many ways, and yet he was so brave.

Maxim sat in the chair facing the chest of drawers on which the photographs of his parents stood. He looked at them for a few minutes, before he opened the letter from his mother and began to read it.

Paris
March 10th, 1939

My dearest Maxim

I go back to Berlin with the realisation that I may never see you again. Yet I return with a lighter heart than I have had for a long time, because I know you will soon be safe in England with Teddy. And there no harm will come to you. Your well-being and happiness have always been of paramount importance to Papa and me, and you must always remember this.

The only reason I go back to Berlin is to help Papa with your grandmother, and to bring her out of Germany to safety.

Papa and I waited for such a long time for you, and the day you were born was the happiest day of our lives. You are growing up to be such a fine boy, Maxim, and Papa and I are so very proud of you.

If we do not come to England, Teddy will look after you until you are grown up. Trust her judgement and wisdom, and love her always, as she loves you.

Whatever happens, know that Papa and I love you very much. You are the best part of us.

I hold you in my heart always, Mein Schatzi.
                    Your loving and devoted
                    Mother

He put the letter down and fumbled for his handkerchief. He wiped his streaming eyes, then stuffed the handkerchief back in his pocket. He sat for a long time in the chair, hurting inside, feeling as if part of him had been cut away.

Finally, he slipped the letter from his mother back in its envelope, stood up, walked over to the chest. Opening the drawer, he took out his father's wallet, tucked the letter inside, then placed the wallet next to his little carved wooden horse, and closed the drawer.

Mutti, Mutti, he whispered, filled with yearning, aching for her. He could not bear that he would never see her again, never hear her voice, or nestle in her arms and smell the perfume, lilies-of-the-valley, she had always worn. He could not believe that he would never go walking in the woods with his father again, or sailing with him on the lake, and that they would never work together in the Westheim Bank when he was grown up, as they had always planned. *Papa, Papa,* he cried out silently, and he felt as if his heart was being squeezed and squeezed. He closed his eyes. And in his head he heard his father's music, heard the tinkling of the piano in his father's house on the Tiergartenstrasse . . .

He picked up the photograph of *Mutti* and Papa in evening dress and stood looking down at it, and fresh tears splashed onto the glass. And Maxim suddenly understood that the sadness inside him would never go away. It would always be there. For the rest of his life.

PART 4

My beloved spake, and said unto me, Rise up, my love, my fair one, and come away. For lo, the winter is past, the rain is over and gone. The flowers appear on the earth; the time of the singing of birds is come, and the voice of the turtle is heard in the land.

The Song of Solomon: The Bible

THIRTY-EIGHT

She heard the girl's voice as she climbed the broad staircase. It floated down to her on the warm July air, light, lyrical, full of music, a lovely voice all the more captivating because it was so natural and unaffected.

Ideal for stage or screen, Margot Derevenko thought, but thankfully she has no ambitions in that direction. And even if she did, her father would never permit her to become an actress. He knows too much about that tough uncertain world to let her venture into it.

As Margot drew closer to the second-floor landing, she paused to listen, one hand resting on the polished oak banister, the other holding a small basket filled with fresh-cut white flowers from her garden. The girl's words were clearer, more distinct now, and Margot realised she was talking to the dressmaker.

'And so, Marie, I said to the *clochard*, come with me, I know you are hungry. I invite you to the café across the street for lunch.'

Marie sucked in her breath incredulously. 'And did the *clochard* come with you to the café, *Mademoiselle*?' she gasped.

'Of course not, Marie! He looked at me as if I had invited him to a funeral. *His own*. And so I said, all right, if you don't want to take lunch with me in the café, let us go to my parents' house. Our cook, Maruba, will make a splendid lunch for you, anything you fancy. And can you imagine what happened, Marie?'

'No, *Mademoiselle*, I cannot.'

'He *refused*.'

'It is good that he did,' Marie said after a moment, in a dry voice. 'I don't think your parents would be too happy if you entertained a tramp in their beautiful home.'

Indeed we would *not*, Margot muttered under her breath.

Anastasia said nothing.

A moment of silence ensued, and then the dressmaker went on to remark in a genuinely puzzled voice, 'I do not understand, *Mademoiselle*, why did you ask this tramp to lunch in the first place?'

'Obviously because he was *hungry*, Marie.'

'But that is *his* problem. Anyway, these tramps of the Seine are all scoundrels.'

'How can you say a thing like that! It's not their fault they've fallen on hard times, have been reduced to living that kind of life. I talk to them all the time, and visit them, and believe me, Marie, the *clochards* are not a bit happy about living under the bridges of the river, sleeping outside in all kinds of weather, existing on nothing, scavenging for food.'

'They bring on their own misfortunes.'

'*I* don't believe they do, and *I* try to help them.'

When Marie did not respond, the girl rushed on breathlessly, 'And I have succeeded in helping *one* of them . . . a lady *clochard*. She is now on the way to making a good life for herself.'

'*Really*,' Marie said, sounding sceptical.

'Yes, it's true, I *did* help her. I persuaded her to give up the wine bottle, which she did, and she now has a job and somewhere to live.'

'I see. And tell me, *Mademoiselle*, do your parents know about your concern for the *clochards* of the Seine, and your involvement with them?'

'Of course, and they approve.'

We do? Margot thought. Since when, I wonder? She now hurried on up the wide, polished-wood stairs and stepped into the spacious first-floor hall where the Degas bronze of the little ballerina took pride of place to the left of the gouache of ballet dancers in green dresses, also by the great Edgar Degas. He and Monet were her husband's favourite artists, and both were well represented in this house.

The huge, double doors leading into the *petit salon* stood ajar, and as Margot crossed the parquet floor to them and peered inside she paused for a moment before entering, catching her breath in surprise and pleasure.

Her daughter stood in the centre of the room and was slowly turning around, her arms outstretched, so that Marie could make a final check of the evening dress she had finished the day before, and which she was now fitting for the last time. The dress, a gossamer confection of chiffon in a mixture of delicate blues and pale greys, floated around her like wisps of sea mist. If the dress was superb, then the girl was perfection itself.

The room was flooded with morning sun which poured in through the tall windows and bathed the girl in its soft light. Her pale blonde hair, falling to her tiny waist, seemed to be full of sunlight and shimmered around her exquisite heart-shaped face. This gleamed like smooth, polished ivory, while her eyes, set wide apart and heavily lashed, were a lovely misty blue-grey colour. Of medium height, and slender, the girl had long and graceful limbs; the floating, cape-like sleeves of the dress fell away from the prettiest of shoulders and arms, whilst the pointed handkerchief hemline showed off her shapely ankles and dainty feet.

So beautiful she doesn't seem real, Margot thought, but then she never did, not even as a child. She's too exquisite and far too sweet and gentle for her own good. Idealist, romantic dreamer. Whatever am I going to do with her? She's much too impractical and trusting for this hard world we live in today. Sighing to herself, Margot pushed open the door and glided into the room.

'There you are, Anastasia!' she exclaimed, smiling at her eighteen-year-old daughter.

'Look, Mummy, isn't it gorgeous?' As she spoke Anastasia held out the skirt of the dress, did a little pirouette and ended up facing her mother, looking at her questioningly.

Margot nodded in approval, and swung her eyes to the dressmaker. 'Good morning, Marie. I see you have created another triumph.'

'*Bonjour, Madame*. It is not I that did that, but you,' Marie replied, looking pointedly at Anastasia. Nonetheless, the compliment about her work pleased her, and she smiled at Madame Derevenko.

'I'm afraid I can't take all the credit for Anastasia,' Margot said with a chuckle. 'I believe her father had something to do with producing her.'

Anastasia laughed with her mother. It was a light, tinkling laugh, which like her voice was as clear as a bell. 'The dress really is divine, isn't it? Marie truly has outdone herself. *Merci beaucoup*, Marie,' she said and made a small curtsy.

The dressmaker's face filled with happiness. She liked nothing better than satisfied customers, and most especially the Derevenko women, who were her favourites. She had made a great many clothes for them over the years, although recently they had been mostly for Anastasia. Madame favoured *haute couture* more than ever these days. But what a joy it was to sew for this girl who did the garments such justice with her incredible beauty, slim, willowy figure and perfect carriage.

Margot was studying her daughter thoughtfully, and now exclaimed, '*Opals!* That's it! You must wear my opals with the new gown. They will go beautifully with the blues and greys in it.'

'Oh Mummy, thank you! How lovely of you to lend them to me.'

'You're going to look ravishing. You'll be the proverbial belle of the ball.'

'Hardly. Yvette will be the star turn, and so she should be. After all, it's her special day,' Anastasia pointed out.

Margot merely smiled, and then glanced around the small sitting room. Solange, the maid, had placed bud vases filled with water on the various occasional tables for her; now she moved around the room with her flower basket, placing blooms in the various little cylinders and pots, then stepped back to regard them, her fair head on one side, giving them critical appraisal.

Anastasia watched her mother, thinking how talented she was when it came to such artistic matters as flower-arranging and table-setting and picture-hanging. She was full of admiration for her.

Margot suddenly swung around and directed her hazel-eyed gaze at her daughter. 'Day-dreaming again?'

'No, Mummy,' Anastasia laughed. 'And I'd better go and change out of this dress. Marie, will you come and help me, please?'

'Of course, *Mademoiselle*.'

'Lunch at one in the garden, Anastasia.'

'Yes, you've already told me,' the girl said, and floated out on a cloud of chiffon and Ma Griffe scent.

The *hôtel particulier* owned by Alexander and Margot Derevenko was on the elegant Faubourg Saint-Germain, only one of a number of beautiful private houses standing on this street behind forbiddingly high stone walls. The Faubourg Saint-Germain was in the seventh *arrondissement*, one of the most celebrated districts on the Left Bank, a district at once both aristocratic and a haven for students, artists and writers.

In the vicinity of the house were the Rodin Museum, the Sorbonne, the French Academy, the École Militaire, the Luxembourg Palace and Gardens, and the Hôtel des Invalides, wherein lay the tomb of Napoleon I, and the tombs of other French leaders. Quite aside from these historic buildings, there were charming little bistros, antique shops and art galleries located in the area, as well as two of the most famous hangouts for writers and artists in Paris, the Café des Deux Magots and the Café Flore, once the haunts of Ernest Hemingway and other celebrated authors.

The Derevenko house was hidden from pedestrians by massive dark green doors which fronted onto the street. Behind them was a small concierge's cottage in a courtyard of typical Parisian design, cobbled, with a fountain in the centre and a horse chestnut tree near one of the ivy-clad walls.

The house itself was elongated and had a front facade of classical design, with many tall, shuttered windows and wide stone steps leading up to a double front door. Inside were numerous spacious rooms with high ceilings which were airy, full of light; they owed their elegance and graciousness to Margot Derevenko's impeccable taste in antiques and furnishings. Her flair and talent at combining and arranging these elements were in evidence throughout.

The entrance hall on the ground floor led straight out to the garden through a series of glass doors, and the garden itself was something of a masterpiece, lovingly and painstakingly created over the years by Margot and various gardeners. Although she had lived in France since her youth and had been educated at the Sorbonne, Margot was English by birth and upbringing. And so it was to one of the great English gardens that she had turned when seeking ideas for her own in the heart of Paris, drawing inspiration from the famous 'White Garden' at Sissinghurst Castle. Like the one in Kent, this much smaller garden sitting under the shadow of the Hôtel des Invalides was a mingling of green foliage and green lawns, flowers and flowering bushes of only one colour – white. It was the simplicity and purity of this green-and-white theme which gave the formal Parisian garden its sense of coolness, serenity and elegance.

A lily pond surrounded by flagstones sat at the edge of the lawn, and the latter was encircled by luxuriant borders and beds filled to overflowing with white flowers of all kinds: azaleas, roses, tulips, narcissi, chrysanthemums, and snowdrops, depending on the season of the year. Beyond the flower beds were lilac and horse chestnut trees, and flowering bushes such as rhododendrons and hydrangea, and surrounding the entire garden were high, ancient stone walls covered with glossy, evergreen ivy.

A flagstone terrace stretched the length of the house and overlooked the garden, and it was here that Margot and Anastasia sat having lunch at a wrought-iron garden table, shaded by a large sun umbrella. Maruba, their North African cook, had prepared a simple meal of grilled fish, a green salad, and fresh sliced peaches soaked in champagne.

Between mouthfuls of fish, Margot said, 'I wasn't eavesdropping before, but I couldn't help hearing your conversation with Marie when I was coming up the stairs earlier. You must stop spending time with the *clochards*, you know. It's simply not right.'

'I'm only trying to help them, Mother!'

'You can't help them. It seems to me that they have chosen that kind of life.'

'How can you say such a thing? You sound like Marie! Anyway, who would choose to live in such extreme conditions?'

Margot shook her head. 'Oh darling, don't be naive . . .' Her voice trailed off, and she was thoughtful before saying, 'Your father and I worry about you. I don't think you realise how lovely you are, and who knows about these tramps – '

'They're gentle folk!' Anastasia interrupted swiftly. 'And not dangerous at all, which is what you're implying. They're not going to attack me, or try to rape me. You mustn't worry, and please don't be angry with me. I can't bear it when you and Daddy are cross.'

'Good heavens, we're not angry, only concerned about your welfare.' Margot smiled at her daughter warmly. 'Actually, your father and I are very pleased with the way you've passed your *Baccalauréat* with honours, and been accepted at the Sorbonne. In fact, I would say we're *more* than pleased, darling. However we – '

'I know what you're going to say, Mummy,' Anastasia exclaimed, cutting in again. 'You don't want me messing around with derelicts.'

'*Exactly.*'

'Those poor souls. I can hardly bear to think of their suffering, the way they live.'

'Yes, it is sad, Anastasia. But the world *is* full of the most awful inequities, and it always has been. There is little you or anyone else can do to help those poor creatures, I'm afraid.'

'I don't believe that, Mummy. In my opinion *one* person can make a difference.'

Margot looked at her daughter swiftly, and was about to disagree with her, but changed her mind, refrained from commenting. She realised it would be wiser to let this subject rest for the moment. As sweet and angelic as Anastasia was, she was nobody's fool, was rather clever and quick-witted. And also extremely stubborn by nature. If she continued to berate her for her concern about the tramps the girl would only dig her heels in defiantly, refuse to budge from her position. They were leaving in a few days to spend the rest of July and part of August in their villa in Cannes, and then Anastasia was going to London to stay with her grandmother. She would be far away from her *clochards* and in the autumn she was starting at the university, and the work schedule there would more than preoccupy her and fill her time.

And so Margot changed the subject, and said, 'I am going shopping with Lucrezia this afternoon. Would you like to join us, darling?'

'Thanks, but I can't. I want to go and look for several history books I need. Yvette told me I would most probably find them at the old bookshop near the Quai Saint-Michel.'

Margot nodded. 'Don't forget, you're joining us for dinner tonight. Your father has people here from Hollywood.'

'He told me. Where are we going?'

'Tour d'Argent.'

'It's going to be full of rich foreign tourists. You know what it's like in July.'

Margot smiled. 'But it's still very beautiful. Think of the gorgeous views of Notre Dame and the Seine. And the gorgeous duck. Besides, that's where the Hollywood people want to go.'

'They always do,' Anastasia murmured succinctly, then asked, 'Is Daddy doing another American movie?'

'It looks like it. Drinks here at the house at eight o'clock, and then we'll wander over to the restaurant about nine.'

'Don't worry, Mummy, I won't be late. I know how important these business evenings are to Daddy. And I promise to be on my best behaviour.' She gave her mother a sly little look and her mouth twitched as she added, 'And I won't mention the *clochards*.'

Margot burst out laughing. 'Well, I must say, I'm glad to see your newly-developed social conscience hasn't affected your sense of humour.'

THIRTY-NINE

Maxim walked at a leisurely pace along the quais of Paris which ran parallel with the Seine, enjoying a stroll on this pleasant afternoon.

He had just finished lunch with an American business associate who was on a trip to France, had concluded an excellent deal, and he was delighted. His first day in Paris had turned out exceptionally well.

When he came to the Quai Voltaire he paused, glanced up a narrow side street on his right, hesitating, wondering whether to wander into Saint-Germain-des-Prés for a cup of coffee at the Deux Magots, and then decided against it. He was making for a particular corner of the city, and he did not want to sidetrack himself.

And so he strode on purposefully, heading in the direction of the Cathedral of Notre Dame, whose imposing early Gothic spires were like giant sentinels silhouetted against the azure summer sky, perfect today and full of that soft filtered light beloved by painters and which was so unique to Paris. It was a light reflected in the waters of the Seine, trembling in the hazy sunshine trickling through the leafy branches of the trees that lined the river's edge.

Paris was Maxim's favourite city. He preferred it to London where he lived and worked, New York where he frequently went on business, and Berlin where he was born. Whenever he came back it always looked more beautiful than he had remembered it to be, forever took him by surprise.

He had first seen Paris in the early part of 1939, when he and *Mutti* and Teddy had been fleeing Nazi Germany, and he had never forgotten that time of his childhood, those gloriously happy weeks with his mother, the last he had ever spent with her. A multitude of images was engraved on his mind, and the memories had remained ever constant, would be forever part of him.

Thirteen years had passed before he had visited the city again. He had first returned in 1952 to celebrate his eighteenth birthday; the trip had been Mark's idea, who had thoughtfully invited Stubby to join them as his guest. They had all had a wonderful time together, and Teddy, in particular, had thoroughly enjoyed herself. She had given birth to her second child in February of that year, a boy they named David, after Mark's brother who had been killed in the war, and the prospect of a long weekend in Paris had excited her.

'It's just what I need,' Teddy had exclaimed, when Mark had told her what he was planning for Maxim's birthday. 'I looked like a whale in a tent for so many weeks of my pregnancy, I can't wait to buy some smart new French clothes, now that I've got my figure back. So Paris it is!' she had enthusiastically agreed. But deep down inside, Teddy had always understood how much Paris meant to her beloved Maxim, knew that he held joyous memories of the months he had spent there with Ursula, and, in actuality, this was the *real* reason she was glad they were going. And so for once she had not fussed about leaving their two-year-old daughter Kay in the care of the nanny and Mark's mother. She had even handed over the new baby with a smile on her face. Maxim's eighteenth birthday celebration and the trip to Paris took precedence over everything. She loved Maxim deeply, as she had loved him from the age of one. He was like her own child, and she thought of him as such, considered him to be her son. He was, and always would be, her pride and joy; he could do no wrong in her eyes. And that was the way it was always to be. He was her favourite.

As it turned out the trip to Paris in 1952 had been truly memorable. But Maxim's birthday had not been the only thing they had celebrated that particular June. He and Stubby had spent some of their time whooping it up and congratulating each other because they had concluded their first successful business deal.

A month before Maxim's birthday they had sold the land they owned in the East End to one of the big London builders, and had made a tidy profit for themselves in the process.

This business venture had originally come about quite by accident, because of Mrs Threscoe, the Trentons' charlady.

Stubby and she had had a soft spot for each other since his childhood, and over the years Stubby had become her most trusted confidant. In 1950, when her husband had been knocked down by a lorry and had subsequently died of his head injuries, Mrs Threscoe, who was childless, had come weeping to Stubby with her problems. Seemingly Jack Threscoe had left very little money; all of his savings were tied up in a piece of land in the East End, a bomb-site which he had purchased in 1946. With Jack gone, she was now ready to sell the land, *needed* to sell it, Mrs Threscoe had explained to Stubby. But to her immense dismay nobody seemed to want it.

When Stubby had told his best friend the story, Maxim had mulled it over for a couple of days, and had then suggested that they look at the land themselves. 'If we're going to be businessmen, now's the time to start,' he had said to Stubby, and had pointed out that rebuilding was going on in various parts of London. 'That land might have possibilities. Perhaps we *should* buy it, Stubby. We'd be helping Mrs Threscoe out, and, with a bit of luck, it could prove to be a good investment.'

As it turned out, Maxim was right.

Before the sixteen-year-old boys had purchased the Threscoe bomb-site, Maxim had asked the opinion of Henry Rossiter, who was still in charge of his money. The merchant banker had called in his real estate experts, who had gone to look at the land; after receiving their report, he had informed Maxim that it would be a safe investment.

'You probably won't make a great deal of money on it when you sell, which obviously you will do one day, but you certainly won't lose,' he had assured Maxim, and he had then purchased the land on their behalf. Mrs Threscoe had asked for five thousand pounds, which gave her a decent profit; the boys had agreed to her price without haggling and had split the cost down the middle, so becoming partners. Maxim had used money from the Westheim funds, which were in Henry Rossiter's control; Stubby, with permission from his father, had plonked down the entire legacy his uncle had left him, plus three hundred pounds contributed by his doting mother.

Two years later they had sold the Threscoe bomb-site for twenty-five thousand pounds, and had made a straight profit of twenty thousand, much to their surprise. And everyone else's, in fact.

They were supposed to have started university that year, having graduated from St Paul's School in July, at the age of eighteen. But they had rejected Oxford. Instead they had started their own company with the profits from the Threscoe deal.

Teddy had objected initially, and so had Stubby's father, but they had both been won around in the end, thanks chiefly to the intervention of Henry Rossiter.

'Forcing them to go to Oxford now is rather like closing the door after the horses have escaped,' Mr Rossiter had said to Teddy and Mr Trenton with a chuckle. 'It seems to me that these two young bucks have embarked on commercial careers already, and rather *successfully*, I might add. So why stop them now? I think they're going to do very nicely for themselves.'

Mark had tended to agree with the merchant banker. His endorsement of the scheme had ultimately convinced Teddy that she was not making a mistake by permitting Maxim to go into business, rather than continuing his higher education. And she had given him her blessing.

Maxim had planned to be a financier, and had never intended to open a real estate business, and if it had not been for Stubby he would not have done so. But because the East End property had turned such a good profit, Stubby had persuaded Maxim to stay in this field, at least for a while. They took offices in Jermyn Street, formed a company called Westrent, which was a contraction of their last names, and started to buy bomb-sites wherever they could find them.

For the most part they concentrated on major industrial cities in the provinces, which had been heavily bombed by the Luftwaffe during the war. They concentrated on Leeds, Bradford, Sheffield, Coventry and Birmingham, managed to find suitable tracts of land at decent prices, sites which they considered to have great potential for future building projects. Once they had had the land cleaned of rubble and fenced in, they had sensibly held onto the sites until really good bids had been made. In some instances they had had to wait several years to make the right sales; ultimately, Westrent was in profit largely because of the post-war building trend which suddenly boomed in England in the mid-fifties.

1952 was also the year Maxim had decided to change his name legally. When he had first mentioned to Teddy that he wished to anglicise Westheim, by dropping the *heim* and calling himself West, she had agreed it was a good idea, and as his guardian had given her consent. 'Your parents planned to do that anyway,' she had informed him. 'In fact, your mother brought the matter up to me several times when we were in Paris in 1939. You know how much she loved England, wished us all to become English. She would be so pleased if she knew you intended to do this, and so would your father. He had wanted to adopt West as the family surname even before we left Germany, but the prince didn't think Admiral Canaris could get new passports.'

Eventually he *had* changed his name – and his nationality as well. He had become Maximilian West, naturalised British subject, with a British passport and the right to vote in the elections.

And in the ensuing years since his eighteenth birthday Maxim had not looked back.

When wheeling and dealing in real estate had become less challenging, and had actually begun to bore him, he had purchased several small, unprofitable companies: a printing plant in Wakefield, a bus company in Bristol and a brick yard in Nottingham. In a relatively short span of time he had put them on their feet, through a bit of brilliant reorganisation and with the help of the new management teams he had sent in. Subsequently he had sold them, making excellent profits on all three. And thus a second company, Westinvest, was born.

Aside from his business acumen and his brilliance with figures, Maxim had the ability to read, understand and assess a balance sheet and all its ramifications immediately with the greatest of ease. He also had imagination and vision. And then there was his gut instinct, which he always relied on, sometimes sweeping away analysts' reports and recommendations in favour of his own instinctive reaction to a deal, the 'feel' he had for it. All of these elements were important factors in his success, were to stand him in good stead for the future.

Now, at the age of twenty-five, he was managing director of Westrent and Westinvest, owned an elegantly furnished flat in Mayfair and a sleek new wine-coloured Jaguar, and belonged to some of the best private clubs in town. He cut quite a swathe in smart London society, escorted numerous beautiful young women, including a couple of well-known starlets, and was considered to be something of a playboy by the British press.

The gossip columnists loved him, although he failed to see the reason why, and were forever exclaiming in print about his dashing good looks, his elegance and his style, his gorgeous female companions, the parties he gave, his wealth.

He considered the parties and the women and his social life in general to be all so much folderol, the fluff of life, and therefore of little value or consequence. The only thing which truly mattered to him, really interested him, and gave him genuine pleasure, was his business.

Maxim's success as a businessman was of paramount importance to him, ruled his life, and he was constantly telling Stubby that he intended to make a million pounds by the time he was thirty. Stubby never once doubted him. Nor did Maxim doubt himself, and making that million was the yardstick by which he judged himself and his achievements. And so it drove him.

Five years to go, he thought, as he came up into the Place Saint-Michel, and stood at the edge of the pavement, waiting for the lights to change. A little smile struck his mouth; he was quite confident he would achieve his goal.

As far as Maxim himself was concerned, the real secrets of his success were single-mindedness of purpose, dedication, hard work, and the ability to put in very long hours without suffering from fatigue. He was fortunate in that he had immense stamina, only needed about five hours' sleep; he usually rose at four in the morning, was at his desk in the flat by four-thirty, where he did paperwork until seven, when he left for his office in Jermyn Street where he put in a full day. He thought nothing of working seven days a week, for weeks on end without a break. Maxim had long acknowledged that he was a dyed-in-the-wool workaholic, which was why he guffawed when the papers called him a playboy.

He thought of this now, and chuckled. *Some playboy*, he muttered under his breath. *If only they knew.*

The truth was, the beautiful women he took out were merely decorative accessories to wear on his arm. Of course, he *had* fallen in love several times. And out of it, rather rapidly. In between he had had numerous affairs. But none of the women had lasted very long with him. Simply put, he had never managed to find the right woman. He wondered sometimes what he was looking for *exactly*. *Perfection*? But he was smart enough to understand that there was no such thing as a perfect woman. Or man, for that matter. In any case, he did not want a paragon.

Still, true love *did* seem to elude him.

The lights changed to green, and Maxim crossed the Place Saint-Michel and headed towards the Rue de la Huchette.

Within seconds he was sauntering down that narrow old street, experiencing a sense of nostalgia as he glanced around. Here on his left was the Hôtel Mont Blanc, where he and Stubby had stayed on a couple of occasions, and immediately opposite was the El Djazier, the North African nightclub which they still frequented sometimes, going there to drink mint tea, ogle the exotic belly dancers, and eat *couscous* with harissa, the hot piquant sauce which blew his head off, but which he nevertheless enjoyed. And a few yards further along were the famous jazz joints, where some of the American jazz greats came to play and musicians of all nationalities to listen, as did he and Stubby from time to time.

He paused when he saw the Rue du Chat Qui Pêche.

It was only a little alleyway, but he had never forgotten this street because the name had so delighted him when he was a child. 'It means the *Street of the Cat Who Fishes*,' *Mutti* had said, translating the French for him. Filled with glee, he had laughed out loud, tickled at the idea of a *cat* who *fished*.

They had been on one of their outings, he and *Mutti* and Teddy. 'Investigating the quaint bits of Paris,' *Mutti* had called their wondrous excursions, and ever since those days this picturesque area had remained a favourite, and he often returned to walk around these narrow cobbled streets, to browse in the bookstores and galleries.

Maxim went on walking up the Rue de la Huchette, past the little Greek and North African restaurants, until he came at last to the top of the street, and into a wide, open area like a square called the Rue de la Bucherie. Here he headed for one of the cafés which fronted onto a series of little gardens and faced the Cathedral of Notre Dame which stood on the Île de la Cité, the small island in the Seine.

He found a seat at a pavement table, and when the waiter came to take his order he asked for a *citron pressé*. The afternoon had suddenly become very warm, and he leaned back in the wicker chair gratefully, loosened his tie, opened the top button of his shirt, trying to cool off.

Within seconds the lemonade arrived, and Maxim sipped it, relaxed, and let his thoughts drift for a while. It was odd how childhood places always tugged at him, pulled him back. Whenever he went to Berlin, whether on business or to see Aunt Irina, he usually made a point of passing by the Tiergartenstrasse and the Tiergarten.

The lure of childhood, he thought, how strong it is with me ... I wonder if it is with everyone else? Or is it because I lost so much when I was a child ... had such irretrievable losses? Do I come back to Paris and Berlin in the hopes of finding something which escaped me long, long ago? Am I on an eternal quest? What is it I hope to find?

The answers to his questions were elusive, as they always were ...

A short while later Maxim paid and left the café, ambled off to Shakespeare and Company. This was a secondhand bookshop nearby, run by a friendly American called Bill, with whom Maxim had been acquainted for the past few years. After staring in the window for a couple of seconds, he finally went inside, and asked for the owner, only to be told by the American girl working there that Bill would not be in the shop before six.

'Any message?' the girl asked, smiling broadly, showing her perfect white teeth.

Maxim shook his head. 'Just tell him Duke stopped in to say hello, and that I'll try and swing by tomorrow.'

'Okay, Duke,' the girl said, and went on arranging a number of books on a shelf.

Maxim watched her for a moment, fascinated by her choices. They were an esoteric selection: novels by Richard Wright, Henry Miller, Lawrence Durrell and Anaïs Nin. These writers, all of whom he had read, had absolutely nothing in common with each other, as far as their writing was concerned. He could not for the life of him understand why the girl was placing them together. And then he remembered that they had all lived in Paris at the same time, and were old friends. Obviously she saw this as some sort of link between them. *The Paris Clique*, he thought, and smiled.

Maxim browsed in Shakespeare and Company for a while, and to his delight he spotted a copy of *The Young Lions* by Irwin Shaw, his favourite writer. He looked inside the book and discovered it was a first edition, published by Random House in 1948. He bought it at once, and left the shop clutching it, well pleased with his find. He had a whole shelf of first editions at the flat in London, and this copy of early Shaw would make a wonderful addition.

Crossing the square, Maxim went past the Hôtel Notre Dame, headed down the Quai Saint-Michel, walking in the direction of another second-hand bookshop, one of a slightly different nature. Arcel and Fils sold antique books, some dating back to the eighteenth and nineteenth centuries, and many were rare, others first editions, yet others genuine collectors' items.

At the sound of the door opening, the owner swung around from the shelves where he was standing, and peered down the shop. His face lit up at the sight of Maxim.

'Monsieur West, *bonjour! C'est un grand plaisir pour moi de vous voir.*'

'And it's a great pleasure for me to see you, Monsieur Arcel,' Maxim replied, walking forward, thrusting out his hand cordially.

The owner of the shop shook it vigorously. 'The book I wrote to you about is in the back room. I will get it. Please excuse me for a moment.'

'Of course,' Maxim answered. He was looking forward to seeing this rare volume on antique jewellery, hoped that it really was as special as Monsieur Arcel had indicated in his letter. If it was, it would make a nice present for Mark.

Maxim slouched against the counter, leaning on one elbow, and glanced around the shop.

It was then that he saw the girl.

He straightened, looking at her alertly, his attention caught.

She stood at the far end, silhouetted against the window. The light of the late afternoon sun surrounded her like an aureole, turned her long blonde hair into tresses of spun gold. Her face was in profile, and it was exquisite. He noted the smooth brow, the small straight nose, the chis-elled chin, the long neck rising from the white silk shirt she wore with a navy-blue cotton dirndl skirt. She was slender, willowy, bare-legged, and her feet were in sandals. Yet despite her casual dress there was an elegance about her, an aristocratic dignity.

Maxim was fascinated. He wondered who she was.

As if she were aware that someone was scrutinising her she turned slowly.

Their gaze met.

Maxim saw that her eyes were large and luminous, a light grey-blue in colour. A dreamer's eyes, he thought, unable to tear his gaze away from hers, mesmerised by her beauty. And yet there was something else, something more than her beauty which captivated him. There was a mysteriousness about her and it made him catch his breath.

The girl suddenly smiled at him.

It was the loveliest of smiles, lifted the corners of her pretty mouth in a tantalising tilt, dimpled her cheeks, brought a sudden gaiety and laughter to her sparkling eyes.

Maxim smiled back.

Unexpectedly, he felt very happy, almost light-headed with happiness. He knew it was her smile that made him feel this way . . . it seemed to fill all the empty places of his heart.

They just stood there staring at each other and smiling.

'Here it is, *Monsieur*,' the owner of the shop said, hurrying back from his private quarters, the antique book in his hands. 'It is unique. And the illustrations are . . . *wonderful.*'

With great reluctance, Maxim pulled his eyes away from the girl.

He swung to face Monsieur Arcel, and glanced down at the book which the Frenchman had placed on the counter in front of him.

'Look at the paintings,' Monsieur Arcel exclaimed, opening the leather-bound volume at random, pointing to a page.

'Yes, I see what you mean,' Maxim murmured, and then, unable to resist, he swung his head, looked over his shoulder, his eyes seeking the girl again. To his surprise and dismay she was no longer standing near the window. She had vanished.

Maxim turned to Monsieur Arcel. Urgently, he asked, 'The young woman who was standing there near the window, did she leave?'

'Why yes, Monsieur West, she slipped out a moment ago. When you were perusing the book.'

'Excuse me.' Maxim rushed to the door, wrenched it open, ran out into the street, looked up and down anxiously.

He spotted her a little further along the quai. He was just in time to see her stepping into a taxi.

'Wait!' he cried.

She did not hear him. The sound of the traffic drowned out his voice.

Helplessly, Maxim stood and watched the cab slide into the swiftly moving line of cars on the Quai Saint-Michel and disappear from sight. A sigh trickled out of him and he swung around and went back into the shop, a sense of dejection descending on him.

'Do you know the girl who just left, Monsieur Arcel?' Maxim asked, striding back to the counter.

The old Frenchman shook his head. 'I am so sorry, I do not. It is the first time I have seen her. Ah, but she *is* lovely, eh, Monsieur West?'

'She's the most beautiful girl I've ever set eyes on,' Maxim said.

'I've never seen you looking so morose, Duke. Not for years,' Stubby murmured, peering at Maxim across the dinner table. 'For God's sake, do cheer up.'

Maxim chose not to comment. He picked up the glass of good burgundy, which Stubby had ordered earlier, and took a swallow.

Stubby also drank, observing his friend over the top of the glass, his eyes thoughtful.

The two men were sitting at a corner table in Chez André, an excellent bistro on the Rue Marbeuf, not far from the Plaza-Athénée Hôtel where they were staying.

Ever since he had returned to the hotel at six-thirty Stubby had been disturbed by Maxim's glum face and even glummer demeanour. He took another sip of the red wine, put the glass down, and remarked, '*You* look as if it's the end of the world.'

'That's how I feel.' Maxim returned Alan Trenton's steady gaze, then muttered, 'I'll never find that girl again.'

'I can't believe it!' Stubby cried, his blue eyes widening. He was incredulous. '*You*, of all people, going on this way about a bloody female! *You!* And imagine, all these years I've believed that the only thing which really excited *you*, gave *you* pleasure, was business. It just goes to show what an idiot I am, doesn't it?' Stubby shook his head. '*You've* certainly fooled *me*, Duke.'

Seeing the humorous side, Maxim had the good grace to laugh. 'I am behaving out of character, aren't I?'

'I'll say.'

The noise of the bistro swirled all around them. They did not speak for a while.

Maxim drew closer, leaned across the table, and asked, 'Can I let you in on a little secret?'

'Why not? You've been telling me your secrets since you were eight. Why stop now?'

'I think I'm in love.'

'Oh come on!' Stubby exploded. He was aghast. Then a shout of laughter burst out of him and he sat staring at Maxim, but quite suddenly his laughter died in his throat, and he said in a sober voice, 'Good God, I think you mean it! But how can you have fallen in love with a girl you haven't even *spoken* to? You, Maxim! Women are usually the last thing on *your* mind.'

'I know. And you're right, of course, Alan,' Maxim said quietly, now feeling more than a little shamefaced. 'I am being stupid, aren't I? *Crazy.*

Let's forget about the girl and all that silliness, which is what it is, actually. Pure silliness. How did your meeting go?' he asked, changing the subject.

'Okay. More than okay. The French group are keen to do a deal. It was well worth my while, driving out to Versailles to see Monsieur Verland. They do have North African oil interests. Libya, I think. The bottom line is this: Monsieur Verland is prepared to come to London for talks, when Dad gets back from Hong Kong, so I think the old man will be pleased with the way I've handled things.' Stubby sat back in the chair, gave Maxim a faint smile. 'But I can't help wishing I was still in business with you, old chap.'

'So do I, Stubby. Come back! Tell your father the oil business bores you, that you want to work with me in Westrent again.'

'I wish I could, but you know very well I can't. Dad's just not up to snuff these days, and if I did a bunk . . . it'd kill him, actually. He really needs me in the business with him.'

'I know. But remember, you're always welcome . . . I miss you.'

'I feel the same way, Maxim. We've always been good sparring partners, haven't we?'

'The best.'

Stubby looked thoughtful. 'The girl . . . how old was she?'

'Seventeen or eighteen, thereabouts. Why?' Maxim lifted a brow.

'She's probably a student. I bet she bought books at Arcel's shop, and that she'll go back. Why don't we stop in there tomorrow? It's Saturday, we've nothing better to do.'

'Why? To what purpose?'

'We could ask old Arcel a few pertinent questions. He might know more than he realises. We could jog his memory. You never know, she might have given him a clue to her identity, and he just doesn't realise it.'

'Oh, Stubby, that's so far-fetched . . . it's clutching at straws . . . ' Maxim's voice trailed off lamely, and he fell silent. The impact of the girl was still fresh in his mind. He would give anything to know who she was, and to find her again.

FORTY

Anastasia saw him before he saw her.

He stood with his back to her, but then he moved his head slightly and she caught a glimpse of his face and her heart missed a beat. She did not have to look twice to recognise the man who had stared at her so penetratingly in Arcel's bookshop yesterday.

That he was a guest at the party celebrating Yvette's engagement to Philippe Arnaud was surprising in itself. But that she had spotted him amongst the two hundred people present, and so early in the evening, was remarkable. Even more amazing was the fact that he was actually talking to her *mother*. At least, the blond young man with him was engaged in conversation; *he* just stood to one side, listening politely. And his companion and her mother appeared to know each other quite well, if their animated expressions were anything to judge by.

Anastasia hovered a short distance away, at the other side of the dance floor. She was standing next to an enormous potted orchid, one of the many exotic floral decorations used to enhance the tented gardens of the de Millinets' house in Neuilly-sur-Seine, near the beautiful Bois de Boulogne.

She stepped behind the plant so that she was partially hidden from view herself but able surreptitiously to observe her mother and the two young men quite clearly.

Anastasia and her parents had arrived at the supper dance about half an hour ago, and, after greeting their host and hostess, and congratulating the newly engaged couple, they had stood chatting to each other for a few minutes, sipping champagne from crystal flutes, admiring the lovely setting and elegant guests. The men were in black tie. The women wore evening gowns and were much bejewelled. It was an extremely chic gathering; the *crème de la crème* of Parisian society mingled with movie people and members of the jet set.

After a while the three Derevenkos had separated and had wandered off in different directions. Alexander Derevenko had caught sight of some of his cronies from the picture business, and had loped off to hobnob with them near the bar. Margot had glided across the dance floor to join her friends Lucrezia and Sophie. Anastasia had drifted about aimlessly, seeking her own friends. Somewhat to her surprise not many of them were in evidence, certainly none of the girls to whom she was especially close. She felt rather lost, especially since Yvette clung to the arm of Philippe, her betrothed. There was such a scarcity of young people, she began to wonder if this was going to turn out to be a boring party – for adults only. Perhaps the de Millinets had invited more of *their* contemporaries than their daughter's special chums. That was not uncommon on these sort of occasions.

And then a split second later, she had seen *him*.

Instantly, she had thought: *Fate. We were* fated to meet again. I just knew it was so last night.

She had not stopped thinking about *him* since yesterday afternoon. The minute she had arrived home she had regretted her hasty flight from Monsieur Arcel's little antique bookshop on the Quai Saint-Michel. But the dark and handsome young man had had such an aura of sophistication and self-confidence about him, and he had stared at her so suggestively, and with such intensity through those dark piercing eyes, she had felt suddenly frightened. And somewhat inadequate. Shy, gauche, schoolgirlish, and most certainly out of her depth. She was very inexperienced when it came to men.

And so she had fled, run out into the street and hailed the first taxi she had seen.

But last night, when she had been dressing to go out to dinner with her parents and her father's Hollywood associates, she had decided to make herself look more grown up, older. Practising, she had muttered to herself as she had piled her hair on top of her head, put on pink lipstick, dressed in one of her new and more sophisticated outfits, a black silk two-piece, and high-heeled black patent shoes.

Her father had looked slightly startled when she had joined him and her mother and their guests for cocktails in the garden. He had murmured that she looked chic, a word he had never used in relation to her before, and her mother smiled and nodded in agreement. Later, at Tour d'Argent, she had noticed that quite a lot of people glanced her way, admiringly, and she had been pleased.

Last night she had been testing the waters, preparing herself, wanting to be ready when she saw *him* again. She was positive that their paths would cross; she had simply not known how quickly.

It was meant to be, Anastasia thought, staring at his well-defined profile. She wondered what to do. She acknowledged to herself that she ought to go and speak to him immediately, whilst her mother was engaged in conversation with the blond young man, so that her mother could introduce her to *him*.

She hesitated, and in that moment she saw that her mother was nodding graciously and walking away, moving across the floor to join another group of friends nearby.

Now, Anastasia instructed herself. *Go now. Go before it's too late, before he disappears in the crowd.*

Skirting the edge of the dance floor, where people were already beginning to dance, she walked over to the other side of the tented garden, and drew to a standstill immediately behind him.

He was tall. Taller than she had realised. At least six feet, and quite broad.

'Good evening,' she said.

He swung around and so did his companion. They both stared at her.

But she heard *his* quick intake of breath, observed his shock and disbelief registering, then saw pure pleasure invading his face.

'It's *you!*' he exclaimed.

'Yes.'

He thrust out his hand. 'I'm Maximilian West. Tell me your name before you disappear again.'

She took hold of his hand. It felt smooth, dry, and his grip was strong. 'I'm Anastasia Alexandrovna Derevenko,' she said.

'What a lovely name. And hello, Anastasia. Hello. *Hello.*' He swung to his friend. 'Alan, this is Anastasia. The young lady from Arcel's bookshop.'

'So I gather,' Stubby said. 'I can't begin to tell you what a pleasure this is, Anastasia. You *are* Madame Derevenko's daughter, aren't you?'

Anastasia nodded. A small frown furrowed her brow. 'Have we met before?'

Alan grinned. 'My parents have a villa in Cannes, and they are friends of the de Millinets. And yes, I think we did meet once. Rather fleetingly, a long time ago. You were about twelve, I believe.'

'Oh,' Anastasia said and smiled at Alan. He smiled back. They all smiled at each other.

Alan said, 'Excuse me, you two. I see an acquaintance of mine over there. Camilla Galland, the actress. I think I'll go and talk to her. She seems to be all alone, looks a bit forlorn. See you later.'

Stubby sauntered off nonchalantly.

'I thought I'd lost you,' Maxim said with breathtaking candour, staring at her, continuing to cling to her hand. 'I thought I'd never find you.'

'I knew we'd meet again,' she responded with the same brand of unselfconscious honesty.

'You did?' He sounded surprised.

'Oh yes, I was certain.'

'Why? I mean, what made you so sure?'

'It's Destiny.'

'Oh.' He paused, peered at her. 'Are you saying that I am your destiny, Anastasia?'

'Yes. And I am yours.'

'I hope to God you are.'

She half smiled, stood looking up at him, her eyes growing dreamier than ever. He was even more handsome than she had realised yesterday: his face was strong and masculine, his dark eyes brilliant, his nose straight and well-shaped above a mouth she could only think of as being beautiful. It was wide, full and generous. There's nothing mean about him, she thought, he's a man of great heart. She could tell this from his eyes and his mouth, the expression on his face. His dark brown hair had a slight wave in it, was brushed straight back from a broad brow. Straight away she noticed how immaculately dressed he was. His dinner jacket had most obviously been cut by the best tailor in Savile Row and the dress studs down the front of his pleated voile shirt were small cabochon sapphires set in gold. Discreet, and expensive, as was the paper-thin gold watch on his wrist. His impeccable clothes and grooming pleased her. She liked men to be well dressed, just as her father was.

For his part, Maxim was staring down into a face that had haunted him for the past twenty-four hours. It was a face of infinite beauty and sensitivity, with that hint of mystery he had noticed yesterday. The face of an angel, he thought. A Botticelli angel. It was the eyes, of course, which so captivated. They were so luminous and light-filled they appeared to be transparent, and they were a lovely hazy-blue in colour. They reminded him of *Mutti's* eyes.

It struck him that the girl appeared more grown-up tonight. It was the hairdo to a certain extent, upswept as it was into a coil of plaits on top of her head like a small coronet. Plus the touch of pink lipstick, the mascara on her thick blonde lashes. Yesterday she had not worn any makeup at all. The chiffon gown she was dressed in tonight and the delicate opal-and-diamond jewellery also enhanced her natural loveliness.

Finally, he spoke. 'What do you do, Anastasia?'

'I go to school. Or rather, I did until I passed my *Bac* earlier this summer. I shall be starting at the Sorbonne in the autumn.'

He nodded. 'How old are you?'

'Eighteen. And how old are you, Maximilian?'

'Twenty-five, and call me Maxim.'

'All right, *Maxim*. And what do you do?'

'I'm a financier.'

She laughed. 'At twenty-five!'

'Of course.' He grinned at her. 'I'm very clever.'

'I'm sure you are.' She laughed again. 'Could we dance? I like this song.'

'What's it called?'

'*Darling Je Vous Aime Beaucoup.*'

'It seems appropriate, let's dance.'

Still gripping her hand, he put his other arm around her shoulders, and led her to the dance floor, where he took her in his arms. For a moment he did not move, just held her very close to him, and she could feel his heart beating very rapidly, as hers was. They stood clutching each other for a little longer, and then he guided her onto the floor, staring down at her, smiling.

'It's a charming song,' he said as they began to dance.

'A friend of my father's wrote it,' she told him. 'Anna Sosenko. She's also in show business.'

'Does that mean your father is?'

'Yes, he's a film producer.'

Maxim merely nodded.

Once they fell into the rhythm of the music and were moving perfectly in step, Maxim slid one hand down her back, and pressed her body into his, and Anastasia welded herself to him. They danced on in silence, cheek to cheek, and she wished the dance would never end; and so did he.

Maxim kept her on the dance floor for several numbers, wanting to hold her in this intimate way, reluctant to let go of her. But at last he said, 'Let's sit and talk, Anastasia.'

FORTY-ONE

They sat at a table for two, hidden away in a corner near a bank of massed hydrangea, tulip and azalea plants, sipping champagne.

Maxim said, 'I enjoyed meeting your mother, she's very charming. Is your father here tonight?'

'Oh yes, he's standing over there near the bar with that group of men. He's the one with the blue cornflower in his buttonhole.' Anastasia smiled as she spoke and her face dimpled prettily. 'Daddy always wears a flower. It's sort of . . . his trademark.'

Maxim followed the direction of her gaze, craned his neck. 'Ah yes, I see him. He's a very handsome man.' Turning to her he remarked, 'Your name is Russian, but I presume your father has lived in France for a long time?'

'He was born here. In 1918. My grandparents are White Russians who came to Paris in 1917, at the time of the Revolution, and they've lived here ever since.'

'From speaking to your mother, I gather *she* is English.'

'Yes, but her father had a French mother, and she's got French blood, and therefore so do I. Well, a drop anyway, and Russian and English; actually, I'm a bit of a mongrel.'

'A thoroughbred, I would say.'

Anastasia flushed with pleasure at this compliment and murmured, 'And you're English, aren't you, Maxim?'

'By upbringing, education and citizenship, but I was born in Germany.'

'Were you really! I would never have guessed that.' She leaned across the table eagerly. 'But you do live in Paris now, don't you?'

'No, London. *Unfortunately.*'

'Why do you say unfortunately?'

He gave her a long, speculative look. 'Because you're not there.'

She stared back at him and her luminous eyes danced. 'I love London, and I go often to visit my English grandmother.'

'We'll see each other when you next come.'

Anastasia nodded. 'Granny's expecting me in August.'

'I'll collect you at the airport.'

'That'll be wonderful.'

Maxim looked at her carefully. He said, 'Will they let you get married?'

'When?'

'Now.'

'No, not yet. When I'm twenty. *Perhaps.* In two years.'

'Next year?'

'Maybe.'

'I'm serious, Anastasia.'

'Oh I know you are. So am I, Maxim.'

They sat staring at each other, their eyes locked, and they did not speak for the longest time, reflecting on each other's words.

Suddenly Anastasia said, 'Come and meet my father.'

They rose together, and Maxim took her hand and they walked across the tented garden to the bar on the other side.

Alexander Derevenko's eyes lit up when he saw his daughter approaching; it was quite obvious from the expression on his face that he adored her. Derevenko was tall, well built, an imposing-looking man, with dark curly hair, light-grey eyes and a somewhat broad Slavic face. He was dressed in a beautifully tailored silk-mohair dinner jacket; a deep-blue silk handkerchief flared in his breast pocket, matched the small fresh flower in his buttonhole.

'Anastasia!' he exclaimed, smiling at his daughter warmly. 'Where have you been for the last half hour?'

'Dancing . . . talking . . . with Maxim, Daddy.' She glanced at Maxim, then back at her father, and went on, 'I'd like to introduce him to you. Maximilian West . . . Alexander Derevenko.'

'I'm very pleased to meet you, sir,' Maxim said, taking her father's outstretched hand.

'My pleasure, Mr West. Let me present my friends and associates, Ilya Lopert, Gregory Ratoff, Anatole Litvak, and Sam Spiegel.'

Maxim shook hands with the four men, who greeted him most cordially, before turning their collective attention on Anastasia. She was obviously a favourite of theirs, and they appeared to be extremely fond of her.

Alexander addressed Maxim. 'Do you know the de Millinets from Paris or Cannes, Mr West?'

'From Cannes. But actually I don't know them very well, sir. They're friends of the Trentons, who are the parents of my best friend, Alan. I came with him tonight.'

'Oh, are the Trentons here?' Derevenko asked. 'I'd like to say hello to them. I've met them from time to time, over the years, mostly with the de Millinets in Cannes. Charming couple.'

'They're in Hong Kong, Mr Derevenko. That's why Alan and I popped over from London for the weekend. To attend Yvette's engagement party in their place, and also to do a bit of business.'

'What type of business are you in, Mr West?'

'Finance. I'm a financier.'

'Are you really, how interesting,' Alexander Derevenko said.

Anastasia slipped her arm through Maxim's and announced, 'We'd better go and find Alan. We did *promise* to sit with him for dinner.'

'Oh. Oh yes, that's right,' Maxim said, quickly catching on, understanding that she wanted to escape.

With a huge smile, Anastasia blew her father and his friends several kisses, and then glided off on Maxim's arm.

'I'm sorry I had to tell a white lie,' she whispered as they moved away. 'But if we hadn't escaped *then* my father would have engaged you in an everlasting conversation about film finance, and all that sort of boring business stuff. I saw the gleam enter his eye when you told him you were a financier.'

Maxim grinned. 'But I don't finance films.'

'*He* doesn't know that, and in any case, we didn't want to get stuck with Mummy and Daddy for supper, did we?'

He shook his head. 'And that was a good idea of yours. I do think we ought to look for Alan, find out what he's up to with Camilla Galland.'

'Do you know her?' Anastasia asked swiftly, looking at him through the corner of her eye.

'No. I've never met her. But I did see her last play in the West End. She's really rather a good actress.'

'I think she's supposed to be in a film for one of Daddy's associates, Pierre Petrovicci, so perhaps that's why she's here tonight. Pierre is a close friend of Jacques de Millinet, whose bank finances a lot of movies, and especially for Daddy's little clique.'

'Who *are* those four men I just met? What do they do?'

'They're lobby sitters,' Anastasia replied, her eyes full of sudden merriment. 'My mother says they're the *greatest* lobby sitters of all time.'

'I'm not following you,' Maxim frowned in puzzlement. 'Why does she say that about them?'

'Because they're always sitting in the lobbies of the best hotels around the world. The George V and the Prince de Galles here in Paris, Claridge's in London, the Excelsior in Rome, the St Regis in New York, and the Beverly Hills in Beverly Hills,' she explained, laughing. 'Having their endless business confabs. Talking picture deals.' She laughed again and finished, 'But joking aside, they are rather important men in the film industry.'

'But what do they *do*, actually?'

'Sam Spiegel's a wonderful producer. He made *The Bridge on the River Kwai*, and *The African Queen*, to name only a couple of his great films. And now he's thinking of making one about Lawrence of Arabia, so Daddy tells me,' Anastasia said. 'Grisha Ratoff and Tole Litvak are both directors, and Ilya Lopert is a producer, like Daddy and Mr Spiegel. One of his last pictures was *Summertime*. Daddy took us to Venice when they were making it, that's my most favourite place. Anyway, the film was lovely, very romantic. Perhaps you saw it?'

'As a matter of fact, I did. Katharine Hepburn and Rossano Brazzi, right? And what about your father? What I mean is, would I have seen any of his films?'

'I'm sure you must have. His last one was called *Eyes of Love*.' There was a little pause before Anastasia added, 'Camilla Galland was in it, although she wasn't the star. Janice Mills was the leading lady.'

Maxim said, 'I did see it, and it was terrific, a wonderful story. So you must know Camilla.'

'Not really, but I have met her.'

'I haven't. Shall we go over and say hello to her? Look, she's standing over there and she's still with Alan. She seems to have attached herself to him. Or vice versa.' Maxim looked at Anastasia and winked, his expression turning wickedly suggestive. 'Good old Stubby, I'm delighted he's found himself a girl for the evening.'

'Stubby!' Anastasia exclaimed, staring at him. 'What a peculiar name.'

Maxim couldn't help laughing at the look of disbelief on her face. 'I suppose it is,' he chortled. 'And it's my fault. I once called him that at boarding school when we were about eight or nine, and I'm afraid it stuck.

In retaliation, he nicknamed me Duke, after Duke Maximilian of Austria, because he said I was imperious.'

'Are you?'

'Sometimes. At least, Stubby says I am.'

She was reflective for a moment, then declared, 'Duke is certainly a better name than Stubby.'

'That it is,' Maxim agreed. 'Come on, let's join them.'

'Hello, Anastasia, it's so lovely to see you again,' Camilla Galland said, smiling sweetly, leaning forward and pecking her on the cheek.

Anastasia said, 'It's nice to see you too. I'd like to introduce Maximilian West, he's a friend of Alan's.'

Camilla and Maxim shook hands, and exchanged greetings.

Alan told them: 'We were just about to come and look for *you*. I think we ought to find ourselves a table and commandeer it. People are already beginning to sit down.'

'Yes, we should do that,' Anastasia concurred. 'Yvette told me there wouldn't be any place cards this evening, so we can sit wherever we wish.'

'That's a cosy table for four over there, let's grab it,' Maxim said, as usual taking charge in his masterful way. He immediately guided Anastasia towards it, saying quietly, 'I picked a small table because it's more intimate. Having just found you again, I don't want to share you with a lot of other people.'

She gazed at him through solemn eyes and admitted softly, 'And I don't want to share you either.'

They stood staring at each other, oblivious to everyone else, and Maxim had to resist the temptation to kiss her. She took his breath away, made him forget everything. Swallowing hard, he propelled her forward, wondering how and when to get her alone.

Once they were seated at the table, Maxim reached for her hand, held it tightly, and said, 'I believe it was most fortuitous that Stubby and I came to this party tonight.'

She nodded in agreement, sat looking at him through eyes grown dreamy, thinking how wonderful he was. She wished they were alone so that he could kiss her. She knew he wanted to, just as she did.

Camilla and Alan joined them at the table, took their seats, and Camilla immediately engaged Maxim in conversation.

Stubby turned to Anastasia and said, with a friendly smile, 'Your mother told me you have a new villa in Cannes.'

'Yes, in the hills above the town. It's very beautiful, and my mother loves it because the grounds are much larger, and she can garden away to her heart's content. I suppose your parents still have a house down there?'

Stubby nodded. 'They bought another place a couple of years ago, too. Listen, maybe we can all get together later this month? Maxim and I are planning to be down there at the end of July. Will you be in Cannes then?'

'Oh yes.'

Maxim, who had been listening to their conversation with one ear, whilst talking to Camilla, squeezed her hand and glanced at her quickly. He said, 'I'll need your phone numbers in Paris and Cannes, and I'll give you mine, Anastasia, so that —'

'Now I realise why I think I know you, Maximilian!' Camilla cut in, and rushed on, 'I've seen your picture in the newspapers, in fact I see it all the time. You're very popular with the press.'

Maxim hoped the actress wouldn't say anything about his reputation for being a playboy, which was untrue and undeserved. Much to his relief Camilla did not mention this. Instead she said, 'You're a friend of Faith Carr's, aren't you?'

'Yes, I am. So is Stubby. Her boyfriend, John Fuller, used to be at boarding school with us. Is she a friend of yours?'

'One of my closest,' Camilla answered, smiling at Maxim.

'Good old Johnny-boy, he's quite the lad,' Stubby cried, grinning, and the three of them launched into a long discourse about the engaged couple and their stormy on-again, off-again relationship.

Anastasia sat back in the chair, and sipped the iced water a waiter had just poured, listening to her companions with only half an ear. Her thoughts were focused on Camilla Galland. There was something about her she did not like. Yet she could not put her finger on exactly what it was about the girl which so disturbed her. All she knew was that she felt slightly uneasy in Camilla's company tonight, as she had when she had met her in the past. Consequently, she was on her guard, wary.

The other three were laughing uproariously about something and there was quite a lot of frivolity between them at this moment, and Anastasia found herself growing suddenly quiet and withdrawn. She felt like being the observer rather than a participant, at least for now.

Maxim was busy talking; he did not seem to notice her constraint, and for this she was thankful. The last thing she wanted was for him to think she was aloof or snobbish. She was not; it was Camilla's presence which made her feel cautious, and watchful. Once again Anastasia wondered why this was so. She hardly knew the English actress, had met her only a couple of times before, when Camilla had been in the movie her father had made last year. And if she was honest with herself, the young woman had always been cordial and pleasant.

As she had been so far this evening, Anastasia had to admit, and glanced across the table at her, thinking that Camilla was rather pretty in an understated way. She was very English-looking with her reddish-blonde hair, translucent complexion and light-green eyes. Anastasia knew she was about twenty-six but she looked younger than this, despite the rather sophisticated black-lace, halter-necked gown she was wearing and all the costly jewellery.

I wonder who gave her the diamonds? This thought made Anastasia sit up in the chair with a small jolt. And then something immediately clicked in her mind. Only last summer she had heard her mother and Aunt Lucrezia talking about Camilla Galland in the garden of Lucrezia's villa in Cannes. They had been speculating who Camilla's current 'protector' was, and discussing her extraordinary collection of jewels, and Lucrezia had said, 'She looks as if butter wouldn't melt in her mouth, doesn't she?' Both women had laughed knowingly, and her mother said, 'She bears watching, that one.' And they had laughed again, and gone on to talk about the painting her father was thinking of buying.

Is that it? Anastasia now asked herself. Am I leery of her because of the things my mother and Aunt Lucrezia implied, or is there something else about Camilla Galland which bothers me? She was not sure.

Maxim said, 'You're awfully quiet, Anastasia, and I can't say I blame you. Here we are, talking about people you don't know, and excluding you. How very rude of us.' He stared into her face. 'And you look so very pensive. What's the matter?'

'Nothing, really,' Anastasia reassured, turning to face him, smiling into his powerful dark eyes.

'Come and dance with me,' he said, rising, helping her out of the small, gold-painted chair.

Once again Maxim held her very close on the dance floor, and she responded by clinging to him tightly. It was obvious to them both that they shared the same overwhelming attraction for each other and identical feelings.

They had only been dancing for a few seconds when he murmured against her ear, 'Yvette is your friend, so you must know this place well. Can't we escape for a while, to be alone? Go for a stroll somewhere? When we arrived tonight I couldn't help noticing that the grounds of this house are very extensive.'

'They are, and yes, let's go for a walk, get a little air. It's stuffy in the marquee.'

Hand in hand, Maxim and Anastasia left the dance floor.

She led him through the tented parts of the garden, and out into the grounds, which were not covered by one of the three giant marquees erected specially for the engagement party.

It was a beautiful night, warm, balmy, gentle. The ink-black sky was sprinkled with dozens of stars and there was a hazy full moon, and the air was heavy with the scent of honeysuckle and roses and the profusion of other summer flowers which grew in great abundance here.

Maxim breathed deeply of the soft air, and murmured, 'It's such a beautiful evening, and you're so beautiful, my wonderful, incredible Anastasia.' He put his arm around her shoulders and kissed her cheek lightly and they walked on in silence towards the old walled rose garden. Yesterday when she had smiled at him he had experienced a sudden surge of unprecedented happiness and he had understood immediately that there was, for him, something very special about her. And since setting eyes on her tonight he had felt almost lightheaded. She was a most wondrous girl and his euphoria knew no bounds. He felt happier than he had since he had been a small child, and the sadness inside him, ever constant, seemed to diminish a little when he was near her.

They wandered through the rose garden and sat down on a rustic iron seat. With one hand, Maxim turned her face to his and looked deeply into her eyes, then found her soft lips with his mouth, kissed her ardently. She responded with equal fervour, and their mutual excitement mounted as their kissing grew more passionate, and they were entranced, lost to the world in each other's arms.

Anastasia was trembling inside, and swamped by fierce and overpowering feelings. She wanted to be with Maxim always, never to leave him again, and inexperienced though she was, she knew in the innermost part of herself that he was the right man for her. The only man she wanted. The only man she would ever want. She had understood this last night.

Maxim broke away from her gently and brought her head onto his shoulder, and, as if he had read her thoughts of a second ago, he asked softly, 'What made you say earlier that we were each other's destiny?'

'It was a powerful feeling I had after I'd seen you in the bookshop. I was absolutely positive we would meet again. I often get strong feelings about certain things, they're almost premonitions. My mother says I'm psychic, my father says I'm a witch.' She sighed lightly, and stroked his cheek, and then whispered, 'Que sera sera.'

'What will be will be,' Maxim translated, bent over her and kissed her gently, and he held her very tightly in his arms. He never wanted to let her go. They belonged together she and he. Two halves come together to make the whole.

And in the rose garden at that moment something was settled between them, and they both understood this, unspoken though it was.

FORTY-TWO

'I'm going to marry my beautiful dreamer,' Maxim announced suddenly, turning slightly in the plane seat to face Alan Trenton. The two men were on the early morning flight to London on Monday morning, following their long weekend in Paris.

Stubby returned his friend's unblinking gaze, and eventually said, 'Yes, I know. In fact, I knew on Saturday night.'

'Good God!' Maxim exclaimed, 'we were that obvious?'

'To me at least. I can recognise love at first sight when I witness it . . . a *coup de foudre*, as the French say.'

'Struck by lightning is right, old son. I've fallen terribly in love with her. I want her to be my wife, and the mother of my children, and I fully intend to spend the rest of my life with her. I'll let you into a secret, Stubby, the thought of being apart from her makes me feel genuinely quite ill.' Maxim shook his head. 'I've never felt like this before, I'm afraid I've fallen very *hard*.'

'I can understand why, Duke, she's a beautiful girl, and she has a lovely warm and outgoing personality.' Stubby hesitated a moment, and then he added quietly, 'She *is* very *young*, of course.'

'That's true; on the other hand, at eighteen she's still malleable.'

'I wouldn't be too sure. Anastasia might not be quite as pliable as you imagine her to be.'

Maxim raised a dark brow, gave Stubby one of his sharp and penetrating glances. 'What makes you say that?'

'From what I observed on Saturday night. For one thing, I think she has a lot of character, and strength of will . . . I bet you anything she's as stubborn as hell. Also, the girl's clever, brilliant actually. A lot of things came back to me this weekend, things I'd heard about the Derevenko girl, indirectly, from my parents. She's apparently an outstanding student, remarkably intelligent, and she's also artistically talented like her mother, who by the way is a very well-known and highly thought of interior designer in Paris, in case you didn't know.'

'Anastasia didn't mention that. I suspect we were too busy talking about ourselves.'

'In short, the girl is *exceptional*, Maxim. I'm certain she's not the submissive type.'

'Oh I agree with you, Stubby, and I'm glad she isn't. Submissiveness is not a trait I especially require in a woman, you of all people ought to realise that by now. When I used the word *malleable* what I meant was a woman who was not set in her ways or rigid, one who was flexible, ready to learn. I want a woman who can keep abreast with me, grow as I grow. I don't want a woman made of putty, one that I can mould into exactly what I want her to be.'

Don't you? Stubby wondered, but said, 'Then I believe that in Anastasia you have found your ideal woman.' Stubby shifted slightly in his seat, leaned closer, and asked, 'You say you're going to marry her. But what about her parents? I mean, won't they feel she's a bit young to be getting married this year?'

'Absolutely. But Anastasia thinks we can plan it for next year, when she's nineteen.'

'So you've already proposed?' It was Alan's turn to raise a brow.

Maxim chuckled. 'More or less, in a slightly flippant way on Saturday night. But she knew I meant it, and I knew *she* meant it, when she said she was as serious as I was. We have an understanding, Alan. We really do.' Maxim paused to glance out of the plane window, instantly swung his eyes back to his friend and finished, 'It's a quite extraordinary thing, but she and I are truly on the same wavelength.'

'Lucky blighter! I hope I can have that sort of relationship with a woman one day, feel so close and involved.'

'You will, I've no doubt. What about Camilla Galland? You seemed quite cosy with her on Saturday night, and then you had a date with her on Sunday. Aren't you interested in *her*?'

'I could be, given half the chance. But she's not champing at the bit as far as I'm concerned.'

'Is there a man in her life?'

'I gather there isn't, and that there hasn't been for a long time. Seemingly she was involved with someone, and very much so. But he died. Suddenly, unexpectedly. She's an interesting woman, Duke, and not at all like one might expect, given her glamorous looks and all that jazz. She's rather deep and reflective, has quite an intellectual turn of mind, and I discovered this weekend that she's very sensitive in so many different ways, not a bit the dumb blonde starlet.'

'I didn't think she was. She's far too good a stage actress to be dumb. Anyway, since she's not involved with anyone, you could ask her out again, couldn't you?'

'I have issued another invitation,' Stubby confessed, grinning sheepishly, 'and she accepted. We're having dinner at Les A. on Friday.'

Maxim punched his arm lightly and laughed. 'Now why did I ever think you'd let the grass grow under *your* feet, you Don Juan you!'

'Hang on a minute, I'm not the playboy, you are!'

'That's pure invention on the part of the British press, and you know it!' Maxim protested with quiet vehemence, giving Stubby a fierce glance. He resented terribly this label which had been erroneously pinned on him, and always reacted defensively even when it was mentioned in jest, had not yet developed a sense of humour about it.

'I know, I know,' Stubby exclaimed swiftly, sounding apologetic, 'don't get your knickers in a twist. I was only kidding. And when are you going back to Paris to see your lady love?'

'This weekend. But not to Paris. To Cannes. Anastasia and her mother are going down to their villa on Wednesday, so I thought I'd hop on a plane myself on Friday morning, pop down to the Côte d'Azur for a long weekend.'

'Are you staying with them?'

'Wasn't invited, Stubbs.'

'You can stay at my parents' villa if you wish. After all, it's standing there fully staffed, and with no one in it.'

'Thanks, I appreciate the offer, but no thanks. I'm going to book a suite at the Carlton Hotel. It's more convenient.'

'If you change your mind, let me know.' Stubby leaned back in the plane seat and then abruptly sat up, looked across at Maxim and said, 'How can you leave on Friday morning? I thought you had an appointment in Sheffield that day, with the managing director of Hardcastle Silversmiths? About buying the company?'

'Yes, I do, but I intend to change it. I'll go up to Yorkshire on Thursday. There won't be a problem.'

Stubby exclaimed, 'That clinches it then?'

'What does?' Maxim looked baffled.

'The fact that you're putting a woman before a business deal. You've never done that before in your entire life. So Anastasia *must* mean the world to you.'

'She does, Stubby. And anyway, if I don't see Anastasia this weekend, I won't be able to do so until early August.'

'Why? Aren't you coming to stay with us in Cannes in July after all?'

'I'm afraid I can't make it until the first week of August now, Stubby. I'm sorry about that, but it just can't be helped. I have to go to Berlin to see Aunt Irina, and then from Berlin I'm flying to New York for three days. I have a meeting with some Wall Street bankers.'

'It sounds as if you have a tough schedule this month, Duke.'

'Oh it's not that bad, and to be honest I sort of thrive on it.' There was a small pause, as Maxim eyed Stubby, and then said, with a huge grin, 'You will be my best man, won't you?'

Stubby grinned back. 'Did you have to ask?'

Maxim sat waiting for Teddy in the Grill Room of the Savoy. The hotel was one of her favourite places, since it had such romantic connotations for her, which was the main reason he had chosen it. He wanted her to be in the right frame of mind when he told her about Anastasia.

He arrived first, and when she appeared in the entrance to the Grill a short while afterwards he could not help but admire her. At forty Teddy had become a truly lovely woman. The years had treated her kindly, and her good marriage to Mark showed in her face, which had the bloom of happiness on it. There was an air of confidence, fulfilment and glowing contentment about her, and her eyes sparkled. Teddy, he thought, my dearest, dearest Teddy. Whatever would I have done without you? When I was growing up you were the rock of my life, and you've always been there for me, no matter what. He loved her very much, and her approval was very necessary and important to him.

Maxim rose as she came towards him, escorted by the head waiter, and he noted how chic she looked in her beautiful navy-blue linen Givenchy suit with a floppy silk rose on one shoulder, a smart little white hat and white gloves.

'You look stunning, Teddy,' he said as she came to a standstill, and he kissed her cheek.

'Thank you, Maxim dear,' she answered with a bright and loving smile, sitting down, pulling off her kid gloves. 'And you don't look too bad yourself. You must have had a restful weekend in Paris.'

He smiled. 'What would you like?'

She eyed his glass. 'If that's tonic water, which I feel certain it is, I'd like the same, please.'

After ordering the tonic water for her, he leaned closer and said, 'I'm going to see Aunt Irina in about a week. Would you like to come to Berlin with me?'

'Oh Maxim, I'd love to!' Teddy exclaimed and then made a small moue with her mouth. 'And I really do wish I could. But I can't. Mark and I have had a little holiday planned for ages. Just the two of us, without the children. We're going to Donegal, to stay at Dromlochan. You know, the Pells' house where we spent our honeymoon. The dates will clash, I'm afraid. But I have a couple of things for Irina, if you wouldn't mind taking them with you.'

'Of course not.' He cleared his throat, looked at her closely and said, 'Teddy, there's something I want to tell you.'

He sounded so serious she stared hard at him and a small frown puckered her brow. 'What? What is it? Is something wrong?'

'Not at all . . . I've met someone. I'm going to marry her.'

Teddy's face lit up. 'Oh darling, I'm so happy for you. Who is she? And why haven't *we* met her, if you're so serious about her? Why haven't you brought her home to Eaton Square for dinner?'

'I only just met her, Teddy.'

'When?' She sat back slightly in the chair, her head on one side, and looked at him quizzically.

At this moment the tonic water was placed in front of her by the waiter, and Maxim waited until they were alone before he responded to her question.

He said, 'It all happened this past weekend. Friday. Well, I *saw* her on Friday, I didn't actually meet her until Saturday.'

'But it's only Wednesday!'

'Nevertheless, I know what I feel. It's something I've never felt before. She's the one. The only one.'

Teddy was so flabbergasted she simply sat staring at him; there were no words.

Maxim said, 'You're going to love her, I know you are, Teddy. She's just the sort of girl you've always wanted for me.'

'Oh Maxim darling, it's so . . . so . . . *fast*. How could you possibly know, or be sure . . .'

'How long did it take *you* to realise what you felt about Mark, when you met him?' Maxim asked softly, giving her a pointed stare.

She was silent, thoughtful for a long moment. 'Well, you have me there, I suppose. Just a few hours . . . well, a few days at the most.'

'Exactly! One always knows how one feels about another person within a short time, Teddy. A very short time in my experience.'

'That's true.'

'And in any case, I'm not planning to marry her tomorrow, so we'll have a chance to get to know each other better.'

'When *are* you thinking of getting married?'

'Next summer. We have to wait until then. You see, she's only eighteen.'

Teddy was even more startled, although she tried to conceal this. But she did not succeed very well, and after taking a sip of the tonic water she put the glass down on the table, and gave Maxim a very direct look. 'Who is she?' she asked at last.

'Her name is Anastasia Derevenko,' he began, and then proceeded to tell Teddy how they had met, and everything there was to know about Anastasia.

When he had finished, Teddy said, 'I can't wait to meet her. She is obviously a very exceptional young woman, from what you say, and comes from a very good family. I –'

'They're not Jewish, Teddy,' he said quietly, quickly cutting in, 'Just in case you think they're Russian Jews – Ashkenazim – they're not.'

'Oh.'

'I hope that's not going to upset you, or trouble you.' Maxim put one hand on her arm as he spoke, and his dark eyes, levelled on hers, were searching.

Teddy sat very still, returning his piercing stare. Finally she said slowly, 'No, I don't suppose it does disturb me too much. I would have liked you to marry a Jewish girl, of course. It's always so much easier bringing up children when the parents are of the same faith, but to me your happiness is more important than anything else. If Anastasia is going to make you happy, then so be it.' Her smile was full of love, as she added, 'After all, you could marry a Jewish girl and end up being miserable. It's better that you marry a Gentile girl and have happiness.'

Maxim filled with relief, and the strained look of a moment ago instantly left his face. 'I knew I could count on you, my darling Teddy. I knew you would view the situation most intelligently, and not let religion cloud the issue. After all, you never pushed it down my throat when I was growing up, and Mark isn't particularly religious, is he?'

'No, nor has he ever been, as you well know. He never insisted that you be *Bar Mitzvahed*, for example. Still, even though his parents are Reform, they are quite religious, traditional. And you *know* Aunt Ketti is, Maxim. But let's not worry about them, you're twenty-five years old, and if anybody knows what they're doing, it's you.' Besides, she said to herself, I don't give much thought to religion these days. Not after what God has done to us. God abandoned the Jews a long time ago. *If* there is a God, and I can't but ponder that, when I think about the Holocaust.

Maxim reached out and squeezed her hand. 'Thank you, Teddy. And thank you for being you. There's just no one like you, there really isn't.'

'I can say the same about you, darling. And so, getting back to Anastasia, I give you my blessing, and so will Mark, I know. Now, most importantly, when are we going to meet her?'

'In August. She's coming to stay with her grandmother who lives not far from you, in Chester Street. I thought you could give a little dinner at home, just the four of us. Unless you want to go out somewhere?'

'We can decide that later, can't we?'

Maxim nodded. 'Are you busy immediately after lunch?'

'Not really, why do you ask?'

'I'd like to get into the safety deposit box at the Rossiter bank, to look at *Mutti*'s diamond ring. Perhaps Mark could have it cleaned and remounted. You see, I'd thought of giving it to Anastasia as her engagement ring.'

'What a lovely idea, Maxim. We can go to the bank straight from here, and whilst we're there today I wish you'd take over that box. I've been asking you to do so for ages, I don't know why you won't.'

'It's such a nuisance, I prefer to leave it in your name, Teddy.'

'The box should be in yours,' she insisted.

'Oh all right then, since you're making such a fuss. We'll do it this afternoon.'

'I'm glad. You should also take a look at your mother's other jewellery. You may want to give that to Anastasia as well.'

'Good thought. Now, shall we order lunch?'

'I think perhaps we'd better, if we want to get to the bank before three.'

Maxim motioned to one of the waiters hovering nearby, who instantly came to the table, proffering the menus.

'Thank you,' Teddy said, as she took hers. She buried her head behind it, thinking not of food but of Ursula's letter written in Paris twenty years ago. Teddy had never been able to give the letter to Maxim, or reveal the contents to him, not even when he was twenty-one. It was still in a second safety deposit box at the bank; long ago she had taken the precaution of separating it from Ursula's jewellery.

If he's old enough to marry he's old enough to have the letter, Teddy now thought. I *will* give it to him. *I must.* Yes, I'll give it to him before he gets married. She experienced such a sudden surge of relief as she made this decision after years of vacillating, it was as if a burden had been lifted from her shoulders at long last.

Quickly she scanned the dishes which were listed, looked over the top of the menu and smiled at Maxim. 'I'd like potted shrimp to start with, and then grilled sole.'

'Snap!' Maxim exclaimed, laughing. 'I had just decided on exactly the same.'

After he had ordered for them, they went on talking animatedly, and Teddy revelled in his happiness. Caught up as she was in Maxim and his plans, she put the letter out of her mind, knowing she would deal with it later.

She had no way of knowing then that when Maxim did marry Anastasia she would lose her nerve yet again, and that the letter would remain locked up in the Rossiter Merchant Bank in Berkeley Square, still unread by Maxim.

FORTY-THREE

'Maxim's success is remarkable, isn't it?' Margot Derevenko said, looking across at Alexander.

Her husband sat in his favourite chair near the window, at the other side of the *petit salon* in the house on the Faubourg Saint-Germain. It was a warm and pleasant evening at the end of July in 1961, and the Derevenkos were enjoying an aperitif before dinner.

Alexander, who was nursing a scotch and soda, took a swallow, before saying, 'Yes, it's incredible. What an extraordinary achievement it is to have made a million pounds before the age of thirty. One has to take one's hat off to him.'

'He's been good for Anastasia,' Margot murmured, then shook her head, laughed softly, almost to herself. 'And to think I had my doubts about him, when they told us they wanted to get married two years ago.'

'You know very well that *I* never did,' Alexander said. 'And I certainly didn't believe all that nonsense about him being a playboy.' Chuckling, he threw his wife a wise and very knowing glance. 'In fact, to be honest with you, Margot, I rather hoped Maxim *had* sown his wild oats before he met Anastasia, so that he wouldn't be sowing them at some future date, after they were married. I'm a great believer in a man getting all that sort of thing out of the way, before he settles down to matrimony.'

'Oh I agree wholeheartedly there!' Margot exclaimed. She sank into the beige silk of the small Louis XV sofa, crossed her elegant legs and sipped her champagne with a degree of reflectiveness. After a little while, she remarked, 'Maxim is very clever, isn't he, Alex?'

'Clever is a gross understatement, my dear. I believe him to be a genius . . . a financial genius.'

Margot stared at Alexander, her brow knotting in a frown. 'Why? How? I mean, what *makes* him a financial genius, in your opinion? Why Maximilian West, and not someone else?'

'That's a hard one to answer!' Her husband was thoughtful for a few minutes, before he placed his glass of scotch on the antique table next to the *bergère* where he sat, pushed himself to his feet, and hurried across the priceless Aubusson carpet. At the doorway, he swung around and beckoned to her. 'Come here a minute, Margot,' he said, and disappeared into the hall.

Margot was watching him in bewilderment, and she jumped up, hurried out after him.

He stood in front of the Degas painting of ballet dancers in green dresses, and as she drew to a stop next to him, he turned to her, waved his hand towards the painting, and said, 'What is that?'

'A painting, of course.'

'Yes, but it is also the outcome, the *result*, if you like, of artistic genius; and Westinvest, the company Maxim created from nothing, is the *outcome* of financial genius. Do you understand what I'm getting at?'

Margot nodded.

He went on, 'Now I can no more explain to you the creative impulse, what it *is* inside a painter that makes him capable of producing a breathtaking work of art such as this, than I can explain to you what it *is* inside Maxim that enables him to put together an incredibly successful company or a stunning deal.' Alexander shook his head, and smiled a little wryly. 'Nor can I explain to you the genius of Rachmaninoff or Puccini, or William Shakespeare or Emily Brontë.'

'It's a gift!' Margot exclaimed, her face growing animated, her eyes lighting up. 'Artistic genius is a great *gift*! A person cannot acquire it, but is born with it, and it has always been there since infancy, becomes apparent in childhood, and flowers in adulthood. And just as a great artist, writer or composer is born with genius, then so was Maxim born with it. Teddy once told me he was a mathematical wizard when he was six or seven years old. A prodigy, in a sense.'

'Yes, so I remember. But there's a lot more to it than being brilliant with figures, I believe.' Alexander took her arm, and led her back into the small sitting room, where they returned to their seats, and sipped their drinks. Alexander murmured, 'In my opinion, Maxim is preternaturally sharp, has great shrewdness and intelligence, and perhaps, more importantly, extraordinary vision.'

'For someone who said he couldn't explain financial genius, I think you may have just done so,' Margot said, eyeing him lovingly.

'No, I haven't, not really, Margot. I've only scratched the surface, given you a few of his character traits. I won't pretend that I could ever get to the bottom of Maxim, understand what makes *him* tick, because I am fully aware that that is an impossibility.'

Margot gave an understanding nod. 'I'm sure nobody will ever be able to do that. He's far too deep a man, and very *complex*. Even Anastasia has mentioned this to me.'

'*Oh.*' Alexander looked at her swiftly, his eyes sharp. 'No problems, I hope?'

'No, darling, none whatsoever. They're madly, crazily, blissfully in love, but then you know that. It was simply a remark she made to me in passing.'

'With his history, I'm not surprised he's complex,' Alexander muttered, and nodded to himself, and then he glanced across at his wife, and confided: 'I sometimes think Maxim has a genie telling him things. I'll never know where he gets his ideas from, what prompts his decisions, or why he makes his moves when he does, but they are all brilliant. In fact, Margot, everything our son-in-law does in business is dazzling. There are no doubts in my mind that Maxim will amass a gigantic fortune and immense power. Selling Westinvest now, and making himself a clear profit of one million pounds, is merely the beginning. Let's not forget that he's only twenty-seven years old.'

'He's proving to be a remarkable provider,' Margot said. 'And certainly a very loving and adoring husband, so I know he's going to be the best father, Alexander. Nothing less than wonderful. The signs are already there. He simply worships little Alix.'

'And speaking of our baby granddaughter, let's go upstairs and take a peek at her before we go out to dinner, shall we?'

Margot's response to his suggestion was a vivid smile, and she sprang to her feet at once, led the way out of the sitting room. The Derevenkos climbed the stairs to the next floor, where Anastasia's old bedroom was located. This had recently been redesigned by Margot, and was now a nursery for the four-month-old baby.

Jennifer, the English nanny, appeared in the doorway of the room next to the nursery when she heard their steps on the stairs; she stood there smiling, waiting for them to cross the landing.

'May we have a look at Alix before we go out to dinner, Jennifer?' Margot asked.

'Of course, Madame Derevenko. She's sleeping soundly, as usual.' The young nanny smiled. 'She's such a good baby, never a whimper out of her.'

Margot and Alexander tiptoed across the carpeted floor of the dimly-lit nursery, and stood looking down at their grandchild sleeping so peacefully in the pink wicker crib trimmed with pink satin ribbons and bows.

After a moment they raised their heads. Their eyes met across the crib, and they smiled at each other with pleasure and pride. Then they tiptoed out quietly, so as not to awaken the baby.

As they went downstairs to the *petit salon* Alexander murmured, 'I'm glad they've gone to Venice for a second honeymoon. With a little luck perhaps they'll make us another grandchild. A boy this time.'

Margot merely smiled.

*

Venice was like a mirage, floating, dreamlike, blues and greys mingling, soft vaporous mists lifting from the lagoon and the canals. Ancient buildings rising up, inchoate images in the muted light. And everywhere a sense of tranquillity and serenity.

La Serenissima, Anastasia whispered to herself, using the name by which the Venetians had called their city for thousands of years. *La Serenissima* . . . so hauntingly beautiful in its splendid isolation, trapped between sea and sky, her favourite place, which she had loved since she had first gone there as a child. Every aspect of it fascinated and intrigued her; she was forever held in its thrall, a captive to its mystery and everlasting beauty and wondrous dreamlike quality.

Anastasia stood at the window of their suite in the Danieli, staring out across the lagoon, which was still hazy with early morning fog. She so brimmed with happiness and incandescent joy she hardly dared contemplate it, for fear of losing it. Tempt not the jealous Gods, she thought, shifting slightly on her bare feet, moving closer to the window, resting her forehead against the glass, still half asleep as she drifted with her thoughts. Maxim was at the centre of them. He was her dream and her reality. He was her world . . . the sun, the moon, the stars . . . without him she would have nothing.

She sighed under her breath. Soon they would have to leave Venice. They had been here a week already and time was running out; their short summer holiday would soon be over. But every single day had been miraculous, perfect, a replaying of their honeymoon, except that everything was better than before, if that was at all possible. He was a wonder, her beautiful husband, and he filled her with wonder. She loved him so much there were moments when she thought she could not endure it, and she could hardly bear to be away from him, wanted always to be at his side.

A fragment of a verse from the *Song of Solomon* ran suddenly through her mind . . . My beloved is *mine* and I *am* his. That was the truth, that was exactly the way it was with them. They belonged to each other. And then she remembered another line from the same book in the Bible . . . I am *sick* with love. How apt those words were. She quite often felt ill, feverish, weak in the legs, trembling all over, filled with yearning for him. There was never a moment in a day when she did not long for his hands on her body, ache for his presence. He was a most wondrous lover, a wondrous husband . . .

So caught up was she in her contemplation of him, she did not hear him get up off the bed and cross the floor, and she started in surprise when she felt his strong cool hands on her bare shoulders.

'What are you doing up so early, my love?' Maxim murmured against her long blonde hair in his warm and mellifluous voice, and turned her to face him.

'I couldn't sleep,' she whispered, touching his cheek with one hand, staring up at him, her eyes moist with emotion, spilling her love.

He leaned closer to her and so did she, mouth seeking mouth. They kissed, and Maxim pulled her even closer, encircled her with his arms. After a moment of clinging together, he released her, slid his hands down her silk-clad back, let them rest on her rounded buttocks, then pressed her into him. Their bodies fitted perfectly together. He thought: two halves do make a whole. He parted her lips, slipped his tongue into her mouth to touch hers.

Anastasia was overcome with desire for him, and she felt the heat rising inside her. It was a fierce and tingling heat which started in her feet, rushed up her legs into her thighs and her groin, flooded her stomach, spread itself through her breasts, and she even felt the warmth of it in her neck. And then suddenly her faced flamed with the red-hot flush of love and desire and need.

Maxim could feel the heat from her body through their thin night-clothes. He drew back from her, took her hand in his, and led her back to the bed, aware now of how much she wanted him. They sat on the edge of the bed and he brought his mouth to hers, sucking at it gently, and they fell back on the eiderdown, their kisses growing in intensity and passion. He was as hungry for her as she was for him.

But within seconds Maxim curtailed their kissing, raised himself up on one elbow, bent over her, smiling into her luminous eyes. Lightly, gently, fleetingly, he kissed her forehead, her eyelids, her nose and her cheeks. She opened her arms and stretched them out to him, and he came into them, lay against her and suddenly his kisses were as passionate as they had been a few minutes before. He crushed his lips to hers, his teeth grazing against hers as he devoured her mouth. Anastasia's response was ardent, as ever, and she met his passion with a fervour that more than matched his, her whole body quivering for him.

Inflamed himself, he pulled away momentarily, stared down at her, marvelling at her beauty. Her head was thrown back, her long white neck exposed to him. There was something vulnerable and tender about her throat and he brought his lips to it, nuzzled his face against her neck. His hand reached out for one of her breasts, and he began to stroke it tenderly. Within an instant the nipple hardened under his touch, was taut and pointed against the silk of the nightgown.

He felt himself stiffen and his erection was enormous, as it always was with her. A groan trickled out of his throat and he slid his hand down over her flat concave stomach, lifted the filmy silk fabric covering her.

Maxim had learned every part of her body well since their marriage and now he sought the centre of her, found it at once, let his fingertips flick delicately against the core of her.

Anastasia moaned and arched slightly towards him, all of the heat of her body centred in the core of her womanhood.

To Maxim the moist warmth of her was irresistible. He wanted to sink himself into her, take her to him, possess her completely with every bit of his strength, yet he held back, needing to give her pleasure first. He pulled at her silk nightgown. It slipped off her shoulder and he reached for her breast, cupped his hand around it. Her flesh was pearly-tinted in the pale light of early morning, and cool as marble to his mouth. She sighed deeply, as he let his lips linger on her flesh. Unexpectedly he sat up abruptly, lifted her bodily and pulled the nightgown over her head, then shed his pyjamas, his movements swift and urgent.

Naked, they stretched out together on the bed, lying on their sides so that they faced each other, their bodies barely touching. His brilliant dark eyes impaled hers, and he said in a hoarse voice thickened by desire, 'I love you, Anastasia, you'll never know how much, my darling. I can't find the words to tell you. To say *I love you* just doesn't seem *enough* somehow.'

'I know, I love you in the same way,' she whispered, stretching out her hand, stroking his cheek lovingly, wanting him.

He turned her onto her back, raised himself above her, looked down into her huge grey-blue eyes. 'You're my life,' he said.

She half-smiled at him, stretched her body voluptuously, slightly parting her legs, and closed her eyes, and he leaned over her long slender body, enjoying its perfection and youthful beauty. He began to give her pleasure, kissing her breasts, first the one and then the other, until the nipples stood high and the breasts were taut. And then he brought his mouth onto her stomach, trailing his lips down and down and down until they came to rest between her thighs. He caressed her lightly with his tongue and fingers, and she opened herself to him, flowed out to him, and after a moment he felt her stiffen and begin to spasm as she called his name over and over.

He braced himself above her on his hands, and she took him into her lovingly, her face full of adoration as she gazed up into his eyes. She ached to possess him now, just as he did her.

Maxim let out a long sigh as he thrust deeply into her, and she cleaved to him, then wrapped her legs around his back. He put his hands under her body, lifted her closer to him, and they instantly found their own rhythm as they had since the first night of their marriage. They were finely tuned to each other, and they soared upward and upward together as their passion mounted, and as he came to her finally he cried out her name in his need, and they fell away into infinity together.

Later, as they lay in each other's arms, Maxim said, 'Last year when we were here you became pregnant with Alix. I hope we've done it again, my darling.'

'You and Daddy both,' she laughed, resting her head against his chest, throwing one arm over his body possessively. She turned her eyes up to his, said with mock solemnity, 'Unfortunately, I don't think we *have*. Not yet. Shall we do it again? It's wonderful, trying to make babies, I really can't think of anything I like doing better.'

Maxim smiled against her hair, forever enchanted by her. 'You're insatiable, Mrs West.'

'If I am, it's your fault. You're the one who has led me into my wicked ways, taught me everything I know.' She let out a tantalising laugh, slid her hand over his thighs, took hold of him gently.

'And what a willing, enthusiastic and able pupil I've had,' he murmured thickly, every part of him wanting her again. He lifted her face to his, kissed her deeply, and began to make love with her once more.

At noon they took a boat to Torcello, one of the many islands in the lagoon, which had once been a fishing village. They strolled through the ancient streets until they came to their favourite little trattoria and went inside. They were greeted warmly by Giovanni, the friendly proprietor, who knew them, and who led them outside to the gardens.

'Two camparis with soda, please, Giovanni,' Maxim said, after he had seated them at one of the tables.

'*Si, Signore,*' Giovanni said, smiling, bowing, hurrying away.

Their table stood under a wide canopy made of plaited straw matting which covered the spacious loggia, and fingers of sunlight trickled through the woven material, turning Anastasia's hair to mottled gold, casting delicate shadows across her face. Maxim stared at her, and recited, '*She walks in beauty, like the night of cloudless climes and starry skies, and all that's best of dark and bright meet in her aspect and her eyes.*'

'Byron,' she said, looking across at him. 'The only poet one should quote in Venice I suppose, since this was his city. And thank you . . . how you do flatter me, my darling.'

'He might have written those words for you, Anastasia. God you're beautiful! And oh God, how I love you!'

'And I you,' she said, smiling at him, settling back, relaxing in the chair. She loved this small trattoria, so casual and unsophisticated, and charming in its rustic simplicity. The shaded loggia where they were sitting fronted onto wide lawns and many flower beds which were resplendent with honeysuckle, roses and azaleas, the latter the colour of dark burgundy wine. There were trees in abundance, all offering welcome shade in the intense heat of this August day, stately cypress, and willows, and, close by their table, a giant magnolia tree with flowers the size of a man's hand, the dark green leaves so glossy they might have been polished that very morning.

'Oh, Maxim!' she exclaimed suddenly. 'Isn't it beautiful here? So peaceful and relaxed. I've never been so *happy*. Never.'

'I'm always happy with you, *wherever* we are,' Maxim replied, meaning every word. 'You help to make the pain go away.' He regretted these words the moment he had uttered them, having never said anything remotely like this to her before. He tended to keep certain thoughts to himself, was an intensely private man.

She sat staring at him, a small knot of perplexity settling between her eyebrows, and she opened her mouth, was about to say something when a waiter arrived with their drinks.

'*Grazie, grazie*,' Maxim said, and once they were alone he lifted his glass, touched it to hers, then took a swallow. 'That tastes good,' he said. 'Very refreshing.'

Anastasia followed suit, tasted the drink, put her glass down, and gave him a keen look. 'What did you *mean* when you said I help to make the pain go away?'

What a stupid slip of the tongue, he chastised himself, wondering how to answer her. 'I honestly don't know what I meant,' he lied, and then added quickly, with adroitness, 'I was always so disappointed in love, disappointed with the women I took out before I met you. I was a bit lonely I would say, looking back. Yes, that's what I meant . . .' He reached out, squeezed her long, tapering fingers. 'And you have changed all that.'

She beamed at him. 'I'm so glad, Maxim. I can't bear to think that you were ever unhappy or sad. You weren't lonely as a child, were you?'

He shook his head. 'Of course not!' he exclaimed a little too heartily. 'I had Teddy, and good old Stubby.'

At this moment Giovanni appeared and regaled them with the day's specialities, and immediately took their order. When the proprietor had hurried off to the kitchen Maxim started to speak to Anastasia about his impending trip to Berlin to see Irina Troubetzkoy. 'And I thought you might like to go with me,' he finished. 'I plan to leave about the tenth of the month.'

'I *want* to go, and I can't *bear* the idea of being away from you,' Anastasia said with another small frown. 'But I don't want to leave

Alix again. Not so quickly after this trip to Venice. You don't mind, do you?'

'Naturally I mind, but I understand.' He gave her a most loving smile, and his eyes were tender as they rested on her.

Their lunch arrived a few minutes later, and it was delicious. They started with warm polenta, the cornmeal lavished with the tiniest of fried shrimps, herbed and seasoned most delicately. They were slightly oily, and so soft they melted like butter in the mouth. Next, they had fritto misto, tiny little fried fish of all kinds, crisp and succulent; the fish went well with the simple green salad and crisp local bread which Giovanni had sent out to them with the waiter. Maxim had ordered chilled white wine, and it was light, clear, greenish, a young wine and one he had drunk before in Venice, the perfect choice.

'Wasn't that good!' Anastasia exclaimed when they had finished, looking across the table at him. 'But I would still like something else. Do you think I'm eating for two?'

'Possibly *three*, the way we've been going at each other since we got here,' Maxim responded with a wicked smile. 'And I certainly hope so. Twins would please me well.'

She laughed delightedly, and when the waiter reappeared to take their plates away and enumerate the desserts, she settled for *fraises des bois*, the tiny wild strawberries endemic to France and Italy, slightly perfumed and tasting their very best when eaten without cream or sugar. Maxim ordered a sliver of Bel Paese cheese with grapes for himself, and black coffee for them both.

After lunch they took a boat across to the Guidecca at the other side of the lagoon.

They went walking along the street which was called the Guidecca, and which faced towards the Guidecca Canal, and the Grand Canal beyond, the two waterways flowing into the lagoon.

Maxim stood with his arm around Anastasia's shoulders, staring out into the distance. Venice lay across the wide expanse of water, and the whole of the city was stretched out before them – resplendent, glorious, magical, gleaming in the afternoon sunlight.

'It's the most wonderful view I've ever seen,' Maxim said, suddenly turning to her. 'Look at the perfect alignment of spires and towers and cupolas.'

Their eyes swept over the Palace of the Doges and the great palaces of long-dead Venetians, the Palladio churches, and the salt houses, where salt from the lagoon had been dried centuries before. And they were both struck by the breathtaking beauty of Venice which appeared to float on the water before their eyes.

'No wonder Canaletto and Turner wanted to paint Venice,' Anastasia said. 'What artist wouldn't want to capture this splendour on canvas.'

'It does have a timeless beauty. It's unique, there's nowhere quite like Venice in the entire world,' he said, a hint of awe in his voice.

They sauntered on, hand in hand, to the end of the Guidecca, and then retraced their steps, and eventually they took a boat back to the Danieli.

They lay together in the deep bed, reclining on huge soft Continental feather pillows, the kind he remembered from his childhood in Berlin. They were lazy and languorous after their lunch and the boat trips, but the bedroom was cool and restful, shaded from the hot sun by the slatted wooden shutters.

Maxim ran his lips down her bare arm, enjoying the feel of her silken skin, the smell of her. Anastasia's body was fragrant from the sun, and it held a tinge of salt from the sea wind that had blown up on their boat ride back to the hotel from Guidecca Island. Golden skin, the colour of an apricot, and just as smooth, he thought, running a finger from her shoulder to her wrist. But it has the bloom of the rose upon it.

Anastasia turned her huge pellucid eyes to him and smiled lazily: she was satiated from their lovemaking of the last hour, and sleepy from the wine at lunch.

'Have a nap,' he suggested, bending down to kiss her hair.

'Mmmmm, I think I will,' she said, nestling into the pillows, pulling the sheet up over her naked body.

He rested on one elbow, continuing to contemplate her for a while, loving her so much. She was the most extraordinary girl, full of enormous warmth and joy, and so very generous and giving of heart. She was sensual and voluptuous, too, a discovery which had delighted him, given him tremendous satisfaction.

Very erotic, my little Botticelli angel, he thought, smiling inwardly, remembering their honeymoon. Virgin though she had been when he had married her, she had taught him more about sexuality than any other woman he had known intimately. There was no coyness or false modesty about her, and after the first few months of marriage he had come to understand her needs and desires, since she made it clear what pleased her the most. Also, in a curious way she had taught him about his own body, had made it come alive as never before. She adored his body and told him so, took all the pleasure she wanted from it and from the fulfilment he gave her. She pleasured him in return, as no woman ever had, and they cried out in their mutual need, in the excitement and ecstasy of their lovemaking, and there was no restraint between them.

Maxim slid off the bed and walked over to the window, and stood where Anastasia had stood that morning, gazing across the water, marvelling at the incredible beauty spread out before him in the fading light of late afternoon.

He would never forget their times in Venice, would always remember the softness of the air here . . . the serenity . . . the mists and the blue-grey skies the colour of her eyes . . . the balmy nights . . . the lapping sound of the canals as the water slapped against the pilings whilst they slept. And Venice would always be associated in his mind with the exquisite Anastasia, his beautiful dreamer, the girl of his dreams, his true love, his dearest wife, the only wife he would ever want.

FORTY-FOUR

'Thank you for a wonderful lunch. You outdid yourself,' Maxim said, smiling at Princess Irina Troubetzkoy, placing his napkin on the table, pushing the chair back slightly, and crossing his long legs.

'I'm glad you enjoyed it,' she said, also smiling, her bright blue eyes lighting up with pleasure at his compliment.

'I always do, but I still think it was far too hot a day for you to be in the kitchen. You should've let me take you out, as I wanted to.'

'No, no. I insist on making one meal for you whilst you're in Berlin, *Liebling*. You're so good to me, it's the least I can do.'

'But I am taking you out tonight, Aunt Irina. We'll have dinner at one of your favourite restaurants, and then, if you like, we'll go dancing afterwards. I know how much you enjoy that.'

'You spoil me, Maxim – you make me feel young again,' she said with a gay laugh.

'You're not old!'

'I was fifty in March, don't forget.'

'That's still not old, and you certainly don't look anywhere near fifty,' he answered in absolute truthfulness, thinking how beautiful Irina was today, slender and elegant in a delphinium-blue silk dress that exactly matched the colour of her vivid eyes. Her auburn hair was as burnished as ever, and no doubt owed a great deal to the skill of the hairdresser these days, he was quite certain of that. Nonetheless, it did not look dyed, and it was as becoming as it had always been with her clear pink-and-white complexion. But perhaps the most remarkable thing about her was her face, which was still lovely and relatively unlined, despite the very hard life she had had.

'You're staring at me,' Irina said, her expression questioning as she gazed back at him.

'But admiringly so, Aunt Irina. You do look extremely well, you know.'

'Thanks to you and your love and care, and the help you have given me over the years, and Teddy, who has also been so affectionate. You've both been wonderful to me. I can never thank you enough.'

'Thanks are not necessary, we're your family,' he replied. 'Now, how about a glass of lemon tea? After that *Schwarzwälder Kirschtorte* of yours I really need it.'

Irina laughed at his expression. 'I didn't force you to eat it, and it is your weakness, you know,' she said, laughing again. 'You've loved it since you were a child.'

'Chocolate and cherry tart with lashings of cream might be permissible when you're four years old, but it helps to put the weight on when you're twenty-seven.'

Irina frowned slightly, shook her head, said slowly, 'I keep forgetting how old you are. It seems like only yesterday that I held you on my knee and rocked you to sleep, when I used to stay with your parents at the villa in the Wannsee.'

'Time flies, Aunt Irina, doesn't it?'

'It truly does. Just imagine, your father was your age when I first met him. Goodness me, so long ago ... before you were even born.' Irina suddenly averted her face, stared into the distance, then stood up abruptly, unexpectedly. 'I had better go and ask Hilde to make the tea, if you'll excuse me a moment,' she said, hurriedly walking away from the table.

Maxim, who had risen with her, said, 'Let's have it in the living room, shall we?'

'Why not, it's much cooler in there anyway,' she replied as she rushed across the dining room, making for the kitchen.

Conscious of the sudden change in her mood, he stared after her in puzzlement, shrugged, swung around and strode out to the entrance hall, where he veered to his left. The living room opened off the hall through an arched doorway, and it was spacious and airy in feeling, looked down onto the Lützowufer and the Landwehrkanal. He strolled up to the windows and stood staring out across the canal; his eyes focused on the leafy green treetops of the Tiergarten beyond.

He and the baron, Irina's stepfather, had bought this apartment for her in 1956. When he and Teddy had flown to Berlin to see it, both women had laughed because the new building was so close to the spot where Irina's 'little abode' had once been. He had never seen her 'hole in the ground', but he had heard about it from Teddy, and it sounded like an appalling place for anyone to live, especially a Romanov princess.

When he had come back to Berlin for the first time since his childhood in 1950, Irina was already ensconced in the studio off the Ku'damm, a place which Mrs Reynolds had found for her in 1949. This had been merely adequate, in his opinion, and even the larger studio on the Budapesterstrasse, which she had moved into later, had seemed cramped and dismal. And so when this apartment had come up for sale he had been delighted to help pay for it, having always wanted her to have somewhere which was gracious and comfortable, and which she could make into a proper home.

Through an arrangement with the Deutsche Bank in Frankfurt, established by the Rossiter Merchant Bank, he had been sending money to Irina since he was sixteen. She had not asked for anything, nor was she aware that he had anything to give, as far as he knew, but the conditions under which she was living at the time, and her plight in general, had so disturbed him that he had been determined to assist her. Teddy, as his legal guardian, had agreed, and the banks had worked out a way to transfer the money directly to her. Her stepfather, although not a rich man, helped out as well: also, Irina had been earning money herself for several years, had become a respected freelance translator for various German publishing houses. Maxim did not care whether she worked or not. He was delighted to support her. She had been very close to his parents, and he knew his father would have done exactly the same thing under the circumstances, had he been alive.

What gratified Maxim the most was the way she had created beauty, charm and comfort in the flat, using furniture the baron had given her from the castle in the Black Forest – plus much flair and ingenuity. Maxim's eyes swept around the living room and he noticed a few new additions since his last visit: handsome silk cushions on the big cream brocade sofa and several silk-shaded lamps. Also new were the framed photographs of his baby daughter Alix, arranged on the piano along with the other pictures.

Walking over to the piano, Maxim bent forward and peered at them. To one side were replicas of his own favourites, which he had had since boyhood, and which Teddy had copied for Irina years ago. *Mutti* and Papa in evening dress – the famous 'portrait' taken in 1935 – and the family group which commemorated his fourth birthday. The third picture was the one of *Mutti* and Teddy and himself standing outside the Plaza Athénée in

Paris in 1939. His marriage to Anastasia was well represented; he picked up a silver-framed photograph of his wife and himself on their wedding day in Paris, stood looking at it, admiring her, thinking how beautiful she was in her lace wedding gown, flowing white veil and coronet of orange blossoms.

After a moment he put it back in its place and swung around, as Irina came gliding back into the living room, carrying two glasses of steaming lemon tea on a tray.

She set this on the coffee table in front of the sofa, looked across at him, and said, as she sat down, 'I had a rather nice letter from Margot and Alexander Derevenko the other day. They've invited me to stay with them in Cannes . . . the last week of September.'

'I think you should go, it'll do you good,' Maxim told her, walking over, sitting down in one of the two armchairs on either side of the sofa.

'I was going to accept. They're a lovely couple, and I enjoy being with them.'

Maxim said, 'Alexander just bought an extraordinary painting at auction – another Degas. I must say, he is acquiring an impressive collection of art – ' Maxim broke off, reached for the glass of tea Irina had placed in front of him, and took several sips, sat back in the chair. A thoughtful look slid onto his face, and he appeared to be momentarily distracted.

Irina studied him intently for a second, the expression on her face as thoughtful as the one on his. The pause lengthened. Eventually, she said softly, 'You're thinking about the Westheim Art Collection again, aren't you?'

He nodded. 'I don't suppose we'll ever know what happened to the Renoirs, and all the other great works my family collected.'

'I'm afraid not . . . they're gone, lost without a trace. But so many valuable paintings and objects of art belonging to so many people disappeared during the war, Maxim. Some were destroyed in the bombing raids, or were confiscated by the Nazis. *Stolen* is perhaps a better word to use.'

Maxim focused his dark, penetrating gaze on her. 'I'll never understand why my father didn't leave Germany in the thirties, when so many Jews *were* getting out.'

'You've said that to me every year since you were sixteen, and I've never had a proper answer for you, or an explanation. I still don't, I never will.'

'He was such a brilliant man, an international banker,' Maxim muttered. 'And he knew so much about everything. As long as I live, I will never be able to fathom out *why* he lingered the way he did, why he left it until it was too late.'

'So many did, Maxim. Millions of German Jews thought nothing would, or *could* happen to them, especially those of wealth and standing and position. It was a terrible misjudgement, of course.'

'I know, and you've told me that so many times in the past. But I still cannot comprehend how my father could have ignored all the signs –'

'Your father wasn't the only one who miscalculated!' she exclaimed peremptorily. 'Millions made the same mistake. If they hadn't, if they'd left Germany, there would have been no Holocaust.'

'Yes, so I realise.'

'When he did decide to get out, to get the entire family out, we thought there was enough time, Kurt and myself, Reinhard and Renata. We were quite sure we could get you all to safety with the help of Admiral Canaris and Colonel Oster . . . but, of course, I've told you this before.'

'I'm sorry to keep mentioning it every time I come to Berlin. I suppose I just can't help myself.'

'I understand, I really do. There are so many memories for you here, and you're bound to think of your mother and father.' Irina's eyes strayed to the photographs on the piano and she stared at the portrait of Ursula and Sigmund for a long moment, then, with a faint smile, she murmured, 'You look so much like he did when he was your age. He – ' Irina cut off her sentence. Her mouth trembled and tears suddenly brimmed. She brought her hand up to her mouth swiftly, and turned her head away.

'Aunt Irina, what is it?' Maxim asked, filled with concern.

It took her a little while to regain her equilibrium. Finally, she turned back to Maxim and said, in a very soft voice, 'I loved him, you know. Oh please don't misunderstand, there was never anything between us, he only had eyes for your mother. In fact, he never knew how I felt, I kept my feelings very carefully hidden.' She paused, a faint smile flickered. 'We were such good friends, he and I, and that's how he thought of me, only a friend. I was, well, a sort of chum to him. A pal. But I fell in love with him when I first came to Berlin, when I first met Sigi and Ursula. I was so very fond of her too, she was my dear, dear friend.' Irina sighed and looked at Maxim through eyes still moist. 'Your father is the only man I've ever loved.'

Maxim rose, went and sat next to her on the sofa. 'Oh Aunt Irina, Aunt Irina,' he said quietly, taking her hand in his, staring into her face. 'Whyever didn't you tell me before?'

'I don't know. Perhaps I felt it was inappropriate, and anyway it's so long ago now . . .'

'Yes, it is,' he said, holding her hand tighter than ever. 'Now I know why you never married.'

'Yes, you do.'

He put his arm around her and held her close, filled with compassion for her. And he could not help thinking how truly tragic Princess Irina Troubetzkoy's life had been.

After Maxim had left, Irina sat down on the sofa again, leaned back and closed her eyes, hoping to quieten her rapidly beating heart.

Every year that he came to Berlin to see her, Maxim talked to her about the same thing, and every time she answered him in the same way. She forever wished she had new and different answers for him, but she did not. Time changed nothing. And God knows she lived with the same questions herself. There was not a day went by that she did not think about Ursula and Sigmund and their tragic fates: Sigi executed in the most foul way at Buchenwald, Ursula beaten to death in Ravensbrück. She had always been relieved that Teddy had never told Maxim the truth about the way his mother had died, grateful that she had withheld the facts from him. How could the boy then, the man now, bear to hear anything as horrendous as that, cope with such awful knowledge?

Her friend from their resistance group, Maria Langen, who had been in Ravensbrück with Ursula and Renata, had told her many things when she had been released finally in the summer of 1944. Things she could hardly bear to hear at that time, or remember now. Unspeakable things. But remember she did; she could not get them out of her mind.

Maria had told her about a wall in Ravensbrück . . . a punishment wall. Women were taken to it and beaten unmercifully by the wardresses in the camp, beaten senseless, and then they were made to stand against the wall, even though they had no strength left. Maria had told her that their screams and cries and moans went on all day and all night, and that they were left against the wall in the rain and the most freezing weather, were never given anything to eat or drink, not even a drop of water.

According to Maria, Ursula had been taken to that wall so many times and beaten so relentlessly that Maria did not know how Ursula had lived as long as she had. Renata and Maria had crept out to the wall at night, trying to comfort Ursula, bringing her water, tending to her bleeding and battered body as best they could with bits of cloth torn from their own clothing. Every time they did this, they themselves were sent to the punishment wall the next day, and were beaten and left there with Ursula, but they had not cared about their punishment. They had always returned to look after Ursula, and had continued to do so defiantly until the day she had died against the wall in Renata's arms.

They had such courage, Irina thought, unbelievable courage. They were both heroines and they paid with their lives, Renata in Ravensbrück, Maria after her release.

The manner in which Ursula and Sigmund had died was Irina's nightmare, one that never went away. At least, not for very long. And it haunted her, year in and year out; it would continue to do so forever.

FORTY-FIVE

Maxim's mind was focused on Irina as he rode back to the Kempinski Hotel in a taxi cab.

Her confession that she had been in love with his father had initially startled him, then he had experienced a rush of sympathy for her. Unrequited love was such a sad circumstance of life. He had not really known what to say to her, how to comfort her. Perhaps there was no comfort to give after all these years. Certainly she must have learned to live with her pain and disappointment by now.

He glanced out of the window as the cab raced down the Kurfürstendamm.

Berlin, he thought. It was forever nagging at the back of his mind when he was not there. Sometimes he felt that the city held a special secret for him, although in relation to what he did not know. There were times when he believed that he was pulled back because of nostalgia, his memories of his parents, his early life. But he was also aware now that he returned to see Irina Troubetzkoy.

When he had first gone back to the city of his birth in 1950, he had strongly sensed that she needed him. Now he truly understood why. He was the link to his parents, specifically to his father, apparently the love of her life.

In actuality, she represented the same thing to him . . . the link to the past. Irina had been his parents' contemporary, their close friend, always in their company. Therefore she could tell him so much about them. More than Teddy could tell him, in certain ways. Irina and he had always talked about his parents, often at great length, and she frequently reminisced about the times they had spent together, and in a way this kept them alive. At any rate, it made them live again in her mind, and also in his, and thus it gave comfort to them both, and that was all that mattered.

It suddenly struck him that because he was his father's son she might conceivably see him as her own child, the child she might have had with Sigmund, if the circumstances of their lives had been different.

Oh, the complexities of the human heart, he thought, and he was suddenly pleased that he had been taking care of her financially, and coming to see her every year. He was positive he helped her to feel less lonely and alone.

Maxim and Irina spent a wonderful evening together, as they always did when he came to Berlin. They talked and laughed, thoroughly enjoyed each other's company over dinner, and then he took her dancing at one of the clubs on the Ku'damm, as he had promised earlier.

They were still laughing and talking when they left the club at two o'clock in the morning. Maxim took hold of her arm affectionately, and together they strolled along the Kurfürstendamm, enjoying the air. As was usual on a Saturday night, the club had been jammed with people and full of cigarette smoke, and in the last hour the atmosphere had become unbearable in the confined quarters. And even though it was still hot in the streets in the early morning hours of this August Sunday, they were both relieved to be outside.

They walked for about ten minutes, then Maxim hailed a passing cab. It stopped, and he helped Irina in, leapt inside after her. They had hardly settled back on the seat when the driver swung his head, stared hard at them in the dim light of the taxi, and said, 'They're building a barricade.'

'Who are?' Maxim asked, frowning, not understanding what the man meant.

'The East Germans,' the cab driver answered. 'The Communists.'

Maxim felt Irina stiffen on the seat next to him, and he glanced at her quickly, before saying, '*Where?* Where are they building this barricade?'

'On the Potsdamer Platz.'

'We want to go in that direction anyway, so please take us there. I'd like to see what's happening!' Maxim exclaimed.

'Right away,' the driver replied, starting his engine.

The cab rolled down the Ku'damm, making for the Lützowufer, one of the streets leading into the Potsdamerstrasse, which in turn flowed into the Potsdamer Platz, at the juncture of the two zones.

Suddenly Irina said, 'Too many people have been leaving East Germany this past year. Over two hundred thousand actually, and most were young people.'

Maxim looked at her alertly. 'Are you saying what I think you're saying?'

'Yes. They're not building a barricade to keep West Berliners *out*, it's to keep East Berliners *in*, to prevent them crossing into the West Zone.' She laughed hollowly. 'That's the communist regime for you. They have to encircle their people with barbed wire to keep them from fleeing.'

'You're absolutely right.'

Within minutes the cab was cruising down the Potsdamerstrasse, and both Maxim and Irina saw that a large crowd was already gathering in the area; they exchanged worried glances.

'We'll get out here,' Maxim said to the driver, who pulled in close to the kerb and braked. After helping Irina to alight, Maxim paid the cab, and the two of them hurried off in the direction of the Potsdamer Platz.

They were at once startled and dismayed at the sight that met their eyes. As they pushed through the crowds of people milling around, Maxim and Irina saw that immense rolls of barbed wire had been stretched across the square to block all movement between the East and West Zones. Border guards were still in the process of putting the wire in place; they worked to the sound of loud and ferocious jeering and catcalls and derisive whistling from the West Berliners who stood at the other side of the wire in the Western Sector, watching them. The guards erecting the barbed-wire barricade worked by the light of gigantic lamps, and they were backed up by tanks and heavily armed troops, who were now coming in by the truckload.

'This whole thing has the look of a real military operation,' Maxim said, turning to Irina, staring at her in concern.

She clung to his arm and he felt her shivering, despite the warmth of the August weather. 'You can see that they mean business,' she muttered. 'What we're going to have is a totally schizophrenic city. It was bad enough before, but it will only get worse from now on.' She shivered again, clutched his arm more tightly. 'Please, take me home, Maxim.'

'Of course. Come on, let's go, it's getting very late.'

They swung around and walked away from the barricade, making for the Lützowufer.

At one moment Irina came to a sudden standstill, and pivoted to face Maxim. She said in an ominous voice, 'Barbed wire won't be enough for them. You'll see, they'll build a wall to divide Berlin.'

And Princess Irina Troubetzkoy was right; they did.

The Wall stretched for over one hundred miles and was nine feet in height. On one side, in the Eastern Sector, it was painted an antiseptic white; on the other, in the Western Sector, it was covered with colourful graffiti.

Maxim took Anastasia to look at the Wall when she came to Berlin with him in June of 1963. She had not been to Berlin for several years, and so she had not seen it before; like everyone else, she was not prepared for it, or for the feeling of revulsion it engendered in her.

'But it's so wrong!' she cried, glancing from Maxim to Irina, who was accompanying them. 'Totally and utterly wrong.'

'Yes, it is,' Maxim agreed.

'Many people have been shot, trying to escape over the Wall,' Irina explained. 'However, many thousands more *have* made it over safely, *have* escaped to freedom here in the Western Zone.' She shook her head, said derisively, 'Communists! They make me sick.'

'And me, too, Aunt Irina,' Maxim remarked, and said to Anastasia, 'Come on, let me show you the graffiti, I think you'll find it interesting. In places it's truculent, in others disparaging. It's also humorous, sad, defiant. It runs the gamut, really.' He took hold of Anastasia's arm, and Irina's, and together the three of them walked along, inspecting the colourful display.

'The graffiti has been called the longest cartoon in the world,' Irina told her. 'Because, as you can see, it stretches for miles and miles.'

'Some of the items are almost works of art,' Maxim added, 'they have been quite brilliantly executed.'

Since she painted herself, and was artistically inclined, Anastasia was fascinated by the graffiti, and she hovered in front of the Wall for quite a while. Later, Maxim took her up onto one of the viewing platforms which was twenty feet in height, and enabled her to look down into East Berlin on the other side of the Wall.

'How dismal and unfriendly the streets seem,' Anastasia muttered to Maxim, who stood next to her on the platform. 'So desolate and empty. Where are all the people?'

Maxim shrugged. 'I don't know . . . working most probably. And I suppose there's no special reason for those who are not working to be outside. I've noticed the streets every time I've come up here and looked over the Wall . . . so empty and depressing.'

'It's like a No Man's Land,' Anastasia said. 'Different from West Berlin, where there's so much life and activity and excitement.'

The three of them remembered Anastasia's words the following day, when she and Maxim and Irina made their way to the Rudolf Wilde Platz. Maxim's and Anastasia's visit to Berlin coincided with that of President Kennedy, who was on a European tour, and hundreds of thousands of West Berliners were flooding into the streets, also making for the Schöneberg Town Hall in the platz. It was here that the president was going to speak, after his own visit to the Wall and the signing of the Golden Book in the town hall.

When President Kennedy finally came out, accompanied by Mayor

Willy Brandt and West German Chancellor Konrad Adenauer, the crowd
cheered and shouted, clapped and waved, and generally showed their
approval of him. But when he began to speak they fell silent, and there
was not a sound to be heard in the square, except for his words.

Anastasia craned her neck to see the handsome young American president, carefully listened to what he was saying.

Kennedy said: 'I know of no town, no city, which has been besieged
for eighteen years that still lives with the vitality and force, the hope
and determination of the city of West Berlin. While the Wall is the most
obvious and vivid demonstration of the failures of the communist system,
for all the world to see, we take no satisfaction from it . . .'

President Kennedy paused, then concluded dramatically, 'All free men,
wherever they may live, are citizens of Berlin, and, therefore, as a free
man, I take pride in the words *"Ich bin ein Berliner."'*

The crowd went crazy on hearing these words, screaming and shouting
wildly, and many of the West Berliners and foreigners alike had tears
streaming down their faces. Anastasia, Maxim and Irina were also cheering the President of the United States, the three of them as touched and
as moved by Kennedy's speech as everyone else.

But suddenly Maxim sensed a feeling of hysteria growing in the air,
and instinctively, protectively, he put his arms around Anastasia and
Irina, pulled them closer to him. He could not help wondering if he had
been wrong to bring them to this square today, which was jammed now
with hundreds of thousands of people. How easily they could be trampled
underfoot, and hurt, if the crowd went out of control. And it was not until
he had brought the two women safely back to the suite in the Kempinski
Hotel that he breathed easily again.

But a few months later he was to recall vividly those words he had heard
in the Rudolf Wilde Platz in Berlin, and he was truly glad that he had gone
to hear John Kennedy speak on that warm summer day in June.

FORTY-SIX

It was a radiant day.

The sky was a high blue and clear, and the sun was brilliant.

To Anastasia, Manhattan looked as if it had been well and truly polished. The skyscrapers and other buildings appeared to shine on this
crisp Friday morning as she walked across Fifth Avenue in the direction
of Bergdorf Goodman.

Within seconds she was pushing through the swing doors into the exclusive department store, and taking the elevator up to the children's department. Yesterday, when she had been browsing, she had noticed a pretty party dress she hoped would be the right size for two-year-old Alix and several other items that had looked perfect for the new baby. Their son Michael was now eighteen months old and growing rapidly.

Anastasia smiled to herself as she thought of them. The Venetian babies, Maxim called them, since both of their children had been conceived in Venice, Alix on their honeymoon, Michael in August, when they had gone there for a second honeymoon.

She missed her children terribly, even though she and Maxim had only been in New York for a week; she worried about them, despite the fact that they had their nanny, Jennifer, with them, and also Mrs Woodson, the housekeeper-cook who looked after the whole family so well. Plus her mother, who had flown over from Paris to stay at the Mayfair house while she was absent with Maxim on this business trip.

I shouldn't be so jittery, she thought, as she stepped out of the elevator. They're in such good hands. Even so she hated to be parted from her children, who along with her husband were her whole world. She wanted little else except the three of them. She loved them so very much.

To Anastasia's delight the pink organdie dress was still on the display stand, and she stood eyeing it appraisingly for a moment, picturing her blonde blue-eyed little daughter wearing it.

A moment later a sales lady was by her side, confirming that the dress was the right size, and taking it off the stand. While the dress was being wrapped in tissue paper, placed in a silver box and tied with a purple ribbon, Anastasia looked at romper suits and tiny shirts for Michael, and purchased three of each.

Twenty minutes later she was riding down in the elevator carrying two large shopping bags. She glanced at her watch as she left the store. It was a few minutes to one and she would be exactly on time to meet Maxim. They had arranged to have lunch together in the Oak Room of the Plaza Hotel, just across the little square from the store.

As she went up the steps and into the hotel, Anastasia was not aware of the flurry she created, nor did she notice the admiring glances cast in her direction. At twenty-two she was more beautiful than ever, her skin glowing and full of health and vitality, her long blonde hair upswept on top of her head today. She wore a dark ranch mink coat which Maxim had bought her several days ago, high-heeled black patent pumps and long cream suede gloves. Small diamonds sparkled in her ears and a pearl choker encircled her neck.

After leaving the shopping bags and her mink coat in the ladies' cloak-room, Anastasia crossed the lobby of the hotel and made her way to the Oak Room.

Maxim saw her come in and rose as the captain escorted her to the table, beaming at her.

How handsome her husband looked in his dark grey pin-stripe suit and pale blue shirt. He was the best-looking man in the room. And she could tell from the brilliance of his dark eyes that he had had a very successful morning, that his meetings in Wall Street had gone well. And why wouldn't they? Her husband was a genius. Everyone said so; he seemed to have the Midas touch. Whatever business deal he went into, he always made money, lots of it, and came out the big winner. Her father said he was the most brilliant and gifted businessman and entrepreneur he had ever known, and coming from Alexander Derevenko that was praise indeed.

Still smiling, Maxim kissed her on the cheek as she arrived at the table. They both sat down, and he said, 'You look fabulous. You should wear red more often, darling, it really suits you.'

'Why thank you, kind sir,' she answered, giving him a flirtatious look. 'And obviously you charmed your business associates and the bankers, got your own way in Wall Street this morning, from the look on your face.'

He leaned towards her, dropped his voice. 'As long as I get my own way with you, that's all that matters, Stassy, my love. In case I haven't told you lately, I absolutely adore you. I have great plans for this afternoon . . . for *us*. My work is finished for the day, so I'm all yours. After lunch we're going to meander back to the hotel and – ' He leaned even closer, whispered in her ear, 'Make wonderful love together. And who knows, perhaps we might even make another baby.'

She laughed, and a slight flush tinted her face a pretty pink. Her luminous eyes grew more luminous than ever. 'What a gorgeous idea. And I adore you, too.' Reaching out she squeezed his hand, then eyed his glass. 'Is that a drink?' she asked, sounding surprised.

'It is. I know it's not like me to drink during the day, but I ordered a bottle of Sancerre. I thought it might be nice to celebrate my little deal. It's only worth about twenty-one million dollars, but it's just the beginning.'

'Oh darling, how wonderful! Congratulations! And what do you mean, *just the beginning*?'

'Of West Investments in America. Will you have a glass of white wine with me, drink to that?'

'I certainly will.'

Maxim motioned to the waiter hovering a few feet away, and the man hurried over, lifted the wine bottle from the bucket, filled her glass. As he replaced the bottle he asked if they wished to order lunch.

'In a few minutes, thank you,' Maxim said, swung to face Anastasia, raised his glass. 'Here's to the big adventure we're going to have in New York.' He touched his glass to hers.

Anastasia looked at him curiously. '*Adventure?*'

'I want to spend more time in the States, eventually open an office here, perhaps even take an apartment on Fifth Avenue or Park or Sutton Place. Wherever you wish. Would you like to live in Manhattan part of the year?'

She hesitated only momentarily, then said, 'If you want to, then yes, of course. New York is a most exciting city. But . . . look, what about the children? About their schooling? Things like that?'

'Darling girl, they're still babies! We've lots of time to worry about schools and the like. And you're correct, it *is* an exciting place, and in many different ways. It's especially exciting in business. This is where the future is . . . in my opinion. That's what I meant when I used the word adventure.'

'Everyone says you have great vision and wisdom, and I know you do.' She paused, gave him a small smile. 'So I am with you all the way.'

He grinned at her, his expression one of happiness and genuine delight. 'Thank you for that marvellous vote of confidence, my love. You're the best wife I've ever had.'

'And the *only* one you will ever have!' she shot back, laughing with him.

'Perhaps we ought to look at the menus,' Maxim suggested, handing her one.

'Thank you.' She put it down in front of her, said, 'Actually, I know what I'm going to have. Clam chowder and then grilled Boston scrod.'

'I'll also have the soup, but I think I'd enjoy a bit of that roast beef the waiter is carving on the trolley. It looks delicious.'

After Maxim had given the order, Anastasia said, 'You've been very secretive about your new deal. Can't you tell me what it is, now you've closed it?'

'Of course I can. I've bought a company called the Allandale Group, based here in New York.'

'What is that?' She stared at him blankly. 'It doesn't mean a thing to me.'

'The Allandale Group is a company with rather diverse holdings. For example, it owns Marianna Monteveccio, a small cosmetic company, real estate in Manhattan and Long Island, a tool and die company, and a large bakery, one that supplies half the stores in the city and suburbs.

As I said, it *is* rather diverse, and that's its basic problem. I plan to sell off the non-profitable bits, keep only the divisions that make money.'

'Which ones are they?'

'The real estate division and the cosmetic company. Those are the two I'm going to reorganise. I plan to launch the Monteveccio cosmetic line in England and Europe next year. I know it will do well, the product is superior.' He gave her a little smile, one that was full of confidence. 'That's the art of the takeover, knowing what to sell and what to keep.'

'You like these little takeovers of yours, don't you?'

He stared at her. '*Little*. They're not so little, Peach Melba.'

She threw him a sharp look. 'I wish you wouldn't call me that,' she chastised.

'Why it's the perfect name for you. After all, you're good enough to eat.' His charming, lopsided smile flashed and he leaned over, kissed her cheek, then went on: 'The takeover is the most marvellous invention. It's such a fabulous shortcut, saves all those years of slowly building a company, and it yields wonderful profits. It's also very exciting, finding the right company to take over, and then pursuing it.'

'I suppose that's the part you love the most.'

He shook his head. 'I admit it's thrilling, but I like wrestling with the financial problems, and then reshaping the company, being creative, making it into something bigger and better. I'm not a paper-chaser, I don't want to build an empire out of paper. Nor am I an asset-stripper. I prefer to keep the companies I've bought and run them, once the fat's been trimmed. Anyway, I – '

Maxim broke off, as the waiter served the soup, placed a bowl of clam chowder in front of each of them.

'And you think that this cosmetic company has a future?'

'Very much so, here as well as in Europe, actually. You see, it's been mismanaged, and it also needs new packaging, a fresh marketing approach. The product is excellent and – ' Maxim stopped abruptly, his attention caught by a small commotion near the entrance to the Oak Room. Two waiters were speaking to the captain. One was gesticulating excitedly, the other was openly weeping, and Maxim noticed that the captain seemed dazed, had turned as white as chalk.

'How very odd. I think something's wrong,' he said to Anastasia, his brow furrowed. 'Look at the captain. He appears to have had a terrible shock. The waiters don't seem to be helping either.'

'Perhaps someone's been taken ill in the restaurant.' Anastasia swung her head, glanced around. She caught the attention of a waiter hurrying out of the service entrance from the kitchen and beckoned to him.

The waiter came to a halt at their table.

Anastasia could not miss the expression on the man's face. It was grave, and there was a stunned look in his eyes.

'What's going on?' she asked in a low voice. 'Is there something wrong? We couldn't help noticing the – '

'He's been shot,' the waiter told her, his voice shaking, and it broke as he added, 'The President's been shot.'

'The President,' Maxim repeated, peering at the waiter, noting his acute distress. 'You don't mean President Kennedy, do you?'

The waiter nodded, unable to speak. His eyes filled with tears and his face twisted in a terrible grimace of pain, and he turned on his heels and fled back into the kitchen.

Maxim and Anastasia sat gaping at each other, for a moment not comprehending what they had just been told.

But the news was spreading fast through the Oak Room. People were turning to each other worriedly, leaning across to other tables, speaking to strangers. In an instant the room was a babble of voices.

Maxim threw his napkin on the table, pushed back his chair and leapt to his feet. 'Come on!' he cried, and moved across the room with such speed Anastasia had to run to keep up with him.

When he reached the captain, Maxim demanded in a quiet but rasping voice, 'Is it true? Has President Kennedy really been shot?'

The captain's face was grief-stricken. 'In Dallas. At about one-thirty. Bulletins are coming in over the radio in the kitchen.'

Maxim and Anastasia were both speechless, horror-struck.

Reaching into his jacket pocket, Maxim pulled out his wallet, extracted two one-hundred-dollar notes and gave them to the captain. 'This should take care of my bill,' he mumbled, and taking hold of Anastasia's hand he reeled out of the Oak Room, dragging her in his wake.

Maxim and Anastasia stood in the middle of the sitting room of their suite at the Pierre, just across the street from the Plaza, staring at the television set.

Incredulity, shock and disbelief were written all over their faces and they were rooted to the spot as they listened to the famous newscaster Walter Cronkite delivering all of the facts about the shooting of the President.

A muscle in Cronkite's face twitched, and his voice was shaken, solemn, as he repeated what he had just said, apparently recapping the news for viewers who had just turned on their sets.

John Fitzgerald Kennedy, the 35th President of the United States, was dead. The back of his head had been blown off by an assassin's bullet as he had ridden in his motorcade through the streets of Dallas. His body lay in Parkland Memorial Hospital in the Texas city.

Maxim still found it hard to accept. The facts would not quite sink in, and he kept changing the stations, going from CBS to NBC and ABC, and back again, wanting to glean bits of additional information from the other newscasters, who were as stunned and grieving as Walter Cronkite.

At one moment Anastasia glanced down and the skirt of her brilliant red dress caught her eye. She thought: Oh. Oh God! It's the colour of blood! And she clapped her hand over her mouth and fled into the bedroom as the tears began to flow again. She was almost sobbing as she unzipped the red dress, stepped out of it, and quickly put on a dark blue cashmere sweater and matching skirt, and returned to the sitting room.

So absorbed was Maxim in the news on television, she realised that he had not even noticed her brief absence. Moving across to the sofa, she lowered herself onto it. After a moment Maxim joined her, and they sat together watching the ongoing broadcast, holding hands.

He suddenly turned his stricken face to hers and said in a hoarse voice, 'I can't believe it. We just saw him in Berlin this summer, speaking outside the Schöneberg Town Hall. It hardly seems possible that he's dead.'

Anastasia's attention was riveted on Maxim, and she saw that his eyes were full of tears, and she pressed her hand against his. Maxim groped for his handkerchief and wiped his eyes, leaned back against the sofa, feeling suddenly wrung out.

She said softly, 'He looked so young that day in Berlin, and so handsome with his reddish-blond hair glinting in the sunshine. "Ich bin ein Berliner" he said . . .'

'I remember . . . I remember it very well.'

'Why, Maxim? Why? Why was he killed?'

Maxim shook his head. He had no answer, at least not one which would make any sense.

'Why would anybody want to kill Jack Kennedy?' she asked again, more insistently, baffled and frightened by such violence.

'I don't know, Stassy, I just don't know.'

'What a foul and horrible world we live in today!' Anastasia cried.

'It always has been,' Maxim mumbled.

'Yes. Yes, I know, darling,' she whispered, thinking instantly of the way his parents had died, and of the Holocaust.

Maxim and Anastasia sat together in front of the set for many more hours. They did not say very much to each other through their long vigil, caught up as they were in the news, straining to hear every detail of this senseless killing, the most horrific murder in the history of the United States.

Lyndon Johnson appeared on their television screen at six-fifteen that evening of Friday, November 22. As the new President he made his first statement to a grieving nation reeling from the incomprehensible act of violence in Dallas.

'He's dead,' Maxim muttered, more to himself than Anastasia. 'John Kennedy is dead.' And he sighed heavily, finally accepting it.

'Ich bin ein Berliner. Ich bin ein Berliner. Ich bin ein Berliner.'

Maxim awakened with a sudden start, Kennedy's words and voice reverberating in his head. He blinked in the darkness of the bedroom, adjusting his eyes to the gloomy light, glancing at Anastasia, who was on her side, sleeping peacefully, her breathing even. He lay for a moment, trying to go back to sleep. When he realised that he was wide awake, he slid his legs out of bed and padded to the living room, closing the bedroom door behind him.

The sitting room of their suite overlooked Fifth Avenue, and he walked over to the window, stood staring out at the trees in Central Park. He moved his head slightly to the left, focused for a brief moment on the Plaza opposite. The lights from the hotel shone brightly, illuminating the square in front of the wide steps. The streets were deserted, looked bleak and wintry in the pale lamplight.

Maxim sighed under his breath and turned away from the window, walked over to the sofa and lay down, a multitude of thoughts running through his mind.

The assassination of President Kennedy did not make sense, not to him or anyone else, if the television commentators were anything to go by. Had it been the act of a single man working alone? A crazy man? Or had it been a conspiracy? Fascists? Communists? Who could really say for sure? Who would ever really know? But *evil* had run amok in America earlier today, and the country had been savaged by an insane act of the most terrible and senseless violence.

He had always known that evil lurked around corners, even from being a little boy. Somehow he had understood this after Teddy had told him that bad things were done to Jews in Nazi Germany. Teddy was ambivalent about the Germans. But he had no particular feelings, certainly not hatred. Only an insatiable curiosity about them. Furthermore, even as a Jew, whose parents had been victims of the Third Reich, he did not believe this generation should be blamed for the crimes of the last.

Often when he went back to Germany to see Irina Troubetzkoy he would look at people in the streets, or in cafés and stores, filled with bafflement, and wonder how it was that such a strong and noble people as the Germans could have been deluded into following a man like Hitler.

Of course that megalomaniac had blinded them with the power of his personality, his high-flown rhetoric, his promises of economic security, a better life, a strong and stable Germany free of Communism. The majority of Germans had followed him unquestioningly, seeing not the charlatan that he was but a charismatic leader who would lead them to prosperity and glory.

After mathematics and languages, history had been his favourite subject at St Paul's. He had studied it well, had come to understand that Hitler had been the embodiment of pure evil, had created the most evil regime in the entire history of the world, a sinister regime of bigotry, racism, brutality, oppression and murder. For twelve years and four months the Third Reich had trampled over, intimidated and dominated Europe in a reign of terror which had hitherto been unknown to man before. It had been a machine of destruction and death, operated by ruthless and cruel men with evil intent in their hearts and the minds of criminals; gangsters, thugs, murderers, degenerates.

When the criminals take over the prison then chaos and bloody murder reign, he thought. He wondered how it had come to pass . . . he would never know. That was not strictly true. Diabolical men such as Hitler and his cohorts always played on the ignorance, weakness and fear of people. The Germans were such a cultured and civilised race, and yet they had espoused Hitler's policies of anti-Semitism. Maxim sighed under his breath and continued to lie on the sofa in the darkness, his mind racing. Evil men can soon engender hatred and prejudice in others, he thought. He knew that from his history books, which he had studied so diligently and carefully at school. Atrocities had leapt off those pages . . . the Spanish Inquisition, the Russian pogroms, the Turks slaughtering Armenians. Atrocity had been around for centuries, perpetrated by supposedly civilised men against other men.

Who will be next? he asked himself.

Maxim rose, went over to the small sideboard where several bottles of liquor were standing on a tray. He poured himself a brandy, carried it back to the sofa. As he sipped it he acknowledged, with a terrible sadness, that nothing had changed since the beginning of time. And nothing would ever change. There would always be men of evil out to dominate and subdue others. Until one day one of them, caught in the grip of insanity, would push a button and blow the world to smithereens.

As for Jack Kennedy, a young and brilliant man had been cruelly struck down in the prime of his life, and all the world would mourn as America mourned. As he mourned now. Maxim got up and went and turned on the television set. The network was running a film of Jack Kennedy made in Berlin this past June.

There he was on television, standing before Maxim as he had in reality only six months earlier, his hair ruffled by the light breeze, smiling his curious little smile, looking slightly amused, yet detached in a way, but caring and genuine as well. A man capable of warmth and irony and humour.

Maxim felt the tears prick the back of his eyes at the sight of the fallen President as he had been in life. God damn the sons of bitches who did it, he cursed, and slammed his fist into the back of the chair in his fury and grief.

FORTY-SEVEN

'The phenomenal success of the Allandale Group has certainly been an extraordinary achievement for Maxim, hasn't it?' Margot Derevenko said, putting *Time* down on the table and looking across at her daughter. 'This article about him is full of accolades.'

Anastasia was silent.

She sat staring out into the lovely garden which her mother had created so painstakingly over the years, thinking what a haven of beauty and tranquillity it was, and right in the heart of Paris. Peaceful, she thought. So very, very peaceful. Anastasia suppressed a sigh, not wishing her mother to ask if something was wrong. *It was.* She felt so terribly tired, exhausted really, and drained of all energy. She had been feeling like this for the longest time now.

Margot said, 'Darling, didn't you hear me?'

Anastasia roused herself, gave her mother a small reassuring smile, but said, 'I'm sorry, I'm afraid I was daydreaming for a moment.'

'I said the article on Maxim had wonderful things to say about him, and I simply remarked that the success of the Allandale Group is quite extraordinary.'

'Yes, he's turned it into a conglomerate of no mean proportions in the past seven years. But it's also the cross I have to bear,' Anastasia replied in a flat, dull voice.

Margot looked at her, frowning. 'What a peculiar thing to say.'

'It's at the root of our problems – ' Anastasia began, and stopped with abruptness, regretting the remark immediately.

'*Problems!*' Margot exclaimed, sitting bolt upright in the garden chair. 'What on earth do you mean?'

'Oh Mother, I don't really want to go into it, not now. Please, forget I said it.'

'I can't forget it, Anastasia. You haven't looked well this past year, and your father and I have been worried about you, if you want to know the truth. I was delighted when you said you were going to come and stay with us for a few weeks.' She squeezed her daughter's beautiful tapering fingers, and said, 'Please, can't you confide in me? We've always been such good friends.' When Anastasia made no response, Margot added, 'Your father and I feel you haven't been yourself for ages, but we didn't think for one moment that you and Maxim had problems.'

'Perhaps we don't, Mother, perhaps the problems are all in me.'

'What do you mean?' Margot asked, concerned.

'I feel so tired all the time. Debilitated, actually, as if I've been ill. And I don't seem to have any spark left.'

'No spark!' Margot cried, looking at her askance. 'But you're only twenty-nine, for heaven's sake!'

'I realise it sounds ridiculous, but it's the truth. I have no energy, and I'm always depressed these days.'

Margot Derevenko was horrified by this last statement, and she searched her daughter's pale face, saw at once that she meant what she said.

Sympathy quickly replaced incredulity. 'Anastasia . . . darling . . . *you*, of all people, have no reason to be *depressed*. You are young and very beautiful. You have a handsome and charming husband who adores you, one who is a millionaire, who showers you with every possible thing you could want. You have two lovely and clever children, as well as doting parents. Aside from all this, you have a house in Mayfair that is a showplace, a lovely villa in Beaulieu, and an apartment on Fifth Avenue.' Margot shook her head. 'If *you* feel depressed there is obviously something radically wrong. It must be *physical*. I think you ought to see a doctor.'

'I don't need a doctor, Mummy. Frankly, I don't know what I need.' Yes I do, she thought to herself. I need Maxim to be the way he was when we were first married. I can't reach the man he has become. He's not the same any more. I don't know why, but we've lost each other.

'Sometimes depression is caused by a diet deficiency. What about going to a nutritionist?' Margot suggested.

Anastasia shook her head.

Margot's expression became thoughtful, and she reflected for a moment, before saying slowly, 'Now that both of the children are away at boarding school, perhaps you're feeling a little lonely.'

'I don't think it's that.'

'A moment ago, when we were talking about the Allandale Group, you said it was at the root of your problems. Please tell me what you meant, it's the only way I'll be able to help you.'

Anastasia turned to face her mother, and when she saw the love and concern and understanding reflected on Margot's still pretty face, her eyes welled with tears. 'I *am* lonely, Mummy,' she admitted. 'But not so much for Alix and Michael. It's Maxim I miss. He's away so much. Constantly flying to New York and back, it's been like that since he bought Allandale. And then he's always rushing to Hong Kong or Australia or Los Angeles. Or *somewhere*. It seems to me that in the past six years he's never been off a plane, and all because of Allandale. Oh it's the basis of his empire, and he's turned it into a huge success. But at what price?' She sighed, and finished in a low voice, 'The price of our marriage, in my opinion.'

'*Anastasia* . . . I just didn't realise . . .'

'His work comes first. It always has and it always will. It consumes him entirely. I know that now. He's not normal, you know, not when it comes to work. Maxim is beyond a workaholic, Mother. They haven't invented a name for a person who works the way he does. *Around the clock.* He has the stamina of a bull, and the most extraordinary concentration.'

'I don't suppose one can fault him for working hard. However, it does strike me that he may be neglecting you.'

'I suppose he is. Even when he's with me he is preoccupied, lost in his business deals. Oddly enough, he's grown more withdrawn in certain ways, and less communicative,' Anastasia confided.

'But you've always said he was intensely private, a complicated man.'

'That's true.' Anastasia laughed hollowly and shook her head. 'Believe it or not, after ten years of marriage I still don't know what makes Maximilian West *tick.*'

'Anastasia dear, I hope you don't mind me saying this, but perhaps you should travel with Maxim more than you have been doing. Go to New York more frequently, especially now that both children are away at school.'

'My going to New York doesn't change very much, Mummy. Maxim leaves for the office very early, and stays there until all hours at night, and our social life is non-existent. I'm bored when I'm in New York. I don't have that many friends there. And anyway, Maxim's liable to fly off to Los Angeles for a day or two, and then I'm left to fend for myself.'

Margot gave Anastasia a pointed look, and said quietly, 'Are things . . . are things all right between you? I mean in the bedroom . . . *sexually*?'

'If you're asking me if we still sleep together, the answer is *yes*, we do. Maxim is a very physical man, and passionate, and we do make love. Not as frequently as we once did though, even when he is at home.'

'I see,' Margot muttered, sounding and looking suddenly worried. 'You don't think there could possibly be another woman, do you?' she finally ventured.

Anastasia shook her head vehemently.

'Are you *sure* he doesn't have a mistress in New York?'

'I doubt it. Oh look, Mummy, maybe he's had one-night stands, after all he's away from me a great deal, more than half the year these days. But I don't think he's emotionally devious – ' She stopped, bit her lip, glanced away.

Margot exclaimed, 'What is it? You've thought of something, haven't you? Or, more correctly perhaps, *someone*.'

'Not really. It's just that a few weeks ago, when Maxim was in London, I saw him going into Claridge's with a woman. I was passing the hotel in a cab at the time. I suppose he was taking her to lunch.'

'Who was it, do you know?'

Anastasia hesitated then blurted out, 'Camilla Galland.'

'Camilla! But she just remarried recently!'

'Don't be naive, Mother. The marriage vows don't preclude adultery.'

'So you *are* suspicious?'

'I don't know. No, that's not true. I *do* know, and I absolutely give Maxim the benefit of the doubt. I don't think there's anything between him and Camilla Galland. It's just that . . . well, to be honest, I've never really liked her, perhaps because I've never *trusted* her.'

'Don't start building a case against Maxim, just because you saw him entering Claridge's with her. Nobody knows men and their *curious* – for want of a better word – ways than I do. But ever since you married Maxim I've felt he was true blue.'

'Before we married you thought he was a womaniser.'

'That was then. This is now.' Margot leaned forward and squeezed her daughter's arm. 'I'm going to help you to organise your life with Maxim better, and when he comes to the south of France next month, you must tell him you plan to travel with him more often.'

'Oh I don't know . . .' Anastasia's voice trailed off.

'Are you suggesting he will *object*?'

'No, but – '

'No buts with me, Anastasia. The matter is settled.'

It was a hot hazy day, and earlier Maxim had thought the *mistral* might be blowing up, but now the light wind had dropped and the air was balmy, the sea as calm as a pond.

He stood on the terrace of La Serenissima, their villa in Beaulieu-sur-Mer, between Nice and Monte Carlo, looking out across the long stretch of green lawn, past the swimming pool to the Mediterranean beyond.

The month he had spent here with his family had done him good, he knew that. He felt renewed and relaxed, full of vigour and vitality. It had given him enormous pleasure to spend time with Anastasia and the children. After a whole week of doing nothing but lazing around, he had made several quick trips to London to deal with business, but had returned almost immediately. From that point on, he had stayed put, had worked from his office here at the villa. It had just recently been completed for him, and it contained all the latest equipment, and was a communications centre as well, which enabled him to stay in touch with his offices in London, New York, Paris and Hong Kong.

'Daddy! Daddy!'

He turned his head, looking to his right, saw Alix coming up the steps from the beach, swinging a towel and waving to him. Her brother Michael, carrying a bucket and a fishing net, followed closely on her heels.

How beautiful his children were.

At nine Alix was a young replica of Anastasia, blonde and fair of complexion, with the same delicate bone structure as her mother. But her eyes were a smoky grey-green, and she was going to be much taller than Anastasia. She was long and lean and coltish, and something of a tomboy at this age. Eight-year-old Michael was *his* boy, so like him in appearance with the same dark hair and eyes, his build, and Michael would probably be as tall as he was when he grew up. Both children were bursting with health, energy and high spirits; to Maxim they seemed more beautiful than ever with their young limbs tinted golden-brown by the summer sun.

They ran across the lawn, came to a stop at the terrace and stood looking up at him.

Michael said, 'Are we going to have the bonfire, Dad?'

'Of course,' Maxim responded, suddenly remembering the papers he had to destroy. At breakfast he had told Michael he was going to have a fire, since the shredding machine in the office was broken.

'Can I help too, Daddy?' Alix asked, gazing at him appealingly, her head on one side, wrinkling her nose prettily.

'Why not? And I think we'd better get to it well before lunch. I don't think your mother will appreciate a smoky atmosphere when we're eating, especially since guests are coming. Why not go and find Marcel, tell him to start the fire, and I'll go and get the papers. I'll meet you at the back near the little wood in a few minutes.'

'Come on!' Michael said to his sister, and the two of them sped across the lawn at breakneck speed, heading for the back of the villa.

Maxim pivoted and walked inside, crossing the main *salon*, thinking how cool and restful it was, with its mixtures of pale colours – creams and whites and *café-au-lait*, with a hint of peach here and there, and touches of lime green. Anastasia had inherited her mother's flair for decorating, and the entire villa was a tribute to her immense taste and talent.

He ran into her in the marble hall, and caught his breath, thinking how lovely she was this morning.

She wore a pale-green cotton sundress with a ruched strapless bodice, a large cream-coloured straw hat with poppies and cornflowers clustered on the band, and carried a basket of flowers. Her golden hair, lighter than ever from the sun and sea, hung down her back almost to her waist. Her arms and shoulders were tanned golden, as were her legs, her feet in sandals.

She smiled at him.

He smiled back. And then he reached for her, brought his arm around her waist and pulled her to him, held her very tightly. Nuzzling his face against her neck, he mumbled, 'You're very Peach Melba-ish this morning, honeybunch.'

She laughed and pushed him away gently. '*I* have flowers to arrange.'

'And *I* have papers to burn.'

'See you at the pool for a swim before lunch?'

'Absolutely,' he said, winking at her.

They went in different directions. Anastasia walked along the corridor to the kitchen; Maxim veered to his left and hurried into his office. He had been placing the papers in two huge shopping bags for days, and he picked these up and took them out to the back of the house.

Alix and Michael were waiting for him, and Marcel, the gardener, had already started the fire. The four of them stood around it, and Michael and Alix fed the papers into the flames.

'Why are you burning them, Daddy?' Alix suddenly asked.

'Because they're *confidential*,' Michael answered before Maxim had a chance to respond.

'Yes, I know. But why not simply lock them up in the safe, Daddy?' she asked, addressing her father.

'There are too many, to begin with, *Schatzi*. And secondly, I don't need them any more. Rather than having them floating around, it's better to destroy them like this, or in the shredder.'

'I see,' Alix said, and added, 'Because you don't want anybody else to see them or get them, isn't that right?'

'Smart girl,' Maxim said, squeezing her bare shoulder.

'She's the smartest girl *I* know,' Michael announced, sounding proud. 'In fact, she's so smart, Dad, we might even take her into the business with us.'

'It's certainly worth considering,' Maxim said, his mouth twitching with a hidden smile, realising his son meant this seriously. 'If Alix wants to come into the business with us, of course she can.'

'I might,' Alix said, beaming at them both, rather flattered by her brother's unexpected compliments. 'I'll have to think about it. I haven't really made up my mind about a career yet.'

Maxim and Michael exchanged knowing masculine glances, and went on burning the papers.

Later that morning, after he had made his business calls to London, Maxim went swimming with the children in the pool. He adored them, enjoyed being with them, and they reciprocated his feelings; there was a bonding between the three of them which was very special.

When Anastasia came down to the pool an hour before lunch, she stood at the edge, watching them cavorting in the water, smiling indulgently.

'Aren't you coming in, Mummy?' Alix cried, bobbing up and down next to Michael, holding a large rubber ball in her hands.

'Yes, Mums, come on in!' Michael yelled, beckoning.

'I don't think I will, not at the moment, angels,' Anastasia said, and walked over to one of the poolside lounging beds. Taking off her towelling robe, she threw it over the back of the chaise, sat down and picked up *Nice-Matin*, began to read it.

'Do you feel all right, Stassy darling?' Maxim asked a few minutes later, standing in front of her, looking down with a worried frown.

'I'm wonderful, but not up to pool antics, suddenly.'

He flopped down onto the chaise next to hers, and stretched out his long legs, put his hands underneath his head, stared up at the clear blue sky. 'Isn't this weather glorious? And hasn't our holiday been simply marvellous this year?'

'Yes, it has,' she answered, turning to him, giving him a wide and loving smile. She thought: *Thanks to you. The holiday has been perfect because you have been with us most of the time, and not so preoccupied as in the past few years.* The whole of July had been exceptional in every way, as far as Anastasia was concerned. She had not been as happy as this in the longest time, not since *before* Maxim had purchased the Allandale Group.

Lifting her newspaper, she began to read it again, her heart light, her mind at peace.

Maxim closed his eyes, enjoying the warmth of the sun on his body. The sun was like a tonic to him; he could not get enough of it, and the one regrettable thing about England was the poor weather.

His mind turned to the new company he was about to form. He was going to call it West International. It was to be a holding company for future takeovers and acquisitions, and there were quite a few of those on the horizon. One company in particular. One he really wanted, planned to go after.

He was about to make the big leap into the truly big time.

The mere idea of it excited him in a way that nothing else did. In a sense, business was his aphrodisiac. He knew that only too well, and it was something he could not change in himself. If only Anastasia could understand this.

For a split second he contemplated telling her about the new company, and instantly changed his mind. She wouldn't be interested, and in any case, business bored her. It always had. But he didn't mind that it did. She had so many other remarkable attributes, and he loved her so very much.

'Stassy . . .'

'Yes, darling, what is it?' She glanced at him, and put down the newspaper.

'On my last trip to London two weeks ago, I stopped in to see them at Camper & Nicholsons in Berkeley Street.'

'You did! Oh darling!' She sat up straighter on the chaise, then swung her legs over the side and stared at him. 'Are you going to charter a yacht from them next summer? As you've been promising?'

Maxim did not answer. He also straightened up, swung his legs to the floor, and sat facing her. A wide smile slowly spread across his face.

'Tell me!' she cried excitedly, grasping his arm. 'Tell me!'

'I've commissioned them to *build* a yacht. A beautiful yacht for my beautiful wife.'

'Oh Maxim!'

'They have the best naval architects, engineers, yacht stylists, and electrical designers in the world, in my opinion. They've been in business since 1782, so they must be doing something right. In any case, the designs will be done first, for our approval, then they will start building her, once they have the go-ahead from me.'

'When will she be ready?'

'Not for several years. Two and a half, three maybe. And once she's finished, I want you to do the interior design, with your mother's help, if you wish.'

'Oh she'll be so thrilled, Maxim.'

'More importantly, are *you*, Peachy?'

'*Very*.'

He leaned forward, took her face between his hands, kissed her on the lips. Then he leapt to his feet, pulled her up onto hers, walked her over to the outside bar at the far end of the pool area.

'I'm going to crack open a bottle of my best Roederer Cristal to toast the yacht.'

'I'll toast her with you!'

He let go of Anastasia to walk around the bar.

She sat down on a stool as he brought the bottle of champagne out of the refrigerator underneath the bar, carefully began to unwind the metal wire.

'Incidentally, who's coming to lunch today?' he asked.

'Just a bunch of locals,' she laughed.

'Teddy and Mark, I'll bet, and your parents.'

'Correct. And Yvette and Philippe Arnaud. And Stubby, of course, with his latest lady love in tow. He just phoned to tell me.'

'I wish that old reprobate would settle down and get married.'

Anastasia laughed again. 'So does his mother.'

Maxim poured the Cristal into two flutes, pushed one towards Anastasia, and lifted his glass. 'Here's to your yacht, Peachy.'

'To *our* yacht, my darling,' she said, giving him the most dazzling smile.

FORTY-EIGHT

He called her *Beautiful Dreamer*.

She was one of the most magnificent ocean-going yachts ever designed by the best naval architects there were, custom-built to Maxim's precise specifications by Camper & Nicholsons, the great British yacht-builders.

Sleek of line, elegant, and equipped to sail anywhere in the world, her overall length was 213.9 feet and her cruising speed was fifteen knots. Originally, Maxim had intended to have a smaller, shorter yacht designed, at first opting for maximum speed and greater manoeuvrability above size and spaciousness. Rather quickly, he had come to realise that much of the pleasure and fun of owning a yacht was to invite guests aboard to cruise with them part of the time.

With the extended family he and Anastasia had, a large number of staterooms and cabins were an absolute necessity. Aside from Anastasia and himself, and their children, he required comfortable accommodation for those he loved and cared about: Anastasia's parents, Teddy and Mark, and their children to whom he was close, and who were his siblings, in a sense. Kay, now twenty-four, worked for him at West International in London, and her brother David, who was twenty-two, had recently come down from Oxford and was about to enter the family diamond and jewellery business with Mark. David and Kay had always looked up to him, and he was like an older brother to both of Teddy's children. Then there were two other very important people in his life to consider and include – his beloved Irina Troubetzkoy, and his dearest friend, the faithful, ever-devoted Stubby.

When she was completed, after an expenditure of several million pounds, *Beautiful Dreamer* could accommodate twenty people, plus twenty in crew.

She was the ultimate in luxury. Apart from three grand staterooms, there were seven other bedrooms, each one with its own private bathroom en suite, an elegant main salon and a large dining room, both for more formal entertaining, a library, Maxim's study, plus a completely equipped communications centre next to an office for his secretarial staff. A swimming pool and the fore and aft decks provided for swimming, outdoor activities and sunbathing, while the boat deck lounge served as a games room and a place for casual dining. To Maxim a helicopter pad was imperative; this had been included in the ship's overall design so that he could come and go as he wished.

Beautiful Dreamer was almost three years in the building, and it took Anastasia and her mother another year to furnish and decorate her appropriately. When they finally finished their work the yacht was exquisite, stylish and opulent without being pretentious or intimidating. Pale colours, French and English antiques, impressive objects of art and fine paintings abounded. To Maxim's immense satisfaction the interior of the yacht had comfort, great charm and distinction, and was in perfect taste.

He took delivery of her in July of 1974, and when he saw her moored in one of the best berths in Monte Carlo harbour he was overcome by her intrinsic beauty.

Awed, he stood admiring her from the dock, along with Anastasia, Alix and Michael, marvelling at her lovely rakish lines, her high streamlined prow, her overall gracefulness. She gleamed brilliantly white against the glittering deep blue sea in the intense morning sunlight, and as far as he was concerned she was the best-looking yacht in the port of Monte Carlo – the *Atlantis*, owned by Greek shipping magnate Stavros Niarchos, notwithstanding.

'She was worth waiting for, eh, Stassy?' he said as they walked up the gangplank.

'Indeed she was. A great deal of time, talent and love has gone into her creation,' Anastasia replied quietly. 'I'm only sorry she wasn't ready for your fortieth birthday.'

'I think we ought to forget *that*,' Maxim laughed as he stepped onto the deck, swung around to give his hand to Anastasia, and helped her on board. Together they walked forward to greet the captain, who was waiting for them with other members of the crew.

That weekend *Beautiful Dreamer* sailed up the Mediterranean coast, heading for Saint Tropez. Maxim had invited Margot and Alexander Derevenko, Teddy and Mark to join Anastasia, the children and himself on this short maiden cruise. After four glorious days at sea, the yacht turned around and sailed back to Monte Carlo, in readiness for the first party they were going to give on board. It was to be a supper dance for seventy guests on Saturday night.

Anastasia filled the yacht with flowers, decorated it with glittering fairy lights, hired the best trio on the Côte d'Azur, ordered cases and cases of Roederer Cristal champagne, and planned a menu of delicious food with her two French chefs. She then proceeded to throw *the* party of the 1974 season.

Halfway through the evening everyone was already congratulating her, telling her she had *two* grand successes on her hands: the beautiful yacht and the spectacular supper dance.

Anastasia thanked them graciously, smiled, and went on smiling for the rest of the evening, even though her heart ached and she was filled with pain and hurt inside. Things were not at all right between her and Maxim; they had not been right for several years. And tonight, of all nights, she felt as if she was on the verge of a nervous breakdown, at worst some sort of physical collapse.

Now she stood at the far side of the dance floor watching him closely. He was dancing with Chedlya El Bahi, the young Moroccan woman who had been brought by David Maines, a friend of Stubby's who had become part of their crowd. Maxim looked impossibly handsome tonight, his sun-bronzed face, dark hair and brilliant dark eyes emphasised by his cream raw-silk dinner jacket. He was gazing down at Chedlya, chatting and laughing, listening attentively to every word she had to say.

He has time for everyone but me, Anastasia thought bitterly. Charming and dazzling the world at large, with his charisma, his power, his immense wealth. He even paid more attention to my father when we were cruising up to Saint Tropez. He certainly had little to say to me, except to issue orders in his imperious way. Duke Maximilian indeed.

She bit her lip, blinking rapidly as she saw him lean closer to Chedlya, whisper something in her ear. The young woman laughed vibrantly, looked up at him, smiling into his face. There has always been something hypnotic about him, Anastasia thought miserably, a seductiveness. Most people do fall under his spell. To her dismay she noticed that Maxim and Chedlya suddenly appeared to be dancing much closer, were glued to each other. She felt as if a sharp knife was being twisted in her stomach, experienced a swift rush of the most blinding jealousy. It was an emotion that had become only too familiar.

Anastasia had no peace of mind these days. The empty ache inside her was eternally present; she was lonely and depressed, these feelings engendered by Maxim's lifestyle and behaviour, she was fully aware of that. He was absent constantly, more than ever before in fact, always on the run, on the wing, in and out of London and Paris, rushing to New York or Los Angeles or God knows where else. Because of his long absences from her, she found it increasingly difficult to believe that he did not have his flings, become embroiled with some woman somewhere. Casual sexual encounters were probably a part of his life now, the norm, she suspected, while she sat and waited. Waited for him to come home when it suited him.

It struck her that she had been doing a great deal of waiting over the past few years. Waiting for Maxim. Waiting for the yacht to be built. Waiting for the furnishings to be delivered . . . the antiques, the art, the fabrics, the carpets, all the trappings required to create the floating palace he wanted. Waiting, waiting, waiting. And worrying. Worrying herself to death.

She thought back to the summer of 1970, when she had had the heart-to-heart talk with her mother in Paris, and had then spent a lovely holiday with Maxim and the children at the villa in Beaulieu. It had been idyllic. At the end of the summer, following her mother's advice, she had begun to travel with him. At first it had worked; eventually it had become far too difficult for her to sustain. His schedule, the very nature of his wheeling and dealing in the world of big business, had a certain unpredictability. Sometimes they would arrive in New York only to spend a couple of days there, even though their stay had been planned for much longer. Unexpectedly they would have to fly straight back to London. For business reasons. Or they might have to leave for another city in the States. Or Hong Kong. Or Australia. Or some far-flung corner of the globe where he had a deal. She did not have Maxim's penchant for planes, nor his immense unflagging stamina. The strenuous routine soon wearied and debilitated her, took its eventual toll on her health, brought her to a standstill.

Then there were the other demands on her, which necessitated her presence in England and France. A large house in Mayfair and the villa in Beaulieu to run; a variety of staff problems in these homes constantly needing to be ironed out; the children to tend to during half-term and holidays.

After a year she had had to stop being his travelling companion. It had become too much for her. Then before she even had a chance to take a breath there was the yacht to deal with. Countless details needed their attention; she had had to cope with them herself, since Maxim was forever away, in board meetings somewhere in the world.

Inevitably, their separations became longer, and weeks went by without them seeing each other. Frequently the weeks turned into months. If she saw him half of the year now she was lucky.

He's drifting away from me, Anastasia thought, and she was suddenly terribly frightened.

Focusing her gaze on her husband, the man she loved beyond all reason, she saw that he still held the Moroccan girl in his arms. Her stomach turned as she continued to observe him intently. She felt herself beginning to tremble with anger and jealousy, and she had to exercise enormous control to get a grip on her emotions. *In jealousy there is more self-love than love,* she reminded herself, thinking of the line by La Rochefoucauld.

With a flash of clarity and true objectiveness, she thought: Maxim's got the kind of mesmerising charm and devastating looks women find utterly irresistible, fatal. Without him doing anything to encourage them, *they* fling themselves at *him.* And what man could resist that kind of temptation?

And I bet he doesn't, she added under her breath, still quite unable to tear her eyes away from him and from the Moroccan girl, whom she had now begun to detest.

Maxim caught sight of her and smiled, but Anastasia swiftly averted her face, pretended not to have noticed his acknowledgement of her.

She swung around and began to walk away from the dance floor, seething inside, her jealousy rampant, her anger spiralling into genuine rage.

David Maines was making a beeline for her and there was no way she could veer to her right or her left, at least not without giving offence to this very nice man. A screenwriter, and now a best-selling novelist, he had been an acquaintance of her father's for ages, having always been around the film clique in Paris and London. Stubby had taken up with him some time ago, and David had been drifting in and out of their lives for about five years. He always seemed to be in the south of France when they were there, and frequently dined, partied, or played tennis with them. Two years ago they had been his guests at his beautiful villa on the top of a hill in Tangier, where they had spent a long weekend with him. Before the advent of Chedlya.

David drew to a stop in front of her, bowed gallantly and said, 'My friend

Chedlya seems to have commandeered your husband, so I think it's only fair and just that I do the same with you. Please come and dance with me, Anastasia.'

'Oh but I don't – ' she began, then, realising that as hostess she could not be rude to one of her guests, she minded her manners. 'I'd love to, David,' she said.

He led her out onto the dance floor, complimenting her on the fabulous party as they fell into step. 'As for the yacht, it's the epitome of beauty and faultless taste,' David remarked.

'Thank you. The party was a bit easier to produce than the yacht though.' She forced a smile and added, 'My mother should get a lot of credit, you know, she's enormously talented as an interior designer.'

'So are you,' David said, smiling down at her, his eyes full of admiration. Aside from her artistic attributes, she radiated beauty, and he could not help thinking how lucky Maximilian West was to have this superb woman as his wife.

'And I hadn't realised you were a painter,' David remarked, as they glided around the floor. 'I was very taken with the watercolours in the main salon earlier, and Stubby told me *you* painted them.'

'Years ago. I just sort of putter around,' she murmured dismissively, looking over his shoulder, her eyes scanning the area for Maxim. He seemed to have disappeared.

'If that's puttering, then you can putter any time for me,' the writer said. 'Look, Anastasia, if you ever have a show, or if any of your paintings are ever for sale, do let me know. I'd love to buy a few for the house in Tangier.'

'How nice of you, David,' she said distractedly, wondering where Maxim had gone with David's girlfriend. 'But I don't paint very often, it's not even a hobby.' She longed to escape. Her heart had begun to race, and she was frantic, her face taut, her eyes panic-stricken. Had Maxim taken the girl somewhere to be alone with her? To make love to her?

She said a little abruptly, 'David, would you mind awfully if we stop dancing now? I've just remembered something I must tell the chef at once.'

'Of course not, and thank you,' he said, immediately leading her off the floor. 'Ah, there's Chedlya! Obviously looking for me, I've no doubt. See you later, darling.'

Anastasia gave him a small, faltering smile, excused herself and hurried away, wishing the pounding in her chest would cease. Through the corner of her eye she saw Maxim propping up the bar with her father and Stubby, laughing uproariously at some joke, and she felt a surge of relief. Nevertheless, having told David Maines that she had to speak to one of the chefs, there was no possible way she could linger here.

Avoiding the bar, and her mother and Irina, who were both waving to her, trying to catch her attention, she flew along the main deck to their stateroom, and went straight into the bathroom. She was shaking so much she could barely lock the door. After she had managed to do so, she stumbled over to the mirror and looked at herself.

Sadly, she did not see her great beauty, only the panic in her eyes, her grim mouth and strained expression, the beads of perspiration on her face and neck. But in all truth, at thirty-three Anastasia was at her loveliest. Tonight she wore a draped strapless gown of white chiffon, designed by Madame Grès, and a magnificent diamond necklace which Maxim had just given her. Both the dress and the necklace were shown off to great advantage against her golden-brown skin; her blonde hair was swept up in a mass of curls on top of her head, and she had an etherealness about her this evening that was breathtaking.

But blinded as she was by jealousy, possessiveness, anger and hurt she saw nothing as it truly was. All she could think about were Maxim's neglect of her, his protracted absences, his preoccupation with his business, his detached attitude to her well-being, which she considered to be cavalier at best.

I love him too much, she thought. He is my whole existence, but I am only part of his, just a fraction of it really, and that's the basic problem. Tears came into her smoky-blue eyes and she strove hard to push them back, peered at herself in the mirror again. Perhaps there's something wrong with me. Not perhaps; there *is*. I'm sick. *I am sick with love.* For him. She recalled those other words from the Bible: My beloved is *mine* and I *am* his. Except that he's not mine, not any more, she thought. Even though I am his and will always be his.

Oh why couldn't he have been just an ordinary man? Why did he have to be a business genius, this brilliant tycoon of vision and daring? A great sigh slid out of Anastasia and slowly the tears trickled down her cheeks. She wanted their marriage to be the way it had been in the beginning. She wanted all of him. But that was not possible, because Maxim could not give all of himself to her.

She thought: *I can't go on like this. I have to do something. I can't stand the pain of loving him.*

Remembering her guests, she pulled herself together as best she could. Throwing the towel on the washbasin, she reached for a tissue and patted her eyes before hurrying through into their stateroom.

Seating herself at the dressing table, she applied fresh eye makeup and lipstick, sprayed herself with perfume, pushed a curl into place.

Rising, she took a deep breath, managed to summon all of her dignity, and returned to the dance and her guests.

'Congratulations, Peachy,' Maxim said a few hours later. He took off his cream dinner jacket and draped it around the back of a chair.

Anastasia stood at the other side of the stateroom. Slowly she turned around, stood staring at him. She loved him so much, wanted him so much. But it was not to be. She was losing him. Just as she had known when they first met fifteen years ago that it was their destiny to be together, so she now knew that it was their destiny to part. *Que sera sera . . .* what will be *will* be.

She had not been able to stand those women pawing him throughout the evening, clutching at him, flinging themselves at him, draping themselves all over him, kissing him flagrantly when they left at the end of the evening. She hated each and every one of them.

Nausea rose up in her. She thought her legs were going to buckle.

Maxim undid his bow tie, dropped it on the chest, opened the top button of his shirt, continued to look at her. He smiled his charming lopsided smile. 'The party was a spectacular success, the yacht is superb, and the diamond necklace looks gorgeous,' he said, and smiled at her again.

She felt something cracking and splintering inside her, and she reached out, held onto the back of a chair. 'That's all I am to you these days, isn't it? The giver of your parties, the decorator of your homes, the wearer of your diamonds,' she exclaimed coldly.

Maxim was flabbergasted.

He could only gaze at her blankly, startled by her extraordinary words, her curious icy voice. Recovering himself quickly, he said, 'You are also the recipient of my love, Stassy.'

'Recipient of your love! That's a joke. Me and how many others?'

'What on earth do you mean?' he demanded, his tone instantly changing. He gave her a sharp look, annoyance replacing bafflement.

'Oh come on, don't play the injured innocent with me. I know you have affairs with other women.'

'I certainly do not!' he exploded, infuriated by her unjustified accusation.

'You don't expect me to believe that a passionate, very physical man like you doesn't become involved in little liaisons, when he's away from home, do you? I know you very well, Maxim, and sex has always been extremely important to you. Very necessary, I would say.'

'If you can accuse me of philandering, then you don't *know* me at all!' he shouted back, his voice rising to a higher pitch. 'There are no other

women in my life, and there never have been. I have always been true
to you!'

'And what about Camilla Galland, God's greatest gift to the English
stage?' she shot back, her voice acerbic.

'Camilla Galland,' he spluttered and laughed disbelievingly. 'What an
outrageous suggestion. You can't mean that seriously.'

'I most certainly do. Quite aside from the fact that I've seen you with
her over the years, others have spotted the two of you together.'

'You've seen me with her,' he gasped. 'When?'

'In point of fact, this spring, going into the Ritz. And several years ago,
going into Claridge's. You seem to have quite a few luncheons with that
lady. Not to mention dinners in New York. You've been seen, you know,
so don't deny it.'

'I wasn't going to deny it, Anastasia. Why should I? Camilla and I are
friends, have been for years. It's no secret. I have had lunch with her in
London, and I sometimes speak to her on the phone, as you well know.
And I have had dinner with her in New York, yes, when she's been in a
play on Broadway. I've been giving her advice about her investments off
and on over the years. And incidentally, as far as the dinners in New York
are concerned, her husband has always joined us. In case it's slipped your
mind, Camilla married Peter Jarvis five years ago. She's still *very* married
to him.'

'Husbands are generally the last to know about extra-marital affairs!
As indeed are wives. Don't think you can pull the wool over my eyes by
flinging her marriage at me, because you can't.'

Maxim was more furious than ever, took a step towards her, cried, 'Ask
Stubby. Go down the corridor to his cabin *now*, and ask him, goddamn it!
He'll tell you I've been advising her on her investments. He was the one
who suggested it in the first place.'

'*Ask Stubby!*' she exclaimed, her icy voice dripping sarcasm. 'Well,
well, well, that's the joke of the century. *Ask Stubby indeed.* How
preposterous you are, Maxim. Stubby will say anything to protect
you. He'd sell his own mother to protect *you*. Why, Stubby thinks
you're God.'

'What *is* all this about?' Maxim demanded frantically, truly not understanding why she was ranting and raving at him. His face had turned grey
under his tan, and anger had brought goose flesh springing to his face.
'What's brought this on, Anastasia, after our lovely few days together?
And the wonderful party tonight?'

'The party may have been wonderful for you, but not for me. I was left
alone to fend for myself, whilst you paid court to Chedlya and every other
woman present.'

'You're being utterly stupid. I danced with Chedlya *once*. And I was the host, remember. I had to dance with our women guests.'

Anastasia's face suddenly contorted, twisted into an ugly grimace, momentarily obscuring her great beauty.

He sucked in his breath, hardly recognising her. She might have donned a mask.

She cried, 'Things are not right between us any more, Maxim! You're always *away*. You don't share your life with me. You shut me out years ago.' As her pent-up rage flooded her she began to shake uncontrollably, clung to the back of the chair to support herself.

'I have never shut you out!' he protested, his face livid. 'You're not interested in my business, that's why I don't discuss it with you. It bores you. It always has. I do my level best to be with you as much as I can. You don't want to travel with me, because you say you can't take the pace, that it exhausts you. What in God's name do you want from me?'

She did not answer.

'You know I love you, Stassy,' he said, softening his voice and his manner, moving closer to her. 'I've only ever loved *you*. You're the only one I've *ever* wanted. I try to show you how I feel in every way. You yearned for a yacht over the years, so I had one built for you. I called her *Beautiful Dreamer*, because that's what you've always been to me . . . my beautiful dreamer,' he murmured placatingly, his smile loving.

'I don't want your yacht!' she screamed. 'I don't want your diamonds!' Losing control, she pulled at the clasp, wrenched the necklace off and threw it on the bed. 'I don't want it, do you hear!'

Maxim flinched, drew back, gasping at her words.

He felt as if she had kicked him in the stomach, and a terrible coldness swept through him. He genuinely had no idea what this row was about, what had triggered it. All he knew, at this moment, was that he had to get out into the fresh air. He felt the bile rising in his throat, thought he was going to be sick.

Without uttering another word he pivoted and walked out, slamming the door behind him.

'I only want you, Maxim! That's what I meant! I only want you! Material things don't matter to me!' she shouted after him, staring at the door. But he did not come back. She threw herself onto the bed and began to sob, repeating over and over again, 'I only want you, my darling, I only want you.'

Maxim did not hear her words.

FORTY-NINE

Maxim walked down the main deck. It was empty. Everyone had gone to bed. He stepped over to the rail and leaned against it, stood looking out across the dark sea to the dim horizon, taking great gulps of air, endeavouring to still his shaking limbs. He felt unsteady, sickened by her words.

Anastasia had hurt him so much he could hardly stand it. The accusations she had levelled at him were so ridiculous they were laughable. But he could deal with those. What had cut him deeply, like a lash, caused him pain, was the way she had flung the necklace on the bed, screaming that she did not want it.

The diamond necklace was quite extraordinary and it had cost a small fortune. This did not matter to him. What *did* matter enormously was the *love* he had invested in its creation. He had gone to Mark and asked him to make something truly unique for her, and Mark's most gifted designer at Tannen and Graf had created an exquisite design. Then Mark had spent over a year searching the world for flawless blue-white stones. Maxim had wanted the diamonds and the necklace to be perfect for Anastasia, because he loved her so much, and Mark had understood this, had set out to create a masterpiece.

During the entire time the necklace was being made, he had gone to Mark's prestigious jewellery shop in Regent Street whenever he could, wanting to watch the craftsman working, mounting the stones in the intricate lacy web of white gold. He had hardly been able to contain himself until it was finished, until he could finally present it to Anastasia, see it enhancing her beauty.

He had given it to her after they had boarded the yacht for the first time the other day, and sailed up the coast to Saint Tropez. It had looked stunning on her and she had been thrilled, or so he thought. But only a few minutes ago she had flung it back at him. He realised this did not mean much. Her gesture had been one of anger, anger with him, he recognised this. What he did not understand was the reason *why* she was so furious with him, what was at the bottom of it.

Sighing under his breath, Maxim walked over to the bar and poured himself a glass of water, carried it back to the rail where he stood drinking it, trying to sort out his troubled thoughts. Aside from her anger, there had been her outrageous and unfounded accusations to contend with. He could not imagine what had brought on her strange outburst, or prompted her to make the statements she had.

They had had their quarrels in the past, like most married couples, but none of them had ever been quite like this one. He had never seen her so hysterical, so . . . so . . . *irrational*. Her behaviour had been very much out of character. She was normally composed, tranquil, a poised young woman.

She's over-tired, he thought, worn out after all of the work she has done on the yacht in the past year. It *has* been a backbreaking task, even with her mother's help. What Anastasia needs now is complete rest, relaxation, me, and my companionship and love. Yes, she needs me to be with her, to take care of her. She's really quite fragile, my beautiful dreamer.

Maxim was suddenly glad he had planned a cruise to the Greek Islands as a surprise for her. They would be leaving in a few days and would be sailing around the Aegean for about three weeks. It would do them both good, and with a little luck maybe it would be as idyllic a holiday as the one they had had four years ago. That summer at the villa had been so sublime, it had stuck in his mind ever since.

Once the cruise was over he would attempt to structure his life differently, in order for them to spend more time together. He had been planning to do that anyway; he truly wanted to make her happy if he could.

It was a warm night, and Maxim stayed out on the main deck for several hours, endeavouring to sort things out clearly in his head, to make plans for their future.

When he finally returned to their stateroom Anastasia was sound asleep.

He was relieved that she was, for he had not relished another quarrel with her. He crept into his dressing room quietly, took off his clothes and prepared for bed, reassuring himself that tomorrow, after a good night's rest, his wife would be her normal self.

And over breakfast he would tell her about the cruise to the Greek Islands. He knew how much this would please her, and he was looking forward to it himself.

'Daddy! Daddy! Wake up! Wake up!' Alix cried, pummelling his arm.

Maxim sat up in bed at once with a start, and stared at his daughter who stood with her brother at the side of the bed.

'What's the matter?' he asked, their agitation registering with him immediately. '*What is it?*'

'Mummy just left. She's going to Nice airport,' Michael announced, swung his head and pointed to the porthole. 'She's taking off now in the 'copter, Dad.'

As Michael spoke, Maxim heard the roar of the helicopter's blades as it hovered for a moment above the yacht. Throwing back the sheets, he jumped out of bed and raced across the room, peered out of the porthole. To his dismay he saw his helicopter whirling up and away into the sunny blue morning sky.

'She's going back to London, Daddy,' Alix informed him, running to Maxim, catching hold of his arm. 'She was crying this morning,' Alix went on unsteadily, gulping, her eyes filling up. 'You're not going to get a divorce are you, Daddy? Michael and I don't want you and Mummy to get a divorce!'

Maxim was thunderstruck, exclaimed, 'Of course we're not getting divorced! Don't be so silly, *Schatzi*.' He bent down, hugged her, then beckoned to Michael. His twelve-year-old son came running into his arms, and the three of them stood holding each other. He adored his children, and it tore at him that they were upset and disturbed by Anastasia's actions, her sudden dramatic departure.

Finally he straightened, released his children from his tight embrace, and said, 'Everything's going to be all right. I don't want either of you to worry about anything. *Understand?*'

'Yes,' Alix said. 'But why *has* Mummy left?'

'I honestly don't know,' Maxim answered truthfully. 'Now scoot, the two of you, and let me take a shower, shave, and get dressed.'

Michael said, 'What are you going to do, Dad?'

'I'm going to fetch Mummy back. I love her very much. Therefore that is what I *must* do.'

'For God's sake, let me drive, Duke,' Stubby exclaimed. 'You're going to have Margot's Roller and *us* in the drink if you're not careful. *Slow down!*'

Maxim eased his foot off the accelerator of his mother-in-law's new Rolls-Royce, which he had borrowed, and dropped down to a lower speed. 'You're right, Stubby. I don't know why I'm racing like this. By the time we get to Nice airport, the plane Anastasia's booked on will have taken off anyway. If Margot hasn't been able to charter one for me, I'll have to wait for the next commercial flight.'

'I'm certain Margot will have managed to get hold of a private plane for you by the time we get to the airport, even though it's Sunday,' Stubby said reassuringly. 'But in any case, when you get to London, Anastasia will have calmed down, take my word for it. You know what women are. Skittish, like thoroughbred horses.'

'I hope she's more like herself,' Maxim mumbled. 'God only knows what brought this on. I still haven't the slightest idea what the row was about. I'm truly puzzled.'

'She was pushing hard to get the yacht finished for your birthday in June, and even though she didn't succeed, and was late, she worked damned hard. Maybe the pressure and the stress got to her,' Stubby suggested. 'She's probably exhausted, you know.'

'That's what I've been thinking myself.' Maxim tightened his grip on the steering wheel, then confided, 'Stassy accused me of having an affair with Camilla Galland, of all things.'

There was a small silence, then Stubby said, 'You haven't, have you?'

'Oh come on, Stubby, don't be such a bloody fool! Of course I haven't. You ought to know that better than anybody.'

'What I *do* know is that Camilla has had quite a thing about you for years. To put it succinctly, she's had the hots for you, two husbands notwithstanding.'

Maxim threw him a quick glance out of the corner of his eye, snorted in disbelief. 'That's a load of codswallop if I've ever heard anything!'

'Take my word for it, lad. Give her a wink and she's yours.'

'You're wrong, very wrong. In any event, I'm certainly not interested in Camilla, and I never have been.'

Stubby was quiet. After a moment's thought, he ventured, 'You don't think Anastasia's heard gossip about you, do you?'

'*Gossip*? What the hell do you mean?'

'You know, gossip about you and other women.'

'What other women?'

'The ones you've had affairs with.'

'I've only ever had a couple of one-night stands in my *entire* married life,' Maxim snapped. 'That's hardly having *affairs*, as *you* put it!'

'Sally Batterson lasted more than one night, Duke. I remember *her* very well, since I was in New York with you at the time.'

'It lasted a big three weeks! It was a *prolonged* one-night stand, that's all. The whole thing was meaningless. And you, Stubby, my friend, are the only person who ever knew about it.'

'Except for the lady involved.'

Maxim threw him a swift, scathing glance, said nothing.

'Sally knew,' Stubby pointed out.

'*She's* hardly likely to have told anybody.'

'How do you know? Some women like to boast . . . about the notches on their belts. And let's face it, you're worth boasting about.'

'Please believe me, Sally never told a soul about our brief dalliance, such as it was. She was engaged to be married at the time, although I didn't know until a few months later. When I received an invitation to the wedding.'

Stubby laughed cynically. 'Cold-blooded creatures women are at times, don't you think?'

Maxim concentrated on the traffic ahead, braking as they came to a bend in the Lower Corniche, the road running parallel with the sea. Once they had a clear stretch of road ahead of them again, he pushed Margot's Rolls forward, anxious to get to the airport. 'No, Anastasia can't possibly have heard any gossip about me, for the simple reason there is none,' Maxim remarked, after a moment. 'I've led a blameless life for a very long time. In fact, I've always led a blameless life, if you really think about it.' He laughed hollowly. 'I realise there are those who would like to make me out to be a playboy, a cross between Porfirio Rubirosa and Aly Khan, but nothing could be further from the truth.'

'God rest their souls,' Stubby murmured. 'They both died young, but oh what lives they lived!' He sighed, then after a pause, went on, 'I know you're not a womaniser, you don't have to sell me on your fidelity to Anastasia. I've been a witness to it, and you've been nothing if not a devoted husband and father. Hell, I'm sorry I ever asked you to help Camilla sort out her investments. But that twit of a husband was only creating a bigger muddle than she already had.' Stubby frowned. 'By the way, what prompted Anastasia to seize on poor old innocent Camiknickers?'

'She apparently saw me going into the Ritz with Camilla this past spring. We were meeting her accountant there for lunch. Also, I gather some friendly friend told Stassy that they'd seen me dining with Camilla in New York.' Maxim shook his head, grimaced. 'Whoever *that* trouble-maker was forgot to mention Camilla's husband was with us.'

Stubby groaned. 'Just goes to show how careful you've got to be when you're a married man. Thank God I'm a bachelor. And that's the way it's going to remain. Actually, I enjoy being the eternal fiancé.'

Maxim laughed. 'If anybody's the playboy, it's you! I'll never understand why they've always wanted to pin the label on me.'

'You *look* the part more than I,' Stubby pointed out, grinning. 'Dashing, gorgeous, glamorous etcetera. Most people think of me as your bumbling sidekick.'

'Good God, if only they knew! Fast women, fast cars, fast boats, fast roulette wheels. But just watch your step, old son, as far as the fast cars and boats are concerned. I don't want to lose you.'

'Listen who's talking! You're the one who always has his foot down on the pedal. But never fear, I plan to be around a long time.' Stubby settled back in the seat and a thoughtful expression entered his pale-blue eyes.

Maxim drove on in silence for a while.

Suddenly Stubby said, 'She's always been possessive of you.'

'I suppose so.'

'And a bit jealous. I have a deep affection for Anastasia, she is the most wonderful girl, but she gets upset if you even so much as *look* at another woman.'

Maxim glanced at Stubby, swung his eyes back to the road. His brows came together in a puzzled frown. 'Do you really think so?'

'Yes, I do.'

'But surely she knows how much I love her. I've always *adored* her.'

'I know, but women can be funny.' Stubby hesitated, then said, 'There's another thing. She hates you to be away from her . . . this may sound odd to you, but I think she *resents* your business, *resents* the time you devote to it.'

Maxim was startled, exclaimed heatedly, 'But I can't just stop! I've built an enormous empire in the last few years. I have a responsibility to thousands of people – employees, major stockholders, and the public, not to mention myself. I happen to enjoy my work.'

'I'm sure she's aware of that,' Stubby said quickly. 'And I'm not saying she wants you to get rid of your business empire. She's far too intelligent a person to expect you to do such a thing. What I'm trying to say is . . . Well, you *do* spend a lot of time away from her. What woman wouldn't get fidgety?'

Maxim nodded. 'Point well made, Stubby. I must agree. I'm going to have to organise my work schedule a little better.'

He sighed so heavily and looked so worried that Stubby exclaimed, 'Hey come on, Duke, everything's going to be fine. You'll see, when you get home to London, Anastasia will be calmer. This is a storm in a teacup. I'm sure I'll be driving the Roller back to Nice tomorrow, or the day after, to pick you both up.'

'I hope so, I can't stand it when things are not right between me and my girl.'

They patched things up and sailed around the Aegean, and for a while the marriage worked. But within the year it was in trouble again. And for all the same reasons. Inevitably, Anastasia became nervous and run down, her fragile psyche shattered by innumerable problems, some real, some imagined. Without meaning to do so, she created a rift between them, and, unthinkingly, she never gave Maxim a chance to bridge it. In 1976, unable to take the stress and pressure of his life, she insisted on a trial separation. At first he fought it, but finally had to agree. Loving her the way he did, he was afraid of endangering her health.

When Anastasia divorced him in 1977 Maxim was stunned and heartbroken, their children hurt and baffled, their families and friends shocked and saddened.

PART 5

CAMILLA

TANGIER

1981

Wherefore the king said unto me,
Why is thy countenance sad, seeing
thou art not sick? This is nothing
else but sorrow of the heart.

Book of Nehemiah: The Bible

FIFTY

Camilla Galland sat waiting for David Maines in the cool, marble-lined bar of the El Minzah Hotel in Tangier where she was staying.

It was that quiet time of day when the bustle in the streets outside had subsided. The sun was dropping low in the sky, mottling the dark-blue sea with speckles of gold and mauve, and she knew that in a moment night would swiftly descend.

Camilla had always liked this particular hour in North Africa, when it was neither day nor night. The *gloaming* it was called in Scotland, where she originally came from. It was a gentle time.

The silence in the bar was broken only by the muffled whirring of the ceiling fans, the faint plaintive voice of the *muezzin* calling the faithful to prayer from the minaret of the mosque, echoing to her across the *casbah* walls.

In the splintered half light of the bar she saw David walking towards her, tall, thin, deeply tanned from years of living here. Coming to a standstill at the table he reached out, took both of her hands in his and drew her to her feet, hugging her to him. 'Camilla! It's wonderful to have you here in my backyard! Welcome!'

'It's lovely to see you, darling,' she said, meaning it.

They drew apart, sat down at the table, eyed each other appraisingly, then burst out laughing. They had always enjoyed working on movies together, several of which he had written especially for her; in a sense, they shared battle scars, were like old comrades in arms.

'I never thought I'd see you in Tangier alone,' David said, settling back in his chair.

'I'm divorced from Peter Jarvis, you know, and I have been for almost two years.'

'So I read in the gossip columns. What I meant is that the last news I had of you was from Alan Trenton. He told me you were heavily involved with Maxim West. So where is the great Maxim? Off making some stupendously big deal somewhere, I've no doubt.'

Caught off guard, she stammered, 'It must be a while since you heard from Stubby. Maxim and I haven't seen each other for the last six months.' She reached for her glass of wine to hide her confusion, gulped it down.

His quick writer's eye took in everything. 'Oh dear, I've put my foot in it, haven't I? I'm such a clumsy fool. Do forgive me.' He smiled at her warmly, rushed on, 'Let me go and get us a drink, and then we can catch up with all the gossip. Another white wine?'

'Yes, please.'

He strode across to the bar, and she heard him murmuring in Arabic to the barman. In the moment he was away she caught hold of herself, tried to relax in the chair. She wished she had written him a note from Paris before she had left. At least she would have been spared the embarrassment about Maxim, more importantly the painful thoughts of *him*. She could not help but equate him with pain these days. He had hurt her terribly.

'Want to talk about it now? Or shall we leave it until later?' David asked when he came back to the table and lowered himself into the chair.

'I don't mind.' She shrugged her shoulders lightly, made a little moue with her mouth that had a hint of regret to it. 'There's nothing much to tell. I ran into Maxim in New York last September, and we became involved. For three months! Then he suddenly dropped me.' She forced a laugh, shook her head. 'Anyway, *you* know what he's like, after all you've been a friend of Stubby's and his for quite a few years. He's always rushing off to make a big deal somewhere, that's one of the problems.'

'There's no question the man's a workaholic,' David remarked.

'Very much so,' Camilla agreed. 'Anastasia was right about him there.'

David glanced at her sharply. 'Is that the reason they got a divorce?'

'I don't know. Maxim doesn't reveal much. He's the strong silent type. And very *secretive*. Actually, I found him rather enigmatic, hard to get to know, *truly* know. He mystifies me, he really does. Despite our nice friendship over the years, and then our closeness, our intimacy for those three months, I can honestly tell you I have no idea what that man is all about.'

David had seemed puzzled as he had listened to her, but he had asked no further questions, merely said, 'I'm sorry you and he broke up. Maxim appeared to be so lonely after the divorce . . . the loneliest man in the world, to me.'

Camilla made no comment, although she tended to agree.

David said, 'Ah, here's Mohammed with our drinks.'

The smiling waiter placed the glasses of icy white wine in front of them, bowed and backed away.

David touched his glass to hers. 'Down the hatch,' he said, laughed, and winked at her.

'Down the hatch!' She took a sip of the wine, then volunteered, 'Maxim *is* lonely, David. I worry about him, and I still care what happens to him . . . he has that quality.'

'I understand.' David leaned back in the chair, focused his keen intelligent gaze on her, and changing the subject, he asked, 'Tell me what you're doing in Tangier.'

'I'm seriously thinking of buying a house here,' Camilla said. 'I love the climate, it's within easy reach of Paris and London, if I have a film or a play to do, yet it's sort of . . . off the beaten track.' She laughed at David's startled face, and added, 'I'm like you, my darling, I crave a bit of solitude now and again.'

'Camilla, this is wonderful news, and it'll be great to have you here. There's a nice little English-American community, and you'll be welcomed with open arms. But they'll leave you alone when you want peace and quiet. That's the beauty of Tangier. I love the place.'

'I'd hoped you would be able to steer me in the right direction, David, help me to find a real-estate person.'

He grinned, and exclaimed, 'The *right* real-estate person. *That's* very important here. And yes, I know a wonderful French woman who found my villa for me. I'll phone her tomorrow, invite her to lunch with us. I'm presuming you're free.'

'As a bird. But it's your turn now. Tell me all of *your* news. Do you still have that lovely girlfriend? The Moroccan girl . . .'

'Chedlya El Bahi. And no, I don't. She married several years ago. A young Moroccan painter. They live here part of the time, and in Casablanca. I'm fancy free, as they say.' He reached for his drink, sipped it, and continued, 'Actually, I'm enjoying not being involved, for once in my life.'

Neither spoke for a moment, then he said, 'Incidentally, congratulations again on winning the Oscar for best actress. I did drop you a note in April, I hope you received it.'

'Yes, thank you,' Camilla replied, smiling, and then she began to tell him about the making of the movie for which she had won the Oscar. David ordered more drinks, and they sat talking shop and reminiscing for another hour or so, until at last David said, 'Come on, let's get out of here, go to dinner.'

They walked through the dimly-lit, mosaic-tiled lobby of the hotel and out into the main street of Tangier. It was dark. The high-flung black sky looked almost luminous, chipped with thousands of tiny stars and hung with a pale moon.

David lifted his head, touched her arm, pointed to the sky. 'Great set-decorator we have, eh, Camilla?'

She laughed, as always enjoying him, and together they walked down to the sea road, making for his favourite restaurant at the top of one of the highest buildings in the city. 'It's not all that high,' he explained. 'Hardly a Manhattan skyscraper. But the restaurant has a huge plate-glass window, floor-to-ceiling, and you can see the whole of the town, and beyond, on a clear night. It's as if you've been suspended in the sky above Tangier.'

They passed the *Socco Chico* and the *Grand Socco*, the two markets. A few Moroccans sat at one of the cafés, their heads close together as they talked, their *djellabas* pulled closely around them, their glasses of mint tea neglected on the table.

The dark alleys leading into the *casbah* looked mysterious and uninviting. Camilla shivered and drew closer to David. 'Those streets do look sinister,' she said, slipping her arm through his.

He laughed, patted her hand resting on his arm. 'You're with me, Camilla, and we're quite safe, I assure you.'

As they reached the sea road she relaxed. The cafés facing the ocean were in full swing and busy, packed with Moroccans and Europeans. Their coloured lights threw bright rays onto the road, illuminating their way. A huddle of Berber women straggled past, their *haiks* wrapped around them like tight cocoons of brown fabric, their bare feet slapping the sandy road as they made their way back to the hills. A reluctant donkey followed in their wake, his back laden with a precarious mountain of unbelievable parcels.

'It was market day today,' David explained, as her eyes followed the weird little band of women. 'They probably brought down vegetables and flowers. Now they're going back with tea and cloth, and, if they've had a lucky day, sugar and flour.'

'How strange that they're not wearing veils,' Camilla remarked, as she and David caught up with the mule train.

'The country women never do. But they sometimes pull their *haiks* – their robes – around them to cover their faces. Actually, quite a few of the city-dwelling Moroccan women *are* emancipated now, don't wear the veil either these days. Ah, here we are.' He led her forward towards the building where the restaurant was located.

Camilla looked back at the Berber women. They seemed like creatures from another age, their beady black eyes darting back and forth, staring out from their wrinkled brown faces, which she thought looked like polished walnuts. Or they could be baby sparrows, she added under her breath.

David escorted her through the lobby of the apartment building. It was extremely modern, with gleaming marble floors, mirrored walls, and crystal chandeliers. They took the elevator up to the top floor, and went through glass doors into the flower-filled restaurant.

The *maitre d'* greeted David cordially and showed them to a corner table and as David ordered a bottle of white wine, Camilla took in the magnificent view through the wall of glass. By turning slightly she could see the whole of Tangier: the port and the harbour, the strange, cube-like composition of the houses of the *casbah*, the dark hills beyond. And straight ahead in front of her, the sea and sky merging endlessly.

She caught her breath, exclaimed, 'David, it's fantastic!'

'Isn't it just. And it makes you feel like God looking down.' He smiled at her affectionately. 'There's Tangier for you, Camilla, at your feet.'

'I'm so glad I came, David. I think I'm going to enjoy it here. I do hope I'll be able to find a house. The right house.'

'I'm sure you will. In the meantime, I have an idea. Why not move into the villa, stay with me whilst you're here? My place is huge, and rather beautiful, even though I do say so myself.'

'Why, how generous of you . . .' Her voice trailed off, and she hesitated.

He said, 'Go on, say yes. You'd be wonderful company for me.'

'All right then, you've got a deal!' she agreed suddenly, beaming at him.

'Good girl! Now, let's order dinner. I don't know about you, but I'm starving.'

'So am I, to be honest.'

David ordered for them both. He selected a French country *paté* to start with, a local fish baked in paper with herbs and spices, and a selection of steamed vegetables.

They sipped the chilled Pouilly Fuissé as they waited for the food, and David filled her in with details about Tangier and the life he led there. And then during dinner he told her about the screenplay he was writing, and unexpectedly suggested she might like to star in it.

'It's a great part for you, Camilla,' David said, between mouthfuls of fish. 'I'll be honest, I didn't have you in mind when I started it. I didn't have any actress in mind. But now that you're here, and I'm looking at beautiful you, I know how marvellous you'd be.'

'Beautiful me and all of my forty-seven years!'

'But the story *is* about an *older* woman, if you'll forgive the expression,' he explained, grinning at her, thinking how beautiful she did look tonight. She wore a pale green silk dress and emerald earrings; with her reddish-blonde hair, green eyes and pink-and-white skin she was an English rose. What a fool Maxim is to have thrown her over. Aside from her lovely looks, she is a very nice woman, and extremely bright. Some men don't know when they're lucky, he thought.

Camilla said, 'You're staring at me.'

He nodded. 'Yes, I am, and I was just thinking that you could easily pass for thirty-six.' He leaned across the table, fixed his cool grey eyes on her. 'Know what! You might look too young for the part.'

She guffawed.

'I'm being serious. Honestly I am.'

'Shut up and tell me the story,' she answered. 'A good part might be exactly what I need to cure what ails me.'

Later, as she lay between the cool sheets in her bed in the hotel, Camilla thought about the film. David Maines told a story well, and he had intrigued her. Perhaps she ought to let him suggest her to the producer. Yes, it *was* worth considering. And she had meant it when she had said to him that a good part would cure what ailed her.

Camilla Galland loved her work, and her acting career had always been the most important thing to her. Certainly it had given her the most satisfaction, above everything else in her life. Her two husbands had never been able to understand this, hence her two divorces. They had felt threatened by her career, her fame, her immense success. Only Charles Mallingham had understood her acting, her deep-seated need to perform on a stage or in front of a camera, and in so doing enlighten and entertain. She had met Charles early on in her career, and had been engaged to him when he had suddenly dropped dead of a heart attack at the age of forty-nine. She had been twenty-three. But she had never noticed the age difference between them, had been grief-stricken by his death. A prominent investment banker, who was widowed and childless, Charles had left her the bulk of his fortune, had made her a very rich young woman.

Charles had been the only man she had ever loved. Except for Maximilian West. When she had first met Maxim in Paris in 1959 she had been very taken with him, had fallen heavily. But he had never even noticed her, had only ever had eyes for Anastasia. And so, being pragmatic, she had got on with her life, buried her feelings for Maxim, and eventually married two other men. Her first husband had been Roland Vickers, an English actor, her second Peter Jarvis, a stage director of small talent. She and Maxim had become friends over the years, and he had helped her from time to time, giving her advice about her investments. But there had never been anything between them, much to her disappointment. Until September of 1980, just ten months ago, when they had run into each other in New York.

Maxim had asked her out to dinner several times and suddenly, to her enormous surprise and happiness, they were involved in an affair. She had been ecstatic. He had been so warm and attentive, seductive and charming, ever the ardent lover, sending her flowers, books, and he had even given her an expensive piece of jewellery. In December he had sent her a diamond brooch from Cartier, just before flying off to London, where he had gone to spend Christmas with Anastasia and their children.

When he returned to New York in January he had been cool, unresponsive to her, showed no real interest in her any more. Quite unexpectedly, and with an abruptness that was startling, he had explained that it was all over between them. When she had asked for a reason, he had been evasive, had turned icy cold and uncommunicative. She had seen a toughness in him, a ruthlessness even, which had been dismaying. Nonetheless, recognition of these traits had not changed the way she felt about him. But she had had no alternative but to put up a good front for the world and get on with her life.

The play she was starring in on Broadway closed in early March and she had flown to California to attend the Academy Awards. Two months later, proudly carrying her Oscar, she had flown from Los Angeles to Paris, where she had an apartment, and which had been her home for a number of years.

Camilla turned over restlessly. Sleep still eluded her. Again her mind focused on the script David was writing, and she thought: yes, I *am* going to do it, and to hell with Maxim West. At the thought of Maxim her eyes filled with tears, and she began to weep into the pillow, her anguish surfacing. Deep down, within herself, she knew why he had broken off their relationship. He still loved Anastasia. She had known this even when they were romantically involved. He would always love Anastasia and only her.

Impatiently throwing off the bedclothes, she went into the bathroom, where she found a box of tissues. She dried her eyes and blew her nose, splashed cold water on her face, and endeavoured to pull herself together.

Loving a man who did not love her was a waste of time. And she had never quite recovered from the indifference he had shown to her this past January, upon his return from London. To hell with him, she muttered again under her breath, and she resolved to do the film. She would tell David tomorrow when he came to pick her up to move her into his villa.

Work will help to assuage my sorrow, she told herself as she turned off the bathroom light and went back to bed.

FIFTY-ONE

It had been difficult to explain to the taxi driver where she wanted to go. It still had no name yet, this vast white villa on the hill, David's home, filled with his books and paintings and all the other precious trophies he had collected in his world-wide meanderings as a writer over the years.

She paid off the cab and pushed open the huge iron gates. The bell tinkled and she nodded to the *gardien*, who came to the door of his gate house when he heard the chimes.

The old man bowed low, touching his dark-red fez.

Camilla smiled back and nodded, and went up the drive, the gravel crunching under her feet as she walked at a brisk pace.

The villa stood on a rise, its pure white marble columns glinting in the afternoon sunlight, the lawns glistening with water from the many sprays David had installed, the shrubs and trees bright with blooms of vivid colour. She had been staying at the villa for three weeks, since moving from the El Minzah, and she was still not accustomed to the beauty of David's house as it was viewed from the main gates and the driveway.

When she reached the steps that led up to the portico and the front door, she turned, and as usual a smile of pleasure crossed her face as she looked down.

Rolling steeply away from the villa were more verdant grassy lawns, bordered by eucalyptus and orange trees, and beyond the stone wall surrounding the property the rooftops of Tangier were just visible. Still further beyond were the pale sandy beaches of the coastline and the aquamarine Mediterranean.

The villa was silent when she went inside.

She dropped her packages on an ancient pearl-inlaid loveseat in the marble hall, and pushed open the door to the sitting room. The shutters were closed to keep out the bright sun and she blinked as she focused her eyes in the cool darkness.

Camilla had given this room a name when she had first arrived. She had dubbed it the mint-tea room because of its lovely mixtures of greens against the white walls. The latter were offset by pale lime-green silk draperies. Deeper-green rugs were laid on the white marble floor, silk pillows in various shades of green were arranged on the white sofas and French Louis XV chairs, also upholstered in white heavy cotton. Enormous rubber plants and other tropical species with dark green leaves grew in brass tubs standing near the many windows. The only splashes of vivid colour in this cool coniferous room were the modern paintings on the walls, the shelves of books, the masses of flowers in white ceramic urns, picked from the little plantation at the back of the house.

She laughed to herself when her eyes fell on the low Moroccan brass table set with an ancient silver teapot and tea glasses in silver filigree holders.

'You called this the mint-tea room and that's what it's going to be from now on,' David had said to her several weeks ago, and since then either Fatma or Menoubah set the table every afternoon. It was a new ritual obviously meant to be kept, although she and David did not always do that.

Closing the door of the sitting room, Camilla walked along the hall in the direction of David's library. She heard the sound of his typewriter as he tapped out new words for his screenplay. He still wrote on an ancient electric machine; no new-fangled word-processors for this wordsmith.

He was going at full speed and she wondered whether to disturb him, hesitated before knocking. Suddenly his voice rang out through the heavy, brass-inlaid doors as she raised her hand.

'Camilla, come in, I know it's you. I heard your high heels. Fatma and Menoubah just slap around in their bare feet. Unless of course – ' the door was jerked open in her face, ' – I have some unexpected lady visitor.'

'Am I disturbing you?' she asked, staring up at him.

He led her into the library. 'No, absolutely not. And I have very sharp ears, Camilla, and I actually miss the sound of your little feet tapping around this great old place. I just sit and wait for you to come back, when I'm not working.'

'David, you have been so wonderful to me, and this place is so fabulous . . . I never want to leave.'

'You don't have to leave, Camilla. You can stay as long as you wish.'

'That's so sweet of you, darling, but I must find my own house.'

'I know . . . any luck?'

She shook her head. 'Janine is still scouring Tangier. As yet I haven't really liked anything I've seen. But then I'm spoiled by this place, it's so heavenly.'

'The thing is to take your time, you'll eventually stumble on the perfect villa when you least expect it. Now, how about a drink? It's almost six and I was just about to pour myself a *coupe de champagne* . . . Pommery and Greno, pink version. I've earned it after my day in the salt mines – '

'More like the gold mines, wouldn't you say?' she cut in.

'*Touché,*' he laughed, and walked across to the bar at the far end of the library. 'Want a glass?' he asked as he bent down behind the bar and opened the refrigerator, took out the bottle of pink champagne.

'Why not? It sounds like a grand idea, thank you.'

A moment later he came back carrying the two glasses and a packet of the thin black cigarettes he occasionally smoked.

'What sort of *secret* mission took you into Tangier after lunch?' he asked, and winked wickedly as he sat down. 'I know you weren't looking at villas today. Janine told me she was off to Fez with a rich American client.'

She laughed. 'Don't be such a fool! I went to buy a pair of *babouches*, so that I can slide around the house silently like Fatma and Menoubah. And some books.'

'I hope you bought at least one David Maines. I need the money,' he teased.

'No. But I bought a book *for* David Maines, my most generous and loving friend.' She rose and left the library before he could respond, and as she hurried through into the hall she hoped he would like her gift. She had spent most of the afternoon searching the shops and the *souks* for it, wishing to present him with something special to show her appreciation for his many kindnesses to her.

When she returned and gave it to him, he opened the package excitedly like a small boy with his first important gift.

'Camilla, you shouldn't have, but I can't say I'm not thrilled, because I am. The only girl who gives me presents is my twenty-year-old daughter Polly.' He pulled off the last piece of wrapping paper and exclaimed in delight, 'An old Moroccan Koran! Wherever did you find it? I've looked for one of these for years. Why, darling, it's perfectly beautiful.' He looked through the ancient book, turning the pages carefully, fingering the Moroccan-leather binding tooled in gold, appreciating its rarity.

'It *is* old isn't it?' she asked anxiously. 'I did want to find one that was genuine.'

'It is indeed, and it's a masterpiece, in my opinion. It's from Fez, the old university city. Thank you, Camilla, thank you so much.' He put the Koran down on a table nearby, hugged her, kissed her cheek.

'It comes with much love, David.'

He smiled, went and sat down on the sofa again, lighted one of his thin black cigarettes. 'Come on, darling, drink your champers before it gets warm.'

Taking the chair opposite him, Camilla lifted her glass from the heavy mahogany table inlaid with brass, took a quick sip of the pink champagne. 'Mmmm, that's good, it was very hot in the town this afternoon. You were certainly hard at it, pounding away when I came in. How's the screenplay going?'

'Very well, I'm *pleased* with it, Camilla. I should have the first draft finished in a couple of days, and then I want you to read it. I've spoken to Dick Tomlinson, and he's itching to have you star in it.'

'I can't wait to read it, David.'

They sat and talked about the script for a short while, and drank another glass of champagne each, and then David said, 'I forgot to tell you, I'm expecting guests for dinner.'

'Anyone I know?' she asked, looking across at him, lifting a shapely blonde brow.

'No, you haven't met them . . . the Marrons from Casablanca. They're in Tangier for a few days with their son, Michel, and his Moroccan wife, Leyla. They called this morning and I invited them for supper. You'll like them, they're very charming. And, not unnaturally, they're excited about meeting you. They're fans of yours.'

Camilla smiled at him, glanced at her watch. 'I suppose they're about to arrive, and here am I looking very grubby and sticky in an old cotton frock.'

'They won't be here for about an hour and a half. You have plenty of time to get into your best bib and tucker. But I'd better meander into the kitchen and poke old Fatma in the ribs. She's slower than ever these days.' As he spoke he rose, and so did Camilla.

Together they strolled out into the hall. Camilla picked up her bag and the rest of her packages and headed in the direction of the wide, curving staircase.

'See you later,' David said as he went through the door into the kitchen.

As she walked past it she heard Fatma, his cook-housekeeper, chortling merrily at his instructions in Arabic and Spanish.

David had given her the bedroom Camilla considered to be the best in the villa. Large and light, with three French windows opening onto a terrace, it overlooked the gardens and the sea.

At first she had protested, feeling quite certain that she was turning him out of his own room. But he had sworn he had never used it as his, and she had believed him. It was much too feminine for a man. Later he had shown her his own suite, a series of adjoining rooms, rather masculine and furnished somewhat sparsely. They had been designed, like his library downstairs, for writing, his bachelor existence.

He had bought the villa and much of the upstairs furniture from a French banker who had quit Tangier. 'Got it for a song,' David had told her, the first day she had been there. 'Poor bastard! It held too many tragic memories for him. I almost felt guilty, I got it so cheaply.' According to David, the banker had built the villa for his mistress, a young Algerian girl, who had been fatally killed in a motorboat accident in the Bay of

Tangier. The room Camilla occupied had been hers, and quite often, in the weeks since she had been here, Camilla had caught herself wondering about the girl, trying to visualise her face.

The room had a stark, almost virginal quality to it. Vast and high, with white walls and a white marble floor, it was furnished with a large four-poster bed, a huge armoire and a dressing table. All were Spanish in feeling, made of black wood with gilt inlays. The rugs and the draperies were also white, but David had given life to this virginal boudoir with some of his colourful paintings, and Menoubah filled huge Moroccan pottery jugs with fresh flowers every day.

Camilla took a bath in the grand mosaic-tiled bathroom adjoining her bedroom, and thought about what she would wear for the dinner this evening. Being July, Tangier was hot, and so she decided on a short pale-grey chiffon dress that was strapless, had a draped bodice, and a full floating skirt. It was gossamer light, cool.

After her bath, she wrapped a towel around herself and went to the dressing table, where she sat down and brushed her reddish-blonde hair. Once she had swept it up into a chignon on top of her head, she anchored it firmly in place with two antique silver combs she had found in one of the *souks*.

Her weeks in the Tangier sun had given her a light tan, and she needed little makeup, only a touch of brown mascara, silver eye-shadow and bright red lipstick. Once she had sprayed herself with Joy, she put on pale-grey lace underwear, pale-grey stockings shot through with silver, and then the dress. Her shoes matched, were high-heeled grey silk pumps. She stepped into these, wound the long matching scarf around her neck, let the ends fall down her bare back.

Camilla liked the pale grey image of herself that stared back at her from the mirror. It was soft, gentle, and the grey chiffon was perfect with her tan, far more subtle and becoming than white or pale blue would have been. She realised she did not need much jewellery. 'Let's not gild the lily,' she muttered out loud. Large *mabé* pearl earrings and her diamond evening watch were the only pieces she selected from her small travelling jewellery case.

A moment later she hurried out, glancing at her watch as she did so, noting it was twenty to eight. Thankfully, she was only a few minutes late. She loathed arriving after everyone else, making an entrance, because as a famous actress she knew everyone expected it of her. At least, strangers did.

Coming down the wide staircase and crossing the hall, she headed for the sitting room where David usually served cocktails on the long terrace which opened off this room. As she walked in she could see him talking to someone through the French windows which stood ajar.

As she pushed open the doors and glided out, she exclaimed, 'There you are, David, I do hope I haven't kept – ' She broke off and stood gaping at him and his companion.

It was Maximilian West.

Maxim stood there smiling at her, looking larger than life. His lean and handsome face was deeply sunburned, and he wore an impeccably-cut cream silk suit, a cream Swiss voile shirt and a dark-blue tie. Everything about him seemed to gleam, from the tips of his highly polished brown shoes to his dark and brilliant eyes. He was forty-seven and gorgeous, all six-foot-one of him. And, as always of late, he had more the appearance of a movie star than a business tycoon.

Rarely ever at a loss for words, Camilla was speechless. She stood rooted to the spot, gaping at him stupidly, so startled to see him she had as yet not even returned his smile. She began to shake inside and her legs felt unexpectedly weak.

David said, 'Have a nice evening, you two. See you later.'

Finding her voice at last, Camilla exclaimed, 'But David, where are you going?' and she was furious with herself as she heard the shrillness in her voice.

'I have a date,' David replied, winking at her. 'Enjoy yourselves.' With a nonchalant wave of his hand he was gone, disappearing through the French doors.

'It looks as if we're on our own, kid,' Maxim said, bestirring himself from where he stood near the balustrade, walking towards her slowly, his brilliant smile intact.

FIFTY-TWO

'I've been set up!' Camilla said fiercely. 'You and David set me up. That's not fair. In fact, I resent it.'

'No, you don't, you haven't got a resentful bone in your beautiful body,' Maxim said, his smile full of warmth as he sat looking at her across the small table on the terrace. 'And it's not the way it appears, truly it isn't, Camilla.'

'Which *way* is it then?' she asked crisply.

He was silent, and then he pushed himself to his feet, offered her his hand. She took it automatically, without thinking, then flinched inside at his touch, instantly aware that he had the same devastating effect on her as always. Clamping down her feelings for him, she stood up, allowed him to lead her over to the balustrade at the edge of the terrace.

'What do you see out there?' Maxim asked, looking down at her.

'Nothing unusual,' she replied, sounding slightly puzzled, her eyes scanning the garden. 'Lawns, trees, flowers.'

'Beyond the garden . . . look towards the sea.'

She followed the direction of his gaze, and exclaimed, 'Oh! It's your boat, isn't it?'

'Ship,' he corrected with a faint smile. 'Yacht, to be exact. And yes, it's *Beautiful Dreamer*. I was cruising the Med with a few friends, and Stubby had the bright idea of sailing over to see our dear old chum David. As a surprise, so to speak. We finally got here late yesterday, dropped anchor out yonder.'

Maxim waved his hand in the direction of his yacht, and continued, 'Stubby telephoned David last evening, to announce our arrival. And, in typical Stubby fashion, invited us all over here for lunch today. Only to be told, in no uncertain terms by David, that we couldn't come for lunch. Because you were his house guest and he didn't want you upset.'

There was a small pause. Maxim's gaze was very direct as he finished, 'Upset by *my* presence, to be precise.' A mirthless little laugh escaped him, and he added as an afterthought, 'David did call Stubby back to say that I shouldn't take offence.'

'Did you?'

'Not really. But it brought me up short, made me start to think. I realised I did owe you an apology, Camilla.'

'Is that why you're here?'

'Sort of.'

'What does *that* mean?' Camilla probed, eyeing him, all of her senses alerted for trouble. Swiftly she raised her defences. This was the most lethally attractive man she had ever known. Furthermore, she had been in love with him for years. He could quite easily be her ruination. She must be on her guard against him.

Maxim made no response to her question.

In a little while, he said slowly, his voice soft, contrite, 'I am sorry, Camilla, very sorry. I behaved badly towards you, and certainly you didn't deserve to be treated in such a cavalier manner. It was very wrong of me.'

When she remained quiet, he asked, 'Do you accept my apology?'

'Yes.'

Maxim flashed her his lopsided smile, full of charm. 'Then let's kiss and make up.'

'Oh no!' she cried. 'No kissing.' She shrank back, held out her hand. 'Let's *shake* and make up.'

Unable to hide his amusement, he laughed, took her hand in his, shook it rather formally, then unexpectedly he bent his head, kissed her fingers.

The touch of his mouth on her skin unnerved her, and she snatched her hand away, stepped over to the table, reached for the glass of champagne he had poured for her earlier. She endeavoured to conceal her panic, said in a voice pitched unnaturally high for her, 'If David was so adamant about you not upsetting me, then how on earth did Stubby talk him into letting you come over here this evening?'

'Stubby had nothing to do with it,' he said, moving closer to her. 'I phoned David from the yacht early this morning. I told him I wished to see you. I explained that I owed you an apology, that I also wished us to be friends again. And so he suggested I stop by at seven-thirty. For drinks.'

'He agreed as easily as that?' she asked incredulously, thinking that David was obviously a pushover.

'Not at all. He was very tough with me. In fact, I had to do quite a lot of talking, persuading. But he finally gave in.'

Oh yes, Camilla thought, *you can be very persuasive when you want to be. As I know only too well.* But she said, 'I still feel as if I've been well and truly set up by the two of you.'

'Please don't, Camilla. And don't be angry with David. That lovely man is genuinely very fond of you, and he thought he was doing the right thing. He really did mean well, as, indeed, do I.'

The glance Camilla now gave him was cool, appraising. 'When I asked you a moment ago if you were here to apologise you said *sort of*. I'd like to know what you actually meant by that remark.'

'Of course you do. Look here, Camilla, I didn't come here only to apologise. I wanted to see you again, talk to you, and have dinner with you.'

'I'm afraid I can't!' she cried, that sense of panic washing over her once more. 'Quite aside from the obvious reasons, I happen to know that dinner has been prepared for me. I'm dining here. *Alone.*'

He merely smiled at her indulgently.

Maddened, she said in a cold voice, 'Anyway, hasn't it occurred to you that I don't want to have dinner with you?'

Ignoring her question, he remarked evenly, 'David arranged for the cook to prepare *couscous*. It's one of my favourite dishes, and it has been for years. I used to eat it at the El Djazier in the Rue de la Huchette in Paris.' He smiled at her again. 'We're both dining here, actually.'

She took a step backwards, wanting to put distance between them. Glaring at him, she snapped, 'I was right! You did set me up.'

*

It was obvious to Camilla that David had been a willing conspirator with Maxim. As if the villa and the gardens were not beautiful enough in themselves, David had gone out of his way to make the setting even more perfect.

He had arranged for them to dine in the garden by candlelight, where they were served by Aly and Menoubah, his butler and housekeeper. As soon as it had grown dark, just before dinner, Aly had turned on the hidden spotlights, so that the fountains, orange trees and flower beds were illuminated, thrown into prominence in the most spectacular way. The garden became a magical place. Aly had also turned on the sound system, and romantic music, selected by David earlier, played softly in the background whilst they dined.

The circular table had been set up near a cluster of eucalyptus trees at the edge of the lawns, which swept down to the dark sea, silvered now by moonlight. It was a breathtaking kind of evening, the dark-blue sky clear, cloudless, full of stars, the air warm, heavy with the scent of jasmine.

Aly kept filling her crystal goblet with cold white wine, and as she sipped it Camilla found herself starting to relax. She discovered that she was not particularly hungry, ate only a few forkfuls of *couscous* now and again, picked at her green salad.

Against her will and her better judgement, she was falling under Maxim's spell once more, mesmerised by his charisma, and seduced by his charm, his hypnotic voice, his looks and his immense warmth. Having been in love with him for half of her life, since she was twenty-five in fact, she was extremely vulnerable to him anyway. His presence overwhelmed her. There was nobody like him really, and she found herself laughing at his stories, listening to him attentively, and enjoying being with him, swept up by the force of his personality and magnetism.

He was so outgoing with her, so open and honest, that at one moment during dinner Camilla was on the verge of asking him why he had disappeared from her life so abruptly in January. But inevitably she refrained. She was afraid of his answer, did not want to hear it. For she was not sure she would be able to handle it, if he said it was because he was still in love with Anastasia. This thought brought her up short, and she reminded herself that she had vowed earlier not to succumb to his charms. But there was no denying he was at the top of his form this evening. He dazzled her. And so when he kissed her lightly on the cheek, after she had made him roar with laughter about something, and then when he lifted her hand from the table, kissed her fingertips, she did not pull away or protest.

But much later, over the tiny cups of strong, sweet coffee which Aly made, Camilla looked at him carefully in the candlelight, shrewdly assessing him and his motives. He was here for a reason, not just to apologise, talk to her and dine.

After a very long moment, as he returned her gaze unblinkingly, she said, 'What do you want?'

'*You.*'

'For how long?'

'*Tonight.* The next two weeks . . . whilst I'm in these parts.'

'And then?'

'I don't know.'

'At least you're honest, Maxim.'

'I want to be honest with you, Camilla. Nothing less would do for you. Not now. Well? Give me an answer.'

'I want you too, I won't deny it. But . . . I'm afraid.'

'Don't be fearful. I promise I won't hurt you again.'

'You will hurt me if you make love to me, engage my emotions, then go off and leave me.'

He was absolutely silent. Not a muscle moved in his darkly handsome face.

She held herself quite still.

They stared at each other, wanting each other. They recognised this in each other's eyes.

'I won't be your mistress,' she said softly.

'I know that,' he answered, his voice as soft as hers. Pushing back his chair, he rose. 'Let's go for a walk through the gardens,' he said, then helped her up out of the chair.

He took her hand, guided her across the grass, and she allowed herself to be led by him. She felt as if she had no will power as far as Maximilian West was concerned. He stopped walking suddenly, and, putting a hand on her bare shoulder, he turned her to face him, stared down into her face, touched it lightly with his fingers.

'You're so lovely, Camilla, and I want you so very, very much. But I won't force myself on you. It's your decision.'

'I want you too, Maxim,' she whispered.

He leaned into her and kissed her very lightly on the lips, and immediately pulled away. 'Shall we go in?'

Camilla could only nod.

Maxim locked the bedroom door, turned around and leaned against it, staring at Camilla, holding himself in check.

She had walked in ahead of him and stood in the centre of the floor, as unmoving as a statue, caught in the corridor of brilliant moonlight streaming in through the open window.

His chest tightened as he continued to look at her. She was a very beautiful woman, a typical English rose because of her colouring, serene and ladylike in her demeanour. But underneath that facade of gentility she was earthy, sensual, very sexual. It was these contrasts in her which turned him on, started the fire racing through his blood, filled him with excitement. The first time he had made love to her he had instantly understood that she had a strong sexual drive, therefore the power to excite him over and over again.

In the three months they had been together last year, she had satisfied him completely every time they had made love, in a way no other woman ever had except for Anastasia, who was lost to him. He pushed aside the thought of his wife. *Ex-wife.* To dwell on her now would be disastrous. If he carried an image of Stassy across the room, he would be rendered impotent, useless to Camilla. He had not come all this way searching for her, wanting to bed her, to rekindle their liaison, only to flounder because of a power failure on his part. Frustration was the last thing he needed. He had lived with that for the last six months. And, if he was correct in his assessment of her, so had she. Camilla was not a promiscuous woman, and he was certain there had been no other man in her life since him.

'Oh darling . . . ' She spoke softly, holding him with her intense gaze, taking a step forward. Desire for him spilled out of her eyes.

He threw his jacket on a chair, loosened his tie. This followed the jacket and he began to swiftly unbutton his shirt as he walked across the room towards her.

When he came to a standstill in front of Camilla he smiled faintly, then slowly unwound the long chiffon scarf wrapped around her neck, let it fall to the floor, took the silver combs out of her hair, so that it cascaded around her face.

Touching the bodice of her strapless dress, he said softly, 'Take this off.'

Unzipping it, she let it drop to her feet, stepped over it and into his arms, her bare breasts pressed against his bare chest.

Maxim kissed her lightly on the lips as he had a moment ago in the garden, before bending to kiss her breasts. They were small, rounded, taut and high, a young girl's breasts, and he kissed them fleetingly, led her over to the bed. Pushing her down onto it, he leaned over her, removed her shoes, threw them to one side, and slipped off her grey lace panties. He unfastened her suspenders one by one, carefully slid each stocking down her leg, one after the other.

Her eyes did not leave his face.

He said, 'I've thought of you constantly, wanted you constantly. For months. I don't want to rush it now.'

'I feel the same,' she whispered. Her heart was beating at an excessive rate, and she trembled inside. The heat was rising in her as it never did with any other man. Only with Maxim West. He merely had to glance at her to excite her. The manner in which he was removing her underwear, so delicately, so slowly, drove her crazy, heightened her desire for him. She closed her eyes, curbed the moan of desire rising in her throat, not wishing to break the tension mounting in him, in them both, by making the slightest sound. *I want you now*, she thought. *At once. Immediately. Now. Take me. I love you. I love you. Maxim. Maxim. I've only ever loved you. All my life. I've only ever loved you. Take me. Take me.* The words repeated themselves over and over in her head, like a Bach fugue, endlessly, endlessly repeated themselves.

He had been caressing her body; he stopped, moved away from her. She heard him walking across the tiled floor, opened her eyes swiftly, saw him unzipping his trousers. He stood near the chair, undressing rapidly. She watched him closely, sensually savouring every contour and line of his body: the wide shoulders, slender hips, long legs. Naked, he walked back to the bed, and to her. Her heart missed a beat when she saw how excited he was.

Maxim lay down next to her, took her in his arms, kissed her deeply, his warm mouth enclosing hers. She felt his soft, sweet tongue on hers, and she seemed to draw his breath into her deeply as they clung together.

Camilla lay against the cool sheet, luxuriating in the pleasure of him. She had vowed she would never let him near her again. Now she wondered why she had ever made that vow. This was all that mattered really. Making love with each other like this, his mouth on hers, his hands on her body. He had lovely hands. They were sensitive, gentle, fluttering over her, touching her breasts, moving down over her thighs, seeking and loving that most secret part of herself.

She opened her eyes, watching him as he kissed her stomach, her thighs, his lips grazing her gently as they moved on, finally came to rest where they always did. His hands were fluttering once more, joining with his lips to pluck at the kernel of her womanhood, bringing her to climax, and quickly so, as he knew how. But once the trembling started she tried to hold back.

'Don't fight me,' he whispered, lifting his head for a moment, looking at her intently. And so she allowed him to do what he wanted with her, let herself go, felt herself flowing out to him. And no longer able to restrain herself, she cried out in her passion, pleasure and excitement, 'Maxim! Oh Maxim!'

He took her swiftly, fiercely, moving into her hard. As he thrust himself forward, her body arched to his and her arms encircled his broad back.

He slid his hands under her body, lifting her closer and higher to him
. . . higher and higher, and she flung her legs around his waist, welded
herself to him. They moved together in perfect unison.

Every one of Maxim's senses was clamouring for her after months of
longing to hold her in his arms like this. Sex with her was pure pleasure.
Suddenly he had the need to possess her completely; he must drive her
on to that point of physical ecstasy which he was swiftly climbing to
himself. He pushed his body against hers, moving faster and faster at an
accelerated rate and she took his lead, quickening her speed to rise and
fall with him.

Their passion exploded around them suddenly. She cried his name
again, but he made no sound at all as he abandoned himself to her and
fell down into oblivion.

Later, as they lay side by side on the bed, Maxim raised himself up on
one elbow, looked down at her, moved a strand of golden hair away from
her face. '*Would* you have been upset if Stubby and I, and our friends, had
landed on you for lunch today?'

'Yes, I would. But I could've handled it. And none of you would have
known how I felt. I'm a good actress, you know.'

'Not good . . . *great*.' He kissed her nose. 'But you haven't been acting
for the last hour. This was real.'

'It was.'

'I wasn't acting either.'

'I know you weren't.'

Maxim hesitated, said, 'You don't have to believe this, but I haven't
slept with another woman since you. Not since we broke up in January.'

Slightly startled by this admission, she said, 'I believe you. What would
be the point of lying to me now? But why not?'

'I haven't had time.'

'Bastard!'

A mischievous glint entered his eyes. 'That's only partially the truth.
Although I have been swamped with business, I really haven't wanted to
sleep with anyone but you.' He pushed his face into her hair, murmured
against her ear, 'You've really got my number, babe.'

She laughed at this remark, which was so unlike anything he would
normally say, slithered off the bed, padded into the bathroom. She
reappeared with a large towel, paused to turn on the ceiling fan, glided
back to the bed. Clambering on to it she dried his body with the towel,
then wiped her own.

'It's so warm in here, we're both covered with perspiration,' she said.
'You don't mind the fan, do you? I thought it would cool us off.'

'It won't cool me off, babe, not when you're around,' he replied, giving her a cheeky, boyish grin.

A secretive, knowing smile slid onto Camilla's face. She crouched next to him, began to flutter her hands over his body as he had done to her earlier. And slowly, joyously, she began to make love to him with her hands and her mouth, until his breathing became shallow, harsh. And when he could no longer stand her ministrations, thought he was going to explode, he moved onto her with speed, braced himself over her body, and took her again.

'Am I too heavy?' Maxim asked.

'No, I like to feel you on top of me.'

Nevertheless, after kissing her cheek, he rolled off her body, and fell back against the pillow. 'Is there a bottle of water up here, Cam?'

'Yes, I'll get it. I'm thirsty myself.' Camilla went to the chest near the window, opened the bottle, poured two tall glasses, and brought them back to the bed, handed one to Maxim.

He said, after a moment, 'I've a confession to make.'

'What?'

'It wasn't Stubby's idea to come here to visit David. It was mine.'

'Oh.'

'I was in Paris at the end of June. I kept phoning your apartment, before I flew down to Monte to pick up the yacht. I tried for several days. Finally I got your maid. She told me you'd gone to Tangier, that you were staying at the El Minzah. So I phoned the hotel, only to be told by them that you'd checked out. I pressed them for a forwarding address, and they said you were staying with David Maines.'

'Why were you looking for me?'

'Surely you know.'

She did not answer him.

He said, 'You can't deny there's a strong sexual attraction between us.'

'Is that why you came then?'

'Yes.'

'Sure of me, weren't you?' she remarked, staring at him sharply.

'Not really. But I'm forty-seven years old, and so are you, and we're not children. There *is* a tremendous sexual bonding between us. In fact, leave *us* alone together for a few minutes and we inevitably end up in bed these days.'

She continued to stare at him without uttering a word.

'Admit it, Camilla. You know very well how much we turn each other on, satisfy each other in bed.'

'Yes,' she said at last. *But she was in love with him. That was the difference between them.* Still, she had no intention of telling him how she felt about him. Obviously he did not love her. Oh, he was fond of her, she knew. But that was all.

'There was another reason I was trying to find you. I wanted to invite you to join us on the cruise.' He reached out, slid a finger along her cheekbone, gave her an affectionate smile. 'Will you join us for the next couple of weeks?'

'Why?'

'I need you, Cam.'

'But for how long will you need me?'

'I just told you, we'll be sailing around the Med for two more weeks.'

'I didn't mean that, and you know I didn't, Maxim.'

He nodded. 'I understand what you're getting at.'

'I told you earlier, in the garden, I won't become your mistress.'

'It's marriage you want, I realise. I can't promise you that . . . let's go slowly, see what happens, how we get on in close proximity for two weeks on the yacht. So, will you come?'

'I'll think about it.'

He shook his head. 'You're maddening,' he muttered, bending over her, bringing his mouth to hers. And slowly, expertly, he made love to her again.

FIFTY-THREE

'I'm very glad you came with us on the cruise, darling girl,' Stubby said to Camilla one morning, as they sat having coffee in the boat deck lounge. This had become a daily ritual with the two of them, since they both wanted to avoid the glaring morning sun, preferred the cool shade of the lounge.

'So am I,' Camilla replied, smiling at him. 'The last two weeks have been marvellous for me.'

'You've certainly done Maxim good. I've noticed he's much more relaxed when you're around. He's been lonely since the divorce, Camilla. You're very attentive to him, to his needs, you make him feel good, I can tell.'

'I love him,' she blurted out before she could stop herself, then sat back in the chair, shook her head. 'Oh dear, I do have a big mouth, don't I? I didn't mean to tell you that, Stubby.'

'Oh, but I knew, I've known for years. You've been in love with Duke since 1959. Right?'

Camilla was slightly startled by his remark, asked swiftly, 'Has it been so obvious?'

'Not at all. But you were never interested in *me* in those days, certainly not sexually, when we were ... er ... er ... stepping out, shall we say? You were forever asking me questions about *him*. One day the penny dropped. But your secret's safe with me.' Stubby grinned, squeezed her arm. 'You're a good kid, Camilla.'

'Some kid,' she laughed.

'Anyway, I hope you're going to stick around.'

'I'm not sure what you mean by that, Stubby?'

'After the cruise. There *is* life after this, you know,' he pointed out with a chuckle.

'David wants me to star in the film he's writing – '

'I know,' Stubby cut in. 'He tells me so every day at lunch. And I'll say this for him, he's very dedicated, even on the cruise. Locked up in his cabin all morning, every morning, hard at it. However, I was actually referring to Maxim ... what I meant was, I hope you're going to stay with *him*.'

'I have no idea ... I don't know what's going to happen.'

Stubby looked at her carefully. 'Stay with him, Camilla. He needs you.'

Camilla gave her old friend a hard stare, a thoughtful expression crossing her face. Eventually she said, 'I wish I knew what he truly felt about me. Maxim is very close; he doesn't reveal his feelings.'

'He has great affection for you, anyone can see that,' Stubby reassured her. 'The two of you seem to be very compatible and you obviously enjoy being together. Look here ...' Stubby leaned forward, fixed his pale-blue eyes on her, '... if two people are still on speaking terms, after close confinement on a yacht for two weeks, then they've got it made, in my opinion.'

'I notice you haven't mentioned the word *love*, Stubby.'

'Don't quibble. You're not seventeen. Neither is Duke. You're both forty-seven. And, actually, I think you're damned lucky to have what you have together, in this lousy world we live in. The two of you *do* have a lot going for you, which is more than I can say about most couples I know.'

'Hasn't Maxim ever said anything about me to you? Mentioned the way he feels?'

'No,' Stubby fibbed. After a moment he cleared his throat, and said, in all truthfulness, 'Maxim *is* a very private man, he'd never confide anything like that, discuss in detail the intimate side of his life. He's a gentleman, you know.'

Camilla nodded, drew closer to Stubby, murmured, 'It's just ... Frankly, Stubby, I don't want to end up being his mistress. As much as I care for him, that role's not for me.'

'I understand. Still, I do think you ought to stick around. If not for Maxim's sake, then for another excellent reason.'

'What's that?'

'For your own sake, Camilla. He's very good for you too. You're looking wonderful, better than I've seen you in years, and there isn't an ounce of strain left in you. In fact, you're positively blooming. Ask David. He agrees with me.'

'Oh, so you've been talking about me behind my back, have you?' she exclaimed, but there was a hint of jocularity in her voice.

'And very fondly.'

Camilla smiled at him but made no response. She sat quite still, staring through the door towards the deep-blue Mediterranean, admitting that Stubby spoke the truth. Maximilian West *was* good for her. She had never felt as happy in her life. From the moment she had stepped on board *Beautiful Dreamer*, Maxim had treated her affectionately, and with respect, had shown her every consideration. His gallant treatment of her aside, they laughed a lot, talked endlessly about a variety of things, thoroughly enjoyed each other's company. And then there were their nights of passionate lovemaking. His desire for her had not waned – in fact, he did not seem able to get enough of her. She felt the same about him.

She had quickly begun to realise that she had never really known Maximilian West properly. Their friendship over the years had been rather superficial. He had been a married man, not in the least interested in her, and so she had carefully buried her feelings for him. Then again, during the three months they had been involved in New York last year, their time together had been limited. Snatched moments, a night or two a week, Sundays. The chief reason for the infrequency of their meetings was their conflicting hours. She was starring in a hit Broadway play; he was running a billion-dollar empire. As he was going to bed, she was walking off a stage, ready to go out to dine and relax. They had always been out of sync somehow, as far as time was concerned.

But in the two weeks they had been cruising around the Balearic Isles and Sardinia, they had been together constantly, hardly ever out of each other's sight, except when Maxim worked in the mornings, and early evenings before dinner. In consequence, she had acquired a better understanding of him. She had always been in love with him; now she genuinely liked him, saw his many qualities as a human being – his kindness, his integrity, his compassion for people. He was a good man. She was aware that he could be tough and hard-nosed about business, perhaps even a bit ruthless. Nonetheless, he was a man of character and honour, and she admired him.

Maybe Stubby is right, Camilla now thought. *Maybe I should stay with Maxim. He wants me to, he's said so several times. And what's wrong with being his mistress?* *The gossip,* she thought. *I don't want to cope with the gossip, the publicity.* Oh, to hell with all that . . . who cares what the rest of the world thinks? I can't live my life for the world. I must be true to myself . . . *I want to be with Maxim . . .*

'Penny for your thoughts,' Stubby said.

'You can have them for nothing.' Camilla flashed him a lovely smile. 'I was thinking that perhaps . . . Well, I might take your advice, and stick around. After all, who cares what the world thinks?'

Stubby was momentarily startled by this comment. His brows knitted. 'You're too mature to worry about that sort of nonsense, love. Too big. And far, far above it. Besides, Maxim hasn't compromised you in any way on the yacht. You have your stateroom, he has his own cabin – '

'Speaking of that, there's something I've been meaning to ask you,' Camilla interrupted. 'Maxim moved out of his stateroom when I came on board and gave it to me. Which was lovely of him, very considerate. But I don't understand why he doesn't have a stateroom of his own. I thought there were three on this yacht.'

'There are. You have one. Marcia and I have the other. The third is kept permanently locked.'

'Why?'

'It belongs to Anastasia. Only she uses it.'

Camilla stared at him, perplexed. 'I still don't understand.'

'When they got divorced, Maxim said she could have anything she wanted. The house in Mayfair, the villa in Beaulieu, the Fifth Avenue apartment, this yacht. Literally anything. *Everything,* if she so desired. But the only thing she asked for was her stateroom on the yacht. To use when she came on board to go cruising with Maxim and the children. She also told him she would prefer it if no one else used it. He respects her wishes. It's locked. Unless she's around, of course.'

'Why only the stateroom? Why didn't she ask for the yacht?'

Stubby leaned forward, said in a confiding voice, 'Anastasia didn't want *anything* from Maxim, except enough money to live on comfortably. None of the grand homes, nor this yacht. She didn't divorce him because she hated him, you know. She divorced him because she loved him far too much, so she wasn't out to skin him alive. Actually her love was rather obsessive, possessive. Anastasia built her life around him, made him the be-all-and-end-all of it, the centre of her existence.' Stubby pursed his lips, shook his head sadly. 'Not healthy. For anyone concerned. She eventually realised this, and she left him, to save herself, in a sense.'

'But Maxim loved her. Surely she knew that,' Camilla ventured.

'She did. However, she couldn't cope with his life, his business, his work schedule. He's not a nine-to-five man, and he never has been. He's driven, ambitious, and brilliant at what he does – '

'Why does he do it? Why does he keep acquiring more and more companies, expanding his business?'

'He's an empire-builder by nature, the maker of a dynasty. And he can't help the way he's made, Camilla. He's brilliant at it, as I just said.'

'But surely he has enough money by now. He's a multi-millionaire.'

Stubby half smiled. 'It has nothing to do with money. It has to do with his need to create, the excitement of wheeling and dealing, of meeting immense challenges, plus the satisfaction he derives from what he does. Listen, it's rather like asking me why a mountaineer wants to climb Mount Everest.'

'Why does he?'

'Because it's there to climb. To conquer. Maxim has to conquer, too.'

'But didn't Anastasia understand that?' Camilla asked softly, raising a brow.

'I think she did. But understanding didn't make it any easier to accept. At least not for her. I've always felt she has a very fragile psyche . . . I think a woman's got to have a streak of toughness in her to cope with Maxim's way of life.' He paused, then added, 'You could do it. You could cope.'

'Are you saying I'm tough?' she exclaimed, throwing him a challenging look.

'I hope to God you are! Yes, you do have a certain toughness in you, Camilla, you're a survivor. Please don't misunderstand me. When I say *toughness* I mean resilience, strength, the will and the capability to bounce back. Don't confuse the word *tough* with the word *hard*. There's a big difference. A woman who has a bit of toughness in her can also be emotional, feminine, sensitive, soft and loving. All the things you are – '

'Thanks for those nice words, Stubby.'

He smiled. 'On the other hand, a *hard* woman is totally without emotion, or feelings. *Hard-bitten*.'

'What you're saying is that Anastasia wasn't resilient enough to cope with the pressures and stresses of Maxim's life, the demands his business makes on his life.'

'Exactly. Plus his total dedication to it, his absorption in it. But look, that's all water under the bridge. As you probably know, Anastasia had a nervous breakdown just before the divorce, but she's much better now, making tremendous strides.'

'They're friends, he told me . . . '

'Yes. She still loves him, worships the ground he walks on actually. But it's an arm's-length friendship. I think that's the only way she can handle it, loving him the way she does. I'm sure she doesn't want to expose herself to his lifestyle again.'

Camilla nodded, remained silent. She was longing to ask Stubby if Maxim was still in love with Anastasia, but she held her tongue. She preferred not to know what his feelings were about his former wife.

David Maines suddenly walked into the boat deck lounge, exclaiming, 'Good morning! Good morning!' and so curtailed any further conversation about Anastasia.

David said, 'Phew! It's bloody hot out there this morning. *Blistering.* Mind if I join you for a cup of coffee? Or is this a private confab?'

'Of course it isn't,' Camilla replied; rising, she went to the sideboard, poured a cup of coffee for David and brought it to him. She placed it on the table next to him, and he said, 'Thanks, darling.'

'How's the script coming along?' Stubby asked.

David raised his thumbs. 'Pretty terrific. I've discovered I like writing on a yacht. There's a splendid isolation about it, no distractions.'

At this moment, Maxim appeared, stood framed in the doorway, holding a sheaf of documents in his hands. He lolled against the door frame nonchalantly. 'Good morning, chaps. I'm just off to do a few hours' work, but before I disappear I wanted you to know I'm considering extending the cruise for another ten days. Who's game?' Although he addressed them all, his brilliant dark eyes were levelled on Camilla as he spoke.

'I am, darling,' she said at once with a loving smile.

David said, 'Count me in, Skipper.'

'What a splendid idea, Duke!' Stubby exclaimed. 'Marcia and I would love it.'

Maxim beamed at them. 'The Lanes and the Turners are disembarking tomorrow, as planned, to fly back to London and the States respectively. So it'll just be the five of us.'

FIFTY-FOUR

The ten days became two weeks.

Beautiful Dreamer sailed down to Sicily, went on to Malta, and ventured into the Ionian Sea, where she dropped anchor at several Greek islands. Eventually she turned around and cruised back the way she had come, heading in the direction of Tangier.

Now that the other guests had left, it seemed to Camilla that Maxim was even more relaxed and at ease. Furthermore, much to her delight, he was spending a great deal of time with her, did not seem able to get enough of her company. Although he worked every day during the week for a few hours, he was attentive, considerate of her needs, full of warmth. At night, in the privacy of her stateroom, he was as passionate as he had been a month ago when he had first arrived in Tangier looking for her.

One evening after dinner, when the others had straggled off to bed, Maxim lingered longer than usual at the bar on the main deck. Once the crew also retired, and they were finally alone, he said in a low voice, 'I want to talk to you about something, Camilla.'

'Yes, of course, what is it? You sound serious, look troubled, Maxim.'

'No, no, I'm not troubled. But I am serious.' He held her gaze steadily for the longest time, before saying, 'Would you consider marrying me?'

Camilla was thunderstruck. This was the last thing she had expected and she could only sit and gape at him stupidly.

He chuckled. 'You do look startled, my pet. *Speechless*, actually. But before you say yea or nay, let me explain that there would have to be a few ground rules if we married. May I tell you what they are?'

Camilla nodded. She did not care what his ground rules were; she would agree to anything so long as they married. She was so much in love with him she was besotted, had been about to accept him on any terms, to become his mistress, if necessary, rather than lose him.

'If you marry me, I wouldn't want you to give up your career,' he said. 'It's always been a vital part of your life, Cam, and it's very necessary to me that you continue to act. In films, on the stage. Also, I'd like you to do David's film in January.'

'What you're saying is that you'd prefer *me* to be busy, whilst *you're* running your empire.'

'I am. But it's also for *you*, darling. You're a great actress, you're at the height of your talent, your career is flourishing. You're a big name, a very big name. I wouldn't want you to give it up, sacrifice what you've worked for, striven for, all these years – to marry me. I want you to have that success, a sense of fulfilment.'

'I *have* to work, Maxim, just as you have to ... they'd take me away in a straitjacket if I didn't. Anyway, I wouldn't know what to do with myself if I didn't act,' she explained.

'I know what you mean. But to continue, Cam, I need plenty of space. In fact, I must have it in order to do my work properly. I don't want you clinging to me, making me the core of your existence. I have to travel a great deal, and I hope you understand this. Of course, you can come with me on the extended trips. I'd love it, love to have you with me. But not on the short, quick trips. They're too hectic, and I'm always locked up in meetings. I don't want distractions. Or to be deflected from what I have to do – because I'm worrying about my wife. I've always had great direction, concentration. I can't change. Business is a huge and vital part of my life.'

'I know that.'

'Also, there are certain periods when I have to see Anastasia and our children, be with her, Alix and Michael. Birthdays, some holidays. You wouldn't be upset, would you?'

'Of course not. I would think it odd if you didn't see them, under the circumstances. And what *about* Alix and Michael? How are they going to take it, if you marry me? Second wives aren't always popular.'

'There'll be no problem. They're both mature. Alix is twenty now, Michael nineteen, remember. They're grown up.'

She nodded. 'All right, keep going. What are the rest of your ground rules?'

'There are no more ... that's the lot.'

Camilla was silent, looked thoughtful.

'What about you? Perhaps you have some ground rules?' A dark brow lifted quizzically.

'No, I don't, Maxim.'

'Will you marry me?'

'Of course I'll marry you.' She did not say that this was the only thing she had ever really wanted, but she certainly thought it.

His face lit up, and he rose, went and sat next to her on the sofa, put his arms around her. 'I'm not cut out to be a bachelor, you know. I'm far too monogamous by nature,' he said, touching her cheek lightly. 'And I'll always be good to you, Camilla.'

'I know you will,' she answered, her face full of radiance.

He bent forward, kissed her deeply, whispered against her hair, 'Shall I break open a bottle of champagne to celebrate our forthcoming nuptials? Or shall we do that in bed?'

She did not speak. Extracting herself from his embrace, she rose, held out her hand to him, gave him a small knowing smile.

Maxim took it, stood up. Together they walked hand-in-hand to her stateroom.

He could hardly wait to get her undressed and into bed, and he took her very quickly, urgently, without much preamble. His passion for her raged through him, exploded almost immediately he took possession of her, and for the first time, in all the weeks of their lovemaking, he cried out her name as he climaxed and flowed into her.

Much later that night, after he had made love to her again, slowly and more leisurely, and given her satisfaction, he sat up in bed, propped himself on one elbow, looked down into her face. 'Let's not wait, Cam. Let's get married immediately.'

'Whenever you want,' she said, reaching up, brushing his hair back. Her face was brimming with love for him.

'We'll do it tomorrow,' he announced authoritatively with a huge smile. 'Or the day after. We'll be arriving in Tangier in a few hours. The British Consul will marry us. I'll make all the arrangements first thing. Is that all right with you?'

'Everything's always all right with me when I'm with *you*, Maxim.'

It was a golden November day, an Indian summer day.

The sun shone brightly in a perfect sky that was vividly blue, blameless, without cloud. Camilla paused on the steps of Maxim's Mayfair house, where she now lived with him since their marriage, sniffing the air, breathing deeply, thinking what a glorious day it truly was. An ideal day to go to the country.

As she stepped forward, Maxim's chauffeur, Humphrey, got out of the Jaguar and came around to open the door for her. 'Good morning, Mrs West,' he said, with a polite smile as he helped her in.

'Good morning, Humphrey. Isn't it a lovely day? Hardly like winter at all.'

'It's beautiful, Madame.' Humphrey closed the car door, returned to the driver's seat. 'Are we going down to East Hendred again, Mrs West?' he asked, glancing over his shoulder. 'Mr West told me this morning that I'd be driving you to the country today.'

'Yes, we are,' Camilla said, settling back against the seat. 'And we've plenty of time. I have an appointment at the new house with the interior designers, but they're not expecting me before noon.'

'Very good, Mrs West,' he said, starting the engine, pulling away from the kerb.

Camilla's thoughts drifted aimlessly on the drive to East Hendred, the little village in Oxfordshire where she had recently bought a lovely old Queen Anne manor house. She and Maxim had found it at the beginning of September, before they had flown off to New York together on one of his business trips. They had both liked it the moment they had seen it, had decided to buy it on the spot. When she had insisted on paying for it, Maxim had protested, shaken his head, been highly amused at her insistence about this. But she won, and after she had bought the house she had given it to him as a wedding present. He had been deeply touched by this gesture, had accepted her gift with grace.

Even though the manor had stood empty for two years, because the previous owner now lived in Barbados, Lacey Court was in relatively good condition. The interior designers she had hired were already hard at work, creating the comfortable, unpretentious country look she and Maxim preferred. It was going to be a wonderful weekend retreat for them both, especially for Maxim. The way he worked, he needed a place to unwind occasionally in peaceful surroundings.

She leaned her head against the seat, closed her eyes, suddenly thinking of her husband, the man she had loved since she had been a girl, whom she had always believed to be beyond her reach. Never in her wildest dreams had she thought she would ever be married to him. Or be so incredibly happy with him. He was the most glorious man. Deep down inside, she knew he did not love her in the same way she loved him, but this did not matter to her any more. Maxim was passionate in bed, caring and affectionate at all times, generous to a fault. Since their marriage in August, he had showered her with beautiful gifts – exquisite jewels, fine paintings, valuable antiques and silver for the new house.

If there were odd moments when she longed to hear him say, 'I love you,' these had become few and far between. She constantly remembered Stubby's words, when she had mentioned *love* to him on the yacht. Don't quibble, he had said. Be glad you've got what you have. You and Maxim have more than most couples. It was true, they did. Besides, Maxim had started to express his feelings for her lately, murmuring things like, 'I adore you,' or 'you're my special lady,' and when he did so his voice was loving, his dark eyes full of warmth.

Her thoughts shifted to their wedding at the British Consulate in Tangier. If the others were surprised that Maxim had not asked the captain of his yacht to marry them, she was not. He had built *Beautiful Dreamer* for Anastasia. To marry *her* on it would have been inappropriate in his eyes. He was sensitive in so many different ways. And she knew that Anastasia still owned a large part of Maximilian West, and of his heart. The real reason for the location of the wedding had obviously struck Stubby at one moment, for he had looked at her swiftly, and smiled, his eyes conveying his support of her, his understanding. She hadn't minded where they married.

Stubby had also finally tied the knot at long last, his playboy days at an end. The wedding had been in September, after she and Maxim had returned from the States. He had taken the lovely Marcia Bell to be his bride, and the wedding had been at Caxton Hall. Maxim had been best man; she had been matron of honour; afterwards Maxim and she had given the wedding breakfast at the Mayfair house.

Teddy and Mark Lewis had been present at Stubby's wedding, and much to her delight they liked her, seemed to be extremely happy that she had married Maxim. Furthermore, so were his children, much to her gratification. Neither Alix nor Michael had apparently been upset to learn of their father's marriage to her, quite the contrary. And she was starting to develop a lovely relationship with Alix, who was such a beautiful, intelligent young woman.

I'm so lucky, Camilla thought, I'm the luckiest woman in the world. I really do have everything I've ever wanted. Maximilian West. My wonderful career. Even children now, since his appear to have genuinely taken to me. As an only child, whose parents were dead, and childless herself, she felt as if she had a proper family at last.

A radiant smile slipped onto her face without her realising it, and happiness and contentment shone in her expressive green eyes.

Opening her handbag, Camilla took out her small diary, checked her appointments for the rest of the week. She was looking forward to their dinner with David Maines this evening. He had arrived in London yesterday, bringing with him the shooting script of the new film. She had agreed to star in it, and she was anxious now to read the final version.

A little over an hour after Humphrey had driven away from Chesterfield Hill in Mayfair, he was turning into the winding driveway which led up to Lacey Court.

The Queen Anne manor stood in a small dell, surrounded by a copse of trees which grew on a slight rise above it, and it had a lovely timeless quality. This morning its many windows winked in the sunlight, and its ancient stones were mellow and gentle against the dark winter landscape, the backdrop of leafless trees.

Humphrey parked opposite the front door, newly painted a shiny pristine white, and instantly the two young interior designers came rushing out onto the broad front steps.

Never one to stand on ceremony, Camilla opened the door, got out of the Jaguar before Humphrey had a chance to assist her, and hurried forward to meet them.

Alison Dixon and Tony Campbell, the designers she had always used in the past, were full of smiles as they greeted her, escorted her into the house.

'Everything's going marvellously well,' Tony told her, stepping back to let her walk around the large entrance hall. 'And the fabrics you selected are going to look fabulous. It's easier to tell how they're going to blend in now that the walls are painted in all the rooms. The house is really coming together, Camilla, and has a lovely cohesion to it.'

'I can't wait to see everything,' Camilla responded, smiling at the talented young team, glancing around the hall, liking the deep-salmon shade they had used for the walls, the botanical prints in dark wood frames, the gilt Georgian mirror, and antique crystal and bronze *doré* chandelier.

'You're going to get a lovely surprise when you see the rest of the house,' Alison told her. 'We've made tremendous strides this past week.'

Steering her into the library, Alison continued, 'Most of the rooms have been painted, as Tony told you, the wood floors cleaned and refinished – oh, and the beds came from Harrods yesterday. And this room, as you can see, is practically finished. The only things missing are the chesterfield sofa, the books and accessories.'

Camilla stood in the centre of the library, her eyes sweeping around appraisingly, missing nothing. She kept nodding her head approvingly. The panelled walls of the lovely old room had been cleaned and restored, as had the bookshelves; a Georgian desk and chair, comfortable armchairs, a Savonnerie rug, and brass lamps with cream-silk shades were all in place. There was even one of her favourite horse paintings hanging over the fireplace.

'Congratulations!' Camilla exclaimed delightedly, looking from one to the other. 'As you know, this room is for Maxim, and I'm so glad you did it first. At least I know he has somewhere to work, even if other parts of the house have to be completed after we've moved in.'

They took her on a general tour, and then headed back downstairs to the kitchen. Tony said, 'We think we can have the house ready by the middle of December, Camilla, since we're making such good progress.' He held open the kitchen door for her, and as she went in, he added, 'Oh and by the way, rather than go to one of the pubs in the area for lunch, we brought a picnic with us. We thought it would be much nicer, also we can show you some of the fabrics we selected for the antique wicker furniture, and the tiles for the guest powder room whilst we eat.'

'What a good idea,' Camilla said. 'But I'd better pop outside, tell

Humphrey to go and find a pub and have a snack. He can come back for me in a couple of hours, since we've more things to go over. Please excuse me.'

'Will you have a glass of wine, Camilla?' Alison asked, taking the bottle out of the wicker picnic hamper.

'Why not? Thank you,' Camilla said and hurried out.

After dispatching the chauffeur for lunch, Camilla paused for a moment outside, glancing around, thinking that she must engage a gardener as soon as possible. Even though it was late November, when nothing could be planted, the garden was somewhat overgrown, a wilderness that needed sprucing up before the spring. I'll put daffodils over there, she thought, have them planted at random under those trees. And crocuses and snowdrops. And I'll have lilac bushes put in. Maxim loves lilacs.

It would be wonderful if we could spend the Christmas holidays here, Camilla thought, going back inside. Maxim had told her Alix would be with them, while Michael went to Jamaica with Anastasia. She walked along the corridor to the kitchen, paused when she came to the door of the basement, thinking suddenly of Maxim's main Christmas present. She had decided to have part of the basement turned into a fully equipped wine cellar for him, was intending to stock it with the very best wines. Stubby had been helping her to select Maxim's favourites, as well as the champagnes he preferred, which he liked to have as an aperitif rather than hard liquor. Although he was not a big drinker himself, he did insist on serving his guests only the very best vintages. Stubby had already been to one wine auction for her, and they were making excellent progress. The wine racks had been ordered and were due any day.

Deciding to take another look at the basement whilst Tony and Alison were setting up the picnic lunch in the kitchen, Camilla opened the basement door. She switched on the light, started down the long wooden staircase which was shallow and very steeply pitched.

She had only descended a few steps when the heel of one of her shoes caught in a crack on the wooden step. Not realising what had happened she tried to continue down the steps, was jerked backwards as the shoe heel remained stuck in the step. She lost her balance, and as she twisted then catapulted forward she let out a terrified scream, grabbed wildly for the banister which ran down the side wall. It was rotten, came away from the bricks in her hand. She screamed again as she went hurtling on down the steep staircase and landed with a heavy thud on the concrete floor at the bottom. She lay absolutely still.

Alison and Tony heard her scream, came racing out of the kitchen. They flew down the corridor, immediately saw the door to the basement open and went to it. Tony stood on the top step looking down, and let out a cry of horror. 'Oh my God! Camilla's fallen down the steps!' he exclaimed, going cold all over. He went down the staircase gingerly, his heart in his mouth.

He found her shoe, the tip of the heel still caught in the crack on the step, and he knew at once how the accident had occurred.

Alison, who was shaking uncontrollably, was chalk-white. She followed her partner down the stairs, so frightened and upset she could barely walk. When she arrived at the bottom of the steep staircase, which she now realised was dangerous, Tony was kneeling next to Camilla.

Her body lay awkwardly, and looked oddly askew on the basement floor. Her beautiful face was white, her eyes closed. Blood seeped out from underneath her golden hair.

'She's badly hurt,' Alison whispered, her voice barely audible. She crouched down to Tony, trying to control her shaking limbs.

Tony looked ghastly. 'I don't think we ought to move her,' he said unsteadily. 'We might injure her even more. I'll stay here with Camilla. You go and phone for an ambulance.'

Alison nodded, mounted the stairs at a snail's pace, discovering that her legs were as heavy as lead.

Tony watched her disappear through the door at the top of the stairs, then swung his head back to Camilla. Although he had not said so to Alison, he was quite sure Camilla had broken her neck when she fell, and that she was no longer alive.

Maxim could not accept that Camilla was dead.

It was only after her funeral had taken place that it sank in. The finality of her death struck him a hard blow. He could not believe that the lovely, vibrant, gifted and loving woman he had so recently married was gone from him forever.

He was devastated.

It was his daughter Alix who helped him the most, although Stubby, Teddy and David Maines also tried to give him solace in his grief.

The day after the memorial service had been held for Camilla, Maxim and Alix were sitting together in his Mayfair house. Alix put her hand on his arm, and said gently, 'I liked Camilla a lot, Daddy, and we became good friends. She told me she thought of me as the daughter she'd never had, asked me if I minded. I told her I didn't, I was flattered actually.'

Maxim looked at her swiftly but made no comment.

Alix returned his glance, thinking how terrible he looked. Her father was grey under his permanent tan, and his dark eyes, usually so brilliant, were dulled by sorrow. Alix took a deep breath, went on, 'After Mummy, Camilla really was the nicest woman I've ever known. I'm so sorry she had that hideous accident, and I want you to know I'm here for you whenever you need me.'

Maxim was still unable to speak. But he took hold of his daughter's hand, held it tightly. At last he said, 'Camilla was very special . . .'

'Yes. And she loved you so much, Daddy.'

'And I loved her. Not in the same way I love your mother . . . it's just not possible to love two people like that in one lifetime. But I did love Camilla, in a different kind of way, and she was important to me, gave me a lot of happiness these last few months. She helped to make the loneliness go away – ' His voice broke. He was unable to continue.

After a few minutes Maxim regained his composure, and said softly, 'I never told her I loved her, Alix. Not once. I'll never forgive myself for that.' Tears came into his eyes, and he quickly tried to brush them away with his fingertips.

Alix put her arm around his shoulders, rested her head against his arm. 'I'm sure Camilla *knew* you loved her, Daddy.'

'It was wrong of me, I should have told her,' he muttered, his voice a harsh rasp.

'A woman always *knows* whether a man loves her or not. Honestly she does,' Alix soothed, her heart aching for him, going out to him in his pain. 'She feels it in her bones. And anyway Camilla was so happy with you.'

He turned to his daughter, searched her face. 'Do you really think she was, Alix?'

'Yes. *You made her very, very happy.* She told me that only a few days before the accident.'

Maxim leaned back against the sofa and closed his eyes. His daughter's words gave him some comfort, but not much.

Not long after Camilla's death, Maxim disappeared from any sort of public life. He buried himself in his work more than ever before, curtailed his social life completely, saw only his colleagues, business associates and his immediate family. There had been a great deal of publicity about Camilla's death, their marriage, her life, and his, before they had married. It all sickened him. He hired a battery of aides to keep the press at bay and his name out of the gossip columns. He did not relish speculation about his private life.

Maximilian West retreated and pulled the drawbridge up behind him.

PART 6

ADRIANA

NEW YORK

1987

Every wise woman buildeth her
house: but the foolish plucketh it
down with her hands.

Proverbs: The Bible

FIFTY-FIVE

Adriana Macklin West stood in the centre of the drawing room of their Fifth Avenue apartment, surveying it through jaundiced eyes.

She did not like it. She never had, not since the first moment she had set foot in it eighteen months ago. The proportions of the room were superb; it was airy, spacious and light-filled, with extraordinary panoramic views of Central Park. Unfortunately, it had been decorated by his first wife, and she found the furnishings abysmal – old-fashioned, outdated, washed out, and totally lacking in style. She had been itching to redecorate since her marriage to Maxim, but whenever she broached the subject he waved his hand dismissively, told her he liked it exactly the way it was. These days he cut her off every time she mentioned the word decorating, would not even listen to her reasons for wanting to make the changes.

She had even offered to pay for everything herself, but he had told her money was of no consequence, that this was hardly the issue.

Adriana's dark brown eyes swept around the room again, carefully assessing each item as she had done so often of late. The problem with the room was that it was far too austere, almost cold in its overall feeling, with an over-abundance of pale colours, pale fabrics, pale woods, and delicate paintings. What it needed was vibrant colours, rich fabrics, expensive wall-to-wall carpeting, handsome Chinese porcelain lamps, exciting new paintings and eye-catching objects of art. Those things would give it the necessary pizazz, the feeling of glamour she wanted to create, the chic New York look which had always been a feature of her other apartments in the past. It was a look she adored, for it proclaimed to the world that the owner had money, power, success.

Dropping her eyes to the yellow pad she was holding, Adriana began to scribble down her ideas for the renowned international interior designer whom she had hired that afternoon. He had met her in the executive offices of the cosmetic company she owned, Empress Eugenia Beauty, of which she was president and chief executive officer.

She had liked Valentine Lubbock the moment he had walked in, and the feeling had been mutual. They had understood each other within the first ten minutes of meeting. She knew that Valentine had superb taste, since she was well acquainted with his work, and she had absolutely no doubts that he was going to produce the expensive and glamorous ambience she deemed appropriate for her station in life as Mrs Maximilian West.

Valentine did not come cheap, and there was no question that the apartment was going to cost a bundle of money, between four and five million dollars to redesign, revamp and redecorate to be exact. But she could afford it, since she was a millionairess in her own right. If money was of no consequence to Maxim, then certainly it was not to her either. Her second husband, Arthur Macklin, had left her a fortune when he had died four years ago, as well as the cosmetic company, which was one of the largest in the United States.

She had told Valentine Lubbock that she wanted him to redesign every room, not only this one where she now stood. The library, the dining room, Maxim's study, her den, and all of the bedrooms were to undergo a complete overhaul. Valentine was meeting her here tomorrow with his design team, and they were going to spend the entire day going over every inch of this . . . this . . . mausoleum.

She was well aware that Maxim was going to object when she informed him of her decision tonight. But she would explain her reasons, talk him into it somehow. She had a knack of twisting him around her little finger, getting her way with him, especially when they had been in bed. He seemed more open, receptive and vulnerable to her then, certainly easier to handle. She had come to understand he was a difficult man, not easy to know, or live with, and secretive.

Adriana sighed. The problem was that they had not been to bed lately. His sexual interest in her had waned of late, and she did not understand why. When they had first met he had been like a young stud, going at her all the time, unable to get enough of her, and for the first six months of their marriage he had continued to be insatiable. But he had not touched her for months and months now. Of course, he *had* been away a great deal, travelling for business; she herself had had to make several trips to California, Texas and Rome, so they had been separated quite frequently. However, he had now been in Manhattan for the whole month of March, and he had still not made love to her since his return from London. When she had tactfully hinted that it was time they went to bed, he had brushed her off politely with a variety of excuses: he was preoccupied with his latest deal, a major acquisition, exhausted, or not in the mood. And he always retreated to his own bedroom these days, or rather nights, never came to hers anymore. She had not liked the idea of separate bedrooms, had balked at it from the beginning, but he had insisted when they had arrived in New York after their marriage in France.

'My hours are so erratic,' he had said. 'I get up at the crack of dawn to deal with my offices in London and Paris. It's better this way. I don't want to disturb your sleep.' He had kissed her, flashed her his dazzling smile that always devastated her, and had murmured, 'There'll be plenty of nights when I sleep in your bed, Adriana, don't make any mistake about that. But this is the way I've always lived. I need my own room, please don't worry about it.'

Well, she did worry, and she was not sure she believed him when he implied that he had had his own bedroom with his other wives. And he certainly had been coming to hers less and less. If she didn't know him so well, she might start suspecting he had a mistress. But that was not his style. He was such a workaholic he surely did not have time for another woman.

A painting which was slightly askew on the wall caught her attention and she walked across the Aubusson rug, intending to straighten it, but paused when she came to the Louis XV console, stood staring at the silver-framed photograph of herself and Maxim on their wedding day in September of 1985. They had been married in the town hall of the fourth *arrondissement* in Paris because he had been detained there on business. She had worn a pale-blue outfit by Givenchy and afterwards Maxim had given a dinner for ten at Lasserre. She picked up the photograph, thinking how well he looked at fifty-one, the age he had been when they married. So lean and handsome and tanned from the summer sun.

When her investment bankers had tried to buy Marianna Monteveccio from him in 1984, and had failed, she had dropped the idea of expanding Empress Eugenia for the moment. Instead she had gone after Maximilian West, finding him a fascinating and exciting man, not to mention an eligible bachelor. In the summer of 1985 she had managed to manoeuvre an introduction to him in Monte Carlo, through a friend who knew him. To her immense delight and gratification he had fallen for her at once, obviously stimulated by her keen business mind as well as her beautiful face and perfect body. They had had a whirlwind courtship of six weeks, and to the stunned surprise of his family and friends they had married at the end of that summer. She was aware his son and daughter did not particularly approve of her or like her, and she was not overly enthusiastic about them either, considered them to be stuck-up little prigs. As for that ex-wife of his, Anastasia, she was a real pain in the rear end. Always wanting to talk to him about something, or needing to see him about something. And off he trotted, like an obedient pet dog. She had tried to put a stop to those excursions, only to incur his terrible wrath, and he had told her, in no uncertain terms, never to mention the name Anastasia again. That bitch had some sort of hold on him although she had no clue what it was. The children most likely. She often wondered what a man like Maximilian West had ever seen in that faded, wimpish, mealy-mouthed blonde. His second wife, the actress who had fallen down the basement steps and broken her neck, had not been much better looking either.

Adriana placed the frame on the console, stepped over to the small painting by Manet and straightened it, then glanced at her watch. It was almost six o'clock. Maxim had told her that he would be home by seven, and wanted to eat in the apartment. It was Thursday, and both the cook and the butler were off. Usually Maxim took her to Le Cirque, La Grenouille, La Caravelle or the Four Seasons, or some other smart New York restaurant. But before he had left for the office this morning he had explained that he had a mountain of work to get through by tomorrow. And so she had had the cook prepare a cold supper of salad, smoked salmon, cold meats and chicken, cheeses and fresh fruit – the things he enjoyed the most.

Hurrying out of the drawing room, Adriana went down the corridor to the kitchen, opened the refrigerator door, checked that there were several bottles of Dom Perignon on ice, plenty of caviar, then raced back along the corridor to her bedroom.

She took off her dark business suit, hung it in the wardrobe, stripped off her expensive underwear, and went into the bathroom. After flinging handfuls of her own brand of bath beads into the tub, she turned on the faucets, stepped over to the mirror and pinned up her hair, wondering what to wear tonight. Something sexy. She must make herself look tempting and irresistible for her husband, get her own way with him tonight . . . in every way.

Her mind stayed focused on Maxim for a few minutes as she lay luxuriating in the hot perfumed bath. She considered her marriage to him to be the *coup* of the century. And it was. She was the wife of one of the richest men in the world, a billionaire who happened to be in the prime of life, and gorgeous as well as brilliant. Not bad for a rather ordinary middle-class girl from Westchester, who had had a typical middle-class upbringing, a boring first marriage to a childhood sweetheart, a second slightly less boring marriage to a rich, older man.

Her thoughts veered to Arthur Macklin. She had been married to him for ten years before he had died in 1983 of complications following a stroke. He had been seventy, she had been thirty-one. She had been extremely fond of Arthur. He had been her stepping stone into a whole new world.

After her divorce from Larry Tucker, her first husband, she had moved to Manhattan, found a small apartment, and become a model.

Her grasp on success had been swift. After being photographed by Scavullo and becoming a cover girl with her face on every magazine from *Vogue* to *Mademoiselle*, Arthur Macklin had noticed her, had instructed the advertising agency he used to hire her to be the Empress Eugenia Girl.

Six months later her face had suddenly been on hoardings, on television, in magazines and newspapers, and displayed on giant posters in department stores. Her arresting, exotic movie-star looks had been the exact image Arthur Macklin had been seeking to promote his beauty products. Those looks also captivated the owner of the company. The Empress Eugenia Girl became *his* girl. He pursued her, paid court to her most attentively, lavished her with gifts, from jewellery to furs, divorced his wife of thirty years, and married her before she had had time to catch her breath, or shake the Westchester dust off her feet.

She had continued to be the Empress Eugenia Girl for a couple of years, and became the spokesperson for the company. Arthur, a shrewd self-made man, rapidly discovered that his great beauty also had brains. Since he had no children, he brought her into the business, personally trained her to be his successor, and bequeathed the company to her in his will. When he had been felled by the stroke in the spring of 1983 she had looked after him tenderly, diligently, and with kindness, and run the company as he would have done himself. But after his death she had charted a new course, steered Empress Eugenia into the big time. After buying up several smaller cosmetic companies and merging them with hers, she had repackaged the products, had perfumers in France invent several new scents for her, and hired chemists to create a whole line of herbal and natural products. She had called this new line Body Beautiful, had opened Body Beautiful Boutiques all over the country. In the process her company had outstripped many of its competitors, including Marianna Monteveccio, a division of the Allandale Group, which Maxim owned. Once she had wanted to acquire that company, to merge it with Empress Eugenia, but she had no desire for it any longer. The odd thing was, Maxim had lately started to accuse her of being competitive with him, and at first she had laughed, believing him to be teasing her. But she had begun to realise that he was serious. She was competitive by nature, she couldn't help herself, and of course she competed with the Monteveccio line just as she did with Lauder and Arden and Revlon. It was nothing personal. He apparently thought otherwise. Six months ago they had each gone after the same small house that manufactured a variety of products for the hands. It was a sort of friendly rivalry on her part, and she had thought it to be a wonderful joke. He had not. The head of his acquisition team in New York, Peter Heilbron, had been furious.

She sat up with a little start in the bath. Was Maxim holding a grudge? Surely not. She laughed out loud. Surely he wasn't depriving her of sex in the manner of a disgruntled wife who seethed over some imagined insult. No, that couldn't be. He was far too big a man for such silly games. He was not sleeping with her at the moment because of his preoccupation with his current deal. Passionate and highly sexed though he was, he could be remarkably disciplined when he so wished. And he could abstain for months, indeed, *years*. He had told her, in one of those rare moments when he had chosen to confide in her, that he had been celibate for two years after his second wife's death. It had not only startled her, but had illustrated to her the extraordinary will power of the man. *My man*, she added under her breath, and pushed herself up, climbed out of the bath, grabbed a towel, and dried herself quickly.

Walking over to the floor-to-ceiling mirror which she had installed on one of the bathroom walls, she stood regarding herself for a long moment, turning from side to side, checking out her figure. It was still perfect, without an extra ounce of flesh, yet she was not a walking skeleton like some of the New York women she knew. Most of them made her shudder, especially those who put little or no food into their mouths, starved themselves into wraiths.

She had a decent covering of flesh on her bones, yet without being fat. Because she was quite tall, just over five feet eight inches in her stockinged feet, she did not have to panic if she put on an additional half pound now and then. She turned slowly once more, glad that her exercise trainer came twice a week to put her through her paces. She was in good shape. Her breasts were a little heavy, in her opinion, but well shaped, and voluptuous enough to excite Maxim. She had realised when she lost weight last year that he had been turned off by her boniness.

Reaching for the Empress Eugenia lilac-perfumed body lotion she smoothed it all over her body, sprayed herself with lilac perfume, one of Maxim's favourite scents, and brushed her thick dark brown hair. After slipping on a silk robe, she walked into her bedroom.

Adriana seated herself at the dressing table, stared at herself in the mirror, wondering what kind of makeup would appeal to him tonight. Should she create a soft girlish look with a pretty pink foundation, blushes, powders and light pastel-coloured eye makeup, or turn herself into a more dramatic-looking woman?

Leaning forward, she examined herself closely. She had a wide, full face, with a broad forehead, slightly slanting eyes, shapely dark brows, and a rounded chin with a dimple. I'll be myself, she thought, reaching for the pale almond foundation lotion, spreading it on across her high cheekbones. That's who he fell for. *Adriana Macklin*. Anyway, I'm my most alluring when I'm myself. All thirty-five years of me.

FIFTY-SIX

Maxim braced himself before putting the key in the lock of his Fifth Avenue apartment and opening the door. He was intensely preoccupied with business and not in the mood to cope with Adriana tonight. But cope he must.

Apparently Adriana had heard him come in, and was rushing out of the library to greet him before he even had a chance to remove his trenchcoat.

'There you are, angel!' she exclaimed, gliding forward, her exquisite purple-and-gold caftan floating around her like a cloud.

'Hello, Adriana,' he said mildly, putting his briefcase on the small Louis XV bench in the foyer, giving her a half-smile.

She drew to a standstill in front of him, locked her arms around his neck and planted a kiss on his mouth. 'Mmmm. *Yummy.*'

He winced inside, turned away, shrugged out of his coat and hung it in the hall closet, then retrieved his briefcase.

'I have champagne on ice, a cold supper waiting,' Adriana murmured in a silky voice, taking his arm, strolling along the vast hall with him. 'I thought I'd open the champagne now, so that we can have a glass before dinner. Would you like that, honey?'

'Not now, Adriana. I'm going to take a shower, change into something more comfortable, and then perhaps I'll have a drink.' As he spoke he veered to the left, walked towards his bedroom. 'I'll see you shortly,' he added quietly.

'I'll be in the library, angel.' She watched him disappear into his room, frowning to herself. He closed the door behind him, shutting her out rather pointedly, and she stood for a moment staring at it, trying to assess his current mood. Thank God, he seemed less bad-tempered and irritable, which was the way he had been for the past few weeks, since his return from Europe. If he was not in a good mood, he certainly wasn't in a *bad* one. *Neutral*, she thought. *He's in a neutral frame of mind.* She smiled to herself, confident that she would be able to handle him very well this evening. A little tender loving care, soothing words, champagne and caviar, soft music, a few gentle kisses. She would soon win him over about the redecoration of the apartment, she had no doubt about that. Later, once she had him in a mellower mood, she had every intention of taking him to bed.

*

Maxim undressed, went into his bathroom, took a steaming hot shower, stretching and flexing his arms above his head, twisting his shoulders from side to side, moving his neck in circles, attempting to ease some of the tension. It had been building in him throughout the long day at his office. He thought of the last conversation he had had with Graeme Longdon just before leaving tonight. She agreed they should drop the current deal they were working on, although Peter Heilbron had been against making any drastic moves for the time being. 'Let's not be rash,' Peter had said, walking him to the elevator a short while ago. He had told Peter he would sleep on it. What he needed now, after his shower, was total relaxation. He wasn't sure he would get this with Adriana, who was irritating him more than ever these days. But he must let go of this deal mentally, clear his head for several hours. He felt like a few drinks, a bit of mindless television, and six hours of deep sleep. It was imperative that he was fresh tomorrow morning when he was going to make a final decision about his latest business proposition. He was in the middle of a hostile takeover bid for a major American corporation, Palmyra-Kettelson, and suddenly he was not sure that he wished to continue.

Maxim reached for the soap; immediately the perfume of lilacs permeated the shower stall. Adriana really is too much, he thought. He laughed hollowly, acknowledging that she was extremely heavy-handed at times, in a variety of different, not to mention startling, ways. And yet she really was one of the most striking women he had ever seen, and he was unable to deny her dark exotic beauty.

The first moment he had set eyes on her in Monte Carlo he had been captivated, instantly swept off his feet. Her incredible face, so full of sensuality, her perfect body and long shapely legs, and the potent sexuality that seemed to pour out of her had excited him enormously. That summer, a year and a half ago, he had been ripe, an easy target. For the first time since Camilla's death he had been ready to get involved, had truly wanted to bed down with a woman, become completely immersed in her. And this was exactly what he had done with Adriana. On one occasion, during their courtship of six weeks, they had stayed locked up in a suite at the Carlton Hotel in Cannes for three days and nights, unable to tear themselves away from each other sexually.

Adriana had been a departure for him, he had to admit, so very different from the other women he had known and married. He had always fallen for refined, gentle-looking blondes; she was a dark-haired, sloe-eyed siren with truly exotic overtones. And she was different in other ways, too; she had an earthy, almost raunchy, sense of humour, which at first he had found entertaining, but now abhorred, and he had quickly discovered a number of equally dismaying traits. She was opinionated, stubborn to the point of rigidity, abrasive, and even brash. Furthermore, that keen sense of business, her understanding of his world of finance, no longer fascinated him as it had initially. Underneath all that exotic beauty and glamour she was curiously masculine.

Masculine, he repeated under his breath. What an odd word for him to use in relationship to Adriana, but true, nonetheless, he realised with a jolt. Was that the reason he could no longer get an erection with her? Did she turn him off *because* of that streak of masculinity? His raging lust for her had been swiftly satisfied. Six months after their nuptials in Paris their marriage was over, at least as far as he was concerned. Taking her for his wife had been terribly flawed judgement on his part. He ought to have known that the burning rage to bed her, his immense lust fuelled by hers for him, would burn out with amazing swiftness.

His impotency with Adriana had come as something of a shock, and had worried him at first. He had even wondered if he was losing his touch, had considered going to see a doctor. But he had strayed one night with an old acquaintance, had discovered to his profound relief that his touch was as sure as it ever was. When he was with a blonde, he had commented to himself. The fault lie not with him but with Adriana apparently.

Now he no longer felt fragile about his ego. All of his mechanisms were in working order. He smiled to himself. A man never got an erection without having his mind and psyche at the back of that erection, as well as his body. Most men were much more delicate physically than most women, that's why men and women were so different. There had to be at least a little desire in a man in order for him to get an erection, have a sexual encounter. But a woman could make love without desire. All she had to do was lie down and wait for the man to perform. If he couldn't, she blamed him, never herself. Well, rarely herself.

Because he had become impotent with Adriana he avoided any kind of sexual contact with her these days, wishing to sidestep embarrassment. This was difficult, in that she was hot-blooded and forever on his trail, but fortunately he somehow managed to out-manoeuvre her. Most of the time.

A year ago he had thought of announcing his intention of getting a divorce, and then changed his mind. He had still not done so. He travelled a great deal, and was away far more than he was in New York. Having a wife was a safeguard, and certainly marvellous protection against other predatory females. Also, he was too involved and immersed in his business for emotional scenes or upheavals. He would bide his time, deal with Adriana later.

After dressing in dark grey flannel slacks, a black turtle-necked sweater and black cashmere sports jacket, Maxim left his bedroom, crossed the entrance foyer and strolled into the library.

Adriana was nowhere in sight.

Soft music played on the tape deck. A bottle of Dom Perignon stood open in the silver ice bucket on the small chest. The low coffee table in front of the fire burning in the hearth had been set for supper. No doubt Adriana was in the kitchen, preparing a tray of caviar, lemon wedges and toast, which she now served on the cook's night off with boring regularity.

Stepping up to the chest, he lifted the bottle, poured himself a glass of champagne, and took a long swallow, savouring it. He blinked in the dim light, and realising the room was far too dark he walked over to the desk near the window, turned up the lamp. The yellow pad caught his attention at once, and he stood staring down at it, reading Adriana's large scrawl. The name *Valentine Lubbock* leapt out, hit him between the eyes. Lubbock was the most expensive interior designer in the world. Bending his head, Maxim peered at the pad, continuing to read the long list she had made.

At this moment Adriana was returning from the kitchen with the tray of caviar. She stopped dead in her tracks in the doorway, cursed herself silently for being so stupid, for carelessly leaving the pad on the desk. Dismay swamped her, rapidly turned to alarm when he lifted his head and glared at her. His expression was one of such intense dislike it frightened her.

Maxim's brilliant black eyes blazed in his face, which was livid. He waved the pad at her, demanded angrily, 'What's all this? Planning to redecorate, are you?' He threw her a scathing look.

'No, no, of course I'm not. It's just that – '

'Just *what*?' he thundered, and not giving her a chance to respond, he rushed on furiously. 'Under no circumstances are you going to make any changes in this apartment! It is perfectly beautiful, in superb taste, and it suits *me* very well! Not one single item is going to be removed or changed, do you hear me!'

'You don't have to shout. I only wanted to redecorate your *study*. As a birthday present for you,' she said, improvising quickly, sidling into the room, placing the tray on the coffee table. She moved closer to the desk, gave him a wide, flashing smile, added, 'The study is starting to look a bit shabby, Maxim, you must admit that.'

'So what! I don't give a damn. As for redecorating it for my birthday, that's a load of crap! On this – ' he waved the pad in her face again, 'you have listed every room. I'm not stupid you know. My mother-in-law is a decorator – '

'*Ex-mother-in-law!*' she exploded peremptorily, giving him an icy stare.

He ignored her comment, and continued in a frigid tone, 'And through her I know Lubbock, who is also based in Paris. He wouldn't touch *one room* with a barge pole. He only decorates entire apartments!' He flung the pad down on the desk disdainfully. 'You don't learn, do you? I told you, I'm not going to have you turning this apartment into an expensive, over-decorated, glitzy imitation of some garish Miami hotel, with the help of the over-rated, over-priced and under-talented Mr Lubbock! Trust you to pick a flashy, tasteless *shopper* such as him.'

'*He is brilliant!* Anyway, who the hell do you think you are? Suddenly you're the great expert on decorating!' she cried shrilly, losing her temper. 'Some expert! I've only got to look around this cold, colourless, out-dated dump, this mausoleum, to understand you know nothing about decorating.'

He did not deign to respond, merely glared at her.

Shaking with rage, frustrated with him, she hissed, 'It's far too French. It has no style.'

He blinked, did a double-take, threw back his head and guffawed. 'The French invented style, you nit-wit!'

'I fully intend to make some changes in this apartment whatever you say,' Adriana exclaimed, drawing herself up to her full height, hating him suddenly for his superiority and breeding.

He walked over to her and peered into her face, his eyes narrowing, said in the iciest voice, pitched very low, 'If you have this *compulsion* to decorate an apartment, with the help of the over-rated Mr Lubbock, I suggest you find an apartment of your own. *Tomorrow.* You are not going to touch *my* apartment. Never. If and when it needs redoing, my mother-in-law will fly over from Paris, and she and Anastasia will take it in hand.'

'You bastard! Always flinging that ex-wife of yours in my face,' she screeched, all of the colour draining from her face. 'I'm not going to stand for it.'

'And what do you intend to do about it?' He gulped down his champagne, put the glass on the end table, walked out of the library without looking at her again.

She ran after him, followed him down the hall, watched him as he opened the closet, took out his trenchcoat, threw it over his arm.

'Where are you going?' she cried, her eyes widening.

'Out.'

'Where?'

'For a walk. I need fresh air.'

'A walk! I don't believe you. I know you, Maxim, know what a sexy, physical guy you are. You never sleep with me these days, so you must be sleeping with another woman. It's obvious you have somebody stashed away. Some blonde hustler.'

'This town is full of hustlers, Adriana. Blondes, brunettes and redheads. They come in all colours, sizes, and shapes.' He walked out, slamming the door behind him.

His temper cooled within minutes of hitting the street.

He walked down Fifth Avenue at a moderate pace, more annoyed with himself than with her, in a sense, for flaring up in the way he had. Anger was such a waste of valuable energy. He needed his strength for more important things at this moment. A wry smile flickered on his mouth as he walked. *Time*, he mused, a commodity I cannot afford to squander at present. I didn't spend enough *time* with Adriana to get to know her properly. *Marry in haste, repent at leisure*, he added under his breath, recalling Teddy's words after his wedding. Deep within himself he knew that she had not approved of Adriana. But his dearest Teddy loved and respected him far too much to interfere in his life, tell him what to do. I need my brain tested, he thought dismally. I should never have married Adriana Smith Tucker Macklin, and I must extract myself as soon as I've solved my other problems. *That's the bottom line.*

His mind, always sharp, zeroed in on his hostile takeover bid for Palmyra-Kettelson, a gargantuan beauty products company, and a major American corporation, international in scope. He had been buying its stock for some time, now owned twelve per cent of the company and had recently informed the chief executive officer he was prepared to purchase as many more shares as he needed to give him control of the company. The offer had been rejected. The executives had gone into a tailspin. A battle was underway. But he did not want to do battle, despite Peter Heilbron's urging. The head of his acquisition team in New York was encouraging him to continue, predicted he would win, be the *big* winner ultimately.

Turning up the collar of his trenchcoat, and pushing his hands in his pockets, Maxim walked on, lost in concentration, which was one of his most formidable assets, part of his genius.

As he crossed Seventy-Second Street and continued on down Fifth he finally came to his decision. *He would pass.* Tomorrow morning he would phone the president of Palmyra and call off his hostile bid for the company, offer to sell his stock in the company back to them. He had about $500 million invested. He would probably come out with a huge profit, maybe $90 million, and he would probably be accused of greenmail. *So what*. He had to unload. He did not want the company. Peter would be disappointed, but he could not help that. Graeme would be relieved. She was with him on this, understood his reluctance to invest any further in America at this moment.

He had a peculiar uneasiness about the economy here. Leveraged buyouts and junk bonds were beginning to sicken him; junk bonds were going to turn out to be just that: junk paper, worthless in the long run. West International was secure, the Allandale Group was secure, and the two huge conglomerates were profitable, completely in the black. He did not want to extend himself further.

Maxim's mind switched to his personal investments in the American stock market. He had hundreds of millions of dollars tied up in stock in other companies. He would start unloading that tomorrow. Slowly, carefully. He did not want to start a panic in the street. He would sell his shares over a period of months, and by August or September he would be liquid. He had a strong suspicion that the economy in the States might possibly start lurching in the autumn of this year. He did not know how or why he suspected this, because he never knew where his premonitions about business came from. Gut instinct perhaps. And his gut instinct told him to sell. He did not want to be caught if the stock market *should* fail, God forbid.

Suddenly, he felt lighter, the heaviness in his chest dissipating. It came as no surprise. He generally experienced this rush of relief when he had made final decisions about business problems which had troubled him for weeks.

He lifted his head, saw to his surprise that he was at 57th Street and Fifth. He went to the nearest telephone, dropped a quarter in the box, dialled quickly.

'Hello?'

'It's me, darling.'

'Where are you, Maxim?'

'On the corner of 57th and Fifth. I'm coming over.'

'I can't wait. I'll give you a couple of minutes.'

'About twenty. I want to walk to Sutton Place. See you, babe.'

Blair Martin dropped the receiver back in the cradle and spun around. Her eyes took in every detail of the living room which overlooked the garden, the East River, and a portion of the 59th Street Bridge.

She nodded to herself, both relieved and pleased that the room looked perfect. Maxim was such a stickler for neatness, but everything was in its given place; she had no cause to worry. A tranquil haven of soft pastel colours and fine French furniture, it looked particularly lovely tonight, filled with the flowers he now sent her several times a week since they had become lovers. All of the silk-shaded lamps had been turned on, a fire burned brightly in the grate, and there was a warmth and a mellowness to the setting.

Blair walked across the Aubusson carpet, turned to look back before leaving the sitting room, thinking how lucky she was to live in this house. Maxim had bought it for his daughter, Alix, two years ago, as a peace offering after their quarrel in 1985, in the hopes of patching things up with her. Anastasia and Maxim had then decorated the house together; they both had superb taste and that was why the house on Sutton Place was so beautifully appointed throughout.

But Alix had spurned the house, had refused to accept it. Silly girl, Blair thought, shaking her head, as always somewhat mystified by the foolishness and impracticality of others. She was very much a pragmatist herself.

A housekeeper had looked after the house for a while, but had eventually left, finding the existence too lonely, Maxim had explained. He had suggested she move in about ten months ago, not long after they had started their love affair. He had pointed out that quite aside from needing someone to occupy it for security reasons, he preferred her to live in a private house where he could come and go freely and with impunity. The prying eyes of apartment building doormen alarmed him. 'It's much more discreet, better for me, if you live at my Sutton Place house,' he had pointed out. When she had seen the house she had accepted at once. The building where she lived was going co-op and she could not afford to buy her apartment. In fact, she had been in a dilemma about where she would live.

And so the arrangement was perfect for them both.

As she ran upstairs Blair thought of Maxim. She was crazy about him and he was mad about her. Odd that she had known him off and on since 1982, had frequently dated him, but that he had only become involved with her after his marriage to Adriana Macklin. Gorgeous woman, so beautiful, the epitome of glamour. But a bitch on wheels, horrendous, really, and abrasive, with a tendency towards flashiness at times. Blair could not stand women who had diamonds dripping from every pore.

Blair went into the bedroom, stripped off her trousers and silk shirt, raced into the bathroom. After spraying herself with perfume, she brushed her short reddish-blonde curls into a halo around her heart-shaped face, refreshed her pink lipstick, and smeared a little pale grey eyeshadow on her eyelids. This colour always made her blue eyes look bluer. Once she had touched up her blonde lashes with mascara, she returned to the bedroom.

Opening the armoire, she took out a pale-green silk pyjama suit by Trigère, slipped into the wide floating trousers, put on the long jacket, tied the broad sash, and stepped into a pair of matching silk shoes.

After a quick glance at herself in the mirror, she closed the armoire door and headed out of the bedroom, intent on going down to the kitchen. There was plenty of champagne on ice, and she had bought fresh salad and vegetables earlier that day. She was a good cook; he loved her spaghetti primavera. That's what she would make, and they could finish the meal with cheese and fruit. Maxim was a simple eater, not faddy about food, which made life easier for her, since she was a working girl, ran her own small public relations firm.

Halfway down the stairs, Blair remembered her birth control pills. The last thing she wanted was to get pregnant. Swinging around, she sped up the stairs and into the bedroom. Jerking open the drawer of the bedside table, she took out the pills, dropped one into her hand. It was halfway to her mouth when she stopped, stared down at Maxim's photograph on the table, a reflective look crossing her face. Why don't I want to get pregnant? she asked herself, frowning slightly. I'm already almost thirty. I ought to get pregnant, in fact. And there was no good reason why she should not. In fact, she would like to have a baby. She'd also like a husband. Maxim West to be precise. She was beginning to get tired of being his lover, or to use a more old-fashioned word, his mistress.

Taking very determined steps, Blair Martin went down to the kitchen and emptied the birth control pills into the waste-disposal unit. She went back into the bedroom, walked over to the bedside table and closed the drawer.

For a very long moment she stared at Maxim's photograph in its silver frame, one she had taken here in the garden last summer. Then she brought three fingers into the palm of her hand, and pressed her thumb and forefinger together to form the shape of a gun.

Smiling to herself, she aimed her thumb and forefinger at his photograph.

'I gotcha, Maxim. Gotcha, gotcha, gotcha.'

PART 7

A man of many lives. A man who had his own centre, something untouchable about him, something he did not know about himself . . .

Rich: The Life of Richard Burton
by Melvyn Bragg

FIFTY-SEVEN

'I'm so glad you were free, Daddy,' Alix said, smiling at Maxim.

'So am I.' He smiled back, patted her hand, then reached for one of the menus Joseph had just placed on the table. The two of them sat together on a banquette in Mark's Club, where he had brought her for lunch after she had shown up at his office in Grosvenor Square a short while before. 'Now, Alix, do you know what you want?'

'Nothing first, thank you. Then I'll have the liver and bacon, please.'

'I'll join you.' Maxim motioned to Joseph, ordered, and then turned to face his daughter. 'Well, I must say, it's either a feast or a famine with you, *Schatzi*,' he remarked, reverting to his pet name for her from childhood.

'What do you mean?' Alix asked, staring at him in puzzlement.

'For four years you kept me at arm's length and behaved as if I was Attila the Hun. Now I don't seem able to get rid of you. Wherever I am, there *you* are, popping up all over the globe. Just think, on Monday you were in New York, as was I, and now, on Wednesday, here you are in London. I'm beginning to think you're following me, Alix.'

She drew away from him slightly, gave him a sharp look through narrowed pale green eyes. 'Am I being a nuisance? Is that what you're implying?'

'Of course not,' he laughed. 'And don't look so worried. I'm only teasing. You ought to know by now that I love all the attention you've been giving me for the past six months or so. You're spoiling me. I shall miss it, you know, when you up and marry and leave me to my own devices.'

She also laughed. 'I'm not likely to do that. There are no men on *my* horizon at the moment.'

'What's happened? Has the entire male population gone blind?'

Alix shook her head. 'I just haven't met the right man, Daddy.'

'He'll come along, Alix, and when you least expect it. That's the way it usually happens.'

'Talking of men. I've never admitted this to you before, but you *were* right about Jeremy Vickers, he *was* after my money. Of course, I didn't see that. Remember, I was only twenty-three at the time.'

'He was also after *you*, darling girl. You're a pretty tempting package. Young, beautiful, intelligent, and rich. I wouldn't blame any man for going after you. The problem was, Vickers is the worst kind of playboy, and a gambler, to boot. A son of a bitch in general. It was his foul reputation that bothered me ... his reputation for being a rough customer, violent. I couldn't bear that you were entangled with such ... rubbish.'

'He never laid a finger on me, Daddy. You and Michael would have been the first to know about it if he had ever hurt me. Anyway, I'm glad you were so tough about him with me, that you really played the heavy father. Looking back, I realise I wasn't too crazy about your attitude four years ago, but I am now, and I have been for ages. Thanks, Dad.'

Maxim squeezed her hand. 'I always trusted you, Alix, I knew that ultimately you wouldn't do anything silly or rash, behave in a foolish way. But I did have to let you know what my feelings were, tell you how much I disapproved of that man, even at the risk of antagonising you.'

'I know, and your approval has always been important to me. I wouldn't have married Jeremy over your objections. And, actually, I wouldn't marry anyone today if you didn't approve, even though I am now twenty-eight.'

'Sssh! You're making me feel old,' Maxim said.

'Oh come on! You old! *Never*.'

'Have you forgotten I was fifty-five this past June?'

'You don't look it! In fact, you look terrific. Tall, dark, handsome, tanned, and raring to go. That's my *old* dad,' she teased, laughing.

He laughed with her, took hold of her hand, kissed her fingertips. 'You do your old dad's heart good, you really do.'

Alix leaned towards him, kissed his cheek lightly, whispered in his ear, 'Those two men over there are really intrigued by us. I actually believe they think I'm your mistress.'

'I'm flattered they would think an old geezer like me is deserving of a stunning beautiful blonde such as you, Daughter. However, I'd prefer it if you didn't mention the word *mistress*. I'm afraid I break out in a rash when I hear it these days.'

'Oh, sorry, Daddy.' Alix eyed him carefully, ventured in a low, cautious voice, 'If I'm prying you can tell me to shut up, but out of curiosity, what *is* happening with Blair Martin?'

'Nothing much.'

'I meant how is she? What's her attitude to you?'

'Hostile. Naturally. She wants me to divorce Adriana and marry her. Obviously she wants the baby to have my name, and she's very much playing the injured party, the damaged woman, insists that I do the right thing by her.'

'Injured woman! What cheek! Honestly, Dad, nobody has to get pregnant in this day and age. Not if they don't want to ... take my word for it.'

Maxim returned his daughter's loving gaze steadily, and nodded his head slowly. 'I realise that, Alix. I'm not stupid. And Blair and I had an understanding right from the beginning of the relationship. At least, so I thought. She promised to take precautions. Certainly she knew my feelings about that subject very well. When she told me in the summer of 1987, after I returned to New York from London, that she was pregnant, I was dreadfully upset, I even chastised her about it.'

'How did she explain her pregnancy, if she was supposed to be looking after the situation?'

'Her answer was that it took two to tango.'

An angry glint entered Alix's luminous misty-green eyes. 'But it doesn't take two to swallow birth control pills! Or use some other method of protection. I think Blair set you up, Daddy, I really do.'

Set me up, Maxim thought. A strange look glanced across his face, and his eyes suddenly held a faraway expression as he stared into the distance, for a split second lost to Alix.

'What's the matter? Is something wrong?' she asked.

'No.' Maxim smiled faintly. 'I thought of Camilla all of a sudden, just then in fact. *She* once accused *me* of setting her up. In a different way than we were discussing, obviously.'

'Did you?'

'Oh yes, very much so. But I had my reasons.'

'And Blair Martin set *you* up, and *she* had *her* reasons.'

'I believe you're quite correct, Alix . . . I can't begin to tell you how many times I've asked myself lately why I got involved with her . . . I think perhaps because she reminded me of Camilla. Blair does have the same colouring, is a similar type, isn't she?'

'But she's not half as nice as Camilla was! Camilla was a lovely person.'

'How terribly tragic that she died. For all of us,' he murmured, thinking out loud, sorrow touching his face fleetingly.

'Thank God you didn't die, Daddy. As long as I live, I'll never forget the way I felt when you were lying in Mount Sinai, at death's door after you were shot. I was in agony. I realised how stupid I'd been over the Jeremy Vickers situation, understood that you'd only ever had my welfare at heart. All I wanted was for you to get better so I could make it up to you.'

'And you have, darling girl.'

She smiled at him, leaned closer. 'Thank goodness. And you look fabulous. This summer on the yacht did you a lot of good, didn't it?' Alix said.

'I think it truly turned me around,' Maxim replied, nodding. 'I felt very weak after I got out of the hospital in February, even though I didn't say anything to you and your mother, or Teddy. But I'm from strong stock, and I bounce back very quickly. I'm as good as new now. Never felt better, in fact. Ah, here's our lunch, Alix. I don't know about you, but I'm starving.'

After lunch Alix walked with Maxim back to the West International offices in Grosvenor Square. She tucked her arm through his, and shrugged deeper into her thick tweed coat, muttered, 'Gosh, it's cold for October, I hope we're not going to have a bad winter.'

He glanced down at her. 'You sound as if you're planning to stay here in London. I thought Manhattan was now your home. All those rich clients you tell me you have, anxious to give you barrels of cash for art objects and paintings, and old French furniture.'

Alix groaned, shook her head. 'Not any more. Well, I do have my regular clients, the top-drawer interior designers, the old-money, of course. But a lot of my others, the *nouveaus*, fell by the wayside, what with the Wall Street crash in October of 1987, and some of the other Wall Street economic problems. Yuppies aren't such ready spenders any more.'

'I shouldn't think they are.'

'And what about you, Dad? Are you going to be in London for the next few months?'

'It's more than likely. I might make a couple of quick trips to New York, but I won't be staying long. Actually, I'm planning to spend Christmas in London. Care to join me, *Schatzi?*'

'I'd love to, Daddy!'

'It's a deal,' he said, beaming at her, drawing to a standstill in front of his office building.

Alix smiled at him in return, her face radiant. She reached up, kissed him on the cheek, gave him a bear hug. 'I love you, Daddy of mine.'

'And I love you, too, Daughter.'

'Good afternoon, Sir Maximilian,' the uniformed doorman said, holding the door open for him as Maxim hurried forward after saying goodbye to Alix.

'Afternoon, Jim. Everything all right with you? With the family?'

'Very good, thank you kindly, Sir Maximilian.'

Maxim nodded, rushed on, heading for the bank of elevators. He got in, rode up to his executive suite on the eleventh floor.

His secretary, Faye Miller, looked up as he came barrelling through the door, and exclaimed, 'Oh, Sir Maxim! You've just missed Graeme Longdon. Shall I get her back?'

'Not now, Faye, thanks,' Maxim said. 'New York can wait a while . . . until later in the day.' He strode towards his inner sanctum, stopped, and asked, 'It wasn't anything urgent, was it? Did she say what it was about?'

Faye shook her head. 'No, only that you could return the call any time, that it was nothing vital.'

'Fine.' Maxim went inside, closed the door, took off his black trench-coat, hung it in the coat closet.

Once he was seated behind his desk, he glanced at two folders on his blotter, then picked up the phone and dialled his son's extension.

'Michael West here.'

'It's me, Michael.'

'Yes, Dad?'

'Can you please come to my office for a moment?'

'I'll be right there.'

Within minutes his twenty-seven-year-old son was walking into the room, his face as serious as always, his dark and brilliant eyes as compel-ling as Maxim's. He gets to look more like me every day, Maxim thought, studying Michael closely as he strode across the room, lowered himself into the chair near the desk.

Michael crossed his long legs, settled back in the chair and gave his father a direct look. 'What did you want to see me about?'

'These,' Maxim said, lifting the folders, showing them to Michael, then placing them on the desk again.

A dark brow lifted, a gesture unconsciously copied from his father, and Michael stared hard at Maxim. 'What are they?'

'Never mind, for the moment. We'll get to them later. First I want to talk to you about something else.'

'All right, Dad.'

'For the last few years you've been angry with me, disgruntled, hos-tile – '

'Dad, how can you say that!' Michael interrupted, his voice rising slightly, his eyes flashing.

'I can say it because it's true,' Maxim shot back, leaning forward, fixing his steady, unblinking gaze on his son. 'In fact, things were pretty damned difficult between us, even though we both kept up some sort of pretence of cordiality. Until I was shot earlier this year. And when I almost died your attitude changed towards me. Some of your anger seemed to fall away, at least to dissipate. True or not?'

Michael was silent for a moment.

The two men stared hard at each other.

Michael finally said, 'Yes, it's true.'

'But there is still hostility in you, Michael . . . hostility towards me. And that's one of the things I wanted to talk to you about, discuss with you now.'

'I'm not hostile, Dad!' Michael protested. 'My God, I was heartbroken when you were lying there in New York unconscious, when we didn't know whether you'd live or die. I was so desperately worried about you I couldn't see straight!'

There was a short pause. Michael cleared his throat, said in a low voice, 'I love you, Dad.'

'I know you do, Michael, and I love you. Look here, I'm not being critical of you, even though it may sound as if I am. I was merely leading up to something, and it's this – I want to say that I truly understand *why* you've been angry, disgruntled and hostile in the past.' Maxim propped his elbows on the desk, steepled his fingers, looked over the top of them at Michael.

Michael sat perfectly still in the chair, waiting for his father's next pronouncement, wondering what was coming. He was silent. He knew better than to make the slightest sound when his father had that intense, concentrated expression in his eyes.

At last Maxim spoke again. He said, 'You had every right to those emotions, because, in certain ways, I haven't been fair to you over the years. For one thing, I haven't given you enough responsibility, enough power.' Maxim let out a heavy sigh, shook his head. 'I've clutched the power to me, but without realising I was doing so. *Unconsciously*, if you like. Just too preoccupied with all the deals, that's been my main problem over the years. So preoccupied with the deals I've neglected a lot of things I should have paid attention to. In fact, I've been selfish, especially to some people. However, that's another story, we won't go into it. I asked you in here now so that I could tell you things are about to change, Michael. As my only son, and heir to this gargantuan empire, I think it's about time you started sharing more of the workload, the responsibility, the power.'

Michael was flabbergasted. Astonishment swept across his face. He continued to stare at his father disbelievingly.

'Aren't you going to say something?' Maxim asked at last, with a brief laugh.

'Are you serious, Dad?' he finally gasped.

'Do I ever say anything I don't mean, when it comes to business?'

'No. But Dad . . . I mean, gosh, Dad, thanks.' As the facts sank in, a huge smile spread across Michael's face. 'This is fantastic news for me. I *have* been anxious to do more in the company, and I won't let you down.'

'I know that, Michael. And let me just add that you're a brilliant businessman. The problem is, you've been operating in my shadow. Now's the chance for you to go out there and shine.'

'Go out *where*?'

'New York. I'd like you to go to New York and run West International for me. And with me, of course.'

Michael was stunned, but managed to say, 'Dad, this is great, wonderful.'

Maxim tapped the two folders. 'These are the details of the two small deals I've been working on with Grae and Peter, plus a number of memos from me about the New York office – what to expect from certain people.'

Michael frowned. 'But you'll be there, won't you?' he asked swiftly, staring at his father.

Maxim shook his head.

'You mean you're throwing me in at the deep end? Alone? To sink or swim?'

'You won't sink, you'll swim. You're my son. We're winners. I've no worries about you. And don't look so troubled, it's what you've always wanted, isn't it?'

'But Dad – '

Maxim held up his hand. 'That's it, Michael. I've made the decision. You've always wanted the power. And the New York office. Take them both. Grae and Peter will back you all the way. You can trust them, they won't steer you in the wrong direction. In any case, I'll be at the end of a phone.'

'But where?' Michael asked, frowning. 'Where will you be?'

'Here in London. Or on the yacht. Perhaps even in New York, sitting two doors away from you in my office. The point is, I want you to run the American end of West International from now on. Will you do it?'

'Yes, of course I will, Dad. I was only *momentarily* startled. You seem to be giving up so much all of a sudden, and so unexpectedly.' There was a moment of hesitation on Michael's part, and then he said, 'May I ask you why?'

'Of course. First of all, West International will be yours one day. You know the London operation inside out; I think the time has come for you to totally understand the American end of the company. I will guide you, always be there for you, whenever you need me. However, I do want you to start *running* it, Michael. Put very simply, it's your turn now.'

Michael nodded. 'I understand.'

'Secondly, I want to take it a bit easier. I've rushed and pushed and driven myself hard for years and years. Since I was eighteen, actually. I think I should slow down a bit.' A wry smile slid onto Maxim's mouth, and he confided quietly, 'My brush with death made me realise that there are more things in life than big deals.'

'There are, and I'm glad you want to relax, Dad. However, I hope you're not thinking of retiring yet. You're only fifty-five.'

'No chance of that, Michael,' Maxim exclaimed, grinning. 'I'd miss the excitement of wheeling and dealing. However, I don't have to work twenty-four hours a day . . . I've come to realise that.'

'When do you want me to go to New York?'

'Whenever you can clear your desk here. Shall we say immediately?'

'I can leave this weekend. There's not much on the back burners here. Will you be going with me?'

'No, but Graeme and Peter are expecting you, eagerly waiting for you. I'm leaving for Berlin next week, actually. I'm going to see Aunt Irina with Teddy.'

'It's a strange time to go, isn't it, Dad?'

'What do you mean?'

'All the demonstrations, the unrest in East Berlin, in East Germany, in all of the Eastern bloc countries.'

'I think it's a fascinating time! We're going to see some extraordinary changes in the next few months, Michael, mark my words. Russia's in trouble economically, and that's part of what's behind Gorbachev's overtures to the West. He's not so concerned with saving the Communist Party these days, but saving his country, his people. And also his attitude to the Eastern bloc governments is going to lead the way to a great deal of reform. You'll see.'

'Three years ago, when I was with you in Berlin, you told me the Berlin Wall had to come down, and that it would, one day. Do you think that *will* happen?'

Maxim shrugged. 'I don't know. It should come down, it's an abomination.'

'If it did, do you think there would be reunification in Germany?'

'I don't know; that's not as easy as it sounds. It would be pretty complicated to achieve.'

A reflective look crossed Michael's face. 'A reunited Germany? How will people react to that?'

'I don't know. But let's not forget that the Germans of today think of themselves as Europeans, and in 1992 there are going to be *no borders* in Europe. We're going to be as one, in a sense. A sort of united commonwealth.'

'I understand what you're saying . . . however, there will be those who will over-react, who will see German reunification as a threat.'

Maxim laughed. 'I know, but those who think in this way simply don't understand European politics, and, moreover, the European economic situation as it is today. And anyway, the Germans have been bending over backwards to expiate their crimes for the past forty-four years. They're going to be very careful. They want world approval.'

'New generation, new values. Is that what you're saying, Dad?'

'I suppose I am.' Maxim stood, picked up the folders, walked around his desk.

Michael jumped up, took the folders from his father as they were handed to him. 'Thanks for this tremendous vote of confidence, Dad. I won't let you down.'

'I know you won't, Michael. You're my son, a chip off the old block.' As Maxim spoke he put his arm around Michael's shoulders, and walked him to the door.

'Mr Trenton will be coming for a drink before we go out to dinner, Marco,' Maxim told the butler who ran his Mayfair house.

'Shall I serve the usual Roederer Cristal, Sir Maxim?'

'Yes please, Marco. Mr Trenton will be arriving around seven-thirty. We'll have drinks in the downstairs library.'

Marco inclined his head. 'Would you like anything now, Sir Maxim? A cup of tea perhaps?'

'No, thank you,' Maxim murmured, walking over to a chair, sitting down, picking up the *Evening Standard*.

'Very good, sir.' Marco slipped out of Maxim's upstairs study, which was part of his bedroom suite, and closed the door quietly behind him.

Maxim glanced at the front page, and put the paper down, not in the mood to read. He leaned back in the chair, closed his eyes, thought of the day's events. His daughter's sudden arrival in London had been a surprise and a delight. One of the things which had given him the most satisfaction in the past nine months since the shooting was the healing of the rift between them. That had been Alix's doing, who had been at his side constantly during his stay in hospital, and afterwards. He had been about to instigate a reconciliation himself, at the beginning of the year, when he had flown to New York to see her, only to discover she was on the coast. They were truly good friends again, closer than they had ever been. And now perhaps he would be able to enjoy the same kind of relationship with his son. His thoughts turned to Michael, whose stunned shock had been something to behold. He really had been knocked for a loop this afternoon. Maxim smiled inwardly, happy that he had finally handed over some of his power and responsibility. Quite aside from anything else, Michael was deserving. He'll do just fine, Maxim said to himself. He'll truly come into his own, running the New York office.

New York. The thought of the mess there filled him with dismay and apprehension. But it would have to be dealt with sooner or later. Suddenly he remembered something Camilla had once told him years ago. 'We write our own scripts, then act them out,' she had said, and she had been correct. He had written all of those New York scenes himself. There was really no one else to blame, and ultimately he must take the responsibility.

Next week he was going to Berlin with Teddy. From there he would fly to New York. He experienced a surge of relief as he came to this decision. Once in New York he would put things right. He had no alternative but to do that; so many lives were involved.

He had survived the shooting by the skin of his teeth, and he had made a promise to himself to bring order to his unorthodox private life when he was fully recovered. And he had been doing this slowly. His recuperation had taken longer than he had expected; then in June there had been the investiture at Buckingham Palace, when he had been knighted. And after that, following his doctor's advice, he had taken a long cruise on his yacht, sailing around the Mediterranean with his immediate family during July and August: Alix, Michael and Anastasia, Teddy and Mark, the Derevenkos, Stubby, and Marcia . . . those he was closest to, loved and cared about the most, and who loved him. In September he had flown to Japan on urgent business, had stopped off in Australia and Hong Kong, before returning to London.

He had been here for the whole of October, supervising the acquisition of a French perfume and cosmetic company. Then working on his plans for Michael's eventual succession as head of West International a few years from now, when he finally retired. But obviously the time had come to settle matters in New York.

Maxim rose, walked over to the fireplace, stood with his back to it, an abstracted expression filling his face. He was still as tortured by inner conflicts and doubts as he had been at the beginning of the year, before the shooting. His brush with death had only made him more acutely aware of them. Most nights he lay awake, prowling the dark labyrinths of his soul, seeking meanings for his life and all that had happened to him. He still had no answers for himself, no new wisdom.

He had been filled with a deep sadness for years, ever since his childhood. Anastasia's departure from his life had only underscored that sadness, the immense sense of loss he had carried inside him.

The sadness would always be there, he had come to understand and accept that. He could only pray that one day he would find the peace which had eluded him for so long, and that when he did he would be at ease with himself and his life at last.

Maxim heard the doorbell ringing, roused himself from his thoughts, and went out of the study. He ran lightly down the stairs as Marco was opening the door to Stubby.

He's been my friend for forty-seven years, Maxim thought. *My best friend.* Loyal, staunch, devoted and wise. Whatever would I have done without him?

FIFTY-EIGHT

'What time is Aunt Irina expecting us at her flat?' Maxim asked, walking out of the bedroom of his suite in the Kempinski Hotel in Berlin.

'Not for a couple of hours,' Teddy answered.

He glanced at his watch. 'It's only five o'clock. I must have misunderstood you. I had it in my head that we're supposed to be meeting her shortly.'

'You didn't misunderstand anything, Maxim,' Teddy said. 'I did tell you we should be ready by five o'clock. However, we're not going to Irina's just yet . . . I'm expecting a guest.'

'Who?'

'A friend of . . . a friend of *Mutti's*,' Teddy began, and stopped, staring up at him, suddenly seeing him very objectively for once in her life. She could not help thinking what a striking and handsome man he was, and how well he looked after his ordeal. When he had been shot she had been out of her mind with worry. And she who had lost her faith had begun to pray again; she had prayed every night for him, and when he recovered, her faith in God had been restored. Maxim said, 'You're looking strange, Teddy. What's the matter?'

'Nothing. To tell you the truth, I was just thinking how wonderful you're looking at the moment. So very healthy.'

He smiled at her. 'It's the tan. But seriously, I do feel very well, Teddy. But *who* is it that you're expecting?'

'I told you, a former – ' Teddy stopped, stood up abruptly at the sound of knocking, hurried to open the door before Maxim had a chance to do so. 'Good afternoon, thank you for coming,' she said, and opening the door wider, Teddy escorted her guest into the suite.

Maxim stood in the centre of the floor, slightly taken aback when he saw the woman with Teddy. She was a nun dressed in a dark brown habit and a black veil. He was puzzled, and gave Teddy a quick, questioning look.

Teddy said, 'Sister Constanza, I would like to introduce you to Maximilian West. Maxim, this is Sister Constanza of the Sisters of the Poor of St Francis.'

Maxim inclined his head, wondering what the association between *Mutti* and the Catholic sister could have possibly been.

The nun walked forward, smiling, her hand outstretched.

Maxim took it, smiling in return, thinking that he had never seen such a peaceful face on anyone before in his entire life. 'I'm pleased to meet you, Sister Constanza.'

The nun was small, dainty, her eyes warm, her voice gentle when she said, 'I am delighted to meet you at last. Teddy has written to me for many years, and has told me so much about you.'

Maxim's bafflement increased and he stared at Teddy expectantly.

Teddy ignored his quizzical expression, turned to the nun and said, 'Please do sit down, Sister Constanza.'

'Thank you,' the sister responded and lowered herself into a chair.

'Can I offer you some sort of refreshment? Coffee or tea?' Maxim asked, looking across at the nun, and then at Teddy.

'No thank you,' the sister said.

'And what about you, Teddy?'

'Nothing, thanks, Maxim. Come and sit here with me.' Teddy patted the sofa, where he joined her, frowning slightly, wondering what this was all about.

Clearing her throat, Teddy said, 'There's something I've wanted to tell you. For years and years, Maxim.' She held him with her eyes, continued, after a moment, 'And I *should* have told you . . . a long time ago, actually. But I didn't.' She took a deep breath. 'In 1939, before we left Paris, Ursula gave me a letter for you – '

'Yes, I still have it,' he interrupted, a hint of impatience creeping into his voice.

'And Ursula also gave *me* a letter, which I was instructed not to open except in the event of her death. That is the first thing I did when I came back from Berlin in 1945. There was information in the letter which she wanted me to have, something she wanted me to know. She said I had to use my discretion . . . about telling you or not, when you were old enough to understand. But I never did tell you, or show you the letter.'

'What did it say?' Maxim asked, his curiosity fully aroused.

'I'll tell you in a moment,' Teddy replied. 'When you almost died earlier this year I regretted that I had never given you the letter. I suddenly realised how wrong I had been to . . . well, to play God, in a sense. You had every right to know what was in the letter.'

'What *was* in it?' he demanded.

Teddy reached out, took hold of his hand, held it very tightly in hers. She said softly, 'Ursula Westheim was not your birth mother, Maxim. She adopted you . . . she and Sigmund adopted you when you were a day old.'

Maxim sat back slightly, gaping at Teddy. He was stunned by her extraordinary words. Shock flooded his eyes. For a moment he was unable to say anything, trying to digest what she had just said, to comprehend her words.

But at last he managed to ask in an unsteady voice, 'Then who *was* my mother?'

Teddy returned his penetrating stare but did not answer him.

There was a sudden, painful silence in the room.

Very softly, in that same gentle voice, Sister Constanza said, 'I am your mother, Maxim. I gave you life.'

Maxim's jaw dropped. His eyes focused on the nun, remained riveted on her. He was reeling from shock, still unable to absorb the things he was hearing.

'But how can you be my mother?' he gasped hoarsely. 'You're a nun.' He looked from Sister Constanza to Teddy, his eyes dazed.

Sister Constanza said, 'I was not always a nun, and I *am* your birth mother, Maxim, truly I am.'

'But I don't understand!' he exclaimed. 'You are a Catholic, the Westheims were Jews. How did they come to adopt me?'

'I would like to tell you the story,' the nun replied. 'May I?'

'Of course! *I must know . . . everything!*'

'My name before I became a nun was Dorothea Schubert. I went to work for Ursula Westheim in 1931, when I was sixteen, as her social secretary. She liked me very much, and was always very good to me. When I became pregnant out of wedlock, in 1933, my parents disowned me, threw me out of the house. You see, they were staunch Catholics, very religious, and they felt that I had brought terrible shame upon them.'

Sister Constanza shifted slightly in the chair, smoothed a hand over her habit, and continued, 'I had no one to turn to in my terrible distress, no real friends to help me, and certainly the rest of my family were against me. It was Ursula who befriended me, allowed me to live at the house in the Tiergartenstrasse for a few months. During that time I began to realise I could not keep my child, that I would have to have the baby adopted. I knew Ursula was unable to have children. One day I went to her, and I asked her if she would adopt my baby.'

'And my mother agreed?' Maxim said.

'Not at first,' Sister Constanza responded. 'She said she must think about it very deeply . . . mostly because I was Catholic and she was

Jewish. I pointed out to her that we were not talking about religion, but about love. I told her that I knew she and Herr Westheim would give my child the greatest love and affection, and so many things which I could not.'

'And so they finally agreed?'

'Yes. Frau Westheim took a small apartment for me, just off the Ku'damm, so that I could have my privacy away from the mansion. She had Herr Westheim moved to the villa in Wannsee. It was important that neither of us were in the mansion in the city, because of the servants.'

'And then after my birth you gave me to the Westheims immediately . . . Teddy did just say I was adopted when I was a day old,' Maxim stated.

Sister Constanza inclined her head, gave him a long and thoughtful look. 'It was better for everyone to do this quickly. You were such a beautiful boy, I knew I would not be able to give you up if I held you in my arms for too long. They came for you on June the thirteenth, and took you home with them. They were so happy. I told them that I wanted them to have you above any couple in the whole world . . . because I knew what good and wonderful people they were. I knew they would bring you up with love and kindness, and shower you with everything that money could buy.'

'They did,' Maxim said softly, remembering his mother and father with the greatest of love.

Teddy noticed that Sister Constanza looked pale, drained, and she continued her story, said to Maxim, 'Sister Constanza went away from Berlin, Maxim. She had decided to go into a religious order, a nursing order of nuns, and she went to Aachen, to the Motherhouse of the Sisters of the Poor of St Francis, where she became a novice.'

'*Aachen*,' Maxim murmured. 'What a strange coincidence. That was the border town we stopped at when we were fleeing Germany in 1938.'

'Yes,' Teddy said, and went on slowly, 'In Ursula's letter to me, she told me all of this, and gave me the name and address of Sister Constanza, asked me to stay in touch with her, to write to her with news of you. Discreetly, of course.'

'And she did . . . all these years,' the nun added, leaning forward in the chair, clasping her hands. 'I realise you have suffered greatly, and have had great sadness in your life, because of the way you were separated from Ursula and Sigmund. And because of the way your parents died in the death camps. But I believe that I did the right thing for you, in spite of this.'

'Yes, I agree with you,' he said, his voice barely audible, meaning every word. 'You did the only thing you could at the time. You were not to know what would happen.'

'I hope you will see it in your heart to forgive me,' the nun said.

'But there's nothing to forgive.' Maxim gave her a swift glance. 'I loved my parents, and they loved me very much, and that's all that matters in the end.'

'Yes,' she said. 'You speak the truth there.'

'Who was my birth father?' he asked.

'His name was Karl Neuwirth.'

'Was he also a Catholic?'

'Yes.'

'Why didn't he marry you?'

There was a tiny silence before she said, 'He was a married man.'

'Is he still alive?'

'Oh no, he was killed in the war. He was a soldier on the Russian front. And his wife and two children were killed in a bombing raid.'

'I see.' Maxim stared at Teddy. 'Why didn't you tell me years ago?'

'I kept meaning to . . . quite a few times, Maxim. But I always lost my nerve . . . I was afraid, I didn't want to cause you pain.' She cleared her throat. 'I had to tell you finally, because I thought it was wrong to withhold this information from you, as I explained a moment or two ago. And anyway, I felt that at the age of fifty-five you are mature enough to understand everything.'

For the first time a faint smile flickered in his eyes. 'Yes, I think I'm old enough to understand, Teddy.'

At this moment, quite suddenly, Sister Constanza stood up. 'I must leave now,' she announced. 'I have duties at the convent I cannot ignore or neglect.'

Maxim jumped up. 'But can't we offer you tea, something before you leave, Sister Constanza?'

She shook her head. 'You are kind, but I really must get back. I am needed.'

'Do you have far to go?'

'No. It will only take me about half an hour on the train. The convent is just outside the city.'

'Please let me send you in my car – '

'No, no,' she cut in, touching his arm lightly. 'I must lead my life the way I have always led it. But thank you for your kindness.' She stretched out her hand.

Maxim took it, held it in his.

Sister Constanza stared up into his face. Her dark brown eyes were full of love. She said, 'Be at peace with yourself, Maxim. And may God bless you always.'

He felt a stirring in his heart for this gentle, religious woman, who had given birth to him, and he impulsively leaned down and kissed her on the cheek.

Her eyes filled with tears, then she smiled at him, and her face was radiant.

FIFTY-NINE

'Are you angry with me?' Teddy asked a short while later, after Maxim had read Ursula's letter, written so long ago, which he had handed back to her.

'How could I ever be angry with you, my dearest Teddy?'

'Upset then?'

'No.' His expression was as loving and devoted as it always was.

'Then what *are* you feeling?' Teddy pressed, worried about him, concerned about the effect the nun's revelations had had on him.

'*Startled, stunned, shocked.* I think anybody would feel those things under the circumstances, don't you?'

'Yes,' Teddy agreed quietly, continuing to observe him.

'You could have shown me the letter years ago, you know,' Maxim said, returning her gaze evenly, his expression neutral.

'The main reason I didn't, Maxim, is because I thought it would hurt you.'

'What I just heard from Sister Constanza does not change anything in my life, Teddy. *Mutti* will always be my lovely blonde *Mutti*, my fairytale mummy from my childhood. I'll never stop loving her, and the memory of her will remain precious to me until the day I die. And no matter whose male genes I have in me, Sigmund Westheim is still my father. He will always be my father to me. He is the one who gave me love, and my standards, and my code of honour. I have lived by the rules he set out for me when I was a child, to the best of my ability, all the days of my life.'

He paused, gave Teddy a small, almost shy smile, and confided, 'I still have the little bits of paper he gave me when I was four years old. I've kept them all these years. In fact, I copied his words down on white postcards, in order to preserve them along with the little carved horse. And, incidentally, I passed on my father's standards, his rules of conduct, to Michael and to Alix. I gave them copies of his words.'

'Oh Maxim, what a lovely thing to do. You never told me!' Teddy exclaimed.

'I have to keep a few secrets from you,' he replied, his voice lighter, teasing all of a sudden. Teddy studied him for a moment. 'Well, now at last you know who you really are, Maxim, know that you were born a Catholic of Catholic parents.'

'No, Teddy, my parents were Jews. *And I am a Jew.* I was brought up a Jew, I feel like a Jew, therefore, I am a Jew.'

Taken aback momentarily, Teddy stared at him, made no comment. Slowly she began to nod her head. 'Yes, Maxim, you are right. You are a Jew.'

Pushing himself to his feet, Maxim went over to the sofa, sat down next to her. He took her hand in his, looked deeply into her face. She was still a beautiful woman, even though she was now seventy years of age. There were fine wrinkles around her green eyes, etched at the corners of her gentle mouth, and her hair had turned snow-white. But there was a serenity and a loveliness about her that age could never dim. He loved her so very much at this moment he thought his heart was going to burst. She had been there for him every day of his life, his sweet and loving devoted Teddy.

He said, very softly, 'There's something else I want to say to you.'

'Yes, what is it, dear?'

'Sister Constanza may have given birth to me, and *Mutti* will always be so very special to me. *But you are my mother, Teddy.*'

She stared at him speechlessly. Her eyes filled up with sudden tears.

He touched her wrinkled cheek with the greatest of tenderness, remembering all she had done for him for fifty-four years of his life. He told her, 'You have looked after me since I was one year old. You took care of me when I was small, took me to safety in England. Protected my life at the risk of yours, brought me up, raised me to be the man I am today. Whatever good there is in me, I owe to you, Teddy. You're the very best part of me. Yes, my dearest, *dearest* Teddy, you *are* my mother. I love you very much, I thank you from the bottom of my heart for everything you have done for me.'

Profoundly moved, the tears rolled down Teddy's cheeks. She clung to Maxim's hand, and her voice was brimming with emotion as she said, '*I've loved you as my own child.* I never thought of you in any other way. You were always my first born . . . in my heart.'

Maxim put his arms around Teddy and brought her to him. 'Yes, I know that. I always knew it, I think.'

They held each other close, remembering so many little things about the last fifty years, lost for a moment or two in their own private thoughts, bonded as mother and son.

And then Maxim said, against her snowy hair, 'It's odd, but so much has become clear to me in the past few days. I have been so mixed up inside myself, so torn, so full of doubts ... about myself, my life. I haven't been able to see straight. And one night, before the shooting, I had wondered who I was, why I was here on this planet, what the hell life was all about.'

'I know you've been troubled for a very long time,' she said.

'And then last week, a day or two before we left London, I had a flash of insight, a revelation ... You might say it was my *epiphany*. I suddenly understood so many things about myself, understood that I had been yearning after *Mutti* for most of my life, searching for *her* even in other women perhaps. Yes, I truly did understand myself at that moment ... I realised I was the lost boy Hans.'

Teddy eased herself away from him, looked up into his familiar, handsome face. 'What do you mean?'

'When I was a little boy here in Berlin, so long ago now, you read a story to me about a boy called Hans. Do you remember the story?'

'Vaguely.'

'His mother lost Hans, and she could never find him again, so he was lost forever, wandering around the world, with nobody to love him. That story really made an impression on me. When we were in Paris in 1939 I asked *Mutti* not to lose me. And then she did. At least, so I thought, because I never saw her again.' He looked into her face, and finished, 'I've always been the lost boy.'

Sadness fell like a shadow across Teddy's face and her heart ached for him. But she said in the gentlest tone, '*You*, lost. Never.' She shook her head, denyingly. 'You've been mixed up, yes, and your life is now in the most ghastly mess, but I refuse to ever think of you as *lost*.'

'But deep within myself that *is* the way I've felt, although I suppose I only recognised this the other night, when I was having dinner with Stubby in London. He made a remark to me that triggered everything off in my head.'

'What did he say to you?' Teddy asked, her eyes searching his face.

'He said that the women in my life had hurt me badly, let me down, whether they had done so intentionally or not. I asked him what he meant, and he pointed out that *Mutti* was wrenched from me at a tender age, that Anastasia left me against my will, and that Camilla also left me – because she died on me. He then added that Adriana failed me and Blair Martin betrayed me.'

'All that *is* true,' Teddy agreed, thinking that Stubby had acquired wisdom in middle age. She had had a soft spot for Stubby since his boyhood, was very fond of him.

Maxim explained, 'It occurred to me that in the same way *Mutti* was *wrenched* from me, all of the women in my life *abandoned* me, in one way or another.'

'I can't argue with you there.'

'And that same night I understood that *you* were the only woman who had never hurt me, never let me down. You've always been there for me, and you've been my rock. When I was going in and out of unconsciousness in New York, in the hospital in January, I remember opening my eyes at one moment. And do you know what I saw?'

She shook her head, mystified.

'I saw my first wife, my third wife, my mistress, my daughter. *And my mother*. That's what I thought, when I saw you. *Mother*. And then I started drifting off into unconsciousness again, and you, as you are today, as you look today, disappeared. In place of the silver-haired seventy-year-old Teddy, I saw the Teddy of my childhood. I kept thinking that Teddy would come soon, come and save me as she had when I was a child.'

'I would always try to save you, Maxim, but there are times in life when we must save ourselves, when no one can do it for us, and that's the way it is now with you.'

'What are you getting at?'

'I think you must save yourself by clearing up that frightful, upsetting mess in New York. Those women, Maxim. Adriana, Blair. The baby, Viveca. You mustn't let that situation continue to drift the way it *has* been drifting since you were shot. It's simply not right.'

'Oh, I know that. I plan to bring some order to the chaos in my life as soon as possible. I don't love Adriana. She doesn't love me. Only my status. I plan to divorce her, give her anything she wants, if necessary. We have a pre-nuptial agreement, but as far as I'm concerned, I'm prepared to re-negotiate if it frees me.'

'And then what are you going to do? About Blair Martin and her child?'

'I'm certainly not going to marry her, if that's what you're getting at, Teddy. I'm sorry there's an innocent child involved, but I'm not going to sacrifice myself, get myself into another marital trap with the wrong woman. You see, I don't love Blair either. Nor does she love me. Only my money.'

'You'll provide for the baby, even though you have no positive proof she is yours?'

'Why not? I'm a rich man. And what if the child *is* mine? I'd hate to think of *my* offspring in need, wanting for something, wanting for anything.'

'You've obviously done a great deal of thinking in the last week. Things didn't seem quite so clear-cut to you Maxim when we had lunch a fortnight ago. You sounded muddled, and you troubled me, worried me.'

'I told you, the other evening with Stubby gave me such insight . . . it was my epiphany.'

There was a sudden sharp knocking on the door.

Startled, Maxim swung his head, then looked at Teddy.

'I wonder who that can be?' he muttered, rising.

Teddy said, 'Oh dear, I forgot to tell you, I'm expecting another guest.'

'Who?' he asked.

She ignored his question. 'I'm afraid I've been playing God again,' she said.

Striding to the door, Maxim wrenched it open. And for the second time that day his jaw dropped. But with remarkable swiftness he recovered himself, and his aplomb.

A dazzling smile spread across his face. 'Anastasia!' he exclaimed, stepped forward, took hold of her arm and escorted his ex-wife into the suite.

SIXTY

Princess Irina Troubetzkoy greeted them excitedly when Maxim, Teddy and Anastasia walked into her apartment that same evening.

'I'm sorry we're so late,' Teddy began, only to be silenced by Irina's raised hand.

'You don't know, do you? You haven't heard?' Irina cried, her eyes focused on them.

Teddy looked bewildered, Anastasia intrigued. Maxim said, 'Heard what, Aunt Irina?'

'The news from East Berlin!'

'No,' he answered.

Anastasia took charge. 'Let's go into the sitting room, Aunt Irina, and you can tell us about it.' She slipped out of her sable coat, placed it on the bench in the hallway.

'Of course! How rude of me to keep you standing here in the foyer. Please take off your coat, Teddy, give me your mink, Maxim, hang your overcoat in the cupboard,' Irina instructed, bustling around them.

A few seconds later, in front of the fire in Irina's living room, the three of them sat back, stared at her expectantly.

Irina was far too worked up to sit, and she stood near the fireplace, one hand resting on the mantelpiece. She said, in the same tense, excited voice, 'A little earlier today, Günter Schabowski, head of the East Berlin Communist Party, had a press conference. He said that starting at midnight *tonight* East Germans can leave if they want.' Irina's voice shook, tears welled. 'They can leave without special permission . . . for a few hours, a few days, *forever*, if they so wish. They are free! Free at last, out of bondage!' She was so overcome she began to weep, groped in her jacket pocket for a handkerchief.

Maxim went to her, put his arm around her shoulders.

After a moment, she said to him, 'You were always right. The Berlin Wall *is* going to come down, as you predicted it would.'

'I never thought I'd live to see *this* day!' Teddy exclaimed.

'Neither did I, Teddy,' Irina murmured, patting her eyes again, pulling herself together.

Maxim truly had been surprised. He said to Irina, 'Teddy and I have been tied up for several hours, with an old friend of . . . of Teddy's, then Teddy and I had things to discuss, and suddenly Anastasia arrived. I missed the evening news on television. Naturally, we were in the dark when we arrived here. But what wonderful news this is.'

'I've cancelled the table at the restaurant,' Irina said. 'We are going to have dinner here, and later, around eleven, we must go out into the streets. We must be there when the crossing points are opened along the Berlin Wall.'

'That's right!' Maxim exclaimed. 'We can't miss this . . . this historical event. Why, history is shifting under our feet at this very moment. We are seeing history in the making, in fact. Nothing is ever going to be the same again . . .'

'What do you mean?' Anastasia asked.

Gifted as he was with exceptional vision, Maxim had instantly understood the implications, seen into the future, and he said, in a voice as excited as Irina's had been, 'I believe we are about to witness the fall of some of the communist regimes in Europe. You're going to see . . . one by one they'll all come tumbling down. Freedom and democracy are on the march.'

'Do you really think so?' Teddy asked. He was rarely wrong. At least, about business or politics.

'Yes, I do,' Maxim replied. 'It is Mikhail Gorbachev. He has opened the way to this, with his *perestroika*, and by preaching reform. Believe me, it couldn't have happened without him.'

'The wheel of history,' Irina said softly. 'How it turns, sometimes slowly, sometimes so fast. I am seventy-eight, and all of my life I've lived under the menacing shadow of Communism. The Bolsheviks slaughtered my family – my father, my Romanov uncle, Tsar Nicholas, his wife Tsarina Alexandra, my cousins. When I was only a small child I fled Russia with my mother.' She sighed. 'Over seventy years I've waited, praying that Communism would fail ... that somehow the people would rise up, and that in their desire for freedom and justice they *would* ultimately prevail.'

'They *are* prevailing,' Maxim told her. 'For months now there have been demonstrations – in Leipzig and all over East Germany. And East Germans have been pouring out, through Hungary and Czechoslovakia, into West Germany, at an amazing rate. It was only a matter of time before the Berlin Wall came down. But look, what about a drink, Aunt Irina? We must make a toast on this historical occasion.'

'How stupid I am! Hilde put champagne on ice before you came. It's over there, Maxim, on the chest with the glasses. Would you open it, please?'

He strode across the room, opened the bottle, poured the champagne. Anastasia joined him, picked up two glasses when they were filled, carried them over to Teddy and Irina.

'To Freedom!' Irina exclaimed, lifting her glass high.

'Freedom!' Teddy, Maxim, and Anastasia said in unison, raising their glasses.

'It's November the ninth today!' Teddy said, a look of sudden comprehension crossing her face. 'November the ninth, 1989. Fifty-one years ago tonight it was Henrietta Mandelbaum's twenty-first birthday ... and the night the Nazis torched the Central Synagogue. November the ninth, 1938, was *Kristallnacht*. I'll never forget it ... racing through the streets on the back of Willy Herzog's motorbike, fleeing from the raging mob of stormtroopers. Tonight is the 51st anniversary of *Kristallnacht!*'

'How extraordinary that the Wall is coming down tonight,' Maxim said. 'History truly has come full circle.'

Irina nodded in agreement. 'If Hitler had not come to power, there would have never been a war. Berlin would never have been divided into East-West Zones. Nor would the country have been divided; there would have been no communist regime running East Germany. Everything harks back to the Nazis, doesn't it? Only now, as the Berlin Wall crumbles, are we truly seeing the end of the legacy of the Third Reich.'

'*Tor Auf! Tor Auf! Tor Auf!*' the crowds bellowed at eleven forty-five. 'Open the gate!' they repeated over and over again. And they continued to taunt the East German border guards for another fifteen minutes, as they waited for midnight at Checkpoint Charlie in West Berlin's American Sector.

Maxim stood with his arm around Teddy; Anastasia had hers linked through Irina's. The four of them were amongst the thousands thronging the streets, impatiently waiting for the stroke of midnight.

At exactly twelve the crowds went wild, cheering, shouting, and screaming as East Berliners began to stream through the gate at Checkpoint Charlie, many of them coming over into the West Zone for the first time in their lives. The whistling, the shouting, the cheering continued unabated; West and East Berliners hugged and kissed each other, and wept, overcome by joy. They danced in the streets, shared the champagne and beer the West Berliners had brought with them. It was a grand and glorious night as they celebrated freedom.

All manner of mixed emotions crowded in on Maxim as he stood watching the Berliners go crazy around him. Many of them were now clambering up onto the Wall, where so many had died trying to escape to freedom; others had begun to chip away at it with hammers and picks, intent on breaking it down, this hideous wall of shame.

Berlin. The city of his birth and childhood. It had forever pulled him back, and he had always believed it held a secret for him. It had. The secret had been revealed today. He thought of Ursula and Sigmund Westheim, who would always be his *Mutti* and Papa, and the sadness swelled in him when he thought of their persecution, the way they had died in the death camps. Rage swamped him, but he pushed it aside. It served no purpose now. Instead, he clung to the image of them in his mind's eye, saw Ursula's lovely blonde beauty, Sigmund's dark head bent over the piano, heard her laughter, heard his glorious music that had filled the house in the Tiergartenstrasse. They would live on in his heart forever, their memory clear, profoundly pure, intact, unchanged by anything he had heard today. His mind swung to Sister Constanza. He did not believe he would see her again. He was quite certain she had no need or desire to meet him for a second time. She had only come today because Teddy had asked her. The nun had her God and was at peace with herself. He had understood this about her the instant he had met her. Absolute peace dwelt in that innocent, sweet face.

He had told Teddy many things today. *He had spoken the truth. She was his mother. He was her son. He was a Jew.*

It suddenly struck him how curious it was that Teddy had insisted they come to Berlin this week to see Irina; that today, as the Berlin Wall tumbled, the walls in his mind had tumbled.

'It's like New Year's Eve!' Teddy shouted above the noise, clinging to his arm.

'Or Bastille Day!' Anastasia suggested.

'Celebration . . . revolution . . . no matter what we call it, this is a night to remember!' Irina cried. 'The last time we were in a huge crowd like this was in 1963, when we heard President Kennedy speak in front of the Schöneberg Town Hall.'

'*Ich bin ein Berliner,*' Anastasia said, quoting John Kennedy, looking at Maxim as she did.

'If only he were still alive to see this,' Maxim murmured, and then he hugged Teddy to him, brought Irina and Anastasia into the circle of his arms. He thought of the night he had been shot; he thanked God he had survived, that he was alive.

It was almost two o'clock in the morning by the time Maxim, Teddy and Anastasia came back to the Kempinski Hotel, after they had taken Irina home.

At the door of her suite, he kissed Teddy goodnight, and so did Anastasia.

'It's been quite a day,' Teddy said, turning around on the threshold of her room. 'A memorable day. A memorable night.'

'Yes, Teddy, it has, indeed,' he agreed.

Teddy went in and closed the door without another word.

Maxim and Anastasia stood alone in the corridor, staring at each other. 'Where's your suite?' he asked.

'Just along here, not far from yours,' she replied.

They walked down the corridor together in silence. When they came to her suite, she inserted the key, opened the door, swung to him. 'Would you like a nightcap, Maxim?'

'Why not?' he answered, following her inside.

After they had shed their coats, Anastasia went to the small bar. 'What would you like?'

'No more champagne,' Maxim said. 'It's coming out of my ears.'

'How about a brandy then?'

'Good idea. Are you having one?'

'Yes.'

She poured two glasses, carried them over, handed him one, sat down in the chair opposite his.

They raised their glasses to each other, but said nothing.

After a moment, Anastasia remarked, 'Michael told me how generous you've been with him, Maxim. Giving him so much power and responsibility, and the New York office to run. He's elated. Thank you.'

'I suppose occasionally I do do something right.'

'I'm not sure I'm following you.'

'Don't pay any attention to me, forget it,' he mumbled, rose and walked across the room, glanced out of the window into the street. Below, the Ku'damm was still full of milling crowds celebrating. He felt her eyes on him, and slowly swung around to look at her.

She sat holding the brandy balloon, a quizzical expression on her face.

He felt bound to explain his last remark, said, 'I seem to make a mess of things most of the time these days. I've certainly got a mess going for me in New York . . . in my private life.'

Anastasia made no comment.

He said slowly, 'How on earth did I get myself trapped between those two women?'

'I think it was my fault,' she answered without hesitation.

'Now *I'm* not following *you*.'

'I should never have divorced you, Maxim.'

'I agree with you there, Anastasia.'

'It was the biggest mistake of my life.'

'True.' His eyes did not leave her face. 'I've never been in love with any other woman but you.'

'And I've never been in love with any other man.'

'There is only *you*, Anastasia.'

'There's only you . . . for *me*, Maxim.'

'I've just had a wonderful idea, Peachy,' Maxim said.

'What is it?'

He began to walk towards her. 'Come with me . . .'

'Where to?' she asked.

'*Venice*.'

'When?'

'Tomorrow. My plane is at Tempelhof Airport. Waiting.'

Anastasia stood up. 'Yes,' she said as she walked into his outstretched arms. 'Yes, yes, yes.'

She looked up into his face and smiled her incandescent smile.

It filled the empty places of his heart. The sadness inside him slipped away. He knew it would not come back ever again.

ACKNOWLEDGEMENTS

I would like to thank a few people who were involved in this book with me in different ways. Firstly, Joan Blutter of Chicago, a friend of many years, who is always there for me, and who grew to love my characters as much as I love them. Jane Ogden of Naples, Florida, another friend of long standing, who also grew up in wartime Britain, and confirmed that my memories had not been eroded by time passing.

Enthusiasm is not for sale; it is only ever freely given. Susan Schuhart Zito, my assistant, has always had unflagging enthusiasm for my novels. I am grateful to her for helping to prepare the manuscript meticulously and for assisting with some aspects of the research.

Two other friends took the time and trouble to assist me with certain details and I am indebted to them. Bernard H. Leser, President of Condé Nast Publications Inc.; Shirley Burnstein of London.

I would like to express my grateful thanks and appreciation to Trudi Gold of the Spiro Institute in London, who helped me to understand the situation regarding European Jewish immigrants to England in the 1930s and Britain's attitude towards these immigrants.

BIBLIOGRAPHY

Bielenberg, Christabel, *The Past is Myself* (Corgi)

Bolton, Cecil (Editor), *I'll Be Seeing You: Songs of World War II* (EMI Music Publishing Co.)

Burrough, Bryan and John Helyar, *Barbarians at the Gate* (Harper & Row)

Cannadine, David (Editor), *Blood, Toil, Tears and Sweat: The Speeches of Winston Churchill* (Houghton Mifflin)

Clare, George, *Berlin Days 1946–1947* (Macmillan, London)

Collins, Larry and Dominique Lapierre, *Is Paris Burning?* (Simon & Schuster)

Everett, Susan, *Lost Berlin* (Gallery Books)

Fallon, Ivan and James Strodes, *Takeovers* (Hamish Hamilton, London)

Gilbert, Martin, *Winston S. Churchill, Vol. VI, Finest Hour 1939–1941* (Heinemann, London)
——————— *Winston S. Churchill, Vol. VII, Road to Victory 1941–1945* (Heinemann, London)

Irving, David, *Göring* (Macmillan, London)

Johnston, Moira, *Takeover: The New Wall Street Warriors* (Arbor House)

Kaplan, Philip and Richard Collier, *Their Finest Hour: The Battle of Britain Remembered* (Abbeville Press, New York)

Manchester, William, *The Death of a President* (Harper & Row)

Metternich, Tatiana, *Tatiana: Five Passports in a Shifting Europe* (Century, London)

Morrow, Edward R., *This is London* (Schocken Books, New York)

Rosten, Leo, *The Joys of Yiddish* (Pocket Books)

Ryan, Cornelius, *The Last Battle* (Simon & Schuster)

Schlesinger Jnr, Arthur M., *A Thousand Days* (Houghton Mifflin)

Scott, David L., *Wall Street Words* (Houghton Mifflin)

Shirer, William L., *The Rise and Fall of the Third Reich* (Ballantine Books)

Simmons, Michael, *Berlin: The Dispossessed City* (Hamish Hamilton, London)

Solmssen, Arthur R. G., *A Princess in Berlin* (Ballantine Books)

Taylor, James and Warren Shaw, *Dictionary of the Third Reich* (Grafton Books, London)

Toland, John, *Adolf Hitler* (Doubleday)

Vassiltchikov, Marie, *Berlin Diaries 1940–1945* (Random House)

Wasserstein, Bernard, *Britain and the Jews of Europe 1939–1945* (Oxford University Press)

Whelan, Richard, *Robert Capa: A Biography* (Ballantine Books)

Wyndham, Joan, *Love Lessons: A Wartime Diary* (Heinemann, London)
——————— *Love is Blue: A Wartime Diary* (Heinemann, London)

GLOSSARY

Ashkenazi The name applied to the Jews of Central and Eastern Europe; a term used since the sixteenth century.

Ashkenazim As above (plural).

Bar Mitzvah A ceremony in a synagogue in which a thirteen-year-old boy reaches the status of a 'man'.

Bissel A little bit, a little piece.

Bubeleh Term of endearment, like darling, honey, or sweetheart; deriving from *buba*, the Russian–Yiddish word for 'doll'.

Chanukah The feast of lights, a less solemn Jewish festival, which usually falls just before Christmas.

Chollah A braided soft loaf, glazed with egg white.

Chuppah The wedding canopy under which the bride and groom stand for the wedding ceremony.

Chutzpah Audacity, nerve; incredible 'guts'.

Gelt Money.

Gonif Thief, crook.

Goy A Gentile, anyone who is not a Jew.

Goyim As above (plural).

Haimisher Cosy, warm, a person without 'side', unpretentious.

Kaddish A prayer glorifying God's name, usually at funerals.

Kiddush The prayer and ceremony that sanctifies the Sabbath and Jewish holy days. Not to be confused with Kaddish.

Kike An offensive way of referring to a Jew.

Kinder Children.

Kop Head.

Kosher Clean and fit to eat; food prepared according to Jewish dietary laws. Now has wider meaning in slang, ie used to denote something truly *authentic*. For example 'Is this a Kosher deal?' means 'Is it a proper deal?' and 'Is he Kosher?' means 'Is he trustworthy?'

Landsleit As below (plural).

Landsman A person from the same town in Europe, a countryman.

Macher A big wheel, a big man.

Mama-loshen Mama's language; 'Let's talk Mama-loshen' means 'Let's get to the heart of it' or 'Let's talk straight.'

Megillah A rigmarole; a far too long story.

Mensh Someone of consequence, to admire and even to emulate.

Meshuggeneh Crazy, absurd; can be applied to a person or an idea.

Mishpocheh Family or 'clan'.

Oy vey is mir Oh woe is me; truly a cry of distress.

Shabbat Sabbath.

Shabbes Sabbath.

Shadchen A professional matchmaker (as in matrimony).

Shammus Sexton or caretaker of the synagogue.

Shaygets A Gentile boy.

Sheeny A very offensive and disparaging name for a Jew.

Shikker To be drunk.

Shiksa A non-Jewish woman, a Gentile.

Shivah The seven days of mourning for the dead,

beginning immediately after the
funeral.

Shul Synagogue.

Torah The scroll containing the
five books of Moses: Genesis,
Exodus, Leviticus, Numbers and
Deuteronomy.

Trayf Any food which is not Kosher.

Tsuris Troubles, worries, woes.

*Translation of Hebrew prayer: Blessing
over Sabbath candles on page 93.*

Blessed art Thou, O Lord our God,
King of the universe, who hast
sanctified us by Thy commandments
and commanded us to kindle the
Sabbath-light.